About the Authors

"DORIS BETTS has been writing remarkable stories for two decades," according to Washington Post book critic Jonathan Yardley. And each year her audience and her reputation as one of the country's finest fiction writers continues to grow. She has won numerous literary prizes, and *Beasts of the Southern Wild* was a finalist for the 1973 National Book Award. At present she has a total of seven works of fiction to her credit, including *The Scarlet Thread, The River to Pickle Beach* and *Heading West*. She is Professor of English at the University of North Carolina in Chapel Hill.

MARK STEADMAN taught American Literature at the American University in Cairo, Egypt, between 1968 and 1969 and was Fulbright Lecturer in American Literature at Leningrad State University in 1983. In addition to *McAfee County,* Dr. Steadman is author of the novel *A Lion's Share,* which was published in 1976. Professor of English and Writer in Residence at Clemson University in Clemson, South Carolina, he is also the recipient of an NEA Creative Writing Fellowship. He is at work on a new novel.

SHIRLEY ANN GRAU began her writing career in 1955 with almost unanimous acclaim for her first book, *The Black Prince*. She followed that remarkable volume with two novels, *The Hard Blue Sky* (1957) and *The House on Coliseum Street* (1961). Her third novel, *The Keepers of the House,* won the 1965 Pulitzer Prize. An eighth volume of fiction, a collection of short stories, will be published in 1986. Mrs. Grau lives and works in New Orleans and on Martha's Vineyard.

LEWIS P. SIMPSON, one of the leading literary scholars in the country, is Boyd Professor and Editor of the prestigious *Southern Review* at Louisiana State University. He is author of a number of scholarly and critical studies, including *The Brazen Face of History, The Dispossessed Garden* and *The Man of Letters in New England and the South*.

3 BY 3

MASTERWORKS
OF THE
SOUTHERN GOTHIC

BEASTS
of The SOUTHERN
WILD

& Other
Stories

By

Doris Betts

McAfee
County:
A CHRONICLE

By

Mark Steadman

The BLACK
PRINCE

&
*Other
Stories*

By

Shirley Ann Grau

INTRODUCTION BY LEWIS P. SIMPSON

PEACHTREE PUBLISHERS, LTD.

Published by
PEACHTREE PUBLISHERS, LTD.
494 Armour Circle, N.E.
Atlanta, Georgia 30324

Manufactured in the United States of America

First printing

Library of Congress Catalog Number 85-61992

ISBN 0-931948-80-0 Hardcover
ISBN 0-931948-84-3 Trade paper

Contents

Introduction

The authorities disagree. In *American Gothic: Imagination and Reason in Nineteenth-Century Thought* (1982) Donald A. Ringe argues that, following its adaptation by Charles Brockden Brown, the Gothic mode reached its fullest American achievement in the fiction of Poe and Hawthorne. The Gothic influence on American writers in the later nineteenth century was comparatively slight, Ringe says, and it has had no important impact on our literature in the present century. In contrast, a contemporary British student of literary Gothicism, David Punter, contends in *The Literature of Terror: A History of Gothic Fictions from 1765 to the Present Day* (1980) that, after its initial expression in the later eighteenth century, the power of the Gothic increased throughout the next century and has been significantly present in twentieth-century British, Continental and American writing. Such variant conclusions by the experts result from the fact that on the one hand Ringe assumes that the Gothic mode was completely defined in such original examples as Horace Walpole's *Castle of Otranto* (1764), Ann Radcliffe's *The Mysteries of Udolpho* (1794), Matthew Gregory Lewis's *The Monk* (1796) and Frederich Von Schiller's *The Ghost-Seer* (1795). When its characteristic devices — "presentiments, prophetic dreams, the haunted house, the mysterious pictures and assorted apparitions" — yielded to realistic fictional techniques, the Gothic lost its hold on the imagination. Punter, on the other hand — seeing literary Gothicism as centered in a pervasive motive of modernity: the self-conscious terror of existence — defines it not as a fixed but as a plastic, a highly expressionistic, story-telling mode. Never approaching the fixity of a genre, capable of technical virtuosity, the Gothic mode, according to Punter, has had a continuous existence for the past two hundred years.

Students of American literature will find Punter's interpretation of the flexibility and endurance of literary Gothicism compatible with the orthodox interpretation of an aspect of the national letters that has assumed a notable place in this century, namely fiction by Southerners. Not only is Gothic expressionism conventionally regarded as germane to Southern fiction, it is associated with Southern culture as a whole, including both religion and politics. (No one blinked in 1968 when journalist Robert Sherrill published a political analysis of the South entitled *Gothic Politics in the Deep South: Stars of the New Confederacy.*) Yet while Southern writers generally seem to accept, even to encourage, an equation between the Southern and Gothic, some of them appear to have reservations about the relationship. Occasionally, as in the instance of Flannery O'Connor, they have said so. In her well-known essay, "The Fiction Writer and His Country" (*Mystery and Manners: Occasional Prose,* edited by Robert and Sally Fitzgerald, 1961), O'Connor complains that she and other serious twentieth-century Southern storytellers are unthinkingly "considered to be unhappy combinations of Poe and Erskine Caldwell" — creators of "Gothic monstrosities" and of "everything deformed and grotesque" — when their real motive, although seldom overtly religious, is to fulfill an imperative embedded in Southern culture, "respect for the mystery of being." For this reason, O'Connor says, Southern writers have a particular "penchant for writing about freaks." In the South the conception of man is still influenced by Christian theology, O'Connor declares, this region of America being "if not Christ-centered, . . . most certainly Christ-haunted." The freak in Southern literature is, O'Connor implies, a ghost of God, a "figure" of the "essential displacement" of the concept of the "whole man" — of man as a creature wholly the creature of God — by the concept of man as a construct of the social scientists. Afflicted by the "demonism" of the economists, sociologists and psychologists, some Southern writers (presumably the less "serious" ones) constitute a literary "entity" that may appropriately be called the "School of Southern Degeneracy." O'Connor's implication is that the degeneracy consists not in a natural propensity of the writers of the school for the degraded and the obscene but in their inability to transcend a realism based on social scientism. Held in thrall by secular doctrines, they cannot "separate mystery and judgment from vision."

Neither in "The Fiction Writer and His Country" nor in a companion essay on "The Grotesque in Southern Fiction" is O'Connor concerned with repudiating the Gothic. She had indeed firmly embraced the grotesque as the primary mode of her art. Gothic monstrosities result, she says, when the writer, using the Gothic technique in the name of science, is blind to the spiritual efficacy of the freakish and the grotesque. O'Connor, it might be said, wanted to recover the sense of the term the "Gothic" conveys when it is employed, in contrast to the term "Romanesque," to describe the style of architecture and decor associated with the medieval cathedral. With its pointed arches, heavenward reaching spires and dramatic flying buttresses, a Gothic cathedral was once conceived by Western man to be the embodiment of the mystery of being. One prominent feature of the cathedral architecture was gutter spouts, or gargoyles, fashioned in the imagined likenesses of demons and outlandish beasts. As functional entities of the structure, these grotesqueries, representing the dark, subliminal forces that haunt the margins of consciousness, were incorporated into the faith the cathedral embodied. The gargoyles were no more freaks than the stone angels that graced the spiritual edifice. Nonetheless they served to suggest a certain freakish quality in the whole elaborate but precarious design of the cathedral, expressing as it did not only the solidity but the fragility of faith. Even as the "delight of its aspirations is flung up to the sky," Henry Adams observed, the Gothic cathedral acknowledges "self-distrust and anguish" in the "leap downwards of the flying buttresses" to bury the secret of doubt in the earth.

A possible interpretation of the Gothic mode in fiction is to see it as a comparatively minor, pre-Romantic expression of dissatisfaction with eighteenth-century rationalism. Donald Ringe points out that in their use of extraordinary settings, particularly gloomy old castles and a contrived machinery of the supernatural, the Gothic fictionists yet showed a fundamentally rationalistic bent by anchoring the "main events of their books in the world of material reality." But the anchor in the material world is never firmly set. Although the Gothic tale typically exhibits a tension between rationality and irrationality that is resolved when it is discovered, for instance, that a mysterious voice is a trick, the tension between reason and unreason in some stories is resolved by a surprise twist. In Lewis's *The Monk,* the monk is destroyed by a literal Lucifer. Such a moment in Gothic fiction is not, in any simple way at any rate, a reaction to Enlightenment rationalism. It is a kind of tawdry parody of the original Gothic vision of the mystery of existence incarnated in the ecclesiastical architecture of the twelfth and thirteenth centuries; or, it may occur to us, in what is after all the archetypal work of literary Gothicism, Dante's *Commedia.* Eighteenth-century literary Gothicism, in other words, put a final period in the endeavor to assimilate doubt to the great design of faith represented by the medieval cathedrals — a design that expressed faith in the soul's incorporation of a comprehensive structure of the visible and the invisible, the temporal and the eternal. Yet at the same time Gothicism served as the mask of a continuing attachment to the idea of the "whole man."

The contrasting figure of the man of reason, the key figure of the eighteenth-century ideal community of the cosmopolitan, secular mind, is central in the literature of the British colonials who overthrew Church and State in the American Revolution. They justified their action by the political doctrine that the source of government is inherent in the consent of the governed, a doctrine implying the radical notion that ultimate sovereignty resides in the individual self.

Writing in the aftermath of the American Revolution, Charles Brockden Brown and Nathaniel Hawthorne, as well as Washington Irving and James Fenimore Cooper, obviously imitated British and European literary Gothicism, but their novels responded to an emotional and intellectual situation different from that of the Old World. Committed to the autonomy of the individual mind, to the doctrine of the sovereignty of the self — to the dictate of reason that each individual is born with "certain inalienable rights," among these being "life, liberty and the pursuit of happiness" — the American Republic, as Alexis de Tocqueville said, depended on the consonance between its interests and the interest of each citizen. The vanquishment of the tradition of the corporate community in America forebode the final fulfillment of John Donne's seventeenth-century society in which "every man alone thinks he has got / To be a phoenix, and that then can be / None of that kind, of which he is, but he." That in its displacement from "just relation" (as Donne put it) the self could become a freak, a grotesque, was a more distinct possibility in Jeffersonian America than in Jacobean England or even in the England of George III. America as a society, in fact, was under deep psychic distress. In the name of the sovereignty of the individual it had committed symbolic regicide. In the name of the same concept it had abolished the foreign slave trade in its Constitution but had paradoxically remained constitutionally obligated to preserve chattel slavery as a domestic institution.

But the maintenance of this obligation was owing largely to the special interests of the slaveholding citizen of the Southern states. For this reason — while acknowledging the development of an "American Gothicism" in Brown, Irving, Cooper and Hawthorne, we are justified in identifying early on in American literary history the development in the South of a unique version of literary Gothicism. With a certain critical license, this may appropriately be called pastoral Gothic. Deriving essentially from a fusion of the motives of the eighteenth-century Gothic as exhibited by Walpole, Radcliffe and Schiller and an inversion of the motives of the Western pastoral mode (as created in ancient times and reinstituted in the Renaissance), the Southern Gothic mode had its inception in Thomas Jefferson, specifically in the nineteenth Query of his *Notes on the State of Virginia* (1785), in which the man of letters and slave master who composed the Declaration of Independence invokes a powerful vision of Virginia masters corrupted in intellect and spirit by their psychic bondage to their own slaves. A hyperbolic portrayal of plantation life as Jefferson himself knew it at Monticello — or indeed as it existed on any Southern plantation, to be precise, a deliberate fiction — the famous nineteenth chapter of *Notes on Virginia* is the originating image of the familiar plantation Gothic, which depicts a Southern landscape of nightmare, homeland of a decadent aristocracy of slaveholders and of their descendants, prone to neurotic terrors and violence. In spite of the fact that Roderick Usher is not presented as a slaveholder, the forbidding House of Usher, reputedly suggested to Poe by a ruined mansion he saw somewhere in Virginia, is a major feature of this landscape. Before Jefferson the Southern landscape had been imagined in William Byrd II's description in *The History of the Dividing Line* (not published until 1866) of the "lubberlanders" of the North Carolina backwoods. Byrd anticipated the appearance of a backwoods grotesque in the humor of the Old Southwest (the antebellum semi-frontier world of Tennessee, Arkansas, Louisiana, Mississippi, Alabama and Georgia). Reaching its climax in George Washington Harris's *Sut Lovingood: "Yarns Spun by a Nat'ral Born Durn'd Fool"* (1867), this body of humorous writing is a kind of Gothic repudiation of the very world Jefferson offers in *Notes on Virginia* — in a striking counter image to his image of plantation pastoral — as the redemption of history: an idealized pastoral, a nation populated chiefly by small farmers, freed from both European feudalism and urbanism, living a rational, virtuous life on self-sustaining freeholds.

Basically the antebellum Southern Gothic, intentionally so on the part of the humorists, offered an ironic comment on the American vision of, as Alexander Hamilton says in *The Federalist*, a people for the first time in history forming and conducting a national order on the basis of the human capacity for "reflection and choice." The improbability that a nation could not only perpetuate itself in history but redeem the world from unreason by an endless accommodation to a process of reflecting and choosing by each citizen was disastrously confirmed in 1860. Both the North and the South appealed to God to intervene in a history they could not manage and fought one of the bloodiest wars on record. Following the Civil War the Southern literary imagination was confined by the intimidating piety of the Lost Cause and occupied with writing the Southern apologia. In *Adventures of Huckleberry Finn* and *Pudd'nhead Wilson*, Mark Twain, schooled in the pastoral grotesque of the Southwestern humorists, penetrated the darker aspects of the antebellum slave society. But the Southern literary imagination did not make a general exploration of the dark unreason of the Civil War — and of the years leading up to and following the catastrophe — until the second generation of writers after the Civil War. In William Faulkner, the greatest writer of the generation of the First World War, both the plantation Gothic and the comic Gothic — often intermingled in Faulkner but more or less precisely represented respectively in *Absalom, Absalom!* and *The Hamlet* — came to a rich fruition.

The effort by the Faulkner generation (including its younger representatives Robert Penn Warren and Eudora Welty) to discover the meaning of the South as integral with modern history, an effort directed by a complex mingling of piety and irony, continued well past the end of the Second World War. But the motivation of Southern writers whose careers belong to the age after 1945 has been different. This is not to say that post-Faulknerian writing lacks a discernible relation with the older modes of Southern literary Gothicism. Its continuity with the comic grotesque is especially to be noted, as quite clearly not only in O'Connor but in Cormac McCarthy and Mark Steadman. But as the Southern chain of living connection with the Confederacy and the Civil War has lost its last links, the post-Second World War — the post-Auschwitz, post-Hiroshima — Southern writers have had less incentive to recover Southern memory and history than to associate contemporary Southern life with the "absurdity" of human existence in the twentieth century. Still, in adhering to the existential mood, writers in the South have shown a continuity with the Old South Gothic. This is clear in the relation borne by O'Connor, Walker Percy (in *Lancelot*), McCarthy or Steadman to the comic grotesque of Harris and others in the last century. This connection is grounded in the resemblance between the awareness of cultural displacement in Harris and that known to the latter-day Southern writer. The ludicrous and often violent characters and situations in the Sut Lovingood stories do not merely presage the grotesque comedy in O'Connor, Percy and Steadman; they are themselves symbols of the psychic, and the spiritual, dislocation of modern man; who, Albert Camus said, has been "divested" of the illusion of a transcendent significance for either his social or personal existence and so finds himself an "alien, a stranger," an "exile," in the world that had once been his home. The most important prophetic reference of the pervasive mood and mode in the twentieth-century Southern fiction that we imprecisely define as Gothic is, however, Poe; for it was Poe who self-consciously realized that the potentiality of the Gothic lay not in its generic evolvement but in its unfolding as an expressionistic style that would (the comparison is not Poe's but follows the logic of his perception of the Gothic) like Gothic architecture provide a symbolic context for the life of the individual.

Southern literary Gothicism as it is manifested in writers from Faulkner to Doris Betts, Mark Steadman and Shirley Ann Grau in *3 By 3: Masterworks of the Southern Gothic* is ultimately emblematic of the deformation of the soul in its displacement from the culture that conceived the architecture of Chartres or Westminster Abbey to be the witness to generation after generation of the conjunction of time and eternity, the mortal and the immortal. The drama of the estrangement of the soul from the tradition of faith in this conjunction and the soul's transformation into the alien entity of the "self," isolated in the modern society of science and history, composes the underlying subject of modern literature. Placed in the perspective necessary to a true understanding of it, American literature belongs entirely to this drama. Modern literature came into its effective formation not later than the time of Shakespeare and Bacon, when the settlement of the eastern seaboard of the future American nation was just beginning. The self-conscious realization of the role of the New England, and of the Middle Atlantic area, in the drama of modernity produced the "American Renaissance" in the antebellum age. Repressed by the compelling, though anachronistic, historical effort of the South to establish itself as a great modern slave state, the self-conscious recognition of writing in the South as an exemplification of modernity did not come until the present century. When it did arrive, Southern novelists tended to render the image of the South as a symbol of the disorder and depravity of the modern age at its worst, filling their stories with a complete catalogue of the bizarre and the horrible: rape and incest, murder and suicide, lynching (by fire or rope), castration, miscegenation, idiocy and insanity. It is no wonder that many Southerners reprobated what appeared to be the rise of an unrestrained, unfair and even vicious Gothicism in their storytellers. In a recent essay Fred Hobson quotes Gerald Johnson's bitter characterization of the Southern novelists of the 1930s as "merchants of death, hell and the grave," altogether "horror-mongers in chief."

But in detailing life in the South as a horror story all serious Southern writers have, like Flannery O'Connor, responded to the terror and pathos of the self's difficult, maybe impossible, attempt to achieve a meaningful identity. Whether the struggle is considered as involving the recovery of the self as the soul open to transcendence or the assertion of the self's identity even in the face of its immutable enclosure in time, the Southern writer has resisted placing the representation of the drama of the self in a merely sociological and/or psychological context. The consciousness of individual being — of the self as a spiritual entity in the universe — has remained for the Southern writer a mystery beyond scientific analysis.

No more than Faulkner's or O'Connor's writings do the works collected in *3 By 3* indicate a dedication to the Gothic mode as such, still less do they suggest a commitment to a Southern Gothic movement or school. In such remarkable stories as Betts's "The Ugliest Pilgrim," "Beasts of the Southern Wild" or "Spider Gardens of Madagascar"; Steadman's "Daddy's Girl," "Dorcus and the Fat Lady" or "John Henry's Promise"; Grau's "The Black Prince," "Miss Yellow Eyes" or "White Girl, Fine Girl," the present-day Southern Gothic defines itself in examples as a vision of life that blends realism and grotesquery in a manner that we readily grasp as typical of the Southern literary imagination but find almost impossible to explicate critically. At once a harsh but an ambivalent interpretation of Southern life by its own story-tellers — a cultural self-interpretation — the stories of Betts, Steadman and Grau, project a vision of the South illustrative of the bizarre terrors of existence under the conditions of modern history. Yet, at least in moments, their vision intimates the equally bizarre hope of redemption, the imagination of damnation in the South still being inextricably linked to the imagination of salvation.

— Lewis P. Simpson

BEASTS
of the
SOUTHERN
WILD

&Other
Stories

By

Doris Betts

The Ugliest Pilgrim

I sit in the bus station, nipping chocolate peel off a Mounds candy bar with my teeth, then pasting the coconut filling to the roof of my mouth. The lump will dissolve there slowly and seep into me the way dew seeps into flowers.

I like to separate flavors that way. Always I lick the salt off cracker tops before taking my first bite.

Somebody sees me with my suitcase, paper sack, and a ticket in my lap. "You going someplace, Violet?"

Stupid. People in Spruce Pine are dumb and, since I look dumb, say dumb things to me. I turn up my face as if to count those dead flies piled under the light bulb. He walks away — a fat man, could be anybody. I stick out my tongue at his back; the candy oozes down. If I could stop swallowing, it would drip into my lung and I could breathe vanilla.

Whoever it was, he won't glance back. People in Spruce Pine don't like to look at me, full face.

A Greyhound bus pulls in, blows air; the driver stands by the door. He's black-headed, maybe part Cherokee, with heavy shoulders but a weak chest. He thinks well of himself — I can tell that. I open my notebook and copy his name off the metal plate so I can call him by it when he drives me home again. And next week, won't Mr. Wallace Weatherman be surprised to see how well I'm looking!

I choose the front seat behind Mr. Weatherman, settle my bag with the hat in it, then open the lined composition book again. Maybe it's half full of writing. Even the empty pages toward the back have one repeated entry, high, printed off Mama's torn catechism: GLORIFY GOD AND ENJOY HIM FOREVER.

I finish Mr. Weatherman off in my book while he's running his motor and getting us onto the highway. His nose is too broad, his dark eyes too skimpy — nothing in his face I want — but the hair is nice. I write that down, "Black hair?" I'd want it to curl, though, and be soft as a baby's.

Two others are on the bus, a nigger soldier and an old woman whose jaw sticks out like a shelf. There grow, on the backs of her hands, more veins than skin. One fat blue vessel, curling from wrist to knuckle, would be good; so on one page I draw a sample hand and let blood wind across it like a river. I write at the bottom: "Praise God, it is started. May 29, 1969," and turn to a new sheet. The paper's lumpy and I flip back to the thick envelope stuck there with adhesive tape. I can't lose that.

We're driving now at the best speed Mr. Weatherman can make on these winding roads. On my side there is nothing out the bus window but granite rock, jagged and wet in patches. The old lady and the nigger can see red rhododendron on the slope of Roan Mountain. I'd like to own a tight dress that flower color, and breasts to go under it. I write in my notebook, very small, the word "breasts," and turn quickly to another page. AND ENJOY HIM FOREVER.

The soldier bends as if to tie his shoes, but instead zips open a canvas bag and sticks both hands inside. When finally he sits back, one hand is clenched around something hard. He catches me watching. He yawns and scratches his ribs, but the right fist sets very lightly on his knee, and when I turn he drinks something out of its cup and throws his head quickly back like a bird or a chicken. You'd think I could smell it, big as my nose is.

Across the aisle the old lady says, "You going far?" She shows me a set of tan, artificial teeth.

"Oklahoma."

"I never been there. I hear the trees give out." She pauses so I can ask politely where she's headed. "I'm going to Nashville," she finally says. "The country-music capital of the world. My son lives there and works in the cellophane plant."

I draw in my notebook a box and two arrows. I crisscross the box.

"He's got three children not old enough to be in school yet."

I sit very still, adding new boxes, drawing baseballs in some, looking busy for fear she might bring out their pictures from her big straw pocketbook. The funny thing is she's looking past my head, though there's nothing out that window but rock wall sliding by. I mumble, "It's hot in here."

Angrily she says, "I had eight children myself."

My pencil flies to get the boxes stacked, eight-deep, in a pyramid. "Hope you have a nice visit."

"It's not a visit. I maybe will move." She is hypnotized by the stone and the furry moss in its cracks. Her eyes used to be green. Maybe, when young, she was red-haired and Irish. If she'll stop talking, I want to think about trying green eyes with that Cherokee hair. Her lids droop; she looks drowsy. "I am right tired of children," she says and lays her head back on the white rag they button on these seats.

Now that her eyes are covered, I can study that face — china white, and worn thin as tissue so light comes between her bones and shines through her whole head. I picture the light going around and around her skull, like water spinning in a jar. If I could wait to be eighty, even my face might grind down and look softer. But I'm ready, in case the Preacher mentions that. Did Elisha make Naaman bear into old age his leprosy? Didn't Jesus heal the withered hand, even on Sunday, without waiting for the work week to start? And put back the ear of Malchus with a touch? As soon as Job had learned enough, did his boils fall away?

Lord, I have learned enough.

The old lady sleeps while we roll downhill and up again; then we turn so my side of the bus looks over the valley and its thickety woods where, as a girl, I pulled armloads of galax, fern, laurel, and hemlock to have some spending money. I spent it for magazines full of women with permanent waves. Behind us, the nigger shuffles a deck of cards and deals to himself by fives. Draw poker — I could beat him. My papa showed me, long winter days and nights snowed in on the mountain. He said poker would teach me arithmetic. It taught me there are four ways to make a royal flush and, with two players, it's an even chance one of them holds a pair on the deal. And when you try to draw from a pair to four of a kind, discard the kicker; it helps your odds.

The soldier deals smoothly, using his left hand only with his thumb on top. Papa was good at that. He looks up and sees my whole face with its scar, but he keeps his eyes level as if he has seen worse things; and his left hand drops cards evenly and in rhythm. Like a turtle, laying eggs.

I close my eyes and the riffle of his deck rests me to the next main stop where I write in my notebook: Praise God for Johnson City, Tennessee, and all the state to come. I am on my way."

At Kingsport, Mr. Weatherman calls rest stop and I go straight through the terminal to the ladies' toilet and look hard at my face in the mirror. I must remember to start the Preacher on the scar first of all — the only thing about me that's even on both sides.

Lord! I am so ugly!

Maybe the Preacher will claim he can't heal ugliness. And I'm going to spread my palms by my ears and show him — this is a crippled face! An infirmity! Would he do for a kidney or liver what he withholds from a face? The Preacher once stuttered, I read someplace, and God bothered with that. Why not me? When the Preacher labors to heal the sick in his Tulsa auditorium, he asks us at home to lay our fingers on the television screen and pray for God's healing. He puts forth his own ten fingers and we match them, pad to pad, on that glass. I have tried that, Lord, and the Power was too filtered and thinned down for me.

I touch my hand now to this cold mirror glass, and cover all but my pimpled chin, or wide nose, or a single red-brown eye. And nothing's too bad by itself. But when they're put together?

I've seen the Preacher wrap his hot, blessed hands on a club foot and cry out "HEAL!" in his funny way that sounds like the word "Hell" broken into two pieces. Will he not cry out, too, when he sees this poor, clubbed face? I will be to him as Goliath was to David, a need so giant it will drive God to action.

I comb out my pine-needle hair. I think I would like blond curls and Irish eyes, and I want my mouth so large it will never be done with kissing.

The old lady comes in the toilet and catches me pinching my bent face. She jerks back once, looks sad, then pets me with her twiggy hand. "Listen, honey," she says, "I had looks once. It don't amount to much."

I push right past. Good people have nearly turned me against you, Lord. They open their mouths for the milk of human kindness and boiling oil spews out.

So I'm half running through the terminal and into the café, and I take the first stool and call down the counter, "Tuna-fish sandwich," quick. Living in the mountains, I eat fish every chance I get and wonder what the sea is like. Then I see I've sat down by the nigger soldier. I do not want to meet his gaze, since he's a wonder to me, too. We don't have many black men in the mountains. Mostly they live east in Carolina, on the flatland, and pick cotton and tobacco instead of apples. They seem to me like foreigners. He's absently shuffling cards the way some men twiddle thumbs. On the stool beyond him is a paratrooper, white, and they're talking about what a bitch the army is. Being sent to the same camp has made them friends already.

I roll a dill-pickle slice through my mouth — a wheel, a bitter wheel. Then I start on the sandwich and it's chicken by mistake when I've got chickens all over my back yard.

"Don't bother with the beer," says the black one. "I've got better on the bus." They come to some agreement and deal out cards on the counter.

It's just too much for me. I lean over behind the nigger's back and say to the paratrooper, "I wouldn't play with him." Neither one moves. "He's a mechanic." They look at each other, not at me. "It's a way to cheat on the deal."

The paratrooper sways backward on his stool and stares around out of eyes so blue that I want them, right away, and maybe his pale blond hair. I swallow a crusty half-chewed bite. "One-handed grip; the mechanic's grip. It's the middle finger. He can second-deal and bottom-deal. He can buckle the top card with his thumb and peep."

"I be damn," says the paratrooper.

The nigger spins around and bares his teeth at me, but it's half a grin. "Lady, you want to play?"

I slide my dishes back. "I get mad if I'm cheated."

"And mean when you're mad." He laughs a laugh so deep it makes me retaste that bittersweet chocolate off the candy bar. He offers the deck to cut, so I pull out the center and restack it three ways. A little air blows through his upper teeth. "I'm Grady Fliggins and they call me Flick."

The paratrooper reaches a hand down the counter to shake mine. "Monty Harrill. From near to Raleigh."

"And I'm Violet Karl. Spruce Pine. I'd rather play five-card stud."

By the time the bus rolls on, we've moved to its wider back seat playing serious cards with a fifty-cent ante. My money's sparse, but I'm good and the deck is clean. The old lady settles into my front seat, stiffer than plaster. Sometimes she throws back a hurt look.

Monty, the paratrooper, plays soft. But Flick's so good he doesn't even need to cheat, though I watch him close. He drops out quick when his cards are bad; he makes me bid high to see what he's got; and the few times he bluffs, I'm fooled. He's no talker. Monty, on the other hand, says often, "Whose play is it?" till I know that's his clue phrase for a pair. He lifts his cards close to his nose and gets quiet when planning to bluff. And he'd rather use wild cards but we won't. Ah, but he's pretty, though!

After we've swapped a little money, mostly the paratrooper's, Flick pours us a drink in some cups he stole in Kingsport and asks, "Where'd you learn to play?"

I tell him about growing up on a mountain, high, with Mama dead, and shuffling cards by a kerosene lamp with my papa. When I passed fifteen, we'd drink together, too. Applejack or a beer he made from potato peel.

"And where you headed now?" Monty's windburned in a funny pattern, with pale goggle circles that start high on his cheeks. Maybe it's something paratroopers wear.

"It's a pilgrimage." They lean back with their drinks. "I'm going to see this preacher in Tulsa, the one that heals, and I'm coming home pretty. Isn't that healing?" Their still faces make me nervous. "I'll even trade if he says . . . I'll take somebody else's weak eyes or deaf ears. I could stand limping a little."

The nigger shakes his black head, snickering.

"I tried to get to Charlotte when he was down there with his eight-pole canvas cathedral tent that seats nearly fifteen thousand people, but I didn't have money then. Now what's so funny?" I think for a minute I am going to have to take out my notebook, and unglue the envelope and read them all the Scripture I have looked up on why I should be healed. Monty looks sad for me, though, and that's worse. "Let the Lord twist loose my foot or give me a cough, so long as I'm healed of my looks while I'm still young enough —" I stop and tip up my plastic cup. Young enough for you, blue-eyed boy, and your brothers.

"Listen," says Flick in a high voice. "Let me go with you and be there for that swapping." He winks one speckled eye.

"I'll not take black skin, no offense." He's offended, though, and lurches across the moving bus and falls into a far seat. "Well, you as much as said you'd swap it off!" I call. "What's wrong if I don't want it any more than you?"

Monty slides closer. "You're not much to look at," he grants, sweeping me up and down till I nearly glow blue from his eyes. Shaking his head, "And what now? Thirty?"

"Twenty-eight. His drink and his cards, and I hurt Flick's feelings. I didn't mean that." I'm scared, too. Maybe, unlike Job, I haven't learned enough. Who ought to be expert in hurt feelings? Me, that's who.

"And you live by yourself?"

I start to say "No, there's men falling all over each other going in and out my door." He sees my face, don't he? It makes me call, "Flick? I'm sorry." Not one movement. "Yes. By myself." Five years now, since Papa had heart failure and fell off the high back porch and rolled downhill in the gravel till the hobblebushes stopped him. I found him past sunset, cut from the rocks but not much blood showing. And what there was, dark, and already jellied.

Monty looks at me carefully before making up his mind to say, "That preacher's a fake. You ever see a doctor agree to what he's done?"

"Might be." I'm smiling. I tongue out the last liquor in my cup. I've thought of all that, but it may be what I believe is stronger than him faking. That he'll be electrified by my trust, the way a magnet can get charged against its will. He might be a lunatic or a dope fiend, and it still not matter.

Monty says, "Flick, you plan to give us another drink?"

"No." He acts like he's going to sleep.

"I just wouldn't count on that preacher too much." Monty cleans his nails with a matchbook corner and sometimes gives me an uneasy look. "Things are mean and ugly in this world — I mean *act* ugly, do ugly, be ugly."

He's wrong. When I leave my house, I can walk for miles and everything's beautiful. Even the rattlesnakes have grace. I don't mind his worried looks, since I'm writing in my notebook how we met and my winnings — a good sign, to earn money on a trip. I like the way army barbers trim his hair. I wish I could touch it.

"Took one furlough in your mountains. Pretty country. Maybe hard to live in? Makes you feel little." He looks toward Flick and says softer, "Makes you feel like the night sky does. So many stars."

"Some of them big as daisies." It's easy to live in, though. Some mornings a deer and I scare up each other in the brush, and his heart stops, and mine stops. Everything stops till he plunges away. The next pulsebeat nearly knocks you down. "Monty, doesn't your hair get lighter in the summers? That might be a good color to ask for in Tulsa. Then I could turn colors like the leaves. Spell your last name for me."

He does, and says I sure am funny. Then he spells Grady Fliggins and I write that, too. He's curious about my book, so I flip through and offer to read him parts. Even with his eyes shut, Flick is listening. I read them about my papa's face, a chunky block face, not much different from the Preacher's square one. After Papa died, I wrote that to slow down how fast I was forgetting him. I tell Monty parts of my lists: that you can get yellow dye out of gopherwood and Noah built his ark from that, and maybe it stained the water. That a cow eating snakeroot might give poison milk. I pass him a pressed maypop flower I'm carrying to Tulsa, because the crown of thorns and the crucifixion nails grow in its center, and each piece of the bloom stands for one of the apostles.

"It's a mollypop vine," says Flick out of one corner of his mouth. "And it makes a green ball that pops when you step on it." He stretches. "Deal you some blackjack?"

For no reason, Monty says, "We oughtn't to let her go."

We play blackjack till supper stop and I write in my book, "Praise God for Knoxville and two new friends." I've not had many friends. At school in the valley, I sat in the back rows, reading, a hand spread on my face. I was smart, too; but if you let that show, you had to stand for the class and present different things.

When the driver cuts out the lights, the soldiers give me a whole seat, and a duffelbag for a pillow. I hear them whispering, first about women, then about me; but after a while I don't hear that anymore.

By the time we hit Nashville, the old lady makes the bus wait while she begs me to stop with her. "Harvey won't mind. He's a good boy." She will not even look at Monty and Flick. "You can wash and change clothes and catch a new bus tomorrow."

"I'm in a hurry. Thank you." I have picked a lot of galax to pay for this trip.

"A girl alone. A girl that maybe feels she's got to prove something?" The skin on her neck shivers. "Some people might take advantage."

Maybe when I ride home under my new face, that will be some risk. I shake my head, and as she gets off she whispers something to Mr. Weatherman about looking after me. It's wasted, though, because a new driver takes his place and he looks nearly as bad as I do — oily-faced and toad-shaped, with eyeballs a dingy color and streaked with blood. He's the flatlands driver, I guess, because he leans back and drops one warty hand on the wheel and we go so fast and steady you can hardly tell it.

Since Flick is the tops in cards and we're tired of that, it's Monty's turn to brag on his motorcycle. He talks all across Tennessee till I think I could ride one by hearsay alone, that my wrist knows by itself how far to roll the throttle in. It's a Norton and he rides it in Scrambles and Enduro events, in his leathers, with spare parts and tools glued all over him with black electrician's tape.

"So this bastard tells me, 'Zip up your jacket because when I run over you I want some traction.'"

Flick is playing solitaire. "You couldn't get me on one of them killing things."

"One day I'm coming through Spruce Pine, flat out, throw Violet up behind me! We're going to lean all the way through them mountains. Sliding the right foot and then sliding the left." Monty lays his head back on the seat beside me, rolls it, watches. "How you like that? Take you through creeks and ditches like you was on a skateboard. You can just holler and hang on."

Lots of women have, I bet.

"The Norton's got the best front forks of anybody. It'll nearly roll up a tree trunk and ride down the other side." He demonstrates on the seat back. I keep writing. These are new things, two-stroke and four-stroke, picking your line on a curve, Milwaukee iron. It will all come back to me in the winters, when I reread these pages.

Flick says he rode on a Harley once. "Turned over and got drug. No more."

They argue about what he should have done instead of turning over. Finally Monty drifts off to sleep, his head leaning at me slowly, so I look down on his crisp, light hair. I pat it as easy as a cat would, and it tickles my palm. I'd almost ask them in Tulsa to make me a man if I could have hair like his, and a beard, and feel so different in so many places.

He slides closer in his sleep. One eyebrow wrinkles against my shoulder. Looking our way, Flick smokes a cigarette, then reads some magazine he keeps rolled in his belt. Monty makes a deep noise against my arm as if, while he slept, his throat had cleared itself. I shift and his whole head is on my shoulder now. Its weight makes me breathe shallow.

I rest my eyes. If I should turn, his hair would barely touch my cheek, the scarred one, like a shoebrush. I do turn and it does. For miles he sleeps that way and I almost sleep. Once, when we take a long curve, he rolls against me, and one of his hands drifts up and then drops in my lap. Just there, where the creases are.

I would not want God's Power to turn me, after all, into a man. His breath is so warm. Everywhere, my skin is singing. Praise God for that.

When I get my first look at the Mississippi River, the pencil goes straight into my pocketbook. How much praise would that take?

"Is the sea like this?"

"Not except they're both water," Flick says. He's not mad anymore. "Tell you what, Vi-oh-LETTE. When Monty picks you up on his cycle" ("sickle," he calls it), "you ride down to the beaches — Cherry Grove, O.D., around there. Where they work the big nets in the fall and drag them up on the sand with trucks at each end, and men to their necks in the surf."

"You do that?"

"I know people that do. And afterward they strip and dress by this big fire on the beach."

And they make chowder while this cold wind is blowing! I know that much, without asking. In a big black pot that sits on that whipping fire. I think they might let me sit with them and stir the pot. It's funny how much, right now, I feel like praising all the good things I've never seen, in places I haven't been.

Everybody has to get off the bus and change in Memphis, and most of them wait a long time. I've taken the long way, coming here; but some of Mama's cousins live in Memphis and might rest me overnight. Monty says they plan to stay the night, too, and break the long trip.

"They know you're coming Violet?" It's Flick says my name that way, in pieces, carefully: Vi-oh-LETTE. Monty is lazier: Viii-lut. They make me feel like more than one.

"I've never even met these cousins. But soon as I call up and tell them who I am and that I'm here . . ."

"We'll stay some hotel tonight and then ride on. Why don't you come with us?" Monty is carrying my scuffed bag. Flick swings the paper sack. "You know us better than them."

"Kin people," grunts Flick, "can be a bad surprise."

Monty is nodding his head. "Only cousin I had got drunk and drove this tractor over his baby brother. Did it on purpose, too." I see by his face that Monty made this up, for my sake.

"Your cousins might not even live here anymore. I bet it's been years since you heard from a one."

"We're picking a cheap hotel, in case that's a worry."

I never thought they might have moved. "How cheap?"

When Flick says "Under five," I nod; and my things go right up on their shoulders as I follow them into a Memphis cab. The driver takes for granted I'm Monty's afflicted sister and names a hotel right off. He treats me with pity and good manners.

And the hotel he chooses is cheap, all right, where ratty salesmen with bad territories spend half the night drinking in their rooms. Plastic palm bushes and a worn rug the color of wet cigars. I get Room 210 and they're down the hall in the teens. They stand in my doorway and watch me drop both shoes and walk the bed in bare feet. When Monty opens my window, we can hear some kitchen underneath — a fan, clattering noise, a man's crackly voice singing about the California earthquake.

It scares me, suddenly, to know I can't remember how home sounds. Not one bird call, nor the water over rocks. There's so much you can't save by writing down.

"Smell that grease," says Flick, and shakes his head till his lips flutter. "I'm finding an ice machine. You, Vi-oh-LETTE, come on down in a while."

Monty's got a grin I'll remember if I never write a word. He waves. "Flick and me going to get drunker than my old cousin and put wild things in your book. Going to draw dirty pictures. You come on down and get drunk enough to laugh."

But after a shower, damp in my clean slip, even this bed like a roll of fence wire feels good, and I fall asleep wondering if that rushing noise is a river wind, and how long I can keep it in my mind.

Monty and Flick edge into my dream. Just their voices first, from way downhill. Somewhere in a Shonny Haw thicket. "Just different," Monty is saying. "That's all. Different. Don't make some big thing out of it." He doesn't sound happy. "Nobody else," he says.

Is that Flick singing? No, because the song goes on while his voice says, "Just so . . ." and then some words I don't catch. "It don't hurt"? Or maybe,

"You don't hurt"? I hear them climbing my tangled hill, breaking sticks and knocking the little stones loose. I'm trying to call to them which way the path is, but I can't make noise because the Preacher took my voice and put it in a black bag and carried it to a sick little boy in Iowa.

They find the path, anyway. And now they can see my house and me standing little by the steps. I know how it looks from where they are: the wood rained on till the siding's almost silver; and behind the house a wet-weather waterfall that's cut a stream bed downhill and grown pin cherry and bee balm on both sides. The high rock walls by the waterfall are mossy and slick, but I've scraped one place and hammered a mean-looking gray head that leans out of the hillside and stares down the path at whoever comes. I've been here so long by myself that I talk to it sometimes. Right now I'd say, "Look yonder. We've got company at last!" if my voice wasn't gone.

"You can't go by looks," Flick is saying as they climb. He ought to know. Ahead of them, warblers separate and fly out on two sides. Everything moves out of their path if I could just see it — tree frogs and mosquitoes. Maybe the worms drop deeper just before a footstep falls.

"Without the clothes, it's not a hell of a lot improved, says Monty, and I know suddenly they are inside the house with me, inside my very room, and my room today's in Memphis. "There's one thing, though," Monty says, standing over my bed. "Good looks in a woman is almost like a wall. She can use it to shut you outside. You never know what she's like, that's all." He's wearing a T-shirt and his dog tags jingle. "Most of the time I don't even miss knowing that."

And Flick says, disgusted, "I knew that much in grammar school. You sure are slow. It's not the face you screw." If I opened my eyes, I could see him now, behind Monty. He says, "After a while, you don't even notice faces. I always thought, in a crowd, my mother might not pick Daddy out."

"*My* mother could," says Monty. "He was always the one *started* the fight."

I stretch and open my eyes. It's a plain slip, cotton, that I sewed myself and makes me look too white and skinny as a sapling.

"She's waking up."

When I point, Monty hands me the blouse off the doorknob. Flick says they've carried me a soda pop, plus something to spruce it up. They sit stiffly on two hard chairs till I've buttoned on my skirt. I sip the drink, cold but peppery, and prop on the bed pillows. "I dreamed you both came where my house is, on the mountain, and it had rained so the waterfall was working. I felt real proud of that."

After two drinks we go down to the noisy restaurant with that smelly grease. And after that, to a picture show. Monty grins widely when the star comes on the screen. The spit on his teeth shines, even in the dark. Seeing what kind of woman he really likes, black-haired as a gypsy and with a juicy mouth, I change all my plans. My eyes, too, must turn up on the ends and when I bend down my breasts must fall forward and push at each other. When the star does that in the picture, the cowboy rubs his mustache low in the front of her neck.

In the darkness, Monty takes my hand and holds it in his swelling lap. To me it seems funny that my hand, brown and crusty from hoeing and chopping, is harder than his. I guess you don't get calluses rolling a motorcycle throttle. He rubs his thumb up and down my middle finger. Oh, I would like to ride fast behind him, spraddle-legged, with my arms wrapped on his belt, and I would lay my face between his sharp shoulder blades.

That night, when I've slept awhile, I hear something brushing the rug in the hall. I slip to my door. It's very dark. I press myself, face first, to the wood. There's breathing on the other side. I feel I get fatter, standing there, that even my own small breasts might now be made to touch. I round both shoulders to see. The movement jars the door and it trembles slightly in its frame.

From the far side, by the hinges, somebody whispers, "Vi-oh-LETTE?"

Now I stand very still. The wood feels cooler on my skin, or else I have grown very warm. Oh, I could love anybody! There is so much of me now, they could line up strangers in the hall and let me hold each one better than he had ever been held before!

Slowly I turn the knob, but Flick's breathing is gone. The corridor's empty. I leave the latch off.

Late in the night, when the noise from the kitchen is over, he comes into my room. I wake when he bumps on a chair, swears, then scrabbles at the footboard.

"Viii-lut?"

I slide up in bed. I'm not ready, not now, but he's here. I spread both arms wide. In the dark he can't tell.

He feels his way onto the bed and he touches my knee and it changes. Stops being just my old knee, under his fingers. I feel the joint heat up and bubble. I push the sheet down.

He comes onto me, whispering something. I reach up to claim him.

One time he stops. He's surprised, I guess, finding he isn't the first. How can I tell him how bad that was? How long ago? The night when the twelfth grade was over and one of them climbed with me all the way home? And he asked. And I thought, *I'm entitled.* Won him a five-dollar bet. Didn't do nothing for me.

But this time I sing out and Monty says, "Shh," in my ear. And he starts over, slow, and makes me whimper one other time. Then he turns sideways to sleep and I try my face there, laid in the nest on his damp back. I reach out my tongue. He is salty and good.

Now there are two things too big for my notebook but praise God! And for the Mississippi, too!

There is no good reason for me to ride with them all the way to Fort Smith, but since Tulsa is not expecting me, we change my ticket. Monty pays the extra. We ride through the fertile plains. The last of May becomes June and the Arkansas sun is blazing. I am stunned by this heat. At home, night means blankets and even on hot afternoons it may rain and start the waterfall. I lie against my seat for miles without a word.

"What's wrong?" Monty keeps asking; but, under the heat, I am happy. Sleepy with happiness, a lizard on a rock. At every stop Monty's off the bus, bringing me more than I can eat or drink, buying me magazines and gum. I tell him and Flick to play two-handed cards, but mostly Flick lectures him in a low voice about something.

I try to stop thinking of Memphis and think back to Tulsa. I went to the Spruce Pine library to look up Tulsa in their encyclopedia. I thought sure it would tell about the Preacher, and on what street he'd built his Hope and Glory Building for his soul crusades. Tulsa was listed in the *Americana*, Volume 27, Trance to Venial Sin. I got so tickled with that I forgot to write down the rest.

Now, in the hot sun, clogged up with trances and venial sins, I dream under the drone of their voices. For some reason I remember that old lady back in Nashville, moved in with Harvey and his wife and their three children. I hope she's happy. I picture her on Harvey's back porch, baked in the sun like me, in a rocker. Snapping beans.

I've left my pencil in the hotel and must borrow one from Flick to write in my book. I put in, slowly, "This is the day which the Lord hath made." But, before Monty, what kind of days was He sending me? I cross out the line. I have this wish to praise, instead of Him, the littlest things. Honeybees, and the wet slugs under their rocks. A gnat in some farmer's eye.

I give up and hand Flick his pencil. He slides toward the aisle and whispers, "You wish you'd stayed in your mountains?"

I shake my head and a piece of my no-color hair falls into the sunlight. Maybe it even shines.

He spits on the pencil point and prints something inside a gum wrapper. "Here's my address. You keep it. Never can tell."

So I tear the paper in half and give him back mine. He reads it a long time before tucking it away, but he won't send a letter till I do — I can tell that. Through all this, Monty stares out the window. Arkansas rolls out ahead of us like a rug.

Monty has not asked for my address, nor how far uphill I live from Spruce Pine, though he could ride his motorcycle up to me, strong as its engine is. For a long time he has been sitting quietly, lighting one cigarette off another. This winter, I've got to learn smoking. How to lift my hand up so every eye will follow it to my smooth cheek.

I put Flick's paper in my pocketbook and there, inside, on a round mirror, my face is waiting in ambush for me. I see the curved scar, neat as ever, swoop from the edge of one nostril in rainbow shape across my cheek, then down toward the ear. For the first time in years, pain boils across my face as it did that day. I close my eyes under that red drowning, and see again Papa's ax head rise off its locust handle and come floating through the air, sideways, like a gliding crow. And it drops down into my face almost daintily, the edge turned just enough to slash loose a flap of skin the way you might slice straight down on the curve of a melon. My papa is yelling, but I am under a red rain and it bears me down. I am lifted and run with through the woodyard and into the barn. Now I am slumped on his chest and the whipped horse is throwing us down the mountainside, and my head is wrapped in something big as a wet quilt. The doctor groans when he winds it off and I faint while he lifts up my flesh like the flap of a pulpy envelope, and sews the white bone out of sight.

Dizzy from the movement of the bus, I snap shut my pocketbook.

Whenever I cry, the first drop quivers there, in the curving scar, and then runs crooked on that track to the ear. I cry straight-down on the other side.

I am glad this bus has a toilet. I go there to cool my eyes with wet paper, and spit up Monty's chocolate and cola.

When I come out, he's standing at the door with his fist up. "You all right, Viii-lut? You worried or something?"

I see he pities me. In my seat again, I plan the speech I will make at Fort Smith and the laugh I will give. "Honey, you're good," I'll say, laughing, "but the others were better." That ought to do it. I am quieter now than Monty is, practicing it in my mind.

It's dark when we hit Fort Smith. Everybody's face looks shadowed and different. Mine better. Monty's strange. We're saying goodbyes very fast. I start my speech twice and he misses it twice.

Then he bends over me and offers his own practiced line that I see he's worked up all across Arkansas, "I plan to be right here, Violet, in this bus station. On Monday. All day. You get off your bus when it comes through.

Hear me, Viii-lut? I'll watch for you?"

No. He won't watch. Nor I come. "My schedule won't take me this road going back. Bye, Flick. Lots of good luck to you both."

"Promise me. Like I'm promising."

"Good luck to you, Vi-oh-LETTE." Flick lets his hand fall on my head and it feels as good as anybody's hand.

Monty shoves money at me and I shove it back. "Promise," he says, his voice furious. He tries to kiss me in the hair and I jerk so hard my nose cracks his chin. We stare, blurry-eyed and hurting. He follows Flick down the aisle, calls back, "I'm coming here Monday. See you then, hear? And you get off this bus!"

"No! I won't!"

He yells it twice more. People are staring. He's out of the bus pounding the steel wall by my seat. I'm not going to look. The seats fill up with strangers and we ride away, nobody talking to anyone else. My nose where I hit it is going to swell — the Preacher will have to throw that in for free. I look back, but he's gone.

The lights in the bus go out again. Outside they bloom thick by the streets, then thinner, then mostly gone as we pass into the countryside. Even in the dark, I can see Oklahoma's mountains are uglier than mine. Knobs and hills, mostly. The bus drives into rain which covers up everything. At home I like that washing sound. We go deeper into the downpour. Perhaps we are under the Arkansas River, after all. It seems I can feel its great weight move over me.

Before daylight, the rain tapers off and here the ground looks dry, even barren. Cattle graze across long fields. In the wind, wheat fields shiver. I can't eat anything all the way to Tulsa. It makes me homesick to see the land grow brighter and flatter and balder. That old lady was right — the trees do give out — and oil towers grow in their place. The glare's in my eyes. I write in my notebook, "Praise God for Tulsa; I am nearly there," but it takes a long time to get the words down.

One day my papa told me how time got slow for him when Mama died. How one week he waded through the creek and it was water, and the next week cold molasses. How he'd lay awake a year between sundown and sunup, and in the morning I'd be a day older and he'd be three hundred and sixty-five.

It works the other way, too. In no time at all, we're into Tulsa without me knowing what we've passed. So many tall buildings. Everybody's running. They rush into taxis before I can get one to wait for me long enough to ask the driver questions. But still I'm speeded to a hotel, and the elevator yanks me to a room quicker than Elijah rode to Heaven. The room's not bad. A Gideon Bible. Inside are lots of dirty words somebody wrote. He must have been feeling bad.

I bathe and dress, trembling from my own speed, and pin on the hat which has traveled all the way from Spruce Pine for this. I feel tired. I go out into the loud streets full of fast cars. Hot metal everywhere. A taxi roars me across town to the Preacher's church.

It looks like a big insurance office, though I can tell where the chapel is by colored glass in the pointed windows. Carved in an arch over the door are the words "HOPE OF GLORY BUILDING." Right away, something in me sinks. All this time I've been hearing it on TV as the Hope *and* Glory Building. You wouldn't think one word could make that much difference.

Inside the door, there's a list of offices and room numbers. I don't see the Preacher's name. Clerks send me down long, tiled halls, past empty air-conditioned offices. One tells me to go up two flights and ask the fat woman, and the fat woman sends me down again. I'm carrying my notebook in a dry hand, feeling as brittle as the maypop flower.

At last I wait an hour to see some assistant — very close to the Preacher, I'm told. His waiting room is chilly, the leatherette chairs worn down to the mesh. I try to remember how much TB and cancer have passed through this very room and been jerked out of people the way Jesus tore out a demon and flung him into a herd of swine. I wonder what he felt like to the swine.

After a long time, the young man calls me into his plain office — wood desk, wood chairs, shelves of booklets and colored folders. On one wall, a colored picture of Jesus with that fairy ring of light around His head. Across from that, one of His praying hands — rougher than Monty's, smoother than mine.

The young man wears glasses with no rims. In this glare, I am reflected on each lens, Vi-oh-LETTE and Viii-lut. On his desk is a box of postcards of the Hope and Glory Building. *Of* Glory. *Of* Glory.

I am afraid.

I feel behind me for the chair.

The man explains that he is presently in charge. The Preacher's speaking in Tallahassee, his show taped weeks ahead. I never thought of it as a show before. He waits.

I reach inside my notebook where, taped shut, is the thick envelope with everything written down. I knew I could never explain things right. When have I ever been able to tell what I really felt? But it's all in there — my name, my need. The words from the Bible which must argue for me. I did not sit there nights since Papa died, counting my money and studying God's Book, for nothing. Playing solitaire, then going back to search the next page and the next. Stepping outside to rest my eyes on His limitless sky, then back to the

Book and the paper, building my case.

He starts to read, turns up his glitter-glass to me once to check how I look, then reads again. His chair must be hard, for he squirms in it, crosses his legs. When he has read every page, he lays the stack down, slowly takes off his glasses, folds them shining into a case. He leaves it open on his desk. Mica shines like that, in the rocks.

Then he looks at me, fully. Oh. He is plain. Almost homely. I nearly expected it. Maybe Samuel was born ugly, so who else would take him but God?

"My child," the man begins, though I'm older than he is, "I understand how you feel. And we will most certainly pray for your spirit . . ."

I shut my eyes against those two flashing faces on his spectacles. "Never mind my spirit." I see he doesn't really understand. I see he will live a long life, and not marry.

"Our Heavenly Father has purpose in all things."

Stubbornly, "Ask Him to set it aside."

"We must all trust His will."

After all these years, isn't it God's turn to trust mine? Could He not risk a little beauty on me? Just when I'm ready to ask, the sober assistant recites, " 'Favor is deceitful and beauty is vain.' That's in Proverbs."

And I cry, " 'The crooked shall be made straight!' Isaiah said that!" He draws back, as if I had brought the Gideon Bible and struck him with its most disfigured pages. "Jesus healed an impediment in speech. See my impediment! Mud on a blind man's eyes was all He needed! Don't you remember?" But he's read all that. Everything I know on my side lies, written out, under his sweaty hand. Lord, don't let me whine. But I whine, "He healed the ten lepers and only one thanked. Well, I'll thank. I promise. All my life."

He clears his long knotty throat and drones like a bee, " 'By the sadness of the countenance the heart is made better.' Ecclesiastes. Seven. Three."

Oh, that's not fair! I skipped those parts, looking for verses that suited me! And it's wrong, besides.

I get up to leave and he asks will I kneel with him? "Let us pray together for that inner beauty."

No, I will not. I go down that hollow hall and past the echoing rooms. Without his help I find the great auditorium, lit through colored glass, with its cross of white plastic and a pinker Jesus molded onto it. I go straight to the pulpit where the Preacher stands. There is nobody else to plead. I ask Jesus not to listen to everything He hears, but to me only.

Then I tell Him how it feels to be ugly, with nothing to look back at you but a deer or an owl. I read Him my paper, out loud, full of His own words.

"I have been praising you, Lord, but it gets harder every year." Maybe that sounds too strong. I try to ease up my tone before the Amens. Then the chapel is very quiet. For one minute I hear the whir of many wings, but it's only a fan inside an air vent.

I go into the streets of Tulsa, where even the shade from a building is hot. And as I walk to the hotel I'm repeating, over and over, "Praise God for Tulsa in spite of everything."

Maybe I say this aloud, since people are staring. But maybe that's only because they've never seen a girl cry crooked in their streets before.

Monday morning. I have not looked at my face since the pulpit prayer. Who can predict how He might act — with a lightning bolt? Or a melting so slow and tender it could not even be felt?

Now, on the bus, I can touch in my pocketbook the cold mirror glass. Though I cover its surface with prints, I never look down. We ride through the dust and I'm nervous. My pencil is flying: "Be ye therefore perfect as your Heavenly Father is perfect. Praise God for Oklahoma. For Wagoner and Sapulpa and Broken Arrow and every other name on these signs by the road."

Was that the wrong thing to tell Him? My threat that even praise can be withheld? Maybe He's angry. "Praise God for oil towers whether I like them or not." When we pass churches, I copy their names. Praise them all. I want to write, "Bless," but that's *His* job.

We cross the cool Arkansas River. As its damp rises into the bus and touches my face, something wavers there, in the very bottom of each pore; and I clap my rough hands to each cheek. Maybe He's started? How much can He do between here and Fort Smith? If He will?

For I know what will happen. Monty won't come. And I won't stop. That's an end to it.

No, Monty is there. Waiting right now. And I'll go into the bus station on tiptoe and stand behind him. He'll turn with his blue eyes like lamps. *And he won't know me!* If I'm changed. So I will explain myself to him: how this gypsy hair and this juicy mouth is still Violet Karl. He'll say, "Won't old Flick be surprised?" He'll say, "Where is that place you live? Can I come there?"

But if, while I wait and he turns, he should know me by my old face . . . If he should say my name or show by recognition that my name's rising up now in his eyes like something through water . . . I'll be running by then. To the bus. Straight out that door to the Tennessee bus, saying, "Driver, don't let that man on!" It's a very short stop. We'll be pulling out quick. I don't think he'll follow, anyhow.

I don't even think he will come.

One hundred and thirty-one miles to Fort Smith. I wish I could eat.

I try to think up things to look forward to at home. Maybe the sourwoods are blooming early, and the bees have been laying-by my honey. If it's rained enough, my corn might be in tassel. Wouldn't it be something if God took His own sweet time, and I lived on that slope for years and years, getting prettier all the time? And nobody to know?

It takes nearly years and years to get to Fort Smith. My papa knew things about time. I comb out my hair, not looking once to see what color sheddings are caught in the teeth. There's no need feeling my cheek, since my finger expects that scar. I can feel it on me almost anywhere, by memory. I straighten my skirt and lick my lips till the spit runs out.

And they're waiting. Monty at one door of the terminal and Flick at another.

"Ten minutes," the driver says when the bus is parked, but I wait in my seat till Flick gets restless and walks to the cigarette machine. Then I slip through his entrance door and inside the station. Mirrors shine everywhere. On the vending machines and the weight machines and a full-length one by the phone booth. It's all I can do not to look. I pass the ticket window and there's Monty's back at the other door. My face remembers the shape of it. Seeing him there, how he's made, and the parts of him fitted, makes me forget how I look. And before I can stop, I call out his name.

Right away, turning, he yells to me "*Viii*-lut!"

So I know. I can look, then, in the wide mirror over a jukebox. Tired as I am and unfed, I look worse than I did when I started from home.

He's laughing and talking. "I been waiting here since daylight scared you wouldn't . . ." but by then I've run past the ugly girl in the glass and I race for the bus, for the road, for the mountain.

Behind me, he calls loudly, "Flick!"

I see that one step in my path like a floating dark blade, but I'm faster this time. I twist by him, into the flaming sun and the parking lot. How my breath hurts!

Monty's between me and my bus, but there's time. I circle the cabstand, running hard over the asphalt field, with a pain ticking in my side. He calls me. I plunge through the crowd like a deer through fetterbush. But he's running as hard as he can and he's faster than me. And, oh!

Praise God!

He's catching me!

Hitchhiker

She woke that morning angry about something — perhaps a dream? — she could not recall. Her tongue was dusty. She drank two glasses of water with the aspirin. Belching the bitter gas of coffee, she threw her breakfast dishes into the sink and promised herself *no more parties.*

No more losing sleep to hear stupid people talk for a hundred years about things that did not matter. To her, to them, to anybody. No more diluting bad parties with gin and bourbon; after midnight she'd have swallowed gasoline had someone poured it in her glass. Now her whole body was nasty with alcohol. Black slime and swamp gas.

She wrapped herself in dark clothes, stepped into flat shoes, and carried her books to the car, which smelled of rubber and the skin of dead animals. The steering wheel was dimpled underneath to fit her grip. Yet there was no place she wanted to go, least of all to the next city to work. She opened the car door and spat onto the greasy cement a wad of the snot which had leaked into her mouth. Then she pulled out of the garage and hooked her car onto a row of others on the highway, like a link on a chain.

The party. Max had explained Wall Street to her, especially "futures," where men bought abstract bacon they did not want delivered, which — indeed — did not exist; and then sold it again. A lawyer discussed the importance of making demands no court would grant so cases could be settled nearer his real demands. All evening she had crossed and recrossed Max's living room like a languid billiard ball, thumping in one group against Catholicism and the Pill, in another the need of the Vietnamese peace talks to have square or round tables, and in a third an argument about the Apollo space flight around the moon. Someone insisted the astronauts, once out of sight, wheeled patiently in space and sent back false reports as a boost to the nation's self-esteem. An advertising man, it was claimed, had promoted the whole idea of faking three wise men aloft at Christmas. "Oh, for Christ's sake!" she'd said — to a bearded student who turned out to be in seminary.

The string of cars reached the four-lane interstate route, and she pulled out to pass a long metal line. The wind rushed and subsided in a series of gasps as she went by, swung uphill free of them, and turned left onto the narrow road which would take her thirty miles to the Research Company, Inc., where all day she would sit in a frosted-glass box and type polysyllables.

She reached for the plastic jar of aspirins she kept in a niche by the windshield and chewed three. Lyons Motor Court, with its neon lion. The Bar-B-Q Barn. Then she was into wooded countryside on a looping, slow highway the trucks and salesmen avoided, and she could slow down and watch the pines come toward her, split, and pass on both sides. The sun through the window glass melted her flat on the seat, and the regular slap of her tires on the asphalt lines made her drowsy. A young woman tried to wave down a ride, but she did not stop.

Ahead of her, the solid concrete bridge across the first river split at the last minute into two walls, and swept by. There was a woman atop the hill with her thumb out; she wore a red dress. She appeared, tiny in the rear-view mirror, like a blood spot in an egg.

She turned on the car radio. The *Pueblo* had been released by North Korea. American negotiators explained it was necessary to confess the *Pueblo* was a spy ship in order to free the crewmen. The apologetic statement was read over the air, along with its repudiation. As she turned off the news, she saw another woman hitchhiker, also in red, but older than the others. She did not want to get to work, and drove more slowly. The lumps on the steering wheel were sculpted in the wrong places and would not fit between her fingers. She clasped and unclasped her damp palms.

Her name was Duffy. Rose Marie Duffy, although only the last name appeared on the plastic breastpin the gate guard handed her every morning at the plant. She dreaded the pin, the baked parking lot. She dreaded walking down the halls, passing executives who would say, "Good morning, Miss . . ." and squint at her chest before they added, "Duffy." Especially she dreaded all that today, for Friday had been a busy day, and she had bent a key on her typewriter. Friday she had been typing a report in the usual way and had glanced down at the center row of lettered tabs on which her fingers rested as lightly as moths. She could have typed them blind, in the dark, after a hundred years of being away from typewriters. ASDFG might as well have been tattooed across her left knuckles. HJKL; on the right. And suddenly, like a message springing up from heretofore invisible ink, she had read on her own skin, "Ass, Duffy. Go Home, Jekyll." She stared at the — anagram, was it? Cryptogram? Hallucination? Then she had to type the whole page over after jamming the keys. After that the bottom row of keys set up a buzzing hum in her ears. "ZXCVBNM, ZXCVBNM," they said, like beetles.

She stared at the face of the typewriter, and then read in the first two rows:

> Queer tie, you hope
> As daffy go highjinkle

No, that second line was wrong. "As differ gherkin jackels." She started over with the top row of letters. "Kew wert? Why, you, I hope!" Despairing, Duffy felt if she had only known Latin she could have made all twenty-six letters arrange themselves into three lines, like a litany, and it would have been comforting to whisper to herself.

But that was on Friday, and by now Duffy would not have cared if one swipe to clean the typewriter keys had brought forth steam and a genie. She would not have been very much surprised, either.

She drove through Pitchfield, a village with three stores and a bankrupt movie house which had been for sale two years or more. Beyond the town, Negroes lived on each side of the highway in paired rows of black, weathered houses. There were fifty children living on each side of the road, and every time she passed they were all in their front yards, yelling across her car to their counterparts on the other side. Their voices made her feel rained-upon. She passed now their gray church, parked even on weekdays with used cars. Someone was catching a nap behind the church, wrapped in a red cloth and curled on a mat of pine needles.

Duffy drove upward, the land pulling, to the hilltop from which she would see the second river. Every morning she looked forward to the view, as the river wound out of a pasture and forest, churned by a little island it had spit up, and fell down a low man-made waterfall just beyond the bridge. In the fall, the far hillside ran red and gold, and in spring the first leaves made it misty with color that wasn't green yet but soon would be. Now it was green, dulled by the August drought. Duffy rolled up her windows, for the river was the urinary tract for five paper mills and its waters stank.

Then — had she planned it? — she crested the hill, swept down, and at the last minute jerked the wheel to the right and drove straight down the rocky bank into the river.

The current was sluggish and she had no difficulty turning in to it, the brown water halfway up her windows, and heading downstream. It was a great relief to drive at the river's speed, so that she went between the shrouded banks instead of seeing them pour headlong toward her face, and separate reluctantly to let her car pass through. She leaned back and read the dashboard of her car: "Temp," "Fan," and "Def," it said, "Oil," "Gen," and "Speed." The words matched the tune of the Navy Hymn, "Eternal Father, Strong to Save," and she liked them much better and sang as she sailed. The doors were leaking, but she had lived so long with leakage that the rivulets seemed an artistic pattern, streaking the car's lining with an abstract design. The motor gurgled, drank deep, and ended. Duffy laid her head against the seat, watching shadows fall on the water ahead of the car and pour through the windshield, cool on her face. She closed her eyes and could still see them, through her eyelids, like clouds.

When she fell asleep, she dreamed she was working in her cubicle at the Research Company. She had misspelled some long and rippling word. When she erased it, a space appeared in the paper like a small transparent window. Curiously, she scrubbed the eraser on another word and it turned to air. In her dream she laughed, erasing the entire page, paper and all, until there was nothing left but some rubber shavings and, tattooed in midair, a translucent watermark.

When she awoke, the car had beached itself on a sandbar. Her door was jammed and she felt like a biscuit in an oven. Duffy rolled down the window and beat on the hot metal side. She could see nothing but the brown river, forest on both sides. She took off everything but her underwear and wriggled painfully out the window, feet first. She dropped ankle-deep in the yellow sand.

The sandbar was round, not much larger than the car itself. It rose above the water like a bald head with a few tufts of grass around the rim. Duffy circled it, but there was nothing to see except the thick woods. She waded out on the narrow side, but the water rose swiftly and she scrambled back ashore. She tried the horn, but it only sighed. Then she stood by the driver's seat, hands on wet hips, and yelled for help. Because she felt there was something orderly about it, she screamed from the trunk of the car, the other side, the grille, and sent her need radiating in four directions. She lay in the sun and waited for help to come.

At sundown, a fisherman in a motorboat, headed upstream, spotted Duffy's car and picked her up. "I thought it was some TV commercial at first," he said with a laugh, turning the way he had come. "The car set down by a helicopter or something. And you in your underwear — well, what else could it be?" He laughed for miles downstream while Duffy huddled low in the boat, hugging herself and shivering. She wondered where the mosquitoes were. "It's a long ride," he said. "No houses here. People have left the river. I fish it every night, and there wasn't no car stuck out there yesterday. I tell you, I looked everyplace for the cameras."

The water stank so bad Duffy asked him how a fish could live in it, and he said none could; that was his job, rescue work. Getting them into the air. He ran his motor at speed and they flew through the water so fast that Duffy was dizzy. "My daddy used to fish," she said, but he couldn't hear her for the roar.

She was cold in the whipping wind. They seemed to be rushing from day into dark, and the river grew narrow as the trees and their long shadows leaned thicker from the banks. "How far is it? I'm cold." He stared straight ahead. If they struck a rock at this speed, she thought they'd both be thrown, flapping, like water birds. Like terrified water birds. That was a nice word, "terrified." She said it under her breath, because it was what she should have been when she drove off the bridge. Perhaps she could be it yet, by will.

"I hope we get there in time," said the fisherman. She did not know in time for what. They roared downstream a long way before the first lights were seen, a window there, a whole building ablaze. He cut their speed. In the dark she could see nothing but the isolated squares of light, some large, some no bigger than cat eyes.

He said, "You cold?" He handed her something, a garment, sleazy to the touch. Old taffeta, perhaps, or faille. It would not wrap her and she fumbled for its shape. A dress. She shook it out to find the neck and sleeves, then pulled it over her head.

"Now," he said, throwing one arm toward the lights which lay at random on either side. The water was a looping ribbon now, wide enough for two boats if they passed carefully. "I'll slow the speed," he said. "That's all I'm allowed to do. You try to get somebody to see us."

Duffy stood up, spread the skirt with her palms. She waved at the windows and lamps and lights as they went by. The dress was red. She wavered to keep from falling overboard, threw out both arms, and yelled, and on both sides the towns and cities of the earth drove by.

The Mother-In-Law

I cross the alley which runs between the back of the neighborhood grocery and the back of *her* house. I believe it is 1932. Now softly to the lighted bedroom window to part the dry spirea twigs and see through the cloudy pane.

Already yellowing, she rests in the high bed and breathes through her mouth. She is barely forty and her heart does not want to stop; it beats against the cancer like a fist on a landslide.

They sit around her bed. Husband, three sons. Another long evening. They talk over the day like any ordinary family.

There is the youngest boy, Philip. Black eyes and silence. In ten more years, he will marry me.

She does not ask them the only question which still concerns her: Will you look after Ross? So they do not answer. If I could slip into the room and make her hear, I would whisper, "Yes, of course"; but she has never heard of me, and never will.

I am a ghost here and my other self is skipping rope in another state.

Snow on the alley. Nathan, the eldest, hangs back. He feels responsible for everything he sees, and started living through a long lens at an early age. Ahead of him, Ross is scraping fingers in the snow, slinging handfuls behind him. My future husband walks sideways, so he can look ahead and watch Ross at the same time. He lacks Nathan's sense of duty; with him, all is instinct.

They come to the rear of the grocery store, where trucks unload at the ramp and fermenting produce is piled in cans. Since the woolen mill closed, the cans rattle all night. People trot up the alley carrying tow sacks.

With his good arm, Ross makes a snowball spatter on their empty garage. The car has been sold. Nathan tries to decide whether the thump disturbs their mother. My husband throws snow, too, and makes his ball fall short. By instinct.

Nathan stops, points. Above the loading ramp, the grocer has installed two poles with electric lights which will shine directly on the garbage cans. Now the boys must keep their window shades pulled at night to avoid recognizing the fathers of friends.

They turn in the sagging wire gate to their back yard. Under the snow lie *her* crowded iris; the stalks of uncut chrysanthemums rattle when Ross limps through. Nathan reaches out to help him across a drift. Before he can grasp the hand, my future husband has dropped snow down Ross' back; they roll and tussle. Philip gets wetter. A draw — Ross laughs. I am watching the scene with my own hand out; if I were to change this or that?

They walk through my transparent arm and climb the back steps. The pattern is set.

Mr. Felts has asked the grocer not to burn his big lights all night long. "They shine in her window." She sleeps so little now, even with medicine. All night he hears the "sooo — soooo" as she sucks breath through her clenched teeth.

The grocer says the police advised it. His windows, door locks are being broken. Obliquely he blames Mr. Felts for the Depression, because he is an accountant and is still working the town's math when its weaving machines have stopped.

The grocer's son ran a machine. "I better leave them on."

Mr. Felts fastens her window shade with thumbtacks. Still the gold leaks in. The shine frightens her; she knows the back alley has never been bright. If there is a fire, Ross will not be able to get away.

Again Mr. Felts begs the grocer. Those who raid the garbage cans do it hastily now, half blinded, in a clatter. She hears; she sucks air faster. One night a metal lid rolls down the entire alley and spins out with a twang against the corner curb. She — who never missed church until this illness — cries out about Ezekiel's chariot.

Next morning, in full sight of the neighborhood, Mr. Felts heaves bricks at the light until both bulbs are broken. He wants to throw one at the grocer, too, but Nathan stops him.

March. When they come home from the funeral, Ross hurries to the bedroom. He does not understand she will not lie there anymore. Only Nathan was old enough to see inside the box. He takes Ross now onto the back steps and speaks for a long time about death and Heaven. Ross hits him.

In her bedroom, their father pulls outward gently on the shade. One by one, the thumbtacks pop onto the floor like buttons off a fat man. My husband smiles when he sees this; my ghost smiles. How I am going to love him!

Crying at last, Ross slams the back door and screams his name.

"Come here," Philip says. "Help me pick up these tacks."

Ross was born with a bad arm and leg. One eye is fixed and useless; there is slight vision in the other. While there was money, the Felts saw many doctors. Casts and splints were used; his night brace banged the bars of the crib when he dreamed.

His spectacles are plain glass and thick glass, so his brain seems to be bulging out through the magnified eye which strains to see shapes, light, and shadow. Ross is intelligent and, thanks to *her*, well adjusted. She must have bitten her tongue half off the day he climbed onto the garage roof. How her throat swelled shut the first of the hundred times he fell downstairs. But she was successful. All boys fall, Ross thinks.

Summer evenings there was baseball in the vacant lot by the grocer's. Ross batted like a spider, ran bases like a crab. The boys' laughter sounded to him like comradeship. In the bull pen Nathan made sure it was. Philip told me these things.

Now that I have Philip's children, I know how many bloody noses she iced in the pantry. I go into that pantry and watch her from behind the flour bin. She is thinking about the first lumps which have bent her nipple. I understand why she's sure they are harmless; it is not her *turn* for cancer. At night I tap my foot silently by the green chair while she searches her Bible. I'm not a Bible reader myself. I like the Greek myths. She reads St. Paul.

Staring at the green chair, where in more than a decade my other self will sit, she almost meets my eyes, almost pledges to accept any unbeliever who will care for Ross.

"I'm going to be pretty and red-haired," I say — she doesn't care.

"In bed, Philip and I . . ." She can't be bothered.

She dreams beyond me of how Ross kicked against her womb with a foot that could not have been withered. It was Achilles' foot.

Nathan, the dutiful son, has brought her daisies, which she puts absently into a vase. I beg her: Look at my Philip now. He carries no flowers but his black eyes — does she see? Now she embraces Ross and, over his crooked shoulder, gazes deeply at her other sons. She cannot help it; she has begun to bargain. Will they? Can they? Has she prepared them to?

Harmless as marbles, the fragments of her death shift in her breast and another, smaller, rolls in the womb that sheltered Ross and the others. I, Nathan's wife, their children, ours — we hear the bits roll as she looks though time and our faces.

She lets Ross go; the moment passes, will exist in no one's memory but hers and mine.

In 1942, Nathan becomes an army officer. Philip is in high school, unaware that in another state I am in love with a basketball center who owns his own car. We park in it, too; I evade his long arms. Philip's ghost sits in the back seat. I sense him there. I am uneasy, dimly suspecting he exists, fearing his shade is nothing but my frigidity.

This is the year Mr. Felts has almost finished paying the cost of her futile treatment — X-rays and pills — the headstone. He shrinks as the bills shrink; his flesh seems to drain away toward hers. Philip says, "You rest, I'll read tonight." Ross is a college freshman. They take turns with his texts.

The grocery store has been torn down and a warehouse built. Its lights shine day and night, and light up the place in her yard where the iris roots have reared up to lie on the ground like a tumble of potatoes.

At fifteen, I go away to girls' camp in the Blue Ridge Mountains. My parents can afford it. Across the same lake, their church holds summer retreat. Mr. Felts has brought the two younger boys because he promised her. In the dark, Philip smokes secretly after hours and stares over the black water at the lights of the camp where I am sleeping. I can't see what Mr. Felts is doing.

Once, on my horse, I ride across the place where Philip and Ross have had a picnic; they have just gone; maybe no more than a rhododendron bush keeps us from meeting.

Up the hill as they walk away, Ross is asking, "Isn't it time you got interested in girls?"

Now it's time. I go to college in his town. I am eighteen, so ignorant and idealistic that the qualities overlap and blend. My grades are good. I think I will become a social worker and improve the world. I sign up to read for blind students.

(Here I must pause. The ghost of my English teacher protests such melodrama, such coincidence. I, too, protest it. I am a tool of the plot, a flat character rung in on the proper page. I say — with Iphigenia — thanks but no thanks! The blade comes on.)

In no time at all, I move from knowing Ross to knowing Philip. I recognize him. He looks like his mother. While we are falling in love, we take Ross everywhere with us. He can ride a gentle mare, swim an awkward backstroke. In the balcony, we explain movie scenes if the dialogue is vague. He hardly notices when we kiss or touch each other. One night, drunk and tired of trying to work out marriage plans, we let Ross drive down a country road — screaming directions, "Right!" and "Left!" — till all three of us hurt from laughing. I kiss Philip so hard my own teeth bite me.

Secretly, Ross talks to me about wanting girls. I repeat it to Philip, whose black eyes go blacker. Nathan is mailing long letters home about how Ross should save himself for his bride.

In spite of what the basketball center said, I am not frigid. Lost at last under Philip, Philip lost in me. In the silence afterward, the ghost of Ross. We get up and dress and go find him and take him for a long walk. Coming home, we sit with our backs against the warehouse, singing. Soprano, tenor, baritone, under the blazing lights.

We marry and the war ends. Ross has a job running a machine he can pedal with one foot. With his checks he buys radios and phonographs. Every morning, Mr. Felts cooks him Cream of Wheat.

Philip and I live over a beauty shop. The smell of hot hair has got into our linens. Philip finishes college; Nathan comes home and begins.

Saturday nights I go to her house and cook a big pot of spaghetti. I am pregnant with our first. Philip is independent and we have refused to cash my parents' checks, which have grown smaller anyway.

I wash the dishes in her sink. Did she cook spaghetti here? Ross likes it. Yes.

Late in the evening when my back aches, I leave the men talking and lie across her bed. They have painted the window sill, but its frame is neatly pocked where the shade was nailed down. I lie there fearful for my child. I ask her: What were the earliest signs? Did you vomit much? Take vitamins?

But she has slipped into the room where Ross and the others are playing cards.

Our daughter is almost ready for kindergarten. The next one is walking and throwing toys; the third sleeps through the night at last. I have got used to the beauty-shop smell.

The telephone rings. Ross says, "I came in? The coffee wasn't fixed?"

I call to our bedroom, "Philip?"

In my ear the telephone: "I can't find where he's gone."

"I'll come," Philip says.

They find Mr. Felts in the furnace room. The shovel is under the coal, and he has gone down around its handle like a wilted vine. His heart tried to get out; all is stained.

We bring Ross home to our four rooms. Afterward I visit her empty house. Where are you, Mr. Felts? What was it like for you? Why did you never say?

Silence. He was as still as Philip is.

Ross lives with us now. Nathan fills out his income tax. He buys insurance policies for Ross. He never forgets a birthday and they ask Ross to dinner once a month. Nathan's daughters go to orthodontists and reducing salons.

I carry four baskets of laundry up these stairs instead of three. Our children like bread pudding. All four are healthy, make noise, eat a lot. They will have straighter teeth when the second set comes in.

Philip works too hard. Some Saturday nights he sits in the kitchen and drinks whiskey alone until his own limbs seem crippled. I have to help him down the hall. "Something worrying you?"

"What could be worrying me?"

I have stopped asking. What he cannot say, I must not. Mostly we talk over our days like any ordinary family.

Sometimes when our bedspring has stopped squeaking, I can hear Ross's squeak. Do the children hear? What will we do when they are too old to share his room? He never complains of the sweat when the vaporizer steams all night and I come in and out with aspirin. Sometimes he sits up in bed to smoke and wait. I'm afraid he'll set the mattress afire some night when I sleep through the smoke.

"Let me light you a cigarette," he always offers.

I always let him. Philip says Ross needs to give us something back.

Lung cancer? I never say that aloud. Secretly, I flush the butt down the toilet.

"I've got more," Ross always calls pleasantly when I come back into the hall.

Now, while the children sleep and Ross sleeps among them and I sit down at last to wait for Philip to come from his overtime work, somebody rattles my garbage can; somebody breathes on my glass, looking in. Somebody's glance like a blaze of light gets under my shade.

I am mending *his* shirt. I am forty, like *her*.

I say to the black windowpane: Yes, we are. Go away.

She understands and her gaze burns past to where Ross still sleeps in a brace in the crib she bought. I understand her, too. Even on weary nights, I am glad her desire found me, drew me to this room.

He's just fine, I say. He will live a long life.

Then, for one icy moment, the ghost of her envy stares at the ghost of mine.

Beasts of the Southern Wild

...I have been in this prison a long time, years, since the Revolution. They have made me an animal. They drive us in and out our cells like cattle to stalls. Our elbows and knees are jagged and our legs and armpits swarm with hair.

We are all women, all white, bleached whiter now and sickly as blind moles. All our jailers, of course, are black.

So much has been done to us that we are bored with everything, and when they march me and six others to the Choosing Room, we make jokes about it and bark with laughter. I am too old to be chosen — thirty when I came. And now? Two hundred. It is not clear to me what has happened to my husband and my sons. Like a caged chicken on a truck, I have forgotten the cock and the fledglings.

We file into the Choosing Room and from dim instinct stand straighter on the concrete floors and lift our sharp chins. The Chooser sits on an iron stool. Negro, of course, in his forties, rich, his hair like a halo that burned down to twisted cinders. Jim Brown used to look like him; there's a touch of Sidney Poitier — but he has thin lips. I insist on that: thin lips.

They line us up and he paces out of sight to examine our ankles and haunches. He will choose Wilma, no doubt, who still has some shape to her and whose hair is yellow.

The Chooser steps back to his seat and picks up our stacked files and asks the guard a few soft questions while a brown finger is pointed at first this one of us and then that. This procedure is unusual. The dossiers are always there, containing every detail of our past lives. Usually they are consulted only after the field has been narrowed and two finalists checked for general health, sound teeth.

He speaks to the guard, who looks surprised, then beckons to me. The others, grumbling, are herded out and I am left standing in front of the Chooser. He is very tall. I say to his throat, "Why me?" He taps my dossier against some invisible surface in the air and goes out to sign my contract.

"You're lucky," says the guard through his thick lips.

I am beginning to be afraid. That's strange. I've been beaten now, been raped, other things. These are routine. But something will change now and I fear any changes. I ask who the man is who will take me to his house for whatever use he wants, and the guard says, "Sam Porter." He takes me out a side door and puts me in the back seat of a long car and tells me to be quiet and not move around. And I wait for Sam Porter like a mongrel bitch he has bought from the pound.

When the alarm rang, she dragged herself upright and hung on to the bookcase. She loved to sleep — a few more seconds prone and she'd be gone again, with the whole family late for work and school. She balanced on one foot and kicked Rob lightly in the calf. "Up, Rob. Rob? Up!"

Fry bacon, cook oatmeal, scramble eggs, make coffee. There was a tiny box, transistorized, under her mastoid bone. All day long it gave her orders, and betweentimes it hummed like a tuning fork deep in her ear. Set table. Bring in milk and newspaper. Spoons, forks. Sugar bowl, cream.

She yelled, "Breakfast!"

Nobody came and the shower was still running. Down the hall both boys quarreled over who got to keep the pencil with the eraser. When the shower stopped, she yelled again, "Breakfast!" (I'm Rob's transistor box.)

Her husband and sons came in and ate. Grease, toast, crumbs, wet rings on the table. Egg yolk running on one plate, a liquefied eye. If thine eye offend thee, pluck it out.

"Don't forget my money," Michael said, and Robbie, "Me, too."

"How much you need?" She counted out lunch money, a subscription to *Weekly Reader*. Rob said he'd leave the clothes at the cleaners, patted her, and went off to the upholstery shop. She drove the boys to school, then across town to the larger one where she taught English, Grade 12, which she liked, and Girls' Hygiene, which she despised. It was November, and the girls endured nutrition charts only because they could look ahead to a chapter on human reproduction the class should reach before Christmas.

Today's lesson was on the Seven Basic Foods, and one smartmouth, as usual, had done her essay on eating all of one type each day, then balancing the diet in weekly blocks. The girl droned her system aloud to the class. "So on Wednesday we indulge in the health-giving green and yellow vegetables group, which may be prepared in astonishing variety, from appetizing salads to delicious soups to assorted nourishing casseroles."

None of the students would use a short word when three long ones would do. They loved hyperbole. Carol Walsh wanted to say, "There's no variety, none at all," but this was not part of their education. She was very sleepy. When she looked with half-closed eyes out the schoolroom window, the landscape billowed like a silk tapestry and its folds blew back in her face like colored veils.

In the hall later, a student asked, "Miz Walsh? What kind of essay you want on Coleridge? His life and all?"

"No, no. His poetry."

"I can't find much on his poetry." The boy was bug-eyed and gasping, helpless as a fish. Could't find some library book to tell him in order what each line of the poems *meant*.

She said, "Just think about the poems, George. Experience them. Use your imagination." Flap your wings, little fish. She went into English class depressed. There was nothing to see out this window but a wall of concrete blocks and, blurred, it looked like a dirty sponge.

"Before we move to today's classwork, I'm getting questions about your Coleridge essay. I'm not interested in a record of the man's biography. I don't even want a paper on what kind of poet he might have been without an opium addiction." A flicker of interest in the back row. "I want you to react to the poems, emotionally. To do what Coleridge did, put your emphasis on imagination and sensibility, not just reason." She saw the film drop over thirty-five gazes, like the extra eyelids of thirty-five reptiles. "Mood, feeling," she said. The class was integrated, and boredom did the same thing to a black face as to a white.

The Potter girl raised her hand. "I've done a special project on Coleridge and I wondered if that would count instead?"

Count, count. They came to her straight from math and waited for the logarithms of poetry. Measure me, Miz Walsh. Am I sufficient?

She said, "See me after class, Ann. Now, everybody, turn in your text to the seven poems you read by Thomas Lovell Beddoes." They whispered and craned in their desks, although the section had been assigned for homework. Dryly she said, "Page 309. First of all, against the definition we've been using for the past section, is Beddoes a romantic poet?"

Evelina dropped one choked laugh like a porpoise under water. Romantic, for her, had only one definition.

"Ralph?"

Ralph dragged one shoe on the floor and stared at the scrape it left. "Sort of in between." His heel rasped harder when she asked why. "He was born later? There's a lot of nature in his poems, though." He studied her face for clues. "But not as much as Wordsworth?"

His girl friend raised her hand quickly to save him and blurted, "I like the one that goes, 'If there were dreams to sell,/What would you buy?'" In the back, one of the boys made soft, mock-vomit noises in this throat.

After class Ann Potter carried to the front of the room and unrolled on the desk a poster of a huge tree painted in watercolor. Its roots were buried in the soil of Classicism and Neoclassicism: "18th Century,". it said in a black parenthesis. Dryden, Swift, and Pope had been written in amongst the root tangle. James Thomson vertically on the rising trunk. Then there were thick limbs branching off assigned to Keats, Shelley, Byron . . .

When Ann smiled, she showed two even rows of her orthodontist's teeth. "This sort of says it all, doesn't it, Miz Walsh!"

"You could probably be a very successful public schoolteacher."

"It's got dates and everything."

"Everything." Blake's *Songs of Innocence* branched off to one side, where Byron would not be scraped in a high wind. "Tintern Abbey." There was a whole twig allotted to "Kubla Khan."

"I thought you might count this equal to a term paper, Miz Walsh. I mean, I had to look things up. I spent just days on it."

"Ann, why not write the paper anyway? Then this can be extra credit if you need it." She'd need it. There was nothing in her skull but filtered air, stored in a meticulous honeycomb.

"My talents lie more in art, I think. I had to mix and mix to get just that shade of green, since England's a green country. I read that someplace. The Emerald Isle and all. I read a lot."

"It's a very attractive tree."

For last period, Carol Walsh gave a writing assignment; they could keep their textbooks open. Compare Beddoes and Southey. She sat at her desk making bets with herself about how many first sentences would state when each man was born. I'm good at dates, Miz Walsh. That Poe *looks* crazy. Well, Blake had this vision of a tiger, burning bright. He was this visionary. And he wrote this prayer about it.

That night she graded health tests until she herself could hardly remember what part of the digestive tract ran into what other part and whether the small or the large intestine came first. She chewed up an apple as she worked, half expecting its residue to drop, digested, out of her left ear. Who knew what a forbidden fruit might take it in its — in *her* head to do?

"You're going to bed this early?" Rob glanced up from the magazine he was skimming during TV commercials.

"Not to sleep. Just to rest my eyes. Leave the TV on. I might decide to watch that movie." She got into bed and immediately curled up facing the wall. She was drowsy but curious, not ready for sleep; and there was nothing on television to compare with the pictures she could make herself. The apple had left her teeth feeling tender, and she had munched out the pulp from every dark seed, cyanide and all. Once she'd read of a man who loved apple seeds and saved up a cupful for a feast and it killed him.

She smiled when the story started.

. . . The car is moving. Its chauffeur is white, a free white who could buy off his contract. Sam Porter has said nothing. He does not even look at me but out the window. For years I have seen no city streets and I long to get off the floor and look, too; but he might strike me with that cane. A black cane, very slim, with a knob of jasper. The tops of buildings glimpsed do not look new. It's hard to rebuild after revolutions.

We stop at last. I follow him through a narrow gate, bordered with a clipped yew hedge. A town house, narrow and high, like the ones they used to build in Charleston. This one is blue. A white man is raking in the tulip beds — spring, then. I had forgotten. Sam Porter walks straight through the foyer and up the stairs and shows me a bedroom. "Clean up and dress." He opens a closet with many dresses, walks through a bathroom and out a door on the far side. So. Our rooms adjoin. Mine seems luxurious.

I do not look at myself until I am deep in the soapy water. My body is a ruin. No breasts at all. I can rake one fingernail down my ribs as if along a picket fence. The flesh which remains on my legs is strung there, loose, like a curtain swag. I am crying. I soak my head but lice do not drown; and finally I find a shampoo he has left for me which makes them float on the water and speckle the ring around the tub. I scrub it and wash myself again.

The dresses are made of soft material, folded crêpes and draped jerseys, and I do not look so thin in the red one, although it turns my face white as a china plate. He may prefer that. I wonder if there is a Mrs. Porter; I hope not. They have grown delicate since the war and faint easily and some of the prison women have been poisoned by them. I pin up my wet hair and redden my lips, so thin now I no longer have a mouth, only a hole in my jaw. He knocks on the door. "We'll eat. Downstairs." His voice is very deep. I have lived so long with the voices of women that his sound makes a bass vibration on my skin.

Practicing the feel of shoes again, I go down alone to find him. The table is large, linen-covered. I am set at his right. There's soup and a wine. It's hard not to dribble. The white housekeeper changes our plates for fish and a new wine. She looks at me with pity. She must be sixty-five. Where is my mother keeping house? At what tables do my sisters sit tonight?

"Carol Walsh," he says suddenly, looking down as if he can read me off his tablecloth.

The wine has changed me. "Sam Porter," I say in the same tone, to surprise him. He lifts his face and his forehead glistens from heat on its underside. His eyes are larger than mine, wetter, even the tiny veins seem brown.

"What do you expect of me?" I ask, but he shakes his head and begins eating the pale fish meat. I put it in my mouth and it disappears. Only the sweet taste but no bulk, and I am hungry, hungry.

After dinner he waves one hand and I follow him to a sitting room with bookshelves and dark walls. "Your file indicates you are literate, a former English teacher." He has no trouble taking down a book from a very high shelf. "Read to me. Your choice."

I choose Yeats. I choose "Innisfree" and "Sleuth Wood." To him I read aloud: "Be secret and exult/Because of all things known/That is most difficult." He sits in his big chair listening, a cold blue ring on his finger. I turn two pages and read, "Sailing to Byzantium."

When that is done, Sam Porter says, "What poem did you skip? And why?"

I have hurried past the page which has "Leda and the Swan." The lines are in my head but I cannot read them here: ". . . the staggering girl, her thighs caressed/By the dark webs . . ."

I say aloud, "I'll go back and read it, then," but the poem I substitute is "Coole Park," and he knows; he knows. He smiles in his chair and offers me brandy, which turns my sweat gold. He says, "You look well."

"Not yet. I look old and fresh from prison."

He rises, very tall, and does not look at me. "Shall we go up?"

I follow on the stairs, watching his thighs when he lifts each leg, how the muscles catch. He passes through my room and I follow; but he stops at the door to his and shakes his frizzed head. "When you come to me," he says, "it will not be with your shoulders squared."

He closes the door while I am still saying "Thank you." I cannot even tell if what I feel is gratitude or disappointment.

They drove Sunday afternoon to look at a new house in the town's latest subdivision. "Wipe your feet, boys," said Carol. The foyer was tiled with marbleized vinyl, and in the wallpaper mural a bird — half Japanese and half Virginian — flew over bonsai magnolias.

"If the interest rates weren't so damn high," Rob said, muffled in a closet. "That's one more thing George Wallace would have done. Cut down that interest."

"It's got a fireplace. Boys, stay off those steps. They don't have a railing yet."

"Bedrooms are mighty little. Not much way to add on, either. Maybe the basement can be converted."

There were already plastic logs in the fireplace and a jet for a gas flame. Their furniture, all of it old and recovered by Rob's upholsterers, seemed too wide to go through the doorways. He called to her from the kitchen, "Built-in appliances!" She could see the first plaster crack above the corner of the kitchen door. Rob had gone down into the basement and yelled for them to stay out, too many nails and lumber piles. "Lots of room, though," called his hollow voice. "I could have myself a little shop. Build a rumpus room?"

Carol stood in the kitchen turning faucets on and off — though there were no water lines to the house yet — and clicking the wall switches that gave no light. I could get old here, in this house. Stand by this same sink when I'm forty and fifty and sixty. Die in that airtight bedroom with its cedar closets when I'm eighty-two. By the time they roll me out the front walk, the boxwoods will be high.

"Drink of water?"

"Not working, Robbie. See?"

"Well, Michael peed in the toilet!"

"It'll evaporate," she said. They were handsome boys, and Robbie was bright. Michael had been slower to talk and slower to read; nothing bothered him. Robbie was born angry and had stayed angry most of his life. Toys broke for him; brothers tattled; bicycles threw boys on gravel. Balls flew past his waiting glove. Robbie could think up a beautiful picture and the crayons ruined it. She'd say to him, "Thinking's what matters," and doubt if that were true.

"We move in this house, I want a room by myself," he announced now, and punched at the hanging light fixture. "Michael's a baby. Michael wets in the bed."

In the doorway Michael stretched his face with all fingers and stuck out his dripping tongue and roared for the fun of it.

"Michael gets in my things all the time. He marked up my zoo book. He tore the giraffe."

Rob's head rose out of the stairwell. "No harm in asking the price and what kind of mortgage deal we could get. You agree, Carol? It's got a big backyard. We could build a fence."

"Could we get a dog?" Michael yelled.

Robbie pinched his arm. "I want my own dog. I want a big dog with teeth. I'll keep him in my room to bite you if you come in messing things up."

Carol made both boys be quiet, and in the car agreed the house was far better than the one they rented now. Rob smiled and swung the wheel easily, as if the car were an extension of his body, something he wore about him like familiar harness.

"I like that smell of raw wood and paint," he said. "Yesterday we had a nigger couch to cover, a fold-out couch, and it smelled so bad Pete moved it in the back lot and tore it down out there. Beats me why they smell different. It's in the sweat, I guess."

Robbie was listening hard from the back seat, and she was afraid tomorrow he would be sniffing around his school's only Negro teacher. "There's no difference," she said, putting her elbow deep in Rob's side.

"You college people kill me."

They drove in silence while she set up in her mind two columns: His thoughts and Hers. He was thinking how tired he was of a know-it-all wife, who'd have been an old maid if Rob Walsh hadn't come along, a prize, a real catch. With half-interest in his daddy's business just waiting for them. Gave Carol everything, and still she stayed snooty. Didn't drink, didn't gamble, didn't chase women — but by God he might! He might yet! He was two years younger. He was better-looking. He didn't have to keep on with this Snow Queen here, with Miss Icebox. Old Frosty Brain, Frozen Ass. Who needed it?

And Her thoughts, accusing. Who do I think I am? What options did I ever have? Was I beautiful, popular, a genius? Once when we quarreled, Rob said to me, "Hell, you've been in menopause since you were twenty." I'll never forgive him for that. For being mediocre, maybe; but never for saying that.

Turning in to their driveway, Rob said in a sullen voice, "You college people can't be bothered believing your noses. All you believe is books." He got out of the car and went into the house and left them sitting there.

Robbie said to his brother, "I warned you not to pee in that toilet."

After supper of leftover roast, Carol read the boys another chapter from *Winnie the Pooh*. When she had heard their flippant prayers and turned out the light, she stood in the hall and smiled as they whispered from bed to bed. I can love them till my ribs ache, but it still seems like an afterthought. She dreaded to go downstairs and watch the cowboys fight each other on a little screen, one in the white hat, one in the black.

While she was ironing Rob a clean work shirt for tomorrow, she wondered if there were some way she could ask Sam Porter about an odor without offending him. She decided against it.

. . . I have been here two weeks and Sam has never laid a hand on me. Yet I am treated like a favorite concubine. I dine at his table; he dresses me as though the sight of me gave him pleasure. The housekeeper mourns over what she imagines of our nights together. Every evening, I read to him — one night he asked for Othello just to laugh at my startled face. One other evening, he had friends over and made me play hostess from a corner chair. He encouraged me to join in the talk, which was of new writers unknown to me. One of the men — a runt with a chimpanzee's face — looked me over as if I might be proffered to him along with the cigars. Plainly, he could do better on his own. He made one harem joke, a coarse one, and jerked his thumb toward me and up. Sam Porter tapped him atop his spine. "Not in my house," he said. I was looking away, grinding my teeth. To me he said, "Sit straight. There's nothing in your contract which says . . . Some things you need not endure."

"He isn't worth my anger." Sam laughed, but the others worried and took him off in the front hall to offer advice.

Tonight as we sit down with our brandy, he says to me, "You were happy in the old days? As a woman?"

"Sometimes."

"My color and hair. Perhaps they disgust you?"

"No. Although in prison we were often . . . forced. I cannot forget those times."

"And you never had pleasure? From a black?"

"No. None. What shall I read tonight?"

"From yourself, perhaps? Or the women prisoners?"

"Not much," I say quickly, and, "Should we read some of the new things your friends like?"

"What subject did you choose for your Master's thesis?"

By now I know Sam Porter is no quick-rich, quick-cultured black. He is Provost at New Africa University, which I attended under its old name. And my dusty thesis must be stored there, in the prewar stacks. If he wished to know my subject, then he already knows it. I answer truthfully anyway, "John Donne."

He hands me a book of collected writings, from the library at school.

"Perhaps the early work?" I reach for it and my fingers graze his. His hand is warmer than mine — unscientific, I know; but I can feel old sunlight pooled in his flesh and my hand feels wintry by his.

I am sorry to have the book again. The blue veins on my hands are high as the runs of moles; when I held Donne last, I had no veins at all and my skin was soft. I was twenty-three then, and not in menopause, No! I felt isolated from all things and swollen with myself as a tree hangs ripe with unplucked fruit. I was ugly, if the young are ever ugly; and sat alone in the caves and tunnels of the library, at a desk heaped high with Donne's mandrake root. Sam Porter says, "When you tire of staring at the cover, perhaps you will read?"

"The Sunne Rising." I look to a different page and, perversely, read aloud, "I can love both faire and brown/Her whom abundance melts and her whom want betraies."

Sam is watching me; I feel it though I do not look up. Sometimes his eye lens seems wide as a big cat's, and it magnifies the light and throws it in perforations onto me. I swallow, read "Her who loves lonenesse best, and her who maskes and plaies." My voice is thin through my dry mouth. I ask Donne's question, "Will it not serve your turn to do as did your mothers?/Or have you all vices spent, and now would finde out others?/Or doth a fear, that men are true, torment you?"

When the poem is done, there is silence. He drinks his brandy; I drink mine; is it as warm going down inside him as in me? His glass clicks on the table. "You sit awhile. The brandy's there, and the book. I'm tired tonight."

I sit numb in my chair. He passes, then, with one swoop, bends down and touches my mouth with his, and his lips are not thin — not thin at all. He walks out quickly and I sit with the book and the snifter tight in my hands, for there is a smell; yes, it is sweetish, like a wilted carnation fermenting on an August grave. Even a mouthful of brandy does not wash out his scent. My lungs are rich with it. And I do not go upstairs for a long time, until Sam Porter is asleep in the other room.

All evening she had been marking the participles which hung loose in the Coleridge essays like rags; and all evening Rob kept interrupting her work. He talked of the new house and what their monthly payments would be if they took a ten-year mortgage, or twenty. Or thirty — like a judge considering sentence.

"I'm leaving that up to you," she said, trying to figure out on which page Ann Potter had changed Kubla Khan to Genghis Khan in her paper, "The Tree of Romanticism."

Rob said if she'd give less written work she wouldn't have to waste so much time marking papers. One of the themes — George's — appeared to be copied from an encyclopedia. Symptoms of opiate intoxication. There followed a list of Coleridge's poems. "These," George wrote, "show clearly the effects of the drug on his mind." She turned the page but there wasn't a word more.

Rob said, "If the federal goverment would just quit raising the minimum wage. How can I tell how much I'll earn in a year or two years, the way they eat into profits more and more? You know how much I got to pay a guy just to put chairs on a truck and drive them across town?"

"Umm." Ralph's paper was "Nature in Wordsworth and Coleridge" and how Wordsworth had more of it and wrote prettier.

"The harder I work, the more I send to Washington to keep some shiftless s.o.b. drawing welfare," Rob said, and rattled his newspaper. "And next year they raise my taxes to build back the big cities the bums are burning down. So everybody can draw welfare in new buildings, for Christ's sake. My daddy would turn over in his grave."

There's life, she thought, in the old boy yet. She read an essay on an albatross, a harmless bird feeding on fish and squid, and no need for anybody to fear it.

Rob was asleep when she marked the last red letter grades and slipped between the sheets like an otter going under the surface without a ripple. She lay wide-eyed in the dark. The streetlight shone through the window blinds, and threw stripes across their bed and her face. After a while she slid one hand under the covers and closed her eyes.

. . . Sam is sick. The doctor who came was the chimpanzee man and he pinched in the air at me — but I moved. There is something of me to pinch now, after Sam's food and his wines and my long, lazy days in his handsome house. The doctor says he has flu, not serious; and for two days I have been giving him capsules and citrus juices. The housekeeper sees I am worried and has lost all her pity. She turns her face from me when I draw near, as if my gaze would leave a permanent stain.

Last night I sat by his bed and read to him:

> *"Are Sunne, Moone, or Starres by law forbidden*
> *To smile where they list, or lend away their light?*
> *Are birds divorc'd, or are they chidden*
> *If they leave their mate, or lie abroad at night?"*

He fell asleep from his fever and I read alone and sometimes laid my hand on his blazing forehead. Against his color, my hand had more shape and weight than it has ever had.

Tonight he is much better and sips hot lemonade and listens with half his attention to old favorites. "Come live with me and be my love."

He asks once, "You don't sing, do you?"

"No."

He falls asleep. I tiptoe into my own room. Perhaps in the Choosing Room there is someone new, who sings. I pace on my carpet, John Donne's poems open on my dressing table like a snare. He hooks me with his frayed old line, "For thee, thou needst no such deceit/For thou thy selfe are thine own bait." I close the book; I spring his trap; I leap away.

In the mirror I see who I really am . . . my hair grown long and brown, my eyes brown, my skin toasted by the sun on Sam Porter's noonday roof. I will never be pretty, but this is the closest I have ever come, and I pinch my own cheeks and look at myself sideways. I have grown round again from eating at his table, and my breasts are distended with his brandy. I put on the red robe and walk softly into the next room. Sam sleeps, turned away from me, with one dark hand half open on the pillow as if something should alight in it.

I return to my room and brush out my hair. My body has a foreign fragrance — perhaps from these bottles and creams. Perhaps I absorb it from the air.

I pass through to the next room and drop my robe on the floor. I turn off the lamp and he is darker than the room. I slide in against his back, the whole length of him hot from fever. I reach around to hold him in my right hand. His is soft as flowers. He makes some sound and stirs; then he lies still and I feel wakefulness rise in him and his skin prickles. He turns; his arms are out. I am taken into his warm darkness and lie in the lion's mouth.

The bed shook and she opened her eyes and stared at the luminous face of the clock. Rob said, "You asleep?" She lay very still, breathing deep and careful, pressing her hand tight between her thighs as if to hold back an outcry. The air was thick with Old Spice shaving lotion — a bad sign. A hand struck her hip like a flyswatter. "Carol? You can't be asleep." The ghostly face of the clock showed 1 A.M. "Honey?"

She jerked her hand free just in time for his. "Ah," he said with satisfaction against her shoulder blades. He curled around her from behind. "Picked a good time, huh?" She moved obediently so it would be quickly done, and he rolled away from her and slept with one arm over hers like a weighted chain.

. . . Sam bends over the bed where I have been crying and now lie weary,

past crying. "Who was it, Carol? Tell me who it was?"

I roll my head away from him and he kisses one damp temple, then the other. He whispers, "This isn't prison anymore, hear me, Carol? No more endurance is required. Understand that. You are home, here; and that was rape. Whoever it was, I'll punish him."

I am a single bruise. "No." I run my hand under his shirt. "I didn't encourage him, Sam, I didn't. He broke in here — I was alone. I called for you. I never wanted him."

"If you do," says Sam, "I'll tear up your contract and let you go."

"No." I look in his eyes. "He was never my desire. An intruder. A thief. He forced himself on me. I swear it."

"Tell me one thing." He lies by me and his heat comes through the blanket. "Was he a white man?"

"Yes. He was white."

Gently he holds me, says, "I can have him killed, then. You know that. Did you know him?"

"I know his name. That's all we know, each other's names."

His hair is black and jumbled. "If you tell me his name, I can have him killed. But I won't ask you to do that. You must choose. You'll not be blamed if you choose silence." His hands are so pale on one side, so dark on the other.

"Rob Walsh," I whisper. "Rob Walsh."

"We'll hunt him down," he says, and gets up and goes downstairs.

He does not come back for hours and I wake near dawn to see him stripping off the black suit, the black mask, the black cloak. I sit up in bed. "It's done," he says, sounding tired, maybe sick. He comes naked and curly to me and falls away on the far side. "There's no love left in me tonight."

But I am there, my hands busy, and I can devour him; he will yield to me. The room is dark and he is so dark, and all I can see is the running back and forth of my busy hands, like pale spiders who have lived underground too long.

Burning the Bed

Isabel tapped lightly on her brakes to keep from ramming the long ambulance which was bringing her father home. Its taillights winked and the painted cross on the rear doors swayed down the clay road which had washed ragged with winter rains, then frozen in lumps and craters. Now the last snow had sunk into the soil. The mud was cold, rust-colored.

Isabel rolled down her car window, leaned out, pressed her horn. The ambulance turned left. One minute, Isabel thought. That's all it would take to check the mailbox. It seemed to her the aluminum door was cracked, that even as she drove by something white with her name on it could be seen. She braked harder, and the rear wheels floated slightly to one side on the slick mud.

"Goddamnit," she said aloud, pulling into the ruts left by the ambulance. She'd probably have to walk back for her letter, through the mire and after dark.

While she parked in the far corner of the yard, the hospital driver rocked back and forth, then swung in a slippery crescent and backed toward the front steps. Both attendants got out, opened the ambulance doors. Then they looked toward her car.

"I'm coming," Isabel said. She put her key in her pocketbook next to Brenda's postcard. She checked the hand brake.

When she was halfway to the house, the driver said, "If you'll just hold open the front door." Isabel did not like his tone.

Into the ambulance the other man said, "Get you right inside, Mr. Perkins."
They slid him out as carefully as a pane of glass. Isabel was looking down at his
head. A skull thrust through his face.

"How deep was the snow?" he said to them all. His smile looked raw. Isabel
was carrying his false teeth in her pocketbook.

"You rest, Papa."

"A couple of inches." The orderly moved to the foot of the stretcher,
looking at Isabel.

Quickly she said, "It's all gone now except in the shady places." She could
have gnawed off her tongue. Now, of course, he would want the men to carry
him around the north side of the house and show him those last patches.

"Papa!" she said, even while he was pointing. "Lay back and hush! Let's get
you inside. You'll catch your death of cold."

She ran ahead of the bearers onto the porch, held open the door. Her eyes
felt cold in her head, like silver spoons. She could have cried. Turning away,
she looked down the hall where they would carry him, through a doorway to
the old bed which filled the room like an abandoned river barge, washed up
askew and catty-cornered. The counterpane was turned back, the pillow as
white as a square of snow below the eaves, or somebody's flat grave marker.

The two men maneuvered the stretcher past, grazing her waist.

"That room straight ahead," Isabel said, standing thin against the wall. The
men did not like her. She could tell that.

Then they carried him beyond her, toward the bed where he had jerked
with joy when he fathered her, the same bed in which she had been wetly born,
and Jasper, too. Twice her father had stood and looked down into that bed at
what would survive him, and half the time he'd been wrong. Now he had a
month or two of dying to do in that mammoth bed. After that, Isabel thought,
she might burn the thing. Might leave it burning in the back field, below the
old orchard. Might fly through the smoke of it, headed north, and not even
look out the airplane window. She pressed her pocketbook where the
stretcher had touched her, and followed them down the hall. Brenda can help
burn it. Brenda wouldn't let me go through that funeral all alone. I doubt I can
carry the bed outside by myself.

They laid him down and drew the sheets to his chin. Isabel signed the slip
which said Marvin Perkins had been delivered with due care by the county
ambulance service. On the way out, the short man pulled a small jar of pear
preserves from his hip pocket. "Mama sent it," he said, and thrust it toward
Isabel's front. "She's in his church. She said he liked pear preserves."

Isabel caught the jar against her purse. She'd forgotten what Papa liked and
didn't like in the years she had been gone. Between now and Easter, she could

not learn it all again. She was more grateful for the information than the fruit. She wanted to smile at the man, but she was a head taller and he kept his face down.

She held out her hand to the big one. "I believe you were in school with my brother."

"I played basketball with Jasper." The handshake was quick. "Got boys of my own playing now."

"That's fine," said Isabel, though really she thought it was depressing. "Thank you both."

Her father had gone instantly to sleep, the way a tired child will when at last he is dropped someplace familiar. Isabel stopped with her mouth open on the cheery word there was no need to say. On the pillow, his face even looked like a child's face, one which had been slightly crumpled. There were only a few wisps of hair on the pale scalp. Isabel laid his false teeth on the bedside table. He snuffled juicily in his sleep, like a baby or a bulldog. If she hurried, she could be back from the mailbox before he even wanted supper. She set the pear preserves beside the teeth.

The telephone rang in the hall.

It was Papa's preacher. She craned to see the clock. "Yes, he's asleep right now." Isabel felt through both pockets of her corduroy coat but could find no cigarettes. The preacher said something about food left on the kitchen table. By the church-women. Isabel said that was very nice. She braced the telephone on her shoulder and poured out her pocketbook and found cigarettes but no matches. "You'll tell them how much we appreciate it? Since I don't know the names? . . . Oh. Yes. Certainly."

Isabel made an ugly face at the framed picture of "Washington Crossing the Deleware" on the opposite wall. George, the boat, the tumbling waves: all painted in snuff, tar, nicotine. There was a pencil in the clutter from her bag and she wrote on the telephone book names the preacher spelled for her. With the eraser she poked Brenda's postcard into view. Cypress Gardens, for Christ's sake. "Yes." She thanked him again.

In the kitchen she found chicken broth and potato salad, two loaves of yeast bread, jars of beets and spiced apples, a bowl of ambrosia, a tall coconut cake on a cut-glass pedestal. They can't mean all that for a man who has cancer of the stomach, she thought. Most of that is for *me*. Deep in her throat there rose something smooth and solid, like a hard-boiled egg. They must have seen the coffee cups stacked in the sink, maybe even smelled the sticky glasses. What do I care if they poked through the kitchen? At home, Brenda won't even let me make toast.

Isabel poured the broth into a small pan, set it on the front burner of the stove, and looked at it. Globes of fat skated on the surface as if they were alive. Pushing the other food to one end of the table, she took her stationery box from a chair seat. There was a pack of matches inside with her pen. She wondered if the Baptist women had opened her stationery box and read the letter which still lay inside, face-down. She took out the two sheets and, lighting a cigarette and clicking her pen, read what she had written.

Dear Brenda,

Here I am in this ghastly hospital; I wish you could see it. No matter what waiting room I pick, somebody always sits beside me with a running sore, a bloody bandage, or a scar on his face where the skin was burned and snatched off. They don't get sick here, they get hurt. Axes and car jacks and hunting accidents. Even Papa still thinks it was carrying hay bales and feed that gave him his cancer. First he got hernia and then the hernia got mean.

But today they're sending Papa home and I have to feed and nurse him to death. I do believe in mercy killing, I do. How could you watch this day after day and not believe in it? But if I had that power I don't know where I would stop. Two perfectly healthy boys have just walked through smelling of beer and motor oil, and I could poison them both.

I can't tell yet when I can come home. You can't imagine how far away from you I feel. This is some other planet. Papa's preacher is in and out, talking in whatever his language is — it can't be English. I never liked it here and it's worse now, at my age, when I've been living my own life so long. Nights I've been leaving the hospital to sleep in that house I never wanted to live in anymore. It's cold and empty. Everything you do in it makes a loud noise and everything Papa owns is made of tin and falls down in the night.

Nothing here is comfortable to me, and I don't mean the old plumbing or the mattresses that have fallen in. Even the parts of the house I thought I liked aren't there anymore. Four of us lived here and two are dead and one is dying, and it makes me nervous. The people who used this furniture don't use it anymore.

Isabel pinched off a piece of the cake icing and pushed it back in that space on her gum where a wisdom tooth should be. She drew a line across the page, deliberately sloping it upward in case Brenda should be looking for clues about her mood. Then she began to add in a firm, angular hand:

That reminds me of what I wanted to tell you about the bed.

She put out her cigarette. No point in pressing on with this letter when, even now, a long one from Brenda might lie in the mailbox. She buttoned her coat, hurried out the back door. As soon as she had gone halfway, Isabel began to fear Papa was calling, or the chicken broth had boiled all over the stove. She tried to run, mud spattering on her broad shoes and freckling her ankles. I must look like a grizzly bear, she thought, aching. The mailbox was empty.

She took her time walking back. Let him call. He'd be calling in an empty house if she was home in Baltimore where she belonged. Her shoes were such a mess she unlaced them at the back steps and left them there. The broth still waited over an unlit burner on the gas range. Isabel took off her coat. She ate a tablespoon of ambrosia. The linoleum was cold on her bare feet.

It was too soon to tell Brenda about the bed, how they could burn it together in the back field. At night. With Isabel pointing out the constellations. Save that for a surprise. Brenda would say, "What makes you think of such things!" And Brenda would giggle, carrying the slats out just the way Isabel said, and backing downstairs with her end of the stained old mattress.

Isabel sat down again to her letter. "That reminds me of what I wanted to tell you about the bed." She wrote:

Now we're at home and Papa's asleep in his big bed. I've moved it at an angle because the footboard is too tall to see over. God knows what makes Papa so cheerful, even about the snow he couldn't really see from the hospital. He's happy to have me here and says daughters will always come home when you need them. You know what a lie that is. But I want you to see this bed. It's a hundred years old, maybe two, and somebody built it out of trees cut down on the farm. It's put together with wooden pegs and they made it to last forever.

She got up and put some more ambrosia into a bowl and spooned it between sentences. There was a little sherry stirred into the juice.

Brenda, I wish you'd write more often. I need your letters. I don't see why you're going to the movies with Katherine Moose even if she is lonesome and has trouble getting her support checks. When did you ever have anything in common with Katherine Moose? (Which I mean as a compliment to you.) I thought you were going to make a decoupage table while I was gone, for the living room? After this house, I'll be glad to see something colorful. All Mama ever hung on these walls was that fellow hoeing in the fields, the Horse Fair, cathedrals, that St. Bernard in the woods with the children, George Washington, and Gainsborough's Blue Boy. All of them, even the blue boy, painted in brown gravy. I am so depressed. . . .

Papa was calling. Isabel flicked on the gas under his broth and hurried to the bedroom.

"Who's that?" he cried when she came in. More and more, Isabel thought, he comes out of sleep into a world he's half forgotten. Maybe the world was for him like this house to Isabel. Not even the good parts looking like they used to.

"It's Isabel," she said, as gently as she could. She knew her voice was too loud for a sickroom. The nurses had said so. Even the doctor whispered, while touching her father with rapid, hairy hands.

"Isabel? That you?"

"You're home." She eased to his side and laid one hand on his arm, to show she was real. If he asks about Jasper, I don't know what I'll say.

"You've got things fixed up real nice. Even the cobwebs swept down. You've not been washing this old woodwork?" He struggled higher on the pillow. Isabel shook her head. "It looks whiter. What time is it?"

"I'll bring you some soup. You never saw so much food. Mrs. . . . Mrs. Bradford. And two others. And somebody sent you pear preserves." She nudged the jar but he reached beyond it for his teeth in their gauze wrapping. "I'll get your supper now. You need anything first? You need the bedpan?" Isabel didn't know why she asked, since by now she knew he was like any other animal and did not defecate until after a meal. She and Brenda had an Airedale at home the same way. "You get your teeth in," she said, although he was already settling his jaws with a few bites of empty air.

She arranged his tray carefully by the bed, then sat in a chair where the high footboard hid him. She did not like to watch him eat. Tonight she looked at the room itself, improved somehow just because it had Papa to belong to. The wide floorboards had mellowed from years of traffic. Two braided rugs were faded gray. Under the bed the lint curled back, and softly under Mama's treadle sewing machine, behind her domed tin trunk stamped with flowers, then under the bureau with its three-foot mirror.

The mirror was in such a condition nobody was safe looking into it. Its surface had peeled and bubbled along jagged stripes of gold and gray. Isabel had glanced in it her first day home and discovered a face that, for all its broadness, looked frail and insane.

Neither she nor Papa could see themselves in the mirror now, after her struggle to move the furniture. Getting ready to bring him home, Isabel had lain in the big bed where he would lie, just to be certain. No need, she'd thought, for Papa to see how his skin had yellowed, his eyes shrunk away from their bony cups. Papa's fine black eyes lay now in their sockets like two butter beans. Isabel smiled. Brenda wouldn't know what a butter bean was. The Baptist women will bring some when Papa dies; Brenda can taste them then. She'll feel sorry for all I've had to bear these last weeks. She'll be sorry she didn't write more letters.

In front of the mirror on an embroidered spread was Papa's stopped cookie of a watch, two combs, shaving mug, brush. A china heart which held buttons, cuff links, and moldering tieclasps. In the bottom corners of the leprous mirror two photographs were stuck: one of Isabel, age 10, riding a mule; and of Jasper in his army uniform. She'd been tempted to put these in a drawer but decided she didn't have the right. From where Papa lay, they wouldn't look much larger than postage stamps.

Behind the high wall of his bed, Papa said, "How's it feel to be home? Not counting me sick and all?"

"Not the way I remember it," Isabel said. She was glad she could not see the way he siphoned up his soup.

"You never did come home much. You sure you can get off work this long?"

"I'm sure. I'm good at my job, you know."

"I hate costing you money. You was always tight about money, not like Jasper." The slurping stopped. He said, "And that's a good thing. Here you are, independent. No worries. Nobody telling you what to do. I'm that way myself."

He did not know how long ago his insurance money had been used up, couldn't guess how much Isabel had paid the hospital. With her cruise money. She and Brenda had meant to go to Greece this summer. She said, "Your preacher called, wants to come see you. I told him tomorrow morning. Get you over the trip. Get your strength up." She could not tell whether he laughed or choked.

Then at last the question she had dreaded. "When's Jasper coming?" He had already asked it once, just after the operation.

"Papa," she said, but he was ahead of her.

"That's right, Jasper's dead. It's the fault of the medicine. With the medicine I can't tell what time it is."

Isabel said it was seven o'clock. "Soon be time for . . . well, not for bed. For sleep."

"I don't mean clocks," he said crossly, and the dishes rattled when he put the tray on the table. "They's not a thing wrong with my mind and don't you forget it. The medicine flattens things out, that's all. It can send you into any year it damn well pleases."

Isabel thought this was not a good time to remind him to take another dose. She cleared the dishes, slid the bedpan under his blanket, and went to the kitchen to put food away. She carried her cigarettes to the back steps, because when he was awake smoke made Papa cough, and coughing made Papa hurt. The mud had hardened on her shoes like concrete. When she put them on, the earth dragged at her soles. She clumped around the yard. I told Brenda it was like another planet here. Even gravity pulls harder.

She could barely see the mailbox in the growing dark. Tomorrow, at least, one of Brenda's damned postcards. Brenda taught third grade in a private school for Jewish children, and all year long she made them bring in postcards showing vacation spots in fifty states. Brenda would never have to buy a postcard in her entire life. Especially being so stingy with them. So far, Isabel had only received Natural Bridge, Virginia, and the Cypress Gardens, both with a hole where they had once been thumbtacked to a display board. Both said much the same.

Busy at school. Had to get new battery your car. Hope things aren't too bad. Letter follows love Brenda. Can't write going to movie with Katherine but got your letter and will answer soon.

Isabel had jammed that one inside her pocketbook so hard the shiny surface folded and made a long crease up the Southern belle in her hoop skirt.

She flattened her cigarette with a weighted foot. When she padded in bedroom shoes to Papa's room, carrying the medicine bottle and spoon, he was already asleep and the bedpan waited for her on the table, as neatly covered with the napkin as a plate of cooling rolls. It won't be long, thought Isabel, before I'll be giving him a needle in his arm, the way the doctor showed me. "You've got a real knack for this," he had said when she plunged distilled water into the orange. "You'd have made a good nurse."

"I don't talk soft enough," Isabel had said.

She woke her father and made him take the medicine, though he swore he didn't need it tonight. They had an argument. In the end, she jammed the spoon into his mouth while he was still fussing, and made a small reddening dent on his upper gum. He pulled back, stiff, on the pillow and held the liquid in his mouth. His cheeks blew out like a squirrel's.

"You swallow that now," she said. He would not.

"I didn't mean to hurt you. Please swallow it down."

Still he lay rigid, his eyes black, neck hard, chin sharp.

She said, "Jasper would want you to take the medicine." Her father closed his eyes. The bulb jerked in his throat. His face relaxed. Isabel laid her hand on his forehead, but he would not move and he was not going to open his eyes. "Good night, Papa," she said trying to make her voice soft, and thinking,

Goddamn him, damn Jasper, damn Brenda, damn them all.

Jasper's bedroom was the most comfortable place in the old farmhouse and that was the only reason Isabel was sleeping there. A late addition, the room had electrical outlets in the baseboards and less bulky, gloomy furnishings. Jasper's old books still lined the shelves he and Papa had built, and she and Jasper had painted.

A broad map of Korea was tacked on one wall, a green peninsula touching the Sea of Japan, Manchuria, and the Yellow Sea. A snaky line of black crayon marked the places Jasper might have been, battles in which he might have fought. Papa had kept this record against the day Jasper came home to tell them everything. Near Wonju, the black line broke off. Once Jasper died, in February, 1951, the whole Eighth Army, the war itself, stopped dead and hung uncompleted on Jasper's wall.

Isabel looked at the fading map while she put on pajamas. She plugged in Jasper's reading lamp and ran one finger along his books. *Tom Swift*. Zane Grey. *Tarzan and the Jewels of Opar. Kidnapped. Wuthering Heights. Boy Scout Handbook*. Dog and horse stories. True stories of the F.B.I. *Tobacco Road. Dutchess Hotspur*. Frank Harris.

From the flyleaf of *Robin Hood,* she read the blurred lines scrawled across the treetops of Sherwood Forest:

> *You steal my book*
> *And I can tell*
> *You'll go to Hell.*
> *Marvin Jasper Perkins, Jr. Age 9½*

Sometimes on the map of her own mind Isabel tried to draw the rest of Jasper's life — to crayon him home across the Pacific, over the continent to Carolina, to some good Northern college on the G.I. Bill and what money Isabel would have given him. What was a cruise to Greece compared to that investment?

And now Jasper would be . . . forty-one years old, two more than Isabel was now. And they might be sitting here tonight, in Papa's house, waiting out Papa's death together.

She had always been larger than Jasper. By now he, too, would have added weight. Maybe his pale hair would have thinned, the capillaries begun to surface in his cheeks. Her income would have been higher than his — and how Jasper would have hated that! He'd have told her for the hundredth time to let her hair grow long. Isabel took a bottle of Scotch and a glass from a drawer.

They could have shared a drink, talked about things. About Brenda. About whoever Jasper might have had to talk about.

Papa called out. Isabel put her drink behind the photograph of Jasper in his high-school mortarboard. She went to the back bedroom, but he was asleep again from the medicine that could send him into any year it pleased.

"I'm still here, Papa," she said, just in case he could hear.

Then she went to bed.

. . . Jasper moves swiftly ahead of me through the thick forest. Sometimes he swings from vines; at others, he is simply thrown lightly from one great tree to another. I am riding more slowly behind him on the ground, on the back of something shaped like a mule but much larger. Nearly the size of an elephant. I am happy, but I wish he would wait for me. We are going to a cleared space he knows, to build our house. He calls down to me that the Indians are coming. He calls down that we will need help in building our house. I am to choose some Indian to help us. Now I see the line of natives marching, a column in single file. All are women, very dark brown, young, healthy, as tall as the animal which carries me. They wear nothing but short skirts made of black feathers. I pick a girl I think Jasper will like. She looks very strong. Now I see another who resembles her; she says the two of them are sisters. Perhaps they are even twins. I decide to choose both girls to help us in the clearing where Jasper is waiting for me. . . .

When Isabel woke, the thick forest turned into a network of tree-branch shadows thrown by the morning sun on the walls and floor and across the four-legged bed. Her mouth was dry. Her head ached and seemed to be full of fungus. She got up, feeling tired, and put the Scotch back inside Jasper's bureau. She decided to wear her wool slacks because the preacher probably wouldn't like slacks.

She made Papa's oatmeal and soft-boiled egg and woke him. He looked into her face as if he had never seen it before.

She said it twice. "Time for breakfast."

His eyes slowly remembered what breakfast was. She put another pillow behind his head and shoulders. "Want you to eat early and get cleaned up. Your preacher's coming."

"Good morning, Isabel," he finally said. In a minute he smiled.

He ate as if he were really hungry. It depressed her to think of all that good food, falling down into that internal ruin. "You're not a bad cook, Isabel," he said, not noticing, as she did, the oatmeal spilling onto the sheets. "For somebody that always hated cooking. You fix your own meals in Baltimore?"

"Anybody can make oatmeal." She stored his empty suitcase in the closet, under the suit he would likely be buried in. "Maybe we'll have time to change those sheets."

"You should of got married," Papa said.

"I'm better off than plenty married people. Tomorrow you want a poached egg?"

"I never could stand an egg looked like it had just fell out of the nest. You really don't miss it? Your friends married and all?"

"My friends aren't married."

"You're not old yet. Maybe you're courting? You and your roommate go out much? You and Sheila?"

Isabel gave him the yellow capsule. "I haven't lived with Sheila for over a year now. Sheila turned out to be somebody I couldn't respect. I don't even see her anymore. Want some more water?"

"What are you getting so mad for? You and the new one, then. You find any bachelors to take you to supper?"

"Brenda. Her name is Brenda." She decided to brush the sheets off and leave them. Why make the preacher think a dying man was neat? "Anything else?"

"Open the window," Papa said. "Maybe it's started to smell like spring."

Isabel took the preacher to Papa's bedroom, waited politely while they talked about Easter, baseball, plans for the new church — none of which Marvin Perkins would live to see. She had never met so tactless a man as that preacher, and she stood behind the high footboard and made disapproving faces until even her scalp was tired. He kept right on telling Papa what a fine time the youth club would have camping by the river when it got warm, and how they'd moved the revival to August.

At last he began to read Scripture — which was all he was supposed to do in the first place, thought Isabel. He started the Sermon on the Mount, but Papa said he'd like something older than that, something sterner.

"I've got to like the Old Testament again," he said, sounding embarrassed, as if this were a breach of taste. "What I really like is the wars against the Philistines."

"I see." The preacher began leafing back.

"After Moses, though," said Papa. He settled back and spread his arms wide on the counterpane, palms up. Like a horizontal shrug. "I never thought it was right Moses got shut out of the Promised Land."

That would have tickled Brenda! The preacher began to read about armies, battles, the fear of the Lord. Isabel excused herself, took down her coat from its peg in the hall, and went into the yard, knocking clay off her shoes. The jonquils were already up, their buds like cartridges. There were red knots on the twigs of the maple she and Jasper had climbed. Jasper once climbed to the very top of that tree because it had been his ambition to spit down the house chimney; and he did, but he missed.

Through Papa's half-open window she could hear that the story was about Moab, the Canaanites, and Deborah the prophetess: ". . . for the Lord shall sell Sisera into the hand of a woman," the preacher read.

Isabel circled to the back yard. Here the orchard spread downhill to the back field, bottomland, winding creek. There were broken limbs still caught in the fruit trees, jelly-filled wounds in trunks where peach borers waited out the winter. Last year's caterpillar webs flapped on the cherries like wet old flags.

"You've quit tending the orchard?" She'd asked Papa that in the hospital, on some choking, long, steam-heated afternoon.

"Not much point after your mama died. Too much to eat raw, and nobody to make jam or cobbler." Talk of the orchard revived him, though he was very weak from surgery. "I never liked sprays and poisons. Used to go out and kill everything by hand. That way, a worm knew who it was and I knew who I was." His cheeks grew red as apples. At that time, the doctor was saying he would live either a day or two months, depending on which his heart decided and how fast his stomach ate itself. "It still blooms, though, down that whole hillside. Not as much fruit, but how it does bloom!"

Now she paced downhill, wondering if he would wait to see it blossom one more time, ducking her head under the limbs of the Bartlett pear. Bartlett was self-sterile; she'd heard him say you needed another variety to cross-pollinate. He'd set another pear far down the hill. Isabel looked for it, but all the bare trees looked alike at a distance.

When Papa's done with the bed, I'll burn it there. In the bottomland. Primitive ritual, I'll tell Brenda. Like putting a Viking to sea on his flaming barge. It'll be just pagan enough to suit an anti-Semite Jewess like Brenda. She'll shiver while she's laughing. "Isabel, there's nobody like you in the world!" she'll say. But she'll be uneasy about it, too, and we'll need a drink when we get back inside, in Jasper's room.

Then Isabel thought one more step: she saw herself home and telling the other women in their apartment building. Katherine Moose. And Rhonda. She imagined how easy it would be to boast, to repeat when she was drunk and maudlin. "So the country Baptists got the body to bury, but the real ceremony was mine. Father and offspring, just like that." Offspring. I could make a pun on bedspring if I was sober. And Brenda would echo the telling in mock horror. "I said, Isabel, you can't do that! But you know Isabel, she'd been down there till she needed to be *cauterized*, or something, so I took one end and . . ."

In the distance, Isabel heard the preacher's car. Hurrying to the house, she forgot to bend her head and some tree — the pear? — raked a limb through her short hair.

There was still no letter and that night Isabel tried to call Brenda Goldstein. The telephone in their Baltimore apartment was first busy, and later unanswered. She tried the number several times. When she finally got through at eleven-thirty, there seemed to be a party going on.

"Brenda? It's Isabel. What in the world is all that noise?"

"Turn that thing down. Hello?"

"I said it's Isabel! I've been calling for hours."

"I went to an art lecture. What's the matter? Has he died?"

Isabel was angry and said, too loud, "NO, HE HAS NOT DIED!" She wondered if Papa could have heard. "He's about the same. I just wanted to talk to you. I haven't had a letter for two weeks."

"Well, I mailed you one." A crowd was milling around that apartment, talking, laughing, shaking ice cubes.

"Listen, it gets lonesome down here." Isabel decided she must speak softer, much softer. She stared at George Washington, who seemed to her afloat in rapids of Scotch and seltzer. She eyed the canal in Venice on the other wall, painted in shades of bourbon whiskey thinned down with spit. "Listen," she hissed, "where were you all night long with me calling and calling?"

"I told you. I went with Katherine Moose to an art lecture."

Isabel said it sounded like they were having a goddamn party.

"Well, Ron's here from next door. And Sheila. We ran into Sheila at the museum."

Isabel paced up and down on the gleaming heart-pine boards. "It's all right for Rhonda to be there, but you know, Brenda, you *know* Sheila's not to set foot in that apartment! Brenda, you know that! As many times as I've said . . ."

"Yes," came a stiff, polite voice. "It was a *very* good lecture. Manet."

"Oh, Christ," said Isabel. "And Sheila just can't wait to see what changes you've made in the apartment. Rode her home in my car, I'll bet! I can imagine. She can't wait to tell you all my faults while I'm down here keeping a deathwatch. You hear me, Brenda? A deathwatch! I never thought the minute my back was turned . . ."

"Well, you try to get some sleep and not break your own health over it," Brenda said, and hung up.

Isabel couldn't sleep at all. She rolled from one edge of Jasper's bed to the other. She was almost grateful when Papa cried out with pain in the night, but the hurt was gone before she got to him. He was sleeping. The gray folds of skin under his neck hung loose. He breathed in and out, in and out.

I meant to offer him those pear preserves for supper, thought Isabel. I'd have thought of it if Brenda had stayed home where she belonged, and my mind had been easy. In and out he breathed. She moved her arm toward his tall mirror where reflected light showed up her wristwatch. Three-thirty. Isabel wound the watch. She did not look at her image.

She went into the hall and dialed, direct, the number of their apartment. Out of a dry and swollen mouth, Brenda said, "Hello?"

Isabel said nothing.

"Hello? Who is this?"

Isabel breathed heavily into the telephone. In and out. In and OUT.

"What number are you calling?" said Brenda.

(She's sitting up in bed now and reaching for her robe. She covers up with that fluffy robe even to talk on the phone. Her throat's probably scratching. In the morning her head will ache right over both mastoid bones. Oh, I know her. She'll look older than thirty-five in the morning, and there'll be lines on her face where the pillowcase wrinkled. . . .)

Shaking with the laugh she was holding back, Isabel blew two hard puffs of air into the mouthpiece.

Then she heard a second voice, a woman's voice, say, ". . . answers, just hang up."

There was a single click, then the long singing as emptiness rushed along the black highway, beside the asphalt road, by the rutted road, down the wires to Isabel, across the state of Virginia, humming inland over the muddy yard, into the house and through her ear and into her brain, like that old tent peg the Hebrew woman nailed through the brain of Sisera when he took refuge in her tent.

Still Life with Fruit

Although Gwen said three times she felt fine, the sister made her sit in a wheelchair and be rolled to the elevator like some invalid. Looking over her shoulder for Richard, she let one hand drop onto the rubber tire, which scraped heat into her fingertips. Immediately Gwen repeated on the other side, for her fingers felt clammy and disconnected from the rest of her.

"Your husband can't come up for a while, dear," said the sister, parking her neatly in one corner and pressing the Number 4 button. Sister was broad in the hip and wore a white skirt starched stiff as poster paper. "Are the pains bad?"

"No." Gwen sat rigid and cold, all the blood gone to her fingers. There was so much baby jammed toward her lungs that lifting her chest would have been ridiculous. Surely the sister knew enough to say "contraction," and never "pain." For some women — not Gwen, of course — that could be a serious psychological mistake.

Besides, they weren't bad. Maybe not bad enough. Gwen had no fear of childbirth, since she understood its stages perfectly, but to make a fool of herself with false labor? She'd never bear the embarrassment. To so misread the body's deepest messages — that would be like wetting one's pants onstage.

She said uneasily, "I hope they're not slowing down."

The sister's face grew briefly alert, perhaps suspicious. "When's your due date?"

Gwen told her ten days ago, and the sister said, "That's all right, then."

Maybe if Gwen were Catholic, the sister's face would seem kinder, even blessed. That led to the idea — quickly pushed aside — that had she been Catholic, bearing the first in a long row of unimpeded babies, the sister would like her better.

On Ward 4 she was rolled to a special room, told to put on the backless nightshirt and get into bed.

"And drink water. Drink lots of water," the sister said, took her blood pressure, and left her with a thermometer cocked at an angle in her mouth.

Gwen couldn't recall anything in the doctor's pamphlets about drinking water. Maybe in this hospital it was sanctified? She jerked both hands to her abdomen, relieved when it tightened and hardened the way Dr. Somers had been promising for months. She hoped this new pang was on schedule; Richard's watch was still on Richard's arm, downstairs. She felt no pain, since she was a well-adjusted modern who accepted her womanhood. Two months ago, however, she'd decided not to try natural childbirth, mainly because the doctor who advocated it was male. She was drifting then away from everything male. Lately she had withdrawn from everything, period. (The baby has eaten me, she sometimes thought.)

She climbed into the high bed, suddenly angry and alone, and discovered on the wall facing her a bronze statuette of Jesus wrenched on His cross, each shoulder drawn in its joint, His neck roped from pain, His face turned out with agony. It struck Gwen that Catholics might be downright insensitive. The Virgin Mary was one thing, but in this room on this day, this prince . . . this chaste bachelor on his way to God's bosom? To Gwen it seemed . . . well . . . tasteless.

Another sister recorded her 98.6 temperature and drew an assortment of blood samples on glass slides and in phials. She sucked these up through a flexible brown tube and Gwen wondered if she ever sipped too hard and got a mouthful. The sister also wrote down what Mrs. Gower had eaten and how recently, and made her urinate into a steel bowl. "You take a nap, till the barber comes," she said. And giggled.

But Gwen, crackling with energy, doubled her pillow behind her and sat nearly upright, wide eyes fixed on the wracked form of Jesus in a loincloth. They must have already cast lots for His seamless robe (down on the cool, gray hospital tile) but at this stage in the crucifixion no one had yet buried a spear point in His side. He was skinnier than Gwen had always pictured Him.

Ah, to be skinny herself! To sleep on her flat stomach, walk lightly again on the balls of her feet. To own a navel that would be a hole and not a hill! Gwen made herself bear down once, as if on the toilet. No effect at all. Too early.

The labor room, pale green, was furnished in buffed aluminum. Its single chair was dull metal, straight, uncomfortable. Her clothes had been hung in a green wall locker next to Jesus, including the linen dress with the 24-inch waist she hoped to wear home next week. On her bedside table was a pitcher of water and crushed ice, and a glass with a clear tube in it. She drank water as the sister had ordered. Maybe it wet down the sliding ramp where Junior, like some battleship, would be launched to the open sea. He felt to her like a battleship, plated turrets and stacks and projections, each pricking her own organs until they withdrew and gave him room. She sometimes felt as if her lungs had slipped slightly into each arm and her entrails been driven down her thighs.

The next nurse wore black religious garb, its hem nearly to the floor. With a black arm she set her covered tray on Gwen's mattress, said it was time for the first shave in Mrs. Gower's life, and flicked off the sheet. Gwen pressed into the pillow. She had never felt so naked — even after months of probes with gloved fingers and cold entries of the doctor's periscope. It must be a sign of her failing brain that one minute she saw her baby as a battleship; now there were periscopes thrust up his launching ramp. She had not thought clearly since that first sperm hit the egg and blew fuses all the way upstairs. Even her paintings showed it. Haphazard smears on canvas, with no design at all. Richard pretended, still, to admire them. He pretended the thought never crossed his mind that she might slice off one ear. She might have, too, if she could remember where the thing was growing.

It was the stare of a woman which embarrassed her. A religious. The young sister gazed with interest between Gwen's thighs as she made ready to repeat (here Gwen giggled) what Delilah did to Samson. She thought of asking the nun whether work in a maternity ward lent new appeal to chastity.

The nun said brightly, "Here we are."

"Here *we* are?" Gwen laughed again. I'm getting giddy. There must be dope in that water pitcher.

"You're very hairy." The sister couldn't be over twenty years old. Perhaps she was still apprenticed, a novice. Sleeping single in her narrow bed, spending her days with women who slept double and who now brought her the ripe fruits of God. Her face looked pure and pale, as if she were preparing to cross herself in some holy place. So it was a shock when she said, "All beautiful women are hairy. We had a movie star here once, miscarried on a promotion tour, and you could have combed her into ringlets."

Gwen could not match that, so she lay, eyes closed, while the dull razor yanked out her pubic essence by the roots. She could no longer remember how she would look there, bald. She could recall sprouting her first scattered hairs as a girl, each lying flat and separate. Sparse, very soft in texture. Now would she grow back prickly? Now, when she most needed to recapture Richard, would she scrape him like a cheese grater? Five o'clock shadow in the midnight place? When Gwen opened her eyes, it seemed to her Jesus had been nailed at just the right height to get a good view from His cross.

At last the sister's pan was black with sheep shearings. Black sheep, have you any wool? One for the unborn boy, who lives up the lane? Gwen drank more water while the sister took out the razor blade and wiped the last hairs on a cloth.

"When can my husband come?" asked Gwen. She felt her face pucker. "I don't have anything to read."

The sister smiled. "Maybe after the enema." She carried out her woolly pan. Maybe she stuffed sofa cushions. And the bloodletting nun reclined on them and sipped Type O cocktails through her soft rubber tube. Maybe a "hair shirt" really meant . . .

Why, I'm just furious! Gwen thought, surprised. I'm almost homicidal!

The nurse with the enema must have been poised outside the door. Gwen barely had time to test her shaved skin with shocked fingers. Plucked chicken butt. She ought to keep her fingers away — germs. Had she not just lately picked her own nose? Maybe she bore some deep, subconscious hostility against her baby!

She jerked her hand away and lifted her hips, as she was told, onto the rubber sheet. She refused the cheery conversation floating between her knees. Inside her the liquid burned. When she belched, she feared the enema had risen all the way. She might sneeze and twin spurts jet out her ears. She gasped, "I can't — can't hold it in."

Quickly she was helped across the room to the toilet cubicle. God, she would never make it. She carried herself, a brimming bowl, with the least possible movement. Then she could let go and spew full every sewer pipe in the whole hospital. Through the plastic curtain the nun said happily, "You doing just fine, Mrs. Gower?" Now *there* was psychology!

"O.K.," she managed to say. "Can my husband come now?"

"You just sit there awhile," said the nun, and carried her equipment to the next plucked chicken down the hall.

Disgusting how clean the bathroom was. Gwen was a bad housekeeper — as Richard's parents kept hinting — but she couldn't see why. She was always at work, twenty projects under way at once; yet while she emptied the wastebasket, soap crud caked in the soap dish and flecks of toothpaste flew from nowhere onto the mirror. Nor could she keep pace with Richard's bladder. The disinfectant was hardly dry before he peed again and splattered everything. Yet, enemas and all, this place was clean as a monk's or a nun's cell.

Gwen flushed the toilet but did not stand. In case. She had never felt so alone. Ever since she crossed two states to live in a house clotted with Gowers, she had been shrinking. The baby ate her. Now the baby's container was huge but Gwen, invisible, had no body to live in. Today she had been carried to the hospital like a package. This end up. Open with care.

"Ready for bed?"

She cleaned herself one more time and tottered out. The new nurse was in plain uniform, perhaps even agnostic. She set a cheap clock by the water pitcher. "How far apart are your pains now?"

Gwen had forgotten them. "I don't know." She was sleepy.

"Have you had any show?"

Gwen couldn't remember what "show" was. Some plug? Mucus. She didn't know. Was she expected to know everything? Couldn't the fool nurse look on the sheets and tell? She was probably Catholic, too, and her suit was in the cleaners.

"Your husband can visit a minute now. And your doctor's on the floor."

Gwen fell back on the skimpy pillow. She drowsed, one hand dropped like a fig-leaf over her cool pubis.

"How's it going?" Richard said. His voice was very loud.

"Going!" Gwen flew awake. "It's gone!" she said bitterly. "Gone down the toilet! I don't even have any phlegm left in my throat. All of it. Whoosh." Suddenly he looked a good five years younger than she, tanned, handsome. Joe College. He looked well fed, padded with meat and vegetables, plump with his own cozy waste from meat and vegetables. "Where in hell have you been?"

"In the waiting room." He yanked his smile into a straight line. "You having a bad time?"

She stared at the ceiling. "They shaved me."

"Oh." He gave a little laugh nearly dry enough for a sympathetic cluck. Give the little chicken a great big cluck. Ever since they'd moved in with his parents, Gwen had been the Outsider and Richard the Hypocrite. If she talked liberal and Mr. Gower conservative, Richard said nervously they shared the same goals. When he left mornings for work, he kissed her goodbye in the bedroom and his mother in the kitchen. If Gwen fixed congealed salad and Mother Gower made tossed fruit, Richard ate heartily of both and gave equal praise. Lately Gwen had been drawing his caricature, in long black strokes, and he thought it was Janus.

He said, "I never thought about shaving, but it must be necessary. The doctor can probably see things better."

Things? Gwen turned her face away. Cruelly she said, "It's probably easier to clean off the blood."

"Hey, Gwen," he said, and bent to kiss as much cheek as he could reach. She grabbed him. So hard it must have pinched his neck. Poor little man with a pinch on his neck! She stuck her tongue deep in his mouth and then bit his lower lip.

Uneasy, he sat in the metal chair and held her hand. "Whatever they're giving you, let's take some home," he said.

And go through this again? At first, in their rented room, she and Richard had lain in bed all day on Sundays. Sleeping and screwing, and screwing and sleeping. My come got lost in the baby's Coming. I don't even remember how it feels.

But Dr. Somers, when he came in, looked to Gwen for the first time viril and attractive. A little old, but he'd never be clumsy. For medical reasons alone, he'd never roll sleepily away and leave her crammed against the wall with a pillow still under her ass, swollen and hot. With Richard's parents on the other side of that wall, breathing lightly and listening.

She gave Dr. Somers a whore's smile to show him her hand lay in Richard's with no more feeling than paper in an envelope.

"You look just fine, Gwendolyn," he said. He nodded to Richard as if he could hardly believe a young squirt with no obvious merits could have put her in such a predicament. "We'll take a look now and see how far along things are. Mr. Gower?"

Richard went into the hall. She watched Dr. Somers put ooze on his rubber glove. Talking with him down the valley of uplifted knees seemed now more normal than over the supper table to Richard. She had lost her embarrassment with him. Besides, Dr. Somers liked art. He continued to talk to her as if the baby had not yet eaten her painting hand, her eye for line and color. As if there would still be something of Gwen left when this was over.

While he fumbled around in her dampness, he often asked what she was painting now, or raved about Kandinsky. When she first went to his office with two missed menstrual periods, she mentioned the prints hung in his waiting room. "Black Lines" was Dr. Somer's favorite — he had seen the original at the Guggenheim on a convention in New York.

Gwen had not told him when, in her sixth month, her own admiration settled instead on Ivan Albright. Her taste shifted to Albright's warty, funereal textures, even while her disconnected hand continued to play with a palette knife and lampblack dribble. The few times her brain could get hold of the proper circuits, it made that hand pour together blobs of Elmer's glue, lighter fluid, and India ink. *Voila!* Mitosis extended! She had also done a few charcoal sketches of herself nude and pregnant, with no face at all under the wild black hair, or with a face rounded to a single, staring eye.

Oh, she was sore where he slid his finger! Politely he nodded uphill toward her head. "Glaswell has a sculpture in the lobby, did you see it?"

"We came in the other door."

"I was on the purchasing committee. It's metal and fiberglass, everything straining upward. That answered the board's request for a modern work consistent with the Christian view of man." He frowned. "You're hardly dilated at all. When did you feel the last one?"

"I stopped feeling anything right after the enema."

He thrust deeper. "False alarm I'm afraid. But your departure date — when is it? I want you well rested before a long trip."

"In two weeks." Richard was being drafted. Once he left for the army, Gwen would take the baby home to her parents. The Gowers expected her to stay here, of course, but she would not. Last week she had given Dr. Somers all her good reasons, one by one. When the baby came, she planned to give them to Richard. And if he dared balk, she intended to go into a postpartum depression which would be a medical classic.

He laughed. "The baby's not following your schedule." His round head shook, and behind his thick glasses his eyes floated like ripe olives. "It's a false alarm, all right."

"But it happened just the way you said. An ache in the back. That cramp feeling. And it settled down right by the clock." To her humiliation, Gwen started to cry. "I'm overdue, goddamn it. He must weigh fifty pounds up there. What in hell is he waiting for?"

Dr. Somers withdrew and stripped off the glove. He looked at Jesus thoughtfully. He scrubbed his hands in a steel pan. "Tell you what, Gwendolyn. Stop that crying now. It's suppertime anyway; let's keep you overnight. A little castor oil at bedtime. If nothing happens by morning, I'll induce labor."

"You can skip the castor oil," Gwen said, sniffing hard. "It'll go through me like . . . like a marble down a drainpipe." She did not know how he might induce labor. Some powerful uterine drug? She pictured herself convulsing, held down by a crowd of orderlies and priests. "Induce it how?"

"Puncture the membranes," he said cheerfully. He looked so merry she got an ugly superimposed picture: boy, straight pin, balloons. "I'll just have a word with your husband."

An hour later, they demoted Gwen from the labor room and down the hall to a plain one, where she lay alongside a woman who was pleased to announce she had just had her tubes tied. "And these old Roman biddies hate it. Anybody that screws ought to get caught at it — that's their motto."

The Roman biddy who happened to be helping Gwen into bed did not even turn, although her face blotched an uneven red. Her cheeks ripened their anger as disconnected from her soul, as Gwen's painting hand was adrift from her brain. Among the red patches, the biddy's mouth said, perfectly controlled, "I wouldn't talk too much, Mrs. Gower. I'd get my rest."

The woman in the next bed was Ramona Plumpton, and she had four babies already. With this last one she'd nearly bled to death. "This is the best hospital in town, though, and I'm a Baptist. The food's good and it's the cleanest. No staph infections." Behind one hand she added, "I hear, though, they'll save the baby first, no matter what. That puts it down to a fifty-fifty chance in my book. Is this your first, honey?"

"Yes. They're going to induce labor so I can travel soon. My husband's joining the army." She hoped Richard would not mention false labor, not in front of this veteran.

"You're smart to follow him from camp to camp." Perhaps to counteract her hemorrhage, Mrs. Plumpton had painted rosy apples on each cheek. "The women that hang around after soldiers! You wouldn't believe it!"

Gwen thought about that. There she'd be, home with her beard growing out, while Richard entered some curly, practiced woman. Huge breasts with nipples lined like a pair of prunes. Like Titian, she arranged the woman, adjusted the light. She made the woman cock one heavy arm so she could stipple reddish fur underneath.

"Bringing it on like that, you'll birth fast," said Mrs. Plumpton. "A dry birth, but fast. I was in labor a day and a half with my first and I've got stretch marks you wouldn't believe. Calvin says I look like the tattooed lady."

Gwen assigned Mrs. Plumpton's broad, blushing face to the prostitute in Fort Bragg and tied off her tubes with a scarlet ribbon.

Richard came by but said he wasn't allowed to stay. He'd driven all the way uptown to bring Gwen some books — one of Klee prints and a *Playboy* magazine and three paperbacks about British murders. Gwen usually enjoyed multiple murders behind the vicarage, after tea, discovered by spinsters and solved by Scotland Yard.

He kissed her very tenderly and she stared into one of his eyes. The large woman was imprinted there already, peach-colored, her heart of gold glowing through her naked skin.

"It's very common and you're not to feel bad about it."

She touched Richard's mouth with her fingers. Did a dry birth have anything in common with dry sex? It sounded harder. She reached beyond him and drank a whole glass of water.

". . . Dr. Somers says there's nothing to it. I'll be here tomorrow long before anything happens."

"Now don't you worry," Gwen said, just to remind him what his duty was. She got down a little more water.

Richard said his parents, downstairs, were not allowed to visit. "They send you their love. Mom's getting everything ready."

Sweeping lint from under our marriage bed. Straightening my skirts on their hangers. She can't come near my cosmetics without tightening every lid and bottle cap.

"Mom's a little worried about induced labor. Says it doesn't seem natural." He patted her through the sheet. "They've both come to love you like a daughter."

When he had gone, Ramona Plumpton said, "Well, he's good-*looking*." It wasn't much, she meant, but it was something. "Between you and him, that ought to be a pretty baby. You want a boy or a girl?"

"Girl." They had mainly discussed a son, to bear both grandfathers' names. William Everest Gower. Suddenly she did want a daughter. And she'd tell her from the first that school dances, fraternity pins, parked cars — it all led down to this. This shaved bloat in a bed with a reamed-out gut.

She read until the nurse brought castor oil, viscous between two layers of orange juice. It made her gag, but she got it down.

For a long time she could not sleep. Too many carts of metal implements were rolled down the hall; plowshares rattled in buckets, and once a whole harvesting machine clashed out of the elevator.

When she finally drifted off, she dreamed she found her baby hanging on a wall. Its brain had grown through the skull like fungus, and suspended from its wafer head was a neckless wet sac with no limbs at all. Gwen started to cry and a priest came in carrying a delicate silver pitchfork. He told her to hush, he hadn't opened the membranes yet. When he pricked the soft bag, it fell open and spilled out three perfect male babies, each of them no bigger than her hand, and each with a rosebud penis tipped with one very tiny thorn. The priest began to circumcise them in the name of the Father, Son, and Holy Ghost; and when a crowd gathered Gwen was pushed to the rear where she couldn't see anything but a long row of pictures — abstracts — down a long snaky hall.

She woke when somebody put a thermometer in her mouth, straight out of the refrigerator. It was no-time, not dark or light, not late, not early. She could not even remember if the year bent toward Easter or Halloween.

Pressure bloomed suddenly in her gut. She barely made it to the toilet, still munching the glass rod. She filled the bowl with stained oil and walked

carefully back to bed, rubbing her swollen abdomen for tremors. She had not
wakened in the night when the baby thumped, nor once felt the long leg
cramps which meant he had leaned on her femoral arteries. It came to Gwen
suddenly that the baby must be dead, had smothered inside her overnight. By
her bed, Gwen stood first on one foot, then the other, shaking herself in case
he might rattle in her like a peanut. She laid the thermometer on the table,
knowing it measured her cold terror. She thumped herself. Nothing thumped
back.

"Time to eat!" said Ramona Plumpton, peeling a banana from her tray.

Gwen got into bed, pressing her belly with both palms.

A tall black man brought her breakfast tray. He said it was about six-thirty.
She had nothing but juice and black coffee, which she must not drink until a
nurse checked her temperature and said it was fine. "No labor pains?"

"No. And he isn't moving!"

"He's waiting for *you* to move him," she said with a smile, and marked a
failing grade on Gwen's chart. Later a resident pulled the curtain around her
bed and thrust a number of fingers into her, all the wrong size. He said they'd
induce at nine o'clock. She played with that awhile: induce, seduce; reduce,
produce. She folded out *Playboy's* nude Playmate of the Month, also hairless,
with tinted foam-rubber skin. There was an article which claimed Miss April
read Nietzsche and collected Guatemalan postage stamps, preferred the Ruy
Lopez in chess, and had once composed an oratorio. Miss April owned two
glistening nipples which someone — the photographer? — had just sucked to
points before the shutter clicked.

At nine, strangers rolled Gwen into what looked like a restaurant kitchen,
Grade A, and strapped her feet wide into steel stirrups on each side of a hard
table. The small of her back hurt. Gwen wanted to brace it with the flat of one
hand, but somebody tied it alongside her hip. "Don't do that!" Gwen said,
flapping her left out of reach. A nurse plucked it from the air like a tame
partridge. "Regular procedure," said the nurse, and tied it in place.

Through a side door came Dr. Somers, dressed in crisp lettuce-colored
clothes. He talked briefly about the weather and Vietnam while he drove both
hands into powdered rubber gloves.

Gwen broke in, "Is my baby dead?"

Above the gauze his eyes flared and shrank. "Certainly not." He sounded
muffled and insincere.

Gwen let down her lids. Spider patterns of light and dark. Caught in the
web, tiny sunspots and eclipses.

Someone spread her legs wider. She felt strange cold things sliding in, one of
them shaped like a mailed fist on a hard bronze forearm. The witches did that

for Black Mass. Used a metal dildoe. Gwen was not frightened, only as shocked as a witch to find the devil's part icy, incapable of being warmed even there, at her deepest. She cracked her lids and saw the rapist bend, half bald beyond the white sheet which swaddled her knees.

"*Fine,*" said the gauze. "*Just fine.*" He called over a mummified henchman and he, too, admired the scene. Gwen felt herself the reverse of some tiny pocket peep show, some key charm through which men look at spread technicolor thighs, magnified and welcoming. Now she closed the peephole, and through their cold tube they gloated over her dimpled cervix, which throbbed in rhythm like a winking pear.

Helpless and angry, she thought: Everything's filthy.

"Looks just fine," the henchman said, fidgeting in his green robe. Gwen wondered what the sister thought as she rolled an enamel table across the room like the vicar's tea cart. Full of grace? Fruit of *whose* womb?

Dr. Somers said, "There'll be one quick pain, Gwendolyn. Don't jump."

Until then she had given up jumping, spread and tied down as she was. Now she knew at his lightest touch she would leap, shrieking, and his scalpel would pierce her through like a spear. The sweat on her upper lip ran hot into her mouth. Sour.

"Lie very still now," said the sister.

The pain, when it came, was not great. If fluid spilled, Gwen could not tell, since the sharp prick spilled her all over with exhalations, small grunts, muscles she did not even own falling loose. "Nothing to it," Dr. Somers said.

She shivered when the devil took himself out of her.

"Now we just wait awhile." He gave a mysterious message to the sister, who injected something high in Gwen's arm. They freed her trembly hands and feet and rolled her back to the room she remembered well from yesterday.

Everything, magically, had been shifted here — Klee, clock, her magazines and mysteries. Mrs. Plumpton had even sent a choice collection from her candy box, mostly chocolate-covered cherries, which the sister said Gwen couldn't eat yet. Overnight Jesus had moved very slightly on His cross and dropped His chin onto one shoulder. Yet His exhaustion looked faked. Forewarned, He awaited the shaking and dark. He was listening for the swift zipper rent in the veil of the tabernacle, ceiling to floor. Three days from now (count them: three) and the great stone would roll.

Gwen stared at the sister who helped her into bed. Was this the one who shifted the figurines? Did she carry under her habit, even now, the next distraught bronze who, when cued, would cry out about being forsaken?

Politely, Gwen asked, "You like your work here?"

"Of course. All my patients are happy. You should sleep now, Mrs. Gower, and catnap from now on. Things will happen by themselves."

Trusting no one, Gwen opened her eyes as wide as they would go. Her face was one huge wakeful eye, like a headlamp. "Is my husband outside?"

"Not yet," said the sister, smiling. "Can I get you anything before I go? No? And drink water."

The baby might have died from drowning. Unbaptized, but drowned. Gwen was certain she did not sleep, yet Dr. Somers was suddenly there in a business suit, patting her arm. "You've started nicely," he said.

She felt dizzy from the hypodermic. She announced she would not give birth, after all, having changed her mind. Her body felt drawn and she sat up to see if her feet had been locked into traction. Dr. Somers said Mr. Gower had come by and been sent on to work — there was plenty of time. He faded, sharpened again to say Gwendolyn was to ask the nurse when she needed it.

The next thing she noticed was a line of figures who climbed in the window, rattling aside the Venetian blinds and straddling a radiator, then crossing her room and marching out into the hall. It was very peculiar, since her room was on the hospital's fourth floor. Most of the people did not speak or even notice her. A few nodded, slightly embarrassed to find her lying by their path, then drew away toward the wall and passed by, like Levites, on the other side.

One was a frightened young Jewish girl, hardly fourteen, whose weary face showed what a hard climb it had been up the sheer brick side of the hospital. Behind her came an aging athlete in lederhosen, drunk; he wore one wing like a swan's and was yodeling *Leda-Leda-Ledal-lay.* He gave Gwen a sharp look, half lecherous, as he went by her bed, flapping his snowy wing as if it were a nuisance he could not dislodge. A workman in coveralls climbed in next; he thrust head and shoulders back out the window and called to someone, "I tell you it's already open wide enough!" After much coaxing, the penguin followed him in and rode through the room on his shoulder, so heavy the workman tottered under the glossy weight. Several in the parade kept their rude backs to her. Angry, Gwen called them by name but they would not turn, and two of the women whispered about her when they went by.

It was noon when Gwen next looked at the clock. Richard had not come back. Instantly awake and furious, Gwen swung out of the high bed. She nearly fell. She grabbed for the metal chair — Good God! — something thudded in her middle like a pile driver. She felt curiously numb and in pain at the same time. She clumped to the doorway and hung on to the frame. There was a nun at a small desk to her right, filling out charts in a lovely, complex script.

"Going to telephone my husband," Gwen said. Her voice box had fallen and each word had to be grunted up from a long distance.

A chair was slid under her. ". . . shouldn't be out of bed . . . Quickly." The nurse balanced the telephone on Gwen's knees.

She dialed and Mrs. Gower said, "Hello?" Her voice was high and sweet, as if she had just broken off some soprano melody. Gwen said nothing. "Hello? Hello? Is anybody there?"

With great effort, short of breath, she said, "May I speak to Richard Gower? Please?"

"He's eating lunch."

Gwen looked at the far wall. A niche, some figurines, a lighted candle. She took a deep breath. When she screamed full blast, no doubt, the candle would blow out twelve feet away and across town the old lady's eardrum would spatter all over the telephone. But before she got half enough air sucked in, she heard, "Gwen? That's not you? Gwen, good heavens, you're not out of bed? Richard! Richard, come quick!"

Gwen could hear the chair toppling at the table, Richard's heavy shoes running down the hall, and then "Gwen? Gwen, you're all right?"

Wet and nasal, the breath blew out of her. "You just better get yourself over here, Richard Gower. That's all," she wailed. "You just quit eating and come this very minute. How can you eat at a time like this?"

Richard swore the doctor said they had hours yet. He was on his way right now and he hadn't even been *able* to eat, thinking of her.

She told him to hurry and slammed down the phone. The nun was looking at her, shaking her headdress. She half pushed Gwen into bed. "Now you've scared him," she said gently.

Gwen shook free of her wide sleeve. The next pain hit her and this one was pain — not a "contraction" at all. One more lie in a long line of lies. "Long-line-of-lies," she recited to herself, and got through the pain by keeping rhythm.

> "One more lie
> In a
> Long line
> Of lies."

On the next pain, she remembered to breathe deep and count. She needed fourteen long breaths to get through it, and only the six gasps in the middle were really bad.

By the time Richard trotted in, she was up to twenty-two breaths, and most of them were hard ones in the center without much taper on either end. He stopped dead, his mouth crooked, and Gwen knew she must look pale.

Perhaps even ugly. She could no longer remember why she had wanted him there.

"Good," said Dr. Somers. "We were just taking her in."

Richard kissed her. Gwen would not say anything. He rubbed her forehead with his fingers. New wrinkles had broken there, perhaps, like Ramona's stretch marks. As they rolled her into the delivery room, Gwen saw that Jesus had perked up a lot, gotten His second wind. She closed her eyes, mentally counting her pains in tune. One and two and three-three-three. Four-four-four. Five-five-five. Words caught up slowly with the music in her head: Mary had a little lamb. Little Lamb. Little . . .

When they made her sit upright on the table so an anesthetic could be shot into her spine, Gwen hurt too much from the bending even to feel the puncture. They had trouble getting her spread and tied into this morning's position; she had begun to thrash around and moan. She could not help the thrashing, yet she enjoyed it, too. If they'd let go of me once, I'd flop all over this damn sterile floor like a whale on the beach. I'd bellow like an elephant.

That reminded her of something Dr. Somers had said — that in the delivery room most Negro women prayed. *Jesus! Oh, Lord! Sweet Jesus!* And most white women, including the highborn, cursed. Oh, you damn fool, Gwen groaned (aloud, probably). It's *all* swearing.

Oh, Jesus!

Oh, hell!

They scratched at her thighs with pins then combs and then Kleenex, and Dr. Somers said that proved the anesthetic was working. Gwen fell rather quickly from agony to half-death and floated loose, broken in two at the waist.

"Move your right foot," said the doctor, and somebody's right foot moved. He explained she would be able to bear down, by will, even though she would notice only the intent to do so, and not feel herself pushing. So when they said bear down, Gwen thought about that, and somebody else bore down somewhere to suit them.

"High forceps." Two hands molded something below her navel, outside, and pressed it.

"Now," said the mummified henchman.

The huge overhead light had the blueness of a gas flame. She might paint it, staring, on a round canvas. She might call the painting "Madonna's Eye." She might even rise up into it and float loose in the salty eye of the Blessed Damozel like a dust mote.

Suddenly the doctor was very busy, and like a magician, tugged out of nowhere a long and slimy blue-gray thing, one gut spilling from its tail. No, that was cord, umbilical cord. He dropped the mass wetly on the sheet near Gwen's waist, groped into an opening at one end. Then that blunt end of it rolled, became a soft head on a stringy neck, rolled farther and had a face, bas-relief, carved shallow on one side. The mouth gave a sickly mew and, before her eyes, the whole length began to bleach and pinken. Gwen could hardly breathe from watching while it lay loosely on her middle and somehow finished being born of its own accord, by will, finally shaped itself and assumed a new color. Ribs tiny as a bird's sprang outward — she could see their whiteness through the skin. The baby screamed and shook a fist wildly at the great surgical light.

Like electricity, that scream jolted Gwen's every cell. She vibrated all over. "That's natural," said Dr. Somers, "that little nervous chill." He finished with the cord, handed the baby to a man in a grocer's apron, and began to probe atop her abdomen. "We'll let the placenta come and it's all done. He's a beautiful boy, Gwendolyn."

The pediatrician she and Richard had chosen was already busy at another table. Cleaning him, binding him, piling him into a scale for weight. Dr. Somers explained that Gwen must lie perfectly flat in bed, no pillow, so the spinal block would not give her headaches. If she'd drunk enough water, as ordered, the bladder would soon recover from the drug. Otherwise they'd use a catheter — no problem.

The sister, her face as round as the operating light, bent over her. "Have you picked out a name?"

"No," Gwen lied. *She* needed the new name. *She* was the one who would never be the same.

". . . a small incision so you wouldn't be torn by the birth. An episiotomy. I'll take the stitches now." Dr. Somers winked between her knees. "Some women ask me to take an extra stitch. To tighten them for their husbands."

Stitch up the whole damn thing, Gwen thought. They were scraping her numb thighs with combs again.

". . . may feel like hemorrhoids for a few days . . ."

She went to sleep. When she woke, there was a small glass pram alongside, and they were ready to roll her back to her room. Gwen tried to sit up, but a nun leaned on her shoulder. "Flat on your back, Mrs. Gower."

"I want to see."

"Shh." The sister bent over the small transparent box and lifted the bundle and flew it face down at her, so Gwen could see the baby as if he floated prone in the air. His head was tomato red, now, and the nun's starched wide sleeves flew out beyond his flaming ears. A flat, broad nose. Gwen would never be able to get the tip of her breast into that tiny mouth. There was peach fuzz dusted on his skull except in the top, where a hank of coarse black hair grew forward.

Gwen touched her throat to make sure no other hand had grabbed it. Something crawled under her skin, like the spider who webbed her eyelids tightening all lines. In both her eyes, the spider spilled her hot, wet eggs — those on the right for bitterness, and those on the left for joy.

The Glory of His Nostrils

It never occurred to Tom Carter, on the night of June 30, 1969, that somebody's sanity might be running out, even while he sat at the supper table eating too much of Mae's chicken and mashed potatoes. Had he been picking a day to go crazy in, he might have offered Halloween; but all he was really wondering that night was how you could tell if you had an ulcer.

Leaning back in his chair, he said, "I've eat too much. You must have put real cream and butter in the bowl." Mae, who had intended to make potato patties from the leftovers, said nothing.

The heavy meal had left Tom too sleepy to walk downtown and work overtime, but he had to. Tomorrow was the start of the county's fiscal year. Some of the figures in his annual report still wouldn't balance.

"Don't be late," was all Mae said when he grumbled. She stationed herself in front of the television with a second glass of iced tea. When he got to the front door, she called after him, "Is it raining, by any chance?"

And Tom hollered back, "No. Not yet." And burped.

The air was hot and dry. For two weeks there hadn't been a drop of rain in Rich County. No stars showed overhead and the clouds which hid them were lumped and heavy.

"It's cloudy, though!" he called. "Looks right threatening!" He waited, but Mae didn't even suggest he carry an umbrella. The TV's already got her, he thought. She's already busy watching Dr. Casey save some alcoholic.

Tom waddled down his front steps feeling unusually stubby, short, and unappreciated, his paunch bobbing in advance of him like a large stuffed olive. He puffed past four houses on Locust Street before he came to the large blue-gray one where Wanda Quincey, widowed at Easter, now lived alone. Her house, black-shuttered, graceful, trimmed in wooden lace and embroidery, reminded him first of a lady's summer frock. Then it looked cool as a moonlit pond.

Quincey was just my age, Tom thought. He stopped, belched once, and leaned against the maple by the curb while he fished in his pockets for an antacid tablet. That was how he happened to be the last person in Richdale to see Wanda Quincey in her right mind.

As he later told it, the Quincey porch light came on while he was propped against the tree. The house looked real nice lit up, he thought, black floor and ceiling, that curly gray banister, the gray wicker furniture. Quincey had made sure that house was painted every other year, and paid the mortgage off besides. Much good it did him now.

Something live burrowed through Tom's belly like a mole bubbling down its tunnel. He found a loose tablet stuck to his pocket seam. Mae feeds me too much, always has, so I'll go straight to sleep and sleep till morning.

Just then the front door opened and Quincey's widow came out onto her black porch, carrying a copper watering can, which she emptied over a tubbed elephant-ear plant. Tom said afterward it was just like a stage setting — the heroine moving deftly among her bright props, not knowing there was anything at all beyond the footlights, much less a neighbor full of digestive gas.

Watching her, he licked tobacco crumbs off the mint wafer and slipped it underneath his hot tongue. Onstage the widow bent, placing the sprinkler on the steps. She stretched, rubbed one arm, then fitted her back to a porch post almost exactly as Tom himself was propped in the dark against the maple.

Leaning back, Wanda looked up at clouds which were passing across the sky like rolling barrels, tanks, and cisterns. Tom could not tell much about her face, a black-and-gray shape on a black neck, but the rest of her was buttered glossy in the yellow porch light.

She ain't fat yet, thought Tom, and chewed hard on his mint. Lonesome, maybe. Hot night, empty bed. Tom did not feel a bit disrespectful thinking this, although he had known Wanda all his life. He had been one of the pallbearers at Quincey's funeral.

But in this moment he could look at her lighted shoulders, waistline, hips as though they belonged to someone else, some character conveyed to him by stylized movements, with the light deliberately turned on her this way, to produce exactly this brassy effect. She more or less asks for it, thought Tom, and it seemed to him she opened her thighs slightly to his gaze.

Suddenly her shoulders fell forward. Light slid up like a yellow collar on her neck. Her breasts dropped so far he thought she had abruptly tired of having them grow on her all the time, like tumors. She didn't look a bit like herself, Tom thought again, but like some actress in some sad play.

Wanda turned, her pale costume gleaming. Rear stage she exited and the porch light instantly went out.

Without knowing exactly how, Tom Carter was deeply moved. He was never able to tell this mixed part of it: the pity that nearly made him go knock on her door; and the glee that he was here, alive, unseen, full of his wife's fried chicken. Distended with gas and itchy from the tree trunk, he nevertheless felt no older than a bridegroom. He marched briskly to the courthouse, humming to himself:

> "What 'cha gonna do when the meat gives out, Honey?
> What 'cha gonna do when the meat gives out, Babe?"

The janitor said Mr. Carter was surely in a fine mood for somebody having to work extra time; and Tom said that was attitude. Attitude made all the difference.

At seven-thirty the next morning, wearing a plaid robe, Wanda Quincey walked onto that same front porch, picked up her watering can, and threw it into Locust Street straight at Greene's laundry truck. It fell noisily short and took a crooked bounce over the hood and past the windshield. Mr. Greene hit his brakes, which saved him from being spattered when the slung milk bottle broke; but lined him up exactly right for the rolled newspaper, which flew in his front window by his nose and out the other side. He drove away as fast as the old truck would go, and the more he thought about what had happened, the less he believed it.

Inside a week, though, the whole town believed. Wanda Quincey, who on June 30th had been as nice a woman as you could want, had waked up crazy the morning of July 1st. Since that date opened the county's fiscal year (and it rained, breaking a two weeks' drought, besides), it was easy to remember the widow's craziness birthday, and to keep track of the length and degree of her illness.

Tom told everybody he had seen Wanda on the eve of its onset and she looked queer to him even then. "Gave me such a turn," he said in the County Clerk's office, "that I got behind a tree, a maple, and stayed there till she went inside."

"She threw the thing *at* me," said Mr. Greene, looking flattered. "I don't know what to make of it."

Somebody talked the Baptist preacher into paying a call, but Wanda wouldn't let him inside and flared up the minute he said she was looking well. Grief was like that, the preacher concluded, and grief would pass. She didn't seem dangerous.

By the time Dr. Benjamin came to Richdale, Wanda Quincey had been crazy three years, one month, and a week.

He took a giant step off the train, skipping the porter's stairs, and in four huge strides was inside the station asking the telegrapher, "Have you called me a cab?" He slapped a small card through Pete's ticket window. It said:

Dr. O. B. Benjamin
(Courtesy Title Only)

"Uh, say you want a cab?" Pete reached automatically for the buzzer, which rang in the toilet-sized building two hundred yards away, and read the card twice. Courtesy-Dr. Benjamin loomed beyond the metal bars, six and a half feet tall, black-haired, black-eyed, with a mustache above his mouth which was almost curly. He looked, thought Pete, *florid*, a word he could not even define. He wore a ruby-red ring on his little finger and some rumpled flower — an iris? — in his lapel. Pete told him the Owens Cab Company would be right along.

"Just keep my luggage till I send," said Benjamin in his evangelist's voice, took one wide step outdoors, and had his foot lifted and ready when the taxi pulled up in front of him.

"What's the best motor hotel?" he said as he closed the door and slapped one of his name cards on the driver's leatherette shoulder. The driver plucked it down with one hand, frowned, and then shrugged.

"Rich's, I guess."

"That the only one in town?"

"Yeah." He offered to give back the card, but the doctor waved it away, showing his black watch with the white numbers on it. The taxi whipped out of the dusty parking lot, across the tracks, and through Richdale's two-block business district.

"How many people live here?"

"Couple thousand." He thought about the doctor's card. "We got a hospital, though. Forty beds."

"Always this hot in August?"

The driver nodded, but said personally he thought it was good for a man to sweat. Cleaned out his blood. He waited to see if that would bring any professional remark, but the passenger said nothing. Might be a book-type doctor, he thought, and wondered if he could be a college coach.

Just beyond the Pure Oil Station was Richmotor Inn, which was new, built of concrete block, and painted pink. As if he had been thumped on the breastbone, the doctor said *"UH!"* when he saw it, swung out, and threw two dollars into the front seat. "I've got some bags at the station. If you'll bring them in an hour, I'll double this."

"Yes, *sir*, Doctor," said the driver. He tucked the man's calling card into the sweatband of his hat and offered the doc one of his own, "So you can ask for me special anytime you want good service." He sat rubbing the steering wheel while the big man went into the Richmotor lobby, trying to decide if he should have offered extras right away, women or whiskey. A clerk and the stranger passed the window, crossed the lobby, moved out of his sight.

In the hall the clerk was asking Dr. Benjamin if maybe he was from the university? Had he ever been in Richdale before?

"No, I'm not. No, never have."

Chiropractor? Guy that made eyeglasses? Doctor of divinity?

That seemed to tickle him. "No. Medicine."

What kind of medicine did he practice?

"I don't," said Dr. Benjamin. "Not any more."

The clerk laughed pleasantly as he unlocked the room door, flicked on a light, started the window air conditioner. "Great to be retired so young."

"Not that," said Dr. Benjamin, handing him a tip. "Defrocked." He had to force the money into the man's suddenly taut hand. "I'm an abortionist. Or was. Not any more, of course."

"Of course not," said the clerk. Not wanting to back away, he found himself edging sideways like a crab, at the same time smiling widely in case the doctor had made a joke. The doctor himself was smiling, whatever that meant. "You staying long?"

"I might."

The clerk took one despairing look around, seeing the room turned into surgery, the lamp relocated, carpet stained, unspeakable things dropped in the wastebaskets. ". . . nice visit," he said behind the closing door.

When the cabdriver heard about it, he parked the two suitcases outside Dr. Benjamin's room, knocked on the door, and ran without even waiting for his tip. This was not from disapproval but enterprise, and he whistled all the way back to the cabstand. Once, he had heard the perfect businessman would raise rats on household garbage to feed to minks. Then when he skinned the minks for fur, he could feed their bodies to the rats again. As soon as the cycle was working and both flocks breeding steadily, there would be only profits and no expenses. Now it seemed to Delbert Owens — the cabdriver — that from whiskey to whore to unlicensed doctor was a fair imitation of that chain, and he wanted Dr. Benjamin to see early that he wasn't, by nature, greedy.

He called up Christine and Velma and told them to be standing by and, just in case, called up the colored girl as well. Pete said the doctor could have got on that train in Washington, Richmond, maybe even New York; so he added some gin and vermouth to the box he carried in the trunk of his taxi.

When it was fully dark, he called up Dr. Benjamin, introduced himself again, and asked if he could do anything at all to make him feel at home. No? If the doctor was lonesome, he could maybe send over a very reliable friend he knew. . . . Well, listen, if it was variety he liked . . .

Delbert Owens hung up abruptly, shocked.

"What'd he say?" asked Pete from his ticket cage.

Delbert Owens shook his head. "Said he'd seen so many female bottoms, they'd got to look like faces to him. Grinning, frowning, wrinkled, young. Not so young. Said these days it took a face to interest him half as much as a bottom used to. Said the next woman in his life had to interest him from the very top down. You ever heard anything like that?"

"That's really what he said? In just those words?"

"Well, no," Delbert admitted. "He was dirty about it, like Yankees always are."

Though no visitor had been inside the Quincey house for three years, the people of Richdale watched Wanda's actions almost as if she were truly living on a stage. Every morning she rose at six and turned on the upstairs bathroom light. Before seven, a kitchen exhaust fan churned out steam instead of grease — must boil her morning eggs, and hard as stone from the time it took. Thirty minutes after that, although she had a perfectly good sink piped into Richdale's municipal system, Wanda emptied her dishpan off the back porch, hung it on a nail there like a farm woman, and stood on tiptoe, stretching widely in the morning air. Despite her pose, nobody thought of crucifixions. They watched for the way she spread and flexed her fingers and rotated her wrist joints.

The neighbors whispered, "Limbering up for the telephone!"

And when Wanda Quincey went inside they edged toward their own parlors and hallways, waiting to see whose phone would ring today.

Wanda had called almost every adult in town at least once. She no longer opened the calls with who she was — people *knew* — but nowadays launched right away into her purpose. This was always a grievance, and it had something to do with her dead husband.

"Mr. Wheeler? I see by the paper you're thinking of running for constable. I'd like to know if you plan to keep a special eye on the property of poor widow women with nobody looking after them and taxes eating them to death? I never even knew till after Quince died how many people were walking through our yard, throwing balls, letting their leaves blow . . . their trash scatter . . . their dogs . . ."

The burden of Wanda's calls was how cruelly Quince had been treated all his life. Quince had kept this from her protectively, had been too much of a gentleman even to admit it fully to himself. His papers had showed Wanda much of the truth, her insight the rest. Evidence filled his desk: the misplaced insurance premium, canceled appointment, a bill for the dented fender no driver confessed, the stock which declined in value despite a friend's advice, that cardiogram showing a normal heart ten weeks before it clogged and killed him. His name had been omitted from the list of the Richdale High School class of '38. One year the city directory had him spelled as Quincy and another year Quinsy, which was worse. The pattern was obvious. Wanda could not imagine how she had been so blind.

In Quince's strongbox she found four receipts for magazine subscriptions which never came. The bank had numerous times marked him overdrawn when he wasn't. That time he spoke to the Rotary Club, his speech was garbled into Martian by the typesetter, and the news photograph printed above it was blurred and rather fierce. Thinking back on it, Wanda could remember it was Quince's sweaters which shrank at the cleaners, his accounts which were billed twice, the letters he carried to the post office which the post office lost.

No doubt about it, Winslow Quincey had been a saint, while the world tried to break him. Now, in his honor, she telephoned that world.

And how the world squirmed! "Wanda, honey, I wish I could talk more about it but I've got this dentist appointment. . . ."

"I have to leave this minute to open the pharmacy, Mrs. Quincey, but I'll be glad to check that old account for you. I think it was that laxative pill he took and that foot ointment? I'll make sure. . . ."

"I assure you, Ma'am, that we used the same process that we use for everybody. As a licensed mortician, I have certain standards. . . ."

"Yes, Ma'am. Two papers on the roof in the past three months. We'll speak to the boy about it. And of course we'll credit your subscription. . . ."

Between calls Wanda read and reread the Book of Job. She had torn this intact from her King James Bible, leaving Esther right next to Psalms; and when she walked up Locust Street to town she carried pages 370 to 390 in her left hand and read to herself aloud. There was little traffic in Richdale, and drivers looked out for her as she jaywalked in front of them, hissing aloud, ". . . and hath burned up the sheep and the servants, and consumed them; and I only am escaped alone to tell thee . . ." If anyone dared to touch his horn, Wanda Quincey would flap the thin Bible pages in the air as though God Himself were brushing at flies with tissue paper.

She carried Job with her to church, reading all the way there and back and during the sermon as well. The Reverend Snell, praying, raised his voice to cover her sinister sighing from the back row. . . . "They are destroyed from morning to evening; they perish forever without any regarding it. . . ."

That was where Dr. Benjamin first met Wanda Quincey, on the back row at Richdale Baptist Church. It was his first Sunday in town. He had come because he felt as bound to see the Southern Baptists as he would, in Mexico, the Aztec ruins. And he was enjoying himself, singing the hymns with such vigor that people were twisting around to stare.

At eleven-ten Wanda came in, reading strongly, and joined him on the last bench. Brown hair, he noticed, going gray at the edge, and milky skin. Though haphazardly dressed, wearing one silver earring and one pearl, she was so clean that her skin had the fragrance of a baby after its bath. Dr. Benjamin smiled toward that fragrance, but Wanda was reading. He thought about how that cheek would feel to his hand. He offered her a hymnal but she read on, not looking up. Beside him she muttered through the offering and special music by the choir; he had to reach across her to pass the offering plate to an anemic looking old gentleman who rolled his faded eyes.

Just as Wanda finished mouthing, "When I washed my steps with butter, and the rock poured me out rivers of oil," he tapped her on one shoulder.

"Hush up," said Dr. Benjamin, so loud the minister forgot whom he was praying to.

Wanda's mouth opened and hung there. Pink, he thought. Moist. Tasting faintly of strawberries.

She nearly ran to the aisle. Job shivered in her hand. All the way from the bench to the vestibule, Wanda forgot to read, and had to start over at Chapter 1, having lost her place.

Monday morning, following the light, the fan, the water, the dishpan, the exercises, Wanda dialed the Baptist preacher and asked who that stranger was at church, the big man in the back row.

Mr. Snell was so startled not to hear her usual complaint about how Quincey's memorial money was being spent that his silence made Wanda think the line was dead. She hung up and dialed his number over.

"I said, Who was that big man on the back row in church yesterday?"

"Why, Benjamin, I think. He signed a visitor's card."

"Benjamin who?"

"That's his last name. A transient, I believe. No, I don't know where he lives."

After lunch Wanda walked to the Richdale Pharmacy for shampoo and talcum, reading Job's tribulations as she went.

"Yonder she comes," somebody said, giggling, on the courthouse bench. For a change Wanda *heard* it, although she had come to one of the best parts: "When the morning stars sang together. . . . She looked up angrily, but it was only a boy, his elbows out at his sides like a pair of coat hangers.

The same thing happened half a block nearer town. Some high voice snickered, and Wanda looked into the squirrel bright eyes of a blue woman under a velvet hat. She looked like a walking blood disease, and Wanda thought how old everybody was getting in her absence. The woman began a shrill cough and covered up the giggle. Wanda flipped a new page and pinned it with her thumb, reading, "Will the unicorn be willing to serve thee, or abide by thy crib?"

"Will he, indeed?" said Dr. Benjamin. He was in front of the pink motel, right at the edge of its parking lot, sitting in one of the bent fruitwood chairs which belonged in the lobby. "Good afternoon, Ma'am," he said, and touched one forefinger to his thick hair as if he might doff it all in her honor.

Wanda stopped on the sidewalk, her finger caught between the verse about unicorns and the one about peacocks and ostriches. "How dare you speak to me?"

"A poor substitute for the Almighty, no doubt," he said. His smile was the first Wanda Quincey had noticed in three years, and she thought it the size of a slice of watermelon. Through it he said, "I much prefer the Book of Ruth, myself, where widows behave more sensibly."

"Glean in your fields, I suppose," snapped Wanda, for she wouldn't have him think she'd forgotten that part of the Bible she kept at home.

"You must be," he said slowly and thoughtfully, "really paranoid." He shook his head, his tongue clopping softly in his mouth. There were frown lines between his furry eyebrows.

She hadn't a thing to throw at him but twenty flimsy pages. "Mr. Benjamin . . ." she began coldly.

"Doctor. Dr. Benjamin. I'm an abortionist." He tried to hand her a card but she reared away.

"You ought to be locked up."

"I have been," he said. "If you'd dye your hair, you'd look younger. Everybody does that now. I do myself."

Wanda had started to walk on, reading firmly to blot the big man from her mind, and was disgusted to hear her own grand voice announcing, "THE GLORY OF HIS NOSTRILS IS TERRIBLE!"

Dr. Benjamin roared with laughter, throwing back his broad head until his own nostrils were opened to the sun like twin caves, and the bright light could shine all the way up onto the surface of his brain. Wanda walked rapidly from him down the street. Delbert Owens, who had been coasting his cab by them downhill in the dappled shade, scraped half the whitewall from two tires against the curb. "You all right, Mrs. Quincey?" he called when he had finally jerked free of the gutter. She read him some angry, incoherent verse.

When she came back from the pharmacy, Dr. Benjamin was still sitting in front of the motel.

Wanda tucked the paper sack tighter under one arm. She had not bought New Dawn Hair Color, but out of simple interest had opened one of the boxes on the shelf, taken out the printed direction sheet, and slipped that in with her purchases.

"If you'll come in," called Dr. Benjamin while she was more than ten steps away, and loud enough to be heard all the way to the Baptist manse, "I'll offer you a drink."

Wanda began shaking her head without even looking at him. She shook it all the way reaching him, passing him, and going away; and by the time she got to the courthouse bench she was quite dizzy, and had to sit down. On the bench she read, several times, with growing strength, how "Job died, being old and full of days," and after Job was really dead enough, she felt like walking home. She thought it was a shame the coat-hanger boy had missed that fine conclusion.

That afternoon she made no calls. The lines were jammed with people trying to find out who Wanda was calling *now*. She locked herself into the upstairs bathroom and read the folder about shampooing in youth, which would last for forty-two days, with a mixture so powerful plastic gloves were supplied with every bottle.

That night her kitchen fan went on at seven, as usual, but nothing at all blew out except air. The fan whirled all night, forgotten, and sent a pleasant little vibration up and down the neighborhood. One of the neighbors called the Quincey number just to make sure she hadn't fallen down the stairs and died, but hung up as soon as Wanda answered.

Upstairs, Wanda stood in her bedroom in the growing dark, unfastening the back buttons on her blouse. Her eyes flicked from the glass over Quincey's photograph to the glass in which she saw herself reflected. She wondered why the mirror switched her only from right to left but not from down to up. Some night, Wanda suspected, she might be reversed this second way also, and undress while standing on her head. She began her usual conversation.

"Quince," she said, and the portrait dipped politely in its frame. "The queerest thing happened to me today. A man asked a crazy woman to come to his room for a drink. What do you think of that?"

Slightly muffled behind the dusty glass, Quincey said he knew exactly what such a man must have in mind.

"That's what I thought, too." She stepped out of her skirt. "And, Quince, it's been a long time since — well, since I felt that *idea* in anybody. You do understand, don't you? I don't mean to sound disloyal. But somebody else's thought, his thought about you, is almost like some garment. You can't help trying it on. Just to see if it fits."

Quincey's expression had grown rather ugly, as if he might push his face through the glass. "Did it fit?" he said.

"You're not supposed to talk," said Wanda, "except when I ask you questions."

She hung her blouse and brown skirt on the bedpost and turned so she could look over one shoulder at her mirrored back. The nylon clung nicely to her hips, she saw, and she wondered if Dr. Benjamin had thought as much when he watched her walking by. She decided not to mention that to Quincey.

From her nightstand he rasped suddenly, "What are you looking at?"

She said dreamily, "I've been thinking of tinting my hair. Red, maybe. Like a sweet-gum tree in the fall of the year."

"Maple is red," said Quincey, always a stickler for accuracy. "Sweet gums get purple. And no lady would dye her hair red."

"I'm thinking about that too." Wanda unpinned her bun and the hair fell below her shoulders and tickled her spine. It was the color, she thought, of harmless brown garden snakes.

"Quince, how old were you? In 1969?"

"Not but forty-five."

"And I was thirty-six." She wrapped a strand of hair around one wrist. Dr. Benjamin wore a black watch and a red ring. "We could have had babies, Quince, even though we did marry late. You know that? I wasn't too old." There was a rattle. "Don't vibrate, Quince. It scratches the table." She began brushing her hair.

"Children?" said Quincey. "Children to stay home with us when we got old?"

She whispered, "You didn't get old."

"Children to be nurses when we got sick? The way I stayed home with Mama till she finally died? The way you spent years shooting your papa full of insulin so he couldn't die and you couldn't live? We talked about all of that."

"Soon I'll be forty," Wanda said. She folded his stand down and stored him in a drawer. Then she yanked the petticoat over her head and studied herself in the full-length mirror, stripped down to brassière and pants. She could see that thirty-nine years of gravity had weighted her flesh — the stomach was not flat, the breasts no longer high. Everywhere, the cells of her body yearned slightly downward: shoulders, buttocks, even those folds hung under her chin and eyes.

I have begun, she thought, to fall very slowly into Quincey's grave.

Barefoot she padded out of her room, down the narrow stairs, and to her desk telephone. She asked the Richmotor Inn to give her Dr. Benjamin, please.

His voice burst in her ear.

Quickly she said, "This is Wanda Quincey, and I'd like to know who you think I am, asking me up to your room like that."

Now he said nothing. This bothered Wanda not at all, since silence had been tried by telephone subscribers all over Richdale. She leaned back in her chair and placed her naked feet on the desk top. Her legs looked very white and very long.

"If you want to see *me*," she said, and giggled suddenly.

He asked if she'd finished her reading yet.

"If you want to see *me*," she went on, "you can behave like a gentleman and come calling. I live at 402 Locust Street."

"Honey," boomed Dr. Benjamin, "do you like Scotch or bourbon?"

"I've entirely forgotten," she said, and hung up.

Shortly after midnight, August 18, 1972, a tall man with a package tucked in each armpit knocked loudly on the widow Quincey's black front door. When the porch light went on, he was seen silhouetted like something precious displayed in a gray box on a well-lit velvet lining. Old Mr. Wilkie was in his upstairs toilet at the time, wondering if he might have an enlarged prostate, and he saw the door swing wide to the visitor. For a minute it looked as if Wanda Quincey didn't have a thing on but her underwear, but then Dr. Benjamin bowed so deeply she was cut off from view.

The next day Wanda used the telephone only twice: to tell Richmotor Inn Dr. Benjamin was checking out; and to ask Delbert Owens to taxi over his suitcases and another fifth of Scotch. By then she had remembered which flavor she preferred.

All that week, people rode slowly up and down Locust Street to stare at the Quincey house.

Its shades and shutters and curtains were closed. After supper, everybody living in the 400 block sat on his front porch and stared, and some invited friends to come and stare with them, but no lights went on anywhere in the house. Even the kitchen fan had snapped down its door like an eyelid. Neighbors tiptoed and whispered in their houses. Still they could hear nothing. No scream, no voice. Not even a footfall.

"All I know," Delbert Owens said, in answer to the Sheriff's questions, "is that I carried him two suitcases and he walked me back to the cab for change. He didn't have nothing smaller than a twenty."

"And what did he say?"

"Said Wanda Quincey would never have lost her mind if she'd had a husband who shared more with her. His work, his business. Everything. I gave him the old wink then, but he didn't wink back. Said this town was no good for her, either, and looked at me hard."

"Town my ass. And that's all?"

"Said in some ways Wanda was better off when her papa was alive with the diabetes. Gave her a thing to do. Said she had even taught herself how to give him shots by sticking a hypo in a orange."

"No news in that."

"Would have made a good nurse, he said."

"And what else?"

"Nothing else. He was looking a little tired out when I saw him."

"But no blood on him anywhere? No cuts? No scratches? You didn't really see Wanda herself, alive?"

"I didn't see her. All he had was, low on his neck, one big red lump. Had a dent in it." Delbert pushed down his belt and scratched his navel. "A dent just like a tooth makes in a apple."

"Apple, orange, the hell with it," said the Sheriff.

But since his telephone was ringing off the wall with questions, he put on his badge and gun and drove his official car to Locust Street and knocked at the door of 402.

Wanda herself answered. She was wrapped in what was either some flowered robe or a twisted bedspread. Her face was flushed and the tip of her chin was scraped as if she had fallen face-first into a sandpile.

She said, "Good afternoon!" in that perky but vague way children speak when they have had a long fever.

"Wanda? You're doing okay, Wanda?" What really made the Sheriff stammer was that wealth of bright red hair, standing out from her head in all directions like a burning bush.

Wanda looked right through him. "You don't need to break it to me gently, Sheriff. Quince is dead. My husband is dead. I've suspected it for a long time."

She gave a brilliant smile across his shoulder to whatever she was looking at.

"Ma'am, maybe you ought to . . . well . . . come with me now. See a doctor. Nobody's going to hurt you. We'll help you feel better."

"I've seen my doctor, and if I felt any better I would float right up over your head." She put her right hand on that blazing mop of hair and rubbed it gently. He saw that her feet were bare and a kneecap was showing which was bare, also.

The Sheriff didn't know what to do. He had no search warrant. Nobody had signed any papers to commit her. "Uh, Benjamin's staying here, is he?"

"Just till tomorrow. We're going to Chicago. Or maybe to San Francisco, where the bridges are. I'm going to take an interest in his work. I'm going to sit there and wait, and people will telephone me. I'm going to keep his papers in order." She undid one corner of her robe and threw it back in place again in a very queenly fashion. It was a bedspread, after all; part of the fringe was showing.

The Sheriff tried to see beyond her and down the dark hall. "Maybe I could talk to him about that?"

She said haughtily, "Not unless you telephone first." Out of the folds of her flowered wrap she took a Sunkist orange and began thumping it from one palm to another. "I think that's all, Sheriff. Don't you?" She closed the black door with him still standing there trying to think of some crime to charge somebody with.

All the time Wanda and Dr. Benjamin waited in the depot for the north-bound train, Pete tried to get Wanda by herself. He called the doc to the telephone, but Wanda decided to use the ladies' room just at that time. He insisted on carrying their bags personally, even though he knew it was bad for his bursitis. Loaded down, he walked at Wanda's elbow saying "Psst! Psst!"

"Honey," said Wanda to Dr. Benjamin, "I think Pete's talking to you."

"No, no. Just wheezing. Little cold." He loaded the suitcases on the wagon and rolled it over the depot yard by the tracks, to wait for the Silver Meteor.

"When you coming back, Miz Quincey?" he finally decided to ask in front of them both.

"Back where?" she said.

Pete could see Delbert Owens inching his taxicab across the big lot at zero miles an hour, hoping to hear what went on. Finally he parked it nearby and got out and sat on the hood and cleaned his fingernails.

Nervously, Pete said, "Here you was, just stopping off in Richdale on your way to someplace, and look what happened." He looked up at Dr. Benjamin, who now seemed seven feet tall or eight, and then around to see how close

Delbert was if he needed him. "You going home now to your wife?"

"What wife?" Dr. Benjamin laughed so loudly it sounded as if trains were coming headlong in both directions. To Wanda he said in a whisper, "Don't stand too close; you'll get hurt," and, with his fingers, caught her right breast like some kind of handle and pulled her back from the tracks. Pete said it was the damnedest thing he ever saw.

When the train did come bellowing into Richdale, Pete had his only chance. Under its clangor and whistle and spitting, he yelled into Wanda's ear, "He's an ABORTIONIST! He's dangerous. Don't GO with him!"

Dr. Benjamin turned his broad head. "What's that?"

Wanda said, "Pay no attention, honey. Everybody in this whole damn town is crazy."

They climbed onto the train, Dr. Benjamin helping her with one gentle palm at her elbow and a quick pinch elsewhere. Pete and Delbert Owens just stood together in the parking lot, and waited to see the two of them show up in one of the lighted windows in a passenger car, like a tiny film frame in an old-time nickelodeon. When the pair appeared, they walked a little closer to the railway car.

They were lit by that pinpoint light travelers use to read without disturbing other passengers. First Dr. Benjamin came into its shine, and sat down in the plush seat near the window. Maybe he winked at them; Delbert said so, but Delbert was owed one. Pete was never sure.

Then Wanda knelt on the aisle seat beside him and lowered her face against his, so the light flared brightly on her red hair. The train jerked once, northward. She bent forward and brushed her nose against Dr. Benjamin's nose. The train groaned and moved.

The last they saw, Wanda was framed in that lighted rectangle, scrubbing her nose urgently against his big nose, like a speechless Eskimo in a flaming parka.

The Spider Gardens
of Madagascar

After the two cars parked, the state patrolman climbed out of his and opened both black doors of the Ford. From the roof, out of sight behind a chimney, Coker watched his teacher, and his preacher, then his Grandmother Barnes step out. Briefly they put their four heads in a cluster, sometimes glancing toward the house. Grandmother's white hair bobbed ahead down the front walk between two flat rows of pansies. He knew she'd had to drive fifty miles. He could figure out everything from their stiff parade. While the doorbell rang in the empty house, Coker thought about not going down at all, simply to get details.

But all four would just sit on the porch glider and wait for him. Or go indoors and telephone the neighbors.

Coker swung into the sycamore and climbed down his knotted rope to the kitchen door. Inside he called, "I'm coming," so they'd stop ringing the bell.

He didn't, though. He stood by the humming refrigerator and picked his scab. If they're both hurt, he thought, Daddy's hurt the worst. If one is dead, he's the one. If they were both killed, he died first.

Think how cool it would be to climb into the refrigerator and go to sleep with the butter and eggs.

He dragged open the front door. Instantly, their faces dropped. Grandmother's eyes filled up with water. "My son," said the preacher gravely, and dropped on his shoulder an arm of solid lead.

"Coker!" the teacher said with a sigh, and his grandmother yanked him against her and cried on his new haircut.

He said, "They had a wreck?"

More crying. The patrolman took off his hat before he nodded. "Your mother's in the hospital, son. She's going to be just fine."

He saw they were going to make him ask. "And Daddy?"

Grandmother's muffled words fell through his hair roots and dropped cold on his brain. "God took him to Heaven, Coker. You know what that means."

He knew exactly what it meant. His grandmother's bosom smelled like coconut. He feared he might vomit on it. Mrs. Markas, who knew the signs, said maybe Coker-honey ought to sit down. Their fingers nipped at him all the way to the couch.

There was a crowd of hiccups in his throat. From behind him, the patrolman said again, "Your mother is going to be just fine."

All Coker could see was the pipe rack he had made in Mrs. Markas's class and given his father for Christmas. He stared at it until the wood got soft. "Daddy was planning to drive," he whispered.

"Yes. Will was driving and this truck — It doesn't help to think of these things. You daddy would want us to think of your mother now. And look after her." Coker stared into his grandmother's wet eyes. "You can see her at the hospital tomorrow," she said, her white head bobbing. "I'm going to stay here with you until Lillian's well." Between Coker's eyes and hers, Lillian's existence bloomed. Her daughter. Coker's mother. His eyes said: *Mama was screaming at him just before the wreck,* and hers said: *Maybe so, maybe so, but it can't be changed.*

Mrs. Markas advised him to go ahead and cry. "You'll feel better, Coker, honey."

As usual, Coker knew more than she. In her class and the four grades before hers, he'd seen how little teachers knew — reading aloud their sweet books about family picnics and turkey dinners. If crying made you feel good, he'd be Santa Claus by now.

His chest felt bruised. Inside, his throat was swelling. Dead, he thought. All the time gone. Left me to grow up by myself. Left me with *her.*

His throat blew out like a frog's and choked him.

"See?" said the teacher as he began to moan. "You'll really feel better. When we can't change what's happened, we might as well cry."

He cried, instead, for unchangeable things to come. He was ten years old.

It was fifth-grade Science Project time. Coker had so little faith in books, Mrs. Markas asked him to bring in a shoebox of different rocks. "I know things are busy at your house," she said. "Isn't your mother coming home from the hospital this week?"

"She did. Yesterday."

"Oh. Now isn't that fine! I hope she'll soon be completely recovered."

"Yes, Ma'am."

He picked up rocks all the way home from school. Each time he found one larger, or whiter, or darker, he threw his previous choice away, so he had only one in his pocket when he got home. Grandmother Barnes tossed that one into their stony side yard when she was washing his pants.

"How was I to know it was an important rock?" she said when he reappeared in his jeans. "You've already been in to see your mother?"

"Not yet." He climbed on a chair to get the peanut-butter jar.

"Well, do that first. You know she lies there all day waiting for you to get home. Go tell her what happened at school today."

He spread several crackers. "Nothing happened."

"Go tell her that, then."

Outside his mother's bedroom, he crammed his mouth full, knocked, and rushed in with his cheeks puffed out like bladders. His mother lay in the very center of the king-sized bed, her eyes glittering, her broken jaw wired shut. She said between her teeth, "Coker, what took you so long?" Before he could answer, she was into a long, buzzing speech: "I never know where you are anymore and you just come home when it suits you. I'm about to go crazy with nothing to do and nothing to eat that won't come through a straw. You can't imagine how blue I get. And now's the time we've got to draw together, Coker, you and me. Alone in this world. You are the only thing I've got left. And it's not fair to worry me going off wherever you choose and not coming straight home. . . . Are you listening to me?"

Coker chewed. It took a long time to get the crumbs wet and work the peanut spread off his gums. "I had to get stuff for the teacher. Science. At school."

She leaned toward him and pillows fell softly forth on both sides. "Tell me about it," she said, patting the bed. Through her blue lacy top he could see the tips of her breasts, brown as acorns.

"That's all."

"Maybe I'd help. I could make you a poster or paste things in a book. It would give me something to do instead of going crazy." She laughed and immediately quit laughing. "What shall we do? Mount butterflies? I don't think you're even listening. Here I am offering to help, and you just stand there chewing your cud like a cow." She had always nibbled at his father this way. Met him every day at the front door like some starved bird, her white hands plucking loose in the air. *How's the new bookkeeper? If you'd bring the books home, I could check up after her. Don't you look flushed, Will! Is it fever? I bet you didn't eat a thing for lunch. After I fixed it and wrapped everything to stay fresh. You just don't appreciate, do you? I just wish you'd married some woman who didn't care if you got so hungry your blood dried up and when you cut yourself shaving it would blow off your face like dust!*

Coker could see his father still, standing in the front hall, his eyes flicking from one side to the other. Sometimes his mouth would stay open. He looked like a fish deciding if he dwelt in air or water, and how to move next. Deciding he would rather be a fish than a cow, Coker let his own jaw hang loose so Lillian could see the half-chewed food. She was still complaining about the kind of mother he should have had, that let him run wild in the streets. He sat on her bed and let her talk herself into a few tears and then out of them again.

"Kiss me and go play," she finally said. Her cheeks were pink and her blue eyes shone. "Someday you'll be sorry you treated me like this."

He kissed her near the ear, trying to miss the discolored skin. She had been thrown against the windshield, bruised and thrown back again, caught by her safety belt. His father had gone straight through the glass, and looped like a kite in a wind current, before he hit a pine trunk and broke and slid down. Coker had dreamed this scene so often he felt he had been standing by the car when it happened. He even knew Daddy's mouth was open on one word, "COKER!" which meant, "Be careful, Coker, when I'm gone." Or maybe "Come with me."

Grandmother was waiting in the kitchen doorway, a glass of milk in her hand. "You wash that stuff down, and Coker? I'm sorry about the rock. Can you do something else? There's a toad in the yard. I saw him when I was burning trash. You might could find tadpoles in some pond, warm as it's been."

He didn't want a toad.

"Could you find cocoons? Or take down a few mud-daubers' nests. There must be a hundred under the house."

"What kind of bug is a mud dauber?"

"Bee or wasp or something."

He crawled under the back steps, ducking the ghostly touch of spider webs. The mud-daubers' nests were everywhere, long brick-red tubes of clay which clung to the wood like small organ pipes. He broke off a set of four. The next nest was brittle, shattered in his fingers, and spilled out a dozen black balls the size of buckshot. In the dust, Coker rolled one with his finger. It was a curled, dry spider. . . . He picked up a few more and pinched them to powder. Then he crawled out and went to find his grandmother.

"How come there's dried-up spiders inside?"

She was talking on the telephone and shook her head. "A little better, I guess. All things considered. You know Lillian's always had these nerves. She can't help it. Even when she was a little girl? Just a minute." She pressed her fat hand on the mouthpiece. "They eat 'em, I guess, Coker. Now run on. I'm busy."

Coker had never thought a spider had any enemies but people. A spider that didn't get stomped, he felt, would live to old age and die slowly and lazily in the sunlit center of its web. Should any bird eat a spider that bird would choke from its poison and tickle, and fly straight ahead into somebody's window.

He carried two mud nests to his room and got out the six-volume *Picture Facts* set he got for Christmas but had never read. Frogs, toads, and birds — it said — would eat spiders. Also wasps and praying mantises. One wasp invades the burrow of the trap-door spider, paralyzes it with a sting, and lays an egg on the abdomen — which will hatch and feed on its still-living but helpless host.

Coker was shivering; he didn't know why. It wasn't from pity for the spider.

Carefully he broke open another of the hollow clay rods. More shrunken spiders spilled across his desk, sucked dry by larvae which had long since spread wings and flexed their narrow waists and broken free. When his grandmother called supper, he scooped it all into a drawer.

Grandmother had been crying. Her cheeks were patched with red, as if someone had stood near with a file and rasped here and there on her face.

"What's the matter?"

"It's nothing. Your mother's a little upset."

"She's always upset."

"If only you could understand, Coker. You will when you're older. She's high-strung. This accident . . . we have to be patient."

"Daddy was patient."

"He certainly was." She cried quietly, a paper napkin flat on her eyes.

(Daddy was patient and Daddy is dead.)

Grandmother stopped rocking on her heels and joined him at the supper table. "Eat while the gravy's hot." She leaned back, not eating with him. She seldom ate much at meals, though she was very fat. She ate all the time she was cooking and all the time she cleaned up, and out of her apron pocket all day long.

She gave a rustling cough. "Let me put it this way, Coker. If somebody had a weak leg all his life, we wouldn't blame him if he couldn't run fast — right? Lillian's got a weak nature, weak nerves. She had to go to a doctor half of last year — remember that? You don't get cured, exactly. You just keep a weakness from getting worse."

"That's what the doctor said? She was born with some weak part?"

His grandmother slapped more mashed potatoes on his plate and drenched them with chicken drippings. "I don't think," she said angrily, "that doctor had the first idea what was wrong with Lillian." She poured his glass too full of milk. "What did you decide about the mud daubers?"

"I decided on spiders."

"Spiders. H'm. Well. You'll have to be careful. Some of them . . ."

"Bite," he finished.

At lunchtime, Coker hid in the boys' toilet while his classmates thumped down the hall to the cafeteria. Tiptoeing, he found the school library unlocked. He had never liked it, but now that the room was deserted he had a sense of ownership, and marched around giving every globe a twirl. He looked up "Spiders" in the card catalogue, then located 595 on the shelves. For an hour he read. When the librarian came back, he checked out three books and hid them under his shirt; he didn't want his teacher to think she'd won some battle.

In Science period, Mrs. Markas wrote their topics in a long list on the board. Sue would paint oak leaves in a booklet, with different species at different seasons. Clyde was bringing his salamander and Becky her goldfish. Everybody groaned. They were all sick of Becky's skinny goldfish, which had also come to Pet Day and to Show and Tell, and had served as a model for Plastic Arts.

"And Coker Gibson," said the teacher, "is making us a nice rock collection."

"Spiders," Coker said.

The chalk squeaked once and stopped. "Spiders? What do you plan to do, especially, about spiders?"

"Everything."

Becky, who had made a career from the dime-store aquarium, bent over to giggle.

He stood in the aisle and kicked her desk till she hushed. "I'm bringing in webs. And spiders in jars. And egg cases. When spiders catch bugs, they suck them dry and live on nothing but juice. They can change skeletons and go on living. Some make parachutes and float out to ships at sea. Some spiders can walk on top of water. Some grow so big in South America they catch and eat birds." He sat down heavily and jarred his backbone.

The class was silent. Mrs. Markas finally wrote "Spiders" by his name and let loose a nervous laugh. "We certainly don't want any of *those!*" she said. "You must be sure to let a grownup help you, Coker, so you don't get hurt."

She drew a spider (with only six legs) on the board and sketched in an hourglass on its back instead of its belly. Coker knew what it was.

"Don't worry," he said firmly. "My father will help me." When Mrs. Markas turned with her mouth open, he only stared at her, smiling. She hesitated, then let it pass. He guessed she would call up his grandmother tonight and discuss how best to help him. While she was writing the next name, Coker hissed over his shoulder to Becky, "Don't you want a water spider to go in your goldfish bowl?" She did not answer.

Going home that afternoon, he saw hundreds of spider webs he had been walking past all his life. Some looked like hammocks, others like sheets of silk; and the great wheels which floated between bushes, said his book, were the work of orb weavers. A large black-and-gold spider hung in the center of one, like a brooch pinned on a woman's hairnet. When the wind blew, she rode the billowing web in and out as if even empty space could breathe.

Coker half ran home so he could watch his mother's face when he called. "My Science subject is spiders! Want to help?"

Lillian pressed into the headboard of the bed, her closed teeth showing. "Spiders! Lord, no! What kind of thing is that for the school to make you study? What good will it ever do you to know about those nasty things? I don't see a thing wrong with wildflowers. Or birds. Couldn't you put a feeder outside my window and study birds? They'll be building their nests this month and it would give me something to do. Not that you care whether I lay here all day. . . ."

He ran out of her room, not listening but singing over and over in rhythm:

> "Why did the fly
> Fly? Because the spider
> Spied her.
> Why did the fly
> Fly? —"

"You come back here while I'm talking to you, Coker Ray Gibson!"

He swayed downstairs to his tune. Why did the fly fly? Because the spider spied her. . . . That was one thing about Lillian's broken jaw. Bound as it was, she couldn't really scream at anybody in the old way. The doctor had to give her special tranquil pills, Grandmother said, because of those unscreamed screams. Last year she'd taken them, too, as an outpatient. For weeks Coker had thought this term had something to do with her saying so often, "I am out a patience!" Lillian was always out a patience with weather, bills, all neighbors. Arched hairs above her eyes which grew faster than anybody could pluck. The lack of simple appreciation in this world. And Coker.

Once, her patience all gone as usual, Lillian went to P.-T.A., and when Coker interrupted a talk she and his second-grade teacher were having, she slapped him in the mouth. Then she began to cry and the teacher didn't know which one she ought to comfort. After that, Coker stopped bringing home notices about P.-T.A.

Some days, too, Lillian would set out to "make everything up to you, Coker." Those were the worst of all. The dining-room table would wait for him, sagging with cakes in two or three flavors, and his bedroom floor would be waxed so slick he had to walk across with care. Usually there were flowers all over the house — on the window sills and tables, standing in vases and jars and detergent bottles. Once, Coker found a rosebud jammed into every spigot. Daddy's and Coker's chairs in the dining room would be lined with bed pillows, the table set with linen cloth and place mats and napkins and rows of extra forks, with candles burning at just the right height to blind them as they ate two meats, and baked dishes, and vegetables with sauce poured over them, and soup you could see clear through. They would both rave, would praise her, would eat till they bloated; but none of it would do. Never could they eat enough, marvel enough, be grateful enough. In the end, Lillian would run upstairs to cry, the whole house full of dirty dishes, candle wax, wilting flowers. "What did I do?" Coker used to wail. "What did I say to make her cry?" His daddy would grip him inside his hard, warm arm. "It's not your fault. Not anybody's fault. And Coker?" Daddy would make him lift his face. "It isn't her fault either."

He was sorry he had allowed himself to remember that. His father's voice was so real inside his head, he could have sworn it had just poured, living, through his ear. Instead of rising, by magic, inside his brain. Coker began flapping his arms and leaping to blot out that magic.

As he went dancing through the back door (Why did the fly fly? Because the spider spied her), his grandmother called, "That's all the time you're spending with your mother?"

Still reciting, Coker scooted at speed under the back porch and fell belly-down in the cool dirt. It smelled as if a light rain had just ended. He lifted up a board, and hard-shelled bugs fled toward the dark. There was a web overhead with a fragment of brown leaf in it. Coker broke off an anchor line and felt the sticky silk near its base. He reached for another.

The sudden burn on the tip of his forefinger made him jerk back. He drew it close to his face and, in the dimness, could barely see the pinprick where the pain began. Under his eye, the pad of that finger turned numb and his skin seemed to harden down toward the knuckle. The web trembled. He saw a pale brown spider race along one of the threads and hide in the brick pillar. No widow, then. Coker tried to bend his fattened finger but it seemed to be turning to bone. Sticking it deep in his mouth, he sucked hard. He sensed this was an important moment, like those when Indians cut themselves in brotherhood and pressed their wet wounds to each other. He slid near the stacked brick and found the spider, drawn back in a hole in the mortar. She should have been watching him through many eyes, but in the gloom he couldn't count. Coker slid out into the sunny yard, certain that — behind him — the spider had already begun to reweave the framework of her web.

Sucking his swollen finger, he wandered through the large back lot. Grass and dirt in patches, unpruned trees, tangles of vetch and dandelion, privet which had grown into trees, an arbor with its back broken under scuppernongs. There were funnel webs in the weeds and now and then a long silk cable strung so far he had to follow its lead to find the woven snare. Sometimes he could see the folded, silk-lined leaf in which some spider held her trapline and waited.

From his room, Grandmother called out the window, "What's ailing your finger?"

"Nothing." He asked her to throw down his red library book and, grumbling, she unhooked the screen and dropped the book into his hands. Coker stuck it in his belt, climbed his knotted rope, and slid onto the narrow platform he had nailed in the sycamore. He had not read far before he came across the spider gardens of Madagascar where — in the nineteeth century — spiders had been raised to harvest their tough but delicate silk. He had never heard of Madagascar, a red-earth island which (the book said) broke off thousands of years ago from the coast of Africa.

Coker stared from his tree into the wide back yard, its red Carolina clay worn in places as hard as brick. From where he sat, it seemed that every gleam and glisten was the home of spiders who belonged to him, his whole garden ashine with their handiwork. He whispered, "Madagascar," and nipped dreamily at his aching finger.

Then, by will alone, he broke his Madagascar loose from the continent and shoved it out to sea. He leaned into the trade wind which blew smartly through his sycamore, and when Grandmother called him to eat, her voice was almost lost in the pounding surf. There were dark Africans everywhere, barely out of sight in the tangled vines, winding silk strands onto bamboo spindles. Some of them hummed at their work, like bees.

Finally, with one great swoop of his rope, the King of Madagascar swung onto the mainland. Behind him he could hear the blue lapping of the waves and the high sweet whine of a thousand spinnerets.

When Coker was five, the whole Gibson family had come under siege. He could still remember that fear. Some of it had stayed in the house, under the stairs and in the basement, soaked in like stain where no air or light could reach.

The siege began when a parked car on a sloping street shook free of its brakes and drove itself downhill and through the plate-glass window of his daddy's appliance store. "Insurance will cover it," Daddy said in the hall as soon as Lillian would allow him to speak. He hung up his coat and did not see — as Coker did — the quick blanching of her face, nor hear her whisper on the way to the kitchen, "I wonder why They did that?"

Soon Coker could tell that, during the day, his mother heard sounds too dim for him to hear. She would be tying his shoes and suddenly her head would tip back, listening, her neck as hard as the bough of a tree. He was called indoors when people passed their house, and backed against Lillian's legs to watch through the curtains till they were out of sight. Sometimes he woke from his nap to find her sitting guard by his bed, a broom upright in her hand. One night he dreamed animal men were meeting in his closet, each with teeth like the prongs of a dinner fork. He screamed; and when Lillian came to hear his babblings about the closet, she threw all his clothes out onto the floor and, by the time his daddy came, was on her hands and knees rapping inside for secret doors.

Then she went away for two months and came back with some kind of doctor's pills that dulled her hearing, so she could no longer tell enemies were rustling the shrubbery or breathing behind doors. Coker then worried that the attack might come by surprise, so he tried to listen alertly as she had; until sometimes he, too, could hear Them. After a while he forgot, and They left to lay siege to families in other houses.

Now that he was ten, Coker understood They were magic enemies inside Lillian's head, the way Daddy's remembered voice rang so real in his own. But why couldn't Lillian shut them off by will? He could rid his own brain of anything by vigorous running and yelling. Sometimes he wondered if those medieval people in Taranto, Italy, shown in his book bitten by tarantulas and thus hurled into frenzied dancing, did not thus clean their minds down to a healthy blank. After the accident, he even asked his Grandmother Barnes to buy a tarantella record for Lillian's phonograph, but she never did.

Early in May, Lillian was strong enough to come slowly downstairs on aluminum crutches and prop her cast on a hassock and watch television. Her face now was barely dingy with bruises, and her yellow hair grew dark brown near her scalp.

"Here's this good quiz show, Coker. Come watch it with me. We always used to have such a good time watching programs together."

As long as Coker could remember, Lillian had been claiming they used to do this thing and that, none of which he could ever recall. Perhaps that was magic, too.

"I've got to work on my project," he said from his card table in the corner. He had lacquered various spider webs and mounted them on pasteboard. This had taught him that when a web was not snug against the backing, cutting one foundation line would cause the whole thing to disintegrate. In a fishbowl closed with wire screening, he had imprisoned two spiders, a wolf and a crab, the latter able to change colors and match any flower it sat upon. Coker had been feeding them lightning bugs and moths, but his real hope was that one would attack the other while he watched.

"What's in that jelly jar?"

"Egg sac." Inside, perhaps, there were already hundreds of spiderlings, shedding their first skin and growing tiny claws. When they tore their way out, Coker would carry them outdoors and watch them throw out their first silk, like parachutes, and be windblown all over Madagascar.

Lillian said to her mother that the boy was getting creepy. Spiders. That was all he talked about anymore.

"Maybe he'll go into science. A doctor."

"God, I hope not!" Lillian twisted her mouth. "All they give you is words and sugar pills. I need to get away from doctors. Soon as I'm well, Coker and I ought to take a little trip."

"The beach, maybe," said Grandmother, turning all her wrinkled fat upward in a smile. "It would do you both good."

"New York. I've never been to New York. I wouldn't mind living there."

"What would Coker do in a place like that?"

"For goodness' sakes. Art museums, zoos. Central Park. You're just like Will. He never liked big cities." With her remote-control button, Lillian flipped around every TV channel on the dial. "I'd have been happier in a big city, I know that much. I told him often enough. Not that he cared."

Grandmother frowned.

"In New York schools, they probably study space and physics, things like that. Coker could go to a planetarium." On TV a man in a spangled suit was playing the piano. Lillian turned it off. "You should have made me keep on with music lessons."

"You wouldn't practice," Grandmother said. "You used to hold your breath."

"It was your job to *make* me." Suddenly she shivered. "Coker, can't you keep that mess in your own room? I can almost feel things crawling on my skin."

"All right." That's why he hadn't been able to keep the dog, or the cat, or the canary bird. They gave off mites and fleas into the air. As he carried his project upstairs, Coker heard the women arguing about whether Lillian had taken her last pill at the right time.

Late in the night, coming back from the bathroom, he heard her crying softly in her wide bed. He tiptoed in. "Mother?" She reached out her long fingers and pulled him on the bed against her chest. His own sudden need to cry smothered him.

"Will's dead," she whispered. "What will we do?"

He didn't know.

"Tell me you love your mother."

He told her. Something burned sharp in him, like the sting of venom piercing through his chest wall. He could not tell whether it would kill him or change him to something marvelous. "I do love you, Mother, I do!" he cried, digging his face into her neck.

"I'm so lonely, Coker. And can't sleep. Stay here awhile." She helped him into her bed, lacing his fingers with hers. He lay alongside, staring at the black ceiling. His feet reached only to her knees, one of which was cold and hard in its plaster cast. He thought about Christmas morning till his eyes got wet.

Near his ear she said, "We've got to get out of this house, honey. Make a new life. Everything's going to work out for us now. I'm getting well in lots of different ways, Coker. You're going to be able to see a lot of difference in me as the weeks go by."

"O.K." All day Christmas, Lillian had laughed. Sat in his father's lap to light the new meerschaum pipe. The picture, by magic, flared up in Coker's head. He squeezed her fingers.

She jerked his. "Is that all you can say?"

"Whatever you want, Mother."

"Well, don't you even care? Wouldn't you like that?" She rolled away, the broken leg left like a dragging anchor near his bare foot. Into the pillow she said, sighing, "Everybody's so hard to please. I know plenty of boys would get real excited about living in New York with an elevator right by their front door. I guess you wouldn't care if we lived on the dump and you had to wear feed sacks to school."

He slid to the edge of the mattress.

"Plenty of mothers could lean on their sons in a time of grief. Talk things over with them. Make plans." She groaned. "If they'd left me in the car a little longer, I might have burned to death. Sometimes I'm sorry they pulled me out."

"I'm not sorry," he said loudly, getting out of her bed. "I'm really not, Mother. But listen, why can't you? Why can't you? Why can't you?" He could not find the right end to his question; there was no word in the language for it.

He ran into his own bedroom, closed the door, and stared straight at the blazing bulb in his lamp. His eyes stung. When he walked to the window, the glare stayed with him and turned the glass opaque. Beyond it, wakeful spiders fed from their silver nets. When Coker's eyes adjusted, he thought he could see their strands like thin Christmas tinsel.

He tried hard to remember Christmas, but it was nearly Mother's Day. He dragged the glass cookie jar from under his bed and into the light. Under its lid of wire screening, a black spider turned in her web till the lamplight gleamed on the red hourglass low on her fat belly. Twin drops of blood. Coker watched her weave shut the capsule in which her eggs were stored. The silk wrapping was spun tighter and tighter and thicker and thicker. Satisfied at last, she backed into her silken tunnel in the core of her web and looked out where her egg case hung like a small world in a small, strung universe.

Someday soon, Coker was going to have to decide where he would turn her and her children loose — in Lillian's room, or his.

Benson Watts is Dead and in Virginia

After I died, I woke up here.

Or so it seems. Perhaps I am actually still dying, locked in that darkness between one breath and the next, still wearing tubes which leak from my nostrils and drain that long incision. My wife may even yet continue to bend over the high bed to catch the next beat of my heart while the blood jar is ticking down, like a water clock, into my veins. Perhaps that last hospital scene is the only scene and all the rest is a dream in passage.

But the room and her melting face clicked off, I think. Then the smells went. She was saying something; I could still hear that — I stopped hearing it. I unbloated and the queer whistle in my breathing stopped. I could no longer tell the pain from cold. All my circuit breakers opened and sensations blurred. Someone set fire to my hand but it barely tickled.

Through all this, my mind was clearer and more finely tuned than it ever has been. I treasured that clarity, though it had less and less raw material to think with now. I thought: I must withdraw into my brain and hide — there's nothing left outside.

So I did. I backed into my brain farther and farther and got smaller and smaller the deeper I went, until I fell out the other side.

And woke up prone in this yellow grass. The color is important. When they rolled me back from surgery, it was May.

At first I didn't dare move. If I lifted my hand, it might fall through the air and drop back onto a starched sheet. I could not tell what was still attached to me and might clatter if I stirred.

The place where I lay was so . . . so ordinary. A sky as blue as a postcard. Between it and me, one tree limb: oak. White oak, I thought. The grass felt like all grass. When a cricket bounced over my head, I knew for sure we were a long way from the recovery room; they would not recover me. I sat up. I was on a sloping postcard meadow. At the bottom, a narrow stream. Willows. I touched my abdomen, which should have been hot and painful. Dacron trousers instead of gauze. Not mine, though. These were new.

Around my left wrist hung a small bracelet and a yellowish tag which looked like the ivory sliver off a piano key. On it, carved, was the following:

TO AVOID G.B. —

1. Dwell, then travel
2. Join forces
3. Disremember

Very carefully, I got to my feet. It had been a long time since I could move without pain. The cool wind was a shock and made me clap both hands to my head. Bald as an egg! Not even a prickle, a wisp, a whisker. Otherwise I was myself as I had been before the intestinal cancer, even a little younger. I tried to guess by flexing muscles, checking where pounds were gone, feeling my smoother face. A little beard starting down the cheeks. I thought I might be forty again, or maybe less. I tried out my voice. Normal. For practice, I said aloud, "Well, it sure as hell isn't Heaven," and my laugh was normal, too, — forced, but even that was normal. I took a few steps, then ran downhill and splashed into the water in a pair of shoes I had never owned. Everything normal. A bright September day and I was alive in it.

Yet there was something. There was something wrong with my mind. Too quiet up there, not enough panic. Too small a load of bewilderment, not even enough curiosity. Earlier I said of the tree limb, "White oak, I thought," and that wasn't right. I didn't *quite* think. This was spooky. It was more as if Something thought in me. I felt the words were moving by their own choice through my head the way air bubbles slide down the bowel.

I began walking along the stream bank waiting for — I don't know. For my head to clear? I felt aged forty from the neck down. I waited for that age to rise and cover me like water.

I was in Texas when I died. These hills and fields and meadows looked more to me like — what should I guess? — like Virginia. I said this over and over, aloud, "I'm dead and in Virginia," trying to make the sentence taste like mine. It never quite did.

Now and then, beside the stream, I would spot hoofprints. Cattle? Or deer? I saw nothing else alive except me, that cricket, and dozens of yellow birds on quick and nervous flights. Ricebirds in Virginia? They fed off tall stems and some stunted bush with brown catkins on its twigs. I jangled my wrist tag. I'd worn a bracelet there in the hospital, too, with my name spelled out in beads like an infant's. WATTS. Benson Watts. Ben.

I got the first pain, under one ear. Ben Watts. 226 Tracy Avenue . . .

I got the second pain, a needle, higher. I rattled the tag. *Disremember,* it said.

Crossing the stream, I noticed for the first time I was traveling in the direction it flowed — there! You see how my brain was? Unobservant. Unconcerned. At the water's edge was a stretch of pale sand. Beyond that the mud was like milk chocolate. More yellow grass grew on both sides to the edge of trees just turning from solid green to red maples and yellow hickories. The scattered pines were thinning their needles for fall.

I rounded a bend. To my right the land dipped off, and the water turned and ran downhill faster to empty into a long lake I could not see the end of, maybe half a mile wide. Its surface was very still with a skim of reflections. As I got closer, I knew what was wrong with this scenery, so ordinary and yet so unreal; and it came from absence. Everything I expected to see did not appear. No boats or motors, no fishermen, dogs, garbage, foam, signs, fences. No plastic bottles drifting near the shore. My head was aching. The sun was too harsh on my peeled scalp.

Near the water I glimpsed a small house, almost a hut. *Déjà vu.* I spun to the southwest to see if the Fitchburg Railroad skirted the lake. No. Yet it was his house or nearly like it, built beside the pond a hundred years ago for less than thirty dollars. Built yesterday. I began to run through the ripening grass. If I was back in time, was Thoreau inside? Writing in his journal? Or was it possible that each of us died away into our own personal image of serenity and would be tucked there forever like something in a pocket?

Running made my head worse. But that gut I had cursed for a year was now so new and strong I thought it might be turned to gold or silver, and I ran with both palms pressed there to feel each strand of muscle move.

The wooden door was half open, heavy on its leather hinges. I jumped a low stone wall and ran up the path.

One room with an earthen floor, a smaller one beyond in which I could see strings of onions, peppers, and bean pods. I touched the table, chair, bunk, saw that high shelves on both sides of a fieldstone hearth reached over my head. They held a set of books, maybe a hundred, all with the same green binding. I called out "Hello!" to more absence. Nobody answered; though there were ashes in the fireplace, not quite cold, and the charred spine of a book which seemed to match the others.

There was no dust. Under the bunk I found a stack of empty picture frames, white canvases, a wood box of paints and brushes, and I could see the clean squares on one wall where somebody's pictures had hung. There were no titles on the books, and when I pulled one out I found each page was lined but blank — the other books were the same. This time something happened that I expected; I found pen and ink on the bottom shelf.

To enter the back room I had to stoop. It was a pantry with a board floor. Cured hams were hanging from the ceiling over a flour bin. Crocks of meal and dried beans in sacks were under a table on which apples, potatoes, yams, pears, green tomatoes lay in neat rows. One high shelf held what looked like scuppernong wine in gallon jars. The woodbin was behind the door, full of oak logs, with a sack of cedar kindling nailed outside. The pantry was dim and its odors thick as fog.

I laid the wood over the andirons. Matches had been left in a tin by the hearth, and after I lit the lightwood I rummaged in a second strongbox where small jars of spices were jumbled, some without labels. I read once that if a man eats nutmeg his urine will smell like violets. Perhaps I will try it.

Slowly the oak bark caught fire underneath, curled off, till the log smoked and finally burned. Beautiful was the fire. Its colors moved and changed. I sat before it, watching for the sudden lick of blue which would reappear in a new place. So long as I stared into the flames, my head did not hurt. When there were coals, I slid three sweet potatoes in to roast and sat on, dreaming, sometimes tapping the log with a poker so sparks would leap off and shower onto the dirt floor. I must have sat that way for hours.

But the potato hearts were still raw when I peeled and ate them. I rolled the thickest log across the floor and heaved it into place. Then I went to bed though it was barely dark.

In the night I woke to hear rustling beyond me, something large scraping its hide between a bush and the wall of my house. There were no windows. In the red firelight I found the poker and carried it with me and swung open the heavy door. A large deer moved down the path, stepping as carefully as if he had made it, so heavily antlered that he seemed to be holding up an iron grille by stiffening his neck. He bent and drank from the lake, snuffled lightly, moved off along the water's edge. As soon as he passed, the frogs that he left would sing out again, so I could follow him through the dark long after he was lost to sight.

It was the same deer. I put the poker under my bunk with the paints and brushes. Only when I was settled and warm again and had closed my eyes against the glow of the fireside did I wonder: What does that mean? *Same deer?*

I knew suddenly it must be very dangerous to sleep. I might slide back. My gut would reopen; some bastard in a white coat would whisper, "He's coming out of it." I could almost see my wife hunched in her chair, the brown rubber tubes in her hands, waiting for me. And there was a drop of borrowed blood, halfway down, hung there till my arm would be under it.

But in spite of my fear I went to sleep and when I woke up, I was still here.

2

In the morning I could not remember the deer. I could remember getting out of bed in the dark, but not why. I ate an apple, found coffee beans and an old-fashioned hand grinder, and at last boiled the grounds in a cooking pot. The brew was thick and scummy, but its smell was magnificent. I remembered I'd had no cigarettes for two weeks, no solid food for longer than that. When I picked up the apple, saliva ran down my throat in a flood, and I felt my nose was twitching like a dog's.

I had dreamed about a deer. That's it. In the dream, an old stag came into this house and offered to carry me across the lake on his back. He spoke in rather a high voice for so large an animal. He told me that when many deer swam the lake, each rested his head on the haunches of the one in front, and since the one behind did the same, they suffered no trouble from the weight. He said the whole line swam for the far shore with all speed in this linked position, to reach land before being befouled. He would be lead deer on this trip, he said, and would carry me himself.

No. The headache started.

No, there had been a real deer, outside. I saw him by the lake. It was hard to remember the simplest details. Was it a doe, a fawn? I had never seen a deer this close before — that much was certain.

I grabbed one of the green ledgers and began to write down who I was and how I got here and that the deer was real. It was hard to write. My head felt as if something had come loose inside and was banging the bone. I read the entry twice, until I had it all straight and in order. Every day I would do this; every morning I would set down the previous day and read all the earlier entries. This would be good training for my mind, which, I now thought, had suffered oxygen deprivation there at the end. At the beginning? Whichever it was.

My name is Benson Watts and when I died in Houston, Texas, I was sixty-five and had grandchildren — none of whom I liked very much. I also had thick gray hair and brushy eyebrows. When I told my namesake grandson I looked like John L. Lewis, he didn't know who Lewis was. Now I'm twenty-five years younger, in Virginia, and my scalp is like orange rind, nothing but skin and pores; and I don't remember Lewis too well myself except for the eyebrows.

He might have been a principal in some school where I taught. He had the face for the job. For years I taught U.S. and world history in high schools all over Texas, for peanuts, because that left my summers free. Summers I read books, collected stamps, built halves of sailboats in the back yard, took auto trips, sold Fuller brushes (once), and encyclopedias (four times), coached Little League, tried pottery and built my own kiln, got divorced and remarried, and made notes for the book I would someday write on the Cherokee Indian in North Carolina. Here I am at last, dead and in Virginia, with a pen and inkpot and one wall of blank paper handy, and all I can remember is Tsali and the Trail of Tears. Some joke.

Once, too, I thought I might go to graduate school and write a book on the Dark Ages, on the flickers of light in the Dark Ages. By 1969, I thought we might be edging into the shadow of some new darkness, and without a church to persevere. I taught myself Latin so I could read illuminated manuscripts at Oxford instead of translations in Texas libraries. *Illuminated* manuscripts. What a good phrase! But I did not write that book, either, and now I cannot call up a single Latin root.

All I can easily remember are random facts about myself, which don't amount to much. Trivia. The substance is missing. Let me write down the details.

Texas is bigger than France. There are four or five Texases to be born in — mine happened to be Beaumont, four years after the Spindletop oil gusher blew in. There might have been 10,000 people there then; the city multiplied itself by twelve in my lifetime. I stopped liking Beaumont when it passed 20,000, finished at Baylor, and started teaching history to conceited teen-agers who — if they owned the world and Texas — would rent out the world and live in Texas. That may be why Lyndon Johnson went to Washington, to see for himself how unlucky everybody else was. He stayed gone a long time.

Most summers I escaped from Texas, and once in the Notre Dame library I read the twelfth-century bestiaries and made notes, later lost in a Southern Railway boxcar. In the thirties I jumped freights and thumbed and left my wives (there were three in all) to go discuss me with their mothers.

The third wife, Grace, sat with me in the Houston Hospital while I died. She didn't shed a tear. Grace came late in my life; she never expected much, so was never disappointed. When I loaded up the car, she'd stand in the yard with her arms folded and just say, "Okay, Sunnybitch, don't leave me no dirty laundry." Grace had Indian blood. I miss her calm ways and her slow talking in an alto voice. I've seen her make a face at a coming tornado and then go inside and forget about it. Nothing affected her much. Even sex. She was a challenge. If Grace had cried — even once — in that sterile hospital room, I might have stuck out a finger; I might have blotted that tear and sucked it off and gotten well, just from the novelty of the thing.

She didn't cry, though, and I had not died off into a medieval abbey or a Cherokee camp. You'd think there'd be some choice. They even claim to give you that in the army.

Outside the hut I sat with my book and pen by the lake in the warm sun, reminding myself how the deer had stood and blown the water. Yes, it felt like September here. Indian summer. And for all I knew some real Indian, even a Cherokee with strings of hickory bark around his waist, might step out of these woods. Wonderful!

Might shoot me with his locust bow strung with bear entrails. Not so good. Could I die twice? Re-die? All that was . . . metaphysics. I could not think about it yet.

Could not. The landscape would not allow me. Virginia was opposed to thinking. While I sat in the brightness, empty as a sack, a praying mantis climbed up a weed stalk and lay along its blade. I bent my face beside that green swaying. Red knobby eyes. The only insect, I'm told, that can look over its shoulder. Maybe when this one died of winter, she would be raised up to my scale; as maybe I — shrunken — was now living on the tip of some weed and my lake was a dewdrop in the morning sun.

Yet none of this interested me. The four spread legs, two bent prayer claws, wings folded in layers on her back — I could have watched these tiny things all day, as I had waited for a blue flick on a burning log the night before.

Once I would have touched the mantis to see where she would spring. It was not necessary. I had been let out of thinking as if thinking were a jail. Nothing expected me to connect it with anything else. Not to anticipate — delicious. I felt that first morning the way a baby feels. *I am here.* Nothing else.

Some days went by. My ledger notes are sketchy. Like Thoreau, I gave time to birds and anthills. One afternoon — feeling so far from my other world that I mistook distance for wisdom — I analyzed completely how Western culture fell apart after World War II, and wrote down how this might have been prevented. My words lacked urgency. Nobody would read them. I bored myself.

After burning that, I tried to put on canvas my nighttime deer bent over a floating picture of himself in the black water. My painting was squat and clumsy, a hog at a wallow.

The fifth morning I was sitting on a log by the lake, watching the mist rise. Every morning it lay over the lake like cloud, then slowly churned to blow up the shore and fade among the tree trunks. I watched it begin to thin itself over the land. Down the lake, the mist suddenly shook like a curtain and I had a glimpse of someone walking by the water's edge.

I ran forward a few steps. Like gauze, the air blew shut. I saw it again. If not a man, a bear, upright and moving toward me.

My eye fixed on the fog, I walked in that direction. Fear? I could not remember how it felt to be afraid. In the thinning haze I saw again a — a polar bear? Impossible. White but too small. We could hear each other now. Crackling brush, dry stems breaking underfoot. I moved faster but those other noises stayed unhurried and regular. The mist was waist-high. I walked beyond it into a field of broom sedge and she, at the same moment, worked out of a wispy alder thicket and stared at me. She had on a white uniform, like a nurse.

I called, "Hello!"

She kept one bent alder limb taut in her hand. She was in her late twenties, red-haired, and pregnant. I saw that not only in her shape but the way she stood, bare feet spread wide, her spine tilted. She stepped forward and the branch twanged behind her. "Who are you?"

"My name is Benson Watts. I live . . ." That verb wasn't right. I jerked a thumb over one shoulder. "I've been staying in a little house by the lake."

"Good," she said. "I've not had anything to eat but persimmons. My mouth has shrunk down to zero." She gave me a normal-sized smile as she passed. "This way?"

"Just follow my track. What are you doing here?"

"Eating persimmons is all so far." Flatfooted, she walked along the swath I had made in the ripe weeds. I could not think of a way to ask a pregnant woman if she were dead. I thought about it, but the question sounded impolite. I followed. She was no more than five feet tall. Her short hair was full of beggar's-lice and sticktights.

I said, "Have you been here long?"

"Don't remember."

Her white skirt was streaked with mud and resin. "What's the last thing you do remember?"

"Spending the night in the woods. Oh. There it is." She made for my cabin in that stride which, from behind, looked bowlegged and clumsy. "What's the last thing you remember?"

I decided to say, "A hospital room."

"You're not contagious, are you? TB or anything?" She looked back and I saw how thickly her face was freckled. "You can see why I've got to ask." She patted her belly with her left hand on which she wasn't wearing a single ring. There was a bracelet, though, like mine. I pulled at her tag and turned it over. *Dwell, then travel. Join forces. Disremember.*

"Where'd you get this?"

"The fairies brought it," she said. "And the baby, too." She led the way into my house, stroked the earth floor with the sole of her foot. "This is nice." The tops of her feet were scratched, some of the marks white, some bloodied. I pointed to the pantry. Quickly she ran up to a dangling ham and laid her face on its salty mold. I said I'd slice and fry some. She poked among the pears until she found one mellow enough to eat.

While I chopped off some meat and set the pan in the fireplace, she finished the pear and bit into a cucumber, peeling and all. "What's in this sack?" she called. I was trying to keep the ham from catching fire. "Peanuts!" She crowed, "Oh, glory! Peanuts!" I heard them rattle in a pot. "Let's parch some." She pushed the pan onto a bed of coals and a little grease popped into it and speckled their hulls. "Smell that ham, honey!" she said — not to me, but to the lump at her middle.

I sat back on the dirt floor and let her tend the skillet. "What's your name?"

"Olena."

I had her spell it. I'd never heard that name before. I think she made it up.

"There's flour but no bread," I said. She didn't offer to make biscuits but sat back with her legs crossed wide under the round bulk of her unborn child. I thought through several questions before I chose, "Is your home around here?"

Olena said, "It never was before. Where's yours?"

"Texas." She plucked the fork from my hand and turned over the ham. I took a long breath and blew out a statement on it, watching her. "I was sick in a hospital and then I woke up here."

Olena said matter-of-factly, "I fell down a flight of stairs and this place was at the bottom."

We stared at each other, then quickly looked away. Each of us stole a glance at the pale tag strung to the other's wrist. With a grunt, Olena got to her feet and went to the pantry to find a plate and cutlery. I warned her pork needed to cook longer than that, but she was already spearing an oily slice. "I don't think you can get worms here," she said, staring at the ham.

"I see plenty of regular insects."

Chewing, she didn't care. "Oh, glory, that's good!" she said, with a sigh. I brought her a salt shaker and a tomato with the top cut off; she buried half her freckled face until its juice ran down her chin. "Can I sleep here tonight?" she asked, swiping a forearm over her mouth. I said she could.

Watching her chew the ham and pull its pink shreds from between her teeth, I tried to decide what accident had sent us both here, what kink in orderly process, whether there was some link between our lives or some similarity in our natures which made us candidates for transport to this place. I asked about the location of the stairs where she fell, and Olena said, "Florida. Fort Lauderdale." All I got out of that was a vague sense of regional districts, but it made me walk to the door and search the edges of the lake for some other Southerner. The mist had cleared.

"What you looking for?"

"Just looking." Somebody else would be coming soon. I felt certain of it. "Olena, is there someplace you're supposed to be? Or be going?"

She finished the ham and raked a pile of peanuts onto the floor to cool. "I guess not."

"We'll wait here a few days, then."

3

The fire kept me awake. Even with my eyes closed, its pattern of light and shadow on my face was a physical touch and moved like warm water across my skin. I rolled in my blanket farther across the floor and turned my back to the blaze. Above me, in the bunk, Olena lay, spread-legged, bulging. The covers seemed draped on an overturned chair. Behind me, the fire crackled. Rain had begun in late afternoon, so we kept the fire going against a wet chill rising through the dirt floor. Olena's snore was soft as a cat's purr.

I dozed, then leaped alert. What had wakened me? Perhaps that deer, passing my door, had ground his teeth? I threw back the blanket and sat up, listening. It must have been nearly dawn, since mockingbirds were taking turns, each song intensely sweet and swelling higher than the last. Barefoot, I crossed the damp floor and stepped onto the path. Raindrops on the weeds looked solid, like tacks or metal pellets, but the sky was full of fading stars. Far down the lake, something large and dark bent in the mist to drink, too wide and bulky to be a stag. My naked scalp prickled, for there had flared through my head the leaves of those old Latin bestiaries, page after page of winged quadrupeds and dromedaries, each fact of natural history bent to reflect an attribute of Christ. Just from Olena's presence, this landscape had become a dream we both were having and, like those books, took on some quality of concealment and mystery.

I started through the wet grasses to surprise the drinking animal, but it melted through the brush and downhill into the woods, looking odd and fictional. The woods were, at the same time, dark and translucent. It seemed to me even the tree trunks were spelling words I could nearly read. I rested my hand on the bark of one, and tried in its cracks and lichen crusts to make out the Braille. Not since I was a child had I felt this expectancy, as if at last I were on the verge of seeing everything unveiled. Most of my life I'd been certain there was nothing *to* unveil. A bit of lichen, like tough lace, came loose in my fingers.

Quietly, I walked inside the hut, dried my feet, and slid again into my blanket roll. Olena had turned her face to the wall and her back took on a woman's curves. I was fearful of desiring her. I slept and dreamed that my mother was lying on her deathbed and the doctor took a large white bird out of his satchel and wrapped its claws on the brass bedstead. "If the bird turns to face her," he said, "this is not a mortal illness, but if he keeps his back turned there'll be nothing I can do." The bird unfolded extra wings and feathers after being cramped in the leather bag and seemed to grow larger and larger. One at a time, he uncurled his feet and shook them, then flapped once around the room. Each wingbeat sounded like an oar slammed flat against the water. At last the bird lit facing away from my mother, who gave a great cry. I ran forward to beat at the big bird but I could not make it move or even look at me, and its yellow talons were wrapped on the metal rail as if molded there.

At daylight, we were wakened by loud thumps on the wooden door. Olena sprang half out of bed, one of her feet touching the floor.

"Don't worry," I said. "It's another one."

She whispered, "Another what?"

"Another one of us." I jangled my bracelet in the air between us and stepped into my shoes. I dragged open the heavy door.

He was ugly. Malformed — not deformed but *mal*formed — six feet tall and the parts of his body mismatched. Hips like a woman and a head flattened on both sides. I could not see a bracelet under the black sleeve of his suit. I pictured him yanked from his mother's womb, not by forceps, but with a pair of cymbals clapped over both ears. His face, driven together by the blow, was long and its features crowded. The nose, buckteeth, popeyes had all pushed forward when the doctor first compressed his skull. "Come in?" he asked softly.

"Of course." Another Southerner — Georgia Cracker by his drawl. "Are you hungry?"

Thinking about it, he rubbed his temples with both thumbs. "I think I just ate," he finally said, and spotted Olena waiting by the bed. "Good morning, Ma'am."

I introduced Olena and myself. He wasn't curious. "Melvin Drum," he said, and wrapped my hand in a long set of fingers. He was too thin for his black suit and the pale bow tie made his Adam's apple look red and malignant. He said politely, "Hate to wake you up."

"We've been expecting you." That puzzled him. He took a seat and stared at his knuckles while he popped each one.

"This is a funny thing," he said mildly. "It might be amnesia. But look here." He leaned his head forward and his longish tan hair divided into two hanks. "You see a knot there? Anything?"

I felt his scalp. "Nothing."

He leaned back and his eyes — which I had thought were blue — glowed green as a cat's. "Maybe I've gone crazy," he said, obviously pleased. "They say religious people do."

Dryly I said I thought Mr. Drum would find he had passed beyond all need for religion now.

He did not hear me. "It's hard to tell nuts from saints," he explained to Olena, "except for God, of course. He can divide them up left and right in the twinkling of an eye. The twinkling. Of one eye." Smiling, he tilted his chair onto two back legs and I grabbed for his sleeve where something gleamed.

"Can you explain this?" I said, shaking my own tag. "I can accept it," he said. He pulled his cuff over the third bracelet. "We've all passed on and these are our instructions."

"Passed *on*?" said Olena. She crossed to the pantry, carried back a skirtful of yellow apples, and sat on the floor to share them. "Are you certain you're dead, then, Mr. Drum?"

"That was the last promise I heard." His rabbit teeth bit out a sharp triangle and he talked over the sloshing noise of apple in his mouth. "I turned down an alley — there were three men bent over somebody. I tried to run. They grabbed me; one of them put a flashlight on my face and said, Oh, Lord, it was Willy and Willy had a big mouth. The one I couldn't see said, 'Willy's a dead man, then.'"

"Who's Willy?" I asked.

"God only knows." He read the carving softly: " 'To avoid going back — dwell, then travel. Join forces. Disremember.' Anybody want to go back?"

I pictured myself hooked up to tubes, pumps, catheters, filling and emptying at the nurses' convenience. No.

But Olena had pressed two freckled hands on her abdomen and was staring at them while her eyes filled. She sounded hoarse. "How did you die, then, Mr. Drum? After that promise?"

Tire iron, lead pipe, he wasn't sure.

"But you were cured of your final . . . condition. Your head wound. And you, Mr Watts, of yours. Does that mean? Do you think I?"

We tried not to look at what her hands were cupping. Melvin Drum leaned forward and his face shifted in some way I could not see; his tone dropped down an octave and he got older and almost dignified as he laid his thin hand on Olena's red hair. "Sister," he said, nearly rumbling, "leave it to God."

Water ran down her nose and hung there. "This baby's alive," she burst out. "You hear me? When the time comes, you'll have to help me birth. I won't leave that to God." She shook her head loose from under his hand.

"Yes, you will," he said, but I told her we'd both help and maybe by then we'd find a doctor, too.

Melvin Drum tapped his bracelet. "We've joined forces, then," he said. "When does the travel start?"

Tomorrow, we decided. We'd pack food and bottle water. Olena would rest today and we'd swim, clean our clothes. I wrote these things down in my green-bound book. "Which direction shall we take?"

Melvin said east seemed appropriate. I wrote that down.

In the afternoon, he and I floated on our backs in the lake while Olena hung our clothes on the sunlit bushes. My younger body was a joy to me, moving easily, stroking well. Melvin had a large genital and as we drifted I would sometimes see it shift in the water like a pale fish. "Were you married, Melvin?"

He said no. I thought he must be over thirty. "Were you queer?"

Laughing, he had to gargle out some water. "Very," he said. I don't think he meant for boys.

4

"I'm already tired," Olena complained. "Why must you walk so fast?" On her short legs, she had to make three steps for every one of Melvin Drum's. I was winded, too, and the sun stood directly overhead. "Why hurry?" she puffed, pushing swags of honeysuckle to one side, "when we have no destination and no deadline?"

"None that we *know* of," said Drum, leading the way like the major of a band.

Over her shoulder to me, Olena said, "This is silly. There's no time in this place." Overhearing, Drum pointed straight up at the blazing sun and kept marching. She poked him in the spine above his belt. "Disremember," she said.

We walked noisily, single file, through woods which were thick and shady, their fallen leaves ankle-deep; and the sun slid with us, shooting a ray through a thin branch now and then.

Olena carried the lightest pack — raisins, dried beans and figs, the peanuts she brought over our objections. Drum and I had mostly ham and wine and water jars. The kitchen knife I'd strung at my waist had pricked me half a dozen times climbing uphill from the lake. The land was level forest now, with no sign of paths or trails.

We rested by a shallow spring with a frog in it. I asked Drum, "You hear a river?" He said it might be. Olena stuck her red hair backward into the spring, so the ends uncurled and hung wetly down her back and dripped on the leaves in front of me when we walked on again.

"I'm ready to unstrap this blanket and leave it on some tree."

Drum told her for the third time we'd need blankets later.

"He thinks we'll still be hiking in December," she grumbled. "He's got a new think coming." She passed me a pocketful of peanuts to crack and eat as we walked. She wouldn't give Drum any.

The river still sounded far away when we saw it flowing low between walls of thicket and vines which had briers under their heart-shaped leaves. Drum stopped, and we stepped to either side of him and looked downhill. The water was brown and sluggish, with small sandbars in the middle. "Want to camp here?"

"Won't there be snakes?" But Olena let us lead the way and reach our hands back for her when the slope grew slippery or jagged. Rows of black willows kept us from the water's edge, but upstream Melvin Drum broke through to a slab of gray rock which jutted into the current and had built behind it a sandy pool. Olena unlaced my borrowed shoes and slid her feet into it. "Glory, that's cool!" she said and slipped forward until her white hem turned gray in the water.

"It's a good place to build a fire," Drum said, "But we might want to sleep on higher ground."

"I'm so tired all I'd ask a water moccasin is not to snore," she said, lying back and letting her toes float into sight.

Melvin and I dropped our packs to gather firewood and haul it to the rock. I nudged Olena's shoulder once with my toe. "All right?"

"Sleepy," she said. I climbed uphill for another load, thinking that was Drum who thrashed ahead of me through the bushes in the gathering dusk. I squatted to rip lightwood from a rotted stump. Suddenly, from behind, he spoke my name and I jumped up, pointing uphill at the moving underbrush. We watched the dark leaves stir.

"There?" said Drum softly. I saw only a dim trunk of a thick shrub; then it moved and grew a snout. I could make out between twigs the animal's long outline, lean and low to the ground, with a tail curved around its hind-quarters. He whispered, "Dog?"

"Wolf," I said. Lupus. Very still, like a carving or a piece of statuary. In slow motion the wolf began to back away uphill, and at one point I could see the whole arch of his back and the curve of his tucked-in tail. Once he stepped on a twig which snapped, and he punished his own paw with a nip. I saw the sharp flash of teeth. He turned then, and went up the slope in three long bounds.

Drum's breath blew out on the back of my neck. "A real wolf? Here?"

I didn't think it was a real wolf. More like an animated artwork I had seen drawn somewhere, and I said so. "Didn't you see how the shape was exagge-rated? It looked so . . . so stylized."

Drum sniffed at his armpit. "Well, I'm real enough. I'm organic and I stink and there's a blister on my foot."

I wanted to tell him about a pictured Lupus who could only copulate twelve days in the whole year and whose female could not whelp except in May and then when it thundered; but that was like saying a twelfth-century picture book had come alive before our eyes, and the Psalter or Apocalypse might be next. For all I knew, Melvin Drum had dream beasts in his own head to which I had yet to be subjected.

We carried down the remaining firewood, pulled the small bag of white beans out of its river soak, and boiled them slowly with a chunk of ham fat in our only pot. While they were cooking, I asked Melvin just how religious he had been.

"The last five years I thought of nothing else." He stretched out on the rock. "It's a shame I'm dead," he said, " because someday I would have finished the stealing and had it all."

"Stealing what?" asked Olena, stirring a peeled stick through the beans.

"Religion. I went in every church I could. Catechisms, hymnals, prayer books, rosaries, creeds — I stole them all. Went on field trips to the Mormons and Christian Scientists. I stacked all that stuff in my room. You could hardly walk for candles and books and shawls." Olena speared a bean for him but he shook his head that it was too hard to eat. "I was in Los Angeles at the end," he said. "On the way to visit the Rosicrucians."

She snapped, "What on earth was it for?"

He smiled at the rising moon. "You ever seen a big set of railroad scales? Where you keep adding weights till the arm is perfectly balanced? When I got all the stuff together, when I had collected the right balance . . . weight . . ." Suddenly he giggled toward the darkening sky. "It sounds dumber now than it did then."

I leaned toward him on both my gritty palms. "Doesn't your head hurt when you remember things like that?"

"No. Does yours?"

Olena said hers hurt, too, just behind both eyebrows. She spoke in a fast singsong: "So I've quit remembering I was a beautician and having a baby and he was already married and I didn't care and one day I fell down the steps of my apartment building all the way to the washing machines in the basement and the woman folding towels just stood there and hollered all the time I came rolling down and all I could see looking up was her open mouth and fillings in every tooth in her head." She grabbed her forehead. "Whew! That's the last time, damn it." She turned away and for a while the three of us lay flat on our backs on the hard rock, not saying anything, while the sky got darker behind the stars.

The beans took a long time to soften. We got our spoons out of our pockets and tried them and lay down again.

I was almost asleep when Drum said, "Why don't we use the river?"

"Use it for what? To travel, you mean?"

"Beats walking," Olena said.

"If we knew anything about boats or canoes," said Drum.

I sat up. "It happens I know a little." I told them how the Indians would burn down a big tree or find one struck low by a storm, and put pine resin and tree gum on one side and set fire to that, chopping out the charred wood and repeating the blazing gum, until they had burned the log hollow. "Some of their dugouts would carry twenty men."

"Won't that take a long time?" One of Olena's hands climbed up by itself and rubbed her belly.

"We have a rock, water, matches, trees . . ."

Olena pointed her finger at me. "Hah! Why didn't your head hurt? Talking about the Indians, why didn't your head hurt then?"

"I think," said Drum thoughtfully, "it must not hurt if the things you recall are useful to you. Useful now, I mean."

Which, in view of his vague religion, made us stare at him.

It was late when we spooned our mushy beans in the dark and rolled up in our blankets, tired enough to sleep on solid stone. If snakes crawled up at night, we never noticed. The last thing I thought was that any serpent I saw in this place would be like the one Pepys claimed could feed on larks by spitting its poison into the air, and for that one I would send forth a weasel, since — as the monks wrote in their illuminated manuscripts — God never makes anything without a remedy.

For all I knew, somewhere in Melvin Drums's last rented room there were stacks of medieval books full of viper-worms and amphisbaenae, and perhaps even stories of the Cherokee Thunders, who lived up in Galunlati, close to that great Apportioner, the Sun.

And Drum was right — thinking of all these things, my head never hurt at all.

5

After that come repeated entries in my ledger: "Worked on boat today."

I don't know how long it took. We had one hatchet and we used sharp rocks. My knuckles bled, made scabs, and bled again.

I slipped into a way of life I seemed to know from the bone out. Squatted in the woods, wiped with a leaf, covered my shit. I peed on tree trunks like a hound — it's instinct, I think. We're meant to give back our excrement to plants. We washed in the river. Even Olena, after a while, bathed with us and I stopped staring at her stretched white skin and the brown mat of hair below. My beard grew out itchy; there were welts across my chest and the beans made gas growl inside us all. One night I spotted the wolf's eyes shining near the rock and I called to him, but the lights stayed where they were. When the ham got moldier, we lived off fish. My fingernails smelled like fertilizer.

Olena kept saying the boat was done, but I wanted the shell thinner, lighter, and we chopped through the heartwood and sanded the inside down with stones. We pointed the stern and rounded the bow. Even after dark, we'd sit scrubbing her surface absently with rocks until she felt smoother than our calloused hands.

"She's ready," Melvin Drum said at last. "Admit it, Ben. We can go on."

I did not want to stop. It seemed to me there was grace in the log we had not yet freed, shape that was still unrefined. But finally I gave in. I crushed pokeberries in my palm and wrote on her side with a finger, *"Escarius."*

They made me explain. A labrus fish, thick-lipped, called by Sylvester "Golden Eye." The monks had thought the Scar clever, since, when it was trapped in a fish pot — they wrote — it would not dash forward but would turn around and undo the gate with frequent blows of its tail and escape backward. Other Scars, if they saw him struggle, were said to seize their brother's tail with their teeth and help him back loose to freedom.

We loaded *Escarius,* even filling our water bottles, though we would be afloat in water. We still had beans and damp peanuts, and we opened a jar of grape wine on the rock and poured some on the boat and each spat a swallow into the river — I don't remember why.

Pushing off from the gray rock, we started down the river, Drum and I trying our new poles and paddles. Olena sat amidships and let her fingers trail. She was singing. "Shall we gather at the river? The beautiful, the beautiful river? Gather with the Saints at the river that flows by the throne of God?"

Into the current we moved and skirted the sandbars, slipped silently past the drooping willows, and began an easy drift. The knobs of turtle heads dropped below the water as we drifted by, and floated up again when we had passed. We may have looked majestic, moving downstream in a boat so much longer than we needed. *Escarius* tended to wallow to this side and that, but we learned how to balance with our oars. Our rock went out of sight and the water seemed thick and reluctant and bore us without interest, slowly, while the river spread wider and showed us floodplains and sycamores with watching squirrels.

I felt like a man on a color calendar, poised with my oar level, going off the page and out of sight.

"She's all right," called Melvin Drum. "She rides fine."

Sometimes a snake would drop limp off a low limb and lie on the water like a black ribbon. Olena stopped worrying, since they seemed to fear us and would at the last glide toward the shallow edge and blend with tree roots there. "We're dreaming," she said, turning her face to me. "Even the snakes are dreaming."

The first set of rapids was shallow and we bumped down it like a sledge. Late in the afternoon we pulled up to a low bank under pines and slid the hull over brown needles and braced her ashore with stones. Olena found a tick on her ankle but said it was still a fair place to sleep. My shoulders ached. I walked up the small creek to relieve myself, and on its far side saw the bent tail and stiff fur of the same gray wolf as he slunk away. He could not be the same wolf, yet I was sure he was.

With darkness, the air turned cool and rain spattered overhead. We huddled together under our three blankets but slowly the wool soaked through. Then we just pressed together to outlast the rain, Olena with her back against a pine trunk, Drum and I on either side. Her knees were up, her face down. "I hate it here," she suddenly said. We leaned closer. "I hate it." Putting an arm about her shoulders, Drum and I got tangled with each other, and once I slapped at the wet shreds of his sleeve. "I could have been married by now," she said between her knees. "And had regular customers on my sun porch and bought myself a dishwashing machine." Rain poured over us. "I could have joined the Eastern Star," she wailed.

Trying to rub our foreheads on her soaked hair, Drum and I bumped skulls, and he said angrily, "You let me do all the work today!" Which wasn't so.

When at last the rain stopped, what could we do? We went on sitting there while the moon started down. We were soggy and chilled and had wet wool in our lungs.

In the morning nobody spoke. We spread our clothes to dry and tried to nap but the bugs were too bad.

"We might as well go on," I finally said. I felt resigned. There was nothing at the end of this river but a sea waiting to drown us. It would pull us home like caught fish on a line.

In silence, Drum wadded our wet blankets into the boat. Olena waded out and hoisted herself aboard, and without a word we pushed loose into the current. I was lonely and the river seemed hypnotic, just fast enough not to need our thrust. For a long time we sat with our oars laid in our laps. If Drum watched one bank, I stared at the other, and when his attention shifted I crossed mine over, too.

Once Olena said we should capture the next snake, lift him into the boat, just to see what would happen. Maybe, she said, if one of us was bitten he would move on another layer to someplace else. "We might wake up in the pyramids."

Or Bethlehem, she hoped. I stroked the water hard. Drum grabbed at blackberries hanging from the bank until his hands were purple. I said, "Am I using my paddle enough today? Are you satisfied?"

He said, "It was raining, Ben." We drifted on.

By night we had passed into drier land and could build a fire and string our clothes nearby. We heated a cup of wine apiece. I asked him, "Is there a God? Now? What do you think now?"

"It's hard to think here."

"You can remember, though, better than we can."

The tin cup covered half his face. "I'm like every other expert," he said. "In time, I got interested in the smaller sects. I specialized. Osiris or the voodoo drums. I went to the Hutterites and Shakers. Once I met Frank Buchman and I couldn't see anything special about him. A man had the Psychiana lessons, all twenty-four. It had cost him twenty-six dollars during the Depression; I won't tell you the price he wanted. I didn't pay, of course. I stole the set and hid it in my mattress." He finished the wine. "If a snake bit me, I'd wake up in Moscow, Idaho, asking about Frank Robinson." He said to Olena, "I'd just as soon be here. You feeling better?"

She had fallen asleep, mouth open, the edge of her teeth in view. I knew that I wanted to put my tongue there. I jumped when Drum said, "One thing we mustn't do is fight."

Swallowing, I nodded. He rinsed his cup in the river, stared across its lighted surface. "My brother used to have dizzy fits and he said he dreamed like this. Always of journeys and trips. Mostly he rode on a train that went very fast and roared. He was always on top of the engine, holding to the bells, and the whistle would go right through him, he said. If a tunnel could feel a train go through it, he said he could feel the sound of that whistle, boring, passing." Away from the fire, Drum looked taller. "The dream was always dark except for the engine lamps."

"Where did he go?"

"He woke up too soon."

"Is your brother dead now?"

Melvin Drum laughed coming back into the firelight. He couldn't stop laughing. Even after we had curled up in the damp blankets, I heard him laughing in the dark.

6

How was it possible to dream in that place? Yet I went on dreaming, every night, inventing an overlap of worlds which spun out from me without end. I dreamed of a life in an Indian village ringed by sharpened stakes, where my job was to be watchman over the fields of corn and pumpkins and to run forth with screams and rattles to drive off crows or animals. I dreamed of being alone on a sandy plain, lost, staying alive by eating fly larvae scraped from the surface of alkaline pools.

Drum said he never dreamed. Olena did; she tossed and grunted in her sleep but claimed she could not remember why in the morning.

We blundered on down the river, shipping water, overturning once in white froth when *Escarius* scraped a jagged rock.

"If we took turns sleeping, we could travel at night, too," Drum said; but what was the point now that time did not rush from left to right? Only the river moved — for all we knew, moved forever.

Finally the banks began to withdraw and the wider current slowed. We seldom had to use oars or poles. Early one morning, the shores were suddenly flung outward and we were afloat in a wrinkled lake which seemed without end. Drum said it might be an ocean sound at low tide, since the waves were light but regular. We turned south to keep a shore in view. Soon Drum thrust down with our longest poplar pole and struck no bottom. It flew under the water like a spear and bobbed up far away, beating slowly and steadily toward the sandy bank. Under the hot sun my brain cooked like stew in a pot.

Olena had been silent for a long time. Suddenly she burst out, "You two might be dead but I'm not." Perhaps the child had moved in her, or she imagined that it moved.

Over her head, Drum said to me, "Shall we keep on?" For the first time, he sounded tired.

"Olena?"

She jerked her face away from the disappointing shoreline, so plainly empty of other people like ourselves. Her freckles were wet and her sweaty forehead flamed. "There's nothing here," she said, almost whining. We stroked the water. "You, Melvin Drum, you made us leave that house too soon. Somebody else might have come if we had just waited awhile."

Or, by now, why hadn't we caught up with whoever had burned his books in that fireplace? Yet, I thought, Old Lobo might be the fourth one in our group, and I eyed the shore as if I might spot his gray head sliding through the water, parallel.

The sun had started down the sky when we landed on a small and wooded island pocked with crab tunnels. Drum built a fire and dropped a dozen crabs into boiling water. We carried them in cloths, like hot spiders, up the beach and into the shade of high bushes.

"I'll fix yours," Drum said, breaking off claws, throwing the flippers downhill on the sand. He separated back from body, then gouged down to a paper-thin shell. "Hand me your knife, Ben." He scraped out white meat for Olena and offered it in his palm. She ate bits with her fingers. I cleaned my own. In case there should be some later use for them, we scrubbed the pink shells with sand and set them to dry in the sun. Then, while Olena lay resting under a tree, Drum and I explored the narrow island. There were so many loud birds inland that every tree seemed to scream. We found one pool of brackish water and wild grapevines which still had late fruit, although some had fermented on the stem. We could barely see the shore from which our river had issued, but on the island's far side there was only water and some shadows which might be other islands.

Before dark, the waves grew higher and crabs at their foaming edges carried off the claws and flippers we had thrown. Olena felt pain during the night. Her heavy breathing woke us.

She sprang up and began walking on the damp sand, hunched over.

"She's aborting," Drum said, watching her pace.

Olena heard him and screamed that she was not.

"It isn't her time. She's not big enough for that," he added.

I called to her, "When were you due? What month?" But she would not answer.

Drum asked, "How long have we been here, anyway?" I looked back through these moonlit pages trying to count days, but it was hard to estimate.

I kept glancing at Olena. Drum jerked impatiently at my book. "Is it forty-nine days? Is it close to that?" I didn't know. He said something about people in Tibet once thinking it took forty-nine days for the passage between death and further life; then he clapped both hands to his head. I stared, for at last there was some piece of remembering that made Drum's head hurt. Good, I thought. I wanted his jaw-teeth roots to burn like fire.

I left him and crossed the sand to Olena. "I'll stay with you." The moonlight turned her hair black and skin gray and sank her eyes into pits. Together we marched on the cool sand. When the pain eased, we dragged her blanket closer to mine and I could feel the knob of her bent knee low in my back like something growing on my spine.

She had rolled to the other side when I woke at sunrise. I turned also, and fitted myself to her back. She only murmered as my arm dropped over her. Our parts were sweetly matched as if she were sitting in my lap; under the curve of her hips I could feel my stiffening heat. My fingers slid past her collar to her loose breast until they could play on her nipple like tongues.

Drum coughed. Over Olena's red curls I saw him watching my busy hand, staring at the cloth where it was moving. I pulled on her skin till the breast budded, all the while letting him watch. Olena was awake now. The cells in her body came alive and caused my own skin to prickle.

Now I yanked my blanket and threw it over both of us, taking care that Drum could see, and that he knew I saw him see.

Under the blanket, creating bulges for his following eye, I ran my long arm over the swell of Olena's child until my thumb was centered low in her body hair and my fingertips pressed on. She moved to help me. I heard her breath. Her leg slid wide and dropped back over mine until I was touching her at last. The hot grasp was too much for me and my spasm came while she was simply widening and making ready for hers. I kept on until she made noises and threw herself on her back, knees up and shivering. Instantly, so Drum could not see her taut face, she jerked up the blanket and pulled it to her eyebrows.

Drum never moved. I gave him a long look, but he never moved. I fell asleep with my hand on Olena's thigh and she must have slept also.

In the morning Drum was gone, and the boat *Escarius* was gone, and half our possessions were neatly laid out by the dried crab shells on the beach. There was a moving speck near the mouth of the river, but I could not tell for sure if it was man or animal and, when the sun got higher, could not find it at all in the glare.

7

Sweet days! Long, languid, poured out like syrup.

Olena slept in my arms. No sex in the regular way — because of her coming child — so, like curious children ourselves, we played touching games on each other's bodies.

Our clothes were very worn. I made a loin wrapping from my torn shirt; she sawed my pants off with a butcher knife for herself and left her breasts naked to the sun. We might have been Polynesian lovers from another age except for our bracelets, which, without ever discussing it, we did not discard.

Maybe ten days, two weeks went by. The nights were cooling but our afternoons were still part of summer. For many meals we dug clams from an inland mudbank, steamed them in salty water.

"Wouldn't you give anything for butter?" Olena said. She had persuaded herself the sea waters were supplying her baby rich brain food and protein. She would watch me slide a knife along a fish's backbone as if each filet were preordained to become some tender organ inside her unborn child. Maybe, she sometimes said half seriously, we should powder the fishbones since she had no milk to drink?

In spite of the sweet days and sweeter nights, I began gathering wood, poles, stakes, and lashing them together with strings of our ragged clothes or strips of bark. Olena didn't like the raft. "Where will we go? Not out to sea, and there's nothing ashore but wilderness." She ran a freckled hand around my waist, spun a fingertip in my navel. "You'll help me when the baby comes, Ben. Things will be fine."

But I could hear, in the night wind, winter draw closer than her child. How cold might it get? Which of the fish would stay and what shelter did we have?

She pounded sea oats into flour, mixed that with water, and baked patties in an oven of stones. They were bitter but we ate them for the sake of the different texture. "Now stop working on the raft and let's go swimming," she said. Sometimes I did.

"Isn't it good," she'd whisper to me in the dark, "not to be planning ahead? Saving money? Paying insurance?"

I held her tightly and watched the perpetual sea. "What do you think happened to Melvin Drum?"

Her whole body shrugged. "Who knows?"

Who-knows tormented me more that What-happened. "Maybe," I said, "Drum's found the place by now."

"What place?"

The place it ended. The sweeter Olena felt and tasted, the more certain I was that this was an interlude we would both forget. Our stay on the island was timeless, so I felt certain it could not possibly last. I had even begun to feel homesick for endings, arrivals. Finality.

"Ooh," breathed Olena, grabbing my hand, "Ooh, glory, feel that!" I laid my palm under her ribs. "Feel him move!"

I held my own breath in case there should be some faint shifting at last below her tight skin. "I feel it," I lied.

She rubbed my chest with her forehead so her long red hair tickled. "When Eve had a son, do you think she worried about who he would marry? We're married, Ben. In a way."

"In a way," I said, kissing the peak of her ear.

"Really, you'll be the baby's father."

The word was not real to me, not in this place. I tested it over and over in my head. Fatherfatherfather until the sound was mixed meaninglessness and prayer. Fatherfather.

"We should have asked Melvin to marry us."

I said, "He wasn't a preacher."

"Never did think that mattered much."

What *had* mattered, after all? Damn headache.

"Surely I'll not get much bigger," said Olena, stroking herself. I thought she was the same size as the first time I saw her walking through the mist. We were both browner, though. Her legs were hairier; on my face grew a broad beard, still not a hair on my scalp. We cleaned our teeth by wrapping wet sand in wads of cloth, or chewing twigs into brushes. Nails on our toes and fingers were long and tough; my foot sole felt like canvas. Sea bathing had hardened our skin and crusted the smallest scratch into a quick scar. My forearms looked almost tattooed.

Yes, we had changed. But Olena was the same size.

One morning there washed on our beach an assortment of trash which made me shout for Olena. Empty blue bottles, finger-length. A warped black piece of a nameless book cover . . . the foot of a celluloid doll. She grabbed for that — a toy for the baby, she said. I followed the tidemark of seaweed, stirring it with my toes. Rubber tubing. A piece of comb with the teeth sealed by barnacles. A length of wood which had once been fluted, part of a carved chair or table. Olena traced its design with awe, like some archaeologist.

But I was afraid. While she scanned the horizon for sails or a smokestack, I thought of a rent in the membrane between worlds, perhaps the great suck of a filling vacuum which would sweep Olena down more stairs and drop me under another scalpel. When the wind blew, even lightly, it raised goose bumps under my tan. "I've got to finish the raft," I said firmly. All day I watched, while pretending not to watch, for some vessel to follow its trash ashore. The raft grew wide enough for one person. Olena watched openly for a boat. The raft was wide enough for one person and a half. I worked on it constantly. Olena was bored with the building and bracing of its parts, and no longer sat nearby or carried me cooked fish in crab-shell dishes; but sat at a distance on the beach where the flotsam had washed, crooning to the doll's foot and waiting for something to rear up on the line between sea and sky. Some days she did not cook at all. At sundown I would carry food to her. Often she was sitting in an unnatural, stiff position, and kept her hand poised like an eyeshade longer than she should have been able to keep it there.

One evening she used the doll's foot to mash her fish meat into white gruel, then lapped it up with her tongue, I was disgusted and struck her under one eye. I watched tears spill on her reddening cheekbone.

"I'm sorry, Olena. Forget it. Come sleep now."

She shook her head.

"I want you to put your hands on me."

Her eyes were sliding off my face, across the streak of moonlight on the water.

"I'll put mine on you, then," I wheedled.

No. She shrank away on the darkening sand.

When the raft was done, Olena would not climb on. "We're leaving," I said, "even if it is dark." I held the platform still on the water. She would not come and I threatened to hit her again as I had on that other night.

In the moonlight, then, we walked the raft past the low waves till I hoisted her on board and heaved myself beside. Olena wrapped her body and head in a blanket and sat in the middle, a lump, a cargo bale.

"We can cross most of the water in the cool of the evening," I said. All I could see of her was the roundness of one pale heel showing at the blanket's base. I tried to be cheerful. "We might even see Melvin Drum. I bet he made camp on the shore below the river's mouth, and that's right where we'll land." I paddled with wood, with my hands. The raft was slow and awkward and zigzagged on the black water. "Even if Drum moved on, he may have left some clue behind for us. Some message. Why don't you answer me?"

"I don't feel good," said the lump.

We moved very slowly across the wide bay, as if the thick moonlight were an impediment. The edges of the dark water beat luminous on our island and the landfall.

In a loud voice I said, "I couldn't stand just waiting like that. I couldn't keep doing that."

Olena would not move but rode on my labors like a keg under a tarpaulin.

At first light we landed on the same inland shore from which we had come, although the river was out of sight. No sign of Drum — no old campfires, no heaped shells or stones. The sand piled quickly into low dunes, stubby grass, underbrush.

"Why don't you sleep now?"

"I still don't feel good." Olena tottered up the beach and lay down in her damp blanket while I dragged the raft high from the water. There were shallow paw prints in the wet sand, some in a circle, as if the animal had paced.

I squatted by Olena. "Are you hurting?"

"No." On her back, she stared beyond me. The last stars looked like flecks of paper stuck on the blueing sky. "I feel funny, though."

"It's from leaving. I'm sorry I forced you, Olena."

"Doesn't matter," she said. "But it's colder on this side of the water."

I asked if she wanted a fire, but she said no. I curled up with my head laid on her thighs and went to sleep.

The sun was high and warm when I woke, feeling sticky. Again, Olena was too rigid, with one arm raised off the sand and her palm spread open to the sky. I felt for her knee and squeezed it. "Move around some." Her skin felt cool and dry.

I sat up, staring. Overnight her pregnancy had collapsed like a balloon which had leaked out its air. Without even thinking, I patted the blankets in case there should be a loose baby lying there. No. Nothing at all — no baby, no stains.

"Olena?" I got a good look at her face. She was — what else to call it? — she was dead, her eyelids halfway down. I kissed her cold mouth, which felt hard as a buckle. Then again I kissed her, frantic, blowing my breath deep and pinching her nostrils shut. I was trying to cry without losing the rhythm of the breath and my body shook. I thought my forced air might inflate Olena anywhere, blow up her abdomen or toes, because I did not understand how anything functioned in this place; but nothing happened except that my heartbeat got louder and throbbed in my head until even the sight of Olena lying there pulsated to my eye.

She was dead. I walked away on the beach. I covered her with the blanket and sat there, holding her uplifted hand. I walked some more. I took off every stitch of her clothes and, sure enough, her stomach was flat now as a young girl's. She looked younger, too, fourteen at most, but her face was tired.

I dressed her body again and tried wrapping her hand around the pink doll's foot but there was no grip.

Finally, because I could not bear to put her into this ground, to bury her in Virginia, I laid her on the raft in the blanket and spread her red hair, and combed it with my fingers dipped in water. The bracelet looked tarnished and there was rust in the links of the chain. I placed on her eyes the prettiest coquinas I could find, and she seemed to be staring at the sun with a gaze part pink, purple, pearly. Then I saw I could not push her out to sea without crying, so I wrote in the ledger book awhile, until I could stand to do that.

Now it is dark again, and I think I can bear to push Olena off into the waters and let the current carry her down this coast. There have been noises from the thickets at my back. I think the wolf is there.

In a minute I am going to close up this ledger book and wrap it in a strip of wool I have torn off my blanket and put it under Olena's arm, and then I am going to walk waist-deep into the water and watch them both ride away. Who knows where this sea will end, or where Olena will carry the doll's foot and the book? Maybe somewhere there'll be someone to read the words, or someone who dreams he has read them.

McAfee County:
A
Chronicle

By
Mark Steadman

"We blowed out a cylinder head."

"Good gracious! anybody hurt?"

"No'm. Killed a nigger."

"Well, it's lucky; because sometimes people do get hurt."

— Huckleberry Finn

Mr. McAllister's
Cigarette Holder

1963: JUNE.

June.

McAfee County, Georgia, the month of June.

Five minutes before eight o'clock in the morning, and already the air is molasses warm and sticky. Summer comes fierce and early into the coastal counties of Georgia. For four months of the year everything seems to be melting down toward the ground like a landscape made of wax. Then, just before it all fuses together into a lump, the wind shifts around to the northeast and fall snaps in, bringing back the brittleness of October, so that things begin to separate and stand up straight again.

But the melting begins in June.

The McAfee County road-grubbing gang is impervious to it. Almost nothing like that bothers them. The slash pines are melting like candles into the flats on either side of the freshly graded road — the black water in the ditches turning to syrup — and they don't pay any attention at all.

One of the men says, "I seen me a fish coming to work this morning."

The other men look at him, waiting.

"About that high." He holds his hand up over his head to show them. "He's headed *up*," he says, fluttering his hand.

The men are waiting for what it will be.

"Says he's going to find him a *dry* place if he's got to swum to the *moon*."

The men laugh on the *"dry."*

Dropline Richwine, foreman of the gang, stands a hundred yards down the road, squinting under his hand, looks at them milling around, forming up.

"Here, Dewey," he says. He hands the small Negro boy a dime. "Dr. Pepper." The boy snatches the coin and runs away. A little over a mile down the road is a filling station owned by Phinesy Wooton. All day the boy will run back and forth fetching cold drinks for Dropline. Alternating Dr. Peppers and Seven-Ups. For every trip that he makes, he gets a penny tip. He won't earn enough during the day to buy a drink for himself, but will have to borrow the three or four cents from Dropline. By the end of the summer he will owe the foreman two and a half, maybe three, dollars.

Dropline holds his pocket watch out like a starter at a track meet, glancing at it, waiting for the big hand to touch twelve. When it does, he puts the watch into the pocket under his belt, cups his hands, and gives the signal.

"Goooo . . . to GRUBBING!" he says.

The gang spreads out, spans the black earth of the roadbed. Seven men. From the back they look like seven half-men — torsoless legs swinging along in an easy, apelike gait. From the front they look like the celebrants of some arcane and strenuous religious sect. Jackknifed at the waist, their arms hanging loose and swinging. They make scooping motions with them as they move along.

Doing their job.

The grubbing gang follows the patrols — the road scrapers — grubbing out the roots and rocks and things from the topsoil that forms the roadbed, before the sheep's-foot rollers come along and pack it down. The work has to be done bending over. A break-your-back position. It is undignified and uncomfortable, but there isn't any choice. If a man keeps at it for more than a year, something snaps. His backbone takes on a permanent set, and he can't get it out. Young boys come along and work at it for a year or even two and don't seem very much bothered by it. They crouch around for a week or so after they quit the gang to go to work in the mill, or at the filling station, or wherever it might be, but soon they straighten up pretty well — or at least work the slump up into their shoulders, where it won't look so bad. But grown men who do it for more than a year take a permanent hitch. It won't ever come out.

"Shad Goety worked five years on the grubbing gang . . . ," it's their favorite story, the men on the grubbing gang — they tell it around, " . . . then he spent thirty-five years picking fruit — most of it off *high* branches. And when they buried him, they had to hinge the coffin and jackknife it to get him in." They laugh everytime.

Only Mr. McAllister is the exception to the rule.

He is a great, dignified, bear of a man who has worked nearly twenty years on the grubbing gang, but when quitting time comes he stands up straight as an arrow and walks to the truck like a man in a hurricane with the wind at his back. Dignity personified. And dignity triumphant. Even his clothes don't diminish him.

His bib overalls come from Shotford's Grocery Store and Filling Station, and his snapbrim straw hat from the same place. They are the same that everybody else in McAfee County wears, though Mr. McAllister has decorated his hat with a snakeskin band he made himself. Still, even with the band, it is the same kind of hat that stands on the top counter in Shotford's in nesting stacks three and four feet high. He wears no shirt at all for about half of the year. In the fall and early spring he has a long-sleeved flannel shirt that is red-and-black-checkered. For really cold days he puts on a cardigan sweater that his woman knitted for him out of purple wool. Though most of the men grub barehanded, Mr. McAllister wears white work gloves with blue knit ribbing at the cuffs.

Everyone calls him *Mister* McAllister. That's because of his own manner of speaking. "*Mister* Richwine . . . ," he will say. Or, "*Mister* Glanders . . ." Everyone is *Mister* to Mr. McAllister.

Mr. McAllister himself doesn't understand his own dignity. *He* thinks that the thing that sets him apart is his cigarette holder.

It is a cheap plastic one that he grubbed up in the roadbed one day a year or so after he joined the gang. When he first found it, he didn't know exactly what it was.

"What you reckon, Mister Richwine?" he said.

Dropline looked at the red plastic cylinder, holding it at arm's length, then drawing it up close. He pumped it in and out a couple of times, with the other men standing around watching him. "Cigarette holder," he said.

Mr. McAllister's eyebrows went up. "Shit you say," he said. "Red?"

Dropline pumped it in for another look. "Yes," he said.

Mr. McAllister took it back, holding it at arm's length. "Black," he said. "President Roosevelt. He had him a black one."

The only man Mr. McAllister had ever known to use a cigarette holder was President Franklin Delano Roosevelt, and he had had to go back a good many years to his green salad days to dig up that recollection.

Old Mr. McAllister, Mr. McAllister's father, had not been a churchgoing man, and religion had never been a strong part of his early training as a boy — just what his mother could work in on the sly when the father wasn't around. The old man's main interest had been politics. And, next to Huey Long, Franklin Delano Roosevelt had been his man. They didn't have the Praying Hands picture on the wall, or the Blond Jesus, or any of that kind of thing, but over the mantelpiece there had been a likeness of the President, painted on a cedar slab. Whenever he got drunk, old Mr. McAllister would take down the slab and talk to it — telling it his troubles. Mr. McAllister had the idea that his father was praying, and for a while he had gotten Roosevelt and God mixed up.

But God didn't have a cigarette holder.

After he had found the holder in the road, he took it home and polished it up with wax until it looked like new, and from that time on he was never without it. He kept it in his mouth while he was grubbing, for he was afraid that it would fall out of the pencil pocket of his overalls, and that it might get broken if he kept it in another pocket.

Now and then a young boy, new to the grubbing gang, would try to kid him about it, because most of them weren't used to seeing anybody really use a cigarette holder either. Mr. McAllister never lost his temper when it happened. He took them seriously and tried to answer their clatter rather than fend them off. Generally that worked. Just the same, every now and then a really deep-dyed cretin would come along — one who lived ninety percent of his life out of his spinal column — and he would keep it up and keep it up until even Mr. McAllister couldn't stand to hear it anymore.

"Hey, Mr. McAllister," said Dee Witt Toomey, the young boy on the gang in the summer of 1956, "how come you roll your own cigarettes when you got that fine holder?"

Mr. McAllister put the Bugler packet back into the front pocket of his overalls. He held the cigarette daintily in the fingers of his right hand and licked the seam.

"I seen a picture once," said Mr. McAllister, not looking at Dee Witt, but keeping his eyes on the cigarette, "in a magazine. It showed the inside of one of them cigarette plants. All you could see was cigarettes. Looked like they was a million of them. The words under the picture said they made a hundred thousand of them a day."

He put the cigarette carefully into the holder and lit it with a wooden kitchen match, snapped on his thumbnail.

"Anything that they make a hundred thousand of them a day," he said, "I don't want it."

Dee Witt thought this over for a while. Thinking was mostly a physical act for Dee Witt. He had to get his whole body in on it. You could almost trace the progress of his idea as he worked it up his ganglia, compressing and compacting it and squeezing it up toward his brain — getting it into a shape he could recognize. You finally expected to see something pop out of his mouth — like a Ping-Pong ball in a comic magic act.

"I bet they make a million of them Razorback overalls you're wearing every day," he said at last.

"May be," said Mr. McAllister, "but they's all Shotford's got. I got no choice. Don't count when you got no choice. When I got my choice, one of a thing is what I want."

The reply put Mr. McAllister out of Dee Witt's range, so he had to button up and go off without trying to make a reply. But he brooded about it for the rest of the day, and the next day he worked around until he got a chance, then he snatched the holder out of Mr. McAllister's mouth and ran off a little ways down the road.

"I got it now," he said. He held it up where Mr. McAllister could see it, in both hands, as if he was going to break it.

"Mr. Toomey . . . ," said Mr. McAllister.

"I got it now," said Dee Witt. "It's mine. Finders keepers." The way he was holding it, it looked like he was going to snap it in two.

Mr. McAllister had a rock in his hand that he had grubbed up. Before anyone could think what he was doing, he reared back and threw it. It caught Dee Witt just over his right eye with a hard, plonking sound. Dee Witt fell over backward, sprawling out, with the cigarette holder still in his right hand.

Mr. McAllister walked up to him, pulling out a marking stake that he kept in his pocket in case of snakes when he had to go into the woods for a piss call. He reached down and took the cigarette holder gently, lifting it out of Dee Witt's hand. Then he looked at the holder and at Dee Witt, back and forth, with his face swelling up and turning red like a balloon. Finally he raised the marking stake high up over his head and brought it down right in the middle of Dee Witt's forehead. The sound was duller — duller but harder — than the sound the rock had made. Dee Witt flinched his arms and legs when Mr. McAllister hit him, then he just lay there with his eyes rolled up into his head.

Mr. McAllister looked up at the other men, who were all watching him. "He oughtn't . . . ," he said. Then he put the holder in his mouth and walked off into the pine trees.

It took three days for them to find him out in the swamp, and another day to convince him that Dee Witt wasn't dead. If the law had come into it, he would have gone to jail. Dee Witt's eyes didn't roll back down to the right place for a month, and he never did see too well afterward, but other than that he wasn't really put out by it. The men on the grubbing gang decided that anything that happened to Dee Witt's head was bound to be an improvement, and when they saw he wasn't going to die, they handled the whole thing so the sheriff never got onto it, bringing Mr. McAllister out of the swamp and back to the grubbing gang. Good grubbing men were hard to find.

And Mr. McAllister was a good man.

He enjoyed his work. Finding the cigarette holder had opened up the possibilities of grubbing for him, and he began to notice the things that he found in the roadbed. Strange-shaped rocks and pieces of roots, buttons, arrowheads, and bones of animals. Best of all, mysterious objects he had to puzzle over and figure at without ever being able to settle *what* they were.

"What you reckon, Mr. Richwine?" he would say, holding up something that he had found, and turning it around for Dropline to see. "Petrified wood?" Petrified wood was his favorite. "See there. Like it's got a grain in it?" He would trace it out with his finger. "And a knot."

Dropline would take it and look at it. "Could be it was petrified wood, Mr. McAllister," he'd say. "I wouldn't want to say."

So Mr. McAllister would drop it into his pocket and take it home and add to his collection. He had a whole cupboard full of cigar boxes filled with things he had found just like that in the roadbed. One box was filled with arrowheads. Another was filled with buttons. Another was filled with teeth. The best one of all was the one that was filled with things that he never could figure out. That was his favorite. He would often take it down at night and go through the things, trying to decide what they were. Every now and then he would finally classify something — a piece of petrified wood that turned out to be just a rock — and it always saddened him to have to take it out of the mystery box and put it into one with a label on it.

Singularity — that was the quality that he prized above all others. It was the key to his character.

Some people said that the most singular thing he had in his whole house was Dora, his albino woman. She was one of a kind too.

The grubbing gang swore that he had grubbed her up out of the bottoms when the county road went through to Fancy Statin. The truth is that he found her in the Trailways bus depot at Rainbow, broke and crying, sitting on a cardboard box tied up with string. That had been in the early fall of 1956.

"I ain't never seen no eyes like that before," he said, crouching a little as he stood before her, his cigarette holder gripped in his front teeth, the corners of his mouth pulled up tight in the shape of a smile.

She gave him a long, dead look. "You kiss my ass," she said.

"Miss your bus?" he asked.

She shook her head, then looked away from him.

"Stranded?" he asked.

She nodded.

"Broke?"

She nodded again.

"Shit," he said. "Wouldn't you know?"

He stood looking at her.

"Albino," she said.

"What?" he said.

"I'm a albino," she said.

"Oh," he said.

"I'm a albino, so I got eyes like that."

He nodded.

"You satisfied?" she said.

He nodded again. "Yes'm," he said.

He looked at her for a while. "I got no money to help you with," he said. "I could put you up for the night."

She swung her pale eyes back to his. Her face was streaked from the crying. For a long time they looked at each other straight on.

"I ain't gonna fool around with you, lady," he said. "I just wanted to help you out."

She looked at him straight on for a long time again.

"Does it hurt?" he said.

"What?" she said.

"To be a albino," he said. "Does it hurt?"

She looked at him a minute with her eyes wide open. Then she laughed — a high-pitched, tearing sound. "No," she said. "It don't hurt a bit."

He laughed with her. "I thought so," he said.

After a while she wiped her eyes with her handkerchief and stood up. "Well," she said, "it's the best offer I've had. I ain't no Little Miss Fauntleroy. I guess it beats sitting here on my ass watching the cars go by."

"Yes," he said.

She picked up her cardboard box.

"Here," said Mr. McAllister, "I'll take that." He took the box from her arms. "Jesus," he said, "you sure are traveling light. Your clothes don't weigh nothing at all."

"Ain't clothes," she said.

"What is it?"

"Cotton," she said. "Finest long-staple cotton."

"Cotton?" he said. "What for?"

"Stuffing dolls," she said. "I make dolls, and the cotton is what I stuff them with. Good cotton is hard to find."

"I'll be real careful not to drop it," he said.

She looked at him and smiled. "You do that," she said.

"My name's McAllister," he said, shifting the cardboard box under his left arm, and putting out his right.

"Pleased to meet you, Mr. McAllister," she said, shaking his hand. "Mine's Dora."

"Yes," he said.

"How far is it to your house, Mr. McAllister?" she asked.

"Three mile," he said.

"Kiss my ASS," she said, trudging after him.

After they had lived together for about three years — it was the fall of 1959 — Mr. McAllister asked Dora what she thought about getting married.

"I don't mind much one way or the other," she said. "I'll do it if it bothers you."

"We going to get married, we got to have us a ring to get married with," he said. He clamped the cigarette holder in his teeth the way Roosevelt used to do it. His head tilted back a little, the corners of his lips pulled up, showing the teeth at the sides of his mouth. His expression came close to being arch — as close as his dignity would let him. He was not an ironic man.

"How we going to get a ring?" asked Dora. "You going to grub one up out of the swamp for me?"

He had.

"Reckon this would do?" he asked. He held out a gold ring with a Masonic signet on it. "It ain't a wedding ring, but it is real gold. You could turn it so just the gold part showed."

Dora shrank from the ring. "I ain't going to put that thing on my finger," she said.

"What you mean?" he asked.

"That's a Mason ring," she said.

"I know that," he said. "You'd have to turn it around."

"My daddy was a Mason," she said. "He told me what they do to people who learn their secrets and they ain't Masons too."

"You wouldn't be learning no secrets, Dora," he said.

"Same thing," she said, "same thing."

He held the ring out to her, almost in her face. She shrank from it, fending him off with her hand.

"Put it up! Put it up, god damn it!" she said.

"You ain't no Mason!" he said.

"That's it! That's it!" she said.

Mr. McAllister gave the ring a long look, then he put it on the windowsill in the kitchen. He went to bed without saying any more about it.

For a week the ring stayed where he had laid it and for a week barely a word passed between them. Finally, seeing it hurt his feelings so much, Dora braided a cord out of white sewing thread, looped it through the ring, and put it around her neck. She wore it beneath her clothes where no Mason could see it, but it seemed to satisfy Mr. McAllister, and he began to speak to her again.

In the summer of 1963, Dora's birthday fell on a weekend, Saturday, June 22. Mr. McAllister planned a special treat for her.

"Look," he said when he came in from work on Friday evening. In his outstretched right hand were two bus tickets.

"What you got there?" asked Dora.

"Your birthday present," he said. "Two tickets to Tybee Beach. Round trip."

"We can't afford no trip to Tybee Beach," said Dora.

"And that ain't all," said Mr. McAllister. "This is for when we get there." He pulled two five-dollar bills out of his left pocket and waved them before her eyes.

"And this," he said, putting the tickets and the five-dollar bills on the kitchen table, and pulling a half-pint of Hickory Hill bourbon from his hip pocket, "is for when we get back." He put it on top of the tickets and the bills.

Flexing his knees and rocking back and forth slightly, he stood with his hands clasped behind his back.

"Happy Birthday, DORA," he said.

"Kiss my ass," she said.

They walked in the three miles to the Trailways bus depot at Rainbow, starting out at first light, since they weren't sure when the bus would arrive. It came at ten.

Mr. McAllister wore overalls and a red-and-green-checkered sport shirt with a wide collar, buttoned at the neck. Dora wore a purple voile dress. As they walked, Mr. McAllister dropped behind so he could watch her body moving inside the purple nimbus of the dress, silhouetted by the rising sun ahead of her. Every once in a while he would sing the "Happy Birthday Song" to her.

Now and again he would say, "You're a good woman, Dora." And he would add, ". . . for an albino." Then he would laugh.

When the bus came, Mr. McAllister boarded it ahead of her.

"Any special place you want us to sit?" he asked the driver.

"What?" said the driver.

Mr. McAllister took the cigarette holder out of his mouth. "You want us to sit any place special on the bus?" he repeated.

The bus driver looked at him a moment. "No," he said. "You can have any seat you want to."

"Much obliged," said Mr. McAllister.

He walked down the aisle until he found two vacant seats, then he slid into them, taking the one by the window. Dora sat down beside him.

Pretty soon everyone had gotten on the bus. Then the bus driver got on too, closed the door, started the engine, and pulled out onto the highway.

"Tybee Beach," said Mr. McAllister, looking out the window.

The front end of the bus nosed in toward the black shade of the awning outside the drugstore-bus-stop at Butler Avenue and Sixteenth Street. From the cool, green interior of the bus, the passengers stepped out into the yellow-white sunlight, paused for a moment blinking, then slid into the shade.

Mr. McAllister got off first, not looking at Dora behind him. He stepped into the shade and stood looking down the signs over the bars and souvenir shops on Sixteenth Street. At the end of the street, along the seawall-board-walk, bathers counterflowed slowly in the bright summer sunlight.

"You take this," he said to Dora without looking at her, swinging his forearm back to the left, the palm up. The five-dollar bill was folded tightly and held lightly between the hard, swollen thumb and forefinger of his left hand. "I'll pay for the rides with mine." The sunsquint pulled the corners of his mouth up tight.

"You keep it," said Dora.

"You wouldn't spend it if I do," he said.

"I'll lose it," she said.

It seemed that the breeze might snatch the green bill away, so lightly was it held.

"Put it in your bosom," he said. He pronounced it "*boo*som."

"You keep it," she said.

"It's your birthday," he said.

She took it lightly, holding it away for a moment. Then she made a quick, deft loop with her arm, and the bill disappeared into the front of her dress.

They walked down Sixteenth Street toward the ocean.

"Look!" said Dora.

In the window of the store was a seashell and plastic palm-tree tableau, embedded in plaster of Paris, with a crucifix in the middle.

"Ain't that handsome?" she said.

Mr. McAllister looked down at the pale, watery-colored object, covered with dust in the window. Behind it a gaudy terrycloth towel stood improbably erect. Its colors garish and clashing — bright red and yellow and black. "Tybee Beach, Georgia — Come On In."

"What is it?" he asked.

"A Jesus," said Dora.

They stood contemplating it silently for a minute.

"Let's go look at it inside," he said.

The clerk met them at the door. They were the only customers in the store.

"How much is that there Jesus?" said Mr. McAllister.

"What?" The clerk's hair was dark and shiny, thoroughly combed and parted. In the back a few long strands levered up away from the rest, and when he walked they swayed in a gentle countermotion, like the tail of a fish.

"The Jesus," said Mr. McAllister. "The Jesus in the window."

"In the window over there," said Dora, pointing.

Together they pointed the clerk to the tableau.

"Ain't it handsome?" said Dora, looking at it in the clerk's hands. He did not offer to let them hold it.

"It's an excellent piece," said the clerk, "Look here"; he pointed to the plastic palm trees with his little finger, holding his hand palm up, the other fingers delicately curled. "And here"; he pointed out each of the features in turn, cradling the Jesus delicately in his left arm.

"And look," he said, leading them over to the counter. He plugged in the cord that extended from the back of the plaster-of-Paris base. Three red Christmas-tree lights lit up behind the shells in the front.

"Oh, that's handsome," said Dora. "That really is handsome."

"How much is it?" asked Mr. McAllister.

"Look what the red lights do to the flamingo," said the clerk, not answering him.

"It's nice, all right," said Mr. McAllister. "How much is it?"

"It's all handmade," said the clerk. "You really don't see many of them these days."

"It's all real pretty," said Dora, "but how much is it?"

"Five dollars," said the clerk. His voice was very quiet and he looked at them steadily, but moving his eyes from one to the other, cradling the tableau in his arm and swaying back and forth at his knees.

"Well," said Dora, bunching her eyebrows together a little, "that's a lot of money."

"It's your birthday," said Mr. McAllister almost under his breath, drawing his head back a little to look at the Jesus.

"It's a lot of money, though," said Dora, looking at the Jesus, not Mr.

McAllister.

"They're hard to get these days," said the clerk, "because they're all handmade. Not many things handmade anymore." He jiggled the plug in and out so the lights flashed on and off.

"It's your birthday, Dora," said Mr. McAllister. "You want it, don't you?"

"But I think we better look around some more," she said. We just now got off the bus."

"Why don't you just look around some more?" said the clerk, making an expansive gesture with his free hand. "Just go ahead and look around." He slid the Jesus gently onto the checkout counter where they would have to pass it on the way out.

"Oh, it'll be all right for us to just look around," said Dora.

"Don't sell it to nobody before we get back," said Mr. McAllister.

They began to walk slowly down the counters filled with combs and cheap dark glasses and souvenir key chains and ashtrays, spread out in glass-divided compartments in front of the bright beach towels with palm trees and pretty girls and "Tybee Beach, Georgia," printed on them. The clerk hovered along behind them, his shoulders hunched forward, rubbing his hands together.

"Dora!" said Mr. McAllister.

In one of the compartments of the counter in front of them was a pile of plastic cigarette holders, jammed out in different directions — a stiff, shiny nest of them. All with white stems and red, blue, and black barrels. As they looked, Mr. McAllister slowly took his cigarette holder from between his teeth, his mouth going slack. He poised his holder — comparing. They were the same. A pile that would fill two cupped hands.

The sign clipped to the glass divider said "29¢."

"Yes," said the clerk, stepping toward them. "Those are very nice. We sell a lot of those."

Under the awning the wind came in strong and cool from the ocean. Mr. McAllister sat looking at the napkin holder in the middle of the formica-topped table. His hand on the edge of the table. Beside his hand lay the cigarette holder.

"Eat your Corn Dog," said Dora.

"They was just like mine, wasn't they?"

"Ain't no two things *exactly* alike," she said.

"Mine ain't as shiny," he said, looking at the holder.

"Your red is prettier," she said.

"But it's just the same, Dora," he said.

"Well," she said, "eat your Corn Dog."

"I ain't hungry," he said, pushing the napkin with the Corn Dog on it over to her.

"I don't want it," she said, "but I hate to see it go to waste."

The napkin fluttered in the breeze, then wrapped around the Corn Dog.

"I ain't having much of a time," she said. "You want to go home?"

"It's your birthday," he said.

"I know," she said. "But I ain't having much of a time."

"Let's get the Jesus," he said.

"I don't want the Jesus," she said.

"I want you to get the Jesus for your birthday," he said.

"I don't want to go back in the store."

"I'll get it for you," he said.

"I don't want *you* to go back in the store either," she said. "Let's just go catch the bus back to town."

"It ain't much of a birthday," he said.

"I ain't never been to Tybee Beach," she said. "And we still got the Hickory Hill when we get back."

As they walked to the bus stop, Mr. McAllister kept talking to her about the Jesus. "We can't just come on down here to Tybee Beach and get you a Jesus anytime you feel like it," he said. "You don't get it now, and you ain't never going to see it again."

They stood under the awning next to the bus, Dora hugging her arms under her breasts, looking down at the sidewalk.

"Will you please go get the Jesus, Dora?" he said. A passenger brushed Mr. McAllister getting on the bus. "Will you please get it for me for your birthday?"

She hesitated, biting her lip.

"You better hurry, lady," said the bus driver. "Bus leaves at two on the dot."

"What time is it?" she said.

"Eight of," said the driver.

"Get us a seat," she said to Mr. McAllister. "I'll be back in a minute."

"Yes . . . ," said Mr. McAllister, nodding, ". . . and the Hickory Hill when we get home."

The bus was just ready to leave when she got back. In her hand she had a brown paper bag.

"That ain't the Jesus," said Mr. McAllister. "What you got in the bag?"

Dora didn't answer him. Instead she leaned out and slapped the man in the seat across the aisle from her. He jumped up in his seat and looked at her.

"You a Mason, mister?" she asked.

"What?" he said.

"I said, 'Are you a Mason?'" she said.

"No," said the man.

"Too bad," said Dora.

She hooked her finger into her dress and flipped out the cord with the ring on it.

"I'm thirty-five years old," she said, turning to Mr. McAllister. She sounded as though she didn't believe it.

Dora snapped the ring off the cord and put it on her finger.

"My daddy was a Mason," she said. She held up her hand, looking at the ring. "Never would tell us no secrets," she said. "The dirty son-of-a-bitch."

The man across the aisle looked out the window.

"What the hell come over you, Dora?" said Mr. McAllister, whispering.

She dumped the contents of the bag into her lap.

"What'd you do *that* for?" he asked.

She didn't answer. Instead she placed the open bag in his lap, then picked up one of the cigarette holders in both of her hands, snapped it, dropping the pieces into the bag. She kept on until she had snapped all of them.

"Seventeen," she said. "Seventeen of them all together. And I got this with the change." She handed him a piece of bubblegum.

He held it limply in his hand, looking at the bag full of broken cigarette holders in his lap.

Dora sat stiffly, her arms folded under her breasts, staring straight ahead at the back of the seat in front of her.

"Happy birthday . . . TO ME!" she said firmly.

She swung her left arm out and tapped the bag lightly with the back of her hand, not looking at it.

"Now," she said. "Throw that piss-ant out the window."

Mr. McAllister rolled a cigarette and put it into his holder. He leaned back in his seat, the corners of his mouth pulled up in a Roosevelt grin. Outside the windows the pines were sliding by under the summer sun, melting into the flats along the highway. Beneath him, the hard, black surface of the road unrolled eastward under the speeding tires of the bus.

Lee Jay's Chinese-box Mystery

1962: SUMMER

Why'd you have to do it, Anse?" Dee Witt's voice was whiny and high pitched, like an outraged child's. He sounded like he was going to cry. His face was twisted up in a way that made him look like he was going to cry too.

Anse Starkey didn't answer him. He was sitting on the front-porch steps of his house. Dee Witt stood in the yard, facing him.

"I thought it was going to be just you and me," Dee Witt said, still whining. He twisted his head from side to side as he spoke. "Lee Jay ain't got good sense. He's going to spoil the whole trip for us."

"Lee Jay got money," Anse said. He didn't look at Dee Witt as he spoke. His elbows rested on his thighs, hands lightly clasped together. He was looking at his hands.

"He can't have *that* much money," said Dee Witt, still twisting his head.

"Twenty-five dollars." Anse said it flatly. After he said it he turned his eyes up to Dee Witt. Just his eyes. Not moving his head. His eyes were a light, yellowish green, the color of a seedless grape — a cat-eyed, startling color.

Dee Witt stopped sawing his head around. "Where Lee Jay get twenty-five dollars?" he said. Dee Witt's eyes were blue. White-blue. So light they almost didn't have any color at all.

"Won it on the punchboard down at Shotford's." Anse looked away again. At his hands. The hands were stubby and strong. Red and puffy with calluses. His forearms had a foreshortened look, tight and heavy. They were red too, with a thick dappling of freckles and a down of curly, orange hair. From under the bill of his baseball cap a lock of hair, darker red, looped down on his forehead. Slick and wet looking, like it was painted on there, just above his right eye.

"You seen him?" Dee Witt asked.

Anse turned his eyes up to Dee Witt again, then back to his hands. "I seen him," he said. His voice was low and quiet, with a raspy edge on it. Out of the back of his throat.

Dee Witt wore overalls that seemed to be too big for him, breaking over the tops of his heavy work shoes, and hanging in loose folds around his waist in the back. He was too tall to get a good fit — even in overalls. The proportions were wrong. Everything about him was drawn out and attenuated — his arms hanging limply at his sides, his waist, which looked to be two or three inches below the place where it should have been. Even his skull was long and narrow. Set at an odd angle on the end of his ropy neck. There was more bone than muscle to him, with thick wrists and big hands. A large man, awkward and angular, with pasty-colorless hair. Too white and powdery. And eyebrows that were nothing more than white spots on his red face.

"That's a lot of money," Dee Witt said, not sawing his head now.

"Yes," said Anse.

"We got to take him too?" Dee Witt asked.

"You want me to knock him in the head?" Anse asked, looking up at Dee Witt.

"Wouldn't be no trouble for you to figure a way if you put your mind to it." Dee Witt said.

"It ain't worth the trouble," Anse said.

"We been planning this trip for a month," Dee Witt said. "Why we got to spoil it dragging Lee Jay around?"

"Lee Jay won't be no trouble," Anse said.

"Lee Jay ain't nothing *but* trouble," said Dee Witt. "He don't know shit from apple butter. We ain't just going to run in to Kose, Anse. We're going to Tybee Beach. First thing Lee Jay is going to do is fuck up everything and spoil the whole trip."

"That's just it," said Anse, looking at Dee Witt.

"I know that's just it," said Dee Witt. "That's what I'm saying. So why'd you have to go and get him to come along with us? What you mean 'That's it'?"

"I mean Lee Jay's always fucking up, but he does it funny," said Anse. "We're going to have us a good time with him."

"Let's save us the good time for when we ain't going to Tybee Beach," said Dee Witt. "You're acting like it was something we all the time doing. I don't want to take no fuck-up with me to Tybee Beach."

Anse closed his eyes and shook his head in a disgusted way. "We're going to have us a good time with Lee Jay," he said.

"He don't always fuck up funny," said Dee Witt.

"More times funny than not," said Anse.

"What if this time ain't funny?" said Dee Witt.

"I'd want to take Lee Jay along even if he didn't have no twenty-five dollars," said Anse.

"But we're going to Tybee Beach," said Dee Witt.

"I'm going to handle it," said Anse. "You leave it all up to me."

"Tybee Beach ain't no place for no fuck-up," said Dee Witt, still sullen.

"You going to leave it up to me or not?" said Anse, the edge coming back into his voice.

"Shit," said Dee Witt.

"Jesus God, Lee Jay," said Dee Witt. His face was screwed up and his voice whinier than ever. "You ain't going to wear *overalls* to Tybee Beach?" Dee Witt looked at Anse. "He's fucking up already," he said.

Lee Jay frowned, pouting his mouth and looking down at his overalls. "Got 'em brand new yestiddy," he said.

"Ain't you got nothing else to wear, Lee Jay?" said Anse, leaning his elbow on the window of the pickup. He was sitting behind the wheel. Dee Witt had opened his door and stepped one foot out onto the runningboard. He spoke to Lee Jay over the top of the cab, ducking his head down to talk to Anse inside.

"Naw," said Lee Jay, taking the seams of his pants legs between his thumb and forefinger and pulling them out to the sides so he could see them better. "'Cept my everyday overalls and my church-going suit."

"I seen the suit," said Dee Witt, resting his forearms on the top of the cab and putting his head down on his elbow. "Jesus God."

"How about you wear just the pants?" Anse said.

"Ain't that going to look funny?" said Lee Jay.

"I reckon not," said Anse. "Wear your suit pants and your checkered shirt."

"Oh," said Lee Jay.

"Jesus God," said Dee Witt, his head buried in the crook of his elbow on top of the cab of the truck.

"Go get 'em on," said Anse. "We need to be pulling out pretty soon. Going to take us about two hours to get there."

Lee Jay walked back into his house. He had a hunched, swinging walk, and the same kind of angular body as Dee Witt, only two inches taller. He looked like Dee Witt's big brother, but he was five years younger — nineteen.

Dee Witt stepped down onto the ground, one foot still on the runningboard. "I ain't going," he said. "I told you Lee Jay was going to fuck it up."

"We're going to have us a good time with him," said Anse. "I feel it already."

"That ain't what I feel," said Dee Witt. "I feel like I want to put my number-twelve boot up his ass."

"I told you I'm going to take care of it," said Anse.

"I noticed you was taking care of it just then," said Dee Witt.

"It's going to be all right," said Anse.

While they were talking, Lee Jay came back out of the house. He was tucking in his shirt. Orange-and-red-checkered. His pants were dark blue and shiny, with big, purply spots at the knees and on the seat.

"Got the money?" Anse asked from the cab of the pickup as he came up.

"Yep," said Lee Jay, patting his hip pocket.

"You ain't going down to Shotford's store," said Anse. "Better let me keep it for you." He held his hand out the window of the truck.

Lee Jay hesitated. "I can look after it," he said, holding his hand on his hip pocket.

"Sure you can," said Anse. "I know you can do it. But why don't you give it to me just in case?"

"I can keep it," said Lee Jay.

"But this ain't Shotford's store we going to, Lee Jay. We going to Tybee Beach. Tell you what. You give me ten and Dee Witt there ten and you keep five. We ain't all going to get our pockets picked."

Lee Jay frowned. "How come I only get five?" he asked.

"Well, ten, then," said Anse, "and Dee Witt five."

Dee Witt started to say something, and Anse kicked him.

"Well . . . ," said Lee Jay.

"We're going to Tybee Beach," said Anse. "Better be on the safe side."

Lee Jay drew the money out of his hip pocket. He had folded it up in a handkerchief, and they had to wait while he laid it out on the hood of the pickup and opened it, pulling the folds out carefully. He made three piles of bills. As he laid the bills down one at a time on the hood of the truck, they could see his lips moving.

"Here," said Lee Jay, handing the bills to Anse.

"Count 'em," Anse said, holding his hand out, palm up. "You might of made a mistake."

Lee Jay counted them into his hand. There were nine.

"How'd that happen?" he said.

"See?" said Anse. "You'd of thought I was trying to cheat you."

Lee Jay started to take the bills again.

"Lay another one on there," said Anse. "Then count out five for Dee Witt."

Dee Witt watched the counting without saying anything.

Lee Jay started to reach into the cab from the driver's side.

"Go around," said Anse.

He counted five ones into Dee Witt's open palm.

"Now see how many you got left," said Anse.

Lee Jay stepped up to the hood again and counted out what was left of the bills. When he finished he looked up at Anse through the windshield. "Ten," he said.

"Get in," said Anse.

Lee Jay walked around to the back of the truck and climbed over the tailgate. He sat down against the window at the back of the cab. Anse rapped on the glass.

"What?" said Lee Jay, turning to look through the glass.

"Move over," said Anse. "I can't see out of the back."

Lee Jay slid to one side. Anse rapped on the glass again. Lee Jay's head looked in the window. "What?" he said.

"Button your fly," said Anse.

"I want the white one," said Lee Jay. They were standing by the merry-go-round on the boardwalk, waiting for it to stop so they could get on.

"What the shit difference does it make?" said Dee Witt.

Lee Jay looked at him sullenly. "Lots of difference," he said. "The red one looks funny."

"What you mean?" said Dee Witt, twisting his head and whining.

"I don't know," said Lee Jay. "It just looks funny, is all."

"Jesus God," said Dee Witt.

When the merry-go-round stopped, Dee Witt ran ahead and got on the white horse.

"Get off," said Anse, standing beside him. Lee Jay was climbing onto the merry-go-round.

"I got it first," said Dee Witt.

"You going to keep this shit up too?" Anse said, speaking under his breath. "Get off the goddamn horse."

"The red one looks funny," said Dee Witt, sitting straight up on the white horse and looking ahead. "I told you he was a fuck-up."

Lee Jay came up while they were talking. "I wanted the white one," he said.

"The blue one looks good," said Anse.

"It looks funny," said Lee Jay. "Ain't no such a thing."

"How about the black one?" said Anse.

"I want the white one," said Lee Jay.

Anse rapped Dee Witt's leg with his fist. Dee Witt didn't move.

"Come on," said Anse. They walked around the merry-go-round looking for another white horse.

"How about the yellow one?" said Anse.

Lee Jay didn't answer.

On the back side of the merry-go-round they found another white horse, but there was a child on it — a little boy about six years old with a candy apple in his hand. Anse didn't ask him. He just lifted him off and put him on the red horse next to it. The child had his hand stuffed in his mouth, and he looked at Anse with big eyes, but he didn't say anything. Lee Jay got up on the white horse, and Anse went and sat down in the swan chariot just as the merry-go-round started. During the whole ride the child kept looking at Anse with his hand stuffed in his mouth. When it stopped and they got off, Anse saw him talking to his mother and pointing at them.

"I ain't been counting on but one fuck-up," he said to Dee Witt as they walked away.

"I told you," said Dee Witt, not looking at him.

All afternoon they walked around the beach looking at the girls in bathing suits, watching them skating at the rink on the pavilion and in the bowling alleys. Two or three times they went into eating places on the boardwalk and got Corn Dogs and beer. Anse and Dee Witt rented bathing suits and went in swimming. Lee Jay wouldn't go with them because he was afraid of the waves. So he squatted on the beach in his orange-and-red checkered shirt and watched them. Sometimes he walked around looking for shells.

After they had their swim, Anse and Dee Witt took him and let him ride the bump cars and the Ferris wheel. When it started to get dark, they went down to the Brass Rail to see what was going on there.

"This is the best part," said Anse. "Can't come to Tybee Beach and not go in the Brass Rail."

At the entrance to the club was a billboard. On it were thumbtacked glossy photographs of the acts that were performing. There was a rock-'n'-roll band and a piano player and a Chinese dance troupe, "The Dancing Wangs." The photograph of the dance troupe showed one man and three girls, all in very brief costumes. The man was holding one of the girls over his head with one hand, while the other two girls posed with their toes pointed on either side of him.

The three men stood in front of the billboard looking at the picture of the Chinese dance troupe.

"Reminds me of John Fletcher," said Lee Jay.

"What?" said Dee Witt.

"My brother, John Fletcher," said Lee Jay.

"What reminds you of John Fletcher?" said Anse.

"Them Chinese girls," said Lee Jay.

Anse and Dee Witt looked at each other.

"John Fletcher was in the navy," said Lee Jay.

"I know John Fletcher was in the navy," said Anse.

"And them Chinese girls remind you of him?" said Dee Witt.

"John Fletcher is dead," said Lee Jay.

"What are you getting at, Lee Jay?" said Anse.

"When they sent us John Fletcher's things, there was a picture," said Lee Jay.

Anse and Dee Witt looked at each other.

"Yes?" said Anse.

"His buddy sent us his things we'd like to have," said Lee Jay. "His wallet and ring, and all those things like that we'd like to have."

Lee Jay stood looking at the billboard.

"What about the goddamn picture?" said Dee Witt.

Lee Jay frowned. "There was a picture," he said. "Him and a Chinese girl without no clothes on."

"Him and a Chinese girl without no clothes on?" said Anse.

"*He* had clothes on," said Lee Jay, frowning again and raising his voice. "John Fletcher had his navy suit on. The Chinese girl was the one didn't have no clothes on."

"I see," said Anse. He looked at Dee Witt and raised his eyebrows.

"She was kind of squatting down in front of John Fletcher and him standing behind her with his hands on her shoulders with his navy suit on," he said. "She had her legs apart. Just head-on — like that. Pulling at herself with her hands."

"Pulling at herself?" said Dee Witt.

"Yes," said Lee Jay, "pulling at herself. Pulling herself open, you know. It look like it run crostwise."

Anse and Dee Witt looked at each other, waiting for him to go on. Lee Jay didn't say anything. He just stood there looking at the picture of the Dancing Wangs.

"Crostwise?" said Dee Witt.

"Pa said all them Chinese girls got a crostwise cunt," Lee Jay said, looking at the picture.

"I never heard that," said Dee Witt, looking at Anse.

"She wasn't much to look at in the face," said Lee Jay. "Chinese girl. Sure was funny-looking though, with it open crostwise like that. Ma said it were a sin for even a Chinese girl to go showing herself that way."

"John Fletcher's buddy sent the picture to your ma?" said Dee Witt.

"No," said Lee Jay. He sounded exasperated. "He sent it to Pa. In the wallet and things. Ma seen it. She wanted to tear it up, but Pa wouldn't let her. He said he ain't never seen nothing like that before, and, besides, it was good of John Fletcher in his uniform. Ma didn't like it none."

"What did John Fletcher's buddy say?" said Dee Witt.

"He said John Fletcher was dead," said Lee Jay.

"I mean about the goddamn picture," said Dee Witt.

"He didn't say nothing about the picture," said Lee Jay. "He said John Fletcher was dead, and here was his keepsakes."

"What did he die of?" said Anse.

"Caught something in the navy and just died," said Lee Jay. "Pa got a letter telling about it, but we never could none of us make it out. Then Pa wanted to keep the picture and get it framed because John Fletcher was so handsome looking in his uniform. But Ma got the picture and torn it up. We had to all hold him off her when he found out. He ain't got over it even yet."

The three men stood looking at the picture of the Dancing Wangs.

"I'd forgot all about it," said Lee Jay.

"Let's go in," said Anse.

They sat at a table drinking beer and watching the show. After it was over they went outside.

"Could you tell?" Lee Jay asked Anse.

"Looked all right to me," he said.

"They wasn't much to them costumes they was wearing," said Dee Witt, "but it looked all right to me too. Wasn't nothing funny about the man anyways. Did you see the way he throwed them girls around? I wouldn't of thought no Chinaman would have been that strong. Maybe they's a trick to it."

An hour later they were sitting in a Corn Dog place under an open shed on the boardwalk. They had let Lee Jay have two rides on the merry-go-round. Then they had taken him to have his palm read. The gypsy woman had told him that he would take a long trip by water and would meet a dark lady.

"A Chinese lady?" he asked.

Anse and Dee Witt hurried him out of the palm reader's. They had gone into his last five dollars to buy the Corn Dogs and beer.

"Well, look at that," said Anse.

Lee Jay was studying the palm of his hand, tracing out the lines with his finger and mumbling to himself. "What?" he said, looking up.

One of the girls from the Dancing Wangs was passing on the boardwalk. She had on white shorts and a halter, and her hair was in a pony-tail.

"The other two was prettier," said Dee Witt.

"Maybe Lee Jay's going to get his answer now," said Anse, getting up from the table.

"You going to ask her, Anse?" said Lee Jay.

"Maybe better than that," said Anse. "Come on."

They got up and went out on the boardwalk. The girl was a couple of hundred feet in front of them, walking toward the south end of the island where the boardwalk and stores stopped, and the private houses and sand dunes began. It was the place where all the young couples went to do their love-making.

"You going to get your answer, Lee Jay," said Anse as the girl jumped down onto the beach from the seawall at the end of the parking lot and walked off down the dark beach. Anse's voice sounded excited.

The beach was deserted. Behind the sand dunes the beach houses stood dark and silent. Here and there, through openings between the dunes, they could see a cigarette glowing on a screened porch, or an orange window staring into the dark. The wind and the noise of the waves breaking on the beach drowned out any sounds that might have come from them.

When they got down onto the beach, Anse began to walk faster. There was a half-moon, and they could see the white shorts of the girl ahead of them against the darkness of the dunes. Running in the sand, they didn't make much noise, so she didn't hear them until they were already on top of her. She started to scream, but Anse clapped his hand over her mouth, pulling her down into the sand.

"Help me, God damn it," he said to Dee Witt and Lee Jay, who were standing there watching him. "Grab her legs."

Dee Witt dropped down in the sand, pinning her legs so she couldn't kick them. She was small, but the dancing had made her legs strong. Dee Witt had to hold them hard.

"God damn!" said Anse. "You do that again and I'm going to break your neck."

"What is it?" said Dee Witt.

"She bit me," said Anse.

"What we going to do?" said Lee Jay. He was still standing beside them.

"You don't holler, and we won't hurt you," Anse said to the girl. "Now, you don't holler, you hear?" He removed his hand from her mouth and she started to scream again. He clapped his hand back.

"Give me your handkerchief," Anse said to Lee Jay.

Lee Jay reached into his pocket and took out the handkerchief in which he had folded his money. He knelt down in the sand and began to unfold it slowly. Anse snatched it from him, scattering coins and bills into the sand.

"God damn, Anse," said Lee Jay.

Anse balled up the handkerchief and stuffed it into the girl's mouth.

"Roll her over," he said. Lee Jay and Dee Witt sat on her while Anse got out his hankerchief and tied on the gag.

"Give me your handkerchief," he said, holding out his hand to Dee Witt. He tied her hands together behind her.

"Now," he said. They picked her up, he and Dee Witt, and carried her up into the dunes. They put her down in a bowl between high hills of sand that screened them from the beach on one side and the houses on the other.

"Now we'll see," said Anse. He unzipped the shorts and pulled them off. The girl's body looked pale in the dim light from the moon.

"Come look, Lee Jay," Anse said. He held one of her legs while Dee Witt held the other, spreading them apart.

Lee Jay came up and looked, "No," he said.

"You sure?" said Anse.

Lee Jay looked again, leaning down to make sure. "Yes," he said.

"Let me see," said Anse. "Hold this leg."

Lee Jay stood there looking at the girl.

"Take this leg and let me see," said Anse. He jogged Lee Jay to make him move. Lee Jay took the leg.

"John Fletcher's picture was wrong," said Lee Jay.

"Ain't it pretty, though?" said Anse.

The girl arched her forked body, bending her hips backward. "Hold her up! Hold her up!" said Anse. "She's trying to get sand in it." Dee Witt and Lee Jay lifted her legs so her whole body was off the ground. She rested on her shoulders and the back of her neck.

"You try that again and I'm going to stuff a cactus up you," Anse said. A bed of them was growing in the side of the dune. He reached down and picked one to show her. It was small and bladderlike, the shape of a little round cushion. With long, needly spines sticking out of it. The girl's eyes were wide as he showed it to her.

"Just you be quiet and ain't nobody going to hurt you," he said, throwing the cactus down, and sucking his thumb where one of the spines had pricked him.

"Maybe we oughtn't," said Lee Jay.

"You done got your answer, now you keep out of it," said Dee Witt.

"Just hold onto that leg," said Anse. He unzipped his pants and hooked his finger inside the fly. The girl made noises behind the gag when Anse tried to penetrate her, guiding himself with his hand. She twisted to move away.

"Don't get ants in your pants," said Dee Witt.

Anse turned to him quickly, glaring.

"I mean, don't get so excited, Anse," said Dee Witt. "Just don't get so excited. That's all."

"Maybe you oughtn't," said Lee Jay.

Anse turned back to the girl. "It's just so pretty," he said. There was a dead smile on his face. "So pretty."

The girl kept twisting and making the noises behind the gag.

"You're hurting her, Anse," said Lee Jay.

"She's going to be all right," Anse said.

"Hurry up, Anse," said Dee Witt. "You're taking too long."

"Make up your mind," said Anse.

"She's too little, Anse," said Lee Jay.

Anse's breath was coming hard now. They could hear his breathing over the noises the girl was making under the gag.

". . . I'm dropping my leg," said Lee Jay flatly. He stepped back. The girl twisted and then kicked, getting her dancer's leg right up into Anse's crotch, catching him squarely. He grabbed himself and staggered backward, bending over. She flicked her leg again, kicking Dee Witt in the stomach, and he backed up too, dropping her leg. Anse was rolling on the ground, holding himself and moaning. The girl turned over on her stomach then got up running and stumbling up the dune with her hands still tied behind her.

"I told you," said Lee Jay. He picked up the girl's shorts and ran after her.

Going down the dune on the other side, she fell, pitching forward and plowing head-first in the loose sand. Lee Jay caught up with her and held out the shorts. "He hadn't ought to have hurt you," he said.

She lay in the sand, looking up at him.

"I'm sorry," he said. "Don't try and kick me, and I'll turn you loose." She lay still, while he rolled her over and untied her hands. When her hands were loose she pulled off the gag.

"Get away from me," she said.

"Here," said Lee Jay, holding out the shorts.

She snatched them from him. "Don't look at me," she said.

He turned his head to the side while she put them on. Then she turned and ran off up the beach with Lee Jay trotting after her. At the end of the boardwalk a policeman was leaning on the rail with his back to the ocean, trying to light a cigarette. The wind kept blowing out his matches.

The girl went up to him. "He raped me," she said, pointing to Lee Jay.

"I never did," said Lee Jay.

"He helped," she said.

The policeman looked at Lee Jay and then at the girl. "Ain't you working down at the Rail?" he said, putting the cigarette back into the pack.

"Yes," she said. "He raped me. Arrest him."

"He don't look like your type, lady," the policeman said.

"There were two others," said the girl.

"Where?" said the policeman, looking over his shoulder down the beach and drawing his pistol.

"Back down the beach there," she said, pointing. "One got his balls busted."

"I never did it," said Lee Jay.

"All right," said the policeman, pointing his pistol at Lee Jay, "you better come with me." He was not as tall as Lee Jay, but he was heavier, with a moony face and pouting, rose-petal lips. His head was enormous, and the hat he wore was two or three sizes too small for him. It was perched high on his head, barely covering his hairline, as if someone had put it there playing a trick on him, and he hadn't yet found it out. It made him look like a man coming home from a New Year's Eve party.

"What about the other two?" said the girl.

"I got to take this one in," said the policeman. "We'll get the other two."

Lee Jay looked down at the pistol, then up at the policeman. "You wouldn't shoot me?" he said. There was a surprised look on his face.

"You just come along and be quiet," said the policeman.

"When you going to get the other two?" asked the girl.

"We'll get the other two," said the policeman. "One thing at a time, sweetie."

"Don't *sweetie* me," she said.

"Let's go," said the policeman.

She turned and they started off down the boardwalk single file. The girl in front, then Lee Jay, then the policeman.

"I ain't done nothing," said Lee Jay.

"Keep your hands up," said the policeman. He raised his voice, talking over Lee Jay's shoulder to the girl in front. "What was you doing out on the beach with three crackers at this time of night anyway?" he said.

She didn't answer.

"Bit off more'n you could chew, sweetie?" he said.

"I never done nothing," said Lee Jay. He had his arms stuck straight up from his shoulders. "You mean you going to take me to the jailhouse?" he said.

"We'll see about that," said the policeman.

"I be damned," said Lee Jay.

They walked along the boardwalk for a while without saying anything.

"Lady," Lee Jay said. The girl didn't answer.

"I'm sorry, lady," he said.

She still didn't answer.

"You ain't going to *apologize* for raping her, are you?" said the policeman.

Lee Jay turned his head back over his shoulder, speaking to the policeman. "I never did," he said. "We just wanted to see if it were crostwise."

"What?" said the policeman.

"She's a Chinese girl," said Lee Jay.

"She is?" said the policeman.

"John Fletcher's picture showed it were."

"Were what?"

"Crostwise."

"Who's John Fletcher?"

"John Fletcher's my brother," said Lee Jay.

"Oh," said the policeman.

"He's dead," said Lee Jay.

"Chinese girl killed him?"

"No," said Lee Jay. "He got sick in the navy."

"Oh," said the policeman.

"He sent Pa a picture," said Lee Jay.

"All right," said the policeman. "That's enough. Crazy talk. I don't want to hear about it no more."

"But I'm trying to tell you," said Lee Jay.

"Well, quit it," said the policeman. "I don't want to hear about it no more."

They walked in silence for a while.

"Listen," said Lee Jay. "I'm sorry."

"I bet you are," said the policeman.

"I knowed it were wrong," said Lee Jay. "Even for a Chinese girl. I knowed that."

"Just keep on walking," said the policeman.

Lee Jay turned his head back over his shoulder again. "But I didn't know it were against the *law*," he said.

The police station was a small, stuccoed building at the end of the parking lot, just off the boardwalk near the pavilion. There was a high counter on one side and a row of chairs against the wall on the other. Behind the counter was the chief, a small, dapper man with gray hair and a neatly trimmed gray moustache. He was wearing a short-sleeved white shirt with shoulder straps. The shirt was open at the neck, and through the shoulder strap on the left side looped the harness of a black Sam Browne belt. When they came in he put down the copy of *Strength and Health* he was reading, snapped on his white police chief's hat, and stood up.

He looked at the girl, then at Lee Jay, then at the policeman. Lee Jay still had his hands stuck straight up over his head. He was holding them so high that his shirttail was pulling out of his pants.

"God damn it, Flatt," said the chief, speaking to the policeman, "you think you bringing in Jesse James? You got the public enemy number one there? I told you it scares shit out of the tourists. How come you didn't shoot him too?"

He turned to Lee Jay. "Put your hands down, son," he said. "He ain't going to shoot you."

Flatt stood looking down at his feet.

"All right, Lone Ranger," said the chief, "what'd he do? Park overtime? Litter a Dixie cup on the beach?"

Flatt didn't say anything.

"Maybe it was something serious, like screwing the Dragon Lady here under the boardwalk."

Flatt was standing with his arm hanging down, holding his pistol.

"And put that goddamned thing up before you hurt somebody," said the chief. "I told you about that before."

Flatt put the pistol into the holster. "She says he raped her," he said.

"I said he helped," said the girl. "There were two others."

The chief's eyebrows went up, and he looked at Flatt. "She kidding you or something?" he said. "You know who she is, don't you?"

"But she *said* he raped her," said Flatt.

"He helped," said the girl. "The others did it."

"Where the others?" said the chief. "I want to see what they look like. Was they climbing trees and eating bananas?"

"Getting away," said the girl.

"It figures," said the chief.

"I had to bring this one in," said Flatt.

"You didn't even try to shoot the other two?" said the chief. He looked at Lee Jay. "Sit down, son," he said, motioning toward the row of chairs along the wall.

"The other two are getting away," said the girl.

"He shoot any tourists?" said the chief, speaking to the girl. "Last time he had it out of his holster he shot himself in the leg."

Flatt's face began to get red. "I ain't never going to hear the end of that, am I?" he said. "I was practicing the quick draw," he said, speaking to Lee Jay and the girl.

"I'd take it away from him altogether," said the chief, "only he'd quit. It makes him feel like Gene Autry."

"Where you from, son?" he said, turning to Lee Jay.

"McAfee County," said Lee Jay.

"How'd you get here?"

"Rode," said Lee Ray.

"Bus?"

"Anse's pickup."

"Who's Anse?" said the chief.

"He's the one owns the pickup," said Lee Jay.

The chief looked at the girl. "He raped you, eh?" he said.

"I said he helped, God damn it," she said. "The other one did it, but he helped."

"You said there was two."

"One did it and the others helped."

"Two helped?" said the chief. "I wouldn't have thought you'd be that much trouble."

The girl didn't say anything.

"Where's it at?" said the chief, talking to Lee Jay again. "The pickup?"

"There," said Lee Jay, pointing out toward the parking lot.

"Ford? Chevy?"

"Ford," said Lee Jay.

"What year?"

"Red one," said Lee Jay.

"Go watch it, Flatt," said the chief. "Go find a red Ford pickup and watch it. Don't shoot it. Just watch it."

Flatt started out the door.

"Flatt," said the chief, "you got any bullets in that thing?"

"Couple," said Flatt.

"You shoot it, Flatt, and it's your ass," said the chief.

Flatt put his hand on the handle of the revolver and started out the door.

"And, Flatt . . . ," said the chief.

Flatt turned back toward him, holding the screen open.

". . . Get someplace they can't see you, will you, Flatt? Hide someplace so you don't fuck it up this time. Please."

Flatt went out without saying anything.

"Looks like pretty slow company for you, honey," said the chief, speaking to the girl. "What happened? The general down at Stewart put your snatch off limits for his soldier boys?"

"Don't call me *honey*," she said. "They jumped me."

"You said they raped you."

"That's right," she said. "Not this one. One of the others."

"Just like that?"

"That's right," she said.

"I don't know if you can make a rape case stick," said the chief. "Might be I could get a judgment on them for screwing a knothole in the boardwalk out there. Something serious, you know. Judge Lewis ain't going to be too worked up about you getting raped. Couldn't think up nothing better than that?"

The girl didn't say anything.

"Not this one, you say?" said the chief, nodding at Lee Jay.

"He helped," she said.

"What does that mean?" said the chief. "He hold your pocketbook?"

"Very funny," said the girl.

"I'm just trying to straighten out your case for you," he said. "You know Judge Lewis. He ain't going to buy your story worth a shit. We'll see when Flatt gets back with the others."

"If," she said.

In half an hour Flatt came back with Anse and Dee Witt. There was a satisfied look on his face. Anse was walking spraddle-legged and bent over. Flatt had his pistol in his holster.

"I didn't hear no shots," said the chief, looking at Anse. "What's wrong with that one?"

"I kicked him," said the girl. "He's the one. The red-headed son-of-a-bitch. He's the one that did it."

"I want to see what he looks like," said the chief. "Over here at the desk."

Anse and Dee Witt shuffled over.

"You too," said the chief, motioning to Lee Jay and the girl. When he had them all lined up in front of the counter, he asked the girl again. "Now, once more, honey, what happened?"

"They raped me," she said in an offhand way.

"I know that," said the chief. "You said that before. Details. Describe what happened."

She told him what had happened on the beach.

"He *helped* you," said the chief, nodding to Lee Jay.

"Not at first," said the girl.

"How about that, boys?" said the chief. "What you got to say?"

"I didn't never," said Lee Jay.

"But you was in on it," said the chief.

"He's the one," said the girl, pointing to Anse. "The other two helped."

"Ain't you got nothing to say?" said the chief. Neither Anse nor Dee Witt said anything.

"Say something, Anse," said Dee Witt.

"I got to sit down," said Anse. His voice was so strained they could hardly hear him.

"Okay," said the chief. "You can tell it to the judge. But I ain't going in there with you on no rape charge," he said, speaking to the girl. "Judge Lewis'd throw us out of court. I'm booking them on assault."

"It was rape," said the girl.

"You'll play hell proving it," said the chief, "believe me."

"Can I go?" said the girl.

"Where to?" said the chief. "You going out and try to get raped again? Kind of grows on you, don't it?"

"The motel," she said.

"Should have gone there in the first place," he said. "How come you didn't? You taking the night off or something?"

"To tell the truth," said the girl, not looking at him, "I got a little dose."

The chief arched his eyebrows. "I might have known," he said. "Some people got all the luck. Raped a whore, got his balls busted, and a dose of clap all at the same time." He counted them off, touching his fingers with his thumb. "Now he's got to go to jail too. It's your lucky day, son," he said, talking to Anse.

"Can I go?" said the girl.

"Come back in the morning and sign the complaint," he said.

"You damn right I will," she said.

"Well, boys," said the chief, after she had gone, "you stuck your foot in it this time. She can get you on assault anyway. Maybe she'll cool off by tomorrow. Can you pay her something?"

Lee Jay and Dee Witt looked at Anse, waiting for him to speak.

"Empty your pockets out here on the counter," said the chief.

They put their things on the counter. Lee Jay's pockets were full of sand dollars and seashells that he had picked up on the beach. There was three dollars in cash, but the change had been lost, and the handkerchief, when Anse snatched it.

"What are these for?" said the chief. On top of Lee Jay's shells were three Corn Dog sticks.

"They're nice sticks," said Lee Jay.

"Oh," said the chief. He dropped the sticks on the counter.

"Come on and help me count the money, Flatt," said the chief.

Flatt came up to the counter. They opened the wallets and emptied them.

"I thought you said it was gone, Anse," said Lee Jay, looking at the bills on the counter.

"It is," said Dee Witt. "That's *our* money."

"Christ," said the chief. "How much is it?" He counted the bills. Anse had fifteen and Dee Witt eleven.

"Twenty-nine dollars?" He looked at the three men. "Jesus Christ," he said. "For twenty-nine dollars you could have bought it and had it stuffed." Lee Jay and Dee Witt looked at him.

"What you mean?" said Dee Witt.

"Her going price is ten dollars," said the chief. "Short time."

"You mean she's a *real* whore?" said Dee Witt.

"Son," said the chief, "if she had as many peters sticking out of her as she's had sticking in, she'd look like a porkypine."

"You mean . . ."

"Come around next time it's payday at Stewart and look at them soldier boys lined up outside her motel room. When the tide's in" — he made swimming motions with his arms — "the end of the line is treading water."

"Shit, Anse," said Dee Witt, "couldn't you tell?"

"I got to sit down," said Anse. He went over to one of the chairs and lowered himself into it slowly. Just perching on the lip of the seat. Dee Witt went over and sat down beside him.

"They're going to be blue tomorrow," said the chief.

"I ain't never done nothing," said Lee Jay, still standing at the counter.

"Yes you did," said the chief. "You come to Tybee Beach with a couple of fuck-ups."

Dee Witt looked at Anse. "I told you," he said. "God damn it, I told you." He put his arms on his knees and rested his head on his forearms. "Jesus God," he said.

"Well, anyway, Anse," said Lee Jay, "it ain't so bad."

Dee Witt looked at him blankly. "What you mean?" he said.

"Leastways we settled it about the Chinese girl," said Lee Jay.

"That makes it all right, eh?" said Dee Witt.

"It makes it better," said Lee Jay.

"What Chinese girl?" said the chief.

"That Chinese girl," said Lee Jay, looking at him, surprised.

"The one that was just now in here?"

"Yes," said Lee Jay.

"The one got raped?"

"Uh-huh," said Lee Jay.

"Boy," said the chief, "that ain't no Chinese girl."

". . . Wang," said Lee Jay.

"The other three is Chinese," said the chief. "That one's a Jap."

"Jap?" said Lee Jay.

"Jap," said the chief.

"Well," said Lee Jay, "what's the difference?"

All three men were looking at the chief. Flatt was looking at him too.

"All the difference in the world, son," said the chief. "All the difference in the world. I thought everybody knew that." His eyebrows were arched, and he looked from one of them to the other. Then he held up his hand, wiggling his finger in a side-to-side motion. "Chinese girls got a crossways cunt," he said.

The Dreamer

1956: SUMMER

R

oyall Lyme.

John Fletcher unscrewed the cap and held the bottle of cologne to his nose. He had to smell it twice.

It wasn't like lemons at all.

He put the bottle back into the carton and walked down between the shelves to the prescription counter.

Mr. Lane was waiting on a customer. Filling a prescription. The customer was a tall, straight-backed man, with a red, seamed-up face, and eyes that didn't let go the sunsquint, even inside the drugstore with the sun going down behind the building outside.

Mr. Lane stood waist deep behind the counter. A short, stocky man, with thick-lensed glasses that washed and blurred his eyes when he moved his head. And thin black hair that he plastered down and combed forward to cover the bald part of his head in the front.

John Fletcher stood to one side, waiting for Mr. Lane to finish waiting on the farmer.

"One now. Then one before meals and at bedtime," he said. "It's on the label. Right there." He pointed with his finger, holding the box up between his thumb and index finger. He talked as though he hadn't sold it yet.

The farmer nodded. He stood with his arms folded inside the bib of his overalls. "How much will it be?" he said.

Mr. Lane stood looking at the little box on the counter. He drummed his fingers two or three times. "Three-fifty," he said. His voice went up on the "fifty," and he leaned on the counter stiff-armed with both hands.

The farmer looked at Mr. Lane for a minute without saying anything. Then he picked up the little box, holding it lightly between his thumb and first finger, squinting to read the label. His hands were big, with puffy fingers, but he held the box daintily, seeming almost not to touch it.

"Kind of . . . ," Mr. Lane went hoarse and stopped to clear his throat. "Kind of high," he said, looking at the box in the farmer's hand.

"But that's what Smoaks . . . You know, it's got to be the best there is. Smoaks knows his business." He had shifted his eyes to the customer's while he was talking. Now he looked back at the box, poised lightly between the farmer's thumb and finger.

"Three-fifty . . . ," he said, his voice going down.

"Yes," said the farmer, still looking at the box, but holding it at arm's length, not close enough to be able to read the label.

"Three-fifty is pretty damned . . . high . . . ," Mr. Lane said, leaning stiff-armed, looking down at the counter, "But . . ."

The farmer didn't say anything. He was holding the box at arm's length.

Mr. Lane wrote out the figures on the counter with his finger, coming back to put on the $ with a flourish. "Three-fifty . . . ," he said.

The farmer put the box back down on the counter, then fished a wallet out of the hip pocket of his overalls and counted out four ones on the prescription counter, drawing them out between his fingers to take away the creases, and putting them down in a pile, all the same side up and facing the same way.

Mr. Lane rang up the sale on the cash register and took a half-dollar out of the drawer. He put it down on the counter beside the bills, snapping it down flat like a tiddledywink. The farmer took it and put it into his pocket, ramming his hand all the way to the bottom. Then he picked up the pillbox, holding it in the open palm of his hand, close up to the bib front of his overalls, the way he would carry a baby bird. He was looking down into his hand as he walked away.

After he had gone, Mr. Lane picked up the four bills, put them into the drawer of the cash register, and shoved it closed hard, making it bang.

John Fletcher sidestepped over to the place in front of the counter, holding the aftershave carton in both hands. Then he dropped one hand to his side and put the carton on the counter with the other. Jerky movements, as if he were counting off numbers to himself. As he put it down on the counter, he made a small bow, nodding his head to Mr. Lane.

Mr. Lane stared at the carton without looking up at John Fletcher. He was still leaning stiff-armed on the counter. "Dollar and a half," he said.

"I guess he wanted something for nothing," he said. "Like they always do."

"What?" said John Fletcher.

"You get to be a bleeding heart and you ain't going to be in no business around here," he said. "Not for long you ain't."

"Um," said John Fletcher.

"It ain't my goddamned fault his woman's sick," he said. "Smoaks can kiss my ass anyway." He raised his hands to his mouth, making a megaphone. "Kiss my ass, Smoaks," he said, whispering it like a yell, aiming it out though the front windows of the store. "Kiss my ass, Smoaks . . . ," he whispered a second time, ". . . you mother-fucker."

He dropped his hands to his sides. "Smoaks is a mother-fucking son-of-a-bitch," he said to John Fletcher, not whispering it.

"He is?" said John Fletcher.

"Just write it out and send him on in here," he said. "Then it's Lane's goddamn problem. What he wanted was a bottle of Black Draught anyway. Some B-C powders and a swig of Black Draught to wash it down. And after that a spoonful of sugar with some turpentine in it, and a mustard plaster to sleep on. Smoaks knows that, God damn his ass. But he's got to go and write a high-class prescription, so he'll take him serious and know she's sick."

"His wife's sick?" said John Fletcher.

"Ain't I heard that before?" said Mr. Lane. "His wife's sick. His wife's sick. I wish Smoaks would come in here right now," he said. "I wish he'd just come right in through that door right there." He pointed to the glass door at the front of the store. John Fletcher turned to look where he was pointing. "You know what I'd do?" he said.

John Fletcher looked at him a minute. "Beat his ass?" he said.

Mr. Lane looked at him. "It ain't my goddamn fault his woman's sick," he said.

"No," said John Fletcher, looking at the carton of aftershave on the counter, "it certainly ain't your fault."

"Them pills I gave him," he said. "You see them goddamn pills I gave him?"

John Fletcher nodded. "I saw the box," he said.

"Five dollars," said Mr. Lane. He held up his hand, the fingers spread apart. "I can show you," he said. "I should have charged him five dollars. I let him have those pills for cost."

John Fletcher nodded again. "Ah," he said. Drawing it out, "Ahhhh . . ."

Mr. Lane dropped his eyes to the counter again. "Maybe I should have asked him for the five. He'd be going to piss and moan about it anyways. All over McAfee County. 'Five dollars. Five dollars.' I could hear him now."

". . . him now," said John Fletcher, nodding.

"I can show you the invoice. Five dollars is what I'm supposed to charge him. Just what I paid for them. I could get in trouble letting them go at cost like that. That's a fair-trade item," he said, lowering his voice and nodding his head.

"You certainly wasn't obliged to do it," said John Fletcher, nodding with him. "I could see that, all right."

"He wanted to piss and moan over the three-fifty, too. What does he know? Only he wasn't sure."

"Nobody would expect you to give them away," said John Fletcher.

"He'll be back for a bottle of Black Draught and some B-C tomorrow anyway," he said.

". . . anyway," said John Fletcher.

Mr. Lane looked down at the carton of aftershave on the counter. "Royall Lyme?" he said.

John Fletcher straightened up, giving a little bow and nodding his head. He cleared his throat.

"I don't sell much of that," said Mr. Lane. "You out to get you some pussy?"

John Fletcher jumped when he said it. Then scuttered his eyes from side to side and looked down at the counter. He cleared his throat again, but didn't answer.

Mr. Lane unscrewed the cap and held it to his nose. "Can't hardly smell it," he said. He looked at John Fletcher, then held it to his nose again. "Don't smell like lemons," he said.

"I just thought it might be I would try it," said John Fletcher.

Mr. Lane put the cap back on and then he put the bottle back into the carton.

"Royall Lyme is a dollar and a half," he said.

"Yes, sir," said John Fletcher.

"You want something else?"

John Fletcher looked at the carton of aftershave for a minute. He cleared his throat. "Yes," he said, not looking at Mr. Lane. He looked back over his shoulder. There was no one else in the store.

He leaned on the counter with his elbows, his hands clasped together. "I was going to stop at Kasher's," he said.

"What?" said Mr. Lane loudly. "Speak up."

"Kasher's Shell Station . . . out on Seventeen," said John Fletcher.

Mr. Lane stood leaning on the counter, looking at him.

"He's got a machine . . ."

"What are you talking about, John Fletcher?" said Mr. Lane.

"Kasher's . . . ," said John Fletcher.

"I mean what are you *talking* about?" Mr. Lane said, interrupting him. "I know where Kasher's is at."

"Yes," said John Fletcher, giving a nod and working his lips in and out to wet them. "Well . . . ," he said. He looked up at Mr. Lane, then nodded his head down and looked at the aftershave carton on the counter. He was trying to think of another word. "Listen . . . ," he whispered. He was leaning on the counter and talking into the aftershave carton as if it were a microphone. "Listen . . ."

Mr. Lane looked at him thoughtfully. Suddenly his eyebrows went up, making his eyes blossom behind the glasses. "Rubbers . . . ?" he said. "You want some rubbers, John Fletcher?"

John Fletcher looked up at him quickly, then back at the aftershave carton. He curled the fingers of his left hand around his mouth, nodding. "Yes," he said.

Mr. Lane leaned on the counter with one elbow, bringing his head down to a level with John Fletcher. "What you want rubbers for, John Fletcher?" he said. He spoke in a low tone. Conspiratorial.

John Fletcher spoke into the aftershave carton, not looking at him. "Well . . . ," he said. He didn't say anything else.

Mr. Lane looked down at him for a minute. "No, he said. "No. That ain't what I mean. It wasn't that you couldn't have no rubbers. Only I just was wondering what it was you needed them *for*."

John Fletcher looked up at him over the aftershave. "Shit, Mr. Lane," he said.

"No," said Mr. Lane. "I mean all of a sudden. Why all of a sudden you got to have a rubber, John Fletcher?"

John Fletcher didn't say anything. Then he cleared his throat and looked up at him. "I'm going in the navy next week," he said. "Thursday. Next Thursday. That's July . . ." — he counted on his fingers with his thumb — ". . . July twelfth."

"Yes?" said Mr. Lane.

"I'm going to have to go down to Jacksonville and go in the navy next Thursday," he said.

For a minute neither of them spoke.

"I just wanted to get me a . . . rubber," he said. "If it would be all right."

Mr. Lane looked at him a minute. "How old are you, John Fletcher?" he said.

"Eight . . ." — he had to swallow — "teen."

Mr. Lane looked at him for another long minute. He drew an eighteen on the counter with his finger. "Well," he said, "what kind do you want?"

John Fletcher didn't look at him. He frowned, looking down at the counter. "Um . . . ," he said, ". . . um . . ." He looked up at Mr. Lane. "I want the best you got," he said.

"I ain't got nothing *but* the best," said Mr. Lane quickly.

John Fletcher looked at him.

"I got all kind, son," he said. "All kind. You name it. I got it."

John Fletcher stood leaning on the counter with his head tucked down, sucking his lips in and out. ". . . all kinds," he said.

"All kinds," said Mr. Lane. He made flourishes on the counter with his finger. "You name it," he said, punching a dot on the counter, then leaning on his hands with his head tilted back slightly, looking at John Fletcher, ". . . I got it." He thumbed himself on the chest. "I even got some French ticklers," he said, fluttering his finger.

"Ticklers . . . ?" said John Fletcher.

"*French* ticklers," said Mr. Lane.

John Fletcher stared up at him, sucking his lips.

"Listen . . . ," said Mr. Lane, nodding his head and winking, ". . . Trojans."

". . . Trojans?" said John Fletcher, nodding back at him.

"Trojans is a good *man's* rubber," said Mr. Lane.

For a minute neither of them spoke.

"Aaaaa . . . re they made in France, too?" said John Fletcher.

"American made," he said, stabbing the counter with his finger.

John Fletcher looked over his shoulder, sucking his lips.

Mr. Lane waited for him. "You name it. I got it," he said.

"Trojans," said John Fletcher.

Mr. Lane nodded vigorously. "Trojans is good rubbers," he said.

"Trojans will be fine," said John Fletcher.

"Wet or dry?" said Mr. Lane.

John Fletcher looked at him without saying anything. He glanced over his shoulder to see if anyone had come into the store. "What?" he said.

"They come in wet or dry," said Mr. Lane. "Which do you want?"

John Fletcher looked at him. He sucked his lips in and out.

"Wet's messy, but it's good," said Mr. Lane. "Wet's a real treat."

John Fletcher looked up at the ceiling, then down at the aftershave carton. He gave the carton a careful quarter-turn to the right.

"You got to have experience to handle wet," said Mr. Lane. "They're tricky. Why don't you try dry?"

John Fletcher gave the carton another quarter-turn. "Yes," he said.

"That's right," said Mr. Lane. "How many?"

John Fletcher cleared his throat. "One, I reckon," he said.

"One?" said Mr. Lane. "One rubber?" He drew himself up. "I can't sell you one rubber, John Fletcher. They don't come in *ones*." He drew a three on the counter with his finger. "They comes in threes," he said.

"Threes . . . ?" said John Fletcher.

"Threes," said Mr. Lane.

"Well," said John Fletcher, "how much is a three?"

"Fifty cents," said Mr. Lane.

"I'll take a three," said John Fletcher.

"Fifty cents for a three. Dollar and a half for a dozen."

"I don't want no dozen rubbers," he said quickly.

"Fifty cents for a three," said Mr. Lane, " and a dollar and a half for the aftershave is two dollars with the rubbers," He made a two on the counter.

Mr. Lane took a small red, white, and blue Lane's Drugstore bag from the stack beside the register. He worked his hands under the counter out of sight, not looking at them. Folding sounds came up from under the counter, and John Fletcher watched off to the side of Mr. Lane's head as he waited for him to make the package. When Mr. Lane brought his hands up from behind the counter, he had made a small packet with the bag folded around on itself, so it didn't look like anything but just a folded-up paper bag. He sealed it shut with an American-flag sticker out of a little box beside the stack of bags, then put it on the counter beside the carton of aftershave.

"That'll be two dollars," he said.

John Fletcher reached back to his hip pocket before he remembered he had his wallet in his coat. He pulled back the lapel to get it, showing the black lining with a gold embroidered label. The coat was new. He had bought it earlier that summer when he had moved out of the house away from the family and his father, but there had not been many times for him to wear it, and he didn't feel sure of himself in it yet. It was leopard-skin-patterned, a kind of iridescent green-orange color under the black spots, depending on the way the light was hitting it at the time, with the black lining and black lapels. That was the main part of his moving-away-from-home outfit. The rest of the things he had acquired under the impetus of the coat. He had made a clean sweep. Black pants with tight legs and no cuffs. Black Wellington boots. A black tie, tacked with a golden tiger pin. French-cuff shirt, with black Swank cufflinks. Everything depended on the coat, which he was still worried about.

"I ain't never seen no coat like that before," said Mr. Lane, looking John Fletcher over. "Is it real?"

"No," said John Fletcher.

"I thought so," said Mr. Lane. "It's hard to tell. You sure do see some funny-looking things these days. Crazy clothes. Crazy clothes." He sounded as though he were talking to himself.

John Fletcher didn't say anything. He fumbled the wallet open and took out a five-dollar bill.

Mr. Lane looked up into John Fletcher's face. "I don't mean your coat especially, John Fletcher," he said. "You always been a good boy. I was just thinking about *all* them crazy things the kids is wearing these days."

"Yes," said John Fletcher, putting the five down on the counter beside the aftershave.

"Nigger clothes," he said. "We used to call them nigger clothes." He picked up the bill. ". . . you know?"

"Um," said John Fletcher, waiting for him to make the change.

Mr. Lane held the bill by the ends with both hands, the way he would read a newspaper. Then he laid it down on the counter carefully, pressing it out with the edges of his hands. He made a five with his finger on the counter.

"I seen a kid come in here the other day," he said, underlining the five, then looking up at John Fletcher. "Just a regular high-school kid, you know."

John Fletcher looked down at the bill on the counter, waiting with his wallet sprung open in his hand.

"He had on a pair of pants so tight you could count the change in his pocket," Mr. Lane said.

He paused.

"Forty-five cents," he said.

He paused again.

"Forty-five cents . . . ?" John Fletcher looked at him, starting to frown.

"Well . . . ," said Mr. Lane, ". . . anyway. He had on the pants and one of them strapped-around leather jackets with studs and sparkles and hooks all over it." He paused. "I mean just a regular high-school kid. I seen him in here before. Lots of times."

". . . lots of times," said John Fletcher, looking at the bill on the counter.

"Yes," said Mr. Lane, smoothing the bill again. "He picked up one of those girlie magazines off the rack there." He pointed to the magazine stand at the front of the store. "Used to be they'd read *Titter*, but that ain't nothing now," he said. "They got to *see* it."

John Fletcher looked where he was pointing. ". . . titter," he said.

"Used to be a magazine," said Mr. Lane. "*Titter*. That was the name of the magazine. It showed all you could then, but that ain't nothing now."

John Fletcher looked at him, then down at the bill on the counter.

"It was a pretty good magazine," said Mr. Lane. "But it ain't nothing now." He drew a T on the counter.

"I see," said John Fletcher.

"Anyway . . . ," said Mr. Lane. "I didn't say nothing. Just kept my eye on him. Watching. I knowed what it would be. He was standing there with his leg cocked forward like somebody was going to come around and take his picture. You know how they stand like that. Flipping the pages and looking at the pictures. I didn't say nothing. Just watching him. Sure enough, pretty soon — like that!" He made a fist and held his forearm up. "I didn't say nothing," he said. "It hurt me just to stand here and look at him with it all swole up down his leg that way. Tight pants . . . ," he said, ". . . tight pants." He shook his head. "Halfway down to his knee . . . ," he said. "Big as a nigger's . . . You ever noticed, John Fletcher?" he said.

"No . . . ," said John Fletcher, shaking his head.

"You ever noticed how it is a nigger got all that peter and hardly no balls at all? Little bitty" — he curled his index finger into a circle, holding it to his eye — "like it was a couple of acorns."

He leaned both hands on the counter again. "That's a nigger for you, John Fletcher," he said. "All peter and no balls at all."

John Fletcher looked at him, then down at the five-dollar bill.

"Nigger clothes and nigger peters . . . and that Goddamn shake-your-ass nigger music," he said. "It's getting to be a nigger's world, John Fletcher. Everything is getting to be all niggered up." He shook his head. "I done tried it," he said. "Give them something new and clean, and the only thing they are going to do is take it away and nigger it up for you. If it ain't dirty, and dipped in grease, and got a foxtail tied on it, they don't want it.

"I ain't blaming them for nothing like that you understand," he said. "It's just nigger nature. Only you got to know what it is you can count on in this world. That's one thing I learned a long time ago.

"I have dreams about it sometimes," he said, leaning on the counter and lowering his voice. His eyes bloomed and washed around behind the thick lenses of his glasses as he talked.

"I'm out there at Kasher's, and there ain't hardly no traffic at all. Just me. By myself. And then I can hear a noise coming down the highway like singing.

"Humhumhumhumhum . . ." He made the sound in the back of his throat, pulling his chin into his collar, and keeping his voice like it was far away.

"Always from up toward Fancy Station, on the other side of the viaduct. When I hear it so I can tell what it is, it's always 'Mercy, Mr. Percy,' or some other nigger song like that. Can't tell one from another of them anyway. But they all sound alike, so I know it's nigger music just from the way it sounds.

"Then I see them coming up over the viaduct. And it's a big crowd of bucks, singing 'Mercy, Mr. Percy,' or some other nigger song like that, even if I don't understand the words and can't make them out. Because they are kind of slobbering it so you can't really hear the words anyway, except to know it sure as shit ain't no kind of white man's music like 'Stardust,' or something like that. And then they get close enough so I can see them, and they all have on tight pants, too short so their feet stick out like a paddle blade, and wing-tip shoes with the holes cut out. And red- and yellow- and orange-striped coats with all kinds of colored, candy-striped shirts. And big flowery ties. Just looking at them makes my asshole start to sucking on the seat of my pants. And I want to pick me up a tire iron and coldcock the shit out of them.

"Only there's so *God*damn many of the cocksuckers . . .

"And then I see it. What makes me commence to worry, so I break out in a sweat and want to run away.

"They all got their pants unzippered. With their peters sticking out." He lowed his voice. "Just sticking out there on U.S. Seventeen," he said. His eyes smeared around behind his glasses as he moved his head from side to side. "The dirty cocksuckers . . . And they all got a hard-on. Like a big black baseball bat. A yard long . . . or more . . . with the handle end out. Waving around in front of them when they come marching down the highway."

He took off his glasses to wipe his eyes, and he suddenly looked as though his face had caved in. His eyes receded into his head, congealing into tiny blue agates. Too small for his face, and too close together. He looked blank and stark, the kind of face a child might draw with a pencil that has had too fine a point put on it.

"Ain't that just like niggers?" he said.

"It certainly is," said John Fletcher.

Mr. Lane put his glasses back on and continued with the dream. His voice lowered to a whisper.

"There I am at Kasher's," he said. "All by myself. While them black cocksuckers walk up and surround me, pointing all those nigger peters at me and waving them around.

"And their leader — wouldn't you know? Who do you think their leader is, John Fletcher?"

"No . . . ," said John Fletcher, shaking his head.

"I'll tell you who their leader is. It's John Henry. John Henry Greene."

"John Henry . . . ," said John Fletcher.

"Wouldn't you know?" said Mr. Lane. "He's always their leader. He ties a white flag to his peter and steps into the circle and asks me do I want to surrender or be annihilated. That's what he says. 'Annihilated.' I always wonder where the shit would a nigger like John Henry learn a word like that. But that's what he says. 'Annihilated.' Then he tells me I got just one minute to make up my mind.

"And he starts counting me down. 'One . . . two . . .'

"But I got a trick I learned when I was in the hospital with my hernia. I whip out my pencil (Mr. Lane slid his ball-point pen halfway out of his shirt pocket to show John Fletcher) . . . I whip out my pencil, and tap the head of John Henry's peter with it.

"That's the way the nurses do it when you get a hard-on and they're bathing you up or changing your clothes. I learned that when I was in the hospital with my hernia. The nurses told me they never knew a hernia patient get a hard-on so easy as I did. Just every time they come around me, or tried to fluff up my pillow or anything. They couldn't get over it. I never did have no trouble that way. Even after I had the hernia."

He paused and patted his truss with his hand. "Just don't strain nor lift nothing heavy," he said.

John Fletcher rocked up on tiptoes, looking down behind the counter to see the place where the hernia was.

"When I do that," said Mr. Lane, "tap him with my pencil, John Henry's peter begins to go soft, and he drops down on his knees, kind of biting his lip and looking like he is going to die. Then he says 'It ain't no use, Mr. Lane, boss. You may get me, but my men will get you.' He says, 'my men.' That's exactly what he says.

"But I keep on tapping at the head of his peter with my pencil. I know he's the one I got to handle. So I keep tapping.

". . . Taptaptap . . . ," he said.

"Making it go softer and softer. And he sinks lower and lower. But then he says, 'You done had your chance, Mr. Lane, boss. I tried to make you give it up . . . COLORED MEN . . . ATTENTION! . . .' And I look around and all those black peters are pointing straight at me. So I don't see nothing but white teeth and eyeballs and black, nigger peters. And John Henry, he's stretched out on the ground, with his gone all soft like a big blacksnake between his legs, and the white flag still tied to it. Then he says in a gasping kind of voice, '. . . Ready! . . . Aim! . . . Fire! . . .' And I see the black peters are all pointing at me while I stand there over John Henry with only just my pencil."

Mr. Lane stopped. His voice had gotten loud as he came to the climax of his dream, and his hands were gripping the prescription counter so his knuckles showed white. He looked at John Fletcher for a minute; then he relaxed, letting go of the counter and taking the handkerchief out of his pocket again. He took off his glasses, making his face go tight and sharp, swabbing his eyes and around his mouth with the handkerchief.

"And then I always wake up," he said. "I always wake up just when they are about to . . . to . . ." He put his hands back on the counter with the handkerchief wadded up in his fist. "I always wake up just at that point.

"Someday," he said. His voice trembled. "Someday I reckon I ain't going to make it. Someday I ain't going to wake up in time. Like dreaming you are falling out of a building and you don't wake up before you hit the ground. I know it's going to happen one of these nights. Jesus. And them black bastards will go ahead and get me."

He looked down at the counter, gripping it with his hands.

"Oh, Jesus . . . ," he said, wailing it out. He waved the hand with the handkerchief in it, sweeping it around over the counter. " . . . all over . . ." He put his head down and started to cry. ". . . all over . . . I just won't never wake up again . . . Jesus."

John Fletcher stood there at the prescription counter watching Mr. Lane leaning on his arms and crying. His shoulders heaved as the sobs racked him.

Finally he stopped sobbing and stood up again, taking off his glasses and wiping his eyes with his shirt sleeves. "I want you to promise me something, John Fletcher," he said, pulling his shirt sleeves out and drying his eyes.

"Sir?" said John Fletcher.

"I'm treating you like a man, John Fletcher," he said. "This is just between us. You understand?"

"Yes, sir," said John Fletcher.

"Call me Fred," said Mr. Lane.

John Fletcher leaned down on the counter, speaking into the aftershave carton. "Fred," he said.

"Yes," said Mr. Lane. "I want you to make me a solemn promise and swear you ain't never going to have nothing to do with no niggers when you get in the navy. Man to man," he said. "Will you do that for me?"

"Well, it's not that I wouldn't swear, only that's a hard kind of a thing to tell, the way it is now. They don't make them stay off among themselves like they used to."

"Call me Fred," said Mr. Lane.

"Fred," said John Fletcher.

"I know," said Mr. Lane. "I know what you're saying, John Fletcher. But you still got something to say about it. Just promise me you ain't going to sit down right next to one to eat no meal, nor sleep in the next cot."

"I wouldn't do it unless I had to," said John Fletcher, ". . . Fred."

"That's all I wanted to hear, son," said Mr. Lane. "Just keep away from them all you can, but what the government makes you do."

"Well," said John Fletcher, "I could do that."

"Listen, son," said Mr. Lane, standing up straight, with his glasses on again. "I love my country. I fought the Japs in the Pacific. Little slanty-eyed shitasses. I'd of died too, if it had been that way. It was hell. Jungle rot, and them little slanty-eyed shitasses. Three years . . . ," he said, holding up his fingers. His arm was straining so hard his hand shook. "I seen a lot of my buddies died out there while I watched them. And I'd of died, too, if I'd had to.

"Now it's all going to go down a shithole, just as soon as he can do it." He jerked his thumb at the red, white, and blue "Impeach Earl Warren" sign hanging over the prescription counter. He tilted his head back slightly, and his eyes blurred upward behind the glasses. "The dirty cocksucker," he said.

"But for God's sake, John Fletcher," he said, looking at him across the counter, "you got to promise me just one thing for sure." He drew himself up sternly behind the counter. "I been through it," he said. "I know."

"Yes sir . . . Fred?" said John Fletcher.

"You listen to me, son," he said. "I been though it. More than anything else above all. There's just one thing I got to hear you say you ain't going to do."

"Well," said John Fletcher, "I wouldn't if I couldn't."

"You listen to me, son," said Mr. Lane. He leaned forward across the prescription counter, making John Fletcher lean forward to meet him. Their heads almost touched over the aftershave carton and the little package of rubbers in the middle of the counter.

"Stay out of the showers with them, John Fletcher." He spoke past John Fletcher's right ear, not looking at him. "I been there, and I know. Nothing drives them crazy like a white man's asshole. It's almost worse than a white pussy. They'll be on you and up you before you know what happened. I'm telling you, son. I'm telling you for your own good. Watch your asshole, and stay out of the showers with them."

He pushed himself away from the counter, standing up and holding himself at arm's length. "Promise," he said.

John Fletcher stayed bent over the counter, looking up at him from under his raised eyebrows.

"God's listening, son," he said. "God's listening for an answer."

The front door of the store opened, and a woman came in.

"Quick!" Mr. Lane lowered his voice again, bending down toward John Fletcher. "Say it quick."

"Yes," said John Fletcher. "Yes, Fred." His voice was low and whispering, talking into the aftershave carton.

"It'll be all right," Mr. Lane said, slapping him on the shoulder across the prescription counter. "And don't drop the soap for none of them white boys neither," he said. "Some of them got to stick it in every hole they see, too."

He wrote a two on the counter with his finger. "Two dollars," he said. "Two dollars for everything."

With the fingers of his left hand he slid the five-dollar bill back across the counter to John Fletcher.

"This one's on me," he said. "You don't go in the navy every day."

John Fletcher looked at the bill, then up at Mr. Lane.

"Thank you," he said. "Thank you, Fred."

John Fletcher's Night of Love

S eaman Williston. Seaman Williston.
Seaman Williston."

It wasn't just then that he hated the voice. Earlier, he had. And, later, he would. But this time — not yet. Somewhere under the mucous, adenoidal surface of the words there was a grace note, a muscial quality, coming on toward the top. He homed in on it, letting the words float off down the windows of the ward.

He had an ear for grace notes.

"Time to take your temperature, Seaman Williston," she said.

"Up yours, Lieutenant," he thought, ". . . ma'am."

Her hand looked enormous. Man-heavy and freckled. The thermometer — like the kind banks put on billboards, as he would see it from a distance on a hot day. His eyes were squinting. Blurring the hand and the thermometer, and going on up behind them where the high ceilings of the ward receded into the vault of the roof. He could see patches where the plaster had fallen away. And gray continents of mold, like a grainy photograph of the moon. His head rolled sideways on the pillow, making him tighten the squint against the glare from the late-afternoon sun, banging in through the windows on the opposite wall of the ward, like a battery of lemon-yellow klieg lights. A sound of cymbals was in the color.

Still life on chipped porcelain table beside ward bed: Item — glass of water with bent, clear plastic straw leaning; Item — large metal spoon with USN stamped on handle; Item — medicine bottle half full of purplish-pink liquid, handwritten label stuck on crooked.

He framed them in the squint. Watery vermilion of the medicine bottle and the bluish metal of the spoon on the white porcelain tabletop. Part of the spoon handle jagged behind the water glass. The USN magnified through the glass on the offset part.

He moved his eyes toward the foot of the bed, picking up the projectile-shaped container, suspended upside down in a wire frame. Half full, the thick, clear liquid making runs on the sides as the level went down. Rubber tube connected to it underneath into the blocky metal cap. More plastic straws jointing the black rubber tube, with adhesive tape wrapped around the joints. Awkward. But efficient-looking. By tightening the squint he could see a foamy trace of bubbles moving down the clear plastic parts of the siphon into the black rubber tube. The tube falling straight down out of the heavy metal cap of the container, going out of sight toward the floor, then looping back beside the bed where he wasn't seeing it.

He moved his arm slightly, feeling the sting of the needle planted in the vein of his right arm. A vague pain, as if his arm were lying two or three beds away down the ward. He closed his eyes, listening to the sting of the needle in his arm.

"Seamanwillistonseamanwillistonseamanwilliston." Slimy membrane of words, with a grace note lifting and swelling underneath.

The hand and the thermometer came back into focus again. The thermometer looked too big — too big to lift. He was thinking that she might let it fall on him. It would hurt.

"Buh . . . buh . . . buh . . .," he tried to tell her, pumping his tongue in his mouth aimlessly. A furry Ping-Pong ball he would have liked to spit out.

The thermometer rattled on his lower teeth, jabbing up into the soft, thin place under his tongue. He closed his mouth on it, to stop the jabbing.

His head rolled on the pillow, eyelids fluttering. Everything winging in and out of focus, until he was looking again at the projectile-shaped container hanging in the frame by the bed, and feeling the sting in his arm. A bulletlike container, still half full, with the clear runs down the sides, like a glass of Cointreau half-finished.

A bubble big enough to see by itself floated up from the liquid bottle, the bank of windows on the other side turning it yellow.

Yellow.

Yellow.

Now paling as the sun died, going away. Turning the liquid a pure, translucent lime.

He tightened the squint, moving inside the glass bullet of the container, inside the bubble. Rising and turning. Seeing only the pure, pale, green-yellow of the color itself.

... lime ...
　　　 ... lime ...
　　　　　 ... lyme ...
　　　　　　　 ... ROYALL LYME ...
　　　　　 ... Royall Lyme ...
... Royall Lyme.

Not Mennen's. The usual.

Not Old Spice. For special occasions.

This, now. This was a *very* special occasion.

The shape of the bottle. Well, he didn't care much for the shape of the bottle. Too crude-looking where the seams met, and bigger than it should have been for the shape it was. He needed to be ten feet tall before he could use it. Something about the perspective made him feel his size. A small bottle. Better a small bottle, he thought.

And the crown cap looked dull, leadlike. Which worried him. For a crown.

But all the way from the Bahama Islands. He couldn't get over that it was made from limes in the Bahama Islands.

He unscrewed the cap and held the bottle to his nose. It wasn't like lemons at all.

He put the bottle into the carton and started the car. On the way out he stopped by Kose's sometime picture show — the Vanguard Theater — to get his passes signed by Floyd Wehatchett, the manager. The passes went with his usher's job — four a week. He thought that he would put them into the envelope with the money as a kind of bonus for Nettie. The idea of paying her at all worried him — the fact of it. He didn't want to just hand over the money to her — plain bills. So he decided to get around the problem by buying her a greeting card, something with an appropriate verse on it, and putting the money into that. It would make things seem less like a business transaction. The passes to the picture show would be a bonus. He knew she came there a good bit, since he saw her two or three times a week. Never by herself, it's true. But then, if she didn't need them herself, she could pass them on to John Henry as a kind of bonus to him for his part in arranging things.

Floyd's hair was reddish brown, long on the sides and duck-tailed, but crew-cut on top. John Fletcher looked down into the pink shine of his scalp while he waited for him to sign the passes. The manager was thin in an unhealthy, cadaverous way, and to cover it up he bought his coats a size too large, with padded shoulders. If he had worn a big manila envelope, the effect would have been the same — like a two-button sandwich board. He had to walk kind of sideways, with one shoulder down and leading him — as if he couldn't move head-on because of the wind resistance. When he leaned over the desk to sign the passes, his buttoned coat hung away from him so John Fletcher could see right down to his belt buckle.

"Could a colored boy use them?" John Fletcher asked.

Floyd looked up at him from the other side of the desk that filled most of the tiny manager's office. He had a cast in one eye, so his glance forked all over the office. John Fletcher could never tell for sure which eye was doing the looking, and their conversations always made him nervous.

"I don't give a shit who uses them," he said. "Niggers sit in the balcony."

"Yes," said John Fletcher. "I just thought I'd ask."

Selecting the card had taken time. He had canvassed the drugstores in all the towns for twenty miles around. In the end he had gotten one of the first ones he'd looked at in Mr. Lane's Rexall store.

It was a large card with a stuffed red satin heart in an inset. With a good bit of lavender and some yellow, and a dusting of silver glitter scattered all over. Inside there was another heart. Not a stuffed one. There was also a cupid drawing a bow getting ready to shoot an arrow into it.

The verse started with a silver capital, then flowed on down the page in a liquid script. It read:

> *Some girls remind me of mother,*
> *With loving hearts so true.*
> *Some girls remind me of sister,*
> *For the very sweet things they do.*
> *Some girls make me feel sadder*
> *Than a worn-out, discarded old shoe.*
> *Some girls make me feel "gladder"*
> *Than boys could ever do.*
> *There are girls of all stripes and colors*
> *Every kind of hue.*
> *But the girl who is everything to me,*
> *Is the girl who is known as YOU.*

Across the bottom of the card, he had written in purple ink: "*July 3, 1956 — A night I will ALWAYS remember.*" He had signed it "*John Fletcher Williston.*" The envelope he had addressed to: "*The Incompareably Lovely*

Miss Nettie Oatley." He slipped the passes into the card, along with the check
— he had thought a check more refined than cash money, and had written it
out, also in purple ink, tearing up three checks before he got one on which the
handwriting suited him just right. The card was in his inside coat pocket,
along with the new black Swank wallet.

It was full dark by the time he got home. The headlights of his 1949
Studebaker swept the oaks lining the road. He got a good feeling looking out
at the trees as they rushed into the beams of the lights over the nacelles of the
hood and fenders which characterized the futuristic automobile. Driving it
was like what he imagined it to have been to fly a P-38 in the war.

Some of the trees — the ones leaning out too far into the roadway — had
white trunks. The county gang painted them as a warning to drivers. It was a
narrow road anyway, and they were dangerous. Everywhere you went at
night in McAfee County the low, spreading branches of the water oaks, with
the moss hanging down, made you feel like you were driving in a cave. It was
lonesome.

As he drove, he sang. ". . . Soooftly . . . as in a MORNNNing SUNNNrise
. . ." He had learned it in the high-school glee club, but had never gotten to
sing a solo because Mr. Forne, the director, had kept those to himself — except
for the girls. It was his favorite song.

He pulled off the dirt road into his front yard, not swept, but intended to be
— bare dirt, with two big oak trees flanking the entrance, and others here and
there closing in on the house. He parked his car right up next to the porch,
leaving enough room so the second car coming in wouldn't be cramped or
have difficulty turning around.

His voice filled the darkness, ". . . SAAWFT — ly, as in an EEEVE — ning
SUNNN — set, our love will faaaade aaaa — WAY." He was holding onto the
"WAY," but going up the front steps he saw a shadow on the porch. He clipped
off the note.

"Who's there?" he said.

"Is she with you, John Fletcher?" The voice out of the shadows of the porch
was raspy and high-pitched. The voice of an old man with too few teeth.
Slobbery and wet.

"Pa?" said John Fletcher.

"Is she with you?" he said, stepping out of the shadows and into the
moonlight of the porch. A small, gnomelike man in overalls. His lower jaw
hooked up, caving in his mouth where the teeth were missing — all the
uppers. His hair was sparse and wispy, plastered down in sweaty, black
tendrils, as if a small octopus was trying to climb over him from the back. His
hands were folded inside the bib of his overalls.

"Why'd you have to come over here tonight, Pa?" he said.

"Is she coming on later?" said Pa.

"You got to go home, Pa," said John Fletcher.

John Fletcher and his pa didn't get along. Never had gotten along. Since he was ten years old John Fletcher had known there was some kind of unbridgeable gulf between them, but his pa never found it out. All he knew was that they were father and son — root and branch. "You and me's two of a kind," he would say. He didn't notice that John Fletcher's mouth went tight, and that he always turned around and walked away whenever he said that to him. Most things he didn't notice. His son had been out of the house and gone for more than a week that summer before he missed him. "John Fletcher ain't here, is he?" he said.

No one had ever known Dorcus Williston to have a steady job, though he was pretty good at thinking up get-rich-quick schemes. Some of them were really good in an overall way. But all of them eventually fell through because Dorcus never could get around to working out the details. So it had been Minnie Williston — the mother — who had kept the family together, feeding them and putting clothes on their backs. The old man drove all of them to distraction from time to time. But John Fletcher *stayed* that way. Being the oldest, he had it harder than the other three boys. Dorcus was all the time meddling in his business and getting in the way, putting his arm around his shoulders and offering him homey but stupid advice that he had recognized as disastrous from the very beginning.

So when he got the usher's job at the picture show that summer he talked to Case Deering about the tenant house and moved into it to get some peace and rest.

"I wasn't going to get in the way or nothing," said Dorcus. "I just thought I would stay around and see what she looks like. You know. I had two nights with Maggie Poat once, and I wanted to see if Nettie was like her ma. Maggie was the best there is."

"Pa," said John Fletcher "this is costing me money."

There was a silence.

"It ain't free, Pa," he said. "I got to pay for it."

"How much a girl like that cost?" said Dorcus.

"Enough," said John Fletcher. "Enough so I don't want you sitting around watching us like it was a picture show."

"I wouldn't do no more than just to watch," said Dorcus. "I just ain't never seen a girl like Nettie close to."

"You seen Nettie plenty of times," said John Fletcher.

"With her clothes on," said Dorcus. "I mean I ain't never *seen* her."

"You saw her ma, you said," said John Fletcher.

"Shit, John Fletcher," said Dorcus. "Twenty years ago. Ain't no piece of ass good enough a man is going to keep it in mind *that* long. I just wanted to see what Nettie looked like. You know . . . *tonight*."

John Fletcher looked at him. "I ain't going to share my time with you, Pa," he said. "Get you some money and you can buy her to look at all you want to."

"How much?" said Dorcus.

John Fletcher looked at him. "Twenty dollars," he said.

Dorcus whistled. "Twenty dollars!" he said. "That must be *some* pussy. Maggie was five. I *got* to see what it looks like now."

"Not on *my* time," said John Fletcher.

"I wouldn't disturb nothing," he said.

"Yes, shit," said John Fletcher. "Go home, Pa."

"I ain't only just going to watch," said Dorcus.

"You ain't going to do nothing," said John Fletcher.

"Aw, son," he said.

"Aw, shit, Pa," said John Fletcher. "Save up your money. You can pay for it yourself."

"Twenty dollars?" said Dorcus. "Time I scratched me up that kind of a pile, I wouldn't give a shit no more. It always did take the lead out of my pencil — worrying about money."

John Fletcher didn't answer him.

"Maybe I could get took sick and drop dead tonight, John Fletcher," he said. "Then what?"

"I ain't never been that lucky," said John Fletcher.

"That's a hard thing to say, John Fletcher," he said. "I'm going to be took sometime. It might could be I'd be took this very night. Dead in the morning, and how would you feel then? You got to look at it every way you could. Might be it would happen. You'd be sorry as hell for it in the morning when I was done dead and gone. Too late then."

"Pa," said John Fletcher, "this ain't the kind of a thing that you go and share it with somebody. You sure as hell don't go and share it with your own pa."

· There was a long silence.

"It'd be a piss-poor last thought to have of you anyway," said John Fletcher. "I wouldn't want to remember you horny."

"You'd be sorry just the same," he said.

"Go on, Pa," said John Fletcher. "Get the shit out of here. I ain't kidding."

"Jesus, son," said Dorcus. "You got a hard heart."

"I ain't kidding, Pa," said John Fletcher.

"Shit," said Dorcus.

"Pa . . . ," said John Fletcher.

There was a long pause.

"When you going in the navy, son?" he said.

"Jesus wept," said John Fletcher.

"I'm going on home now," he said, though he didn't make a move. "Your ma wants to know. She worries about you, son."

"We talked about it already. She's going to see me off at the bus when I go to Jacksonville."

"She worries about you, son," he said. "The only mother you got."

"Go on home, Pa," said John Fletcher.

"You want me to take a message, son?" he said. "To your ma?"

"Just go on, Pa," said John Fletcher. "I told her already."

For a minute he didn't say anything. "Is this your first time, son?" he said.

"Shit, Pa," said John Fletcher. "Just shit."

"It was just that I thought you might need some advice from an old experienced hand. Somebody to show you the ropes."

"Don't show me no ropes, Pa," said John Fletcher. "Don't show me nothing at all. Just please get the shit out of here."

"All right," he said. "I'm going. Going home right now."

He started down the steps, then paused, scratching his head. "I never told you nothing about none of this," he said, not looking at John Fletcher.

John Fletcher didn't answer him.

"One thing I always found worked for me pretty good. You should blow in her ear. That drives them right out of their mind. I done it to your ma when we was courting . . ."

"Pa," said John Fletcher, "I don't want to hear it about Ma."

". . . She chased me right up that chinaberry tree in her daddy's front yard . . ."

"Pa . . . ," said John Fletcher.

". . . chinaberry," he said. "Lucky. I wouldn't never have made it up no oak. Drove her right out of her mind."

"Pa . . . ," said John Fletcher.

"Just blow in her ear," he said. He tapped his ear with his finger.

"I'm *paying* for this, Pa," said John Fletcher. "I ain't going to have to blow in nothing."

"Yeah," he said. "I just thought you might like to know about it for some other time. In the navy." He paused, looking down off the porch into the yard. "Cigarette ashes," he said. "Cigarette ashes in Coca-Cola. That's high-powered stuff. You got to be careful with that. I knowed a girl torn herself up on a gearshift once." He looked at John Fletcher. "When you get real hard up you can try that. But you got to be careful." He stopped and scratched his head again. "Ain't none of the cars got floor shifts no more anyway," he said.

"Go on, Pa," said John Fletcher.

The old man walked down the steps slowly, putting both feet on each step. When he got to the bottom, he stood there a minute. "Anything you want me to tell your ma?" he said. "She's the only ma you got," he added.

"You going to tell her about this, I suppose," said John Fletcher.

"Jesus, son," he said. "You want me to tell her you're fucking Nettie Oatley?" He looked up at the porch. "I wouldn't of thought you'd of wanted her to find out about that."

"I just figured you was going to do it," said John Fletcher. "It's just about your idea of good news, ain't it?"

"I wouldn't never mention no names or nothing about a thing like that," he said. "I got some sense."

"When did that happen?" said John Fletcher.

"I know how to handle things," he said. "You don't need to worry about me none."

"Just tell her *one* of her sons is fucking Nettie Oatley?" he said.

"I ain't going to tell her nothing," he said.

"Come on, Pa," he said. "You try to hold that in and you'll blow up like a two-dollar tire."

The old man held his finger up to his mouth. "She ain't never going to know," he said.

John Fletcher looked at him standing in the yard at the bottom of the steps. "Just go on, Pa," he said. "Tell Ma I'll be over to see her tomorrow, or the next day."

"Okay, son," he said. "Never a word. Have you a good time." He turned to go, then turned back. "Wash yourself up real good after you finished," he said. "You don't want to go in the navy all clapped up."

"I'll tell you about it, Pa," he said. "Maybe I'll tell you about it."

The old man looked up into the shadows of the porch. "Yes," he said. "That would be nice."

John Fletcher stood looking down at him in the yard. "I might send you twenty dollars, Pa," he said. "After I get in the navy."

Dorcus looked up into the shadows. "You wouldn't really do that, would you, son?"

"You leave me alone tonight," said John Fletcher. "I might do it."

"You could do it with your navy money?" said Dorcus.

"I don't want to be spoiling my evening looking out the windows for you all night," said John Fletcher.

"You got the money?" he said.

"I'll get it," said John Fletcher.

"You figure you going to make some money in the navy?" he said. "That picture-show job don't pay you enough so you could be taking out high-class whores like Nettie Oatley all the time."

"I'll do it," said John Fletcher.

"Nettie Oatley?" said Dorcus. "You talking about Nettie Oatley? Not some flappy-twatted old fartbag out of one of them piney-woods roadhouses? I done already laid enough pipe in that kind of snatch to run a pissline from here to Daytona Beach."

"I'm talking about twenty dollars," said John Fletcher. "If I see hide or hair of you around this house tonight, you wouldn't get a nickel."

"You wouldn't fuck me up, would you, son?" said Dorcus. "You wouldn't fuck up your own father, would you?"

"You going to fuck *me* up?" said John Fletcher. "I'll do you as I'm done by."

They stood for a minute in silence.

"I don't know whether I'd be up to Nettie Oatley," he said.

"Pa," said John Fletcher, "get the hell out of here. *Now*. Will you, Pa? Before she comes?"

"I trust you, son," he said. He gave an imitation of a salute and began shuffling off toward the road.

"Hey, Pa!" said John Fletcher, shouting from the porch.

"Yeah?" he said, stopping in the yard and turning back toward the house.

"Pa, tell Ma I'll be over for supper tomorrow night, will you?"

"Yes," he said. He put his finger to his mouth again. "Not a word," he said. "Remember. Blow in her ear. Just to prove it works. Don't put no cigarette ashes in her Coca-Cola, though. You wouldn't believe what it would do."

"We ain't going to have no Coca-Colas," said John Fletcher.

"Just as well," he said. "Not the first time, anyways. You got to know what you're doing."

He saluted, then turned and shuffled out of the yard.

John Fletcher watched him out of sight, then turned and went into the house.

All the tenant houses were alike. Functional. This one wasn't in such bad condition, though it was warped over to the side, like it was beginning to want to lie down. Case Deering tried to keep up his houses. Most of the windowpanes were still in, and the front porch sagged only a little. By being just normally careful, you could avoid falling through the rotten planks.

It was built well up off the ground on brick pillars. High enough that a good-sized child could walk under it without stooping over. Outside, it was unpainted clapboard. Inside, the walls were covered with sheet rock, with wide taped joints showing under the paint — salmon pink in the front room, blue in the bedroom, green in the kitchen. All of the colors were pastel and pasty-looking, as though they had been worked into a base of vanilla ice cream. The walls were all furry with a coat of grease and dirt now, with patches here and there where the sheet rock had started to turn to powder and disintegrate. The floors were covered with linoleum rugs — bright yellow, with red and blue triangles that intersected each other. When all the lights were on the glare tended to get up back of your eyes and blind you. In one corner of the living room was a coal stove, painted salmon pink to match the walls. The pipe elbowed out through a flange. It was painted salmon pink too, with weeping black stains at the joints, and more black stains running out from under the flange and down the wall.

The furniture was plain and cast-off looking. An overstuffed couch of coarse cloth, gray with a green fleck in it. One overstuffed chair that looked like the next year's model from the rival company of the one that had made the couch. Darker gray with a brown fleck. End tables at the couch, veneered in some blond wood. One of them had a long sliver of veneer stripped away, leaving the glassy-brown glue showing beneath. Lamps on the end tables. One homemade, from a quart bourbon bottle filled with sand, the shade tan with red and blue ships on it. The other was a vanity lamp, of white plastic that looked like milk glass until you got close enough to see the line of flash along the seam. Potbellied and knobbed. With a white shade, gathered with a pink ribbon at the top. On the wall behind the couch was a large picture in a plastic frame. The lights from the end-table lamps bouncing off it made it difficult to see what it was. A landscape with big patches of blue in it.

John Fletcher had tried to fix the room up a little, though he couldn't afford to spend much money on it. He had draped a crocheted afghan over the back of the couch. His mother had made it, black-bordered squares sewed together, with bright-colored centers. It blotted out pretty much of the gray with green flecks. There were two pillows stuffed into the corners — red and blue satin — souvenirs from Stuckey's, with the "Welcome to Florida" turned to the back. Two ashtrays on the end tables — one from Stuckey's that was chocolate brown with gold lettering, part of the verse to "America the Beautiful," the other from the ten-cent store, a ceramic skull with places in the eye sockets to hold the cigarettes.

He had also added some pictures on the walls — a couple of three-sheet posters from the picture show. One was from a Marilyn Monroe picture that showed her getting her skirts blown up, and trying to hold them down. One was from a Rex Harrison movie, showing him in a dressing gown, with one hand in the pocket, the thumb hooked out. And one was from a Japanese horror movie, showing a giant lizard stepping over a city that was on fire, holding a train over his head in his front paws, and kicking down a bridge with one of his feet. In the foreground a pretty Oriental girl was cringing and looking up at him. The lizard was looking down at her with the red whites of his eyes showing, and a kind of smile on his face. A rapy kind of look.

He had improved on the room as much as he could for this night. Brought a card table out and set it up in the living room for them to eat on, with two kitchen chairs — one straight-backed and wood, the other tubular with yellow formica seat and back — and a checkered tablecloth. He didn't like the color of the room and had decided to cover it up by eating by candlelight. He wanted a wine bottle to hold the candle, but didn't have one, except the wine for supper, which was full. So he used a syrup bottle that had something of the look of a wine bottle about it, he thought. It had a long neck. He soaked the label off, and it didn't look too bad with a red candle in it.

He had set out flowers, red zinnias and marigolds. But the marigolds smelled so bad he had to throw them out. Except for the pink walls, the zinnias looked pretty good. He had sprayed the room with Evening of Paris cologne that he had borrowed from his mother. To cover up the marigolds.

On the end tables he laid out magazines that he had collected for the occasion — *Time, Look, Life , The New Yorker,* and a *National Geographic* that he had found in a trash can behind the library. A couple of paperback books — *Rivers of Glory* by F. Van Wyck Mason and *Sangaree* by Frank Slaughter. Frank Yerby was his favorite, but his copy of *The Foxes of Harrow* had disintegrated and wouldn't make much of a show. On the couch he spread a Sunday edition of the Atlanta *Journal-Constitution,* turned to the book-review page. He had circled a review of a book on Chinese porcelain, making marginal notes like "very good" and "I agree."

He had debated about whether or not to leave the bedroom door open. It wasn't much of a room, and he couldn't afford to redecorate the whole house for just the one evening, but the blue was the best color of the three. Finally he decided against it, though he hedged by leaving the door cracked open just a little.

The supper menu had given him trouble. Finally he had decided on Salisbury-steak TV dinners. He liked the sound of "Salisbury steak." They would have wine with the meal — Roma burgundy — and coffee after. No dessert. He had a little speech about that. The third draft went: "Sweets I have in great abundance. Nettie Oatley, you are a sugar lump in my eye." He had bought a box of chocolate-covered cherries, in case she wanted something more substantial than the speech.

He lit the oven, then read the directions on the TV-dinner cartons and put them in.

Back in the living room he sat down on the sofa and smoked a cigarette. When he finished, he went into the kitchen and emptied the ashtray and rinsed it out. Then he put it back on the end table. He hadn't thought about it before, but he decided now that he should put out some cigarettes too, so he went and got a juice glass and emptied half of his pack of English Ovals into it, and put that on the end table too. He tuned his transistor until he got some slow music, then put it under the couch, thinking that would be a nice touch — to have the music coming from nowhere.

He lit another cigarette and looked at his watch. Nine-thirty. She had been due at nine o'clock. When he finished his cigarette, he took the ashtray out to the kitchen and washed it again. As he came back into the living room he heard the car and saw the lights sweep the front of the house. He put the ashtray back on the end table and turned off the lamps. Then he lit the candle. It took him two matches to get it burning. Before he finished, Nettie was knocking at the door. She knocked twice, then opened it and let herself in.

John Fletcher was in the middle of the room when she came in. He put his right hand into his coat pocket with the thumb hooked out, dropping the match on the floor and looking at her. He was trying to get a debonair expression onto his face. When Nettie first looked at him she thought he had probably cut a fart.

"Welcome," he said, speaking out of the corner of his mouth, "to my humble abode."

From where she stood at the door, she could see the Rex Harrison picture on the wall behind him. "It ain't so humble," she said, looking at the picture and then at John Fletcher. Her dress was blue. Filmy and low-cut. When she came close to him he smelled magnolias.

Nettie was a good-looking girl. Dark hair, almost black. Thick and long. Her eyes were yellow. Not brown, or light brown, but a golden honey color with sharp green flecks in it. Like a cat's eyes, but not quite as hard. The rest of her facial features were finely drawn, even a little sharp. In fact, her face seemed out of place on her body. Above the neck she was a kind of clingstone-peach soufflé; below it she was all meat and potatoes.

"Come in," he said, going over and closing the door, still keeping his hand in his pocket.

She walked over toward the sofa, pausing at the table for a moment and laying her fingers on it gently. "Very nice," she said.

"Have a seat," said John Fletcher. "And let me get you some wine."

"Wine too?" said Nettie, sweeping the papers into a corner of the couch and sitting down. "You *are* putting it on, ain't you?"

"There is nothing that is too good for a beautiful woman," he said. He didn't look at her when he said it. He looked at the candle. There was a rather long silence, during which he put his left hand into his pocket too, and rocked on his heels slightly, pulling his chin into his collar. "Nothing in this world," he said.

Nettie looked at him. "This is going to be one hell of a night," she said.

John Fletcher stopped rocking and smiled. "I'll get the wine," he said, going out to the kitchen. He still had both of his hands in his coat pockets.

He poured the wine into glasses that he had bought at the ten-cent store, and brought them back out to the living room. Nettie was sitting on the couch smoking one of the cigarettes when he returned.

"I like your coat," she said, taking the glass. "Is it real?"

"No," he said.

"It *looks* real," she said.

"Thank you," he said.

He handed her the glass in his left hand, then put the hand back into his coat pocket. He looked at her for a minute, then raised his glass and toasted her. "To the beautifully . . . To the beautiful Nettie Oatley," he said. He looked down at her. His left eyebrow was raised slightly. She thought he had farted again.

"Shit I reckon," she said. "This is going to be one hell of a night."

She raised her glass to his, tapping it hard enough that some of the wine spilled down her arm. "You can lick it off later," she said, and laughed.

They sipped the wine.

Nettie smacked her lips. "Makes you pucker, don't it?" she said.

John Fletcher gave a number of short smacks. "A little persimmony," he said.

"It's wine right on," she said, taking another sip.

John Fletcher sipped his with his hand in his coat pocket. Every now and then he would take it out, but then he couldn't think of anything to do with it, so he would end up putting it back in again.

"Come on," said Nettie, giving the couch a slap, "sit down and let's us get started."

John Fletcher looked at her. "How about supper first?" he said.

Nettie looked at the table. "Well," she said. "I had me a steak just before I left to come over here. I hate to work on a empty stomach. I get gas something awful." She patted her stomach. "I'm afraid I couldn't eat nothing else. What you got?"

"Salisbury steaks," said John Fletcher. He pronounced it *Sal-is-berry*.

"What kind of steak is that?" said Nettie. "Something fancy I bet."

"Not really," said John Fletcher. "I thought you might like to try them."

"I'll try anything once, buddy," she said, leaning over and slapping him hard on the thigh.

John Fletcher flinched, spilling wine in her lap.

"You can lick that off later, too," she said.

She reached out and felt his thigh where she had slapped him. "You ain't too solid, are you?" she said. "Kind of pony size."

John Fletcher didn't say anything. He took his hand out of his pocket, then put it back in.

"Don't let it worry you none," she said. "I had all kinds. It don't make no difference to me. Ponies and racehorses and mules. They's all the same."

John Fletcher stood there with his hands in his pockets, looking down at her. He didn't say anything.

"Let's have supper," he said.

He went out into the kitchen and got the TV dinners out of the oven. He wanted to put them on regular plates, but was afraid he would make a mess of it if he tried. So he brought them in to the table in their aluminum trays, with a plate underneath.

"*TV* dinners?" said Nettie, looking at them.

"Yes," said John Fletcher, smiling with his eyebrows up. "I'm not much of a cook."

"The meat's all right," said Nettie, "but the vegetables taste like shit. I'd as soon eat the box it come in as those green peas there."

"The steaks are good, I hear," said John Fletcher.

"I already had me a steak," she said. She held up her hand, the thumb and forefinger two inches apart. "That thick," she said. "With onions and french fries."

"Well," said John Fletcher. "I hear they're very good."

"Get me some more of that wine," she said. "Maybe a couple more shots of that and I'll get hungry again."

John Fletcher reached for her glass, but she held it away. "Just bring in the bottle," she said. "No need to keep running back and forth."

John Fletcher went out into the kitchen and got the bottle.

She had two more glasses quickly.

"Come on," she said. "We'll try your Salisbury steaks." She got up and went to the table. John Fletcher tried to put his glass down and get there in time to pull the chair out for her. He spilled more wine on the couch, and when he got to her and tried to help, she was already sitting down. She heaved up the chair, getting closer to the table, and put one of the legs down on his foot.

"You got to move fast to keep up with me," she said. She slapped him on the leg again. "Maybe you ought to eat mine too," she said. "Put some meat on your bones. You ever tried taking any kind of a tonic?"

John Fletcher was getting into his chair. He hit the table, and the bottle with the candle turned over. When he lit a match to look for it, it was lying in his plate.

"Now you got to take mine," said Nettie. "I done had me a steak tonight anyway." While John Fletcher got the bottle up and the candle relit, Nettie swapped plates with him.

"How about vitamins?" she said.

"What?" said John Fletcher.

"You ever take vitamins to try and make you gain some weight?"

"I'm bigger than my pa," he said.

"Jesus," said Nettie, "your pa ain't hardly five feet tall."

"But it's in the family," he said.

"Lee Jay is going to be a big man," said Nettie.

"Lee Jay is weak in the head," said John Fletcher.

"Well," said Nettie, "I just wondered. It don't make no difference to me. Big or little. I seen all kinds. You ever tried Hadacol?"

"Pa tried it," he said. "We had to take it away from him."

"It's good stuff," she said.

"Pa quit eating," said John Fletcher. "He was drinking four bottles a day. Staggering around the house telling everybody how good he felt and trying to get Ma in the bedroom with him. We couldn't afford it. He never did put on no weight."

"You ought to try it sometimes," she said. "Or some vitamins. Just to see."

"Well," said John Fletcher.

He began eating his Salisbury steak in silence.

"Give me some more of that wine," said Nettie. "It sort of grows on you. It don't feel like my mouth is turning inside out no more." She held out her glass to him. He poured it full.

While he ate, she sipped the wine and looked around the room. "It ain't much of a place you got here," she said. "The pictures is nice." She raised her glass toward the Rex Harrison picture.

"Yes," said John Fletcher. "I got them at the picture show."

"I can't never remember," she said, nodding toward the Rex Harrison picture, "what's his name?"

John Fletcher looked around at the poster. "Rex Harrison," he said.

"He looks kind of fruity," she said, sipping the wine. "All right in the face, you know, but . . . something . . . fruity is what it is. Like he's got lace on his drawers." She emptied her glass and put it down on the table. "Myself," she said, "John Wayne . . . that's my type. Big Boy Williams . . . he's cute too."

John Fletcher didn't say anything.

She picked up the bottle and poured herself another glass of wine. "Want some more?" she said, looking at John Fletcher. Before he could answer, she poured the rest of the bottle into his glass. "That's all she wrote," she said. She drained her glass and slapped it down onto the table. John Fletcher caught the candle before it toppled over again.

"You go on eating," she said, standing up. "Got to put some meat on your bones. I'm going to get more comfortable."

She walked over to the couch, kicking off her shoes as she went. Then she peeled off her dress, pulling it over her head and dropping it on one of the end tables. She had on black underwear. Across the front of the panties was written in red, "Friday." It was Tuesday. With her back to John Fletcher, she unfastened her brassiere and dropped it on her dress; then she massaged her breasts, kneading them together and pushing them up from underneath. "That feels good," she said, looking back at him.

She took off the panties. Flexed her knees and made a downward motion with her arms; then she was stepping out of them. John Fletcher couldn't follow the motion. Just suddenly she didn't have them on.

He sat at the table watching her with his mouth sprung open, the fork poised in midair, trembling, the peas falling off into his lap.

After she had got her clothes off, Nettie gave an angular pirouettelike spin — she had a baton twirler's grace, had been one in high school — and collapsed backward onto the couch, her legs spread wide apart and sticking out stiff in front of her, her arms raised and hugging the back of her neck.

"You about ready to commence?" she said. Her head was thrown back, and she looked at him under lowered lids.

John Fletcher lowered his fork slowly, not looking where he was putting it. It dropped off the plate and into his lap. He rose slowly from the table, his right hand in his pocket, his left adjusting his tie. He spoke with a croak. "Maybe . . ." He cleared his throat. "Maybe I ought to clear away the dishes," he said.

"Not now, John Fletcher," she said. With her knees locked stiff, she raised and lowered her legs, drumming the floor with her heels.

John Fletcher took a step, kicking the table and overturning the candle. He lit a match.

"Whyn't you turn on the lights?" said Nettie.

"The pink is shitty looking," he said.

"What?" she said.

"It's a shitty-looking pink," he said. "The walls."

The match went out, burning his fingers. "Jesus," he said. He lit another and set the candle upright on the table again.

"The candle is better," he said.

"Come over here, pony boy," she said.

He walked over with his hand in his pocket.

"Sit down," she said, slapping the sofa.

John Fletcher stood looking down at her. "Why . . ." He cleared his throat. "Why . . ."

She looked down at herself. "Do it every day," she said. "Shave all over. ALL over." She rubbed her hands up her legs and over her belly. "Started with a fella I used to go with once. He said he was paying to see it all, and he was, by God, going to *see* it. He done it himself with a *straight* razor. That was one hell of a sensation, I can tell you. I was afraid I'd twitch the wrong way and he'd put me out of business. But it come out all right. He never even nicked me."

She locked her fingers together and pushed them away, cracking her knuckles. "He had a nice touch," she said.

"When it started to grow back, it scratched so much I had to keep up the shaving. I figure it's a good idea anyway — kind of a conversation piece."

She laughed. "How about that?" she said. "Conversation *piece* . . . Get it?"

John Fletcher rocked on his heels and giggled.

"Anyways," she said, "it keeps down the crabs."

"It certainly does," he said.

She raised her hand and tried to unzip his fly. He looked up at the landscape painting. When she touched him, he flinched his hips backwards, pulling away from her.

"Hadn't we ought to go in the bedroom?" he said.

"You're the doctor," she said.

She stood up, running her hands up her body, massaging her breasts and holding them with her hands cupped under them. "That feels so good," she said. She twisted from side to side, rubbing them against him.

John Fletcher stood with his hands in his coat pockets, jumping his eyes up and down from her face to her breasts and back again. "It certainly does," he said.

They went into the bedroom. It was lit by a bare sixty-watt bulb hanging from a long cord in the middle of the room. The blue walls were better than the pink or the green, but still depressing. The bed was a massive walnut one — a lathe turner's dream come true, with posts that looked like strings of shiny black croquet balls. Festoons of smaller turnings had been worked into every available space. A bulbous tour de force. It filled two-thirds of the room. A matching wardrobe of the same massive design stood on one side. Something about its proportions was reminiscent of a 1940 Wurlitzer jukebox, though not so gaudy, of course. The two pieces of furniture accounted for most of the available floor space. Jammed between the bed and the wall there was an upended orange crate that served as a bedside table. On it was an autographed picture of Rex Harrison. *"Best wishes,"* it said. There was also another chocolate-brown Stuckey's ashtray.

"You know that fruity guy?" Nettie said, pointing to the picture.

"Not really," said John Fletcher.

"How'd you get the picture?" she said. "He wrote on it for you."

"Just sent him a letter and asked him for it," he said.

She leaned over and looked at it closely. "I wonder if John Wayne would send you a picture if you asked him?"

"Yes," said John Fletcher. "They all do."

She stood up, spread-eagled her arms, and fell backward onto the bed. "Let's commence," she said.

John Fletcher turned the picture face down on the table, gently. Then he went over and turned out the light.

"Hey," she said. "You can't see."

"There's enough light from the other room," he said, coming over to the bed. He stood looking down at her. "You're a beautiful woman, Nettie," he said.

She worked her right leg between his and moved it in and out. "You're all right yourself, pony boy," she said.

She sat up on the edge of the bed and unzipped his fly. Then she undid his belt and peeled down his pants and underpants.

"That's as pretty as ever a one I did see," she said, holding him in both her hands. One hand underneath, one on top, stroking him.

". . . thank you," he said.

He cleared his throat. "I thought . . . ," he said, ". . . I was afraid . . ."

She looked up at his face. "What?" she said.

". . . you seen all kinds," he said. ". . . It's . . . little . . . ain't it?"

She looked back down at him. "It's pretty," she said. "It don't go by the yard."

"I thought . . ."

She looked up at his face, then back down, "Don't worry, John Fletcher," she said. "I'd lot rather be tickled to death than choked."

John Fletcher didn't say anything. She went on stroking, sitting on the bed while he stood over her, his hands in his coat pockets, looking across at the wall over her head. With a slow, steady motion he began sinking at the knees, thrusting his hips forward and biting his lower lip. He reached down quickly, grabbing her hands with both of his.

"No," he said, holding her tight.

"Well," she said, looking down at him. "I *said* let's commence."

He looked down at her, opening his eyes. She was sitting with one hand cupped in her lap, the other poised, fingers spread, holding it away.

"Is it over?" he said, licking his lips.

"It's only just started, John Fletcher," she said, looking up at him. "Where's the bathroom?"

"There," he said, pointing.

She got up and walked over to it, still holding her hand cupped. As she went by the door to the living room, she flipped on the light. He heard the water running, then the toilet flushing.

While she was gone, he wiped himself off with a handkerchief and pulled his pants and underpants back up.

She looked at him when she came out of the bathroom. "You ain't had enough?" she said.

"You said we'd only just started."

"Why'd you cover up?" she said.

"It bothers me," he said, not looking at her.

"I know," she said. "You'll get used to it. It's better bare assed."

He looked at her.

"It's pretty as a picture," she said. "Believe me. I know. They don't come no prettier."

She walked over to him. "I'll help," she said, reaching for his fly again.

"I'll do it," he said, catching her hand and holding it.

He began by taking off his coat, getting a coat hanger out of the wardrobe, and hanging it up. He took off his tie and began to unbutton his shirt.

"Why don't you go on back in the other room?" he said.

"I don't bother you, do I?" she said.

"You bother the shit out of me," he said. "Go on back in there, and I'll be along in a minute." He had to go to the bathroom and was afraid she would follow him. He couldn't make water with other people standing around. At the picture show he had to watch the rest room and go when nobody was in there, or go in right behind somebody else and hope he wouldn't use the booth.

"Second time is better," she said, going out of the room.

He went to the bathroom, then came back into the bedroom and undressed down to his underpants and socks. He didn't want to go barefoot, but had nothing else to wear.

Then he went back into the bathroom again and got a towel, wrapping it around his waist to cover his shorts. When he went back into the living room, he found her dancing around to the transistor music. She had put her high-heel red shoes on, but nothing else. He went to the couch and sat down, watching her.

"I bet you cheated," she said, dancing over to him on the couch. She twitched the towel away, revealing him in his Jockey shorts. John Fletcher sat with his arms resting beside him on the couch, hands gripping the edge.

She danced away from him.

"Nice music," she said. "Where's it at?"

"I thought you'd like it," he said. "Under the couch."

"I like to dance," she said.

"You certainly are a beautiful dancer," he said.

Her dancing was like a provocative calisthenics exercise. As long as she kept her arms and legs in close, it went okay. But she kept flinging them out and striking angular poses, like a cheerleader practicing her cheers. She had gotten the wine down a little too fast.

John Fletcher sat watching her. After a while he crossed his legs. Once he drummed with his fingers on the cushion.

"Take your socks off," she said, dancing by him.

"I've got ugly feet," he said.

"They look funny," she said. "Not your feet . . . the socks."

John Fletcher tried to stick his feet under the couch.

She danced over beside the Marilyn Monroe poster and imitated the pose, mashing her breasts together with her arms.

"Sometimes people say I look like her," she said.

"Yes," said John Fletcher, shifting his eyes back and forth from the poster to Nettie. "Better," he said.

"Except for the black hair," she said.

"I like black hair better," he said.

The music changed. A slow tune. "Sentimental Journey." Nettie moved around more gracefully. Not kicking so much.

"How about some coffee?" said John Fletcher.

"Where's it at?" she said, stopping. She weaved a little standing there in the middle of the floor.

"I'll get it," he said.

"Woman's place is in the kitchen," she said.

"Some women," he said.

""Where's it at?" she said.

"It's on the stove," he said.

She went out to the kitchen and turned on the burner; then she came out and danced a fast song and two slow ones until it was ready. She poured it in the kitchen and brought the cups into the living room, sloshing coffee into the saucers.

"Let's sit at the table," he said.

He lit the candle and turned out the end-table lamp. This time he helped her into the chair. Then he sat there across from her, looking at her naked in the candlelight. He wanted to get down and look at her under the table, too.

"My table. My house," he said.

"What?" she said.

"Nothing," he said.

"Let's dance," she said. The music was all slow now.

"I don't dance very well," he said.

"I'll teach you," she said.

They tried it once or twice around the floor. She stopped and kicked off her shoes. "Here," she said, holding him at arm's length. "Watch my feet." She did the step for him. Then they tried it together again. "Count," she said. "One-two-three-four . . . one-two-three-four." They moved around the floor. When the music stopped he stepped back from her.

"You'll catch on," she said. "You got rhythm."

"I have?" he said.

"You got natural rhythm," she said.

They tried two more slow dances. "Try counting to yourself," she said.

He stepped on her foot. "I'm sorry," he said.

"Don't apologize," she said. "Keep counting."

He stepped on her foot again. "Let's sit down for a while," he said.

They went to the couch. For a while they just sat there side by side, not talking. Listening to the music. At eleven o'clock the music program went off and the news came on. Then the weather.

"Ninety-eight in Savannah today," said the weatherman. "Humidity eighty-nine percent."

"Ninety-eight degrees," said John Fletcher. "That's hot."

"I'd have died if I'd known it was that hot," said Nettie. " 'Course, I slept most of the day."

"Yes," said John Fletcher.

"It ain't the heat anyway," said Nettie. "It's the humidity gets you down."

"Ninety-eight is pretty hot," said John Fletcher.

"Yes," she said.

"Being in the picture show, I can't tell much about how it is outside," said John Fletcher. "It's always cool in the picture show."

"That's the nice part about working in the picture show," she said. "It's always air-conditioned."

"Sometimes it breaks down," said John Fletcher. "Not very often."

"That must be pretty bad when it does," she said.

"It certainly is," he said.

"It must be bad when you come out at night," she said. "That would make you feel it all the more."

"It certainly does," said John Fletcher.

After the weather report, the farm-and-home news came on. "Cotton is one hundred and sixty-three dollars the bale," said the announcer.

"Did he say a hundred and *sixteen* dollars?" said Nettie.

"Sixty-three," said John Fletcher.

"It sounded like sixteen to me," she said.

"I think it was sixty-three," he said. "I could have been mistaken."

"That's still low," she said.

"Maybe it was *two* hundred," he said.

"That's too high," she said. "Cotton wouldn't be going for no two hundred dollars."

"I thought it was a hundred," he said.

After the farm-and-market news, the obituary program of the day came on.

Organ music swelled in the background, playing "Rock of Ages," then the announcer's voice came on. "On the Other Side . . . ," he said. "Time, ladies and gentlemen, to pause for a moment in the hustle and bustle of weary workaday, and give a thought to those who have left us for a better place . . ." — the music swelled behind him, then died away — ". . . on the Other Side. This memorial program is brought to you by Fenway Brothers Mortuary. On the square in Kose. Your grief is in good hands at Fenway Brothers Mortuary." The music swelled again and died away.

"It's creepy sounding," said Nettie.

"The music is pretty, though," said John Fletcher. "Sometimes they play 'Softly as in a Morning Sunrise.'"

"What?" she said.

"The song," he said, " 'Softly as in a Morning Sunrise.'"

"He sounds happy about the Other Side," she said.

"He's got a good voice, though," said John Fletcher.

"Let's get something else," she said.

"Just a minute," said John Fletcher. "Softly as in a Morning Sunrise" would have made his cup run over. The song did turn up pretty frequently on the program.

The music continued softly behind the announcer's voice. "Mrs. Roscoe Powers passed away this morning at ten-forty-seven," he said, "after a lingering illness. She was in her eighty-ninth year, and had been bedridden since nineteen-forty-nine, in the loving care of her devoted daughter, Miss Glendanna Powers of four-twenty-three Swamp Street in Kose. The body is at rest for viewing at Fenway Brothers Mortuary in Kose. On the square. Graveside services will be held tomorrow at eleven o'clock at Dorchester Memorial Gardens."

"Get something else," said Nettie. "That's creepy-sounding."

"Maybe they'll play 'Softly as in a Morning Sunrise,'" he said.

". . . eight sons and three daughters, twenty-six grandchildren, and seven great grandchildren . . . ," said the announcer.

"Where's it at, John Fletcher?" said Nettie. "Come on and get something else." She was bending over and reaching under the couch. John Fletcher got down and took out the transistor. She took it away from him, tuning it herself. Bill Haley and "Rock Around the Clock" came on.

"That's more like it," she said.

She got up and began dancing again by herself. "Watch this step," she said. She glided away, keeping her legs close together and wagging her behind at him. John Fletcher watched her going away.

She picked up the coffee cups and wiggled out into the kitchen.

"Nigger work is what I'm best at," she said, dancing back in.

He didn't say anything.

The music changed to a slow one. "Blood will tell," she said, lighting a cigarette from the candle on the table, then sitting down backward in the tubular steel-and-formica chair, facing him.

"Don't talk about it," he said.

"Everybody knows anyway," she said. "Why not?"

"Don't keep doing it," he said.

"I don't keep doing it," she said. "I just said it once."

She inhaled a long drag from the cigarette and tapped the ashes onto the floor. John Fletcher handed her the Stuckey's ashtray.

"You don't need to keep talking about being a nigger," he said.

She took another drag on the cigarette. "You the one's keeping on," she said. "Anyway, I am."

"You're light as I am," he said.

She flipped the ashes off her cigarette, not looking at him. "Shit, John

Fletcher," she said.

"You could pass anywheres," he said.

She looked at the burning tip of the cigarette. "Maggie was a sixteenth," she said. "That makes me a thirty-second." She looked at him. "Everybody knows that."

"Everybody in McAfee County," he said. "You're going to be a nigger long as you stay in McAfee County. You could pass anywheres else." He was watching the cigarette smoke. "Anywheres," he said.

"Well?" she said. "What am I going to do that would make it stop?" She drew her hair back over her shoulders by moving her hand beside her neck. The light of the candle behind her made it more black and shiny-looking. Thick. "It's not me that needs to keep it going."

"And it doesn't hurt the busines none, does it?" he said.

She looked at him for a long time, tapping her cigarette. "I always did hate a smartass," she said.

"Well," he said, "why don't you move out of McAfee County? Go down to Jacksonville, or Savannah, if it bothers you?"

"It don't bother *me* any," she said. "*You* the one seems to be bringing it up and wanting to talk about it."

"But *that* bothers you, don't it?" he said. "What about Brunswick, maybe? They got a navy base in Brunswick."

"You trying to get me some work lined up, John Fletcher?" she said. "Or you trying to get me straightened out? What the hell are you trying to do for me?"

"I was just thinking," said John Fletcher.

"I don't need no more business," she said. "I'm starting to walk spraddle-legged from the business I got now. Being a white nigger has got its advantages. It kind of helps keep everything under control. You know?"

"It ain't much of a life," he said.

"What ain't?" she said. "It's a hell of a life, buddy. If I was just a plain little white twat, with my looks I'd have been knocked up and married off ten years ago. I wouldn't have had no chance. By now I'd have me a house full of kids. Streaks on my belly from swelling up with them, and my tiddies sucked down so I'd be dumping them in my lap every time I sat down." She hugged her breasts, looking down at them. "No thank you," she said, putting out her cigarette, "I'm doing just fine."

"You'd make more money in a big town."

"I got to hire me an accountant to figure my income taxes now," she said. "If I went to Jacksonville, I'd be clapped up and out of business inside of six months. Don't do me no favors. And quit worrying what it's going to be like the day after tomorrow. You got *this* whole night ahead of you."

"But wouldn't it be better without all this nigger talk?"

"That's part of it," she said. "Besides, nobody don't bring it up but rarely, John Fletcher."

"I couldn't think what it would be like," he said.

"It ain't your problem," she said. "So why don't you just put it out of your mind?"

"But I just can't think what it would be like," he said.

Neither one of them said anything for a while. She kept looking at him, but he looked away.

"What the hell is it, John Fletcher?" she said. "You figure you got it coming for what you're going to pay for this here night of love?"

He didn't say anything.

"It ain't that much *to* being a nigger," she said. "Not if you don't look like one."

"But don't you worry none?" he said. "Think what you could have been."

"I could have been ugly," she said. "Now *there's* something to make you sweat."

He didn't answer.

"How much you figure on giving me, anyway?" she said.

"Forget about it," he said in a low voice, still not looking at her. "Just forget about I ever asked you."

"You going to lay another five on the twenty you was figuring on to make it all worth my while?" she said. "Or maybe you was going to start to fall in love with me to pay it off. Or propose to go and marry me until you leave and join the navy next week? Maybe it was going to be something really serious like that. How much was it going to be worth to you to hear me tell that story about my nigger grandmammy?" She counted off on her fingers. "My great, great, *great*, nigger grandmammy, Coretta?" She looked at him over the back of the chair, resting her chin on her arms. "Coretta was Colonel Fanshawe's nigger slave," she said. "For poontang in particular."

John Fletcher wasn't looking at her. He was looking at the pictures behind her.

"*Pure* nigger," she said.

He flicked his eyes at her, then away.

"It was in December of 'sixty-four," she said. "Sherman was just about to come down and take Fort Moultrie." She stopped and looked at him. "Are you listening?" she said.

He looked at her.

"I ain't going to tell this but one time," she said. "Is it okay so far? That's the way you heard it, ain't it?"

He didn't say anything.

"It was December of 'sixty-four," she said, going on. "Colonel Fanshawe took Bascombe in — that was his youngest son, Bascombe — to let him blow his cherry on Coretta like the other three Fanshawe boys done before they went away to the war. Bascombe was fourteen years old," she said. She took a drag on her cigarette and put it out in the Stuckey ashtray. "She got took with his child."

"All right," said John Fletcher. He looked at her, then he looked away. "All *right*," he said.

"But you ain't never heard *me* tell it," she said. "You're paying for it, ain't you?"

He didn't say anything.

"It was December of 'sixty-four. . . . I said that," she said. "Then Fort Moultrie got took the next day by the Yankees, because the Colonel forgot they could come from behind where he couldn't aim his guns. So he had to surrender the fort. Then he took Bascombe into the magazine and blowed his brains out for him. Just before he blowed out his own brains." She paused. "Them Fanshawes was a stupid bunch of farts," she said. "Too stupid to live if you ask me. I hate to claim kin with a stupid bunch of farts like that."

"All *right*," said John Fletcher. He looked back at her again.

"You wanted it," she said. "What was it you was going to do for me to make it up? Something I wouldn't never forget? Was you going to pay me or thrill me, John Fletcher?"

"Excuse me," he said. His voice was low and courteous, the way he would ask her if there was something he could do for her. He stood up and leaned over toward her. Then his hand swept in a wide motion, coming around hard so that Nettie's head flicked under the impact of the blow. After he slapped her, her head didn't seem to have moved. She sat there staring at him over the back of the chair.

"Shit on your story, Nettie," he said. "I already heard it from everybody *but* you anyways."

"God damn," she said, lifting her hand to her cheek, touching it gently with the fingers. "God damn, you got a heavy hand, John Fletcher."

"Well," he said, not looking at her, "I'll give you five dollars extra." He lit a cigarette. "I'll give you five dollars extra, and I'll marry you to boot." He blew a big mouthful of smoke in her direction. "And if you try to tell me that goddamn story" — he blew another mouthful of smoke in her direction — "I'm going to beat your ass with a hairbrush and wash your mouth out with Octagon soap."

She looked at John Fletcher "Let's get back in the bed," she said. "We was doing all right before all this ever come up."

John Fletcher looked at her. "Sit down," he said. "We'll get back in the bed directly. I ain't finished smoking my cigarette yet."

"Jesus Christ," said Nettie. "You're a crazy fucker, John Fletcher."

John Fletcher looked at her. She was feeling her cheek with the tips of her fingers.

"Don't call me that," he said.

"Well, you are," she said.

"I don't mean 'crazy,'" he said. "You can call me that. Only don't say 'fucker.' It don't sound right. You ain't got the face to say 'fucker.'"

"What the hell you think I am, John Fletcher? The Rose of Tralee or something? I been saying 'fucker' all my life."

"Well, just don't say it tonight where I can hear it," he said. "You ain't got the face for it. I'm paying you not to say it."

They looked at each other across the back of the chair for a while.

"And don't say 'shit' no more, either," he said. "I'm paying you not to say that too."

"You just got to hear me tell it, ain't you?" she said.

John Fletcher didn't say anything. ". . . Sometime," he said.

"You got any more of that wine?" she said. "I need me a drink."

"No," he said.

"Well, I can't just sit here not saying 'fucker,'" she said. "We got to *do* something."

He didn't answer.

"Come on," she said. "Let's dance." She stood up, reaching over and taking his hands to pull him up.

They danced a couple of slow ones. Then a fast one came on, and they had to go sit on the couch. While he was stooping to sit down, she stripped his shorts off down to his knees.

"Damn!" he said, standing up. "It sticks you, don't it?" He rubbed his backside where the coarse material on the couch had scratched him. Then he sat down, turning to the side slightly and raising his leg to cover himself.

"It's more fun, ain't it?" she said.

"Not yet," he said.

His shorts were still down around his ankles. She bent down and he let her strip them off. She started to strip off his socks too.

"My feet're ugly," he said, holding her hand.

"But it looks funny," she said, "with just nothing but the socks."

"I could get another color," he said.

She looked at him without saying anything. Still bent over. He let go her hands, and she stripped them off. Then she got up onto the couch beside him and pulled him down on top of her. He tucked his feet down between the cushion and the arm of the couch so they wouldn't show.

"Second time is better," he said after a while.

"Yes," she said.

For a while they didn't say anything. Just lay there holding on and listening to the radio under the couch.

"You going in next week?" she said.

"What?" he said.

"The navy," she said. "You going in next week?"

"Thursday," he said.

"You'll like it," she said. "Navy boys has lots of fun."

"Poontang," he said.

"What?" she said.

"Poontang," he said. "I just had me some poontang."

She didn't say anything.

"I like that word," he said. "Pooooon — taaang."

"That's what you had, John Fletcher," she said. "Like the story says. It's true. I got to tell it to you sometime," she said. "Really tell you."

"Sometime," said John Fletcher. "Maybe I shouldn't have said that," he said.

She didn't say anything.

At two o'clock they had another cup of coffee. Then John Fletcher went and got the envelope, with her card and the check and the passes in it.

"What's this?" she said.

"It's for you," he said.

She opened the envelope and took out the card. The check and the passes fell out in her lap. She picked up the passes.

"Passes to the picture show?" she said.

"Extra," he said.

She looked at the check. "What's this?" she said.

"Your check," said John Fletcher.

"My check?" she said.

"Yes," he said.

"Where's the money?" she said.

"That's it," he said. "I made you a check."

"I don't want no check, buddy," she said. "Cash money. That's what I want."

John Fletcher looked at her. "I ain't got no cash money," he said.

"My business is always cash money," she said, holding out her palm and cutting across it with the edge of her other hand. "Right on the line," she said.

"I don't like that cash money," he said. "Not for this."

"Funny," she said. "I seem to of heard that before." She held out her hand, palm up. "Twenty-five dollars. Lay it right there."

"John Henry said twenty," he said.

"You said five extra," she said. "That's what the check says anyway." She held the check up for him to see.

"I was *giving* you that," he said. "Extra."

"I need the cash," she said.

"I just ain't got it," he said.

"You better have it," she said.

"The check is good," he said.

"Ain't they all?" she said.

"Well," he said, "what're we going to do? I ain't got it. I just ain't got it."

She looked at him a minute. She stood with her weight on one hip, her right hand extended palm up, her left holding her right elbow, bracing under her breasts. Then she turned and went to the couch, getting her things. He watched her as she got dressed.

"I'm going to get me some security," she said. "Not that I don't trust you, John Fletcher." She looked at him for a long minute. "Maybe one of your balls," she said. "Or that pretty little talleywacker of yours."

John Fletcher stood in the center of the room, one foot lapped over the other, covering it. His hands were clasped in front, hanging down to cover himself there.

She turned on her heel and went to the couch. Getting down on her hands and knees, she reached under and pulled out the transistor radio. The farm-and-market man was back on. ". . . here's good news for hog growers . . . ," he said. She cut it off.

"This'll do for part of it," she said.

She looked around the room. "Jesus God, John Fletcher," she said. She looked at him. "I'm going to need a bushel basket. Ain't you got nothing *little* that's worth something?" She looked at him for another long minute. "I mean besides your talleywacker," she said. She strode past him into the bedroom. John Fletcher stood there not moving, holding himself.

When she came back out of the bedroom, she had the cufflinks and tie pin in her hand. Also the black Swank wallet. She was holding the wallet open. "Five dollars," she said. "You're right. You ain't got that kind of money. Shit, John Fletcher, you ain't got no money at all." She took out the five and put it into the front of her dress. "For my tip," she said.

While she had been in the bedroom, John Fletcher had gotten his shorts and socks and put them on. He was standing by the couch.

"Turn on the light," she said.

He switched on the bourbon-bottle end-table lamp.

She put the things down on the card table and looked at them — totaling them up. "It ain't enough," she said.

"It cost more than twenty dollars," he said.

"Twenty-five," she said.

"You got the five," he said.

"I thought that was my tip," she said.

He didn't say anything.

"Anyway," she said, "it ain't worth it to me."

She looked at the things for a while. Then she looked at John Fletcher. She turned and went back into the bedroom. When she came out she had his coat.

John Fletcher took a step toward her. "Not the coat," he said.

She held out her hand to stop him. "You'll get it back when you pay me," she said. "It's just for security. Believe me, I'd rather have the money — even if it was real."

"I'll pay you in the morning," he said.

"You'll get your stuff back in the morning," she said.

She put the things in the pockets of the coat, then slung it over her shoulder and started out the door.

"Wait," said John Fletcher.

She stopped and looked at him. "That's all," she said. "You ain't all of a sudden found you some money, have you?"

"Take the card," he said. He picked it up off the table and handed it to her.

She looked at him from the doorway. "Save it for Valentine's," she said.

He held the card out, looking at her. "It's for you," he said.

"I don't want it," she said.

He slipped the passes out of the envelope and held them out to her. "Take these anyways," he said.

She looked at him.

"Give them to John Henry if you don't want to use them," he said.

She stood at the door while he came over and gave them to her. After she took them and put them into the pocket of the coat, she started out the door.

"Maybe I'll see you again," he said.

"I'd better see you in the morning," she said.

"Yes," he said. "Maybe when I come home from the navy."

She looked at him, holding back the screen. "Maybe," she said. "If you save up your money. Ain't all poontang cheap."

"I'll see you in the morning," he said.

"Yes," she said. "You'd better . . ."

Then he thought about the other present he had gotten for her. "Wait," he said.

"What?" she said.

"What would you say about a chocolate-covered cherry?" he said.

She looked at him hard for a minute. "Good night . . . white boy," she said. She went out the door, letting the screen slam shut behind her.

Six days later he himself walked out of the door to catch the bus for Jacksonville and the navy.

The first move was to the south, but all those that came after were to the west. The remainder of his short life consisted of a series of removes, each more Hesperian than the last.

Great Lakes Naval Training Station and Chicago . . . San Francisco . . . San Diego . . . Tijuana . . . Honolulu . . . Guam . . . At each stopping place he found someone — some girl, each more exotic than the last — who would dally with him at a sailor's price.

A mulatto whore in a red-headed wig in Chicago. In San Francisco a girl who claimed distant Kiowa ancestry, and wore a headband to prove it. A Nisei waitress in San Diego, who kept a naked Samurai sword across the foot of her bed, and made him beat her with the flat of the blade before she would have intercourse with him. A *mestiza* that he bought out of a Tijuana bar (she slept with him one time, and gave him his first dose of clap — he felt a kind of gentle affection for her on account of it). In Honolulu, a Chinese girl with a speech impediment. And on Guam a gentle, sarong-wearing Micronesian, who seemed to come to him always fresh from the sea, wearing a hibiscus in her hair.

He missed most of the fine points. But he had the sense that the tendency was the right one. Westering. The Pacific. It was the place he had always wanted to be — in atavistic flight from civilization, like a color-blind Gauguin, without brush or canvas.

Through the whole journey he carried the recollection of Nettie Oatley's honey-yellow eye. Flitting in the darkness of his mind like a spectral firefly, leading him on, to strand and beach him under the high, flaking ceiling of the ward of a navy hospital, set on a green-and-purple island in the middle of the Great South Sea.

As he was lying on the bed in the ward, Nettie's eye would rise behind his retina. A gigantic golden circle — green-flecked, with a center velvet black —

like the mouth of a tunnel of love, into which he glided on a float shaped like a swan. Through the yellow gate and into the velvet darkness. The light going away as he drifted through . . . gray . . . gray . . .

. . . the bubble turned slowly, quivering, compressing and elongating as it rose . . . turning gray in the pale green-gray liquid . . . a thick, steady movement . . .

"Seamanwillistonseamanwillistonseamanwilliston . . ." The voice went dying away.

. . . he cartwheeled slowly . . . holding to the bubble . . . rising through the thick green-gray liquid in the pale lime-gray silence of the dying sun . . . sun dying outside the windows of the ward . . .

". . . willis . . . willis . . . willis . . ."

. . . turning . . .

. . . turning . . .

. . . he wedged himself tightly . . . hearing far away the soft hissing sound of the trace of bubbles in the tube . . . sighing at the sun going black outside the windows of the ward . . . leaving him with only the hissing sound of the trace of bubbles in the tube going into his arm . . . going out of his arm . . . under the vaulted moonscape ceiling of the ward . . . coming down onto the bed itself to wrap him around . . . until even the faint hissing of the bubble trace in the tubing went away . . . leaving only . . . . the perfect . . . . . velvet . . . . . . blackness . . . . under the vaulted ceilings of the ward. . . . . . .

Daddy's Girl

1956: SPRING & SUMMER I

t has to be did," he said, speaking the words under his breath, as if he were afraid someone would hear them.

First light would come soon, the east was just beginning to turn gray, but the low moon still let him see the black outline of the house — dark now. He had turned out the light in the kitchen when he had come into the yard.

He worried about the lantern, was afraid Frances might see it — though he knew she couldn't see it from their bedroom window. She would have to get up and come into the kitchen. But she might do that. She would have been missing him from the bed all night now, and it might have waked her up and started her looking for him.

He began by actually cutting some pieces of kindling — thinking and planning after it was too late to do any good. He had burned a hole in the sheet with a cigarette. Walking the glowing tip around the spot. Tomorrow he would tell Frances it had been an accident, while he was talking to Jackie. She wouldn't think anything about it.

He stood the lightwood on end on the stump that he used for a chopping block, splitting off the pieces in long, jagged splinters, trying to make them come off clean. He had a deft touch, but he was nervous now in spite of himself, thinking ahead. He would have to use his left hand, and he might blink, too.

"It's got to be did," he said again.

He had trouble getting the position right, at first propping it up over a piece of the lightwood. But it didn't feel steady enough to him, so he put it down on the block itself, curling the other fingers back out of the way, extending them along the sides of the stump.

He held the ax close to the head, not raising it very high because he was afraid that he wouldn't be able to control it. Then he thought that it might not come clean, and he would have to try more than once. He braced the handle of the ax along the inside of his arm, clamping it into his side with his elbow, still thinking he was going to miss. He was afraid that if he thought about it too much he would begin to tremble, that he might falter at the last minute. The main thing was to make it clean — a single stroke. It would be hard enough to explain anyway, but he thought he could manage if he did it clean.

He counted to steady himself. "One . . . two . . . three . . ."

The blood welled at the stump of the finger, a swollen red bubble, shiny, pumping off big, slow drops. He closed his eyes, holding the wrist tightly in his left hand, squeezing it to stanch the flow of blood and slow the pumping of the bubble. Behind the lids he could see the other eyes, staring at him open and wide in the moon-filled room. He could feel the other hands on his wrist, locked and still. Holding on — the way you would hold on to a spear thrust into your body, not wanting it to move. Just about able to bear it, if only it wouldn't work in the wound. Not even wanting it out, but just wanting it not to move.

He let the bubble drop onto the block, then another, and another. Covering it. Covering the block and the ax head.

"Call Dr. Smoaks, Frances," he said. His face was chalky white and dead looking, and his eyes seemed to be receding into their sockets, like lead cooling in a mold.

"Good God, Henry! What you done?" said Mrs. Sipple.

"Call Dr. Smoaks," he said. "Then get me a rag or something to tie it up."

When she left, he took it quickly from the block. Still holding the wrist tightly. He went to the pumphouse and put it on the shelf where he kept the tools for the pump, laying it in the back where it wouldn't be seen. Then he walked back to the house and sat down on the steps to the back porch, not wanting to drip blood on the floors inside the house. He was sitting there when the sun came up.

Later, in the afternoon, he went back down to the pumphouse. He worried about putting it there, thinking he should have left it on the stump. The ants had gotten to it, and he let them take it. He didn't know what to do about it now anyway. Frances hadn't asked. She had been too worried about him for that. The next time he looked, it was gone. A rat probably. He had seen one at the pumphouse now and then.

And so it ended like that. With the rat taking it away.

"It's a girl." Dr. Smoaks stood in the Sipple kitchen. It was a cold October night and the windows were sweating, running in black streaks on the black panes.

Mr. Sipple stood by the table, frowning slightly. "Well . . . ," he said.

"Don't act that way, Henry," said Dr. Smoaks. "And don't let Frances see you. It takes a real man to blow the balls clean off."

"First one ought to be a boy," said Henry, not looking at him.

"First one ought to be what it is," said Dr. Smoaks. "It ain't for you to say."

"I was counting on a boy," said Henry.

"You ain't got no right to count on nothing," said Dr. Smoaks. "Now give me one of them cigars and a cup of coffee." He sat down at the table. Henry pushed the box of King Edwards toward him. Dr. Smoaks opened it and took out a cigar. He rolled it around the edge of the flame to get it started even, puffing the smoke up toward the ceiling. Mr. Sipple brought the coffeepot from the stove and poured.

"Frances had a hard time, Henry," said Dr. Smoaks, fanning at the blue cloud that enveloped his head.

"She's all right, ain't she?" said Henry. He stood holding the pot in his hard, balled fist.

"Well, but she had a very hard time." Dr. Smoaks took another pull at the cigar, then sipped the coffee, holding the cup in both hands.

"Is she tore?"

"Always tears a little."

"But is she tore bad?"

"Pretty bad," said Dr. Smoaks, sipping the coffee. "I want you to stay away from her till I tell you not to."

"How long?"

"Can't tell exactly. Seven or eight weeks anyway."

"Well, but she's going to be all right?"

"I think she's going to be all right, but you got to keep away from her. Till I say so."

The two men sat at the kitchen table drinking coffee and not looking at each other.

"It ain't going to be *that* long," said Dr. Smoaks. "It was going to be six weeks anyway. It's always six weeks."

Mr. Sipple didn't say anything.

"It could have been worse," said Dr. Smoaks. "Think about Dero Mullins.

Mae nearly died when Annie came last spring. Dero ain't been able to lay a finger on her . . . not nothing else either . . . for," — he counted on his fingers — "six months now. Six months, Henry. You think about that."

"You sure she's going to be all right?"

"I'm sure. I just don't know how long, is all. I'll tell you what," said Dr. Smoaks, "if it's got to be longer than seven weeks, I'll get you fixed up with Maggie Poat."

Mr. Sipple looked at him.

"'Course, you needn't go telling Frances I said that," he added. "That's privileged information. I'm *your* doctor too."

The corners of Mr. Sipple's mouth were pulling up in a little smile. "You think you could maybe arrange that?" he said. "Pull some strings and fix it up? Maggie ain't bad. You going to fix it so I wouldn't have to stand in line or something?"

"I'm not talking about what I'd do for Maggie. I'm talking about what I'd do for *you*. Maggie's the best there is," said Dr. Smoaks.

"Reckon it's the nigger blood?" said Mr. Sipple.

"I wouldn't say so," said Dr. Smoaks, "though I wouldn't say no, either."

"She's a lot of woman," said Mr. Sipple.

"She's the best there is," said Dr. Smoaks.

"I'd of thought when Nettie come it'd of loosened her up too much. Put her out of business."

"Needn't be," said Dr. Smoaks.

"Nettie was a big baby."

"Don't make no difference," said Dr. Smoaks. He looked at Mr. Sipple. "You ain't worried about Frances that way?" he said.

"Well, no," said Mr. Sipple. "It crossed my mind."

"Don't you worry about Frances," Dr. Smoaks said. "Just stay away from her till I tell you to. You couldn't even tell the difference. It's going to be better than ever. Maybe by Christmas."

"Is this one big as Nettie?"

"Nettie was a big baby."

"How big is this one?"

"Seven and a half, I'd say. Just guessing. Seven and a half or seven and three-quarters, something like that."

"She look all right?"

"Ain't none of them look too good just at first. She's all right."

"Nettie is going to be a better-looking woman than her ma."

"Looks ain't all."

"She's going to have some of the other, too. Plenty of it."

"God damn, Henry, how you think you can tell that? She ain't but five years old."

"You can tell."

"Not me," said Dr. Smoaks. "I can't tell nothing at all. Just looks like a five-year-old girl to me. Little skinny."

"Look at her face," said Mr. Sipple.

"Freckled," said Dr. Smoaks. He looked at Mr. Sipple for a minute without saying anything. "I didn't know you had the gift of prophesy, Henry," he said. "I sure as hell didn't know about that. You speak in tongues too?"

Mr. Sipple didn't say anything.

"Good," said Dr. Smoaks.

"What?" said Mr. Sipple.

"I said, 'Good,'" said Dr. Smoaks. "When Osie brings that daughter of yours down here for you to look at, you can show me how you do it."

Mr. Sipple looked at him.

"You know," said Dr. Smoaks. "Look at her face — or whatever it is you got to look at to get it straight — and tell me how she's going to be when she gets to be a grown-up woman."

Mr. Sipple looked away. "Anyway . . . you can tell," he said.

"Oh, I believe it," said Dr. Smoaks. "I ain't doubting your word. Only I just ain't never seen it done before."

"All right," said Mr. Sipple.

"Yes," said Dr. Smoaks.

They sat in silence for a while.

"While we're just sitting here waiting for Osie to bring her down so you can settle all this business for her and set my mind to rest, would you care to tell me just one other little thing? It ain't hardly worth your time, I know, it being so simple and all, but you got to get it cleared up sometime."

"What?" said Mr. Sipple.

"Would you care to tell me what your child's name is going to be? Or is that kind of fortune-telling too easy for you, and you only pay attention to the hard stuff, like how she's going to be in the bed when she gets to be a grown-up woman?"

Mr. Sipple looked at him. "What?" he said.

"What you going to name her?" said Dr. Smoaks.

"I ain't thought about no names for girls," he said. "I knowed it were going to be a boy."

"Well, you better start," said Dr. Smoaks. "She ain't. You wasn't telling that fortune worth a shit."

"If it were a boy I was going to call him Jack," Mr. Sipple said. "You know,

John. John Sipple. Jack for short."

"That won't do," said Dr. Smoaks, sipping his coffee and pulling on the cigar.

"Jackie is all right," said Mr. Sipple. "Jackie Sipple. Sounds all right to me."

"Why don't you give her a real girl's name?" said Dr. Smoaks. "Annie, or Sue Marie, or something like that?"

"What's the matter with Jackie? There was Jackie Fitzgerald. And Jackie Sue Womack. I've knowed lots of Jackies."

"But you're still thinking like it was a boy," said Dr. Smoaks. "Think like she's a girl. Which she is. How about Sue Marie Sipple? Sounds good to me."

"Jackie," said Mr. Sipple. "I like Jackie Sipple."

"What kind of a middle name you going to put with that? Sue Marie goes together real good. What you going to put with Jackie?"

"Jackie Sue," said Mr. Sipple. "How's Jackie Sue?"

"Sounds tacky to me," said Dr. Smoaks. "I never could stand that Womack child. Can't you do no better?"

"Well, why don't *you* try then?"

"I ain't interested. If it's *Jackie,* it's going to be up to you. How about Caroline Ann?"

"How about Caroline? Jackie Caroline Sipple. Caroline was Frances' mother's name. They come from Carolina, too."

"Too long," said Dr. Smoaks.

"But they come from Carolina," said Mr. Sipple.

"And she come from Two-Oak," said Dr. Smoaks. "If information is all you're after, why don't you name her *Two-Oak, October twenty-seventh nineteen-forty female Sipple?* It's got to *sound* right too, Henry."

"It don't hurt none to show where you come from."

"Better you'd show where she's going," said Dr. Smoaks. "But I forgot. You already taking care of that too."

"Jackie Caroline. Jackie Caroline," he said.

"See?" said Dr. Smoaks.

"Jackie Lou?"

"Sounds too close to Jackie Sue. How about Sue Ann?"

"Jackie Ann," said Mr. Sipple. "Jackie Ann Sipple."

"Dr. Smoaks didn't say anything. He blew a ring with the cigar smoke, and then tried to blow another ring through it.

"Jackie Ann Sipple," said Mr. Sipple. "Sounds all right to me. I don't care about nothing but the *Jackie* anyway."

"Do what you want about it," said Dr. Smoaks. "You owe me five dollars for my fee."

"I'll pay you Saturday," said Mr. Sipple.

"That's tomorrow," said Dr. Smoaks.

"I mean *next* Saturday."

"See you do," said Dr. Smoaks. He took out his prescription pad and scribbled something on it.

"What's this?" said Mr. Sipple, looking at the piece of paper.

"MAGGIE POAT — ONE TIME," the prescription said.

"Just in case," said Dr. Smoaks, smiling. "But you got to wait seven weeks first. It'll be my Christmas present to you if Frances ain't right by then."

Mr. Sipple folded the piece of paper and put it into the pocket of his overalls.

"Hide that where Frances ain't going to see it," said Dr. Smoaks. "I don't like my patients discussing their treatments with each other."

They sat there in the kitchen, waiting for Osie to bring the baby down, listening to the radio and smoking cigars, trying to blow smoke rings. Smoaks was better at it than Mr. Sipple. The news came on, and the announcer told about how the Battle of Britain was going.

"Look at that one," said Mr. Sipple.

The two men watched the smoke ring float off wiggling toward the ceiling. It went all the way.

"That's the best one I ever seen," said Mr. Sipple.

"Ain't she little, though?" Mr. Sipple had paused on his way through the kitchen and stood looking over his wife's shoulder at the tiny girl in the basin on the kitchen table. Frances cradled the child's head gently in her left hand, leaning over to make it more comfortable for her, and giving more support with the forearm along her side. With her right hand she would scoop water and let it run down on her, sometimes holding her fingers and thumb together, pointing down, and letting the water drip, to be more gentle.

Henry was amazed at the tiny, female body in the basin. The small, inverted purse of flesh between her legs, hairless and naked, made him embarrassed, so that he would look away and then back again and away. She took him unawares. He had never seen her naked before that. It was too much of a revelation, because he hadn't been prepared for a girl anyway. But it fascinated him and worried him both, and he never again stopped to watch her having her bath. The nakedness of the girl child jangled his nerves.

When the sons came, they didn't distract him from the daughter, though he actually spent more time with them than he did with her. But wherever she was around the place, he seemed to be always aware of her. In part that was a response to her awareness of him.

From the very beginning, Jackie seemed to know how to have her way with her father. When the younger brothers began to appear, three of them, in stepped progression, regularly every two years or eighteen months, her tie with her father seemed to be strengthened with each new addition. And this without separation from the mother — nor division between them. They were the women of the house and he the man; the one Henry's woman, the other daddy's girl.

At first none of the sons were there to run and meet him when he came home from work in the evenings. Then it was Jackie who won the race to his outstretched arms. When the boys got big enough to beat her, she would stand on the porch, outrunning them with the look in her eyes, one finger poised on her lower lip, taking the prize as the father collected the boys into his arms and onto his shoulders and walked across the swept dirt of the yard up to the porch. Then unloading them and stooping to let her put her arms around his neck and kiss him on the cheek and walk with him into the house.

Once, when she was ten, Mrs. Sipple caught her playing doctor with her brothers — two of them. She told Henry when he came home. It was his duty as man of the house to punish them, and he took the boys into the bedroom and beat them on their bare behinds with a belt. He had done it — had to do it — many times before, and he was comfortable at it, though he didn't enjoy doing it. But Frances insisted that Jackie had to be punished too, which was true. She was the oldest, and she had started the game. It was the first time that Mr. Sipple had ever had to do that, and he took her into the bedroom too, without thinking, before he realized what it was. That this was Jackie, and that he couldn't carry it through. He left her standing by the bed and went back out to talk to Frances.

"You got to do it," he said. "It ain't fit I should beat a daughter."

"You the one swings the belt in this house," said Frances. "You got to cut her too. 'Twouldn't be fair doing it to the boys and not her too. They'd never get over it. It were her doing. They ain't old enough."

"Couldn't you?" he said. The belt was still in his hand, and it wiggled limply at the gestures he made as he talked.

"It wouldn't be the same. Just go on in there and get it over with. You ain't going to really hurt her."

"But I can't," he said, pleading.

"Well, you got to," Frances said.

He looked at her helplessly.

"Face up to it, Henry," she said. "You got two minutes to take it onto yourself and do what you got to do. Then I'm going to take the belt and go in there and do it for you. And you wouldn't never get over that. You the man of the house. And it's got to be did."

He couldn't face up to his wife too, so he went back into the room and closed the door. The late sun was coming in through the window, and it lit up Jackie's hair in a gold nimbus where she was still standing by the bed.

"It's got to be did," he said. "It wouldn't be fair to your brothers."

"I know it," she said. She was sniffling and crying, and the tears were already running down her cheeks.

"I'd give anything not to, but I got to do it," he said.

She nodded. "I know it," she said. "Just get it over with."

"Lean across the bed," he said. She did as he told her. To make it proper, so the blows wouldn't be softened, he raised her skirt a little, carefully, baring the backs of her legs and tucking it under her to hold it just right. Her legs were skinny and frail looking, and he tried not to look at them. The tendons behind her knees stood out where she had drawn up waiting for the blow.

He swung the belt, bringing it down with a fast swishing sound, not looking at the place where the blow fell. In his nervousness he hit her much harder than he had meant to. A great red welt marked the place where the belt had struck. Jackie let out a long wail, then buried her face in the bed clothes. He looked at the red streak on the backs of her legs. The scream startled him, and he couldn't raise the belt again.

"That's all," he said, throwing the belt on the bed. "Don't never do it again."

She looked at him over her shoulder. One side of the skirt came untucked, and it fell down, covering the welt on one side. She was still teary eyed, but she wasn't crying now.

"You give Sid and Gilmore eight apiece," she said. "I counted them."

"I hit you harder," he said. "It's your first time. Now, tell me you ain't never going to do it again." The other side of her skirt came untucked, covering the welt completely.

"I won't never," she said. "Ain't Sid and Gilmore going to be mad?"

"It's your first time," he said. "I made you holler louder. Counting the licks ain't all there is to it."

She nodded, wiping her eyes.

"Now, mean it when you say you ain't never going to do it again," he said. "I couldn't stand to give you another beating, and if you do it, I'll have to."

"Not never," she said. "I promise not never."

"Nor nothing like it neither," he said.

"No," she said.

"Mean it, honey," he said. He leaned down, and she put her arms around his neck, hugging him.

"I do," she said.

He went back out to the kitchen and sat down at the table. "I kept my part of the contract," he said, digging the heels of his hands into his eyes. "I couldn't do no more. If it ain't enough, you got to go in there and finish it up yourself."

"It had to be did," she said, drying her hands and coming over to him. She put her arms around his neck and kissed him. "It were the only fair thing."

He rested his hand on her arm. "Yes," he said, "but I hope to God she don't never do it again. I couldn't carry it off no second time."

"You done what you had to," she said.

"But not no more," he said.

"Yes," she said. She stood behind him with her arms around his neck, putting her cheek against his while he rested his hand on her arm.

As Jackie passed into her teens, her relationship with her father underwent a subtle change, which he wasn't fully aware of at first, though he noticed something and started to puzzle out what it might be. She still sought him out for his approval, was loving and attentive to him, but her interests were widening, turning outward and away from him, to boys nearer her own age. It was a hard time for Henry, for she would alternately be his and not his — aware and coquettish, distant and unconcerned. It made him love her more than ever.

She would come to him for reassurance and approval, putting her arms around his neck and sitting in his lap — playfully, as she had done when she was a little girl. But he began to see more and more that she was practicing on him — at least that was partly it — while saving a secret part of herself for others, whom Mr. Sipple could almost see and hear and smell waiting for her in the darkness outside the house. He grieved for the secret part.

First he forbade her to cross U.S. 17 to the Camp Stewart side — hoping to forestall that calamity — the bane of all the fathers of daughters in the six counties surrouunding the army base. But he couldn't lock her into the house and forbid her to go out with the sons of neighbors — people he had known for years and saw every day. Though the very sight of their pimply faces and the sound of their high-pitched, cracking voices made him grit his teeth and talk out of the back of his throat. He wanted to chase them off with a hoe. Finally he began to worry that he might forget himself and kill one of them.

And Jackie seemed to distinguish among them, showing preferences. That was the worst of all. It made him realize how little he knew his own daughter — how unbridgeable was the gulf that separated them. She liked some better than others. What was the basis of her choice? To him they were an aggregate, a concatenation of fluty, prancing gamecocks, dressed in too-tight Levis and

T shirts — a constant, undifferentiated presence ringing the house, homing in on his daughter like a pack of hounds on a bitch in heat. And Jackie, whom he could not conceive to be aware of it, was being driven, aware or not, along the periphery of that dance of life, despite all he could do to thwart and prevent it. He had never seen a chastity belt, never even heard of one, but he groped for the concept, and, given enough time, might have conjured it up and locked her into it out of the depth and desperation of his anguish. Only time was the one thing he did not have.

And the thought that made him most frantic was the suspicion, enforced by his wife's equanimity, contrasted with his own anguish, that Jackie did have a woman's awareness, below or beyond conscious recognition of that awareness, of what it all meant and led to. And not only that, but that she was enthusiastic about it. There came to him the realization that woman's knowledge was going to beat him in spite of all that he might plan and actually worry into fruition. If he had been able to conjure into substance the chastity belt, he would have found that they, his wife and his daughter, would have already conjured into substance the key.

"Ain't it nice Jackie is so popular?" Frances said to him as his daughter left on a walking date to BYPU, going out of the yard on the arm of one of the pimply-faced, tight-Levied, cracked-voiced bantams, whose neck he had wanted to wring.

He realized that it was a losing battle, but that he would have to fight it anyway.

Frances didn't even notice that he had not answered her.

His anguish turned to agony when Jackie accepted a date with John Fletcher Williston, an older boy who told her that he would be around to pick her up in an automobile.

"You got to talk to her, Frances," he said.

"About what?"

"About not getting in trouble. About how the boys are going to act and what she needs to do."

"We done had that out before."

"But you need to do it again."

"Jackie knows about it. We talked it over."

"But she ain't only fifteen. And she's going out in a automobile."

"It'll be all right. John Fletcher is a good boy."

"Ain't none of them that good. Don't I remember about it myself? And in a automobile."

"It'll be all right. She's rode in a automobile before."

"You ought to remind her."

"You going to put her in mind of it anyway if you keep on talking about it all the time."

"Won't you talk to her?"

"All right. But the talk ain't going to do no good one way or the other if she ain't got sense enough by now anyway."

"It'll remind her."

"Maybe it'll remind her of the wrong thing."

"I'm going to telephone Dorcus Williston and tell him I'm holding him accountable for that boy of his."

"You out of your mind, Henry? You ain't going to do no such of a thing. John Fletcher is a good boy. I told you. It's going to be up to Jackie with him. If she ain't got sense enough, it'll be her own fault. But talking to her tonight ain't going to make her sensible, though I'll do it just to calm you down. You stay away from that telephone."

"I wish I could talk to her."

"Why don't you?"

"I wouldn't know what to say."

"You wouldn't know how to say it, you mean."

"And what to say, too."

"You go on out in the kitchen and get you some coffee and a piece of pie or something. I'll go speak to her."

"Mr. Sipple was sitting at the table in the kitchen when she came back. He had cut himself a piece of pie and was stirring a spoon in a full cup of black coffee.

"What'd you say to her?"

"We talked it over."

"But what'd you say to her?"

"I couldn't say it to you. It's woman's talk."

"But what did you say?"

She looked at him. "You say what you wanted me to say, and I'll tell you if I said it."

They looked at each other a minute, and then he went back to stirring the coffee. He wished he had put his ear to the door and listened.

"You think she understands what we mean?" he said.

"She understood already. Like I told you. I just reminded her about it."

He didn't reply.

She came over and put her arms around his neck. "Don't worry, Henry," she said. "Jackie's a good girl."

Mr. Sipple wouldn't come out of the kitchen to speak to John Fletcher when he came to the house, so Mrs. Sipple had to sit in the front room and talk to him while Jackie finished getting ready. Before she left with him, she came into the kitchen and kissed her father good-bye, pecking him on the cheek.

"You be in by eleven o'clock," he said.

"Eleven-thirty, Daddy," she said.

"You be careful, and make him drive that car right," he said.

"Don't worry, Daddy," she said. "John Fletcher is a good driver."

"Eleven-thirty," he said.

She kissed him on the cheek again and went out of the kitchen, half running.

"You be careful," he said.

The swinging door flap-flapped, fluttering closed.

When he heard the screen slam he got up and went into the front room, looking out the window at Jackie and John Fletcher going out of the yard together.

"Where the hell he get a coat like that?" he said. "Zebra skin?"

"Leopard," Mrs. Sipple said. "It ain't real. All of them wear crazy things these days."

"Looks like it ought to be hanging on the wall," he said. "And him with it."

John Fletcher opened the door for Jackie and helped her into the car.

"He's got good manners," Mrs. Sipple said.

"He knows I'm watching," said Mr. Sipple. "I ain't worried about what he's going to do when he knows I'm watching."

"Come on, Henry," she said. "Don't worry about Jackie. She's a good girl. And John Fletcher is a good boy."

Mr. Sipple didn't answer. He stood behind the curtained window, watching the car going out of his yard.

"I'm going on to bed," she said. It was nine o'clock. "You going to wait up to see she gets in on time?"

"She better get in on time," he said.

"Well, no sense both of us losing sleep. I'm going on to bed."

"I couldn't sleep nohow."

"Don't shame her in front of John Fletcher, Henry. You got anything to say, you wait till he's gone."

She kissed him and went into the back of the house.

He sat in the front room listening to the radio. At ten-forty-five he cut out the lights, sitting in the dark. The car pulled up at eleven o'clock, but Jackie and John Fletcher didn't get out. Through the open window he could hear the occasional murmurings as they talked. He saw a match flare inside the car, lighting up their faces — Jackie was smiling — then the glowing ends of two cigarettes, moving in the darkness. At eleven-thirty-one the door on the driver's side opened and John Fletcher got out. He was not wearing his coat, and had taken off his tie. He went around and opened the door on Jackie's side, taking her hand as she got out. They walked up to the house holding hands and swinging their arms between them, like two small children. Midway to the house John Fletcher stooped and picked up a stone from the yard. He threw it away over the oak tree in the front of the road; then he said something to Jackie, and they both laughed. All the way across the yard they were mumbling to each other, but Mr. Sipple couldn't make out what it was they were saying.

They came up the steps onto the porch and out of his line of sight. There was no talking now, though he could hear their breathing and every now and then a shoe scraping on the boards of the porch. He tiptoed out of the front room and into the hall. Through the curtained window in the front door he thought he could make out Jackie. She was leaning her back against the door. John Fletcher stood on the other side of her. Their arms and hands seemed to be moving, but he couldn't tell about the movements through the curtain of the window.

At last Jackie moved forward and turned to open the door. Mr. Sipple stepped quietly into the front room.

"All right," she said. "Good night."

He couldn't hear what John Fletcher said.

Jackie came into the house quietly, closing the front door behind her without making any noise. He barely heard the click as the latch fell.

Mr. Sipple stepped into the hall.

"You're late," he said.

"What time is it?" she said.

"Quarter to twelve," he said.

"We was back at eleven," she said.

"I said in the house," he said.

She didn't say anything.

"You been smoking cigarettes," he said.

"No I ain't," she said.

"Don't lie to me," he said.

"I ain't smoked no cigarettes," she said.

"I seen you," he said.

She didn't answer.

They stood facing each other in the darkness for a minute. Neither one spoke.

"What else you been doing you wouldn't want to tell me about," he said.

"I ain't been doing nothing I wouldn't want to tell you about," she said. "I ain't been doing nothing at all."

"Like you ain't been smoking cigarettes?" he said.

She didn't reply.

"Didn't your mother talk to you about how you was to behave?"

"Yes," she said.

"She say it was all right for you to go smoking cigarettes and standing around on the porch in the dark?"

"No," she said.

"What else was you doing out there on the porch anyways? Something else you wouldn't be wanting me nor your mother to know about?" he said.

"We wasn't doing nothing."

"Like you wasn't smoking no cigarettes?"

She didn't say anything.

"You tell me," he said. "Tell me what else your mother said you wasn't supposed to be doing."

He could hear her breathing in the darkness of the hall. She didn't reply.

"You done told me one lie, which I wouldn't have known no better than believe, except I seen it with my own eyes. How many more lies you going to tell me tonight?"

"No lies, Daddy," she said.

"I couldn't trust you," he said. "I wanted to trust you, but I couldn't do it no more. You shouldn't have said 'No' about the cigarettes."

"That's the only time," she said. "I'm sorry about that. But it's the only time."

"But I can't believe you no more," he said. "I just got to see for myself from now on. I ain't going to be able to ask you no more."

She didn't reply for a minute.

"I'm sorry," she said.

"Be quiet and come in your room," he said.

He tiptoed down the hall behind her. When they had gone into her room, he closed the door gently so as not to wake his wife. She turned on the light, and the room was lit by a bare bulb, hanging at the end of a long cord from the ceiling.

"Turn that light out!" he said.

She flicked the switch, and the room was dark again, except for the patches of moonlight falling onto the floors through the windows.

"Now," he said, "get your clothes off and get in the bed."

She didn't speak.

"I ain't going to watch," he said. "I can't see nothing in here anyway, but I'm going to turn my back. You do as I say."

"What you going to do?" she said.

"You just do as I say," he said.

In the darkness of the room he could hear the sounds her clothes made as she undressed. The sounds made him nervous, and he talked to cover them up.

"I want you to be a good girl, Jackie," he said. "You go telling lies, and I can't believe nothing you say. Why'd you have to lie to me about that cigarette? You must have knowed I seen you?"

She didn't reply. He began to be aware of something trying to come around from the back side of his mind, but he didn't know what it was. He listened for it for a minute. Then the silence began to make him nervous again, and he started talking to cover it up.

"Just one lie, and now I can't believe what you tell me. I ought to just ask you, and now I can't."

"I'm ready," she said.

"You got your gown on?" he said, not turning around.

"Pajamas," she said.

"Where's your gown?" he said.

"I don't wear a gown now," she said.

For a minute he didn't speak. "Take off the bottoms," he said.

"Why?" she said.

"Take them off," he said. "I ain't going to look. Then get in the bed and pull the covers up."

He heard the clothes sounds again, then the squeaking of the bed and the rustle of the sheets as she got in. It was still trying to come around, but he didn't know what it was.

"You ready now?" he said.

"Yes," she said.

He turned and went to the bed in the darkness. The moonlight came in through the windows, giving enough light for him to see the objects in the room. He took her clothes from the chair and went to the window with them, examining them in the moonlight. She watched him from the bed as he came back from the window, laying the things carefully across the back of the chair.

He sat on the side of the bed, not touching her.

"I'm going to try one time," he said. "You answer me and tell me the truth."

"Yes," she said. She had the sheet pulled up, holding it tight around her neck.

"What happened in that car?"

"Nothing," she said.

"You smoked a cigarette," he said. "That happened."

"But nothing else," she said.

"I'm trying to believe you, girl," he said. "Now, you tell me the truth. Didn't nothing else happen?"

"No," she said.

He sat in silence for a while. The thing was still trying to come around out of the back side of his mind, and he was listening for it, but it wasn't there yet.

"Why'd you have to lie about the cigarette?" he said. "Maybe I'd have believed you if you hadn't lied about that."

"I'm sorry about the cigarette," she said. "But ain't nothing else happened. That's the God's truth."

He sat in silence for a while. "What else you know about that might have happened?" he said. "Why don't you tell me that? What'd your mother tell you about?"

She didn't answer.

"He had the zebra coat off, and his tie, when you got out and come in the house," he said.

"It's hot out tonight," she said.

"What else he have off in that automobile?" he said.

"What you mean?" she said. "He didn't have nothing else off. What you think?"

"And what did you have off?" he said. "Anything you had off in that automobile?"

"Pa," she said. She touched his hand with hers. He took the hand and squeezed it, hurting her. He thought he could feel it coming around again — but then it wasn't — and he squeezed her hand.

"You hurting me, Pa," she said.

"I just got to know," he said.

"Turn loose, Pa. You hurting me," she said.

He let go her hand. "Tell me again," he said. "Tell me ain't nothing happened in that automobile tonight. One more time, so I might believe it."

"I told you," she said. "I told you — I told you — I told you." She started to cry.

"You lied," he said. It was coming around again — almost . . . Almost — and then it wasn't. "You lied," he said.

He put his hands on her shoulders and pumped them up and down on the bed. She fought back, neither of them making any sounds in the dark stillness of the room. Only the creaking and groaning of the springs of the bed, going faster and faster.

His hands were still on her, not just her shoulders, and they were thrashing around on the bed together, fighting each other, the sheets twirling and billowing, wrapping them around and tangling. She moved under him and against him, fighting his hands. Not scratching or trying to hurt him, but reaching and countering his moving hands, fending them off.

He caught one of her hands and held it. Then the other. Holding both of them in his one, his other hand free. Only for a moment. He could have counted to five, just that long before she broke the one hand free and caught his wrist, squeezing it tight so it wouldn't move.

She gave a small, sharp cry.

"Pa," she said, speaking just the one word. And then the movement stopped.

He saw the wide, staring eyes in the darkness of the room and the underlip held in the teeth. He hadn't felt it. But then he did. Like putting his hand into a spider's web and not knowing he had touched it until the hand drew back, collapsing the latticed pattern. He felt her hands locked on his wrist, frozen there while they looked at each other, staring through the dark. The billowing sheet settled around them as they knelt facing each other in the disorder of the bed.

His eyes slid off to the side, going out of focus, and he could feel it beginning to come around now, almost swinging into his consciousness. He moved slowly, twisting his wrist out of her grip, pulling her arms up toward him before the fingers came loose and she fell over on her side with her knees drawn up, locking her hands between her legs.

He rose beside the bed, standing quiet in the dark. "It was . . . ," he said, ". . . you lied about the cigarettes. You know you done that." He cupped his hands together over his nose and mouth, rubbing his fingers along the sides of his nose. Then he put his hands on his hips, standing with his shoulders hunched forward and his head hanging down.

"Well . . . ," he said, ". . . well . . ." He laced his fingers together in front, pushing them away, cracking his knuckles.

Then he went out of the room into the kitchen. He sat in the dark in the kitchen for a long time, staring out the moonlit windows. Sitting at the table, he felt it again, swinging around on the dark side — not there yet, but coming.

He turned on the light and lit the burner under the coffeepot. While it was heating, he went to the shelf to get the sugar bowl. Beside the bowl he saw the cigar box. There were three others, scattered around the house, filled with old Christmas cards and sewing things, buttons and the like. This one had been the first.

When he saw the box, it came swinging around out of the darkness, and he knew what it was.

"Smoaks . . . ," he said, croaking it out of the back of his throat. He was looking at the King Edward box. "Call Smoaks," he said. "God damn it to hell. I should have called Smoaks."

He lifted the cigar box gently from the shelf and put it on the kitchen table. With his little finger he lifted the lid, turning it back gently. A thimble, a pincushion — like a furry, red tomato, studded with the heads of straight pins — and a tangle of ribbons. He looked at it for a minute, then he went and cut off the burner under the coffeepot and came back to sit down at the table. He pulled the open box over in front of him and took the things out of it, putting them on the table.

"Smoaks . . . ," he said, looking into the empty box, ". . . Jesus God."

After a while he went back into her room and burned the spot out of the sheet. Not a large hole — a half-dollar would have covered it. When he put out his hand to move her, she scurried away from his touch. He didn't look at her when he lit the match so he could find the spot.

"I'm . . . ," he said. He didn't finish.

"Go away, Pa," she said.

He went back into the kitchen and sat down at the table with the empty box in front of him. Afterward he shook a single ribbon out of the tangle. It was a pink one, twisted and creased. He dropped it into the box and closed the lid. Then he turned off the light and went out of the house, carrying the box in both hands.

On the back porch he stopped to take the lantern from the nail. He didn't light it, worrying about Frances. At the pumphouse he stopped again to get the shovel. Then he went on into the woods.

When he was far enough from the house that the trees would hide him, he lit the lantern and hung it from the limb of a pin oak, putting the box down gently to one side. Then he scooped a shallow hole in the ground and put the box into it. With the first scoop of dirt on the shovel, he stopped, looking down at the box, pausing. He shot the dirt out of the shovel to the side of the hole and slid the blade under the box, lifting it out gently and putting it down on firm ground beside the hole. He raised the shovel high over his head, holding it by the very end of the handle in both hands and arching his body to keep from going off balance backward. Then he snapped forward, doubling up and bringing the flat of the blade down on the box, smashing it, so that it made a sound like a paper bag bursting, a small, brittle explosion.

He hit it two more times, splintery-sounding swats. Then he scraped the pieces into the hole and covered them over with dirt, pressing it down with his foot and kicking pine needles over the fresh earth to cover the place.

He took the lantern off the limb and walked back to the house, not putting it out this time. When he got back to the pumphouse, he leaned the shovel against it and took the ax. The woodpile was on the opposite side of the house, where he didn't think Frances would see him.

"She's staying out too late, Henry," Frances said. Jackie had just left the house, going off in a pickup with two boys from Kose. They had said there would be another girl — Annie Mullins. They would pick her up going out.

"Well," said Mr. Sipple, "maybe you better talk to her some more. I don't see nothing else I can do."

"You could tell her to come in earlier," she said, "Or not to go out at all."

"But, like you said, it's still up to her," he said.

"Well, but it seems like there ought to be something you could do."

"Nothing for me," he said. "I already done everything I could do. It's up to her now."

"But she's only just fifteen," she said.

"Yes," he said. "Nearly sixteen. But we can't do it for her. She's a big girl now."

They sat across from each other at the kitchen table. Both of them sitting very straight and looking into the center of the table. It was quiet in the kitchen. The coffeepot was sputtering on the stove. Then, across the ceiling, over their heads, they could hear a rat scurrying in the attic.

Mr. Sipple folded his arms and hugged himself, his eyes turned up toward the ceiling, listening to the rat. The bandage was off the stump of his finger, but it was still angry-looking, red and purple. Dr. Smoaks had said it was going to be all right. But for now the empty space between his fingers, splayed out against his upper arms, was very noticeable. He worked the fingers, feeling the absence of the missing one in the empty space there on his arm. A positive feeling of nothing where something ought to be. He sat straight in the chair, feeling the loss in the space between his fingers and listening to the rat scurrying in the attic.

Smoaks, Deering,
Maggie Poat, and the Shark

Threh Rainbow Fishing Camp is located one and two-tenths miles from Kallisaw Sound — that's as the crow flies. But you can't go that way, not without webbed feet you can't. It's straight across the marsh. Nothing but slick, blue-brown mud and marsh grass. Like wading through lard. Every step, you sink in up to your crotch. It won't suck you under like quicksand, but you can't do anything with it. You have to go out in a boat through Half Moon Creek, a tidal estuary that takes its time — over four miles — swinging in a wide, arcing turn through the brownish-green spears of the grass. At low tide the creek is just a trickle of water between mud banks, pocked with the holes of fiddler crabs. The banks look and smell like putrified black flesh.

There isn't much to the camp itself. Just one clapboard building with a shed over the front. Coca-Cola signs nailed all over it, a couple of NuGrape Soda ones — they sell more Dr. Pepper than anything else in the soft-drink line, but there isn't a single Dr. Pepper sign on the place — and some Roosevelt posters left over from the campaign of year before last. McAfee County always goes Democrat, but in nineteen-thirty-two everybody voted.

The Rainbow Fishing Camp is owned and operated — half-heartedly — by Mansfield Whitmire. No entrepreneur. A small, peppery man, with gray hair, a stubble of beard, gray too, and a face that looks like it was stuffed in a cheesecloth bag and baked in a brick kiln. The business end of the enterprise consists of a rickety dock that spans the marsh on the rim of the creek and juts out into the stream itself for perhaps twenty feet. A treacherous causeway of weathered, gray wood, most of it rotten looking, with a floating dock bobbing at the end. There is a walkway down to the floating dock — a ramp with rollers on the bottom end, and hinges on the upper, narrow cleats nailed across for steps. But at low tide it hangs almost straight up and down, and is impossible to use. It is easier to jump. Around the floating dock are tied six flat-bottomed bateaux, all painted dark green, with the paint flecking off, and white numbers on the bows where the names ought to be.

At the end of the bluff, where it drops down into the marsh and the dock begins, there is a sixty-gallon drum with a hose draped into it for fishermen to flush out their outboard motors when they come in. Inside the wooden building with the Coca-Cola and NuGrape signs is a room that takes up most of the space of the building. There are two long trestle tables with benches on either side, and along one wall is a counter, about half of it taken up by glass display cases containing hooks and lines and various patented gadgets guaranteed to help catch fish. Mansfield doesn't try to sell them, so over the years the cases have taken on the forlorn and neglected appearance of a display of artifacts in a museum of natural history.

Mansfield isn't married. It would have cramped his style. Occasionally he will have in a woman for a while to cook for him and keep him company — generally in cold weather, when the camp isn't doing much business anyway. Sometimes she will stay on for a month or two. "Trying her out," Mansfield says. But it never works. Always there is a fight over something trivial, and the girl — they are mostly women now — will be off for the parts unknown from which she came, or toward which she was heading when Mansfield waylaid her. When this happens, Mansfield will begin to show up at Maggie Poat's roadhouse again on Friday and Saturday nights. For two years now he hasn't had anyone in there with him at the fish camp at all. The Depression has slowed everything down.

Number-four bateau nosed in toward the floating dock. Standing in the bow, ready to fend her off when she bumped the edge of the dock, was a tall, William S. Hart-ish man. Six feet two or three, with a healthy-weary leanness. Slightly round shouldered, in profile he was reminiscent of the Indian in *The End of the Trail*. He wore a gray felt hat with the brim flopped down all around.

The man at the oars backed water carefully, trying to bring the boat up to the dock gently. So gently that the tall man in the bow wouldn't be able to feel the moment of impact. Not the slightest jolt.

When the bow touched, the tall man flinched slightly, rocking down on his leg braced in the bow. He stepped onto the dock with the line and dropped it over a bollard. The second man shipped the dockside oar, then pulled on the other, moving the boat ahead against the line secured to the bollard, and bringing it in alongside the dock. The tall man stooped down and put his hand on the gunwale, drawing it up against the fender. While he held the boat, the second man shipped the outboard oar, then stood up. He had the body of an overblown two-year-old. Chubby and rotund and spraddle legged. But a big man too. Just over six feet. He looked a lot like Wallace Beery, with a fleshy, lopsided face. On his head was a battered white yachting cap.

"You hold the boat," he said. "I'll get them out."

"Don't show off, Case," said the tall man. "I'll give you a hand."

"Just hold the boat, Smoaks," he said. "I can get them out."

He stooped over, reaching down into the bottom of the bateau, then stood up with a galvanized washtub in his arms. It was half full of water, which sloshed around, making it hard to balance. Staggering a little, he stepped out of the boat, took three choppy, waddling steps, then put the washtub down carefully on the dock. The shrimp made zinging sounds against the sides of the tub.

"Get the net," he said.

Smoaks reached into the boat and took out the shrimp net. It had been carefully folded, the line wrapped around it neatly and tied. When he dropped it, the sinkers on the skirt made a loud thump on the dock.

"Think they'll be enough?" said Deering.

Smoaks looked at the tub. "The three of us couldn't eat all those shrimp in a week," he said.

"I hate to run short," said Deering.

They heard an outboard motor in the creek.

"Mansfield," said Smoaks.

"Yes," said Deering. "He ain't never going to tune that Johnson."

They looked up toward the sweeping curve in the creek where the Sound was. Mansfield came around the curve, crouched in the stern of number six. The bow of the bateau canted high out of the water, so it came plowing along on its transom, rolling the water up in front, until Mansfield seemed to be pushing the whole creek ahead of him as he came in. He half-stood in the rear of the boat when he saw them, not letting go of the steering arm of the motor, and began waving. They could see his mouth working too, but the sound of the motor blotted out whatever it was he was saying.

"Worked up as hell about something," said Deering.

They made fast the stern line of number four to another piling off to the side of the floating dock, then stood looking at him as he came up. He cut the motor and coasted in to the side of the dock.

"Big bastard," he said, standing up, and then sitting down again before the bateau bumped the piling.

"What?" said Deering.

"Big bastard," said Mansfield. "Biggest one I ever seen."

"Biggest what?" said Smoaks.

"Shark," said Mansfield. He stood up again and grabbed the dock, beginning to walk the boat around to the cleat on the end.

"Give me the line," said Smoaks.

"What?" said Mansfield.

"Give me the line and I'll bring you around," said Smoaks.

Mansfield gave him the line and stood up while they led it around to the front of the dock. Smoaks began to make it fast to the cleat.

"Don't do that," said Mansfield.

Smoaks looked at him.

"What?" said Deering.

"Get in," said Mansfield. "We got to go get him out."

"We can't go now," said Deering. "We got to get the shrimp down to Maggie's."

"Shit on the shrimp," said Mansfield. "I tell you, this is a big bastard."

"Maggie's expecting us," said Smoaks.

"I can't get the bastard out by myself," said Mansfield.

Smoaks and Deering looked at each other.

"They'll be all right," said Smoaks. "We'll fill the tub with water."

"I hate to keep Maggie waiting," said Deering.

"You don't catch a big bastard like this every day," said Smoaks.

Smoaks took a bucket that Mansfield used for bailing the boats and scooped water into the tub. Deering stood on the dock watching him. When he finished filling the tub, they got into the boat, Smoaks first, then Deering. Before they could sit down, Mansfield gave the starting rope a pull. The Johnson didn't catch.

"Shit," said Mansfield, "wouldn't you know?"

He wound the rope around the starter again and gave it a second pull. It caught with a roar, nearly dumping Mansfield out of the boat. He never would sit down to start a motor.

Getting out of the creek was slower than coming in — the tide was on the flood. With Smoaks and Deering in the bow, the bateau plowed into the water, washing waves up onto the banks as they passed, making the marsh grass whip and sway. They had to work out against the tide. A curve to the left, then a long, widening curve to the right, and around the last bank of marsh grass they saw the open gray-green expanse of Kallisaw Sound. Mansfield turned to the right, heading for the public landing. He put his shark line out there, anchoring it to a piling that he had driven into the sand.

Smoaks and Deering could see the line stretched out from the shore. It wasn't moving much — just stretched out taut. They tried to follow it out into the water, but lost it against the movement of the waves. So they looked for the gallon jug that was the standard float for a shark line. While they were looking, they saw it bob to the surface with a blue-green wink. The line dropped into the water for a moment, then sprang taut again as the jug went under.

"Big bastard," said Mansfield.

He ran the boat up onto the shells at the public landing, and they got out. The line was three-quarter-inch manila. Bigger than it needed to be, but Mansfield didn't want to take any chances of losing one when he did get him on the hook. The jug would bob to the surface every now and then and the line would go slack. The movement wasn't frantic, just strong and regular. He had been on the hook for several hours.

"Help me," said Mansfield, going over to the line and taking it in his hands. The two men went over and took hold.

"When I count three," said Mansfield. He wasn't looking at them. He was looking at the piling in the sand behind them.

"One . . . two . . . three. . . ." On the "three" they all put their backs into it and started off up the beach. They made three steps before the line went taut again and stopped them. They could feel the size of the thing on the other end.

Smoaks and Deering looked at each other. "Jesus," said Deering. "It *is* a big bastard."

Mansfield grunted behind them. "I told you," he said. "I told you it was a big one."

For a minute they stood there, all three of them, straining as the big fish stood them off. Then they began to gain on him slightly. The feet that had been poised in the air went down onto the ground, and they made two more steps before it stopped them again.

"How big?" said Deering. They were all straining on the line.

"What?" said Mansfield. He was leaning back on the line, his face going red, while he looked toward the piling in the sand where the end was tied.

"How big?" said Deering.

"You feel him," said Mansfield. "That's how big. Big bastard."

"You ain't seen him?" said Deering.

"I *felt* him," said Mansfield.

They made four more steps.

"What the shit is he doing?" said Mansfield. "He ain't really fighting us none. Just ain't moving."

"You sure it's a shark?" said Smoaks.

"He ain't even seen it," said Deering.

Mansfield looked away from the piling at them. "What the shit else would it be?" he said.

"A big ray will sound like that. Lay himself down on the bottom, and there ain't no way to get him loose," said Deering.

"I hadn't thought about no ray," said Mansfield. "He's moving around too much for that. A ray sucks himself down on the bottom."

"A shark ought to move around more," said Deering.

"I think it's a shark," said Mansfield.

"Well," said Smoaks, "let's get it out. You don't ever know for sure till you get it out so you can look at it."

"Anyway, it's a big bastard," said Mansfield. "Something that big, I'd want him out of the water just the same. Whatever it is."

"Yes," said Smoaks. "You're right about that."

They took two more steps; then the line went taut again, and they lost two.

"Hold it good," said Mansfield. He let them brace themselves; then he dropped the line and ran to the piling, where he took up the slack and put a clove hitch around the piling to hold it. Then he went back and helped them walk six more steps of slack into the line.

"Hold it good," he said.

"How much line you got?" said Smoaks, his face red, leaning back against the pull on the line.

"Thousand feet," said Mansfield.

"Jesus," said Deering. "It ain't going to take but all summer."

"Why don't you go get your car?" said Smoaks. "We'll tie it to the bumper, and you can just drive off and haul him out that way."

"Pull my bumper off, you mean," said Deering.

"You said it was going to take all summer to do it this way," said Smoaks. "You're right."

"What time is it?" said Deering.

Smoaks pulled out his pocket watch. "Five-thirteen," he said.

"Maggie's going to think we died," said Deering.

"Maybe you'll see somebody back at the camp," said Smoaks. "Get them to tell her we'll be late."

"Shit," said Deering.

They left Smoaks to watch the line while they went back to the fishing camp in the boat to get the car.

After they had gone, Smoaks sat down on the beach beside the taut line. The gallon jug would dip under from time to time, catching glints from the sun going down behind him, and winking its blue-green eye at him. Between the dark line of trees on Kallisaw Island and the beach where he sat, the gray-green water of the Sound moved in a gentle, restless chop. It was a hot day, and working on the line had drenched him with sweat, but he didn't even think about going into the water to cool off. No one in McAfee County went swimming in the open sea. Not that Smoaks was a spooky man. Not at all. He was steady and solid. But he had seen the things that got dragged out of the water on the ends of fishing lines. No one who had seen would want to get down into the water with them.

He sat motionless, watching the jug at the end of the line and trying to form an air-lighted image of what was going on in the depths of the gray-green water. Trying to see the great, silent shape moving there in the darkness under the water. Pulsing like the heart of the Sound itself on the end of the line.

He gave it up. It wasn't dark, but it was getting dark. The trees on Kallisaw Island were turning black.

He thought of the other lines like this one, scattered up and down the coast. Catching them at the back of his eye and seeing them wave slowly in the gray-green darkness of the seabed. Each baited with the pale body of a chicken, or a great chunk of rotten meat. Inside the bait, the hook, buried like a hard, inverted question mark. Many of them forged by hand and big as a man's arm from elbow to wrist.

Every one of the brutes fished out of the water was one less to worry about — one to the good. He and Deering had had a moral duty to help Mansfield get his out, a duty that increased in direct proportion to the size of the beast. They had known that at the beginning. The other had just been talk.

But there was no end to it, this fishing for monsters. No matter how many they caught, they could be sure that another — maybe even bigger, maybe a thing more unspeakably obscene — would be waiting for them under the green water. Perhaps next time it would rise to the bait and be pulsing there on the end of the line when they came back — in a day, or a week, or a month — to pull it out.

Smoaks lit a cigarette and hugged his knees. The sweat drying out of his shirt made him cold.

It was over an hour before he heard the sound of the Ford's engine coming down the oyster-shell road toward the landing. Twenty-eight minutes after six. At ten minutes to seven Mansfield arrived in the bateau, keeping in as close to shore as possible, staying away from the jug, where it winked in the water. The sun was getting low behind the marsh to the west, but there were two hours of light left before dark.

Mansfield made Deering back the car up to the piling; then he took the loose end of the line and looped it over the bumper.

"No, you don't," said Deering. "He'll pull the bumper off." He cut the engine and got out of the car. "Give it to me," he said. He took the end of the line and passed it through the rear windows of the Ford, making a harness. "He ain't going to pull off the whole top of the car," he said. "He ain't that big of a bastard."

"Okay," said Mansfield. "Now you-all get a good hold on it while I let off the end from the piling here. Then we'll just walk out the slack until the Ford is taking the whole load."

Deering and Smoaks took up their positions, digging their heels in and hauling back so the end of the line between them and the piling fell slack. Mansfield lifted the clove hitch off the piling in two deft movements, then ran up and took his place in front of them on the taut part of the line.

"Now," he said, "we'll walk out the slack easy and let him pull on the Ford for a while."

Deering kept looking back at his car as they walked it out. It rocked when it took the whole strain, but it didn't move.

They had to get out into the water a little way before the line was taut again.

"I don't like it," said Mansfield.

Deering went and got in the Ford. He started it, put it in gear, and began to roll up the oyster-shell road.

"Hold it," said Mansfield. "Let me look at the line. I don't want to break it and lose the son-of-a-bitch."

He satisfied himself that it was going to hold. "Pull away," he said.

"It ain't scraping the paint, is it?" said Deering.

"No," said Mansfield.

Deering eased the Ford off in first, bringing the line with him.

It came out of the water hissing, squeezing the water off in a mist as the shark surged on the end. The Ford rolled off slowly down the road.

"There he is!" said Mansfield. He and Smoaks both saw the big fin as the fish rolled, coming into the shallower water. "I told you it was a shark," he said.

"He's a big bastard," said Smoaks, speaking low, looking at the great fish pulsing at the other end of the line.

"Help me guide the line," said Mansfield. "He's going to tear himself open on the shell rake out there. Stop the car!" he yelled to Deering. Deering had the door open, watching as the line came in. He stopped the car and put on the brake.

"He's a big bastard," he said, looking at the water, where they could see the fish rolling.

"We'd better bring him in the rest of the way ourselves," said Mansfield. "He's going to cut himself to pieces on the shell rake out there."

In shallow water now the big fish had lost most of his fight. But he was so big that as he came out of the water he got harder and harder to move.

"You got a gun in your car?" said Mansfield.

"Pistol," said Deering.

"Get it," said Mansfield. "We got to get too close to him. I want him dead before we drag him out."

Deering walked back to the car and got the pistol.

"Want me to do it?" he said as he gave the pistol to Mansfield.

"He's my fish," said Mansfield.

"I know that," said Deering. "Do you want me to shoot him?"

"I'll shoot him," said Mansfield.

He took the pistol and went to his boat, shoving it off the sand and into the water. "Hold the line," he said, "and keep him headed away from me if he tries to go for the boat."

"He's worn out," said Smoaks.

"He's a big bastard anyway," said Mansfield. "Don't fuck around, now."

The boat was drifting, and Mansfield took an oar and paddled out to the shark. The boat bumped him, and he thrashed his tail, rolling over and splashing water into the boat.

"Sit down," said Smoaks. "You want him to knock you out of the boat?"

Mansfield sat down. He pointed the pistol, holding it with both hands, and fired all six bullets into the head of the shark. There was a thrashing and rolling; then the water was still. The gray-green turning red.

"Okay," said Mansfield. "Pull him in."

"What?" said Smoaks.

"Pull him on in," said Mansfield.

"You going to leave him here?" said Smoaks.

"I want to *see* him," said Mansfield. "Then we can take him back to the camp."

"We got to get him out twice?" said Smoaks. "How much you think he weighs?"

"He's a big bastard," said Mansfield. "You felt him on the line. How much you think?"

"Once is enough," said Smoaks. "You can see him when we get back to the camp. We can all see him."

Mansfield looked at him for a minute.

"Bring the boat on in," said Smoaks.

Mansfield paddled the boat back to the landing. Smoaks got in and pushed it off, coasting out toward the shark.

"What you better do is tie him on behind the bateau and tow him back to the camp," he said.

"Um . . . ," said Mansfield, looking at the shark. "Ain't there no other way?"

"No other way I can think of tonight," said Smoaks.

Mansfield looked up at the sky, then back at the shark in the water. "It's coming on dark," he said.

"Yes," said Smoaks. "Won't be anything left of him by tomorrow if you don't get him out of the water."

Mansfield stood in the boat looking at the hulk of the shark. "I don't want to be towing that thing in the water in the dark," he said. "No telling what might come after it."

"I'll be riding with you," said Smoaks.

"Can't think of no other way?" said Mansfield.

"He's dead, Mansfield," said Smoaks.

"I know he's dead," said Mansfield. "I just don't like it with it coming on dark and all."

"I'll be with you," said Smoaks. "He's not going to get us."

Smoaks took the hook out of the side of the shark's jaw and put it back in the center, so he would tow more easily. Mansfield made the chain leader fast to the stern of the boat.

"Not too short," said Smoaks. "Give him the whole chain. He'll tow easier."

"We'll see you back at the camp, Case," he said to Deering.

"What if you don't make it back?" said Deering.

"That's the kind of talk we need," said Smoaks. "You want to get to Maggie's tonight?"

"See you back at the camp," said Deering. He got into the Ford, started it up, and drove off down the oyster-shell road.

"Come on," said Smoaks.

Mansfield pulled the starter rope. The Johnson kicked off on the first pull.

"It's an omen," said Smoaks.

"Sit down," Smoaks said.

Mansfield kept standing up to look at the shark in the water behind the bateau. The hook in his lower jaw pulled his head up, holding his snout out of the water. A little wave rolled up and went streaming off out of the corners of his mouth. The tail waved slowly from side to side in the wake of the boat. It looked like he was reaching up out of the water toward the boat.

"He looks like he's trying to bite the boat," said Mansfield.

"What?" said Smoaks. He couldn't hear over the sound of the motor. "Sit down before you fall out."

Mansfield looked at him, then twisted the arm of the motor, cutting it off. The bow of the bateau dropped into the water, and it rapidly lost way. The shark nosed ahead, gliding toward the boat, bumping into it, its head slowly sliding under the water as the strain on the leader went off. The boat lurched when it hit, and Mansfield lost his balance, almost toppling over the stern on top of it. He caught himself on the motor, burning his hand.

"God damn," he said, jerking his hand away.

"It's dead, Mansfield," said Smoaks.

"It looks like he's chasing us," he said.

"*You* shot him," said Smoaks.

Mansfield stood looking over the stern at the hulk of the shark in the water. He held his left hand to his mouth with his right hand, licking it to stop the burning.

"All right," said Smoaks. "I'll show you." He moved to the stern. "Sit down," he said. "Sit down, and I'll show you."

He put his hand on Mansfield's shoulder, pressing gently. Mansfield sank onto the seat, still sucking on his hand. Smoaks sat down on the seat opposite him, looking at him.

"Now, watch," Smoaks said.

He pulled on the chain of the leader until the shark's snout came out of the water. Streams of water rushed out of the corners of its mouth. Smoaks snubbed the chain over the stern with his left hand, then thrust his right hand into the shark's mouth, pushing it all the way to the elbow. He had to lean out over the stern, so his forehead was resting on the tip of the snout.

Mansfield watched him, his eyes going big.

"See?" said Smoaks. "He's dead. He's a big bastard, but he's dead, Mansfield."

"I know he's dead," said Mansfield, his voice loud and whiny. He took his hand out of his mouth. "I shot him, God damn it."

"Well?" said Smoaks.

"He just looks like he's going to take a bite out of the boat when we're pulling him."

Smoaks took his arm out of the shark's mouth and let go the leader. "Get up in the front," he said.

Mansfield put his hand back to his mouth, then stood up and moved to the bow.

"Sit down," said Smoaks.

Mansfield stood looking over the stern of the boat. "I wish it wasn't coming on dark," he said. "I can't make out none of the trees on the shore."

"Sit down where you can't see it," said Smoaks. "I'll take it in the rest of the way."

Deering was waiting for them on the floating dock when they got back to the Rainbow Camp. They rigged a block and tackle to a davit that Mansfield used to haul his boats out of the water to clean and paint them. Putting the hook of the tackle through the eye of the shark hook, the three of them got on the fall of the tackle and hoisted the shark out of the water.

It was the first time they had seen all of it. It was enormous. Gray-white and sleek — not like the brown, wide-headed sand sharks they usually caught. From nose to tail, it must have measured nearly twelve feet. Because of the block and tackle, they couldn't tell how much it weighed. Half a ton perhaps.

"Look at them teeth," said Mansfield. "Nothing but teeth. He's got a hundred of them."

Deering looked up at the great crescent mouth, standing on the belly side of the fish — not too close. "Makes you cold just to look at it, don't it?" he said.

"He's a big bastard, all right," said Smoaks. "Biggest one I ever saw."

It was getting very dark now. Seventeen minutes after eight. The sun was down, the marsh going black.

"Look," said Mansfield. Hanging from the davit, the shark was eviscerating through his anus. On the dock was a pile of slippery-looking intestines, like a mound of wet, purple macaroni.

"No bones," said Smoaks. "Turn him up like that, and everything just drops out where it can."

"He's shitting his guts out," said Mansfield.

"In a manner of speaking," said Smoaks. "Hang him the other way, and they'd come out through his mouth."

"Ain't he a big bastard, though?" said Mansfield.

"We get us a piece of him tomorrow," said Deering. "Don't forget to tell everybody we helped."

"What you want?" said Mansfield.

"I want me some teeth," said Deering.

"You name it. You got it," said Mansfield. "What you want, Smoaks?"

"I'll think it over," said Smoaks. "I'll think it over and let you know in the morning."

They gathered up their washtub and the shrimp net, emptied most of the water out of the tub, then carried the shrimp out and put them in the back seat of the Ford.

"Don't let him get away from you," said Deering. "I want a picture of me with him in the morning."

Mansfield wasn't listening to him.

"How's your hand?" said Smoaks.

"What?" said Mansfield.

"Let me see your hand."

Mansfield held it out, and Smoaks looked at it. "Not too bad," he said. "Put some butter on it. You'll have a blister there in the morning."

They got into the Ford and drove off. Mansfield stood on the edge of the bluff, by the sixty-gallon drum, looking down at the dock, where the enormous fish hung pale silver in the moonlight.

Maggie Poat's roadhouse — that was all anyone in McAfee County ever called it; no one from outside McAfee County ever had any occasion to refer to it at all — was a wooden building set back off U.S. 17 in the live oaks. It had been there for fifteen years or so. No one recalled just exactly when it had been built. Sometime after World War I. Nineteen-eighteen or -nineteen. Its original purpose wasn't very clear, because there had been no U.S. 17 at the time. Just a dirt road that wandered around in the pines and oaks, starting at Midway and eventually ending up at Darien. The building was a monument to some forgotten and misguided entrepreneur — an unsuccessful visionary — who had tried to set up a business in this unlikely spot. Whatever the building had been intended for originally, it was not a dwelling. The rooms were too big for that, and it had no screened porch in front. Probably it had been a store — with the big room for merchandise in front, and rooms at the back where the family lived. Only a family man would have been desperate enough to plan and pursue his fortune in such an out-of-the-way spot. It had to be a project born of desperation.

Subsequently, it had served for a store — so its appearance might have been due to alterations made by Bancroft Davis. He had moved into it sometime around nineteen-twenty-four or -five. Then he had moved out after the stock-market crash of nineteen-twenty-nine. Not that the crash had anything to do with the move, really. People in McAfee County kept hearing about how terrible it was over the two or three radios that served the county in those days. It made some of them nervous to think that something terrible was going on, but actual repercussions were very dim there. It certainly didn't affect Bancroft's business, which had never amounted to much anyway. But Bancroft had a feeling for dramatic moments, and he was fed up with the business, which was really no business at all. So when the crash came along, he took it as an opportunity to go ahead and unload — the way he had been planning to do.

Maggie Poat bought it off him for two hundred dollars cash and a Model T Ford. She had been operating around the county for four or five years — she must have been about twenty-one or -two at the time — and had just gotten tired of moving so much. It looked like an ideal setup to her. The big room for entertainment, and the little rooms in the back where she could take the customers. She kept the kitchen the same size, but partitioned the other rooms, so she had four small ones. On weekends she would have in two or three girls to help her out with the customers. During the week she worked the whole thing by herself, with only one Negro girl to do the cooking and housework.

Maggie took over the business at a bad time, considering. But President Roosevelt helped her along in nineteen-thirty-three by setting up a CCC Camp down in the woods near Fancy Station — about three miles away. Once the word about her place got out, she drew the payroll for the whole camp every Saturday night. Incidental customers would wander in from time to time, whenever luck went their way and they got their hands onto some money. Business became so brisk that she would have a little band come in on Saturday nights to liven things up.

The Dorchester Swamp Stompers was a three-piece outfit — drums, accordion, and banjo — played by Gordon and Folger Gramling and Hewlitt Gay. Folger actually carried the melody on his accordion, but Hewlitt had gotten the group together, and he insisted on fronting it. He was the one with the artistic temperament — high strung and nervous, with a permanent note of insistence in his cackling voice. Gordon and Folger didn't much care. The brothers were phlegmatic to the point of imbecility, and as long as they made a little money on Saturday nights, and got to perform to an appreciative audience, they didn't notice that Hewlitt was having his way. His banjo had a palm-tree beach scene painted on the head in black; and red, yellow, and green light bulbs inside that would blink off and on while he played. "Red Sails in the Sunset" was his showpiece. He would wrap himself around his instrument, playing with his left hand way up on the frets near the head, and his right whipping up and down in a blur, drawing out the chords *legato e molto espressivo*. Sometimes he would get himself so worked up there would be tears in his eyes when he finished.

Smoaks and Deering stayed away on weekends, but they put in a good deal of time around the place from Monday to Thursday — especially Thursday, which was usually quiet, since payday was Saturday, and everyone would be broke by that late in the week. They didn't either one of them have much money to spend — doctors were paid with goodwill and produce in McAfee County, and farming had gone to hell everywhere — but they were good company. And they were always bringing her little presents of one kind or another — fresh vegetables out of Case's garden, or some shrimp or crabs they had caught. Every now and then a bottle of perfume from Smoaks, who did get a cash fee from a patient once in a while. They would take her out to ride in their cars. And she liked tooling around on the dirt roads, scaring the niggers and raising hell.

They had all known each other for a long time. Since they were children. And had gone through school together.

Smoaks and Deering pulled around into the back yard and parked the Ford under one of the big oaks. They still had their fishing clothes on. Maggie was sitting on the kitchen steps, waiting for them when they got there, and the pot was already going, with a fire under it, out in the middle of the yard. Two Negro children, boys, eight or nine, stood near the pot.

"Thought you wasn't coming," she said from the steps, not getting up.

"Mansfield caught a shark," Deering said, getting out of the Ford.

"What?" she said.

"Mansfield Whitmire caught him a shark on his line. We had to help him bring it in," Deering said.

"Mansfield's crazy," she said.

"It's a big one," said Deering. "Biggest bastard of a shark I ever seen."

"How big?" said Maggie.

"Fifty feet?" said Smoaks, talking to Deering. "You reckon it was more than that?"

"What you mean?" said Deering. "Sixty at least. I seen shrimp boats wasn't that big."

"At least sixty," said Smoaks, talking to Maggie.

"You boys got the beer, I see," she said.

"I swear," said Deering. "Ain't that right, Smoaks?"

"He's not lying to you, Maggie," said Smoaks. "Biggest bastard I ever saw."

"Did you get the shrimp, too?" she said.

"Let's get it out, Smoaks," said Deering. Together they got the washtub and brought it over to the fire. They poured off the water onto the ground, then started scooping up handfuls of shrimp and throwing them into the pot. The two Negro boys helped them.

"What's Mansfield going to do with it?" said Maggie.

"Maybe he ain't going to do nothing with it," said Deering. "He's scared of it. He was only looking at it when we left him."

"It's dead, ain't it?" said Maggie.

"Hanging up on his dock," said Smoaks. "But that don't matter to Mansfield."

"I bet he locks his doors tonight when he goes to bed," said Deering.

"Really, now," said Maggie, "how big?"

Deering and Smoaks looked at each other. "We'll go over and look at it after we eat the shrimp," said Smoaks.

"I always wanted a sharktooth necklace," she said.

"Why didn't you tell us about that before?" said Deering. "Smoaks and me would have gone out there to Kallisaw Sound and got you one with our bare hands."

"I never thought to bring it up before," she said. "First time."

"How about a whole jawboneful?" said Smoaks. "You could wear it on your head for a hat, or a crown maybe."

"Well, but what I always wanted was a necklace," said Maggie. "I never thought about a whole jawbone."

"Smoaks and me helped Mansfield get him in. We got a claim on him for anything like that, I reckon."

"Besides," said Smoaks, "he won't go near the thing by himself anyway. We'll just go down there after we finish eating and get you whatever pieces you want off him."

Smoaks went and got the beer out of the car. "It's not cold," he said. "We stopped for the ice on the way from Mansfield's."

"Long as it's not hot," said Maggie.

Smoaks opened the bottles with an opener he had on his key chain. They all three sat down on the steps to drink their beer and wait for the shrimp to get done. Maggie sat on the top step. Deering and Smoaks sat on the bottom one, where they could see up her dress.

They talked of various things. The weather: Hot and dry. Roosevelt: He was the first President the three of them had actually voted for, and they felt a personal interest and responsibility for what he did. So far they were satisfied with him.

They also talked about the upcoming Baer-Carnera fight.

"The wop's just so goddamn big," said Deering. "How you going to knock out a man as big as that?"

"Size isn't that important," said Smoaks. "Look at Dempsey. Carnera's too big to handle himself right. Baer is going to kill him."

When the shrimp were ready, they scooped them out of the pot with a dipper, putting them on newspapers, then shelling them by hand and dipping them in the sauce made with Worcestershire and catsup. Smoaks opened more beer.

"Mansfield sure as shit was scared," said Deering, chuckling.

"How big was he, really?" said Maggie, holding the bottle in both hands and resting her elbows on her knees.

"Sixty feet," said Smoaks. "I told you."

"Okay," she said. "I was just asking."

"Big enough to scare the shit out of Mansfield," said Deering.

"He was a big bastard," said Smoaks, sipping his beer.

"Yeah," said Deering, laughing and slapping his leg. "Scared the shit out of Mansfield. He'll lock his doors tonight."

"Well, it *is* scary," said Smoaks. "I got to thinking about it sitting there on the beach while you and Mansfield went to get your car."

"Mansfield sure had the shit scared out of him," said Deering, slapping his leg again and taking a swig out of his bottle of beer.

"Okay," said Smoaks.

"You notice how he wouldn't get close to him when we got him back at the dock?" said Deering. "Poor old Mansfield. Scared of his shadder."

"Wasn't his shadow he was scared of," said Smoaks, not looking at Deering.

"Wouldn't no man take on like that over no dead shark," said Deering. "Not no *real* man wouldn't do it. Not over no live one neither, for that matter."

Smoaks didn't say anything. The light from the fire lit up the festoons of Spanish moss above the pot and around. They hung suspended, dropping out of the darkness into which the light from the fire did not penetrate — like stalactites in a grotto.

"Mansfield's crazy," said Maggie.

"Mansfield thinks funny," said Smoaks, "but he's not crazy."

"Scared the shit out of him," said Deering, taking another pull on the beer.

"Mansfield's been fishing the Sound for a long time," said Smoaks.

Deering looked at him. "What's that supposed to mean?" he said.

"Nothing," said Smoaks. "Just that he has."

"Okay?" said Deering.

"Nothing," said Smoaks. "Mansfield had the shit scared out of him."

"That's all I said," said Deering.

"Yes," said Smoaks.

"Well, God damn it, he did."

"I said he did," said Smoaks. "Just let it go."

"What are you getting at, Smoaks?" said Deering.

"Nothing," said Smoaks. He looked into the fire for a minute. "I was scared, too, God damn it," he said.

"What of?" said Deering. "It was dead."

"I know the shark was dead," said Smoaks. "It wasn't the shark so much I was scared of." He looked into the fire for a minute again. "He was a big bastard, though."

"Shit," said Deering. "You sound crazy as Mansfield."

"You ever been swimming out in the Sound?" said Smoaks. "I mean, right out in the middle?"

"What the shit has that got to do with it?" said Deering.

"Have you?" said Smoaks.

"No," said Deering, looking into the fire.

They sat for a while without saying anything. Deering looked at Maggie. "You think I'd be scared?" he said.

"What?" said Smoaks.

"You think I'd be scared to go out there in the Sound, don't you?" said Deering.

Smoaks didn't answer him for a minute. "I never really thought about it, Case," he said. I wasn't thinking about you. You *ought* to be scared."

"Shit if that's so," said Deering. "I wouldn't be scared worth a *God* damn."

"Okay," said Smoaks.

"No," said Deering. "You think I'd be scared, don't you?"

"I told you I wasn't thinking about you anyway," said Smoaks. "Why don't you just let it go?"

"Yes," said Maggie. "Let's talk about something else."

"No," said Deering. "No, I ain't going to just let it go." He stood up. "I ain't scared, Smoaks," he said. His assertion had the air of a challenge.

Smoaks looked up at him in the firelight. "Sit down, Case," he said. "Sit down and shut up."

"Don't say 'shut up' to me, Smoaks," said Deering. "I ain't scared."

"Just sit down," said Smoaks.

"For Christ's sake, yes," said Maggie. "Sit down, Case. We've heard about enough of it."

"Say it," said Deering.

"Say what?" said Smoaks.

"Say I ain't scared." Deering weaved a little from side to side as he stood there above them. The fire lit up his face from below, making black holes where his eyes should have been.

"Sit down," said Smoaks.

"Say it," said Deering.

Smoaks looked into the fire. "Okay," he said at last. "Okay. You ain't scared. Now, will you sit down?"

Deering looked at him. "You don't believe it, though," he said. "You don't really think I wouldn't be scared."

Smoaks didn't say anything.

"Come on," said Deering. He began walking away from the fire.

"What?" said Smoaks.

"Come on," said Deering.

"Where?" said Smoaks.

"So I can show you I ain't scared."

"Jesus, Case," said Maggie. "Won't you let it go?"

"No," said Smoaks. "No, he ain't going to do that." He stood up and started after Deering. "Come on," he said to Maggie. "You're through eating, ain't you? You can see the shark anyway."

"This is crazy," said Maggie.

"Yes," said Smoaks. "Yes, it is."

"I hate it when he gets his ass on his shoulders that way," she said.

Deering had the engine of the Ford running. "Come on," he said.

They got into the car and drove to the camp. Mansfield's house was dark, and no lights came on when they pulled up in front.

"He's got his doors locked," said Deering.

"Drive on down there closer to the dock," said Smoaks.

Deering pulled down where the path went out onto the causeway leading to the dock, cut off the engine, and pulled up the brake.

"Come on," said Deering, getting out of the car. "We got to get us a boat."

"Jesus," said Maggie.

"It's a nice night," said Smoaks. "Come on, Maggie. You and me can neck. Case likes to show how good he can row."

They walked down to the dock. The moon was bright, and they could see the great silvery hulk of the shark still hanging on the davit. The pile of intestines glistened in the moonlight.

"He's a big one, all right," said Maggie.

"Sixty feet," said Deering. "Just like we said."

They walked out onto the dock.

"Jesus," said Smoaks. "Look at that. Why'd he want to go and do that?"

A hatchet stuck out of the shark's head. They could see a number of great, bruised gashes where Mansfield had hacked at him. There must have been fifteen or twenty of them.

"What the hell got into him?" said Maggie.

"I told you it scared the shit out of him," said Deering. He stood beside the shark, looking up at its mouth and patting it with his hand.

"Must have stuck in the cartilage in his head, and he couldn't get it out," said Smoaks.

"Maybe he got scared and just ran away," said Deering.

"Maybe," said Smoaks.

"I ain't scared," said Deering. He slapped the great fish with his open hand. A sharp, solid sound. The fish didn't move. "Come on," he said, and walked out onto the floating dock. When they didn't follow him, he made a big follow-me motion with his whole arm. "Come on," he said, "follow me."

"We got to do this, Smoaks?" said Maggie.

"It's a nice night," said Smoaks. "Not too much of a moon, but it's a nice night."

They walked down onto the floating dock.

"Help me get it loose," Deering said, working on the line to number-four bateau.

Smoaks helped him get the bowline off; then they all got into the boat, and Deering took the oars and started to turn the bow out into the stream.

"Let me cast off the other line," said Smoaks.

Deering rowed them out of the creek and into the Sound. He headed for the public landing, keeping well out from the shore. When they got to the public landing, he turned the bow into the Sound and rowed it straight out for two or three hundred yards.

"Is this it?" he said.

"Is this what?" said Smoaks.

"Where the jug was," said Deering. "Mansfield's line?"

Smoaks looked back toward the shore, then around the Sound, getting his bearings.

"Okay," said Deering. He shipped the oars, then stood up and stumbled into the bow. He fumbled around for a minute before he got the flywheel that served for an anchor; then he swung it over the side, slinging it into the water.

He watched the line as it paid out. "Won't reach bottom," he said, looking at the line hanging off the bow. "Okay," he said, turning to Smoaks, who was sitting in the stern with Maggie. "This is about the right place."

"Okay," said Smoaks, looking around. "Looks like about the place to me."

"I'm ready if you are," said Deering.

"Me ready?" said Smoaks. "Ready for what?"

"We'll see who the yellowbelly is," said Deering.

"I ain't in no contest with you," said Smoaks. "This was all your own idea. You just go right ahead."

"Ain't you man enough for it?" said Deering.

Smoaks didn't say anything.

"Calling me yellow, when you ain't man enough for it your own self," he said.

"Nobody called you yellow, Case," said Smoaks. "This whole thing is your own idea. The Sound scares the shit out of me in the *daytime*."

"Are you coming or not?" said Deering.

Smoaks sat looking at him for a long time. "He's crazy as hell, Maggie," he said. "We never should have let him have the beer."

"Come on, Case," she said. "I'm getting cold out here."

"It's me and you, Smoaks," said Deering. "You got the guts for it?"

"Maggie's cold," said Smoaks. "Do it. Or let's go on back and finish the beer."

"It takes a yellowbelly to call a yellowbelly," said Deering.

"That's not quite the way you ought to put it," said Smoaks.

"You're a yellowbelly, Smoaks," said Deering. "Don't tell me. I may be going to have to beat your ass too, after we get back."

"Yellowbelly . . . ," said Smoaks. He stood up in the stern, rocking the boat. "That's the kind of a mind he's got," he said, speaking to Maggie. "I'm not ever going to hear the end of it if I don't. You know?"

"It's crazy as hell," said Maggie. "Let's go on back in. I'm getting cold."

Smoaks patted his stomach with both hands, looking up at the sky. "It's a nice night," he said. "I'd lots rather neck."

"Yellowbelly," said Deering. With both of them standing up, the boat had begun to rock, so it was difficult to keep their feet.

"You see?" said Smoaks. "He's going to remember this tomorrow. He wouldn't never let me forget about it. It wouldn't be a joke after a while. I'm just not up to hearing him run his mouth for the rest of my life."

"We'll see who the yellowbelly is," said Deering. He began to take off his clothes. "We'll both of us go in the water" — the boat rocked and he nearly fell out — "we'll swim out from the boat a ways. Last one has to get back in the boat wins."

"You know . . . this whole thing is crazy as hell," said Smoaks. "Let's go on back and finish the shrimp and beer. The Sound scares the hell out of me in the *daytime*." He looked around him at the black water. The boat rose and fell gently in the swell.

Deering didn't say anything. He swayed, pulling off his undershirt, and almost fell out of the boat.

"Turn your back, Maggie," said Smoaks.

"Jesus Christ," said Maggie. "After all these years."

The men stripped off their clothes, then jumped into the water.

"Kind of warm once you're in," said Smoaks, swimming away from the boat.

"Can I look now?" said Maggie.

"I saw you peeking," said Smoaks.

"This far enough, Case?" he said. They could see the boat, but they couldn't see each other.

"I can't see you, yellowbelly," said Deering.

"You let us know, Maggie," said Smoaks.

"Out a little further, Case," she said.

"This okay?" said Case.

"Little further," said Maggie.

The water was dark and warm. When he moved, Case could see his limbs outlined in phosphorus. Now and then a small fish would dart by, making a phosphor trail in the water — coming up to him, then darting off. The water was very warm.

"Wonder what the little fish are?" said Smoaks, yelling so Case could hear him.

"Don't say nothing," said Deering. "That's part of it."

The gentle swell lifted them from time to time — a rhythmic, pulsing movement. The moonlight made the boat, with Maggie in it, look bigger than it was. But it also made it look farther away.

"This is what I call a hell of a way to spend an evening," said Maggie from the boat.

"No talking," said Smoaks. "We got to concentrate on all those sharks that're swimming around here trying to get us."

Deering didn't say anything. He was treading water, watching the phosphor trails that his legs made in the water beneath him. He didn't like that sparkly light. Moving his arms in paddling motions, he saw them outlined in the silver bubbles too. Now and then more small fish would dart up to him for a moment, hover, then dart away. He moved his hands to fend them off. Looking down into the water, he could see other trails of phosphorus moving below him. Whether they were little fish just beneath his legs, or big ones farther down, he couldn't make out for sure. He didn't want to watch them, but he couldn't make himself look away. He began to remember the shark's crescent mouth.

Case had the skin of a farmer. Red face and V at the neck. Red arms to the elbows. Everything else was dead white. His legs pumping the water below him had the waxy paleness of a plucked chicken — pieces of dead meat.

A shrimp nipped his back, and he thrashed in the water.

"Don't splash," said Smoaks, his voice floating in over the crest of a swell; "that's what gets them interested."

Deering didn't answer him. He moved his arms and legs more slowly.

Another shrimp nipped him on the back, and he jumped — trying not to splash. He watched his white feet moving, trying to look behind them, still seeing the row on row of triangular teeth, stuffed in the white gums.

He looked up into the sky, pale violet, lit by the moon. But then he looked back down into the water again. He couldn't help himself.

He felt his stomach muscles contract. His breathing began to be labored. The water was warm, but it sapped him, drawing the heat out of his body. He felt a chill coming on, hitting him in the stomach in waves. His teeth began to chatter, and his stomach muscles contracted, making him pull his head down into the water. He threw his head back, doubling up his legs, trying to float that way, keeping his nose and mouth out of the water. The spasms of the chill kept hitting him, faster and faster, drawing him into a ball to hold in the heat. His head kept going under water. When it did, he would see the mouth. A hard, white crescent. Open eyes, big as silver dollars, staring into him with a cruel, glazed idiocy. The shape of the fin and the tail waving slowly in the water.

And behind all of these, there was another shape. Which was not the shark, but something else. Moving in a gray-green light, with no real shape at all.

"What's the matter, Case?" Maggie was standing in the boat.

"Something wrong?" said Smoaks.

"Something's the matter with Case. He's rolling around in the water."

"Row the boat over and see if he's all right," said Smoaks.

"I can't row the boat," she said.

"Where is he?"

"Over there," she said, pointing.

Smoaks began swimming in that direction, climbing the black swells.

"That way," she said.

He looked where she was pointing, then corrected his direction. He heard him, and swam to the sound.

"You all right, Case?" he said.

"Chchchchiilll . . . ," said Case. His teeth were chattering, so he could hardly talk at all.

"We got to get you back in the boat," said Smoaks. "You'll have a cramp if you keep balling up like that."

"IIIIIIImmmmmmm aaaallll rrrrrright," said Deering, barely getting the words out through his clenched teeth.

"Like hell you are," said Smoaks. "You're going to drown. I got to get you out right now." The swells rolled under them, throwing them up toward the pale half-moon, bringing the horizon into view all around, then pulling them back down into the black trough.

Smoaks got his hand under Deering's chin and began to tow him toward the boat.

"LLLLeeeeaaaavvvveeee mmmmeeee aaaalllloooonnnneeee," said Deering.

"You lose," said Smoaks. "Face it like a man."

Deering didn't say anything.

Smoaks towed him in toward the boat.

"Is he all right?" said Maggie.

"Help me get him in the boat," said Smoaks. "Hold him." He started to pull himself over the side, but Deering held on to him.

MMMMeeeeffffiiiirrrrssssttt," he said.

"Come on, Case," said Smoaks.

"IIII . . . llloooossseee . . . ," said Deering.

Smoaks looked at him for a minute, then hoisted himself into the boat. Together he and Maggie lifted him in.

They went back out through the fishing camp, up the ramp from the floating dock, by the dead shark without looking, to the car. Mansfield didn't wake up, or at least didn't come out to speak to them. His house was a dark shadow under the trees.

When they got back to Maggie's, Smoaks fanned the embers of the fire back into flame and piled wood on until they had it roaring. Maggie went into the house and got a blanket to wrap around Deering. Then they all sat down in the red light of the fire under the festoons of Spanish moss hanging down out of the darkness, and Smoaks opened bottles of beer for them.

"I seen the mouth," Deering said, holding his bottle of beer and looking into the fire.

"What?" said Smoaks, not looking at him.

"I seen the mouth," said Deering. "The shark's mouth."

No one spoke.

"It was white," he said.

Smoaks took a sip of beer, looking into the fire.

"First time I ever been in the water out in the Sound," Deering said. "Not even in daylight."

"It was bad," said Smoaks.

"You wasn't scared," said Deering.

"Who said?" said Smoaks. "I was pissing in my pants the whole time."

Deering looked at him, then back at the fire. "I seen something else, too," he said.

"What?" said Smoaks.

Deering didn't speak for a minute. "It wasn't the shark," he said.

"Oh," said Smoaks. "You shouldn't have had those beers before."

Deering looked at Maggie. "It wouldn't have made no difference. Would it, Maggie?" he said.

She didn't answer.

"Maybe I wouldn't have gone at all without the beers," he said.

He stood up, holding the blanket around him; then he reached out the one hand holding the bottle of beer, turned it over, and poured the beer onto the ground. When it stopped splashing, he opened his fingers and let the bottle drop. "Well," he said, throwing off the blanket. He turned and started walking toward the car.

"Where you going?" said Smoaks.

"I reckon I'd better be getting along," he said.

"How am I going to get home, then?" said Smoaks.

Deering stopped, turning back to look at him. "Come on," he said.

"Let me finish my beer," said Smoaks.

"Finish it," said Deering. He stood looking back at them by the fire. Not moving.

Smoaks looked at him, then back at the fire. "Go on," he said. "I'll walk." He tilted the bottle up and took a swig, popping it away from his lips.

Deering turned and walked to the car. Neither Maggie nor Smoaks watched him as he started the car and drove away. Both of them were sitting looking into the fire.

When Smoaks got home, he didn't go to bed. He sat around for a while on his front steps. Then he got into his car and drove down to Mansfield's fishing camp. The house was still dark, and Mansfield didn't come out to meet him. He took his black bag, getting out of the car and walking down to the dock where the shark was. It looked huge and silver in the moonlight.

He cast off the clove hitch on the tackle and slowly lowered the big fish onto the dock, snubbing the fall around the davit. It was a struggle to do it by himself, keeping the thing from sliding off into the water. He grabbed the hatchet handle and used it to lever him into position. Finally getting him down and stretched out on the dock.

Bright as the moon was, there still wasn't enough light. So he went up to the house and rummaged around until he found a kerosene lantern. He took it back down on the dock and lit it, putting it down by the big fish's head. It made him look orange, with a red point in his eye.

He heaved the shark over onto its back.

Then he took his tools from his bag and went to work inside the mouth.

Not just taking the first one he came to, but picking and choosing — so he got what looked like the three best teeth in the bunch. There were so many of them, it was hard to tell which were *the* three best. But he got three good ones, cutting them loose until he could pull them out with his hands. It took a little while for him to do it.

After he had gotten them out, he swabbed them with alcohol and wrapped them in cotton. Then he put them away into his bag, and put the bag into his car.

He pulled out his watch and looked at it. Five-twelve. He went to the house and banged on the door until Mansfield stumbled out and answered.

"I got my teeth," he said.

"What?" said Mansfield. His sounded dry and sleepy.

"I said, 'I got my teeth,'" he said.

"Smoaks?"

"Yes," said Smoaks. "I got my shark's teeth. I just took three of them."

"Take all you want," said Mansfield.

"Three's enough," said Smoaks.

There was a silence.

"Is that all?" said Mansfield.

"I wanted you to know who'd done it," said Smoaks.

"Help yourself," said Mansfield. "The bastard's got enough of them." He was yawning as he spoke.

Later Smoaks took the teeth into Savannah to a jeweler's, where he got them set as key chains — sterling silver. He gave one to Maggie, and one to Deering, and he kept one for himself.

"I know you wanted a necklace," said Smoaks. "Maybe Case can get some more for you. The carcass is still down there in the marsh somewhere. Mansfield just rolled if off the dock for the crabs to get."

"It don't make any difference," said Maggie. "I shouldn't have said anything. The key chain's fine. I'll wait on the next one for the necklace."

"I'll go look and see if I can find it," said Deering.

"The key chain's fine," she said. "Thank you."

They kept on seeing each other from time to time during the summer, but they didn't have the good times they used to have. Smoaks was the only one going into the house with Maggie now. It was embarrassing. In August a new roadhouse opened up, closer to Fancy Station, and the CCC Camp men didn't come around to Maggie's so much. She had to let the Dorchester Swamp Stompers go, and it worried her so that she stayed preoccupied most of the time and wasn't much company, even for Smoaks. When the cotton started to come in, Case had to spend all of his time seeing to it, and getting in his other crops. And Smoaks got busy with a flu epidemic, so they just kind of drifted away from each other.

By fall it was pretty well over. Then the wind shifted to the northeast, and the winter came in with the rain.

Just after New Year's, Maggie moved to Jacksonville. In April Smoaks went down to help her with the baby. Just before that — toward the end of March — Case began keeping company with Cora Dekle in a serious way. He proposed, and they were married in the following fall.

Maggie came back two years later with the baby, moved into her old roadhouse, and started up her business again.

They would meet occasionally here and there around McAfee County, and they were always too hearty with each other. Self-conscious and forced.

Smoaks kept his sharktooth key chain in his doctor's bag and used it for the ignition keys to his car. He still has it, worn and yellow now, and no longer sharp. Maggie lost hers while she was in Jacksonville. The day before Case Deering married Cora Dekle, he rented bateau number four from Mansfield Whitmire, rowed it out into the middle of Kallisaw Sound, and dropped his over the side into the deep green water.

After John Henry

1956: JUNE & JULY

Put it down, honey. You drop it and break it, and I have to punish you."

"I wouldn't never. You know I wouldn't." The voice had a sullen quality. It had been corrected too many times.

"You wouldn't never mean to do it. And you'd be sorry when you did. Then I'd have to go and do something mean and ugly. That would make us both mad. So you just put it down. Set it on the table there. You can look at it, and I won't have to worry you'll drop it. Come on, now, honey. Do as I say."

He put the mason jar on the porcelain-topped kitchen table. Leaning on the edge, his chin propped on his forearms, he watched the suspended helix of the objects in the colorless liquid.

The light from the window came in golden yellow through the liquid in the mason jar. It cast a translucent orange shadow on the porcelain of the tabletop.

The road gang from the county farm was working on the bridge. It was a small bridge, just big enough for the logging trucks coming in and out to go one at the time.

Most of the men just stood around leaning on the concrete railing. A few of them with swing blades moved their blades with listless, pendulum motions, brushing the weeds on the shoulders of the fill. It was hot now. They had been out since just after sunup. Dinnertime was coming soon. Back down the dirt logging road, under some trees, the cook, Jessie, had two fires going. On one of them was a pot of beans, on the other was a pot of grits. Jessie was a trusty, an old man who was no longer any good for road work. He was doing five years for stealing a pig from Case Deering — the fourth time he had been on the road gang. The men could see him moving in the shade under the oaks and tending the pots. The day was too still to smell the beans.

Sweat poured off John Henry. He was digging with posthole diggers. A hole to put the supports for the forms in. The muscles in his upper arms bunched and jumped as he worked the diggers. He grunted softly as he speared them down into the hole. When they hit the bottom, his muscles locked; then they strained and locked again as he spread the handles and raised them out of the hole. Some of the men leaning on the railing were looking at him. They liked to watch John Henry work.

In the middle of the road, just off the bridge, Gunther Coleman stood. He was a small man, five-feet-six or -seven, but he stood with his shoulders pulled back and erect. Most of his face was lost in the shadow under the brim of his straw hat, but his chin shot out forward and up. It was square and firm, with a dimple in the middle. There was a stubble of gray hair on it. The thumb of his left hand hooked into his belt, and a double-barreled shotgun was cradled in his left arm, the muzzle tilted down toward the road. His right hand rested on the handle of a pistol slung low on his right hip. The holster of the pistol was tied with a piece of leather bootlace around his right thigh. He stood with his left leg shot, resting his weight on his right.

He was watching John Henry too.

Suddenly Gunther drew the pistol. A whispery blur of a motion, and there it was in his hand. "Okay, boy," he said, "you be careful of them diggers."

John Henry looked at him between the spread handles of the posthole diggers. His arm muscles bunched, and the sweat dripped off his elbows. He was smiling. The blue-black skin made his teeth look very white. He liked Mr. Coleman, but he could never tell for sure. Mr. Coleman was holding it too lightly. It was a big gun — he couldn't shoot it with his arm bent that way. But the black muzzle looked very big, even at that distance. He could see the shells in the cylinders.

"Yes, boss," he said, not moving.

Gunther eased the hammer down with his thumb and put the pistol back in its holster. He continued to rest his hand on the handle. Under the brim of his straw hat, his eyes squinted out of the shade. Light blue eyes — young looking — set in a face that was red and crinkled from the sun. Kind eyes, too. The kind, youthful eyes of a boy.

Gunther loved the pistol more than anything else he owned. It had cost him a month's pay to buy it, and he couldn't shoot it very often because the bullets cost so much — the county wouldn't give him anything but shells for the shotgun — but he loved to wear it and take it out and point it around every once in a while. It was a Colt .45. Nickel-plated, with pearl handles. He had wanted one ever since the Gene Autry movies at the theater in Kose on Saturdays. But he had never actually shot anyone with it. Not a person.

The sound of the dinner gong came out of the trees down the hot, dusty road. The men lined up and filed back where Jessie had the fires going. They walked on the shoulder. Gunther and the other guards walked behind them and to the side.

They sat around under the trees eating the beans and grits. The guards ate beans and grits, too, but for dessert they had bowls of blueberries that Jessie had picked for them, and cold milk. The men in the gang sat on the ground. The guards sat on boxes that Jessie had gotten out of the truck for them. After they finished, the men lay around on the ground, some of them smoking. Jessie sat between the roots of a big oak tree, his legs spraddled out in front of him, his back resting against the trunk of the tree.

"Look out!" Gunther yelled. He was looking at Jessie. His voice was so sudden that everybody jumped. Before Jessie could move, Gunther had quick-drawn his gun and let off a shot at the tree trunk just above his head. The bullet knocked a chunk of bark and wood off as big as a man's fist.

"Lord God, boss," said Jessie, "I ain't done nothing."

"Not you," said Gunther. He walked over beside the tree and picked something up off the ground. It wiggled in a stiff kind of way and then went limp. A lizard. His head and one of his front legs were gone. He was light tan and a little longer than a man's hand.

"Thought it was a scorpion," said Gunther. "It's just a plain old lizard."

"That was *some* shooting," said Jack Inabinet, the chief of the gang. "Took his head clean off. Clean as a whistle. God damn, that was *some* shooting. I ain't never seen nothing that quick."

Jessie giggled, and the other men on the gang murmured to each other. All of them kept looking at the scar where the bullet had hit the trunk — a big white pit in the gray bark of the tree.

"If it had of been a scorpion, he'd of sure saved your life, Jessie," said Jack Inabinet. "One of them bites you, it's worse than a moccasin."

"Yes, sir, boss," said Jessie. "I sure am much obliged to you, boss."

Gunther put his hand back on the handle of the gun and walked around in circles looking at the ground. Every now and then he would look back at the scar on the tree trunk. When he walked he swung his right hip lower, almost limping on the gun side. It had been a good shot, and he didn't get to shoot often — not at anything *real*, he didn't.

"I hope all you boys seen that," said Jack Inabinet. "In case you got any ideas about slipping off sometime, just remember Mr. Coleman here and what he done to that lizard." He patted Gunther on the shoulder, then pointed with his long, angular arm to the scar in the tree trunk. Jack always rolled the sleeves of his shirts up too high, way up above his elbows, nearly to his shoulders. He was proud of his arms. The muscles on the front looked good, but on the back they were dished-out and stringy, and his elbows stuck out too far.

John Henry looked at Gunther and smiled a big smile. Gunther looked off to the side, like there was something way off down the road that he was trying to see. The corners of his mouth turned up a little, and he had to keep swallowing to help pull them back down.

Riding back to the camp that night, Skoad Farley talked to Jack Inabinet. Gunther was in the trailer that hooked on behind the truck. It was his job to be sure that none of the gang got out through the wire doors. The trailer was a little box, like an outhouse on bicycle wheels, open in the front so he could watch the back of the truck. It wasn't very comfortable to ride in it.

"I never seen no shot like that," said Skoad. Skoad was thirty, just starting out, the youngest guard in the camp.

"Best shot I ever seen," said Jack, nodding gravely. "Coleman is a damn good man." Jack was a good, steady driver, and riding the trailer wasn't too bad when he was at the wheel.

"Did you see how them niggers rolled their eyes when he made that shot?" said Skoad. "Even John Henry, too."

"They'll think about that for a long time," said Jack, holding the steering wheel in his right hand and leaning his left arm on the window. "A shot like that keeps the itch out of their feet for a long, long time."

"Even John Henry," said Skoad.

"John Henry get the itchy foot, he gets his ass blowed off same as any other nigger," said Jack.

"I was watching him work the diggers today," said Skoad. "He got a hell of a arm on him. He throwed them diggers like they's a couple of toothpicks. Up and down and up and down. And them arms just a-working."

"John Henry's a good worker," Jack said flatly, whipping the wheel a little to make his arm muscles jump.

"And ain't he got a hell of a arm on him?" said Skoad. Then added flatly, looking out the window on his side. "For a nigger, I mean."

"Shot me a lizard today," Gunther said to his son, Ransome, that night when he got home. "Good, fast shot. Right off the hip." He demonstrated, using his hands.

"Uh-huh," said Ransome, putting the dishes on the table. He looked up at his father for a moment.

"Right in the eye," said Gunther, laying his finger on his cheek under his eye.

Ransome didn't say anything. He went to the stove and stirred the pot of grits, then opened the door of the oven and looked at the biscuits.

"Little bitty one," said Gunther. "Right in the eye."

Ransome stood beside the stove looking at his father. He wiped his hands on his apron, working them slowly in the stained and greasy folds. He was a big man, but shapeless — a head taller than his bantam father, with a high waistline, and most of his weight in his hips. The apron seemed to be tied halfway up his chest, and when he turned around his pants showed puckered and gathered under the belt. His hips were so big that he couldn't get a good fit in the waist, and he had to pull his belt in tight to keep them from falling off. He had on a white, short-sleeved shirt, open at the neck, with collars that fanned out wide, like the collars on the shirt of a small boy. His eyes were blue and darting — piglike — protruding a little and surrounded by a small, puffy lobes of fat, set in a face that was too round and babylike. The lashes were so long he looked like he was wearing eye makeup. His skin had a dirty pallor, like biscuit dough that has been kneaded too much, and his face and arms glowed with a faint, waxy sheen. The dome of his head was plastered with a sparse thatch of greasy hair. In another five years he would be bald — now he had the head of a newborn black-haired baby. About him wafted an aura of Evening in Paris cologne, which almost overcame a thick, rank undertone of creased and folded flesh and dirty underwear.

"Right in the eye," said Gunther again, turning over his plate without looking at his son.

Ransome served them out of the pots, mincing back and forth from the table to the stove. Gunther watched him moving about the kitchen. Somehow Ransome gave the impression he was skipping. It made Gunther tired to watch him.

"Lord . . .," said Gunther, resting his forehead on his clasped hands, his elbows on the table, ". . . for what we are about to receive, make us truly thankful. In Jesus' name. Amen."

"Amen," said Ransome. He sat with his head bowed on his chest, his hands folded in his lap.

After grace, they ate in silence, Gunther hunching forward over his plate, his face almost in it, scooping the food into his mouth with his fork — held the way he would hold a poker to stroke up a fire. Ransome sat straight in his chair, taking small, dainty mouthfuls.

"You're a good cook, son," Gunther said flatly. "And that's a fact." He sat sucking a toothpick and watching Ransome clearing away the supper dishes. He seemed to walk on tiptoe, making movements that were too light and airy for such a big man. Ransome didn't answer.

"It's about the best shot I ever made," Gunther said at last.

"That's good, Pa," said Ransome. He was washing the dishes at the sink, and his back was to his father as he spoke. He didn't turn around.

Gunther pulled the toothpick out of his mouth and looked at it. "You don't give a good God damn, do you, boy?" he said. His voice was soft and even, without tightness. There was no tone of accusation in it. He was just stating a matter of fact.

Ransome didn't answer.

Gunther put the toothpick back into his mouth and leaned on the table with his elbows. "Where your balls, boy?" he said.

Ransome stopped washing the dishes and turned his head to him over his shoulder. His pale, dimpled face was smooth under the overhead light in the kitchen, cupid lips sucked up in a red pout. Gunther wasn't looking at him. Ransome's face flushed, and he turned away.

"No," he said softly, talking into the window above the sink. "No, Pa, I don't . . . give a damn," he said.

"What *do* you care about, son?" he said. "Not my shooting. Not nothing I can talk to you about — like my shooting — nor nothing else we could talk about. Not women . . ." The inflection on the last word went up, as though he expected his son to interrupt him.

Ransome stopped moving his hands in the water in the sink.

"Why couldn't you have some kind of meanness in you I could understand and we could talk about it sometimes? Some kind of meanness I could figure out," he said, going on. His voice was flat, toneless. "Wrecking cars, or shooting niggers, or chasing women . . ."

He sat at the table, leaning on his elbow. Folding the napkin into smaller and smaller triangles with his right hand. Turning it down and creasing it to make it stay.

"I just don't know, Ranse," he said, looking at the napkin. "I just don't know what to do for a pussy."

Ransome stopped moving his hands in the water. "Don't call me that," he said, talking out the window. His mouth pulled up tight and the words coming hard.

Gunther looked up at his son's back, then down at the napkin again. "You like pussy things, you got to be a pussy," he said. "I don't know no other word for it, son. It's just the only word I know." His voice was quiet.

For a while neither of them spoke. The water in the sink made a heavy, sloshing sound.

"What am I going to do, boy?" Gunther said, his voice quiet, talking down to the napkin on the table. "What am I going to do, son? Get you a dress and marry you off?"

Ransome turned from the sink, looking his father in the eye. He leaned back against the rim of the sink, kneading his hands in the apron.

"I'm sorry I'm a fat ass," he said. "I'm sorry I ain't got no big muscles and I'm a fat ass, Pa. Me and my fat ass, we're sorry for it all." His eyebrows were drawn up like he was hurting somewhere and was going to cry about it. "But don't call me a pussy," he said. "Think of something else."

They looked at each other across the kitchen table for a minute.

"That's all," said Ransome, shrugging his shoulders. "There ain't nothing else to say about it," he said. "There just ain't . . . nothing else to say about it."

He turned back to the sink.

Gunther looked at the back of his son's neck with his dead, blue eyes. There were two grayish-pink rolls of fat just above the boy's shirt collar. Dark sweat stains spread below his armpits, and his hips jiggled as he stirred his hands in the water of the sink.

"It ain't just no fat ass," said Gunther.

Ransome didn't answer him.

Gunther rose from the table, scraping the chair backward. "No," he said. "No, there ain't nothing else to say." He put his hands in his pockets and went out of the room. The water in the sink sounded heavy and oily.

Gunther watched the gang taking their Saturday bath under the bucket shower in the yard. John Henry's muscles bunched and jumped as he soaped himself under the cold water. It was warm in the yard, but the water was from an artesian well. John Henry danced and jiggled, first on one foot, then on the other. The muscles in his arms balled up like oranges.

"Hey, boy," said Gunther as John Henry started back to the shed, drying his head. "Hey, boy, come over here.

"You a good strong hand, boy," he said. "How much time you got left?"

"Two weeks, boss."

John Henry's eyes were black. The whites were clear, and he looked at Gunther with his eyes straight on and open. A look that was too steady.

"When you finish your time, you come around and see me," he said. "You come around and see me, and I see about you getting a job. A little time on the gang won't hurt you none. Do you good if you let it. A real strong hand don't have to go hungry in McAfee County."

"Yes, sir, boss," said John Henry. "Yes, sir, I sure will do that."

He walked away, rubbing his head with the towel.

Gunther watched him going away. He watched John Henry's shoulder and arms moving the towel around on his head. Big bunches of muscles jumped out on his neck and shoulders.

"Biggest arms I ever seen on a buck," said Skoad.

"He's a good boy," said Gunther.

After two weeks they turned John Henry loose. Gunther waited for him to come around and see him.

Case Deering had done well as a farmer — he was a little more successful than the average for McAfee County, at least. He had some money, and worked hands on his place, so that most people in the county, the ones who didn't live in Kose, looked up to him. He was stable, deliberate, and generally respected — he was also a fair man, after his own sense of justice — though he was not universally well liked. Positions of authority came to him naturally as a result of his status and manner — both of them inspired confidence. Whenever an organization of any kind began to form up, Case had the refusal of head man for it. During the nearly twenty-one years of his childless marriage, he had been forced more or less to look for outside interests to keep himself going. Cora was a dull, dry woman — proper and selfish.

Two of the many positions that had come to him he took more seriously than the others: deacon and treasurer of the Two-Oak Missionary Baptist Church, and Grand Cyclops of the Two-Oak Klavern of the Ku Klux Klan.

"John Henry been peeping on white women," Mrs. Deering said to him at supper.

Mr. Deering looked at his wife. "Who said?" he asked.

"Grace June Folsom seen him," she said. "And Aggie Dekle." She sopped a piece of bread around her plate on the end of her fork. "I seen him, too," she said.

Mr. Deering pushed his plate away and put his glass of buttermilk in front of him. He was crumbling cornbread into the glass.

"When?" he asked, looking at the glass.

"Yesterday evening," she said.

He looked up at her, then back at the glass.

"I took me a sponge bath in the kitchen. John Henry come up to the window by the stove. I hollered at him, and he run off. I seen him out the window."

Mr. Deering turned the glass slowly between his thumb and index finger.

Mr. Sipple was panting hard as he lifted the shotgun down from its rack in the living room.

"What you doing, Henry?" said Mrs. Sipple, coming in from the kitchen, wiping her hands in her apron.

Mr. Sipple didn't answer her. His breath came in hard, heaving gasps, and he seemed to be about to collapse.

"You been running, ain't you?" she said. "Man your age running around here like that. You sit down and get your breath, Henry. Then you tell me what you been running for."

Mr. Sipple fumbled for the shells. His missing finger made him clumsy. He wasn't adjusted to it yet. Finally he got two shells out, spilling others on the shelf and floor. He held the two between the fingers of his hand, the gun cradled under his arm.

"Sit down, Henry," Mrs. Sipple said again.

"Get back," Mr. Sipple said, his voice dry, panting, with his mouth open. "Get back in the kitchen."

He brushed the catch, and the gun broke across his forearm. He dropped the two shells into the chambers and snapped it closed. Then he went out of the house. At the foot of the front steps he stopped, pressed his hand to his chest, and sat down heavily on the bottom step. He tried to get up, straining, and flopped back on the step.

"Henry . . .," said Mrs. Sipple, coming out onto the porch.

"Get back in the house," he said, his voice strained and panting, "Get back in the goddamned house."

Mrs. Sipple hesitated a moment, holding the screen door back with her hand. Then she stepped backward over the threshold and let the door slam to in front of her.

He was still sitting balled up on the bottom step when the girl came into the yard. She was young, but nondescript, with lank, colorless hair. When she saw him huddled on the step, the gun across his knees, she stopped. "Pa," she said. "What's the matter, Pa?"

Mr. Sipple looked up at her. His voice was still dry and strained, but he wasn't panting so much. Mrs. Sipple stood behind the screen door.

"I seen it," he said. "I seen you down there by the bottoms."

The man and the girl looked at each other across the swept dirt of the yard. "Oh," she said. "Seen what?"

"I'd a been back and blowed his brains out," said Mr. Sipple, looking down at the ground, "only I got a catch in me — here. . . ." He still hugged his chest, pressing in with his left elbow and right hand.

The girl didn't say anything.

"He raped you, didn't he?" he said, looking down at the dirt between his shoes.

The girl looked at her father, then at her mother behind the screen door. Her arms folded, hugging her breasts, her fingers biting hard into the flesh of her upper arms.

Mr. Sipple raised the gun until it was level with his daughter's chest, staring at her out of his tight, blue eyes. His nerve failed him, and he lowered the gun again, looking at the ground.

"He raped you, didn't he?" he said, louder this time. ". . . Jackie?"

"I ain't the first one, Pa," she said, her voice going up, beginning to sound like she would start to cry.

"Frances," he said over his shoulder, "get your daughter inside the house and see to her."

Mrs. Sipple came out of the house, closing the screen door quietly behind her. She put her arm around her daughter, who was crying now, and went back into the house with her. Mr. Sipple staggered to his feet, and he and his wife looked at each other as she went by him into the house with their daughter. She didn't understand yet.

"He raped her," Mr. Sipple said. There was a tone of finality in his voice. He stood bent over, hugging his chest with his left elbow and right hand, the shotgun tilted toward the ground.

"Where you going, James Lee?" she said. The air in the shack was close and rank, smelling of kerosene. The light from the lamp made the newspapers in the window look orange.

"I just going out for a while," said James Lee. He was tall and lanky, with a long, skinny neck. His skull was long and gourdlike, and the back of his head protruded grotesquely.

"You better stay home after dark," she said, looking at the kerosene lamp by the bed. "Ain't nothing good for you out there in the dark."

James Lee hesitated at the door. "I just be going to get me a Co-Cola," he said. "We just going to go down to Shotford's and get us a Co-Cola. I be back directly."

"You better stay away from John Henry," said the woman. She sat stiffly in her chair, looking at the lantern and talking to her son behind her.

"We just going to get us a Co-Cola down to Shotford's, Ma," he said, his voice whining. "I be back directly."

"You go out in the dark with John Henry sometime and you ain't never coming back," she said, sitting straight in the chair, her voice low and level. "John Henry have hisself a big time, you and John Henry. He have hisself a fine big time. And all the colored folks going to pay up for him sometime. John Henry be gone pretty soon now. Very soon. And we be paying up his good times after he gone."

"Ma," said James Lee, wavering.

"You come back and stay with your ma, James Lee," she said. "I make you a glass of sugar water, and you stay here with me."

"I don't want no sugar water," said James Lee sullenly. "I want me a Co-Cola."

"White man going to get John Henry," she said, her voice dropping lower. "You go in the dark with John Henry, white man going to get you too."

"Aw, Ma," said James Lee, whining. He came back into the room and sat down on the bed. "Aw, Ma . . .," he said, ". . . I want me a Co-Cola. . ."

Behind the Two-Oak Missionary Baptist Church is a grove of oak trees. In the grove is a picnic area. Almost every Sunday the church has a picnic, until the weather gets too cold in the winter. The oaks are tall, with big, spreading limbs, and the ground underneath is open and sandy. Under the trees are four big tables, made of concrete slabs, gray and heavy. The men's Sunday-school class made them as a project one summer, and the forms they used weren't fancy. But they are very sturdy tables. Every now and then somebody after church will back a pickup into one of them and just bounce right off, with maybe a little chip knocked out. It took the whole county gang all of an afternoon to set them up. Before the concrete hardened in the forms, Brother Fisco wrote a motto on each one: "Blessed *are* the meek," "Blessed *are* the merciful," "Blessed *are* the pure in heart," and "Blessed *are* the peace-makers."

"They's there to stay, boys," said Brother Fisco the afternoon he held the dedication.

To this grove they brought John Henry.

They pulled some cars and pickup trucks up under the trees and parked them with their lights on, facing toward the tables.

John Henry had a gag in his mouth, and his hands were tied behind him. His eyes were open and staring, and his muscles bunched and twisted under their hands. Four of them carried him and put him down on the "Blessed *are* the pure in heart" table — on his back. Some others stepped up to help hold him down.

"Get his pants off," said Mr. Deering in a dull, matter-of-fact voice. He had a toothpick in his mouth.

They pulled them off, then tied his legs down, passing the rope under the heavy slab of the table so that the edges cut the backs of his knees.

"Let Mr. Sipple up front," somebody said, and they pushed him up to the table. He looked down at John Henry without saying anything.

John Henry made strained, grunting noises inside the gag. He tried to roll off the slab, but they held him down.

"Let's get it over with," said Mr. Deering. He took the toothpick out of his mouth and spat between his shoes.

Anse Starkey stepped up to the table. In his hands he held a pair of long-handled pruning shears. He opened the handles into a wide V and put the bill carefully down between John Henry's legs. John Henry strained and twisted away just a little.

"You better be still, boy," said Anse. "You going to lose more than you need to."

John Henry kept on twisting. Choked, straining noises came from behind the gag. The muscles of his legs flicked and jumped.

"Somebody better hold them," said Anse. "I can't see nothing in this goddamn light anyway." He looked around at the crowd. "Stand back," he said. "Get off them tables and stand back so I can see what the hell I'm doing . . . Hold them, Dee Witt," he said.

"Don't cut my finger off," Dee Witt said.

"You wouldn't miss it that much," said Anse, putting the bill of the shears in again. "Keep it out the way."

He levered down on the handles of the shears carefully, moving them partway closed and holding them. Then he looked closely at the bill of the shears, putting his head down so he could see better. He rocked back, braced himself, then flexed his arms, pushing the handles. They closed smoothly. The men bore down on John Henry to keep him still.

Anse looked at Mr. Deering. "That all?" he asked.

"Leave him something to play with, God damn it," said a voice from somewhere in the crowd.

Mr. Deering nodded his head and spat between his shoes.

"Ain't enough," said Anse. "Where's Mr. Sipple? Mr. Sipple!" he yelled.

Mr. Sipple had moved back behind the lights. They pushed him up to the table again.

"Ain't enough?" asked Anse. He worked the shear open and closed.

Mr. Sipple didn't say anything. He just stood looking down at John Henry on the slab.

"Take it all," said Anse. "Take it all, and he won't never forget it."

"It's enough," said Mr. Deering, looking at Anse.

"Mr. Sipple's to say," said Anse. Mr. Sipple stood by the table staring at John Henry.

"Hold it up, Dee Witt," said Anse, opening the shears again.

"That's enough," said Mr. Deering, taking a step forward.

Anse levered the handles closed again, and John Henry strained and croaked in his throat under the gag.

Mr. Deering came up and jerked the shears away from Anse. "You wasn't going to be satisfied, was you?" he said.

"You getting to be a nigger-lover, Mr. Deering?" said Anse, a faint smile on his face. He jumped away into the darkness behind the lights when Mr. Deering raised the shears as if to hit him.

Mr. Deering looked down at John Henry, holding the open shears by one handle. "Put some turpentine on him," he said. "Then untie him."

He turned to go.

"You want them?" Dee Witt asked.

Mr. Deering looked at him in a cold sort of way. "Leave them there," he said. "Leave them there on the table."

They untied John Henry. He lay there with his legs hanging off the sides of the slab. His breath was heavy and rasping in the back of his throat. When they untied his arms, he moved them down slowly and held himself.

"It had to be did," said Mr. Deering, looking down at him. "It's just one of them things had to be did." He turned and went away. The cars and pickups backed out and drove off down the road in front of the church.

Gunther met the line of cars coming down the road from the church.

Mr. Deering came into the house through the kitchen door and sat down at the table without taking off his hat. He was still chewing on the toothpick.

"Where you been?" Mrs. Deering asked.

He looked at his wife, then back at the table in front of him.

"I wondered where you was off to," Mrs. Deering said. "Where you been?"

"Don't talk to me, Cora," he said, not looking up at her. "I'll be all right after a while. Just don't talk to me right now."

"John Henry?" she said.

"God damn it, Cora, I said don't talk to me." He got up and went out of the kitchen into the yard. At the foot of the steps he saw a toad hop. He drew back his foot and kicked it into the darkness.

Gunther found him spread out on his back, holding himself, the blood dripping off the end of the slab and soaking into the sand.

"Come on, boy," he said quietly, trying to get his arm under John Henry's shoulders to help him up. "Come on, so we can get you to a doctor."

"Don't move me." John Henry's voice was a low, rasping croak. "It hurts."

"You don't get to a doctor, you going to bleed to death," he said.

"I can't move," said John Henry. "Don't make me move."

Gunther leaned both hands on the slab, looking down at John Henry.

"Boss," John Henry whispered.

"What?" said Gunther. John Henry spoke so strained and low he couldn't hear him.

"Boss," said John Henry, "I going to die."

"You ain't going to die, John Henry," said Gunther. "Doctor fix you up. Doctor fix you up good as new. . . ." His voice trailed off.

"I going to die. And I need to do it. Let me do it, boss," said John Henry, holding himself.

"You ain't going to die," said Gunther.

"Give me your gun, boss, so I can do it," said John Henry.

Gunther looked down at him on the slab.

"Boy," he said at last, "ain't no nigger never had that gun in his hand. Ain't but one white man had it, and never no nigger."

"Please, boss," said John Henry, with his eyes closed.

Gunther looked at him for a long time. Then he drew the pistol out of his holster. He held it in front of him and looked at it.

"You ain't no good for a cut shoat," he said. "Not you, John Henry. . . . *I'll* do it," he said, holding the gun to John Henry's head.

John Henry opened his eyes, staring straight up into the branches of the trees over the table. "Yes," he said, "but I need to do it. Me. Let me have the gun, and I can do it. . . . I ain't no shoat, boss," he said.

Gunther looked at him on the slab for a minute. Then he turned the gun and held it to John Henry, handle first.

"You wasn't going to die, boy," he said. "But you be better off anyway."

John Henry looked at the pistol with his eyes, not moving his head. He reached up to take it in his hand, holding himself with the other hand.

Gunther held the gun away. "Wipe the blood off your hand," he said.

John Henry wiped his hand on his shirt, then took the gun.

"You always was good to me, boss," he said. "I sure did always admire your gun and the way you treated me nice."

He lay with the gun in his hand, resting on his chest.

"You sure was good to me, boss," he said again.

Gunther turned to step back from the table. As he did so, John Henry raised the revolver and fired into his chest. Gunther reeled backward under the impact of the bullet. The second shot hit him in the shoulder and spun him around. The third knocked off his hat. The last three whistled off into the branches of the tree.

"I sorry, boss," he said. "I sorry it you . . . I had to get me one . . . I had to get me one."

They found him off to the side of the table next day, lying on his face. John Henry was gone. After they moved him away, there were two dark spots in the sand made by the blood. They never did get it cleaned out where it had pooled in the "Blessed *are* the pure in heart."

John Henry still had the gun with him when they found him.

They gave it to Ransome.

The light from the window came in golden yellow through the liquid in the mason jar.

"They look kind of purply and gray," said James Lee. "I'd have thought they'd be bigger, too."

"Maybe they've shrank. I don't think so. That's probably just the way they look, honey. Like that, I mean."

"They don't move at all," he said. "Just stay there." He took the mason jar in his hand and swirled it.

"God damn it, honey, I told you to leave it alone. You going to go and break it, and I'll have to do something mean to you."

"I just can't stand it when they stay there like that."

"I'm going to put it up so you'll quit worrying about it."

"Not yet, Mr. Ransome," he said. "Don't put it up yet. I won't touch it no more."

"Get temptation out of the way, is what I say. Get temptation out of the way, and then you don't never have to be sorry."

He took the mason jar from the kitchen table and opened the cupboard.

"Let me see the gun, Mr. Ransome," he said.

"Jesus God," said Ransome, "ain't you never going to be satisfied, James Lee?"

"Just let me see it a minute, Mr. Ransome. All I want is to see it just a minute."

"James Lee, honey, I don't even like you looking at that gun. It makes me nervous for you to just look at it."

"Just a little look, Mr. Ransome. Just one little look, and I wouldn't ask you no more. Not no more at all."

Ransome hesitated, with the cupboard door open. He didn't like to look at the gun himself. It made him nervous just to open the cupboard door and see the bundle of rags wrapped around it. It made him go all cold inside, just seeing the rags and knowing that the gun was wrapped up inside them.

"Just one look, James Lee," he said, putting the mason jar on the counter. "Just one look, and then I better not hear no more about that gun. Not no more never. You hear, honey?"

James Lee nodded stupidly, his lower jaw sprung and his mouth hanging open.

Ransome took down the bundle of rags and opened them up on the counter under the cupboard, his back to James Lee. James Lee leaned against the edge of the kitchen table, his hands gripping it tight.

"There," said Ransome, turning. The fingers of his right hand were extended together. The pistol lay on his fingers in his open palm.

"Lawd, ain't it pretty?" said James Lee under his breath. "It looks just like Mr. Autry's. . . . Lemme hold it just a minute, Mr. Ransome," he said. "I give it right back. I just got to hold it in my hand a minute, Mr. Ransome."

"God damn it!" said Ransome. "Didn't I know it? You and every other nigger in McAfee County just got to get this gun in his hand."

James Lee made a tentative move forward from the table.

"Right there!" he said. "You hold it right there, honey."

"Please, Mr. Ransome," he said. "I be real friendly for you, do you let me hold that silver gun in my hand."

"I love your black ass, James Lee," said Ransome, "but I'll blow it off for you, first step you take for this gun."

"Don't you try to fool me now, Mr. Ransome," said James Lee. "Ain't no bullets in that gun. I see it from here."

"Maybe just one you don't see," he said.

They looked at each other for a minute, then Ransome wrapped the gun back up in the rags and put it on the shelf. Then he put the mason jar back on the shelf beside the gun and closed the cupboard.

He sat down on the couch.

"Now, you just forget about that old gun, and come sit down here by me, honey," he said, patting the couch beside him. "Come on over here and sit down and be friendly, James Lee, honey."

James Lee stood looking out the window. The back of his long head swelled out above his thin neck. "Time I be getting home," he said.

"You ain't going to leave me now, are you, honey?" said Ransome. "After I done showed you the gun and all. Come on over and sit here by me."

James Lee stood looking out the window. "Coming on sundown," he said. "Ma don't like I should be out after it get dark."

"Just a minute, honey," said Ransome. "I show you something else. Something better than the gun. Get you a Coca-Cola."

Ransome went into the bedroom. When he came back, he had a deck of cards in his hand.

"Come here, honey," he said, patting the couch.

James Lee came over, wiping the mouth of the Coca-Cola bottle, and sat down beside him. Ransome flipped the deck of cards and looked at James Lee. Then he turned over the deck of cards and showed James Lee the top card.

"Jesus God, Mr. Ransome," said James Lee, staring at the card. "Where'd you get them picture cards at?"

"Ain't never seen nothing like that before, have you, James Lee, honey?" said Ransome. He put his arm around James Lee's shoulder. With his other hand he patted his knee. "You forget about the old gun and John Henry's jewels," he said, squeezing James Lee's shoulder, his cheek almost touching the boy's.

James Lee's mouth was hanging open as he looked at the cards. One by one he slipped them over, carefully, making a new pile on the couch beside him.

"Just look at them pictures, James Lee, honey," he said. "Just look at them pictures and forget all about that gun."

The smell of Evening in Paris cologne was strong in the room.

James Lee didn't say anything. He just kept turning the cards.

Annie's Love Child

1956-1957: FALL,
WINTER, & SPRING

Best your ma didn't live," he said, looking at the girl sitting across the kitchen table from him. "Best your ma died before ever she should live to see that this day should come."

The girl sat with her hands in her lap, motionless; her torso also motionless above the yellow-oilcloth cover of the table. She was a healthy-looking girl, sturdy and well formed. Her breasts were large and pendulous, outlined under the limp cloth of her dress. The dress itself was shapeless, of purple cloth with pink flowers on it. She wore nothing underneath it, and the limp material crested at her nipples, falling straight down in two small, peaked folds. She was a tranquil, healthy-looking girl.

"And you ain't going to say?" he said. The girl didn't answer. "Just somebody come along and it happened. Just somehow it happened — and you ain't going to say."

"Wouldn't do no good," the girl said. "He's long gone anyway. It wouldn't do no good."

"It would do me some good," he said. "It really would do me a whole lot of good." The girl didn't answer. "Where is he long gone to?" he said. "Where to, and where from? Annie, you answer me. You answer me and tell me who."

The girl didn't speak.

"Somebody from the carnival through here in August?" he said. "Some soldier boy from Stewart, maybe? Some kind of a traveling man selling things out of a suitcase, with black, shiny shoes and a automobile?"

The girl didn't speak.

"I'm going to find out sometime, Annie," he said. "You might as well tell me. Sometime I'm going to find it out anyway. Make it easy on yourself."

She didn't answer.

Everything about her tended downward. The small, indistinct festoons of the purple and pink flowers falling from the nipples of her breasts; her shoulders, downward-sloping but sturdy; her lank, colorless hair, hanging straight down along the sides of her head, breaking into thin cascades at her shoulders and fanning slightly over the swell of her breasts. Her arms immobile at her sides, disappearing under the table.

Her eyes, too, were downcast. Fixed on a spot in the middle of the yellow-oilcloth table cover in front of her.

The father sat across from her. Not looking her in the eye, but meeting her gaze at the spot she had selected on the yellow-oilcloth cover of the table and bouncing his father's indignation up under her lowered lids off the shiny yellow surface of the table. He sat with his elbows and forearms on the table before him, his hands clasped. His voice was high, with an edge on it.

"If she had of lived, she would have died this day," he said, talking into the yellow shine of the oilcloth. "This day, and the shame of it, would have been her last, had she lived to see it."

The girl's lips were relaxed. They looked like the soft, relaxed lips of a sleeping child. The man's mouth was hard, his lips thin. His lower lip projected slightly, as if he had an undershot jaw, curving back to meet the thin upper one. His mouth looked hard and dry. When he talked, his lower teeth showed.

"How could you have done it, Annie?" he said. "How could you have done such a thing like that? Such a sinful thing?"

She pursed her lips slightly. Not nervously, but just pursing them slightly.

"I ain't real sure yet," she said. Her voice was low, with a masculine tone in it. "Just almost two months," she said. Her lips barely moved when she spoke. "Just hardly two months. It ain't enough to tell," she said. "Not for sure."

"Tell what?" he said in his high voice. He raised his watery blue eyes to look at her face. She continued to stare at the spot in the center of the yellow table. "Tell what, when you done already told? Ain't no more telling to it. You done it, and that's all. You done it, and the shame ain't going to go away. Not in two months, not in three months, not in three years. Annie, it ain't never to go away."

He moved his eyes down to the table again. Trying to get at her. Trying to get under the lids of her eyes to move against that rooted and vegetable passiveness.

"You think it's going to be all right if you don't have the child?" he said. "You think you can come up with your woman's blood, and it just late a little, and that woman's blood is going to wash it all away?" He worked the fingers of his hands as he talked, clasping and unclasping them on the table. "Woman's blood wouldn't do it," he said. "Woman's blood wouldn't wash it away like it never was. You can bleed yourself out for the next ten years, and it wouldn't do it.

"You sinned," he said. "You sinned, Annie, and wallowed in the filth of it. Ain't nothing going to take that away. Ain't nothing going to make it clean and take that away like it just hadn't never been.

"That's too easy," he said. "That's just too easy. If it were so, I'd go get me a swab and boil me some lye and swab the filth out of you. Swab it out and scrape it clean with a wire brush and boiling lye. I'd open you up and scrub the corruption out of you till you was white and dry inside. White and dry and dead, and clean of the corruption." His fingers bit white into the backs of his hands. "If it were only so. If it were only so, and just so easy."

When he finished speaking his shoulders drooped and he began sawing his head from side to side. For a long while he sat like that, looking down at his hands clasped on the table, his head sawing from side to side.

The girl looked at him calmly across the yellow oilcloth of the table. "You sound like a preacher, Pa," she said. "Church talk."

He looked up at her, working his mouth, compressing the lips. Then he looked back down at the table without saying anything.

She rose from the table and began to clear away the dishes. Her hands moved surely as she picked up the plates. The movements of her hands and arms were deliberate and unhurried as she cleared away the table things, taking them to the sink. Her eyes were still downcast. Not out of shame, and not out of remorse, but out of an inwardness. As if she were looking into herself and listening to something inside, something that spoke a secret to her that she already knew but wanted to hear anyway.

The man sat at the table, not looking at her.

"Leave the dishes alone," he said. "Leave the dishes alone and listen to what I got to say."

"Got to be did sometime," she said, not looking at him.

"Sometime. Some other time," he said. "Sit down, Annie. Sit down and listen to me."

She sat down in the chair across the table.

"What're we going to do?" he said. "What're we going to do if the baby is going to come?"

She looked at him a moment. He was still looking at the table, not seeing her eyes. Her eyes were calm, the lids not raised and not lowered now. Just looking at him calmly. "We're going to wait and see," she said flatly. "We're going to wait and see, and if the baby is going to come, that's all there is. We'll just have to wait and see."

"You ain't going to have no love child, Annie," he said, his mouth tight. "For your mother's sake and her rest and peace, I wouldn't let you do it."

She didn't reply.

"We're going to wait a little while more," he said. "Just a little while more to be sure. And if the baby is still going to come, we are going to do something and stop it."

He looked at her, and their eyes met.

"You ain't never going to have no love child, Annie," he said. "It ain't never going to happen."

Josey stood on one side of the kitchen table, her arms folded under her breasts. Mr. Mullins sat at the table on the other side. He looked at the spot in the center of the table. Sometimes he looked up at her. She stood erect, her head wrapped in a blue headcloth, thrown back a little, looking at him steadily.

"You too late," she said, her voice flat but distinct, not loud. "Three months is too late."

"I had to be sure," Mr. Mullins said. "Can't hardly be sure in three months."

"I could of done it with a coat hanger," said Josey. "Boiled it and scraped it right out, and no trouble. But not now, it's too late." Small, wiry gray hairs had sprung from under the headcloth around her ears. Her apron was worn but clean. A big yellowish-brown stain splotched under the pocket, but the folds were crisp and pressed looking. She wore men's high-topped work shoes. Out of the tops of the shoes her thin shanks rose, bowing slightly up under the crisp apron.

"Three months is too long," she said. "Two is bad enough."

"We done tried the quinine," said Mr. Mullins. "And chopping wood. And I run her up and down the steps till I got tired watching her."

"Ain't nothing I going to be able to do," said Josey. "Ain't nothing I going to be able to do, 'cept the quinine. And that ain't going to work."

He sat looking into his hands on the tabletop as if he had the answer cupped inside them.

"Go get me Dr. Smoaks," he said, talking to the top of the table, then looking at her. "Go get me Dr. Smoaks and bring him out here, and we'll see what he's got to say."

"Same thing," said Josey. "He ain't going to do nothing neither. It too late for me, and too late for him too."

"I done got your say," he said. "Three months may be right. But you get Dr. Smoaks anyway. I want to see what a white man's got to say."

Josey didn't reply. She turned and walked to the kitchen door, knocking the screen open with her shoulder without unfolding her arms.

"Three months is too late," said Dr. Smoaks. He and Mr. Mullins sat at the yellow kitchen table. They were drinking coffee. Beside his cup was his black bag. Josey stood at the end of the table, her arms still folded under her breasts, moving her eyes slowly from side to side as the talk shifted between the two men.

"Maybe we could give her more quinine," said Mr. Mullins.

Dr. Smoaks lifted his cup smoothly but daintly. He sipped it, taking small sips, watching Mr. Mullins over the rim of the cup.

"Quinine ain't enough," he said. "Quinine ain't enough, and it won't do it." He held the cup by the handle, bracing it lightly between the thumb and forefinger of the other hand. "You can give her a gallon of it a day," he said. "Pour it into her with a funnel. And chopping wood won't do it. And running her up the steps. Ain't nothing going to do it," he said. "Why don't you just face it, Dero? Annie's going to have that baby."

"No she ain't," said Mr. Mullins. "It ain't never going to happen."

Dr. Smoaks put the coffee cup back into the saucer, resting his forearm on the table. "Look at her, Dero," he said. "Just look at her and think about it. Nothing we're going to do would make her turn loose of it. Can't you just look at her and see that? You couldn't even stick your hand in there and grab it and pull it out. Like as not, if you tried to do it, she'd just pull down on your arm, and hold on, and bring it to term along with the baby."

Dr. Smoaks pulled his watch out of his vest pocket and looked at it perfunctorily. Then he wound it and put it back into the pocket.

"Only way to get it out is to cut it out," he said. "And I wouldn't be able to do that."

Mr. Mullins looked at him. "You could do it that way?" he said.

"No," said Dr. Smoaks. "I said to cut it out was the only way it can be done. But I couldn't do it."

"She ain't but just barely sixteen," said Mr. Mullins.

"God damn it, Dero, it's against the law," said Dr. Smoaks. "I wouldn't care if she was just twelve. The law won't let you go and cut out a baby just because you feel bad about it."

He stood up and put his hand on the handle of his bag, looking down at Mr. Mullins on the other side of the yellow table. "I feel bad about it," he said. "I really do feel bad about it, but I can't cut her for you just for that."

Josey watched the two men, standing at the end of the table with her arms folded.

"What if she's going to have trouble?" said Mr. Mullins.

"She ain't," said Dr. Smoaks. "I can tell about that too. She ain't going to have no trouble at all."

"But she ain't never going to get over it," said Mr. Mullins.

"You mean *you* ain't never going to get over it," said Dr. Smoaks.

"I mean she ain't never going to get over it too," said Mr. Mullins. "Her with a baby and just barely sixteen."

"Don't nobody have to know," said Dr. Smoaks.

"How is it nobody is going to know?" said Mr. Mullins. "You can't keep no secret like that."

"Maybe," said Dr. Smoaks. "Maybe so."

"How you going to keep something like that a secret?"

"I would say she had the rheumatic fever," said Dr. Smoaks. "Josey could look after her. You would keep her up in the house."

The two men looked at the woman.

"Can't no nigger keep her mouth shut," said Mr. Mullins. "I don't mean you in particular, Josey," he said, talking across the table to Dr. Smoaks, not looking at her. "Just that it ain't possible for no nigger to do it."

"Well," said Dr. Smoaks, "what choice you got? I can't do no better than that. You better think on it awhile."

"And what're we going to do after?" he asked.

"I'll take care of after," said Dr. Smoaks.

"And ain't that against the law, too?" asked Mr. Mullins.

"Well, yes," said Dr. Smoaks. "Well, yes, it is, only not as much. I would take care of after for you. I would do that."

For a while neither of them spoke.

"No," said Mr. Mullins at last. "No, it won't do. It's too risky. I guess you better cut her."

"I told you I can't cut her," said Dr. Smoaks. "God damn it, Dero, get your head out of your ass and listen to me. There's a law says I can't cut her. And if I go ahead and cut her anyway, there's another law says I go to jail for it. And it probably says you go to jail for it too. And Annie."

"And the law don't care that she ain't hardly sixteen?"

"Dero," said Dr. Smoaks, "the law don't give a God damn how old she is. Nor me. Nor you. Nor Josey there."

Mr. Mullins sat thinking for a minute. "Then," he said, "I don't give a God damn for the law.

"I want you to cut her, Smoaks," he said, his hand clasped on the table in front of him. "I want you to cut her and take the child."

"I told you I can't do it," said Dr. Smoaks. "It's against the goddamn law."

"If you don't do it . . . I will," said Mullins quietly.

Dr. Smoaks looked at him across the table. A quick, sharp look. "You want to kill her?" he said.

"She'd be better off, if it come to that," said Mr. Mullins, not looking at him.

"That's crazy talk, Dero," said Dr. Smoaks. "A strong, healthy girl like Annie. You sound like it ain't never happened before. Like Annie done outraged the whole of McAfee County this way."

"It ain't never happened before in *this* house," said Mr. Mullins. "I mean it, Smoaks, if you don't cut her, I will."

Dr. Smoaks looked at Mr. Mullins across the table, gauging him. Mr. Mullins had his head down, not looking at him. His hands were clasped hard in the middle of the table.

"You reckon he means it, Josey?" he said, not looking up at the woman.

She looked at Mr. Mullins. When she spoke, her voice was flat and low. "He might could do it," she said. "He feel it enough so he might could do it. I wouldn't want to say."

"You're just about that crazy," said Dr. Smoaks. "Just about crazy enough to get it started anyway. That would be enough. You might change your mind, and then she would bleed out right there in the bed. And you standing by wringing your hands, and wishing the hell you hadn't never started in on it in the first place. And being sorry as hell after."

Mr. Mullins and Josey didn't speak.

"He might could do it," said Josey.

Dr. Smoaks didn't look at her. "You know what it looks like on the inside?" he asked. "You'd sure wish to hell you hadn't never started on it. I know that's the way it would be after it was too late. And I know you are sure as hell going to do it too, ain't you? God damn it, I told you it's against the law. You want me to get my license taken away?"

"No," said Mr. Mullins. "Only I'm going to do it if you don't. Josey here will help me."

He didn't look at her, and she didn't speak.

"Yes," said Dr. Smoaks. "Oh hell yes. That'll be a fine team, sure enough. Then you can both of you stand there and keep each other company while you watch her bleed to death. That'll fix it up all right."

He stood with his hand still on the handle of his bag for a minute. Then he took it off and put it in his pocket.

"Just keep him at the table till I get back," he said, speaking to Josey. "Ain't no rush," he said. "You got six months to go."

He went out of the kitchen screen door into the dark, leaving the black bag on the yellow-oilcloth table.

Mr. Mullins and Josey waited in the kitchen while he walked it out. He sitting at the table, his hands clasped in front of him. She standing at the end with her arms folded.

"All right," Dr. Smoaks said, letting the screen door slam to behind. "All right, God damn it. But if it ever gets out, I'm going to come down here some night and do me some more cutting . . ." — he pointed his finger at Mr. Mullins —" . . . on *you*.

"And the same for you Josey," he said. "I mean that thing."

They both loked at him, their eyes dead and waiting.

"Get some water boiling," he said to Josey. "I got to go back to my office and get the things. And make him understand he's going to watch it. He's going to watch every bit of it. He'll get himself a lesson out of this anyway. If he don't watch it — and I mean watch every bit of it — I ain't going to do nothing."

He picked up his black bag and went out of the screen door, letting it slam to behind him. They heard the motor of his car roar when he started it, and the wheels spun and slung stones as he lurched it out of the yard.

Annie didn't think too well of it when Dr. Smoaks came back to see her the second time that night. And when he pulled out the needle and wanted to give her a shot, she didn't like that at all. So Mr. Mullins and Josey and Dr. Smoaks — all three of them — had to sit on her to hold her down while he put the needle in and gave her the anaesthetic. It took effect almost right away.

"All right," Dr. Smoaks said, dropping the syringe back into his bag. "All right, Dero, you're going to have a front-row seat. Right there where you can see all the blood and everything." Mr. Mullins was standing beside the bed. Between the bed and the wall. "All the blood and everything else. And when I cut it out, I'm going to put it in your hand, and you're going to take it out in your hand in the backyard, and dig a hole and bury it. And first time you close your eyes not to see, or say something, or just even make a noise, I'm going to stop right there and sew her back up, and that'll be the end of it. You understand?"

Mr. Mullins didn't say anything. He stood in the small space between the bed and the wall, looking down at his daughter on the bed. She looked like she was asleep, except her face was pulled down a little bit more than usual.

"You stand right there, Josey," Dr. Smoaks said. "And when I ask for something, you give it to me right away." He looked at her. "And you listen good so I ain't going to have to say it but one time."

Josey stood at the head of the bed, on Dr. Smoak's right-hand side. A chair was pulled up with its back against the wall at the very head of the bed. The instruments were laid out on it on a towel.

Dr. Smoaks leaned over and raised Annie's nightgown. Josey had to help him, lifting her legs so they could work it up over her stomach. Josey turned it back down again at the top, tucking it under her chin so her face wouldn't be covered.

Mr. Mullins stood by the bed, looking down at his daughter. His hands were clasped in front, hanging down, and he leaned backward slightly, bracing his shoulders against the wall.

"I ought to shave her," said Dr. Smoaks, "but I ain't got the time. Get some of that boiled water and a rag, Josey, and wash her off good with soap."

Mr. Mullins watched.

Annie's thighs were full and slightly apart. He could see the soft rolls of flesh high up and inside them. Her stomach rose in a gentle swell. Over the fronts of her thighs and on her lower abdomen there was a down of fine white hair. The light from the lamp beside the bed caught it from the side and turned it silver. Under Josey's scubbing the skin turned pink, and the blond patch between her thighs turned dark from the wet, dark golden brown, with glinting highlights from the bedside lamp.

Josey toweled her dry, and her skin had a soft, powdery texture.

"Go get some more water," said Dr. Smoaks. Josey left the room. "You swab her down with this," he said to Mr. Mullins, handing him a wad of cotton and a bottle of alcohol.

Mr. Mullins clamped the cotton to the mouth of the bottle, then upended it. He swabbed in small, rapid circles, having to lean far over the bed, because they had moved Annie near the edge on the opposite side, where Dr. Smoaks could work on her better. The circles grew larger and slower. Every now and then Mr. Mullins would douse the cotton from the bottle of alcohol. When he had swabbed her good with the circular motion, he began at the top of her abdomen, working down with overlapping swipes across from the side. He had moved one knee up onto the bed, leaning on his left hand. When he finished, he stuffed the saturated ball of cotton into the mouth of the bottle.

"Just like Mae," he said, looking down at his daughter.

"What?" said Dr. Smoaks.

Mr. Mullins looked down at his daughter's body on the bed. It was shining a little in the places where the alcohol hadn't dried yet. It had turned more pink than ever under the swabbing.

"My wife, Mae," he said. "She looked just like that. I'd forgot. Same white hair and all." He leaned back on his heel, bracing both arms on the bed. "Twelve years," he said. "I wouldn't of thought I'd forgot." He reached out his hand as if to lay it on his daughter's stomach.

Dr. Smoaks caught it quickly. "Not no more," he said. "Nothing that ain't been sterilized. Give me the bottle, and stand back there against the wall."

Mr. Mullins stood between the bed and the wall, slouching his shoulders and bracing them lightly against the wall, his hands held together in front.

Josey came back into the room with a pan of water which she set down on a second chair, beside the one with the instruments on it. Steam rose from the pan.

She and Dr. Smoaks washed their hands in the pan, lathering them and rinsing them, then lathering them and rinsing them again. After he dried his hands, Dr. Smoaks took a bottle of Merthiolate with a glass wand on the cap and drew a long red line with the wand diagonally across Annie's stomach. It was a very long line, and Mr. Mullins looked at it intently. The pink in Annie's skin was fading now. She began to look pale. The red scar across her stomach was vivid against the paleness.

"What's that?" asked Mr. Mullins.

"I cut to that line," said Dr. Smoaks. "I put the line there and cut to it so I don't forget what I'm supposed to do in the middle of it." He looked at Mr. Mullins across the bed. "I ain't no goddamned surgeon," he said. "I ain't no goddamned high-price surgeon, and it ain't every day I get to cut somebody. I figure I better draw me a picture to go by."

Mr. Mullins looked at the long red scar. "Ain't no growed man you got to take out of there," he said, his hands clasping tightly as he held them together. "Just a little bitty one. Hardly just big enough to see."

"You going to tell me all about it?" Dr. Smoaks asked, looking at him hard across the bed. "Why don't I just sit here and listen while you explain all about it to me?"

"It just don't hardly seem like you got to cut her that much," said Mr. Mullins.

"No telling what I might have to take out after I get her open," said Dr. Smoaks. "Might be I got to take out all kinds of things after I see what she looks like inside there."

"You ain't never said nothing about that," said Mr. Mullins.

"I told you I didn't want to cut her," said Dr. Smoaks.

"But only the baby," said Mr. Mullins. "You never said nothing about taking something else."

"Can't tell," said Dr. Smoaks. "Might be I got to take out lots of things when I open her up. You never can tell about that kind of a thing."

Mr. Mullins looked down at his daughter's body on the bed. The red line was very long and ugly. Sweat beaded his upper lip, and he swallowed as though his throat was dry. Annie's skin had gone white again, powdery soft looking, except where it was raked by the red line of the Merthiolate.

He reached his right hand out toward her stomach, an involuntary movement. Dr. Smoaks struck it away hard, firmly and quickly.

"I told you, 'No,'" he said.

"She's *my* daughter," said Mr. Mullins, looking down at Annie, not at Dr. Smoaks.

"You give her to me," said Dr. Smoaks. "I didn't want her, but you give her to me."

Mr. Mullins looked up at him. "When you get through with her, she's going to look like the end of a feed sack," he said.

"You wanted her fixed for the baby," said Dr. Smoaks. "I didn't never say I was going to make her look pretty."

Mr. Mullins looked down at the white, dry belly of his daughter. The fine, pale hair glowed again silver in the light from the bedside lamp. "She's just like her ma," he said. "Just like Mae used to be. I never seen it till now."

"Give me the scalpel." Dr. Smoaks spoke to Josey. She looked at him as he spoke, not moving. "That there," he said, pointing to the instruments on the chair.

The shaft of the bright silver instrument was poised in his hand. He held it deftly, seeming to touch it only with the tips of his fingers. Mr. Mullins clasped and unclasped his hands, licking his lips and swallowing as he watched the hand, and the instrument in the hand. The dainty silver point came to rest at the upper end of the long, red slash, making a tiny dimple in the skin. Dr. Smoaks's left hand moved to rest on Annie's hip, bracing to steady himself. He held that position, not moving for a moment. Then he made a sudden, sweeping stroke, the scalpel point just barely touching her skin. Blood started all along the red line. A string of darker beads inside the bright red of the Merthiolate.

"No . . . ," said Mr. Mullins.

He looked up and found Dr. Smoaks looking at him hard. "I ain't hardly started yet," he said. "That's just to mark the place."

"No," Mr. Mullins said. He reached down, and his fingers closed around the hand that held the instrument, lifting it away.

Dr. Smoaks didn't speak.

"You get through with her, and she's going to have a belly looks like a goddamn feed sack," he said. "Stitched and puckered like a goddamn feed sack."

"You going to change your mind, Dero?" said Dr. Smoaks. "You think you're going to change your mind now?"

"Put them up," said Mr. Mullins. "Put them back in your bag and just go on."

"You wanted it, and I'm doing it," said Dr. Smoaks.

Mr. Mullins still held his hand. He tightened his grip. "You move it, and I break it," he said. "You start to move it, and I break it right off."

They stood like that for a long time, reaching each other across the bed, and across the dry, white belly of the daughter. Across the long scar, stepped off with beads of dark blood inside the brighter red of the Merthiolate. Josey had folded her arms under her breasts, and she stood to one side, looking at them.

"It's going to cost you anyway," Dr. Smoaks said at last. "You wanted it, and I was set to do it. I would have done it, too. So you're going to pay for it."

"Put them in your bag and go," said Mullins.

"But it's going to cost you," said Dr. Smoaks.

"Yes," said Mr. Mullins. He let go of the hand. Dr. Smoaks tossed the scalpel lightly back onto the chair. "Bring them downstairs, Josey," he said. "Bring them downstairs and get me a cup of coffee." As he walked out of the room, he rolled his sleeves down. He didn't look back at Mr. Mullins.

Mr. Mullins lowered his open hand, placing it on his daughter's stomach. The red Merthiolate scar and the dark beeds of blood ran out from under his fingers. Under his palm, her skin was soft and dry. He removed his hand and wiped the blood on the leg of his pants.

Josey was collecting the things and putting them into the bag. "Give me the rag," he said to her. She handed him the rag from the basin.

"Get some soap on it," he said, handing it back to her.

She soaped it and handed it back.

Mr. Mullins took the soapy rag and rubbed it along the Merthiolate scar. The beads of blood disappeared, and the bright red of the mark faded a little. But it did not disappear. Her skin turned pink again under the scrubbing.

"It go away after a while," said Josey, looking down at him.

He looked up at her and nodded. She handed him the towel, and he gave her the rag. After he dried Annie, she helped him get her nightgown back down and pull up the covers. When she took the black bag and went downstairs, she left him sitting on the edge of the bed patting the covers over his daughter's stomach. He didn't look at her as she went out of the room.

When she got to the kitchen, Dr. Smoaks was sitting at the table. He had gotten his own coffee.

"Hardest case of rheumatic fever I ever diagnosed," he said, holding the cup in both hands as he sipped. "And rheumatic fever is always hard," he added.

Josey put the bag down on the end of the table and looked at him. She didn't say anything. When he finished, he rose, taking his black bag, and went to the door. Going out, he stopped, holding the screen open with his hand.

"Tell him that's going to be five dollars," he said. "Five dollars, whether I did it or not. Just for my time," he added. "I would have done it too," he said, not looking at her.

Josey watched him as he went out the door.

Annie took her confinement calmly, growing even more passive as the weeks went by. Mr. Mullins insisted first that she not go out of the house, and then that she not go out of the bedroom, for fear someone would see her. Neighbors' houses were not nearby, and the loblollies screened the house from all save the few who took it in mind to make a deliberate visit, so that keeping the secret was not so difficult after all. One or two delegations of women from the neighborhood came to call, being met once by Mr. Mullins when he was home, and then by Josey when he wasn't. Holding them there on the porch and explaining that Miss Annie was *poorly*, and that Dr. Smoaks wouldn't allow her to have any visitors, since what she had might be catching. The delegations were curious, but not persistent. They soon dropped away and didn't come back.

Josey saw to the house and fixed the meals.

After she was confined to her room, Annie sat for long hours in a chair pulled back from the window — Mr. Mullins wouldn't let her come too close even there, for fear she would show herself and let the secret get away — in an attitude of listening. Tracing the progress of the thing closed up inside her. Concentrated and intent on the augmentation going on inside herself, as if she were to be called on later to give an accounting for it, cell by cell.

Mr. Mullins did not try to break in on her. The night in the bedroom seemed to have cast the die for him, and he was now resigned to the fact of his daughter's condition, sin and all. But her air of listening and waiting quickened him to expectation himself, and his expectation increased as her term drew to a close. Perhaps that too came out of a remembrance of what he had gone through, with Mae, sixteen years ago.

"A week, maybe," said Dr. Smoaks. They sat again at the kitchen table, covered with the yellow oilcloth, Josey standing at the end of the table with her arms folded.

"She's not to have nothing," said Mr. Mullins. "No shot nor nothing to help the pain. This will be for her to learn her lesson."

Dr. Smoaks looked at him over the coffee cup. "She'll learn her lesson," he said, looking into the tilted cup. "Don't you worry about that."

"Not real hard," said Mr. Mullins. "Not real hard, so as to hurt her bad. But enough for her to remember it. Just so she will learn her lesson and remember it for a while."

"She'll remember," said Dr. Smoaks.

They wouldn't let him into the room. So he sat at the kitchen table with a cup of black coffee getting cold in front of him, his hands clasped in front of him on the table, the cup of coffee between his forearms getting cold with a film of oil on top.

Every so often Josey would come down into the kitchen to do something — get some more hot water, or some towels, or something, and they would look at each other, but without speaking.

Finally he heard the crying. A sharp cry once, then a couple of little ones. Then nothing. He never did hear Annie making any noise.

Josey came down into the kitchen and got some more water, cold water this time, and some more towels. They looked at each other hard as she turned from the sink to go back upstairs.

"She be all right," Josey said in a flat, low voice. She didn't look at him when she spoke. From the foot of the stairs she gave him a second long look. Then she went up to the bedroom.

In a few minutes Dr. Smoaks came down the steps. He came down them slowly, rolling down his sleeves, and walked over to the table and sat down across from Mr. Mullins.

"Coffee?" Mr. Mullins asked.

Dr. Smoaks looked up at him briefly, then back down at the table. He nodded.

Mr. Mullins got up and poured a cup of coffee at the stove. Then he put it down in front of Dr. Smoaks and went around and sat down across the table from him.

"Was it hard?" Mr. Mullins asked.

Dr. Smoaks looked up at him, then back at the table, "No," he said. "It wasn't hard. I didn't deliver it. Just caught it. It just dropped right out in my hand."

"I never did hear Annie," said Mr. Mullins.

"Annie's all right," said Dr. Smoaks. "I told you that. I told you Annie would be all right."

"I'm glad she's all right," said Mr. Mullins.

They both sipped their coffee.

"Dero," said Dr. Smoaks.

"Yes?" said Mr. Mullins. "Yes, what is it?"

Dr. Smoaks didn't speak for a minute. "It's a boy, Dero," he said, sipping his coffee. He put the cup down in the saucer carefully, looking into it. They sat for a while across the table.

"God damn it, Dero," Dr. Smoaks said. He swung himself sideways in the chair, looking out the screen door of the kitchen.

"God damn it, Dero . . . ," he said again, looking down toward the floor, ". . . it was a nigger."

Mr. Mullins looked at the side of his face across the table. "What?" he said.

Dr. Smoaks didn't look at him. He was looking out the screen door again. "I said it's a nigger," he said. "A fine, bouncing nigger baby," he said. "Annie gave birth to a fine, bouncing nigger baby," he repeated, ". . . a nigger baby boy."

Mr. Mullins looked at him across the table. His hands were stretched out in front of him limply, and his mouth was hanging open.

"What . . . ," he said, his jaw working slowly, ". . .what did you say . . . ?"

Josey came down the stairs and into the room. She stopped at the foot of the stairs and looked at the two men.

"She wants to know can she have something to drink," she said.

"What?" said Dr. Smoaks, looking at her.

"Miss Annie want to know can she have something to drink. She say she thirsty, and she want to have something to drink," she said. "Something cool."

"Get her a glass of water," said Dr. Smoaks. "She can have a glass of water." He was looking out the screen door again.

"Why'd you do it?" said Mr. Mullins, his voice almost too low to hear. "Couldn't you just dropped it or something?" he said. "Couldn't you just dropped it on the floor?"

"I didn't think to do it," said Dr. Smoaks. "I would have done it if I had thought to do it. But I was too surprised to think about it, I reckon," he said. "It was just that I had it in my hands, and then it was breathing on its own. And it started to holler, so I couldn't think what to do until it was too late. It was really hollering, and it was too late."

"What you mean, it was too late?" said Mr. Mullins.

Dr. Smoaks looked at him. "I mean it was *too late*," he said. He didn't explain.

"It ain't too late for me," said Mr. Mullins. He scraped back his chair and rose from the table.

Dr. Smoaks looked up at him across the table. "She ain't asleep," he said. "You said she wasn't to have nothing, so she ain't asleep. You're going to play hell getting it away from her."

Mr. Mullins stood in front of his chair.

"Anyway," said Dr. Smoaks, looking away again, "it ain't that easy. Even if you do get it away from her," he said. "It ain't that easy."

He rose, scraping back his chair. "Well," he said, "anyway, I'm through with it — finally."

"What?" said Mr. Mullins. "You said you was going to take care of it." He looked at Dr. Smoaks.

"I can't get rid of no nigger baby," he said.

"You said you was going to fix it up and take care of it," Mr. Mullins said.

"Not no nigger baby," said Dr. Smoaks. "I can't get rid of no nigger baby. See Josey," he said. "Maybe she'll get rid of it for you."

"I'll get rid of it," Mr. Mullins said, not looking at Josey.

"All right, if you can," said Dr. Smoaks. "You take care of it if you can. It ain't that easy. Not even a nigger baby is that easy."

He rose, taking his black bag in his hand and going to the door. He stood with the door held open a little, not looking back at Mr. Mullins.

"You owe me a dollar," he said, standing in the door. "My fee for delivering a nigger baby is one dollar," he said. "So you owe me one dollar."

He went out of the house, letting the door slam behind him.

He bowed the hickory stick between his hands, standing at the foot of the bed, watching Annie nurse the baby. She watched the baby, not looking at him.

"You going to give it up," he said. Bowing the stick out in front of him. "I don't mean you going to give it up next week," he said, his voice breaking into the darkness of the room. "Not next week, nor some other time," he said. "I mean you going to give it up *now*."

Annie watched the brown head against her breast. It made her breast look even whiter, with the pale blue veins just under the skin.

Mr. Mullins whipped the stick across the end of the bed. It sounded like a rifle going off in the still room. Annie flinched, but she didn't look at him.

"I mean *now*," he said, louder.

He struck the bed again. Not hitting anything, just the bed. He whipped the stick down again and again, the tempo increasing and the noise of the slaps getting louder. Saying, "Now . . . Now . . . Now!" And the stick hitting in between. Annie flinched every time the stick hit the bed. But she didn't look up at her father. The stick broke, and Mr. Mullins tried to whip the bed with the stump. It was too short, and he threw it against the wall.

"NOW!" he said.

"Let her finish with the baby." Josey spoke from the doorway of the bedroom. "She be through in a while," she said. "That be time enough."

He stood at the foot of the bed watching. His eyes held tight on the brown head against the blue-white of Annie's breast.

Josey spoke again from the doorway. "Whyn't you wait till she be sleep? She got to go to sleep sometime," she said.

Mr. Mullins paid no attention to her. "He's through," he said after a while. He came around to the side of the bed, keeping his eyes on the brown head as he moved. "He's through, ain't he?" he said, looking down as he stood by the side of the bed.

Annie didn't look at him. The baby didn't move. The nipple had come half out of his mouth, and his eyes were closed.

"You got to take him?" Annie's voice was low, and there was just a little quaver in it. She didn't look up at him.

"Yes," he said, "I got to take him now," he said.

He reached down and lifted him up. Annie's arms were limp outside the covers. She didn't move to cover her breast, and after he moved the baby away, Mr. Mullins stood looking down at the whiteness of his daughter's breast, with the nipple still moist and pink from the sucking, the veins pale blue just under the skin. He held the baby away, one hand under its head, and the other under its hips, looking down at her in the bed.

"He's too little," she said.

"Cover yourself," he said.

She drew the sheet over her breast, pulling it up to her chin. "He's too little," she said again.

"You got to give him up," he said, holding the baby away and looking down at her. "You got to give him up now, because you ain't going to want to do it no more tomorrow, nor the day after, nor any other time. Now is the best time," he said.

"Same as killing him," she said.

"It'll be on me," he said. "All of it'll be on me."

He continued to look down at her.

"You knowed you wasn't going to keep it anyway," he said. "Not if it had been like I thought, you wasn't going to keep it. And you sure as hell knowed you wasn't going to keep it like it is."

He started toward the door, still holding the baby away from him. Holding it in his hands so it wouldn't lie against him and touch him.

"Pa," she said from the bed. He turned, and she was looking at him now. "Pa," she said again, still looking at him. "His name is John Henry." After she said it, she looked away from him.

Mr. Mullins looked at her for a long minute, then shook his head slowly from side to side. "Jesus God," he said.

"Pa," she said, looking at him again. "Josey," she said, looking away. "Make him put the bunting on him, Josey. So he don't catch cold."

"Yes, child," said Josey from the doorway.

He walked out of the room and down the stairs, still holding the baby away in his hands to keep it from touching him.

It was getting lighter all the time, and still he hadn't made up his mind. He would have to make it up soon, though, since he had to get done with it and back to the house before it was good light.

The bank dropped off steeply in front of him. The black water undercut the bank, and little eddies floated by in an arc, reaching in toward the roots hanging down into the water. Mr. Mullins was sitting and looking down into the water, his back propped against a tree. Beside him the baby lay on the sack. The sack was spread out on the ground, but there was a bulge in the bottom of it where he had put the rocks. The baby fidgeted, but it didn't cry. Every now and then it would flinch its arm or its leg and screw its face up, but so far it hadn't cried. Mr. Mullins kept thinking that if it would only cry he could do it. And he got mad, since the baby wouldn't cry. He sat there leaning against the tree and getting madder all the time. Looking at the black water swirling past under the bank.

Mr. Mullins would look at the water, and then he would look at the baby beside him. Streaks of mist hung under the trees along the opposite bank. The water looked cold, but he knew it was warm. He had reached down and put his hand in it to see.

"Shit," he said finally, standing up. "Shit on it anyway."

"Out of the county," he said, handing the baby to Josey in the kitchen. It was full light now. He had taken a long time getting back, because he had to stay away from the cleared land for fear someone would see him. "That's all I give a good God damn about," he said. "Just make sure you get him out of McAfee County."

"Yes, suh," said Josey flatly, taking the baby from him and cradling it in her arms. "I see to it," she said.

He went to the cupboard and took out a Prince Albert tobacco can. "Here," he said, handing her the money. "Two dollars is all I can spare. You do it for the two dollars, you hear?"

Josey took the money without speaking, but she nodded her head.

"I ever see him again," he said, "and I'm going back to the river. I'm going to take him back to the river and do it," he said. "Wouldn't happen twice."

Josey nodded and turned to leave, the baby cradled in her arms. "And Josey," he said. She turned to him. "Better not nobody ever find out," he said. "Better not nobody ever find out, or I take you with me when I go back to the river."

She looked at him for a minute, then turned and went out the kitchen door.

"You better get back in that bed," he said. Annie stood at the foot of the stairs. He sat at the kitchen table, his forearms stretched out on the yellow-oilcloth top, his hands clasped together. He looked at her, then back at the table. "You get back in the bed, you hear?" he said. "You get back there and stay till you get your strength back. Then we see what we're going to do."

"He was too little," she said, looking at him from the foot of the stairs. "You wasn't even going to use the bunting till I said it," she said. "If you just could have waited a little bit."

He didn't look at her. "Won't you *please* get back in the bed, Annie?" he said. "We're going to have to talk about it later on. But won't you *please* get back in the bed right now?"

She looked at him from the foot of the stairs. Her bare feet were planted on the floor firmly, and with her hand she reached out, just barely touching the newel. Her lank hair was hanging down over her breasts, and she looked pale. Under her hair the milk was making two long, weeping stains down the front of her nightgown.

"His name is John Henry, Pa," she said, her voice low and level, from the bottom of the stairs. "I give him his name," she said, "and his name is John Henry."

He didn't look at her. "Won't you *please* get back in the goddamned bed?" he said. He put his head down on the edge of the table between his elbows. His voice was muffled and low. "Won't you please, Annie, get back in the goddamned bed?"

She looked at him a minute, then turned and walked slowly up the stairs. Leaving him resting on the shiny yellow table in the kitchen.

John Henry's Promise

Ashutter was clicking away inside Nettie's head, keeping time with the slap of the tires on the asphalt of the highway. Sixty-five . . . seventy . . . the toes of her bare right foot curling around the top of the gas pedal, jamming it down, making the yellow Pontiac stretch itself out and lay down on the highway. It was a good road car, heavy and steady. She liked to run it hard.

"Niggers," she said. "*God* damn. What are you going to do about niggers anyway?"

She had had to argue with Josey every step of the way. First about the coffin. Fifteen hundred dollars for mahogany.

"I don't know, Miss Nettie . . . ," said Josey, her voice getting whiny, making Nettie's hair prickle along the back of her neck.

"Shit on you, Josey." She hadn't said it. The shutter clicked open, black on an empty frame. "It's *my* goddamn money. What is it *you* don't know, anyway?"

She had gone ahead and gotten it just the same — mahogany, with a bronze plate and handles. Beckworth had made a special trip in to Savannah to bring it out in the hearse — not charging the fifty cents a mile. All Josey could do was shake her head and whine. "I don't know, Miss Nettie . . . I just don't know . . ."

"Niggers . . ."

She didn't see the speedometer. Curling the toes of her bare right foot over the top of the gas pedal, laying the yellow Pontiac down on U.S. 17 until she could almost feel it stretching itself out, streaking into Savannah through the pine flats and marsh. There were things floating around inside her head with the clicking. Scenes that would suddenly stop and come into focus like pictures in a frame.

The colors were bright blue and green — the muddy brown of the river and marsh — and the shiny blue and red of the crabs.

Nettie thirteen years old. Standing on the Altamahatchee River bridge, watching as the crane hauled the white Ford out of the marsh, with the water pouring down from the half open windows. Then moving along the rail closer to watch as they pried open the doors and pulled Maggie out of the car — Smoaks cursing and picking off the blueshell crabs with his hands, throwing them down onto the bridge and stomping them with his feet. The Ford had gone over into the water the night before. There wasn't much left of Maggie to claim, because of the blueshell crabs. Nettie had gotten sick watching Smoaks pulling them off.

Then they wouldn't let her bury Maggie in any of the white cemeteries, since the sixteenth part of nigger blood was too much.

"I be *God* damn if I'm going to put her out in a nigger graveyard," said Nettie.

So she and Josey took Maggie in to Savannah to have her cremated, and she went by herself to sprinkle the ashes into Famous Creek, down in the woods behind the house. Afterwards, she kept the urn to put on the mantelpiece in the front room, filled with a spray of sea oats.

The shutter clicked again, and she was seeing the trees and the moss of the cemetery. John Henry's mahogany coffin, with the dull-shining yellow of the bronze plate, spooling down into the open grave. Beckworth himself had been there to help with the fifteen-hundred-dollar coffin, his foot tapping the lever that started the spools to spinning as the coffin went sucking down between the chrome bars on the edges of the grave.

She had been hugging Josey and crying. Both of them crying. Watching the big red-brown box going away.

Then, later, she had had to argue with Josey all over again about the stone. After the funeral, after the red-brown box had sucked down into the black shaft of the grave with the mechanism whirring inside the chrome bars, after Beckworth had taken his equipment away — after it had all been over, she had remembered. There weren't any markers on the graves. Just homemade things that fell apart and got stepped on until the weeds and honeysuckle grew over them. She had remembered that later. And then she had had to argue about it.

"I don't know, Miss Nettie." Josey shaking her head.

"Shit." Not saying it. "What is it *you* don't know, Josey? It's *my* goddamn money. Mine for the coffin and mine for the stone."

Saying instead, "We owe him that, Josey. That much. I'll pay for it."

"I don't know, Miss Nettie. Folks might . . . I don't know . . ."

Thinking, "Folks will . . . John Henry? Yes, yes, you're goddamn right . . . Folks sure as shit will . . ."

"I'll buy it, Josey," she said. "Wouldn't nobody say nothing, because I'll be the one to buy it. Everybody knows about me and John Henry. It'll be all right."

"I don't know, Miss Nettie . . . I just don't know . . ."

"Shit . . . ," she thought, " . . . niggers . . ."

Too late Saturday when she thought about it after the funeral on Friday. She had to wait for Monday, with the stone getting bigger and bigger inside her head all day Sunday. "Gigantic . . . something gigantic," she was thinking. "It's going to be . . . oh, God damn . . . gigantic."

She put all the money she had into the barrel of the flashlight. Three battery-sized rolls. Twenties, mostly twenties. Two thousand, one hundred and eighty dollars. Then she jammed the flashlight under the front seat of the Pontiac and wedged it with rags.

The Oconee River bridge was a blur. Going over it at seventy miles an hour, the tires whining up at her from the metal plates of the center span. Mist hung blue-gray along the shore, rolling up under the branches of the trees. The river hardly seemed to be moving at all. There were great sick-looking patches of algae, lying green-yellow on the still surface.

It was beginning to get hot. Six-fifteen. The Negro men were starting to come up out of the woods to the highway. She passed two of them walking on the shoulder of the road. Their shacks were built back out of sight in the woods, at the ends of the two sandy tire tracks, parallel traces with stunted Bermuda grass plats in between, running off into the pines and Spanish bayonets. Now and then something like little settlements had crept up out of the woods to the highway. A compound of three or four houses, with hard, swept yards, a sagging cat's cradle of clothesline wires running back and forth from house to house, holding the settlement together. In the open spaces between the houses, the big black iron pot would be sitting on a pile of ashes.

The houses were unpainted, some covered with brick-patterned tar paper, leaning and collapsing off the brick and piled stone piers, with dark open rectangles where the doors should have been and floursack curtains waving out of the open windows. Traces of blue breakfast smoke were rising out of the chimneys.

In one of the settlements — three houses set close together, two breasting the highway up close, the third set farther back between them — there was a woman tending a fire at the pot, stuffing pieces of wood under it, turning her face away from the heat of the fire. On the porch of the middle house was a mound of faded clothing.

There were children in the yard — small, toddling age, a few older — stirring up swirls of dust as they chased each other around among the houses. A boy toddled toward the pot with the fire under it. The woman rammed the fire with a piece of yellow kindling, her head turned toward the highway, shielding her face from the heat of the fire with her hand — not seeing the child. He must have been about two or three years old. His shirt was too big for him — red and white checkered, flapping under the blue-black shine of his morning-washed face.

Nettie caught him out of the corner of her eye. He couldn't have been closer than fifteen feet to the pot. There wasn't any danger. The woman would see him, or he would feel the heat of the fire and would veer off himself before he got too close.

The shutter clicked, framing the picture there inside her head — checkered shirt and the black iron pot with the fire going underneath, pink flame licks beginning to curl up the sides, the woman with her face turned away, her hand up, yellow palm outward, shielding her face.

Nettie hit the brake, and the car veered sharply, catching the right-front tire in the rut formed by the edge of the asphalt on the shoulder of the road. She whipped the wheel back to the left to break the wheel out and onto the road, her right hip jammed against the back of the seat, locking her leg on the brake. The car hopped, making a long, looping skid. It came to rest in the left-hand lane, facing back toward McAfee County.

The shutter closed — black — and the picture was gone again.

Over the hood of the car she saw the boy stop and look at her; then he put his hand into his mouth and ran away toward the house, going in and under the front steps standing up. The woman tending the fire was standing beside the pot looking at her, the stick of yellow wood in her hand held slightly away from her body in a limp gesture.

Nettie rested her head on the steering wheel for a minute; then she looked up to see that the Negro woman had started walking toward her. There was no trace of the boy. She ground the gears into reverse and backed off onto the shoulder, turning the car at right angles to the highway. Without looking to see if the highway was clear, she slapped the car into low and gunned the engine, leaping onto the road and heading for Savannah again. When she looked into the rearview mirror to see where the woman was, she saw her standing on the shoulder, still holding the piece of wood in the dainty way.

Nettie watched her in the mirror for a long time as she pressed her bare foot down on the gas pedal.

Josey jammed the piece of wood under the pot, shielding her face with her hand. Then she stood up and walked away, going to get the clothes off the back porch. The water in the pot bubbled and steamed, the steam mixing with the blue smoke from the fire.

"Look out, John Henry!" Nettie was only four, but a year older than the boy. She was bossy, and she treated him as if he were her child, ordering him around and laying hands on him because she had made him her care. There were just the two of them to roam around the yard together, and looking after him gave her something to do. He didn't like it.

She rushed over to stop him, making a big show of it. In trying to help him, she knocked him down, and he started to cry.

"Nettie help you," said Josey. "You ain't going to cry, and Nettie trying to help you? Hush up that crying, John Henry."

Nettie forced herself onto him, straddling him and trying to help as he was getting up, but getting in the way and keeping him from doing it. He bawled, wrestling around in the dirt, getting his checkered shirt dirty, the shirt riding up and exposing the shiny black swell of his belly. He fought to pull it down, covering himself.

"Hush up, John Henry," said Josey. "Hush up that bawling. Don't no manchild cry like that." She came over and helped Nettie, getting her out of the way so John Henry could get up. He ran off toward the porch, with Nettie following along with him, trying to put her arm around his shoulder to comfort him.

"Fire," she said. "Burn up John Henry."

When she said that, John Henry bawled louder than ever, twisting and trying to get away from her. She hugged him harder, mothering him anyway.

"Nettie," said Josey, "come here, Nettie. You help me put in these here clothes."

The girl looked at her, her arm still around the boy, holding him back, the boy twisting to get away.

"Come on now, Nettie," said Josey. "You be a good girl and help me with these here clothes."

She looked at Josey. "Nigger job," she said. "That there's a nigger job."

Josey looked at her. "Come on now, Nettie," she said. "Don't you talk to Josey thataway. I going to tell you mama about how you was talking to Josey."

"That there's a nigger job," she said. She kept her arm around John Henry's shoulder. "I'm taking care of John Henry."

"I be going to tell you mama on you," said Josey. "What you said." She started toward the back porch of the house.

Nettie took her arm away from John Henry's shoulder and gave Josey's back a hard look. "Nigger job, Josey," she said, yelling.

Josey kept walking toward the house, not looking at her.

Nettie dropped her arm and called. "Josey." Josey kept walking toward the house. "I'm coming, Josey," she said, her voice going up. "Don't tell Mama." John Henry started to run away toward the porch steps of the shack. Nettie reached out and gave him a slap on the back of the head. "Bad boy," she said. John Henry gave a loud bawl. Josey stopped and turned toward her.

"I'm coming, Josey," she said. "I don't care. I don't care when John Henry burn up in the fire."

"You be a sweet girl, Nettie," said Josey. "You be a sweet girl and help me with them clothes."

"I be sweet," said Nettie.

"And, Nettie," said Josey.

"Yes," said Nettie.

"Don't you say 'nigger.'"

"Yes," said Nettie.

" 'Nigger' is a hard word, Nettie," said Josey. "Don't you never say that word no more. You hear?"

"Yes, Josey," said Nettie. "Never no more." She walked slowly toward the pot as the woman came back with the clothes.

"Niggerniggerniggerniggernigger . . ." she whispered.

"You be a sweet girl, Nettie," said Josey.

"I be sweet," she said.

The Pontiac sped down the highway, the yellow-white-yellow stripes of the centerline snaking in and out under the left fender.

A boot in the right-front tire clicked on the asphalt, the whirring clicks of the boot working with the clicks of the shutter inside her head, framing pictures. . . .

Playing at Famous Creek that ran into the Dorchester Swamp, down in the woods behind the house. Nettie eleven. John Henry ten.

She had the story about Cleopatra. She had gotten onto it in the tent show. Seven days of double features — Charlie Chan seven times, Charles Starrett and Lash LaRue five times, building to the climax of the last two nights, *Cleopatra* and *The Sign of the Cross* by Cecil B. De Mille. *The Sign of the Cross* playing on Sunday night by special permission.

That summer they played Cleopatra.

"We got to have us a barge," said Nettie. "You reckon you could build us a barge, John Henry?"

"What kind?"

"Cleopatra had her a barge."

"Would something like a raft be a barge?" he said. He was getting taller than she was now. Beginning to fill out with muscles that weren't little boy looking anymore. He could swing an ax and cut kindling as well as Josey could. Next winter he would start splitting the logs for the fireplace.

"Something like," said Nettie. "You could make it fancy?"

"We could fix it up some," he said.

"I'll draw you a picture," she said.

"Not real fancy," he said. "Some."

He made the raft for her, trimming the logs so the front end came to a point. Then she wanted a divan on it, so he made a border of logs and they filled it up with moss and covered it with a quilt. He made a roof for it out of bamboo; and they covered that with a sheet.

Nettie had him cut a palm frond for himself to fan her with, and he used a long bamboo pole to push the barge around in the creek. They spent the first week just getting ready to play Cleopatra. Nettie had to collect some things for herself — earrings and bracelets and necklaces. Then she had to make herself a crown and paint it out of a bottle of gold paint she got at the ten-cent store in Kose. When she had finished with her own costume, she worked up one for John Henry.

"These go on your arms — up here," she said. She handed him bracelets made of strips cut out of tin cans and painted gold.

"What for?" he said.

"Because that's what you wear," she said.

"Oh," he said. "It ain't going to do much good wearing them up there."

"Well," she said, "all I know is what I seen in the picture show."

"Why you reckon I got to wear them?" he said. "It ain't going to do no good wearing them way up there."

"I don't know," she said. "That's the way they showed it. You're going to be the eunuch. Eunuchs always wears them gold bracelets on their arms."

"I see," said John Henry. "Does the eunuchs wear beads?"

"No," she said. "I'm the one wears the beads."

"Oh," said John Henry. "What else does the eunuchs wear?"

"What?" said Nettie.

"What else does the eunuchs wear to push the barge around?"

"Well," she said. She hesitated. "You're going to wear you a piece of white cloth out of a sheet," she said. "I'll show you." She drew him a picture of a big black man in a turban and a white loincloth like a diaper. "It's pure white, John Henry," she said.

"That's two pieces," he said.

"What?" said Nettie.

"One on my head, and the . . . other one."

Nettie looked at the picture. "Yes," she said. "I forgot. Two pieces."

"What about my overalls?" he said.

She looked at him. "You ain't going to wear no overalls," she said.

He looked at the picture. "Just that there little bitty thing is all?"

"Two pieces," she said.

"I need to wear my overalls too," he said.

"That'd spoil it," she said. "Didn't no eunuch wear no overalls."

He looked at her a minute. "I ain't going to be no eunuch," he said.

"I ain't never heard nothing about no eunuch that he was wearing overalls," she said. "I ain't never heard that in my life, John Henry," she said. "We're talking about Egypt. Wasn't no overalls in Egypt. No such of a thing."

He didn't say anything. "What if somebody is going to see us?" he said.

"You got the cloth on," she said. "There ain't nothing to that. Wouldn't nothing show."

"It ain't like overalls," he said. "I wouldn't want nobody to see me."

"Ain't nothing going to show," she said.

"You ain't seeing what it is I'm trying to tell you," he said. "I better wear my overalls."

She looked at him. "We can't play Cleopatra then," she said. "I ain't going to do it half-assed."

"I done made the barge," he said.

"Too bad," she said.

"Well," he said.

"It's pure white," she said. "You going to look good in it."

John Henry didn't say anything.

"You ain't seen what it is I'll be going to wear," she said. "I gone to lots of trouble."

He looked at her. "What were you going to wear?" he said.

"Beads," she said.

"I know," he said. "What else?"

"Hardly nothing," she said.

"Maybe we ought not be playing Cleopatra," he said, "What else you going to wear?"

"Hardly nothing except the beads," she said. "A crown. It's hard to tell about it. You'd have to see it."

"I don't know," he said.

"We got to play it like it was," she said. "Or I ain't going to play it at all."

"You going to wear beads?" he said.

"Lots of beads," she said. "We're going to play 'Going to Meet Mark Anthony.' That's the way she done it. Mostly beads — and the crown."

"Who's Mark Anthony?" said John Henry.

"He's the one she went to meet," she said. "He couldn't hardly believe it."

"I reckon not," said John Henry. "Was he a eunuch?"

"No," said Nettie. "He was a Roman."

"What did he wear?"

"Mark Anthony wore him a uniform. He had on a helmet."

"How come I couldn't be the Mark Anthony?" he said. "A helmet sounds better than the eunuch suit. I look good in a helmet."

"We got to playlike for Mark Anthony," she said.

"Oh," said John Henry. "How come it was I couldn't be the Mark Anthony?"

"I'm trying to tell you," said Nettie. "He was a Roman. Mark Anthony was a Roman general."

"Oh," said John Henry.

"You couldn't be Mark Anthony," she said. "You got to be the eunuch."

"Oh," he said. "I couldn't be Mark Anthony?"

"A Roman is like a white man, John Henry," she said.

"Oh," he said.

"An eunuch is a Egyptian," she said. "They stand around and wear a pure white cloth and wave a fan over me and push my barge around. The eunuch is more important than Mark Anthony, really," she said.

"Yes," said John Henry.

"No," said Nettie. "I mean it. We can playlike for Mark Anthony, but I got to have me a real eunuch to push the barge around and fan me with the palm leaf."

"A eunuch is a colored man?" said John Henry.

"A *Egyptian* colored man," said Nettie.

"Yes," said John Henry. "A eunuch couldn't wear no helmet," he said.

"That's what the Roman generals wears," she said.

"Yes," he said.

John Henry pushed the barge. Sometimes he fanned her with the palm leaf. There wasn't much to her costume — the bottom piece from her bathing suit, a hollow rubber ball cut in half and the halves painted gold, with a lot of beads and bracelets.

They would meet down at Famous Creek, going off from the house separate ways. The game itself caused them to do that, and the costumes, though pushing the barge around was all there was to it.

The third week they had been playing Cleopatra John Henry came down and found Nettie waiting for him on the barge. She was lying on her side on the divan, her head propped up with an elbow.

He looked at her, then he looked around to see if anyone might be coming out of the woods down where they were.

"Put your clothes back on," he said. "What if somebody was to come around down here and seen us? These here little white pants is bad enough."

"*That's* the way to catch you a Roman," she said. "They couldn't put it in the picture show."

"I reckon not," he said, turning away from her, not looking. "That's the way to get me kilt," he said. "Put your clothes back on. It's bad enough anyway. Please, Miss Nettie."

She rolled over onto her stomach, pouting. There weren't many beads in the back. John Henry looked down at her lying on the divan. From the back Nettie was beginning to look like a woman.

"We got to play something else," she said, not looking up at him. "I need me a real Mark Anthony. This here has done played out."

"I ain't going to stay around you like that," he said, "I got to get on back to the house and get my overalls on."

"Ain't nothing going to happen to you, John Henry," she said. She got up and put on her bathing-suit bottom and the rubber-ball halves. "A eunuch just ain't enough. We got to get us a Mark Anthony too."

She brought Vincent Demott, a thirteen-year-old who lived down the road, getting him to be the Mark Anthony. There wasn't time to make a real costume, so she got him to wrap a towel around his waist, and he used a gold-painted football helmet and a sword she had John Henry make for him.

They played "Going to Meet Mark Anthony" for a while, and then Vincent called John Henry a nigger instead of a eunuch, and they started to wrestle. But Vincent was too much older and bigger, and Nettie helped him so they could hold John Henry down and take off his loincloth.

"They ain't much of it," Vincent said when they had gotten the loincloth off.

"He ain't but ten," said Nettie.

"He's a nigger, though," said Vincent. "I'd of thought a nigger had a bigger one than that."

"Let him up, Vincent," said Nettie.

Vincent looked at her; then he reached across and grabbed one of the rubber-ball halves and yanked. Both of them came off. A necklace broke, and beads poured down on John Henry's chest.

"Look out," said Nettie, "you broke my beads."

"Maybe I would be going to break something else," said Vincent.

Nettie looked at him. "Don't break my beads," she said. She stood up and took off the bathing-suit bottom and the beads; then she ran into the water of the creek. Vincent chased her, and they came out on the opposite bank and ran into the bushes. John Henry put on his loincloth and sat on the bank to wait for them. While he was waiting, he picked up Nettie's beads. After about a half an hour, Nettie came out by herself, wading across the creek.

She and John Henry talked it over sitting on the bank.

"You was gone pretty long," he said.

"Yes," she said.

"Just you and Vincent."

"Yes," she said. "I didn't mean to help Vincent against you."

"I hope you had yourself a good time. You and Vincent," he said. "It took you long enough."

"You ain't old enough," she said. "Vincent is thirteen. I told you I was sorry."

"You don't think so?" he said.

"I'll tell you about it sometime," she said. "You wouldn't understand nohow. You ain't old enough."

"I ain't?" he said. "You had to help Vincent. Just a Roman was all you needed. You couldn't use no eunuch."

"We wasn't playing Cleopatra," she said.

"I know you wasn't," he said. "You got to have you a eunuch for that."

"Yes," she said.

"You better put your clothes on," he said. "Vincent done gone home now."

She put on the bathing suit and the rubber-ball halves.

"Here," said John Henry. He held out his hand to her.

"What?" she said.

"I picked up your beads for you while you was over there with Vincent."

She took them from him, pouring them back and forth from one hand to the other. "I let Vincent pee a baby in me," she said.

John Henry looked at her. "What did you say?" he said.

"That's the way you do it," said Nettie. "The boy takes his, and he pees a baby inside you."

"Yes," said John Henry.

"It hurts some," she said.

John Henry looked down at himself. The loincloth was dirty where she and Vincent had wrestled him around on the bank pulling it off. He looked back at Nettie. "He pees?" he said.

Nettie nodded her head. "Yes," she said. "That's the way to make a baby."

"Pees?" said John Henry.

"Vincent peed a baby in me," she said. "I told you."

"Well," said John Henry, "what is Maggie going to say?"

"Maggie ain't going to find out about it," she said. "I ain't old enough to really have a baby. That's the way you do it."

"Did it hurt Vincent?" he asked.

"No," she said. "It didn't seem to hurt him none."

For a while John Henry didn't say anything. "Would you let me?" he said.

Nettie looked at him. Then she looked away. "You ain't old enough," she said.

"I can pee," he said.

"That ain't all there is to it," she said. "You ain't old enough anyway."

"Maybe you could let me try and see if I was old enough," he said.

She shook her head. "It wouldn't be right," she said.

"I known you better than Vincent," he said. "How come it's all right for him and it ain't all right for me?"

"That ain't it," she said. "I know Vincent don't know me the way you do. But it wouldn't be right. I told you, you wasn't old enough."

"I'm old enough to pee," he said.

"That ain't it," she said.

"I pushed your barge around," he said. "I pushed your barge around and fanned you with the fan. I done all that. Let me do it, Nettie," he said.

She was still sifting the beads from one hand to the other. She didn't look at him. "I couldn't let you," she said. "I couldn't let you pee no nigger baby in me, John Henry."

"Oh," he said.

"It wouldn't be right. You see that, don't you?"

"I hadn't thought," he said.

"Maybe we can find you a colored girl so you could pee a baby in her."

"Yes," he said.

"I could help you find one."

"Yes," he said.

"Come on," she said. "Get the palm leaf and fan me. We got to play Cleopatra some more."

John Henry got the palm leaf.

"Don't feel bad," said Nettie. "You're a good eunuch, John Henry."

"Thank you," he said.

"The Romans got to be the Eye-talians," she said. "They ain't much no more."

"Yes," he said.

They didn't play Cleopatra anymore after that. Nettie got to meeting Vincent down at the creek on a regular basis, and then he brought along some friends. She never did help John Henry find himself the colored girl.

That was their last summer of playacting. Nettie grew up the next winter and began keeping company with boys out in the open. Wearing lipstick and high-heel shoes. Maggie didn't care for it, but she wasn't able to do anything about it. Then John Henry went to work for Case Deering, so he and Nettie became just good friends.

In the spring of 1954, just before he was eighteen, John Henry got arrested on suspicion of stealing forty-nine dollars from the Harold Brown Esso Station in Kose. After the trial, he took his turn on the county road gang. His sentence was for two years. While he was doing his time, Nettie would come down with Josey occasionally and bring him things to eat. Once she knitted him a white wool cock warmer with a red head, but he hid it from the other boys on the gang because he was afraid the guards would find out. Most of the time it was too hot to wear it, and even in cold weather the wool tickled and made him itch.

Two years; most of his friends were doing time too. It kept him out of the draft. When they let him go in June of 1956, Nettie and Josey came down to meet him at the gate. Nettie drove him home in her new Pontiac.

At the house Nettie got him aside and told him of her plan. She had been thinking it over and had decided that she owed it to him one way or another. She had never helped him find the colored girl like she promised — and she always tried to keep her promises. That time was past now, but she had thought of something better.

"What picture show you seen that at?" he said, after she explained it to him.

"I got it all fixed." she said. "You got to go through with it. I done it for you mostly, anyway."

"I couldn't do nothing like that, Nettie," he said. "I couldn't go through with it nohow. Somebody would find out pretty soon."

"I tell you, I got it all set up," she said. "You got to go through with it. How many times you reckon a colored boy is going to get him a chance like that?"

"I couldn't go through with it," he said. "You better go see you another picture show. I just couldn't go through with it."

"Ain't a jigaboo in McAfee County wouldn't give his right ball for a chance like that," she said. "It's all set up."

"You going to have to set it down," he said. "I couldn't go through with it."

"No?" she said.

"No," he said.

"Let me explain it to you," she said.

"You done explained it to me already," he said.

"I been working on it all spring," she said.

After she showed him the costumes, explaining it over twice, he said, "What am I going to do when I couldn't go through with it?"

"I got it all figured out," she said. "You're going to wear this. I had Fred vulcanize it out of a inner tube down at Kasher's. He sure as hell couldn't figure it out. I told him it was for a horse I was going to buy. He looked at me funny, but he let it go. You strap it on. If you get buck fever and can't get up yourself, you can use it instead. If it's all right, you can pull it to the side and go ahead anyway. It's the idea that's important."

"What idea?" he said.

"Fixing you up," she said.

John Henry looked at the black tube in his hand. "Ain't that going to hurt them?" he said.

"They'll know they been screwed," she said.

"You going to get me killed, Nettie," he said.

"I'm going to get you a white piece of ass," she said. "Two pieces. What kind of nigger are you going to be to turn down two pieces of white ass? I been working on it all spring. You never did appreciate nothing I done for you, John Henry."

"It ain't going to be like you think," he said. "Why don't you take that thing and use it on them yourself?"

"I told you," she said. "It's the idea of it. You got to be the one."

He looked at the black tube in his hand. "Where you see a picture show like that anyway?"

"It's all set up now," she said. "You can't back out."

He didn't answer.

She got him to carry the black iron pot down into the woods at the place she had set up. Then she got the costumes and the white bantam rooster and took those down herself. At sundown she and John Henry went together and got the fire started under the pot so the water would be boiling when the girls got there. They put in some big pieces of moss to make it look better when the water started to boil. Then Nettie put in some mint and sage and other spices she had brought with her, and a packet of red Rit dye.

"I got them so worked up they couldn't hardly wait for you to get off the gang," she said. "They're stupid, but they're white. White every way there is. I was being careful about that. You ain't going to have that many chances. Not for two, you ain't."

"I ain't sure I can go through with it, Nettie," he said. "Even with this here rubber thing." He held the tube in his hand.

"Stuff it with moss," she said. "It looks like it's ninety years old."

"It ain't that easy for a man," he said.

"It'll be all right," she said. "It's the idea of it, anyway. That rubber doohickey is going to let you bring it off."

They got into their costumes. Long black robes that Nettie had gotten up for them. Just before St. Patrick's Day she had found a shamrock-green top hat — they were selling them in stacks in the ten-cent stores in Savannah. John Henry was wearing the hat in addition to the robe.

"How come a green one?" he said.

"They didn't have nothing else," she said.

"I don't like it," he said.

"I couldn't get nothing else," she said. "That's all they had."

"I don't mean the hat," he said. "I mean all of it."

"You look fine," she said. "You're a fine-looking Lord Redwine."

He didn't say anything, trying to get the hat adjusted on his head.

"That's your name to do it with," she said. "You'll be Lord Redwine."

"Lord Redwine?" he said.

"Yes," she said. "Can you remember?"

"How does the hat look?" he said.

"Fine," she said.

"Ain't it too small?" he said.

"It looks just fine," she said.

"I better wear my pants," he said.

"You ain't going to have time to take them off," she said.

"It don't feel right without my pants," he said.

"You can hold the cloak to in the front," she said. "It would take you too much time to get the pants off."

"You got it all figured out, ain't you, Nettie?" he said.

"I been working on it three months," she said. She looked at him steadily. "I'm going to take care of you, John Henry," she said. "I promised myself. I ain't going to run out on you. I keep my promises."

"Yes," he said.

She gave him instructions about the ceremony, telling him where he was to stand, the way he was going to fold his arms and hold his head up, not looking. And when he was to raise up his arms and throw back the robe. She made him walk through the motions twice. Except for throwing back the robe.

The sun was down and the pot was at a hard, rolling boil when the girls arrived. Over their arms they carried the white robes that Nettie had instructed them to make. John Henry sat on a stump before the fire, his arms folded, not speaking, the way Nettie had told him.

"You can go over there to get dressed," said Nettie, pointing to the big oak tree. The girls looked at John Henry without speaking.

"Get your robes on," said Nettie.

They went behind the tree. Nettie and John Henry could hear Jackie talking.

After a while they came out from behind the tree in their robes. John Henry cut his eyes toward them once; then he stared into the fire under the big clothes pot. Nettie arranged them facing each other across the boiling pot, standing in front of John Henry. Their faces and the robes were orange-red in the firelight.

"Now, you all got to do what I say," she said. She stood on the far side of the kettle, facing John Henry. "For this ceremony, we're going to change names. That there" — she pointed to John Henry — "he's Lord Redwine, Prince of the Outer Darkness." The girls looked at John Henry. He sat with his arms folded, not saying anything.

"John Henry?" said Jackie.

"Lord Redwine," said Nettie.

"Yes," said Jackie.

"I" — Nettie gestured to herself, making the black cape billow and swirl — "I am Sheena, Queen of the Night."

"Sheena is Queen of the Jungle," said Jackie.

"I'm giving the names," said Nettie. "You ain't supposed to talk."

"Did you get this out of a *funny* book?" said Jackie.

"There ain't going to be nothing funny about this," said Nettie. "You'll be seeing about that. Don't you say nothing else."

She waited for a minute to make sure that they were paying attention to her. Then she gestured again. "You" — she pointed to Annie — "you're going to be Nefertiti, Goddess of Virtue." Annie nodded solemnly.

"And you" — she gestured to Jackie — "will be Hatshepsut, Goddess of Virtue too."

"Hot-shit-what?" said Jackie.

"Hot SHEP . . . Hot SHEP . . . ," said Nettie. "Hatshep*sut*. You going to keep this up?"

"Suit," said Jackie.

Nettie looked at her sharply.

"I ain't never heard of Hatshepsut," said Jackie. "How come I couldn't be Nefertiti?"

"I'm going to call the whole thing off if you don't shut your mouth," said Nettie. "I looked for them names all last spring. Hatshepsut is plenty good. Too good for you."

"I heard of Nefertiti once," said Jackie. "How come I ain't never heard of Hatshepsut?"

"Lots of people never heard of Nefertiti," said Nettie.

"I heard of Nefertiti," said Jackie.

Nettie looked at her for a long time without speaking.

"Hot-shit . . . ," said Jackie, ". . . suit."

For a while nobody said anything.

Nettie went on, talking to Annie, "First I got to rub you with oil and spices," she said. "Hold up your gowns."

The girls obeyed.

"Hold it up dainty, Hatshepsut," she said. "Not like you was going to take a crap."

She went to Jackie first. "Hatshepsut, I put this oil on you in the name of the Powers of Outer Darkness. Hocus . . . pocus . . . diamond ocus." She poured oil on Jackie's head, then massaged her body with it. Jackie squirmed.

"Tickles," she said.

"Hold still," said Nettie.

"My daddy'd shit a brick," said Jackie. "Hot shit."

"Hold still," said Nettie.

"Suit," said Jackie.

"I ain't going to tell you again," said Nettie.

Then she rubbed Annie with oil.

"Now," she said, throwing away the oil bottle, "you got to light candles and make your oath to the Dark One."

Jackie looked at John Henry. "He sure is," she said. "Black as the ace of spades. He ain't Lord Redwine. He's Lord *Blackwine*."

"You going to be sorry when I turn him loose on you," said Nettie.

"He is," said Jackie. "How long before you're going to turn him loose? It ain't been nothing to it up to now. I didn't know you was going to have so much ceremony."

"Shut your mouth," said Nettie.

"I'm getting tired," said Jackie. "I want to *do* something."

"Repeat after me," said Nettie.

"How am I going to repeat with my mouth shut?" said Jackie.

"Figure it out," said Nettie. "You're smart enough to hear about Nefertiti, you're smart enough to figure it out."

The girls stood holding candles in both hands. "I ain't never heard of Hatshepsut," said Jackie.

"Repeat after me," said Nettie. She hesitated a moment, looking at them. 'Flesh and blood, muscle and bone, body and soul, heart and hand and all I am, I give to the Prince of Outer Darkness. Lord Redwine, to thee.' Then you bow down."

The girls repeated.

"Now we got to sacrifice the rooster," she said.

"Jesus," said Jackie, "couldn't we skip the rooster?"

Nettie went and got it, holding it by its wings to keep it from flapping. She gave the butcher knife to John Henry, then held the bird's neck out so he could cut it. "To Lord Redwine," she said, bowing her head. John Henry sliced it neatly, and the head came off, Nettie spreading her arms wide, then holding up her hands, letting the blood run down her arm.

"Now you got to anoint the virgins," she said, speaking to John Henry. "On your knees," she said, speaking to the girls.

"You getting ready to turn him loose?" said Jackie.

"On your knees," said Nettie.

"He going to put the chicken blood on us?" said Jackie.

"More ways than one," said Nettie. "More ways than one."

"You're pretty strong on rubbing, ain't you?" said Jackie. "Got to be the chicken blood, I reckon?"

"Just get down on your knees and keep your mouth shut," said Nettie. "We're just about through getting ready."

"What about the candles?" said Jackie.

"Keep hold of the candles," said Nettie.

They knelt down.

"Hands and knees," said Nettie. "Facing each other." She threw their robes up over their heads. Then she helped John Henry, motioning him what he was supposed to do, and he smeared the girls with blood from the rooster.

"Lord Redwine?" said Jackie, her voice muffled by the robe. John Henry didn't say anything. "It's getting better," she said. "You got a nice touch."

"Just a minute now," said Nettie. "You going to be sick, Annie?"

"I'll be all right," said Annie.

"You let me know if you feel like you're to be sick, you hear?"

She waited a few minutes.

"Well?" said Jackie, looking back over her shoulder.

"Just a minute," said Nettie.

"Turn him loose," said Jackie. "We done had enough hocus pocus. I'm done wore out and rubbed out too. Turn that black man loose and let's get on with it."

"Now we're ready," she said.

"Hot shit," said Jackie.

She blindfolded them and made them lie down on their backs, head to head.

"Can you do it?" she said to John Henry, whispering.

"I think so," he said. "They going to stay blindfold?"

"Yes," she said. "Rub them some more with the blood if it'll help."

"I'd rather rub them with the oil," he said.

"Oil's gone," she said.

"It'll be all right," he said, "if they's going to be blindfold."

"What you whispering about?" said Jackie. "Stop that whispering and turn him loose."

"Jackie first," said Nettie.

"Yes," said John Henry. "You can go now," he said, speaking to Nettie.

Nettie looked at him. "What?" she said.

"I be all right," he said. "You can go on. 'Bout a half-hour. Maybe forty-five minutes."

Nettie looked at him. "I set it up," she said.

"Yes," he said. "Much obliged. I couldn't never done it by myself."

"Yes," she said. She made no motion to leave.

"Better make it forty-five minutes." he said.

"I set it *up*, John Henry," she said.

John Henry stood looking at her. His skin gleamed orange in the firelight. "What you mean?" he said.

"Get on with it," she said.

"You wasn't going away?" he said.

"I set it up," she said.

"*You* ain't blindfold," he said.

"Wouldn't none of this happen, except I set it up," she said. "I had to work on it all spring. I worked on it like a dog."

"You mean you going to *watch?*" he said.

"Not you," she said. "Them."

"You going to close one eye?" he said. "What you mean *them?*"

She didn't answer.

"I couldn't figure that," he said. "What kind of man you think I am, taking them women and you standing around watching?"

"It ain't *you*," she said. "It's *them*."

"I'll have to tell you about it later," he said.

"I known you all my life, John Henry," she said.

"Jesus Christ, Nettie," he said. They had been whispering, but John Henry's voice was beginning to rise. "You got to go off and leave it to me. You got to leave this to me."

"Good God Almighty," Jackie said, "it ain't going to take this long to get me into heaven. What the hell part of a ceremony is this?"

"Put that blindfold down," said Nettie.

"You think I'm some kind of a prize bull that you got to make sure about the bloodlines?" said John Henry.

"I told you," she said. *"They's* the important ones."

"You got to go," he said. "You got to go off and leave me."

Nettie looked at him. She made no move to leave.

"I might have knowed," he said. He reached inside the black robe. "Here," he said. He handed her the rubber tube. "You going to have to do it yourself. Then you can be sure."

"What?" said Jackie. "What did you say?"

Nettie looked at it without speaking. John Henry dropped it onto the ground. "Lord Redwine is through," he said. "Go get your clothes on," he said, speaking to the girls.

Jackie sat up, pulling the blindfold away from her eyes, "Jesus Christ," she said. "You mean you're calling it off? Now? After you done rubbed the chicken blood on me?"

"Put that blindfold back on," said Nettie.

"Why don't you go off and leave us alone anyway?" said Jackie "You ain't doing nothing but holding things up."

"Ain't Lord Redwine," said John Henry. "You wouldn't want to do it with John Henry Greene."

"I knowed it was you John Henry," said Jackie. "I knowed it was you all along."

"Get back down," said Nettie. "I'll leave you alone. You ain't going to walk out on me?"

"I got to get my pants on," said John Henry. "I told you it wasn't going to be the way you thought."

"I worked on them three months," she said. "You ain't going to get buck fever and walk out on me now?"

"You girls get your clothes and go home," he said. "It wasn't what you thought."

"It sure as hell wasn't," said Jackie, getting up.

"Stay where you are," said Nettie. "John Henry . . ."

"You going to set it up again," he said. "Work on it some more. Next time you hang that thing between your legs and do it yourself so you can be sure. It's a black one too."

"You ain't walking out?" she said.

"I need to get my pants," he said.

"That's all she wrote," said Jackie. "I wouldn't care if he had to carry it around in a wheelbarrow. It just ain't worth it. Come on, Annie, let's you and me get us a bath."

"I ain't going to let you walk out," said Nettie.

"You ain't going to do nothing else," he said. He turned to the fire, put his foot against the pot, and shoved it over. The red water and moss splashed onto the ground with a hissing noise. The moss looked like a possum after the cars have been running over it on the highway for two days. "This here ceremony is done over," he said. "No more Redwine."

"John Henry . . . ," said Nettie.

"Stay away," he said. "You stay away from me. I ain't your boy no more."

She looked at him across what was left of the fire.

"This here is John Henry Greene," he said, speaking to the girls. "This ain't Lord Redwine, this is John Henry Greene. I'm going to tell you. Tuesday night. I be down to this very spot on Tuesday night," He looked at Nettie. "By myself," he said. "You ain't swore nothing to John Henry Greene."

"John Henry," said Nettie.

He walked away into the dark.

Jackie watched him across the fire as he walked away. "That's *some* nigger," she said.

Nettie was sitting on the steps waiting for him when he came into the yard. "John Henry," she said.

"Yes," he said.

"I kept my promise, John Henry?" she said.

For a minute he didn't answer. "Yes," he said. "Yes, you did, Nettie."

"I ain't never broke a promise," she said.

"I ain't never said you did," he said.

"I ain't never," she said.

For a while neither of them spoke.

"It wasn't them, was it?" he said.

"What?" she said.

"It wasn't them, was it?"

She didn't answer. After a while she said. "I meant to keep my promise."

"Yes," he said.

Then she went into the house and left him sitting on the back steps in the dark.

The yellow-white-yellow centerline snaked in under the left fender. "He had it," she said, speaking out loud to herself. "I kept my promise, and he had it. But he ain't never had it all."

Far ahead down the road she saw a figure, a Negro man in overalls. He was walking on the right shoulder, carrying a brown-paper lunch bag in his hand. "Can't teach them," she said, looking at the figure as it got bigger with the car speeding into it. "Right shoulder."

She passed the man, slowing down, and he looked into the car. The shutter inside her head clicked, opening a blank frame, catching the look from the man on the shoulder of the road. She put her foot on the brake and cut the car onto the edge of the road. The man came up on the highway side of the car, going past. While she was watching him in the rearview mirror, she could see him looking at her through the back window of the Pontiac.

"Hey, boy," she said. She was resting her elbow on the window, looking off down the highway as she spoke. "Where you going?"

After she spoke, she looked at him, tilting her head to one side and hanging it down, looking up at him out of the window.

He stopped beside the car, looking into the empty back seat behind her, over her shoulder; then he took off the railroad cap he was wearing. "Down the road," he said. He pulled his eyes back out of the car, looking down at the edge of the road at his feet.

"Hot to walk," she said.

"Yes, ma'am," he said. He looked up and down the highway, then back at his feet again. "Gonna be hot today," he said.

"Get in," she said. "I'm going that way."

He looked up and down the road again, then back at Nettie, over her shoulder at the back seat. "Much obliged," he said. He started to open the back door on the highway side.

"Come around," she said. "You better sit in the front."

He looked at her, looking into her eyes this time. "No, ma'am," he said. He took his hand off the door handle.

"Come around," she said.

"Thank you, ma'am," he said. He put his railroad cap back on and started to walk away down the road.

Nettie blew the horn, and he flinched.

"Get in," she said. "Sit on the other side where I can see you."

He went around the car and got into the back seat.

She put the car into gear, then pulled out onto the highway, not driving as fast — forty-five and fifty. About half a mile down the highway she came to a dirt road running off into the pines and Spanish bayonets. She slowed and pulled off onto the dirt road. The man looked at her, watching her face in the rearview mirror. She was looking at him with her head tilted slightly. He turned and looked out of the window at the pines on his side of the car. "I ain't going thisaway," he said. Saying it low, whispering. Nettie didn't answer. The road was rutted and narrow. As the car moved along down it, it lurched and bumped, scraping the sides on the spikes of the Spanish bayonets. They didn't come to any houses.

"You going to ruin . . . you car," he said. The lurching made it difficult to talk.

Nettie didn't answer.

"Scratching the paint off with them bayonets."

"You know where this road goes?" she asked, looking in the rearview mirror.

"Down to the landing," he said. He couldn't open the door and jump out into the bayonets. The sound was like fingernails scraping across glass.

"Is there a store or something down there?" she said.

"No'm," he said. "Ain't nothing. Just where they goes fishing."

"Colored folks?" she said.

"Mostly," he said.

"Trash fish?" she asked.

He didn't say anything.

After a while she came to a little clear place where she could pull off. She turned the car into the pines and cut off the motor. The man was sitting forward on the edge of the back seat, with one hand on the back of the front seat and the other hand on the door handle. He watched her watching him in the rearview mirror. Then he looked out the window on his side into the pines.

"You got to do something for me," said Nettie.

The man sat looking out the window. "This ain't the way I go," he said. "I got to be to work at seven-thirty."

"You *got* to do it for me," she said. He wasn't looking at her.

"What time is it?" he said.

"Listen to me," she said. "I said you *got* to do it."

She took his hand, pulling it over the back of the seat and putting it over her breast outside her dress. His hand touched her for a moment; then he pulled it back. He opened the door and stepped out of the car.

"Not me, white lady," he said. "I got to be to work."

"Get back in the car," she said.

"It's broad daylight," he said. He pulled the bill of his railroad cap. "Time I be getting on to work," he said.

She got out on her side, looking at him over the top of the car. "You ain't going to say no to *me*," she said.

He looked back for a minute, then he looked away.

"I'll pay you," she said.

He didn't answer.

She hiked her dress up and pulled it over her head.

"No," he said, not looking at her. Then he looked at her over the top of the car.

"I mean what I'm saying," she said. "I got to have me a black man."

He looked away, then flicked his eyes toward her over the top of the car. She walked around behind the car, getting between him and the road.

"Not me," he said.

"Twenty dollars," she said. She reached both arms up behind her, taking off her brassiere as she came around the car. He stared at her sliding it down her arms and dropping it off on the ground.

"Listen," she said, "I got colored blood in me too. Nigger blood."

He flicked his eyes away, then back, looking at her breasts. "Not . . . not . . . not me, white lady," he said. Her nipples were pink-brown — large.

"Look at me," she said. He looked at her. "I got nigger blood — couldn't you tell?"

His eyes went up and down, looking at her. "All right," he said. "I ain't your man. You ain't nigger enough."

"Black man," she said, coming toward him, "you got to screw me." She moved up to him, standing toe to toe. He wouldn't look at her. She put her arms around his neck and pulled herself up, kissing him on the mouth. "I'm good poontang," she said.

When they were starting to get back into the car, she stopped him. "I ain't paid you," she said. "Twenty dollars."

He looked at her, standing with the back door of the car open, his foot inside. "You don't owe me no twenty dollars," he said. "You don't owe me nothing. I got to get to work."

"You can use it, can't you?" she said.

"Always use twenty dollars," he said. "What time is it?"

"I said I'd pay you," she said. "I keep my promises." She reached into the car and got her pocketbook. "How much nigger blood you think I got?"

"Some," he said. "It'll do."

"Not enough to show," she said. "Enough to make it?"

"That's right," he said. "What time you say it getting to be? I got to be to work at seven-thirty."

She took the automatic out of her purse. When he saw it he stepped back away from the car, not trying to run. She put three shots into him before he knew what was happening. After he flinched his hands down to protect himself, she put three more shots through the backs of his hands, keeping count. She saved the last shot until after he was down on the ground; then she stepped up close and drilled him right between the eyes.

"Not that much nigger blood," she said. "You wasn't nothing of a Roman, neither, boy."

Then she got into the car and drove back to the highway and on into Savannah.

She didn't know just where she was going, but she seemed to home in on it like she was following a radar beam — the Savannah Monument and Stone Works. The yard in front looked like a foreshortened graveyard, the stones and monuments on display crowded up on the grass with just enough space to walk between. They had what she was looking for at the back of the yard. A small obelisk, black granite, with a shaft about four feet tall, rising off a big solid base where the inscription would go. Altogether it was about six or seven feet tall.

She made a cash deal with the man on the condition that it would be delivered right away.

"Can't be tomorrow," he said. "That's Tuesday."

"What about Tuesday?" she said.

"My man don't work on Tuesday," he said.

"Wednesday, then," she said.

"He'd have to work Tuesday for you to get it Wednesday."

"He's going to have to work tomorrow," she said.

"I told you," he said. "He don't work on Tuesday. That'd be extra."

"Why Tuesday?" she said.

"It's his religion," he said.

"What the hell kind of a religion is it won't let him work on Tuesday?" she said.

"I don't know," he said. "He says it's his religion. Stonecutters ain't that easy to find. I can't afford to ask him. He works first-class the rest of the time."

"Does he work on Sunday?" she said.

"That's *my* religion," he said.

"You got a red-hot business going here, mister," she said.

"It works out pretty good," he said.

"He's going to have to work *this* Tuesday," she said. "I got to have it Wednesday."

"That'll be extra," he said. "I can't guarantee it, but it'll be extra."

"You're getting enough now," she said.

"I can't make it Wednesday," he said.

"How often you sell one of them?" she said. "I mean a big one like that. Fancy."

He looked at the stone without answering her.

"I just can't make it Wednesday," he said. "I couldn't afford to make him mad. Stonecutters ain't that easy to find."

"There ain't that much lettering," she said.

"Too much for Wednesday," he said. "It's his temperment. You try to push him, and you can't get him to do nothing at all."

"Here's ten extra," she said, handing him the bill. "You can handle him. Tell him you *got* to have it by Wednesday."

"He thinks he's an artist," he said.

"It's got to be done good," she said. "Twenty?"

"Well," he said.

"I ain't going to be took too much, mister," she said. "Twenty is tops. You get his ass moving for twenty, or that thing can set out there for another year. You ain't going to tell me you sell one every day."

He looked at the bills. "Wednesday afternoon," he said.

"Just so it's Wednesday," she said.

She wrote out the inscription on a piece of paper he gave her.

"With an *e?*" he said.

She looked at him. "What else you think it might be?" she said. "You ain't going to screw this up, mister?"

"That's the reason I wanted to be sure," he said. "It's a hell of a job erasing."

"Just the way I got it down there," she said, giving him the paper. "Space it out so it looks pretty."

He took the paper and put it into his vest pocket. "I told you he was an artist, madam," he said.

After she left the monument works, she drove to the sheriff's office. The deputy on duty was a young man with a tanned face. He was wearing a Stetson tilted back on his head.

"Yes, ma'am?" he said, coming up to the counter.

"I want to see the sheriff," she said.

"He ain't in right now," said the deputy. "He's out on a call. What could I do for you?"

"I'd rather see the sheriff," she said.

"He ain't going to be back before this evening," he said.

"Well," she said. "I really thought I better see the sheriff."

"I could do the same thing for you," he said.

She looked at him for a minute. "You next in line to him?" she said.

"You might say," he said. "I been here two years."

"Well," she said, "All right. It's serious."

"I been here two years," he said.

"I killed a nigger," she said. She looked him in the eye when she said it.

The deputy looked at her. "How'd it happen?" he said. "Hit him with your car?"

"I shot him," she said.

He looked out the window; then pulled his hat down on his forehead and looked at the counter. "You shot him?" he said. He looked back up at her.

"Seven times," she said. She reached into her purse and got the Beretta, putting it up onto the counter. "That there is what I shot him with."

The deputy looked at the automatic, then back at her. "Seven times?" he said.

Nettie dropped her eyes. "He tried to rape me," she said.

The deputy looked at her across the counter. "I better get the sheriff," he said.

The monument was delivered late Wednesday afternoon. Nettie met the truck to direct them where to set it up.

"That's a nigger graveyard," said the man who was driving the truck.

"I got it marked off with string," she said. "You set it up over there where I marked it off with the string."

"I ain't never set up no monument for no nigger graveyard," said the driver.

"You put it down easy," she said. "If you chip it, I ain't going to pay for it. The writing faces this way."

On Wednesday night she got John Fletcher to take her picture on it. She sent him a copy, and used it to pass around for advertising. Finally just about every man in McAfee County got hold of one.

The flashbulb lit up Nettie and the obelisk, but it didn't reach into the background, which was black, except for some pieces of moss hanging down into the top of the picture. Nettie was standing with her side to the camera, one foot on the base, and the other leg lifted and wrapped around the shaft of the obelisk, hugging it with her arms. She had high-heel shoes on, but nothing else. Her arms were reaching up, so her right breast was mashed against the granite, swelling it out, with the nipple showing. Her head was tilted to one side, and she was looking into the camera and smiling.

John Fletcher took the picture on Wednesday night before he left to go in the navy, using up two rolls of film getting it right. More than half of the prints were blurred where the camera shook.

After the pictures were developed, seeing herself and the monument framed by the open blackness of the flash, the clicking in Nettie's head went away — freezing the shutter on an open frame.

For a week after the monument was set up, people from all over the county made special trips to the Golden Rainbow African Baptist Church graveyard just to look at it. Blacks and whites coming together. Finally the novelty wore off, and they stopped coming. But it is still the biggest monument in any of the McAfee County graveyards, except the big Baptist graveyard in Kose.

It is still a fine-looking monument, though the color is graying out in the weather, and the shaft of the obelisk is almost covered with honeysuckle. Jessie Wight keeps the vines pulled back off the base so the inscription will show.

It is very impressive.

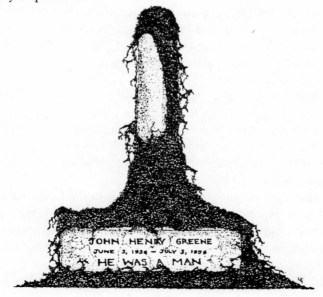

Dorcus and the Fat Lady

1954: LATE SUMMER

The Ferris wheel spun over the midway — pinwheels of light, going around and around. Behind it the night sky swelled high and black, making the spinning lights stand out — red and white — wheeling over and collapsing in on themselves.

Lee Jay stood watching it with his mouth open. Beside him, just inside the entrance, Dorcus stood counting the change from the tickets. He slid the coins out between his thumb and index finger, milking them off into the open purse. The last one dropped, and he flourished his empty hand open.

"Sixty-five cent is a lot of money for a carnival," he said. "Just to get inside. You be sure you ain't going to miss nothing, Lee Jay. Don't no carnival come around just anytime."

"Yessir," said Lee Jay. The top of his head came almost to his father's shoulder — powdery white hair that stayed in his face most of the time. He had developed a permanent crouch trying to see out from under it.

"What's that, Pa?" he asked, pointing to the Ferris wheel.

"We'll see it all," said Dorcus. "That's the Ferris wheel. You ride it."

"Yes," said Lee Jay. "Yes*sir*."

"Here," said Dorcus, putting four quarters into the boy's hand. "That's four big rides, or six little ones. Spread them out. I can't give you no more."

Lee Jay looked down at the four coins in his hand. He had never had more than fifteen cents to himself at one time in his life. "All of it?" he said, looking at his father.

"Yes," said Dorcus. He tried to pat him on the head, but the boy was so tall that he had to reach up to do it. It was awkward. Lee Jay's hair waggled into his eyes under the patting.

"That's a dollar," said Lee Jay, holding his palm out flat with the coins spread on it.

"Don't no carnival come to McAfee County just every day. You got to pay for it," said Dorcus.

"Yessir," said Lee Jay. He closed his hand on the coins.

Together they started down the midway toward the Ferris wheel. Everything was bright and noisy — loud, popping music that changed every thirty feet they walked. Now and then somebody would lean at them out of a red-and-white-painted stall and ask them to step up and do something.

"Keep wallking, son," said Dorcus. "They'll get your money, and you wouldn't see doodley shit. I done tried them games."

Lee Jay hooked his finger through the hammer loop on his father's overalls and put his hand with the money in it into his pocket.

"What's they for, Pa?" asked Lee Jay. He pointed to a row of Kewpie dolls on a shelf back of the counter of one of the red-and-white stalls.

"You win them," said Dorcus.

Lee Jay looked at them for a minute. "How you going to win them?" he said.

Dorcus looked into the stall. "See yonder?" He pointed to a pyramid of three wooden milk bottles at the end of the tent. "You knock them down."

"Them bottle things?" said Lee Jay.

"Yes," said Dorcus. "You throw a baseball and knock them down, and you get you one of them there dolls. They ain't real bottles. They's made of wood."

"Just for throwing a baseball?" said Lee Jay. He was looking at the dolls.

"You think that's real easy, don't you?" said Dorcus.

"Just for throwing a baseball?" said Lee Jay.

"You thinking about how easy it looks, ain't you?" said Dorcus. He closed his eyes and shook his head slowly. "You going to be able to shit a yaller posthole digger sooner than you going to hit them there bottles," he said.

Lee Jay looked at the bottles. They were so close it seemed to him that he could almost reach out and knock them over with his hand.

"It don't look like they's nothing to it," he said.

"That's the way they *want* it to look," said Dorcus, nodding again. He looked at the man in the booth. "How much is it for a try?" he asked.

"Fifteen cents," said the man, who looked like he didn't much care whether they tried or not. His right hand throbbed in the pocket of his seersucker pants where he was scratching himself. He didn't look like he cared much about that either.

Dorcus looked down at Lee Jay; then he reached into his pocket and took out his purse. "I'm going to learn you a lesson," he said, slapping the fifteen cents down on the counter. "Give him a ball and let him try."

The throbbing stopped while the man took his hand out of his pocket and put two baseballs on the counter.

"I get *two* balls?" said Lee Jay, looking back at Dorcus over his shoulder.

"That's a man's share," said Dorcus. He laughed and looked at the man behind the counter. The man had his hand back in his pocket again, and he acted as though he hadn't heard anything.

"Just go ahead and thow 'em," said Dorcus to Lee Jay. "You going to see."

Lee Jay picked up one of the baseballs, holding it between his thumb and the first two fingers of his right hand. He rolled it around looking at it. "Looks all right," he said.

"Just go ahead and thow it," said Dorcus. He folded his arms and looked at the pyramid of milk bottles.

Lee Jay twisted the baseball in the palm of his hand and leaned over to take a long look at the pyramid, crouching down to see under his hair. Then he placed his left foot and turned side-on. He wound up very slowly and elaborately before starting his delivery. As his swing developed, he hopped up into the air and untwisted his body with the motion of his arm coming around, making the shift with both feet up off the ground and coming down squarely with them just reversed — right foot forward and left foot back. It was a crazy, spastic kind of a motion, and a person seeing him do it from a long way off would have thought he was trying to not step on a snake. Sometime before he came back down on the ground, his arm gave a whiplike motion, and the ball went zinging off — right through the center of the pyramid. The two bottom bottles leaped off to the sides — left and right, and the upper one spun in the air while Dorcus could have counted to five.

"Son-of-a-bitch!" said Dorcus, looking at the place where the bottles had been. Lee Jay was frozen in his follow-through position — feet planted firmly on the ground, his arm still extended out toward the bottles, looking down in front of his right foot. His stance was something like that of *The Discus Thrower*.

"Son-of-a-bitch!" said Dorcus again. "You hit 'em!" He slapped the counter with his hand. "Hot damn!" he said.

"I was feeling it," said Lee Jay. He looked up at the place where the bottles had been.

"Right on, Right on," said Dorcus. "Hit 'em right on."

The man behind the counter looked at the bottles sourly; then he went and set them up again.

Lee Jay looked at Dorcus.

"You got another ball," said Dorcus. "But it'll never happen. They got it all figured out." He folded his arms again.

Lee Jay picked up the ball and went through his windup. The second ball went into the pyramid more solidly than the first one had, bouncing bottles off both sides of the tent and the ceiling.

"I be *God* damned," said Dorcus. "Twict. I be God damned."

"What am I going to do now?" said Lee Jay.

"Give him his doll, mister," said Dorcus.

The man was looking at the bottles with the sour expression still on his face.

"I want that one," said Lee Jay. He pointed to a golden, glittery doll, with blond hair and a crown. "That there princess doll."

The man slouched over to the shelf and got it down for him.

"Let me see that there doll," said Dorcus. Lee Jay handed it to him. "Sometimes they's cracked," he whispered. "Yes," he said, holding the doll off and looking at it. He gave it back to Lee Jay. "You wouldn't do it again in a hundred years, Lee Jay," he said. "I hope you done learnt your lesson."

"Yessir," said Lee Jay.

"That's a nice-looking doll," said Dorcus.

"Yessir, it is," said Lee Jay.

Dorcus and Lee Jay walked down the midway, Lee Jay holding the doll in both arms to keep from breaking it. A few booths down from the baseball stall they came to a "Dunk-the-Nigger" booth. As they were passing, the man throwing hit the target on the arm of the seat, and the black man collapsed into the tank of water. When he stood up in the tank he held his skinny arms out limply, blinking his eyes to get the water out of them.

"Ain't that James Lee?" said Lee Jay, pointing.

The Negro was trying to set the trap on the seat, but he couldn't figure it out, so finally the man who ran the booth had to come over and do it for him. When he climbed back onto the seat over the tank, his arms and legs were thin and spidery in the wet clothes, and he looked like a big cricket sitting there inside the chicken-wire cage.

Dorcus stopped and looked. "James Lee?" he said.

James Lee blinked out of the chicken wire, looking to see who was calling him.

"What you doing, James Lee?" said Dorcus.

"Dunkin'," said James Lee. He smiled broadly and waved. "I get me fawty-five centa hour," he said.

"Jesus God," said Dorcus. "Fawty-five centa hour? How'd you get you a job like that, James Lee?"

"Just got it," said James Lee.

"Fawty-five centa hour?" said Dorcus, talking to the man behind the counter.

The man looked at Dorcus, but he didn't say anything.

"He ain't *doing* nothing," said Dorcus.

"You want to throw a ball at him?" said the man.

"No," said Dorcus. "How much is it?"

"Twenty cent for three," said the man.

"No," said Dorcus.

"I done made me two dollahs awready," said James Lee. He gave a high, cackling laugh. "Fawty-five centa hour and free Co-Colas too." He had begun to shiver a little, but he gripped the ends of the slat on which he was sitting, and smiled. "I done had me three Co-Colas and a cigyrette," he said.

Lee Jay held up his princess doll. "Look, James Lee," he said. "I won me a doll."

"That all he does?" said Dorcus. "And you paying him fawty-five centa hour . . . for that?"

"Used to be we could get them for thirty-five," said the man, "but they won't none of them work for that no more. Everything come high these days. Generally they want fifty."

"How deep is that there tank?" said Dorcus.

"Thirty inches," said the man.

"Couldn't nobody drownd in nothing that shaller," said Dorcus.

"Not hardly," said the man.

For a minute neither of them spoke.

"Lost a nigger once in Folkston," said the man. "Hit his head on the side of the tank, I reckon. Never did come up again. I reckon he hit his head on the side of the tank. Couldn't even a nigger drownd hisself in no thirty-inch-deep tank of water."

"No," said Dorcus, "Not even no nigger couldn't do that."

For a while neither of them spoke.

Dorcus cleared his throat. "Got to be a nigger, I reckon?" he said.

"What?" said the man.

"I said, I reckon it's got to be a nigger," said Dorcus. "You wouldn't want a white man for no job like that?"

"No," said the man. "I couldn't use no white man."

"No," said Dorcus. "Not even though he'd work for *fawty* centa hour?"

The man looked at him. "No," he said.

"Yes," said Dorcus.

He looked at James Lee in the cage for a minute. "He doing all right?" he said.

"What?" said the man.

"He doing all right with the job?" said Dorcus.

"Yes," said the man. "Why?"

"If you want to know the truth," said Dorcus, "he's the dumbest shitass in McAfee County."

The man looked at James Lee. "If *you* want to know the truth," he said, "I figure he's the dumbest shitass in the *world.*"

Dorcus looked at James Lee and nodded. "You seen a lot, I reckon," he said.

"I thought I'd done seen them all," said the man.

"Yes," said Dorcus.

"He's doing all right now," said the man. "He wanted to hang on the bar so he wouldn't fall in the water at first. What you reckon he thought the forty-five centa hour was for?"

"Takes a while to catch on, I reckon," said Dorcus.

The man didn't say anything.

"Yes," said Dorcus. "It takes a while to catch on, I reckon."

"Not much to it," said the man. "You know how a nigger is. Don't want to go in the water. You got to kind of get them used to it."

"Yes," said Dorcus. "It's too bad you couldn't use no white man. Then you wouldn't have to worry."

"Yes," said the man.

While they were talking, James Lee got down off the bar and started to get out of the cage.

"Where you think you going?" said the man.

"I just be going to get me a Co-Cola," said James Lee.

"Get your ass back in that cage," said the man. "You done had four Co-Colas already."

"Three," said James Lee.

"Get your ass back in that cage," said the man.

Dorcus looked at James Lee getting up on his perch like a big, shiny spider. "Don't drownd yourself, James Lee," he said.

"Can I thow a ball at James Lee, Pa?" said Lee Jay.

Dorcus looked at him. "Not for no twenty cent for three you can't," he said. "After this here carnival is gone, you can give him a nickel and he'll let you thow at him all day long."

He and Lee Jay started off down the midway.

James Lee waved to them. "Fawty-five centa hour," he said. "Co-Colas extra, too."

"Niggers got to rub it in," said Dorcus to Lee Jay.

After they had gone, a stocky red-haired teenager with pale green eyes stepped up to the counter. "Give me some balls," he said.

The midway was laid out in an elongated horseshoe. At one end was the entrance and a line of concession stands selling hot dogs and candy apples and cotton candy. At the opposite end, on the inside of the horseshoe, were the most spectacular rides — the ASTRO-ROCKET and the MOONTRAIN ROCKET and the DYNONFET ROCKET. On the outside of the horseshoe were shows like PARIS REVUE and BLACK AND TAN FANTASY and GIRLS-GIRLS-GIRLS. On the near side of these was the giant Ferris wheel, folding over on itself outside the pinwheels of red and white lights.

Standing underneath it, Lee Jay thought it seemed to go up forever into the black sky overhead. He hugged the doll to him and looked up at the big machine cartwheeling into the blackness. It made his stomach turn over to watch it, and he thought how it would be if it came loose and rolled away over McAfee County with everybody in it sitting right side up.

"We're going to give it a ride later," said Dorcus. "Not now. We're going to save it for last."

Opposite the Ferris wheel was the freak show. A long platform with pictures behind it of the various freaks that were on display inside. The barker had a little stand in the middle, and next to him on the platform stood a man in blue tights with red trunks on. There was a Band-Aid on his lip, and he was eating a glass lightbulb — just nibbling off pieces of it while the barker explained to everyone what he was doing. He had a careful look on his face, and didn't seem to be enjoying it very much.

"Come on," said Dorcus. "Let's go see us them freaks."

He went up to buy the tickets, which were fifty cents and twenty-five cents for children. At first the barker wanted to sell Dorcus two fifty-cent tickets.

"He ain't but only eleven," said Dorcus.

The barker looked at Lee Jay narrowly. "If he's eleven, he ought to be inside where people could see him," he said, hooking his thumb toward the tent behind him.

"That's the truth," said Dorcus.

"He's too big for eleven," said the barker. "Twelve is fifty cents."

"He ain't going to be twelve until his next birthday," said Dorcus. "That's November sixteenth."

"You mean he's going to be sixteen on November twelfth, don't you?" said the barker.

"No," said Dorcus.

The barker looked at Lee Jay. "How old are you, boy?" he said.

"Tell him how old you are," said Dorcus.

"You stay out of it," said the barker.

Lee Jay looked the barker in the eye. "Eleven," he said. He hooked the doll under his elbow and held up both hands with the fingers spread.

"How many fingers he think he's got?" said the barker.

"He'll be twelve in November," said Dorcus, holding up both his hands with the fingers spread.

"Oh," said the barker. He tore off a child's ticket and handed it to Dorcus. "Seventy-five cents," he said.

Inside the tent there was a platform that was separated into sections by canvas partitions. In each section was a freak sitting on a stool — except that there weren't enough sections to go around, and the Giant and Midget had to share the same one. There was a Monkey Lady, the Giant and the Midget, an Alligator Lady, a Fire Eater who was a Negro, a Thin Man, and an old blue-haired lady in a long red sarong with purple flowers on it who had a big snake wrapped around her neck. After the Snake Lady there was an empty section for the Glass Eater, who was also the Sword Swallower. He hadn't come in from the platform yet.

All of them but the Midget looked sad and mopey and worn out — like they were waiting to be vaccinated in a county health clinic. Even the snake looked droopy — or asleep — with his head flopped upside down and his tongue lolling out of his mouth. He kept sliding off the lady's neck, so she had to be all the time hiking him up and wrapping him back around.

In the middle of the tent was a low platform with a velvet-covered chain around it. In the middle of the platform was the fattest lady Dorcus had ever seen. She sat on a kind of throne made out of gilded four-by-fours, and over her head was a banner — blue cloth with white lettering. It said: FLORINE THE FAT LADY — SIX HUNDRED AND THIRTY-FOUR POUNDS OF *WOMAN*.

Florine had on the sort of short, no-shape dress that Shirley Temple used to wear in the movies, and her hair was done up in the same kind of ringlets. The dress was made of blue satin, cut low and straight across at the top to leave a lot of skin showing, so people would know she was real. Her arms and legs rolled out of the tiny blue dress in wads and folds of flesh like mounds of vanilla ice cream that was starting to melt.

Braced on the floor and leaning back into her lap was a stalk of bananas from which about half of the bananas were missing. Florine hugged it with her left hand. With her right hand she carried a banana back and forth to her mouth in a teeter-totter pumping motion. She wasn't paying any attention to what she was doing — her eyes had a glassy, transfixed look in them — but the motion had the precision and regularity of a metronome. Only her forearm moved, rocking the banana up into her mouth dead center every time. Each time her arm rocked up, about a third of the banana disappeared.

When she finished the banana, she moved her right arm off to the side in another mechanical motion — without looking — and dropped the skin into a galvanized washtub that was sitting on the platform beside her throne. The tub was almost a third full of banana skins. Some of them had caught on the rim, and hung out in looping yellow festoons.

Dorcus stood watching her with his mouth sprung open and his eyes staring wide. "Look at that, Lee Jay," he said, pointing. "Just like a goat eating string."

The barker and the Glass Eater came into the tent, and the barker began getting the people together to see the show. He introduced himself as Garvin Treecastle, and said that he would explain the freaks to them.

Treecastle was a tall, knobby man, with a face like a melancholy bag filled with golf balls. A thin black moustache came winging out from under his nose, V-ing high over his mouth — which looked as though it had been cut with a single stroke of a scratch awl.

He was the saddest-looking person in the tent.

And though the freaks had been despondent enough before, the moment he stepped onto the platform their spirits flagged visibly a further notch or two.

He began his explanations in a mournful voice — not meeting the eyes of the customers, but looking out over their heads toward the front of the tent. His explanations were all scientific and nugatory, as if he were trying to undermine and contradict the promise of the gaudy posters outside. Three of the freaks — the Monkey Lady, the Alligator Lady, and the Fire Eater — were described as victims of "rare skin disorders." Whether it was true of the others or not, the Alligator Lady at least seemed to confirm his diagnosis. The whole time he was explaining her, she stood at the front of the platform, scratching herself and sprinkling the upturned faces of the first row of customers with a fine, flaky dust.

Two other freaks — the Giant and the Midget — he described as having "rare hormone deficiencies," and the Thin Man as the victim of a high metabolic rate.

When he came to the Snake Lady and the Sword Swallower, he seemed to have run out of scientific explanations, but it didn't matter much. By that time his undertaker's voice and the sullen attitude of the freaks had caused most of the customers to lose interest anyway, and they had begun to drift around the tent on their own. Some of them left altogether and went back out on the midway. Only Dorcus and Lee Jay and one or two others stayed on until the end.

For Florine, who was the last of the freaks, the best he could do was to muster up the one word "Glands" and point to the sign over the platform. After which he mopped his face with the red handkerchief that lapped out of the breast pocket of his coat like an inflamed tongue, then screwed a cigar into an amber holder and lit it.

The smoke seemed to revive him, and he turned to Dorcus and Lee Jay. "Poke her if you want to," he said. "She's real."

Dorcus looked at him in surprise. "You mean I can feel her?" he said.

Treecastle blew out a cloud of smoke. "That's what I said, ain't it?" he said. He looked at Florine for a minute. "Anything that big ought to have five legs and a crutch," he said.

Dorcus walked up and poked his finger into her stomach. It sank up to the knuckles. He watched her face to see what would happen. Nothing happened. Her arm with the banana rocked back and forth without a break in the rhythm.

"Come here, Lee Jay," said Dorcus. Lee Jay stepped up, and Dorcus took his hand to guide it into the fat lady. "Feel that?" he said. Lee Jay nodded, his eyes round, looking up at the fat lady. "That's a fat lady," said Dorcus.

"Yessir," said Lee Jay, nodding his head. "That's what it is."

Dorcus poked his finger into Florine again — farther down in her stomach. Florine rocked a banana up to her mouth for the last nip, paused long enough to belch, then dropped the peeling into the washtub.

"I swan," said Dorcus.

After he had felt her, Lee Jay went back to watch the Sword Swallower. Dorcus walked two or three times around Florine's platform, looking at her from all angles. "I seen one before," he said, talking to Treecastle, "but I ain't never got to *feel* one. Don't she mind it none?"

Treecastle looked at Florine for a minute. "Does she look like she minds it?" he said.

Dorcus watched her while she rocked her arm four times and a banana and a half disappeared. "No," he said. "Not hardly."

"Long as you don't get in the way of the banana," said Treecastle, taking another pull on the cigar.

"How many bunches of bananas she eat a day?" said Dorcus.

Treecastle looked at him. "What?" he said.

"I was wondering how many bunches of bananas a fat lady like that would eat a day," said Dorcus.

"Five," said Treecastle, looking at Florine. "Five goddamn bunches of bananas a day. I ought to be running a banana boat."

"That's a lot of bananas," said Dorcus.

"If the price goes up a dollar a bunch, I'm out of business," said Treecastle. "She eats seven when she's upset."

"What?" said Dorcus.

"When she's upset about something, she eats seven stalks a day."

"Seven?" said Dorcus.

"Seven," said Treeecastle.

Together they looked at Florine for a minute without speaking.

"Seven goddamn stalks," said Treecastle.

"I swan," said Dorcus.

"Dolly weighed seven-forty-eight, and she only eat four."

"Dolly?" said Dorcus.

"Dolly was my last one," said Treecastle. "Seven hundred and forty-eight pounds. She didn't never get upset."

"This ain't the only one you got?" said Dorcus.

"Dolly's dead," said Treecastle. "This one's the only one I got now. They don't live long."

"Oh," said Dorcus.

"Glands," said Treecastle. He patted his side.

"Yes," said Dorcus.

"Glands gets them every time."

Dorcus looked at Florine. "How can you tell when she's upset?" he said.

"She eats seven bunches a day," said Treecastle. "I told you."

"You mad about something," said Dorcus.

"No," said Treecastle. "I ain't mad. I'm happy as a goddamn lark."

"I thought you sounded like you was mad," said Dorcus.

Treecastle looked at Florine. "I used to kind of like bananas," he said.

"Yes," said Dorcus. "Bananas is pretty good."

"I'd as soon eat a turd now," said Treecastle.

"I see," said Dorcus. "You can get too much of anything."

"I can't even stand to smell them no more," said Treecastle.

For a minute neither of them spoke.

"It's interesting, though," said Dorcus.

Treecastle looked at him.

"I said it must be interesting working around fat ladies and freaks like that," said Dorcus.

"Used to be," said Treecastle. "I ain't got the balls for it no more. It's driving me shithouse."

"How come?" said Dorcus. "I would have thought it would have to be interesting."

"Well," said Treecastle, "the freak part *is* pretty interesting. Only that ain't all there is to it."

"I see," said Dorcus. "What do you mean?"

"Freaks is easy enough to get along with mostly," said Treecastle, "but you let one of them get his ass in a sling about something, and right away it works around to everybody else."

Dorcus looked along the platform at the freaks. "They look sort of droopy-assed," he said.

"Take Inez there," said Treecastle. He pointed to the Monkey Lady. "She and Harry" — he pointed to the Sword Swallower — "they're engaged."

"Yes," said Dorcus, nodding. "That's interesting."

"Harry tried to eat a forty-watt fluorescent bar a while back. Said he was going to do it in fifteen minutes. Harry's got more sense than that, but he had to show off in front of Inez, I reckon. It like to killed him."

"*Forty*-watt?" said Dorcus.

"That's a yard of glass," said Treecastle. "He had the hiccups for five days. It blowed his nerve. Even after he got over the hiccups he would get to thinking about them coming back on him again — while he had that sword rammed down his throat — and he had to lay off for two weeks. Harry couldn't give it up that long. If he don't stick something down his throat every day, he gets moody. Well, he *couldn't* stick nothing down his throat for nearabout three weeks. It was awful. He took it out on Inez, and now Inez's taking it out on the rest of us."

"That's the way it is," said Dorcus.

"She said she was going to shave all her hair off and get her a straight job." Treecastle shook his head. "Inez couldn't hold no straight job. She's shittier looking with her hair shaved off than what she is with it on. I seen her. She looked like a ugly shaved monkey."

"I see," said Dorcus.

"Something like that throws the whole show off," said Treecastle. "It works around to everybody after a while. Grace there" — he pointed to the Alligator Lady — "she's been talking about going to see a skin doctor. Jesus. She's had them scabs on her since her baby hair fell out, and now she thinks she can go see some quack and get a penicillin shot and it'll go away. They can keep a dose of poison ivy scratching for fifteen years. I seen it happen. One of them sons-of-bitches gets ahold of Grace, he'll be handing her down to his grandbabies to work on. I told her to try Ivory soap and some Vasoline and sulfur ointment

I'd make up for her for nothing. I meant it, but she took it wrong and ain't spoke a word to me for three days."

"Skin doctors is bad news," said Dorcus.

"Yes," said Treecastle.

"The sulfur is good though. I mix mine with lard," said Dorcus.

"Lard?" said Treecastle.

"We got plenty of lard," said Dorcus. "You don't hardly notice the smell because of the sulfur."

"You ought to try Vasoline," said Treecastle. "It's neutral."

"Yes," said Dorcus. "The sulfur is the main thing, though. Sulfur is good."

"Yes," said Treecastle.

He looked back at the platform. "Doloris there —" He pointed to the Snake Lady. "Doloris is scared Jupiter — that's the snake, Jupiter — is going to die. She says she's too old to train her a new one. It ain't nothing only she's feeding him too much to eat. She stuffs him all day long, then can't figure out why he won't wake up for her to do the show. He ain't worth killing now. But you can't talk no sense to Doloris about it."

"It's a nice-looking snake," said Dorcus. "I ain't too much on snakes myself, but I'd say that was a pretty nice-looking snake."

"Handsome *is* as handsome *does,* is what I say," said Treecastle. He took a pull on his cigar.

"Well," said Dorcus. "Is that all?"

"What?" said Treecastle.

"Is that all the trouble you got?" said Dorcus.

"Mister," said Treecastle, taking the cigar out of his mouth. "I ain't only started to tell you my troubles. This here ten-in-one's a trouble *factory.*"

"Well," said Dorcus, "I reckon you must have your share. But it's interesting, though."

"Fred" — Treecastle pointed to the Fire Eater — "that's the nigger there, Fred been reading some of that Black Muslim horseshit. Now he says we got to all call him Ali Baba. *Ali Baba.* Jesus. He says we're all prejudiced and he can't stand working around no prejudiced white trash that they don't know how to treat a nigger right. He says he's going to find him a all-nigger carnival and go to work for it. If he can't do that, he's going to be a missionary out to Africa and save the heathen. I ast him what the shit kind of a church is looking for a halfwit nigger missionary, but he just keeps on saying how prejudiced I am and what would I know about it. He won't hardly talk to me no more. Even when I call him Ali Baba."

"Ain't that just like a nigger?" said Dorcus.

"Fred's all right," said Treecastle, "only I got to get them books away from him."

"A reading nigger ain't worth a shit," said Dorcus.

Treecastle took another pull at the cigar. "Linville" — he pointed to the Thin Man — "Linville's queer."

"The skinny feller?" said Dorcus.

"He run off the Strong Man I used to have, following him around and hanging on him, telling him how pretty his eyes was, and asting him to let him feel his muscles, till he just couldn't stand it no more and he quit the show. Now Linville's gone moody and says he's hungry all the time."

"The tall skinny feller is a queer?" said Dorcus.

"I ain't going to fuck around with Linville none," said Treecastle. "A Thin Man just ain't that hard to find. I'll beat his ass and ram him up a tailpipe is what I'll do."

"I wouldn't blame you for that," said Dorcus.

Treecastle took several deep drags on the cigar, calming himself down.

"Well," said Dorcus, "leastways the Giant and the Midget is all right."

"Yes," said Treecastle, "they's just fine. Only except Goliath is scared shitless of Tiny." He pointed to the platform. "Look how he keeps his eye on him."

Dorcus looked.

"How the hell do you figure that?" said Treecastle. "Something like the way the elephant is scared of a mouse? Maybe Goliath thinks Tiny is going to run up his pants leg and bite his peter off."

"I swan," said Dorcus.

For a minute neither of them spoke.

"Sounds like trouble to me," said Dorcus.

Treecastle didn't answer.

"What about the Fat Lady?" said Dorcus.

"What?" said Treecastle.

"The Fat Lady," said Dorcus.

Treecastle looked at Florine. "Yes, shit," he said, "Florine too."

"What's her trouble?" said Dorcus.

"Well," said Treecastle. Florine dropped a peeling that hit on the rim of the washtub and flopped onto the platform. Treecastle lifted it with the tip of his cane and dropped it into the tub. "Florine ain't been serviced for over three weeks," he said.

"What?" said Dorcus.

"Used to be we'd kind of pass it around the people in the show," he said. "But we can't do that no more. Inez told Harry she didn't care if the whole carny went under, he had to stay away from Florine. I was depending on

Harry, but you know how a woman is when she gets like that."

"Yes," said Dorcus.

"And Linville's queer," said Treecastle, counting them off on his fingers, "and Fred's a nigger, and Tiny — well, you can see how that would be."

"Yes," said Dorcus. "I can see that."

"You ever noticed how it is the women go crazy over midgets?" said Treecastle.

"No," said Dorcus.

"I can't understand it," said Treecastle. "It seems preverted to me."

"Yes," said Dorcus. "I wonder what they see in them?"

Treecastle shook his head. "I never could understand it," he said.

For a minute neither of them spoke.

"What about the Giant?" said Dorcus.

"What?" said Treecastle, "Goliath?"

"The Giant there," said Dorcus, pointing.

"Goliath's *strange*," said Treecastle. "I mean fucked-up strange. I don't have no more to do with him than just what I have to. You don't never know how it is he's going to take something. I'd be afraid to ast him."

"I see," said Dorcus.

"Besides," said Treecastle, "he don't seem to be interested in no women. Probably he just had to give it up. On account of his size, you know."

"Yes," said Dorcus.

"I had me a canvasman used to come in and take care of Florine for me ever once in a while for a dollar. But he quit the show in Pembroke. Now ain't nobody else I can turn to."

Dorcus looked at him for a minute. "Wait a minute," he said. "You mean . . . you mean don't nobody want to fuck the Fat Lady?" he said.

"I mean if don't nobody do it soon, I'm out of business," said Treecastle. "I can't stand no seven bunches of bananas a day." He looked at Dorcus. "How'd you like to be in a business where you had a two-bunches-of-bananas-a-day profit margin?"

"And you got to *pay* somebody to do it," said Dorcus.

"I tried it myself," said Treecastle, "but it weren't no good. I ain't the man I used to be. Besides, like I said, I can't stand the smell of them bananas."

"You mean you got to *pay* somebody?" said Dorcus. "What kind of a man would it be that you'd have to pay him to do it to a Fat Lady?"

"They's all kinds in this world, mister," said Treecastle. "Believe me, they's all kinds."

"I wouldn't have thought it," said Dorcus. "You wouldn't have to pay *me* to do it to no Fat Lady. You wouldn't have to pay me nothing at all."

"You mean you'd like to screw Florine there?" said Treecastle.

Dorcus looked at Florine narrowly, squinting his eyes. "She's *unusual*," he said. "That's the thing."

Treecastle nodded his head. "Yes," he said.

"I done it to a cross-eyed nigger gal had a clubfoot in Jacksonville once," said Dorcus. "She made me buy her a gold tooth first, but it were worth it. That was *some* foot, mister. I ain't *never* seen nothing like that before."

"You did?" said Treecastle.

"And a redheaded hunchback in Waynesboro with a sister was a halfwit. We had to pay her thirty dollars and keep telling her we loved her, but it was worth it too. That hump made *all* the difference."

"*We?*" said Treecastle.

"Yes," said Dorcus, "I had to go halves on that one. That special stuff is too high for me by myself."

"God damn," said Treecastle.

"They's plenty of ugly girls in McAfee County," said Dorcus. "But they ain't any *unusual* ones."

"I see," said Treecastle. "What's your name, mister?"

"Dorcus," said Dorcus.

"Well, Mr. Dorcus . . . ," said Treecastle.

"Dorcus Williston," said Dorcus.

"Well, Mr Williston . . . ," said Treecastle.

"Mr. Treecastle," said Dorcus, "ain't nobody else in McAfee County ever done it to a Fat Lady. I bet you, ain't nobody ever done it."

"I reckon you're right about that, Mr. Dilliston," said Treecastle.

"Williston," said Dorcus.

"Williston," said Treecastle.

"Well," said Dorcus, "I'd be the only one could say he'd fucked a Fat Lady."

"Well," said Treecastle, "yes, you would." For a minute he stood watching Florine eating a banana. She was getting down toward the end of the stalk. "You mean you want to do it?" he said.

"Fuck the Fat Lady?" said Dorcus. "They ain't nothing in this world I'd rather do," he said, looking at Florine. "Nothing in this world."

"Well," said Treecastle, "once you got started on it, you'd have to go through with it. You understand that, don't you? Jesus God, if you didn't go through with it, she'd be eating *ten* bunches a day."

"Mister," said Dorcus, "I ain't never gone back on my word in my life. If I say I'll fuck the Fat Lady, I'll fuck the Fat Lady. What kind of a shithead you think I am?"

"And you say you'll really do it?" said Treecastle.

"I said it'd be a *honor* to do it," said Dorcus. "I'll do it," he added.

"Well," said Treecastle. "It ain't really that bad. I reckon *finding* it is the hardest part."

"Yes," said Dorcus. "I'd be the only man in McAfee County ever done it to a Fat Lady. Think of that."

Treecastle looked at him. "I ain't looking at this from just your side," he said. "The main thing is, you got to promise me you ain't going to try to get out of it at the last minute."

Dorcus looked at him. "You think I'm crazy or something?" he said.

Treecastle looked at Florine for another long minute. "Okay," he said. "But you better not try to get out of it."

"You ain't never going to be sorry," said Dorcus. "I can promise you, you ain't never going to be sorry."

While they were talking, Lee Jay came back from watching the Glass Eater. "He eat a whole light bulb, Pa," he said. "'Cept the screw end. He give it to me for a keepsake." He held up the bulb end for Dorcus to see.

Treecastle looked down at him. "What we going to do about the boy?" he said.

"I hadn't thought," said Dorcus.

"Whyn't you send him on home?" said Treecastle.

"I can't send him home by hisself," said Dorcus. "He ain't but eleven."

"He sure does look older than that," said Treecastle.

Lee Jay held up his hands with the fingers spread. "Eleven," he said.

"He's big for his age," said Dorcus. "Everybody notices that."

"Well," said Treecastle, "we got to do something about him."

"Well," said Dorcus.

"I'm eleven, mister," said Lee Jay, holding up his hands. "Eleven."

"Put your hands down, Lee Jay," said Dorcus. "He knows you're eleven."

Lee Jay put his hands down.

Treecastle looked at Lee Jay for a minute. Then he turned to Dorcus. "There's a fireworks show at ten-thirty. Could you get him to watch that while you come back here?"

"How much does it cost?" said Dorcus. "We're nearbout out of money."

"It's free," said Treecastle.

"It is . . . ," said Dorcus, ". . . free?" He scratched his chin and looked at Lee Jay, then back at Treecastle.

"Yes," said Treecastle.

"Generally a fireworks show ain't free," said Dorcus. "Generally you got to pay to see a fireworks show."

"This one's free," said Treecastle.

"I ain't never heard of no free fireworks show," said Dorcus. "I sure would hate to miss a free fireworks show . . . if it's free."

"Shit," said Treecastle.

"Well . . . ," said Dorcus.

"Forget it," said Treecastle. "I might of knowed."

"You sure it's free?" said Dorcus. "Generally you got to pay to see a fireworks show."

"Forget it," said Treecastle. He turned to go.

"Well," said Dorcus. "I might get me a chance to see a free fireworks show sometime." He looked at Treecastle. "I hate to miss a free fireworks show. What time did you say it started?"

"Ten-thirty," said Treecastle. "You better go on and see the show. You can't make up your mind. I can't take no chance on you if you can't make up your mind."

"No," said Dorcus. "I hate not to see the fireworks show, but it's just everything coming at me at once. I'll take Lee Jay and be back."

Treecastle looked at him. "How do I know you ain't going to change your mind on me again? I couldn't afford the *two* extra banana stalks I'm buying now. I can't take no chance on *five*."

"You could count on me," said Dorcus. "I'm all right now. I wasn't thinking a minute ago." He put out his hand. "Shake on it," he said.

Treecastle came back, and they shook hands.

"I ain't never gone back on my word when I shook on it," said Dorcus.

"The show starts at ten-thirty," said Treecastle. "You be back here then, and I'll have her ready to go in the truck."

"Ten-thirty?" said Dorcus.

"Come around to the back of the tent," said Treecastle. "I got the truck parked out back of the tent. I'll have her ready to go in, but you'll have to help me."

"Ten-thirty," said Dorcus.

"At the back of the tent," said Treecastle.

"Come on, Lee Jay," said Dorcus.

"And, Dilliston . . ."

"Williston," said Dorcus.

"Williston . . . ," said Treecastle.

"Yes," said Dorcus.

"Don't you be late, Williston," said Treecastle.

"Yes," said Dorcus.

"If you're late, it's off," said Treecastle.

"I shook on it," said Dorcus.

Dorcus got Lee Jay settled at the grandstand where the fireworks show was to take place. "It's ten now," he said. "They'll start at ten-thirty, so you'll be able to see real good. Meet me at the freak-show tent when it's over."

The lights were on, but there were not many people in the grandstand yet. Just a dozen or so. Dorcus patted Lee Jay on the head and went away.

Lee Jay sat alone in the stands holding the princess doll in both hands and looking at the screw end of the light bulb that Harry had given him.

Dorcus was waiting at the back of the freak-show tent at ten-fifteen. At ten-twenty-five he heard a sound inside the tent like a steam locomotive pulling into a station. The flap of the tent flew back and Florine waddled into the opening — puffing and sucking, and holding the banana stalk in front of her with both hands, the way a bridesmaid would hold a bouquet. At her side Treecastle staggered, his hat askew, the cigar holder gripped in his teeth.

"Give me a hand, God damn it," he panted when he saw Dorcus. "This ain't no one-man job."

Dorcus helped him get her to the loading ramp of the truck. Beside the ramp they stopped, and Treecastle stood aside to wipe his brow. Florine let the stalk slide to the ground and pulled off a banana.

"Jesus, she's hard to move," said Treecastle. "It's all dead weight."

He put the handkerchief back into his coat pocket and went up the ramp into the body of the truck. Dorcus heard him moving around inside. When he reappeared at the tailgate, he had something in his arms.

"I made it myself," he said. "You should have seen us trying to load her on the truck before."

When he laid it out, Dorcus saw that it was a harness, made up of a heavy leather yoke, which was buckled onto Florine, and ropes that extended from the yoke to pulleys on either side of the tailgate.

When Treecastle tried to buckle the yoke onto Florine, she began making grunting noises and made as if to hit him with the banana stalk.

"She's scared of the ramp," he said. "Come on, Florine. Don't give me no trouble now. We're almost there."

He dropped the harness and took hold of the banana stalk. Florine clung to it, and the grunting noises turned into squeals.

"Come on, God damn it," said Treecastle. He was sweating and panting again. "Give me the goddamn banana stalk." He finally tore it out of Florine's hands and heaved it up onto the tailgate. It struck with a soft, squashy thump.

Florine let out a wail and stretched her arms toward the spot where the stalk lay.

"Now," said Treecastle. He slipped the yoke on and buckled it. "All right," he said to Dorcus, "take the other rope and keep it tight. We got to guide her up. If she falls, I'll have to shoot her."

With Dorcus on one side and Treecastle on the other, they got Florine underway. She walked with her arms outstretched and her legs stiff at the knees, swinging them out to the sides instead of lifting them — like a great mechanical doll. As she waddled up the ramp, she made small, whimpering sounds.

At the top she stopped and tried to reach down for the banana stalk. The whimpering grew louder. Treecastle picked up the stalk and heaved it farther into the body of the truck. The thump echoed off the metal sides, and Florine toddled off after it with her arms outstretched.

Treecastle paused and turned to Dorcus. He pulled the handkerchief out of his coat pocket and mopped his face. "Jesus," he said. "If I ever get anything ahead, I'm going to buy me a fork lift. I ain't up to this kind of shit no more."

"It would of been a help," he said.

"Okay," said Treecastle when his breathing was normal again, "Let's get her clothes off."

They went into the van of the truck, where Florine stood whimpering, trying to reach the banana stalk, and Treecastle began unsnapping snaps. After a while Dorcus sat down to wait for him to finish.

"I think that's all of them," said Treecastle at last, working his fingers to get the cramps out. "Give me a hand."

Taking off Florine's clothes was like striking a tent. What had seemed to be a brief costume when it had been on her took on the dimensions of an awning when they had gotten it off. It covered the whole tailgate of the truck.

Florine stood revealed in all her creased and folded glory.

"Jesus Christ," said Dorcus in a low voice. "I ain't never going to live to see nothing like that again."

"I don't know how to take that," said Treecastle. "You ain't running out on me are you?"

"I just ain't never seen nothing like it before," said Dorcus. "Honest to God."

"We got to get her down," said Treecastle.

At the front end of the truck the floor was covered with straw. It was piled high and loose on the sides, but in the center it was packed into a gigantic crater of a nest. The stalk of bananas lay on the floor at the edge of the straw.

"Now," said Treecastle, picking up the stalk with one hand, and fending Florine off with the other, "be ready. I'm going to throw the banana stalk into the hay. When she starts after it, we'll give her a push. Try to guide her so she falls in the loose part. Be careful. She's got to hit right."

"What?" said Dorcus

"If she don't hit right, it's over," said Treecastle.

"How come?" said Dorcus.

Treecastle looked at him. "This is a *Fat Lady*, buster," he said. "If she don't go down right, there ain't no way you're going to be able to get *at* her — not unless you got a spare yard of peter to snake around. If she lands on her stomach, you couldn't get at her with a drain auger."

"Oh," said Dorcus.

"Just be careful," said Treecastle. "I'll do the guiding."

He fluffed up the hay with his foot. "I'm going to throw it now," he said.

Dorcus crouched behind her, tense and waiting. He gave a short nod of his head.

"Now!" said Treecastle. He tossed the stalk. As Florine started after it, he and Dorcus gave her a push. They were a little off center, and she spun as she fell — daintily, with one leg raised slightly, like a ballerina. Then she toppled sideways, seeming to fall in slow motion. For a moment she lay on her side, thrashing. She could have rolled either way. But Treecastle put his foot on her and gave a shove, and she rolled onto her back.

The two men walked over and inspected her. She lay waving her arms around and trying to lift her legs off the floor.

"Looks okay to me," said Treecastle.

Dorcus was unhooking the straps of his overalls.

"I'll be out by the tailgate if you need any help," said Treecastle. "If you can't manage it by yourself, you call me. You understand, Dilliston?"

"Williston," said Dorcus.

"Williston," said Treecastle. "You understand?"

"I'll manage," said Dorcus. "Ain't nothing to it now."

"There's plenty to it," said Treecastle. "That's what I mean. The light ain't too good in here, and it ain't easy to tell no way. The way she bunches up down there, it looks like a cunt convention. You be sure you get it in the right place. I can't afford no ten stalks a day," he said.

"What you want to do, paint a circle around it?" said Dorcus. He sounded hurt. "I'm forty-six year old, mister. I reckon I know what a pussy looks like."

"I didn't mean to hurt your feelings none," said Treecastle. "But I got a lot riding on this. It ain't easy — even when you got a good light it ain't. Try to be sure. Call me if you ain't." He walked to the tailgate and down the ramp.

In a minute Dorcus called out. "Mr. Treecastle . . ."

"Oh, shit," said Treecastle. "Ohshitohshitohshit."

He looked up to see Dorcus standing stark naked on the tailgate of the truck.

"Mr. Treecastle . . . ," said Dorcus.

Treecastle stood with his head in his hands. "Oh, shit," he said.

"Mr. Treecastle," said Dorcus. "Looks like we done run out of bananas."

The Ferris wheel spun high up into the night, bucking backward as it started climbing, then collapsing in on itself as it came over the curving glide at the top and started down. For a moment before it began to come down, Lee Jay had the feeling that he was going to fly off into the night and roll away over McAfee County. He sat beside Dorcus in the gondola, his eyes wide as two pale blue saucers, wrapping the princess doll in his arms and trying to hold on at the same time. Dorcus sat as he would sit in the glider on his front porch at home — one hand stretched out along the back of the seat, holding Lee Jay, the elbow of the other arm crooked over the side.

"Nothing like riding the Ferris wheel," he said. "Ferris wheels is the way to go."

Lee Jay nodded. His breath was coming in deep gasps that he had to hold on to. He couldn't speak to answer his father.

"I done something tonight you wouldn't believe, Lee Jay," said Dorcus.

Lee Jay held on, trying not to look down.

"I done something tonight I got to tell you about when you get growed," he said.

Lee Jay was holding on to the crossbar. As they started down, his eyes rolled up, looking at the darkness above him.

"I done something tonight even better'n riding the Ferris wheel," said Dorcus. "Better'n a free fireworks show."

Lee Jay was looking up at the gondola above them as they came curving down, sliding backward.

Dorcus reached into his pocket. "Lee Jay," he said, ". . . have a banana."

Anse Starkey at Rest

The raccoon moved back and forth at the end of the tether. Back and forth and back and forth. If you watched it too long, it made you tired. The scope of the chain allowed him a run of only six or seven feet, and he moved back and forth inside it with a continuous motion, anticipating the turns at the ends, and swinging into them almost before he got to them. He moved as if he had contracted to perform a certain number of circuits and was now somewhere past half through — a contract which he felt he had to honor, but had long ago lost interest in. Occasionally he would stop at the end of the run and sit, not resting, just sitting for a short minute — as if the resting too were a part of the contract.

The tether was a piece of light chain, fastened to the raccoon's collar at one end, and at the other to a looped eye in the end of a galvanized grounding rod that had been driven into the ground. He could have roamed all over a circle fourteen feet in diameter — but he didn't do it. Instead he kept his run parallel to the road that passed in front of the store, always holding just enough tension on the chain to keep it from dragging on the ground.

Billy Coon didn't look unhappy. He just looked busy. If he had looked unhappy, Walt Shotford would never have left him out there, because Walt set great store by Billy Coon, and wouldn't keep him doing anything if it made him look unhappy.

Maybe Billy kept so busy on the run because he thought that was what Walt expected of him. The relationship between Walt Shotford and Billy Coon was crazy any way you looked at it, and one explanation was as likely as another.

To begin with, Walt had started to stake Billy out in front of the store because he said it was good for business. But that didn't make much sense. The business he had was going to keep coming, no matter what he did. Shotford's store was the only one in the Two-Oak community — an institution. There wasn't any reasonable way he could have kept his customers *from* coming. If he had locked the door to the store and just wouldn't let them in, it would have *discouraged* them. But, likely as not, they would have stood around until he gave in and opened it up again and let them come, because there was nowhere else to go anyway. The fact was that there was no logical business reason for Shotford to put Billy out there, no matter what he said. Some people had come down to look at Billy and make comments to each other about him at first, but, after all, everybody in the Two-Oak community already knew what a coon looked like, so even that little bit of interest had died out after a week or so, and they almost stepped on him going back and forth to the store, because they had forgotten he was there in the first place.

The real reason Walt kept Billy out there was probably because he had the idea that Billy enjoyed it, although he admitted himself that he couldn't ever really tell what the coon did enjoy. But at least he didn't fight *not* to be put on the leash, the way he had fought not to be put in the pen that Walt had spent two weeks building for him out in the back behind the store. The fact that Billy more or less let it go had to be taken as a sign to the good — Walt interpreted it that the coon enjoyed the chain and stake.

After Walt put him out, it was a couple of weeks before Billy got his routine adjusted like he wanted it. Whenever anything went a way he didn't want it to, he would bristle up and fuss about it, until Walt figured out what he was getting at and adjusted things to his liking.

Billy would get out in the morning and walk the run for about an hour and a half, and again in the evening for a couple of hours. Those were the times that Shotford did most of his business, and it was as if the arrival of the customers put Billy in mind of doing something to earn his keep. In between times, he would loll around in the shade, snatching at flies and bugs, or sleeping on top of the house Walt had built for him. He was never known to set foot inside it, but he liked to climb up on top and straddle the peak of the roof and go to sleep there. At about noon he would start to fussing and squawking, and Maude — Mrs. Shotford — would have to come out and get him and take him into the kitchen and feed him some tidbit — a piece of cheese or a Lorna Doone cracker — to make him stop. Then Billy would climb up in an old rocking chair that was kept on the back porch, with a folded rug in it for a cushion, and go to sleep for a while. When he woke up, the customers would be arriving, so he had to be taken back out front and put on the leash again.

Walt had more patience than sense with the coon. It took him a month to work out the schedule that Billy liked. When he was sure that the arrangement was going to stick, he went in to Darien and got him a nice collar and chain at the ten-cent store — a red leather collar, with silver studs on it. Walt thought it made Billy look very handsome. Billy didn't seem to care.

Leaving the coon out there on the chain at night worried Walt, because he was afraid that sometime the hounds might gang up on him and kill him. But Billy didn't like to stay in the house at night, so Walt gave in and went and got a big Heinz 57 bitch out of the dog pound in Savannah, and put her out with Billy to protect him.

Even though he had wanted a yard dog — one that would stay close to the store and not be following her nose all over McAfee County — Walt was afraid at first that he had made a mistake about Blanche. She was big enough, all right; if she got up on her hind legs, she could have put her front paws on Walt's shoulders and look him in the eye — a kind of cross between a pit bull and a Shetland pony, with short white hair and a big black spot over one eye. But the trouble with Blanche was that she was even lazier than she was big.

For a while it looked like Walt never was going to see what she looked like standing up. Every time he would shoot a glance at her out the window, or when he went into the yard, she would be stretched out on the ground asleep with her hind legs sticking straight out behind her and her head down on her front paws. Or rolled over on her back with her mouth open and her tongue lolling out and her paws flopped up in the air, the flies buzzing in and out of her mouth. When Walt finally got mad about it, and lost his temper and went out and kicked her, she woke up moaning a little. But when she saw who it was, she wagged her stump of a tail, and that was all there was to it. She seemed to be ready for him to kick her to death, and no offense taken. Walt figured that when the other dogs got onto what her nature was, it would be all up with Billy.

Just the same, she had taken up with the coon right away, moving into the house which he didn't use — or rather, moving partway in, since it was too small for all of her, so she had to sleep with just her head and front paws inside the door, and her rear end sticking out in the yard. She ate five pounds of meat scraps a day, and wouldn't have been worth killing for anything else except the job Walt had gotten her for. As it turned out, she was just right for that.

The only thing she took a real interest in was other dogs, and there wasn't a hound in the whole Two-Oak community that could get within five hundred yards of Shotford's store. Whenever she smelled one coming, she would be up on her feet, with the hair down her spine standing straight up like she'd backed under a rake, and a noise in her throat like a dump truck unloading gravel. It made Walt's mouth go dry and his palms sweat the first time he heard it.

He ran out of the store to see what kind of a four-toed throwback had gotten spit up into his yard out of the Dorchester Swamp. He never even thought of Blanche. When he got out there, there she stood, with her back hair up, and the muscles in her shoulders bunched, looking off down the road. About a hundred yards away, in the middle of the road, stood a blue-tick hound, frozen stiff, except for the tip of his tail, which was vibrating from the strain. He was looking at Blanche like he couldn't believe it. They stood that way for about a minute, and then the blue-tick just folded in on himself and stepped off into the bushes at the side of the road, very slowly and deliberately, with his head over his shoulder looking at Blanche and his tail between his legs. Walt knew then that he had picked the right dog.

For the most part, Walt left Billy Coon alone, paying attention to his complaints, and trying to get things fixed up to suit him only when he insisted. For the rest, he would look at him out the window as he passed, waiting on the customers, or glance over when he went out in the front to pump gas. Walt liked having the coon around, but he didn't handle him any, nor did he seem to need to even be close to him very much (Maude was the one who fed him and took up the most time with him directly). Maybe there had been enough of that in the first place. It had cost Walt to get Billy to begin with.

He still had a scar on his finger that Billy had given him when he caught him. Walt had been going out along the logging road to pick blueberries for Maude, because she loved to have them for breakfast in the mornings with sugar and milk. It was the middle of the morning of a Monday in June, and the snakes were out — racers — sunning themselves in looping, black coils on the fence railings. Walt was looking at them, when a movement in the drainage ditch at the side of the road caught his eye. It was a pair of raccoon cubs.

He couldn't help but try to catch them. Before they saw him, he was right on top of them — reaching. They reacted fast — took off scampering in opposite directions — but Walt had gotten too close, and he made a grab for the one of them and caught him. He had to take the cub in his bare hand, and even though he was a little fellow, no bigger than a squirrel, he bit Walt's finger right to the bone. Walt tightened up his fist just enough so the coon couldn't get his head back for a second bite, and walked home with him in his hand — the cub's teeth sunk in his finger — bleeding all the way.

"Get a cardboard box, Maude," he said when he came in the store.

She saw he had something in his hand, and the blood was all over by then, dripping out of his fist, so she didn't ask him any questions, but just went and got the box and brought it to him. Walt opened his fist, and the cub dropped into the box like a wet rag. Then he closed the flaps and put a board on top so he couldn't get out, and some cans from the shelves to hold the board in place.

"Coon," he said to Maude, taking out his handkerchief and wrapping it around his hand, which was covered with blood.

"He bit you bad, Walt," Maude said. She took him in the kitchen and washed his hand off. Then she put some turpentine on the bitten place to keep it from getting infected, and bandaged it with a clean handkerchief that she tore up into strips.

"Always wanted a coon," said Walt, and they went back out where the box was on the counter and took off the board to look in on him. He was still lying there in the bottom of the box, wadded up in a corner. But Walt could see his sides pumping as he breathed, so he knew he would be all right if they could just get him to eat. He had been very careful not to mash him as he carried him back.

He put the board and the cans back on top of the box and went out into the yard and spent the next three hours making a cage for him out of two-by-twos and chicken wire. Then he put a pan in for water, and another one for food, and a piece of a tree limb so he would have something to climb on. When he finished, he brought the cage back in and set it on the counter next to the cardboard box. Then he tapped the side of the box with his knuckle. He could hear the cub scurry around inside.

Walt didn't want him to get away, so he put him into a croker sack, then worked him into the cage from that. The cub tried to get out through the wire all around the four sides, and then he backed himself into one of the corners and just sat there glaring at Walt every time he made a move. He was wild and sad-looking, with his fur all matted and crusty, sticking out in tufts that were black and stiff from the blood.

Walt was afraid he would starve to death if he didn't get him calmed down soon so he would eat. He took him into the back bedroom where it was quiet, and put him in the darkest corner of the room, with some milk in the food pan in the cage. And then he closed the door to the room and went off and left him by himself. When he came back in a couple of hours, the cub was still in the corner of the cage, and it didn't look like any of the milk was gone. That afternoon he went down to the bridge on the logging road where the Negroes came to fish after work, and he traded two cigarettes to a Negro boy for a little bream he had caught. Then he went back and put that in the cage. The next morning most of the bream was gone, and some of the milk.

Walt left him alone all the rest of that day, and when he went back with another bream in the evening, Billy had cleaned most of the blood off, so he was looking more presentable. But he still backed into the corner and glared at him when he opened the door to put in the bream.

The wound in Walt's finger had bled enough that it didn't get infected, but he had to leave the bandage on for a week, and the soreness didn't work out for three weeks more. It bothered him that he couldn't use the hand for that time.

Walt was a big man anyway, and strong. But his hands were strong out of all proportion to his size. They were hard and puffy, with swollen fingers that looked like walnuts on a string — and just about as hard. He had worked a callus on the tip of his right thumb, so he could open a beer bottle with it — holding the bottle by the neck in his hand and forcing the cap off with his thumb. He used to do the trick for the customers every now and then, saying it was good for business. He also had another trick he would do sometimes. Between the first and second fingers of his right hand he would place a pecan, with the fingers sticking straight out from his hand. Then he would slowly make a fist and crack the pecan. He didn't strain when he did it. He would just close his hand, and the nut would crack, most of the time so the halves could be taken out in whole pieces. It wasn't nearly so much of a feat as opening the beer bottles, but there was more showmanship to it, since he didn't have to strain to bring it off. And also, because a number of his customers could almost do it themselves, they tended to pay more attention to it, thinking to learn the technique. The trick of opening the beer bottles was so inconceivable to them that they stopped paying attention to it after a while.

In the evenings the men from the Two-Oaks community would come down to Shotford's store and sit around under the shed in front on upended Coca-Cola cases, drinking Spearmans Ale and talking. While they talked, Billy Coon would be out there on his run, working at the contract, going back and forth, and keeping just enough tension on the chain so it wouldn't be dragging on the ground.

Only two men could stop Billy walking his run in the evenings. The two men were Jessie Wight and Anse Starkey.

Anse had once thrown a firecracker at Billy as he walked by going into the store. It had scared Billy so he had almost broken his neck when the chain caught him running away and slammed him down on the ground. Walt had eaten Anse out about it, so he never threw a firecracker again, but he would often jump at Billy as he walked by, yelling at him and scaring him.

Anse had been mean to animals all of his life. As a child he had always been tying cans and firecrackers to the tails of dogs and cats. Or soaking a corn cob in turpentine and then rubbing it back and forth under their tails to watch them run. Those were common enough tricks for all the boys around the

Two-Oak community, but Anse had a different attitude toward them. The thing was, they never seemed to make him happy. The other boys would laugh and giggle when they sent a hound off up the road with a string of firecrackers going off behind him, because they knew they were doing something that they ought not to be doing, and it made them happy. But Anse never laughed when he did those things. He would just do them, in an offhanded way, as if he wasn't really taking an interest in them, and didn't care one way or the other.

As he got older, he would occasionally trap wild animals — squirrels and possums and sometimes a bird or two — and put them up in cages or tie them to a stake in the yard. He would poke at them with a stick, or mistreat them some other way for a while after he first caught them. But then he would get tired of that and stop paying attention to them, and he would go off and leave them alone. Sometimes they would die, especially the birds that he kept in cages he made out of Popsicle sticks glued together. Most of the bigger things he caught would finally get away and go back into the woods. One possum he kept for almost a year, but then he got mad at it for hissing at him and he beat it to death with a stick.

He never had a pet. Never seemed to need to have one. For about five years, beginning when he was around thirteen or fourteen, there was an old, starved-looking hound that would follow along behind him wherever he went. He never claimed him as his own dog and following Anse around seemed to be all the hound's idea, because Anse never paid any attention to him. No one ever saw Anse feed him, nor pat him, nor show him any sort of kindness at all. But, unsatisfactory as the relationship seemed to be to everybody else, the dog evidently found something satisfying in it, because he continued to hang around anyway.

Once in a while, at Christmas and New Year's and Fourth of July, Anse would tie a string of firecrackers to the dog's tail and send him running off up the road hollering and jumping around, trying to get away from the noise. But after the string of firecrackers burned out, he would be back in the yard like nothing had happened, and Anse would go back to ignoring him again.

One Christmas Anse tied the string on his tail too tight, and the hound couldn't bite it loose after the firecrackers burned out. He went around with the string on until the part of his tail beyond the string died, and the end just dropped off. Before that happened, Anse hadn't called the dog any name at all. When he wanted him to come to him for some reason, he would just whistle and pat his leg and the dog would come, since he was always waiting around for Anse to notice him anway. But after the end of his tail dropped off, Anse started to call him Halfass. Mostly he just called him that to talk about him. When he wanted him to come, he would still whistle and pat his leg.

Halfass went on following Anse around until one day in July when Anse was eighteen and he went down into the Dorchester Swamp, trying to find an alligator, so he could kill it and sell the hide. Halfass got lost in the swamp and never came out.

The men under the shed could tell when Anse Starkey was coming just by watching Billy Coon. He always stopped pacing as soon as he got wind of him. Not at the end of the run where he took his usual rests, but just wherever he happened to be at the time. He would stop and sit back and look down the road. After a while Anse would come in sight, and Billy would keep on watching him until after he had gone into the store and come back out with his bottle of Spearmans to sit under the shed and talk to the men. It got to be such a customary thing that the men would stop talking when they saw Billy watching, and so Anse felt called upon to do something, since they were all looking at him. But he was scared of Walt Shotford, so he settled it by giving a jump at Billy as he went by, making him flinch and rattle his chain. Walt didn't like that either, but he didn't say anything, since it wasn't hurting Billy.

When Jessie Wight was coming, Billy would let them know too, but in a different way. So the men under the shed could always tell which one of them it was. Billy Coon didn't stop pacing for Jessie. But he would shorten his circuit to just a step or two each way, and faster than he usually went. Until Jessie came up out of the graveyard behind the Golden Rainbow African Baptist Church across the road from Shotford's, and then he would stop and sit there waiting for Jessie to come on up and give him his egg.

Jessie was a tenant on Case Deering's place, and he had a henhouse for the extra money he got selling the eggs to Shotford. Every day in the evening he would come down with the eggs to the store, and he always had a nice big one picked out especially for Billy Coon. So the coon would shorten up his circuit when he smelled Jessie coming, and then when he could see him in the graveyard behind the church, he would sit very still until Jessie came up and gave him his egg. He would take it to the pot that caught the drip under the hydrant, holding it in both his hands, and he would wash it off all over and crack the end and suck on the egg. Sometimes Jessie would watch him washing off the egg and then opening it up and sucking it, standing there with his arm hooked through the handle of the half-bushel peach basket that he carried the eggs in.

Then he would go on into the store, and Walt would pay him for the eggs, and Jessie would get himself a Coca-Cola, or sometimes an R-C Cola, and if he had an extra egg, maybe a couple of Lucky Strike cigarettes. Then he would go out under the big live oak tree by the side of Shotford's store with the other colored men and squat down on his heels and drink the Coca-Cola and smoke one of the cigarettes under the shade of the oak tree.

One evening in August the men were sitting around under the shed in front of the store, drinking their Spearmans and talking as they always did, when Jessie came up through the graveyard with his eggs. Anse had come in already and was sitting there under the shed on a crate with his back to the road. He hadn't yet gone in to buy his Spearmans. It was Thursday, and he only had fifty cents until payday on Friday. He was also out of cigarettes, so that meant just the one Spearmans with the package of cigarettes. He was saving it for a little while.

Walt called to Jessie from where he was standing in the doorway under the shed. "Can't stand a suck-egg coon, Jessie. Billy Coon ever gets loose, he'll be heading straight for your henhouse and suck up ever egg you got. It's going to be all your fault when he comes down there and sucks up all your eggs, so don't you come blaming me when it happens. You the one gave him the taste to suck eggs, Jessie. It's going to be all your own fault."

Anse couldn't hardly stand it that Walt showed he liked the old Negro so much.

"Makes my ass pucker like it wants a dip of snuff," he would say.

Jessie had caught Anse once, down in the woods when he was fifteen, pulling himself off, and he had been afraid for years that he would tell on him. He didn't much think he would anymore, because probably the old Negro had forgotten all about it since then, but he had carried the fear and resentment around with him so long that he couldn't shake it off. Whenever the old Negro showed up, the feeling would come on him again, and Anse would get choked and sullen, just looking at the ground and not talking, waiting for the old man to let out the secret and betray him.

After Walt spoke to him, Jessie left Billy and walked over under the shed. Anse wasn't looking at him, and just as Jessie came up, Anse shifted his foot and tripped him. He didn't mean to do it, but it looked like he did. All the men thought it was done on purpose. Jessie fell forward, trying to catch himself with his arms, but the one hooked through the basket caught, and when he hit the ground it sank down into the eggs, breaking most of them.

"God damn you, Anse," said Walt, stepping out from the doorway of the store, "what you got to do a mean thing like that for?"

Anse looked at him, surprised. "I never did," he said.

"I seen you when you done it, damn it," said Walt. "What you mean you never did?"

Jessie was getting up by himself. None of the men under the shed looked at him. They sat there holding their Spearmans bottles in both hands, looking down at the ground between their feet.

"I mean I never did trip him a purpose," said Anse.

"Shit you say," said Walt. "I seen you."

"What'd I want to go and do that for?" asked Anse.

"How'd I know what makes you do any of your mean tricks?" said Walt. "Some people just born with a asshole where their heads ought to be." The men all laughed at that, and Anse glared at them.

Maude had come out to see what was happening. She gave Anse a sharp look. "You hurt, Jessie?" she asked.

"No'm," he said. He was holding the basket in his right hand now. Yellow egg yolks smeared his arm.

She took him into the store.

"How the hell would I know what you got in your mind when you go pulling your shit-eating tricks, like tripping that old nigger there, and fooling around with Billy Coon? You tell me, Anse. How come you always got to be taking it out on somebody, fooling around with Billy there and throwing firecrackers at him?"

"I done that *one* time," said Anse.

"You got to always be jumping at him and scaring the shit out of him," said Walt. "Whyn't you leave the coon alone, Anse? Ain't nothing you do but just make him mad so I can't hardly get near him after you been jumping at him and scaring the shit out of him. I ain't never going to tame him good, long as you got to keep coming up and throwing firecrackers at him and jumping out at him so you get him all excited and scared."

Maude came to the door again. "Jessie's all right," she said. "I sent him in the kitchen to clean himself up some. Ain't many eggs left."

"How much we pay him last night?" Walt asked.

"Dollar," Maude said.

"Give him seventy-five cents," Walt said.

"What about the Co-Cola?" she asked.

"Give him a Co-Cola, too," he said.

After Maude had gone back into the store, Walt looked at Anse. "You wouldn't be feeling like you ought to pay some of that?" he said.

Anse fingered the fifty cents in his pocket, looking at Walt. "Maude's a fine-looking woman," he said, his eyes looking steady at Walt. "How come you got to be always spending your time with that coon when you got a fine-looking woman like that to keep you busy?"

Walt looked at Anse. "Some more of your half-assed bullshit on the way, Anse," he said. "I feel it in my bones."

Anse cut his eyes away from Walt to the men, then back to Walt. "You got some kind of hot pants for that coon, Walt?" he said. "You got some kind of hot pants for Billy Coon, and I'm spoiling your fun? Seems like you ought to be saving it for Maude and not using it up on that coon there. She'll take all you can give her, if you just save it up and don't waste it. Man your age can't waste it nohow. You got to save it up and be careful so you can do Maude like you ought. Lest you want somebody else to do it for you."

Maude was thirty-seven, but she looked like twenty-five. Her face was a little sharp-featured and hard, more like the face of a handsome man than a woman. But the men liked it well enough. All of them thought they could tell she would be good in bed from the way her eyes looked. Walt was forty-nine, and they liked to kid him about it.

"Here it comes, boys," said Walt, stepping up into the doorway. "Get your feet up off the ground. When a shithead starts to running off at the mouth, there ain't but one safe thing to do. Hold your breath and get your feet up off the ground."

Anse didn't say anything.

"Seems like you the one got the hot pants for Billy Coon there," Walt said. "You the one always got to be fooling around with him and wouldn't let him alone. Whyn't you go get you a nanny goat or something, and leave Billy Coon alone?"

All the men laughed. Anse had been caught with a nanny goat once when he was fifteen. Everybody had been shocked and thought of it as queer, even though all the boys in McAfee County sneaked down to the cow barns at night, and some even went into the pig pens. But goats were scarce, and the novelty of it worried them. They were afraid that Anse might be turning into a pervert. Anse didn't like to be reminded of it.

Three things he couldn't stand to be reminded of. The nanny goat, the time Jessie caught him pulling himself off down in the woods and the way the older boys had yelled at him when he was little.

When he was three and four, the big boys found out they could send him home crying by yelling, "Anse, Anse, got 'em in his pants." He didn't know what it meant, but it scared him nearly to death for them to say it. When they did it to him, he would go home crying and tell his mother. She never could take it seriously, because she thought it was funny herself. His father would get mad when he came in crying, and would make him go back out again. So he would crawl under the house and lie there crying to himself, not even able to start to think about what the big boys meant when they said it. Whenever he began to get mad and scared at the same time, he would hear them yelling it again.

"Seems like you the one got the hot pants for Billy there," said Walt. "You the one always got to be fooling around with him and won't let him alone."

Jessie came out with his Coca-Cola. He was also smoking a cigarette.

"You all right, Jessie?" Walt asked.

"Yas, suh," said Jessie. "Miss Maude fix me up so I be just fine." He limped over to the tree where the other colored men were sitting.

"Whyn't you try Jessie's henhouse?" said Walt, watching Jessie limp away. "Whyn't you just go over there and get you one of Jessie's Rhode Island Reds and leave Billy Coon alone?"

"You want to let out a contract on Maude?" said Anse. "I be glad to oblige you if you want to let out a contract on her. Then you can stop saving it up and go spend all your time with Billy Coon."

"Tell you what," said Walt. "Tell you what, Anse. You just go on over there to Jessie's henhouse and pick you out one of them Rhode Island Reds of his, and I'll buy her for you. You can pick out any one you want to, and I'll buy her for you for a present. Then you can take her home with you and leave Billy Coon alone."

"Whyn't you get you one of them Rhode Island Reds for yourself?" said Anse. "Get you one of them Rhode Island Reds and let me have the contract on Maude."

"You can have any one you want to," said Walt, "and I'll buy her for you. Only one thing. You got to pick out a pretty one. I ain't going to pay for no ugly chicken," he said. "You want me to go with you and help you pick out a pretty one?"

"I want you to kiss my ass," said Anse.

" 'Course, when you do come home with one of Jessie's chickens," said Walt, "I reckon that fist of yours is going to just turn green with envy." The men all laughed at that. "Specially if I pick out a real pretty one for you," he added.

"Whyn't you kiss my ass?" said Anse, hunching his shoulders and looking at the ground between his feet.

"Don't know what I'll do about Dee Witt here," said Walt, nodding toward Dee Witt Toomey, who was sitting on a Coca-Cola case, leaning against the front of the store and giggling. "Dee Witt's going to be mighty put out about that red chicken too."

Dee Witt giggled, looking at Walt.

"You going to be jealous of that chicken, Dee Witt?" asked Walt.

"Come on, Dee Witt," Anse said. His voice had an edge on it. "Shut up the goddamn laughing and come on. Sometimes you sound like you ain't got good sense."

"You going to share the chicken with Dee Witt?" someone asked.

"Ain't nobody pulling your chain," Anse said, looking around at the men under the shed to see who it was.

"Maybe Anse'd rather have him a rooster," somebody else said.

"How about that, Anse?" said Walt. "You want me to get you a rooster instead?"

"Then Dee Witt really would be getting jealous," said somebody.

"Goddamn it, shut up that laughing," Anse said, kicking the Coca-Cola case out from under Dee Witt. He flopped down on the ground, still laughing.

"Maybe I'll buy Dee Witt a chicken too," said Walt. "Just so he wouldn't get his feelings hurt."

Anse was standing near Walt, and he suddenly swung his fist at him, thinking to move fast enough to catch him off guard. Walt got his hand up and caught Anse by the wrist. Then he clamped down, and Anse's whole hand began to swell up and turn red. He twisted up his face from the pain, and Walt forced the arm back so he had to drop down on his knees in front of him. Then Walt twirled him around and gave him a kick on the seat of the pants. Anse flopped forward so he was down on his hands and knees in front of Walt, facing away from him.

"You don't move it out of there, I'm going to boot it again," he said.

Anse crawled off a little ways on his hands and knees and then got up.

"You kiss my ass," he said, rubbing his hand to get the circulation started again.

"Whistle, so I'll know where it's at," said Walt.

Anse turned and stalked away, with Dee Witt trailing along behind. The men under the shed were laughing as he went off down the road.

Across the road from Shotford's grocery, in the yard of the Golden Rainbow Church, is a big live oak tree. It canopies almost the whole of the east side of the churchyard, and under it the ground is sandy and bare. On the east side of the tree, away from the church and parallel to the road, a big limb reaches out. Moss hangs down from it, and about twenty feet out from the trunk the limb forks. It is the lowest limb on that side, but still high up. The fork is more than twenty feet above the ground. Once they lynched a Negro from the limb.

It was seven-thirty in the morning, and a small knot of men had gathered under the fork of the big limb. They were looking up toward the fork, and the morning light came in under the limb, lighting up the underside of the tree and falling on their faces, making them squint.

The steel stake with the looped eye was jammed in the fork of the limb. At the end of the chain Billy Coon hung, turning slowly in the air above their heads. His front paws hung down by his sides limply, and his hind legs were drawn up. The red collar was pulled forward on his face, so his cheeks pouched out and his ears canted forward. The chain ran out from the collar under his jaw, and his head was cocked back by it. He looked like he was sitting down and reaching for something, hanging there in the middle of the air above the faces of the men looking up at him as he turned slowly on the end of the chain.

Blanche lay on the ground under the fork, her head resting on her front paws, and her eyes cut back toward Walt, who was standing beside her.

"I know he done it," Walt said. "I know he done it just as sure as I'm standing here."

He kicked Blanche, and she rolled over on her back with her paws flopped up in the air. "How come you let him do it?" he said, looking down at her. She wagged her stump of a tail, scraping it in the dirt.

"He couldn't never get that close to Billy Coon," said Jessie.

"Oh, Dee Witt *done* it," said Walt, "but it was Anse put him up to it."

From the place where the stake had been in front of the store, a mark cut the dirt across the road and up to the base of the live oak tree. Walt looked at the line scraped in the dirt. "Anse done that too," he said, "with a stick, to make it look like Billy got the stake out and dragged it across here himself." He looked back toward the fork where Billy was hanging.

"It's a mean goddamn thing to do," he said, kicking his shoe in the dirt, erasing the part of the scraped line where it went by, going up to the tree. "Mean enough for Anse. Dee Witt don't know no better. Anse put him up to it, God damn him."

He kept looking up at Billy Coon. "What I can't figure out," he said, "is why he went to all that trouble. He must have known we'd figure out he was the one anyway. How come he didn't just walk up there and beat his head in with a stick?"

No one spoke.

"All that trouble," said Walt. "God damn the mean son-of-a-bitch."

"Billy Coon was all right," said Jessie, looking up at the limp, stretched body of the animal hanging there from the fork of the limb. Walt didn't say anything.

"Be all right if I take care of him?" Jessie asked. "I be right glad to take care of him, Mr. Walt," he said.

"Where you going to put him?" Walt asked, looking at Jessie. Then he looked away, saying, "Shit. It don't make no difference."

"I put him over there on the side of the yard," said Jessie. "He be right close there, so you can come see when you would want to."

"It don't matter," said Walt. "You can take him if you want to. You was better to him than anybody else anyway." The men had started to walk off, going down the road in different directions. Walt pulled his hat down and started to walk back to his store.

"He was all right," said Jessie, looking at Walt.

"Yes," said Walt, walking away. He stopped. "I'll give you a package of Lucky Strike cigarettes and two Co-Colas for your trouble," he said.

"Ain't no trouble," said Jessie.

When Jessie was a young boy his grandfather had told him a story about the slave graveyard on the plantation where he had lived. The story had made a deep impression on him, so that he never forgot it. When he had grown up and become a man, he passed it on to other children in his turn.

"Ever now and then one of them there graves would just . . . drop in," he would say, his voice low and serious, so the children would hang on the words and realize what he was going to tell them. "Folks that would come up and look seen the bodies down there in they grave clothes, and the women's hair was growed all the way down to they feets, wrapping them around like it was a nest of black snakes. And they fingernails was all twisty and pale and long as a butcher knife on the ends of they fingers."

It made him sweat all over just to tell the stories again, but he looked on it as his duty and obligation, out of remembrance of the feeling it had given him when his grandfather had told them to him years before. He grieved for the bodies of the dead, wrapped in the choking, snaky coils, and lying, he thought, uneasily under the sandy mounds beneath the moss-draped trees of the graveyard. It made him feel like he wanted to do something about it.

Jessie was a deacon in the Golden Rainbow Church, and because of this he had to go to all the funerals that were held in the graveyard behind the church. Every funeral that he attended brought back to him his feeling of grief about the bodies, and the sense of obligation that he was the one who had to do something about it.

When there was a funeral, the undertaker provided most of the equipment. It made a lovely show — with a dark green canopy over the grave, saying *"Beckworth & Sons, Inc., Funeral Directors"* printed in white along the scalloped edges, and a bright green mat of imitation grass draped over the mound of dirt at the edge of the grave, and folding chairs under the canopy, with a cardboard fan printed with a Bible picture in color laid out on every chair. But the markers that they supplied for the graves were small and insignificant and depressing to Jessie.

At the foot of the mound, after the canopy and the grass mat and the chairs were taken away, was a small aluminum holder, shaped like a harp. Into it, behind a cellophane window, they placed a printed card on which the name of the deceased, the dates of his birth and death, were written with a ball-point pen. At the top was the motto: "Ashes to ashes and dust to dust." At the bottom of the card was the message: "Beckworth & Sons, Inc., Funeral Directors. Fine Funerals at Economical Rates." When the funeral was over, one of the Beckworths would spear this little marker into the ground at the foot of the grave just before they left with the canopy and the grass mat. After the dirt settled into the grave and the mound disappeared, it didn't make much of a show.

John Henry's monument was the only one. And it was so big it just made the rest of the graveyard seem more empty and bare. Having it there made Jessie feel more worried and guilty than ever.

Occasionally a survivor, usually a woman, would try to do something to mark off the last resting place of her kin — bringing a painted oil can with plastic flowers in it, or a Christmas wreath salvaged out of some garbage can. One had outlined her husband's grave with blue Milk of Magnesia bottles, buried neck-down in the sand. But most of the graves just had the little aluminum marker. And pretty soon it would get stepped on, so it couldn't be seen, or it would be lost altogether. Jessie wanted to do something to make it better. But he didn't know what to do.

When they poured the new steps for the church, he found out.

The Men's Bible Class at Golden Rainbow got up a project to replace the wooden steps to the church with new ones of brick and concrete. Fulmer Johnson, who did brickwork for a contractor in Darien, directed the project. He built the brick abutments on either side, and helped them plan and set up the forms for the steps.

The next day after they made the pour, Jessie came down to the church early in the morning to see if the concrete had set up. It had. During the night, while it was still wet, someone had taken a stick and written on the bottom step: FUCK NIGGERS — SEPTEMBER 1956. There was also a rough place where whoever it was had put his initials, then decided against it and erased them.

Jessie felt the step. It was hard. There were the letters frozen into the hard surface of the concrete.

"I be damned," he said, running his hand over the letters. "Whyn't I think about that before?"

His problems were solved.

When Fulmer poured the slabs to put on the tops of the brick abutments at the sides, Jessie watched him carefully as he set up the forms and oiled them. Later that night he came back and printed GOD IS LOVE in the wet concrete with his finger. The next morning it was set up hard. For the first time he was able to think about the bodies in the graves without feeling cold inside.

In a clearing between his house and the graveyard he made a place to work. Then he got Fulmer Johnson to show him how to make a form for the headstone and give him a demonstration on how to oil it and mix the concrete and make the pour, then trowel it off so it would be smooth. From time to time Fulmer would drop by to help Jessie and advise him, until he had gotten straight on all the details. But it didn't take Jessie long to learn how to do it. Eventually he got a headstone made for all of the graves that he or anyone else could identify. There were slight variations in the inscriptions — occasionally some relative wanted something in particular, or the circumstances of the death were unusual — but they were all pretty much the same:

   OR:

After he had made headstones for all the graves he could identify, he began on the others. He had a stock inscription that served them all:

The fact that he had only the one mold didn't seem to worry anyone else very much, though it sometimes worried Jessie.

"Seem like it make 'em all look alike," he would say. Then he would reason it out. " 'Course, they *is* all dead."

He decided that if he started making different ones, then everybody would want one special, and he couldn't ever keep up with that. So he just let it go. Anyway, the survivors would still come down and put their individual touches on the graves — like the blue Milk of Magnesia bottles, or pieces of colored glass, or sometimes just plain rocks laid out to mark off the grave.

Even if they all did look alike, at least the concrete headstones were big and solid. Better than the aluminum holders and the cards from the funeral home, which the rain washed out and people stepped on and bent down onto the ground so they couldn't be seen. It looked like a real graveyard with the headstones, instead of the park it had looked like with just John Henry's marker standing by itself in the middle.

For Billy Coon, Jessie took time out from his farming to dig the grave himself. He decided it didn't have to be as deep as for a person, but he dug it neatly anyway, squaring the sides and getting all the loose dirt out of the bottom. He put Billy in an orange crate, after he had knocked out the divider, laying him on his back and crossing his front paws. He thought that over for a while, since it was a coon — looking down at him in the orange crate and thinking that he should perhaps not put him on his back. But he didn't feel right about having him huddled down there on his stomach, so he decided to do it that way, putting in the red collar and the chain that Walt had told him to bury with Billy. Then he had laid a plank over the top of the orange crate and filled the hole back up, being careful again, and squaring off the sides of the mound when he had finished.

After he buried Billy Coon, he went down to the clearing and poured a headstone for him. He wanted to have a smaller one, which would have suited the grave better, but he couldn't make a special form for Billy either, so he had to use the regular one. When he had troweled it off smooth, he wrote the inscription into the wet concrete with his finger:

After he finished, he washed up his tools and went home to supper. It was coming on dark, and he didn't like to work on graveyard things after the sun went down.

Jessie looked down at the tombstone in the mold. It was too late to do anything about it. The concrete had set up hard. He could fill in the new inscription with fresh concrete, but he couldn't put a new one on. He would just have to throw away the headstone, wasting all the cement, and pour another one.

He sat beside the mold until the new pour had set up too hard to be changed. It was nearly midnight before he went home. Before he got there he had started to remember the snaky black hair and fingernails again.

Jessie worried about Anse making a joke of graveyard things. He thought about it the next morning while he was burying the ruined headstone. The trouble was, Anse was so mean he didn't know what to do about him. He decided to talk to Walt Shotford about it.

"I reckon it's some kind of a joke, Anse," said Dee Witt. They were standing under the big live oak tree where Billy Coon had been found. Right under the forked limb, looking down into the freshly dug grave, and then up to the thing hanging from the fork of the limb overhead. It was just sunup. The first streaks of light were coming out, so Anse and Dee Witt could see better every minute just what was there under the tree, hanging from the limb.

They had been out to the Sportsmans Lodge on Highway 17 until three o'clock that morning. When they left there, they had driven to Anse's house in his pickup. Anse had parked it in the yard and gone into the house to go to bed. Dee Witt had started home, walking down the road. As he went by the Golden Rainbow Church, he had seen the grave and the headstone, and hadn't known what to do about it. He had gone on back and told Anse.

"It's a piss-poor kind of a joke," said Anse. "A goddamn nigger joke is what it is."

Under the limb of the oak tree was a freshly dug grave. It had been dug very neatly, with the sides squared off and most of the loose dirt taken out of the bottom. The mound of loose dirt had been piled on the side away from the road, so anyone passing could see the hole in the ground. At the head of the grave was a concrete headstone:

From the fork of the limb over the grave hung a small doll. It hung by a piece of black fishline that had been tied around its neck, and then to a stick that had been jammed in the fork.

"Nigger joke," Anse said again.

They looked up at the doll, turning slowly at the end of the string. They could make it out clearly now, because it was getting lighter all the time. The doll was crude. It was made out of concrete, with rough places where the fingers that had shaped it had stuck in the concrete and pulled away little peaks and swirls. A big dab of red paint on top of its head identified it. They could see the red on the back of its head as it turned slowly at the end of the fishline.

"Get it down, Dee Witt," said Anse. "I can't stand no nigger joke anyway."

Dee Witt giggled. He looked at Anse, then up at the doll. "He done put the hex on you, Anse," he said.

"I know who done it," said Anse. "I'll fix his black ass. Now get up there and get it down."

"How'm I going to get it down?" Dee Witt asked.

"Climb the goddamn tree," said Anse.

"How come I got to climb the tree when you the one got the hex?" Dee Witt asked. "I near about fell and busted my ass last time."

"Get up there and get it down," said Anse.

"Whyn't you do it?" said Dee Witt, whining. "Maybe I fall and bust my head up there. You the one got the hex on you."

"*Maybe* you fall and bust it if you do," said Anse. "Sure as hell you going to get it busted if you don't." He looked at Dee Witt levelly out of his pale green eyes. "I'm going to count ten," he said. "If your ass ain't up that tree when I get to ten, I'm going to make you wish it was."

"I don't like to climb no trees," said Dee Witt. "Look how high that limb is."

"You going to be a whole lot better off up there than down here when I get to ten. I ain't going to argue with you," said Anse. "One . . ."

"Here," said Dee Witt. "Maybe we can get it down some other way." He picked up a clod of dirt out of the mound beside the grave and threw it at the stick jammed in the fork.

"Two . . . ," said Anse. "We ain't got all day. Sun be up good before long. I want that mother down from there right now. Three . . ."

Dee Witt picked up another clod of dirt and threw it. It hit the stick and dislodged it. The doll fell into the grave. When it hit the bottom, it broke. The head snapped off, and the two pieces lay there in the bottom of the grave, the body on its back and the head turned over to one side.

"Now you done it," said Anse.

"I got the piss ant down, didn't I?" said Dee Witt.

"You busted it," said Anse.

Dee Witt looked at Anse. "You ain't worried, are you, Anse?" he said. "It ain't only just a doll," he said. "You wouldn't worry about no nigger joke like that, would you?"

Anse looked down at the broken doll in the bottom of the grave. He clenched and unclenched his hands, and then he wiped them on the legs of his pants. His eyes darted around, looking over toward Shotford's to see if anybody was coming.

"Get down there and fetch it out," he said.

Dee Witt looked down at the doll and then up at Anse. "You wouldn't really worry about no nigger joke like that, would you?" he said.

"Get it out," said Anse.

Dee Witt stood on the edge of the grave looking at him. "You get it," he said. "You the one got the hex on you. You get down there and fetch it out."

Anse looked at him. "I'm going to knock your half-ass off for you, Dee Witt," he said. "Then you ain't going to have no ass at all. Now get down there and fetch it out. One . . ."

"I don't like to be getting down into no grave," said Dee Witt. "Even if it ain't nothing but only a nigger joke."

"Two . . . ," said Anse.

"Fuck you," Dee Witt said.

Anse looked at him hard. His mouth was still open a little from the "two." "What did you say?" he said.

"I said fuck you," said Dee Witt. "Get it out yourself."

Anse made a move toward him, and Dee Witt ran out into the road. He was talking loudly now. "You got the hex. You fetch it out," he said.

"You going to do what I tell you?" Anse said, keeping his voice down.

"Kiss my ass," said Dee Witt. "I ain't going to get down in no grave."

Anse darted his eyes around. Then he reached down and picked up a clod from the mound beside the grave and threw it at Dee Witt. The expression on Dee Witt's face never changed. The clod exploded on his forehead, spattering dirt over his face and sticking to his lips. His eyebrows were raised a little, and he seemed to be thinking about something a long way off, standing there with his eyes out of focus. He raised his hand slowly, wiping his face, slobbering and spitting out the dirt.

"You scared to do it," he said, talking with his mouth held open, spitting and trying to get the dirt out. "I ain't going to do it for you," he said. "Not this time. You get down there and fetch it out yourself."

Anse picked up another clod. Dee Witt turned his head to the side and hunched his shoulder when he saw it coming. The clod broke on the side of his head. He shuffled off down the road out of range; then he turned back to Anse, making a megaphone of his hands. "Anse, Anse, got 'em in his pants," he yelled.

Anse stood glaring at him down the road, then looked down at the broken doll in the bottom of the grave. He wiped his hand hard across his mouth, his hand balled into a fist. He darted his eyes over toward Shotford's and up and down the road to see if anyone was coming.

"Half-ass," he said under his breath. "Goddamn half-ass."

He picked up a clod from the mound beside the grave and threw it at the doll. It hit and broke, splattering dirt into the bottom of the grave. He picked up another, then another, throwing them down at the doll in the bottom. Every time a clod hit it, the doll would jump. The head rolled away toward the side of the grave. One of the legs broke off.

Anse picked up a double handful of dirt and dropped it on the doll, partially covering it up. He worked fast, scooping up handful after handful of dirt and dropping them into the grave until he had covered up all of the doll.

Then he went around to where the headstone was, and put his foot against it at the top and pushed it over. It fell on its back with the lettering up. So he got his fingers under the edge and heaved it over where the writing wouldn't show.

"I be damn," he said. "How'd he do that?"

The back side had the same inscription as the front.

"Nigger joke," he said, sitting down on the tombstone at the head of the grave and looking into the bottom where the doll was lying covered up with dirt. He hugged his arms around his chest, rubbing his hands on his upper arms.

A clod hit him on the back of the head, exploding dirt down his collar.

"Anse, Anse, got 'em in his pants," Dee Witt sang, yelling through his hands. Then he ran off down the road.

Anse got up and shook his shirt to get the dirt out. He pulled the tails out and jiggled himself up and down, watching Dee Witt run off down the road toward Shotford's store. Dee Witt went into Shotford's side yard. As he passed the shed in front of the store, Anse heard the screen door slam. Shotford stepped out from under the shed, leaning on the pump with his arms folded and looking across the road at Anse.

Anse stopped jiggling, standing there bent forward at the waist by the side of the grave, holding his shirttails out behind him, and looking at Shotford. He looked like he was making a curtsy.

He undid his belt and then turned his back on Shotford, starting to tuck his shirttails back in. Across the graveyard, on the far edge, Jessie Wight was standing. His arms hung down limply at his sides, but one foot was extended a little to the back, as if Jessie had been sneaking up on him, and Anse had caught him at it and frozen him in mid-stride. Anse froze too for a minute, looking at Jessie, with his hand already shoved partway down inside his pants, putting his shirttail back in. He looked back over his shoulder to see if Walt was still there. He was there. Leaning against the gasoline pump with his arms folded, looking at him. Walt's forearms looked enormous. Dee Witt had gone up to the hydrant in the side yard and put his head under it, washing off the dirt from the clods Anse had thrown at him.

Anse turned back around, not watching Jessie or Walt, and finished tucking his shirt back into his pants. When he finished, he took a deep breath, standing up straight and looking up and down the road. There was still no one else coming. He spit on his hands and rubbed them together; then he got down and began to wrestle the tombstone up so he could get it on his shoulder. It was too heavy for him to carry it using his arms alone.

It took a while. The stone was heavier than it looked. Anse guessed two hundred pounds. And it was an awkward size — too short for him to get his shoulder under it without lifting it off the ground. So he had to kneel down and lean it against his shoulder and then pull it up with his arms until he got it in place to balance. He could have done it better, but he had to do it smoothly, since Walt and Jessie were watching. It scraped and tore his shoulder while he was getting it into place.

When he thought he had it balanced, he straightened up, bracing it with his arms, and walked down into the road with it. He made about fifty yards, and then his shoulder muscle rolled out from under the stone and let it come down pinching on his shoulderblade. There wasn't any question of trying to stand the pain. The shoulder just collapsed on him, and he had to let the stone fall. It hit on its side, then flopped down flat in the middle of the road.

He stooped down and tried to get it up again, but the raw place hurt him too much to slide it up. And the arm wasn't any use to him now anyway. So he just had to let the stone flop down in front of him in the middle of the road.

He glanced off down the road, kneeling there with the headstone lying flat in the middle of the road in front of him. Way off, almost as far as he could make them out, two figures stepped up onto the side of the road, then turned, coming toward him, walking on the shoulder. Anse tried to get the stone up again, scraping his hands pulling at it, though he knew before he tried that he couldn't do it. All he could do was raise it up on its side, balancing it on the edge.

Finally he pushed it over flat in the middle of the road again; then he crawled up over it on his hands and knees, his arms straddled out on either side. He knelt there over the stone, panting and looking off up the road at the two men. Then he looked down at the stone beneath him, reading the inscription on it upside down. Over and over again, until his eyes went out of focus, and he couldn't see it anymore. He could hear the two men.

Without looking up, he lowered himself down onto the stone, covering it with his body. He laced his hands behind his neck and clamped his arms to the side of his head, pressing his forehead into the dirt of the road and shutting out the light from the sides. He tried to wrap his body around the stone so that all of it would be covered up.

"Nigger joke . . . ," he whispered to himself, clamping his eyes shut, ". . . half-ass nigger joke."

A Worker of Miracles

T

he Rainbow Pool is a small, open body of water — some forty-five acres in all — that fills a basin on the northwest border of the Dorchester Swamp. The water is dyed black from the saps leeched out of the cypresses and live oaks that grow in it, and from the leaves shed by the live oaks. It is clear water. Scoop up a glassful to look at it, and it hardly seems discolored at all. But the tiny particles, held in suspension, accumulate and make the blackness. Holding your hand just under the surface, you can see it clearly, but if you plunge it deeper, it will fade slowly until you can see it being amputated in the tannin-dyed blackness of the water.

The pool gets its name from the colors reflected on its surface — green and gray and black from the moss-draped live oaks and cypresses growing along its shore and in the water, blue and green and yellow from the patches of open sky that come in through the overhanging branches of the trees, pink and yellow and purple and white from the azaleas and honeysuckle and wisteria on the banks. Because the trees shelter it, the surface is generally smooth as polished glass. You can throw in a stone and watch the ripples spread all the way to the opposite shore. The black undercolor gives back the reflections in a way that makes them more intense. It is a very placid spot.

Brother Fisco uses a small cove just southwest of the Dew Drop fishing camp for the baptizings of his Two-Oak Missionary Baptist Church. Strictly considered, it is not a proper place for baptizing, because of the still water. He has tried spots here and there along the banks of the Altamahatchee and Oconee rivers, but he always comes back to Rainbow Pool. He is a pious man, and he likes the stillness.

"God's down there," he says. "God's down there in the water."

He has not always been a pious man — only for the last nine years. Brother Fisco — Garnet Fisco it was then (pronounced *Gar Net*, as if it were two names) — had gotten religion at a tent meeting in the spring of 1954, when he was thirty-one years old. Gotten it for the fourth time, really. But that was the time it stuck. He stopped drinking, stopped smoking, wouldn't let his wife, Della, wear lipstick or shorts — even though she was a handsome woman — and had torn up the two decks of playing cards they had in the house. He had also joined the Two-Oak Missionary Baptist Church.

For a year he was the most active member of the congregation — sometimes stepping in to deliver the sermon when Brother Campbell, the regular preacher, was called away to remote and more deprived congregations that could not afford a regular preacher every Sunday. Then, in 1955, when Brother Campbell left to go back full time to the mobile-home business in Brunswick, Georgia, Brother Fisco had stepped in and taken over the pulpit. No one objected. Finding a preacher wasn't that easy for a congregation that didn't want to pay one.

For Brother Fisco, preaching is a full-time concern, but not even a part-time means of livelihood. He gets four or five chicken dinners a month out of it, and a certain status in the community. But he has to make his living working, just like everyone else in McAfee County. By trade he is a cabinet-maker — a skilled one. With a toolbox made to display his craft — a hideous and intricate wonder of inlays and marquetry and ornate carving — filled with small saws and chisels that have been dulled to a soft glow with use. Six days a week he follows that trade. Sundays he does God's work in the Two-Oak church. As he fits the intricate joints on weekdays, he thinks of the power he sometimes feels in the church on Sundays, and he longs to be a full-time Man of God. But he is philosophical.

"Thy will be done," he says.

The Two-Oak church is a depressing structure — inside and out. It was built by the congregation just after the Second World War — a white clapboard box, with a steeple, and regular double-hung windows with panes that are painted blue. The light coming in through the blue paint makes the inside gloomy and depressing. The faces of the congregation look like mummies, with an air of settled-in sadness and melancholy. Brother Fisco's face looks like the face of a handsome man with cancer. Ordinarily he looks like a man who is dying. In the blue light of the church — except when he stands to the pulpit for the preaching — his face looks like the face of a man who is dead.

He has used his skill with wood to ornament the church a good deal in the eight years he has been the preacher there. For that alone his congregation should be grateful. He has carved a six-foot-long replica of the Praying Hands, which he painted white and mounted on the top of the steeple. He has made a pulpit that is even more intricate and ornate than his toolbox, with scenes representing the Ten Commandments inlaid in mahogany panels with mother-of-pearl — three months to make each panel. He has also carved a good many miscellaneous scrolls and crosses and plaques with verses from the Bible to decorate the pews and walls.

But his masterpiece is the giant crucifix that looms behind the pulpit, filling the back end of the church. He felled the cypress tree himself, then adzed the beams by hand into twelve-inch-square timbers — twelve feet tall and eight feet wide. With the cross arms fitted in an intricate lap joint, locked with wooden pins, that took him a full day to make. The Christ figure is a mannequin that he found in a trash can in the alley behind Levy's department store in Savannah, patched and restored with spackling compound, and dressed in a flowing garment that Della sewed for it by hand. It is attached to the cross with railroad spikes, fitted carefully through its hands and feet, then driven into the wood of the beams. Red paint marks the nail wounds in the hands and feet, and streams down its face from the barbed-wire crown of thorns.

Still, the blue light from the windows overcomes the grandness of the crucifix — just as it overcomes everything else. And Brother Fisco is happy when baptizing Sunday comes around so he can take his congregation out into the sunlight for a change.

It is not only the cheerful yellow-green morning light, filtering through the branches of the cypress and oak, that makes him love baptizing Sunday.

The relatives always want to be there to see it, so he can count on a good turnout. Nothing like the crowds of sixty or seventy who come for Christmas and Easter and the Fourth of July. But a respectable group of thirty-five or so. Something like a real congregation. Large enough to make him feel he is doing the Lord's work.

And the music. He especially likes the music. Sung haltingly by the group spotted on the bank, dressed in their Sunday clothes, with their Sunday piety to quieten them under the trees. It lifts him and raises him, showing him that the Lord's work is not in vain.

He will stand before them with the child to be baptized, and perhaps Mr. Deering, or some other of the deacons, to help him with the immersion. His coat off, but the good suit pants on. And a stiff white shirt with a tie.

He has to be the one to start them singing, and he puts as much volume as he can into the first two or three bars, straining to pull them after him: "*Sha* . . .

all we . . . ee ga . . . ather at the ri . . . iver . . ."

Just getting them started. Then his wife Della's clear, sweet alto will rise above him back of the group, lifting the burden of the song away, so that he will let his own voice slack off, and with his arm around the child, he will turn and lead her into the black water of the pool, while the chorus on the bank swells behind him: *"The bea . . . auti . . . iful the bea . . . auti . . . iful ri . . . iver . . ."*

Wading out with a little air of expectancy into the black water, wearing the pants to his good suit, feeling the sand and pebbles of the bottom as he slides his stockinged feet along. Not sure but that he will step on something that will hurt him, and knowing that if he does he will have to just step on it and keep going . . . knee-deep . . . thigh-deep . . . until the child is out above her waist, floating on her water-amputated legs — the song arching into the yellow-green light above him and leading him on: *"Ga . . . ather with the sai . . . ints a . . . aat the ri . . . iver . . ."*

Della timing the song so that they get to the last line just as he and the child reach the right depth for the baptizing, then swelling her voice behind the chorus, shooting it out above them like the last roman candle on the Fourth of July: *"That . . . aat flo . . . oows by the thro . . . oone . . . o . . . o . . . of Go . . . od . . ."* Then all standing silent, waiting for him to say the words.

He and the child would be facing them, Deering on the child's left. For a moment he wouldn't say anything, waiting while the song trails off through the cypress trees into the yellow air.

Then he would gather himself, not looking at the ones on the shore, nor at the child standing in the water to his left, but lifting his eyes and raising it up above them there. Saying the words.

" 'Then Peter said unto them, Repent, and be baptized every one of you in the name of Jesus Christ for the remission of sins, and ye *shall* receive the gift of the Holy Ghost.' "

As he speaks, he will raise his left hand gently, holding it in the center of her back, the fingers spread wide to give her support. Then Deering will take his position, ready to help if need be, and he will whisper to the child, "Get a hold of your nose with your left hand . . . Clamp it down tight . . . Cover your eyes with your right hand . . . ," whispering, ". . . *left* hand."

Placing his splayed right hand over the child's two, covering her face under the handkerchief. He can feel her contracting, going small between his hands . . . the size of a child's hollow rubber ball. Beginning to pitch over backward as she'd been told . . . leaning on him.

"I'll tell you . . . ," he would whisper, ". . . it ain't going to be slow."

Then again the words: " 'I baptize thee in the *name* of the Father, and of the

Son, and of the *Holy* Ghost. Amen'"

He would sway her three times, then pause, whispering, "Catch your breath, child," as the congregation responds their "Amen." Then he would be sliding her backward into the black water, watching the streaming hair waving over the white hands and the handkerchief. Only a moment before he would bring her back up sputtering into the yellow air.

The moment he would see her there beneath the water, with the strands of hair snaking across his hand, it would bring a power into him. He would feel that he might squeeze his hands together, make a motion with them, and the child would disappear. Vanish into the black water, like a magician gesturing away a cage with a live pigeon in it, as he had seen on the television.

"I am the Lord's chosen Vessel," he says to himself.

Thinking of what the congregation would say as he raised his empty hands in a *hallelujah* — after the Lord would have taken her away.

Then she would be back up out of the water, rubbing her eyes with her fists and wiping the wet hair away. The congregation on the bank standing silent, until Della's voice would lift behind them, and they would break into the song again as he was leading her to the bank, his arm around her shoulder.

"You done fine," he would be whispering. "You done just fine."

That was baptizing Sunday in the Two-Oak Missionary Baptist Church. The best Sundays of all.

Other Sundays, there would be the same two dozen or so faces, bland in the dead, blue light from the windows. Mostly older women, with a sprinkling of men — all of the men, except Lee Jay, there because they had official duties to perform, taking up collection and ushering. Brother Fisco tried to feel the power, but the faces and the blue light worked against him. In time he grew to hate them both. They became to him a measure of his failure, and a reproach.

The trouble was that he watched other Men of God on the television — Oral Roberts every Sunday, and Billy Graham from time to time — and he could see them moving their thousands, drawing them to the Lord in response to their call. Or he would listen to the Reverend McIntyre on the radio. And he knew that he felt the power too. But who could there be for him to move with it? Just the bland Sunday faces in the open space of the church, most of them huddled up on the first two or three rows, with here and there a solitary one sitting in the blue gloom. He knew that there was a key, but that somehow he was missing it. He should be able to make the power come out and fill the church — fill a tent twenty times bigger than the church. But he couldn't find the key. Meantime, the power went dribbling out over the stiff heads of his congregation, missing its mark and soaking into the ground.

"It ain't easy to be a Man of God," he would say. Eight years. "It ain't nothing easy *about* it."

After the Oral Roberts program went off, Brother Fisco would leave the television on to watch the *Mr. Wizard* program. He admired the cool, knowing way the man had. Feeling in him a certain kind of power as well. Different, but there.

On the first baptizing Sunday in the spring of 1963 the *Mr. Wizard* program was about how to use science to do tricks of magic to mystify your friends. Brother Fisco watched him as he made a candle burn under water. Made an egg drop into a milk bottle. Then Mr. Wizard did a trick that caused a bell to ring somewhere in the back of Brother Fisco's mind. He felt that he had found the key.

What Mr. Wizard did was pour some clear water into a glass and make it turn red. Then he poured it back into another glass and it turned back clear again.

He explained the trick: Water and phenolphthalein salts in the first glass. Baking soda in the empty second glass to make the alkali solution. Vinegar in the third glass to neutralize the baking soda.

"You can do it over and over again," he said.

Brother Fisco sat up. "Water into wine . . . ," he said. "What?" said Della. "It looks like the water into wine," said Brother Fisco. "Like the wedding-feast miracle of the water into wine."

"It's a trick," said Della. "He told you about it. Them chemicals and all."

"But that's the way it *looks*," he said. "Like the water-into-wine miracle."

"Yes," she said.

"I got to do *something*," he said. "They ain't really interested. Only it's habit for them to come."

"What?" she said.

"I'll do 'em a trick, with the water into wine," he said. "To make it interesting."

"You going to tell them?" she said.

"It might be I would," he said. "It's the Lord's work, Della."

"Shouldn't be no trick," she said, "and you not tell them about it."

"The Lord moves in mysterious ways," he said.

"The Lord ain't up to no tricks," she said.

He didn't say anything.

"You be careful," she said.

"I been careful," he said. "Eight years. I'm just where I was when I first started out."

So the next Sunday he was ready with the pitchers and the glasses and the chemicals.

He read the text: " 'And the third day there was a marriage in Cana of Galilee; and the mother of Jesus was there:

" 'And both Jesus was called, and his disciples, to the marriage.

" 'And when they wanted wine, the mother of Jesus saith unto him, They have no wine.

" 'Jesus saith unto her, Woman, what have I to do with *thee*? mine hour is not yet come.' Couldn't nobody never make Jesus do nothing didn't he want to," he said. "Not even his own mother couldn't do it.

" 'His mother saith unto the servants, Whatsoever he saith unto you, do *it*.

" 'And there were set there six waterpots of stone, after the manner of purifying the Jews, containing two or three firkins apiece.' "

Brother Fisco set six iced-tea glasses in a row across the top of the pulpit. "A firkin is nine gallons," he said. "I looked it up. Sounds like it'd be just a little bit, but I looked it up." A murmur ran through the congregation when he brought out the glasses. "Used to be they'd drink them a lot of wine," he said. "In Bible times.

"Not Jesus hisself, of course," he added. "Just them Jews."

The people in the church were sitting up and listening to him.

" 'Jesus saith unto them,' " he went on, " 'Fill the waterpots with water. And they filled them up to the brim.' "

He raised a glass pitcher filled with water from behind the pulpit. Holding it so everyone could see it. The water looked blue because of the light from the windows.

" 'And he saith unto them, Draw out now, and bear unto the governor of the feast. And they bare *it*.

" 'When the ruler of the feast had tasted the water that was made wine, and knew not whence it was:' "

He poured each of the glasses nearly full of the water from the pitcher, and the glasses were filled with purple liquid — like communion grape juice. Not red, because of the blue light from the windows.

The group huddled on the first three rows was leaning toward him, looking at the glasses. The ones sitting in the back got up and moved down to seats closer to the front. Lee Jay stood in a fourth-row pew, leaning on the back of the pew in front of him, looking at the glasses. When Brother Fisco poured the first glass, Lee Jay's eyes got big. "I be a son-of-a-bitch!" he said.

After he filled the glasses, Brother Fisco waited until they had gotten quiet again; then he went on.

" '(but the servants which drew the water knew;) the governor of the feast called the bridegroom.

"'And saith unto him, Every man at the beginning doth set forth good wine; and when men have well drunk, then that which is worse: *but* thou hast kept the good wine until now.

"'This beginning of miracles did Jesus in Cana of Galilee, and manifested forth his glory; and his disciples believed on him.'"

Brother Fisco slammed the Bible closed, making the congregation flinch. Every eye was on him. Lee Jay stood leaning on the pew, his head down and the collar of his coat rising like the scoop of a coal scuttle behind him.

While they waited, Brother Fisco picked up each of the iced-tea glasses in turn and poured its contents back into the pitcher, until it was full of clear, blue water again.

"I be a son-of-a-bitch!" said Lee Jay again — louder. Several of the women looked back at him over their shoulders. "Couldn't even Jesus do that," he said. "Water into wine into *water* again."

"Do it again," somebody said.

So he did it again. And then again once more. Leaving the six iced-tea glasses sitting on the pulpit, but manipulating the two pitchers behind it so they wouldn't see. Lee Jay got up out of his seat and came down the aisle to stand right in front. Watching. His eyes were big as saucers. Brother Fisco's gestures became more expansive as his confidence grew. He embellished his movements.

"Jesus' will be done," he said at last.

"Amen," said the congregation.

"Do it again," said Lee Jay.

"We will now sing hymn number three-seventy-six," he said.

He couldn't hear Della in the singing as it filled the blue light of the church. He never did preach the sermon he had prepared to go with the water-into-wine illustration.

When the singing stopped, he said, "Will you offer up our closing prayer, Brother Williston?"

Lee Jay stood in the fourth-row pew, leaning on the back of the row in front, sinking his head down between his shoulders, so his coat collar rose higher and higher behind his head.

"Lee Jay," said Brother Fisco, "will you offer up our closing prayer?"

Lee Jay's knuckles showed white where he gripped the back of the pew. His face was turning purple under his blue hair.

"Lee Jay . . . ," said Brother Fisco.

Lee Jay clasped his hands. "O Lord . . . ," he said. "O Lord Jesus . . . Jesus . . . Jesus . . ." His coat collar suddenly sank behind his head. ". . . Jesus loves me, this I know . . . ," he said.

"How'd you do that?" said Lee Jay as he shook Brother Fisco's hand leaving the church. "I ain't never seen nothing like that before."

"Come back next Sunday," said Brother Fisco.

"You going to do it again?" said Lee Jay. Other members of the congregation were standing around waiting for the answer.

"Come back and see," he said.

When they were driving home, Della looked out the window on her side of the car. "You didn't tell them how you done it," she said.

"I feel the *real* power, Della," he said.

For the next three weeks he did the water-into-wine trick, with the congregation getting bigger every week as the word spread. Finally people began to come in from outside the Two-Oak community. Two or three came out from Kose. He worked up a sermon on the miracles and the power of faith, and they sat still for it, hoping he would do the water into wine again.

In the meantime he had sent off for a Johnson-Smith and Company catalog of tricks and illusions that he had seen advertised in *Mechanix Illustrated*, and when it came he ordered five dollars' worth of tricks to use with his sermons. By the time the water-into-wine trick began to wear out, he was ready with others.

He did color-changing handkerchiefs to illustrate the "Do-not-let-your-right-hand-know-what-your-left-is-doing" text. And red balls that multiplied between his fingers — from one to four — for the "fishes-and-loaves" miracle. He tried some card tricks, but Della complained about that, because he wouldn't let her have any real cards in the house to play with, so he stopped.

He felt the power more and more.

"There's one thing I got to do, Della," he said. Supper was over, and she was clearing the table. He sat turning his coffee cup.

"What?" she said.

"I feel the power," he said.

"Well?" she said.

"I just been fooling around. They going to get tired of it sometime, and I'll be back with the little bunch of women and Lee Jay again."

"You're getting them to come in there now," she said.

"They got to *stay* in there," he said.

"Well," she said.

"But I *really* feel it," he said. "The *real* power. I got to do something. Something that will make them be able to stick."

She looked at him from the sink. "You got to be careful," she said.

"You done said that already," he said.

She didn't answer.

"I been thinking about it," he said. "You got to *feel* it. Then you could bring it off. Not if you didn't feel it."

"What is it, Garnet?" she said. "What is it you was going to do?"

He waited a minute before he replied. "I'm going to part the waters," he said flatly.

She looked at him. "What waters was it you was thinking about parting?" he said.

He waited a minute before he answered. "Kallisaw Sound," he said. "I could do it when I feel it. I got to be sure."

"Where is it you was going to go when you done it?" she said.

"Kallisaw Island," he said. "I could walk dry-shod to Kallisaw Island."

Della looked at him for a minute. "You going to be in some real trouble, Garnet," she said.

"If I didn't feel it," he said. "I got to really feel it first. Then I could do it."

She looked at him for a minute. Then she filled a cake pan with water from the sink and set it on the table in front of him.

"What's that for?" he said.

"Practice," she said.

He looked at her; then he hit the pan, skimming it against the wall. "God ain't going to be mocked," he said. " 'Oh ye of little faith!' "

" 'Pride goeth before destruction, and an haughty spirit before a fall,' " she said. "You better be careful."

" 'According to your faith be it unto you . . .' 'The woman is the weaker vessel,' " he said. "If you can't think of nothing better to say, you can keep your mouth shut. I got me two verses for every one you say."

She picked up the cake pan and put it on the table again. "You better practice anyways," she said.

"God . . . damn it, Della," he said.

They looked at each other for a long minute.

"I *feel* it," he said. "Ain't I done told you that? I feel it, woman. You can't put no test on the Lord. You got to just go ahead and *do* it."

She stood looking at him, not saying anything.

"I'm going to pray on it," he said, looking into the coffee cup on the table. "I ain't going to do nothing until I prayed on it."

"You better," she said.

"Eight years, Della . . . ," he said.

She looked at him. "You better pray on it good," she said.

The next Sunday he made the announcement.

"Brothers and sisters," he said. "I got something to say to you all this morning, and I want you to listen to me careful, so you are going to hear what I say."

A murmur ran around the church.

"I been your preacher for eight years," he said. "Eight years and two months this Sunday. I keep after it, but it is a discouraging kind of work. Most of you, you got yourself other business on Sunday mornings, so it seems like you can't never hardly find your way to this here church at all. You got to tend to your other business. Out there fishing and hunting and enjoying yourself, and ain't got no time to stop by His house and just drop in to give up a prayer to Him and be thankful for the good things he done give you to enjoy.

"God, He understands that, I reckon. Leastways, He's *got* to be used to it by now. But that don't mean it's right. That don't mean you should be left to walk in your ungodly ways and just get on with it like that. *I* ain't got used to it. I ain't *never* got used to it. I walked them ungodly ways myself for thirty-one years. I know.

"I'm telling you what's a fact, brothers and sisters. I know." He paused, holding on to the pulpit with both hands and nodding his head.

"But I know about something else now too." He stopped nodding and looked at them. "I know about how it is to walk in God's way. How it is to walk in God's sweet way. And that's what I'm here to tell you about this morning."

The congregation shifted uneasily. A murmur ran around.

"I ain't going to do you no tricks this morning," he said. "I been getting you into God's house with a trick, but I ain't going to do you no trick this morning."

"You ain't going to do no tricks?" said Lee Jay.

"Sit down, Lee Jay," he said.

He looked around at them for a minute without speaking. "You knowed it was a trick, didn't you?" he said. "The water into wine, and the color-changing handkerchiefs, and all the rest of it. A trick." He slammed his fist down on the pulpit.

"I got you into God's house with a trick, and that was the idea of it. But I got to tell you now that God ain't no trick. And the time for tricks is done past."

He took the glasses and the pitchers out and put them on the pulpit. "I'm going to show you how I been tricking you into the Lord's house," he said.

"And we're going to bring them tricks to an end."

One by one he explained all of the tricks to them — the water into wine, the color-changing handkerchiefs, the multiplying balls. They sat rapt while he told them.

When he had explained all of the tricks, he looked at them, holding the sides of the pulpit to steady himself. Then he gestured with his right hand, sweeping all the things — glasses, pitchers, handkerchiefs, balls — onto the floor with a crash. The congregation flinched when he did it.

"Now the trick show is over," he said. "God's work is going to be done."

"You listen to me," he said. "You listen to me careful, and I am going to tell you about something I am going to do that it ain't no trick at all. Just God's power and glory. I am going to lay it on the line."

He drew himself up, holding the pulpit in his hands.

"Today is July twenty-first, nineteen-sixty-three," he said. "The year of Our Lord, Jesus Christ, nineteen hundred and sixty-three.

"Next Sunday — July twenty-eighth — at two o'clock in the afternoon, at the public landing of McAfee County, Georgia, I will part the waters of Kallisaw Sound and walk dry-shod across the bed of the Sound to Kallisaw Island. I proclaim this publicly and in the House of God. I am moved by the Spirit of the Lord, and I call on you to witness the same. . . . Ah — men," he said.

The congregation sat stunned.

"What'd you say?" said Lee Jay, standing up.

"I said," he said, speaking slowly, "that I am going to part the waters of Kallisaw Sound next Sunday — July the twenty-eighth — at two o'clock in the afternoon, and that I would walk dry-shod across to Kallisaw Island."

Lee Jay stared at him. "How you going to do that?" he said.

"I am going to do it by the power of God and the strength of faith," he said.

"What?" said Lee Jay.

"Sit down, Lee Jay," he said.

Lee Jay sat down; then he stood back up again.

"And to prove it ain't no trick," he said. "I hereby offer my worldly goods — my house, the land that house is standing on, my nineteen fifty-nine Ford hardtop convertible, got a rebuilt engine . . . all my worldly goods — for sale to the first taker for the sum of one dollar." He held up his index finger.

There was a long silence.

"Your toolbox too?" someone asked.

"All my worldly goods," he said. "My toolbox too," he added.

Several hands with dollar bills in them began to go up, waving above the congregation.

"*After* church," he said. "Now," he said, "any of you that you think you've got the faith that is going to sustain you, he's welcome to come along with me. But if don't none of you come, I am going to do it by myself.

"Let us pray," he said.

Immediately after church, Case Deering bought the property, giving him one dollar in cash for a bill of sale written on a fan. Case then passed the fan to Della for a dollar.

"Just in case," he said. "It ain't that I don't think he's got the power."

"Yes," said Della. "Much obliged."

On the Sunday following, he preached no sermon. Instead, he spent the morning in the sanctuary of the church, kneeling before the giant crucifix and praying. Della sat on the back pew watching him. From time to time members of the congregation opened the door to look inside, but no one came in. At one-thirty he left the church, and he and Della drove to the public landing in his Ford.

The *What's Up Down in Georgia Show,* a local-events program produced by station WSOU-TV of Savannah, carried the event live.

There were two cameras and two sound men, and an announcer in a green blazer with a WSOU-TV crest embroidered over the left pocket.

The show opened with the first camera panning around, picking up the people milling around on the oyster-shell beach of the landing. There seemed to be an enormous number of people. The beach was not very large. Occasionally the camera would find an open space in the crowd through which the Sound itself could be seen, and Kallisaw Island in the distance.

". . . Not only people from the Two-Oak church," said the announcer's voice as the camera panned around, ". . . people from all over this part of Georgia. I have just been told that there is a couple here on their honeymoon from Saginaw, Michigan. Groups from Brunswick, Waycross, Pembroke, and American Legion Post Number 456 of Savannah. It's quite a crowd . . . a very large crowd . . ."

The camera focused on a group of pretty girls in shorts, slid in on telephoto, then out again. ". . . There are reporters here from all the local papers . . . the Atlanta *Journal-Constitution* . . . ," said the announcer. ". . . I've just been told that a man from *Time* magazine is here somewhere. I haven't been able to spot him yet . . ."

The camera panned around the crowd, then tilted up toward the sky. ". . . a beautiful day," said the announcer. ". . . temperature eighty-five degrees here on the McAfee County public landing, an easterly breeze of about ten miles an hour . . . Just a perfect day . . ."

The camera swung and picked up Brother Fisco's Ford edging through the crowd. A shout went up behind the announcer's voice. ". . . I believe . . . I believe . . . I believe Mr. Fisco . . . yes. Mr. Fisco has just arrived . . . his car has just arrived at the landing. We'll try to get a word with him when he gets out of the car. . . ."

A number of reporters — some with microphones — clustered around Brother Fisco as he stepped out of the car.

"Mr. Fisco . . . Mr. Fisco . . . you plan . . . Mr. Fisco, you plan to walk to Kallisaw Island? Mr. Fisco . . . let me through . . . Mr. Fisco . . . when did you first think about doing this, Mr. Fisco?"

The crowd parted to let him through with the reporters and the men with microphones. Several men were holding microphones up to his face.

"God's going to do it." His face on the television screen bloomed large, coming into the camera. Then the landscape tilted, losing the image. When it came back into focus, he was standing at the water's edge, looking out across the choppy waters of Kallisaw Sound. Kallisaw Island was a dark mound in the distance at the top of the screen.

". . . two point three miles from where Mr. Fisco is standing to Kallisaw Island . . ." The announcer's voice whispered in the background behind the picture. The camera swung to pick up the island; then the picture on the screen shifted to another camera directly behind Brother Fisco, looking over his shoulder across the Sound, with the island in the background near the top of the picture.

"We expect Mr. Fisco to begin in just a minute now." The announcer's voice was low, confidential. The noises of the crowd came up behind his voice from the background.

Brother Fisco walked up and down at the edge of the water, looking down at the ground. Just at the edge of the water line, but without getting his shoes wet. The crowd surged along with him, giving ground to make an open place for him to walk. One of the cameramen had to wade out into the water to get the picture.

". . . He made the announcement to his congregation last Sunday . . . two o'clock . . . today at two o'clock. It's . . ." — the crowd noises rumbled in the background — ". . . thirty-five seconds until two."

He stopped walking and turned to face the Sound, still looking down at his feet, standing at the very edge of the water. But not looking at the water. Looking at his shoes.

The picture shifted to the second camera, showing a closeup of his face in profile. His eyes were closed, and his lips were moving.

". . . getting ready . . . ," said the announcer.

Brother Fisco started to speak, and the camera on his face slid back out of telephoto, showing his whole body in profile. He had raised his hands, and stood with his head cocked down, hips swayed forward slightly, his body making a shallow figure S.

" 'And the Lord said unto Moses, Wherefore criest thou unto me? speak unto the children of Israel . . .' "

". . . he's speaking now . . . ," said the voice of the announcer. The crowd noises stopped.

" '. . . lift thou up thy rod, and stretch out thine hand over the sea and divide it: and the children of Israel shall go on dry ground through the midst of the sea . . .' "

". . . lowering his hands now . . . stretching them out toward Kallisaw Island . . ."

There was silence. The camera slid in for another telephoto shot of Brother Fisco's face. His eyes were strained closed, with his head cocked down. The breeze flapped the collar of his white shirt, blowing his tie back under his raised arm. He was wearing his good suit pants.

". . . seems to be concentrating very hard . . . Kallisaw Island is two point three miles across the Sound from this point . . ."

Brother Fisco clenched and unclenched his fists, holding his hands outstretched.

" '. . . Moses stretched out his hand over the sea; and the Lord . . . caused the sea to go back by a strong east wind . . .' "

". . . the wind is blowing from the east *today* . . . ," said the announcer.

" '. . . and made the sea dry land, and the waters were divided . . .' "

". . . the crowd is very quiet now . . . waiting . . ."

" '. . . went into the midst of the sea upon the dry ground: and the waters were a wall unto them on their right hand, and on their left . . .' "

Brother Fisco's head moved, and the camera slid back out of telephoto.

". . . he's walking into the sea!" The announcer's voice went up.

The camera followed him until he was a little over knee-deep. Then the picture switched to the camera behind him, slid in on telephoto, holding the picture on the water washing around his knees. The side camera came in again on his face. He was not looking down. Then he slowly lowered his arms to his sides and stood looking down into the water.

". . . well . . . ," said the announcer's voice. The noises were beginning to come up again from the crowd in the background. ". . . looks like . . . he'll have to try another day . . ."

The camera swung around the crowd, coming in close on their faces.

". . . Mrs. Fisco . . . over there . . . ," said the announcer. Della stood beside Case Deering, her arms folded under her breasts. The wind had blown her hair around across her face.

The camera picked up Brother Fisco coming back out of the water toward the landing.

A young man in dungarees and a checkered shirt ran into the picture, waving his arms and yelling, "I'm going to walk *dry*-shod to Kallisaw . . . Take my picture! . . . Take my picture! . . ." He ran into the water, going hard. For two or three steps he seemed to be walking *on* the water. Then he fell down splashing. Other young men followed.

". . . try to talk to Mr. Fisco," said the announcer. The camera picked him up walking into the lens.

". . . what . . . Mr. Fisco . . . what do you think, Mr. Fisco . . . what happened . . ."

Brother Fisco was still looking at the ground. He mumbled something.

". . . what? . . . Mr. Fisco . . . speak into the microphone, please . . ." The camera jerked around, trying to catch him going by. A hand with a microphone came into the picture.

". . . I felt the real power," he said.

". . . what? . . . Mr. Fisco? . . . What did you say?"

"I felt the real power. I don't know."

"But . . . what do you *think* happened?"

He looked back away from the camera. "I didn't . . . ," he said.

"What? . . . What did you say, Mr. Fisco?"

"I didn't," he said.

". . . Is it true that you sold your house, Mr. Fisco?" said the announcer.

His head stopped, centered in the picture, filling it. He said very distinctly, "Yes . . . all my worldly goods. It was *real*, mister." Then he walked out of the picture.

". . . Mr. Fisco! . . . Mr. Fisco! . . . ," said the announcer.

After he had left, the announcer tried to find Della to get a statement from her. She was nowhere to be found. So he began to talk to people in the crowd, getting their reactions.

"Are you a member of Mr. Fisco's church?" said the announcer.

"Whose?" said Lee Jay.

"Mr. Fisco. Are you a member of his church?"

"I would have thought he could have done it," said Lee Jay.

"Where are you from?" said the announcer.

Lee Jay looked at him a minute. "Kose," he said. He pulled out the bib of his overalls and threw back his head, looking inside. "Kose . . ." — he paused

— ". . . Geor . . . gi . . . a," he said, reading it off the inside of the bib. "AHR
. . . EFF . . . DEE . . . *Two.*" He let the bib go and looked at the announcer.
   ". . . and you are a member of Mr. Fisco's church?" said the announcer.
   "He turned the water into wine." said Lee Jay.
   "What?" said the announcer.
   "He done it with the chemicals," said Lee Jay. "He told us about it."
   "What did you say?" said the announcer.
   "Leastways the *water* was real," said Lee Jay.
   "I don't . . . speak into the microphone, please," said the announcer.
   "Listen," said Lee Jay, "he was *good.* I mean it, mister. He was good. I'd
have thought he was going to do it."
   ". . . yes," said the announcer " . . . let's see if we can get some other
reactions."
   He talked to the honeymoon couple from Saginaw, Michigan. "Have you
ever been in Georgia before?" he said.
   "I never did think he would do it," said the man. He had pale hair and an
unpleasant face. His voice was high-pitched.
   "Yes," said the announcer. "I understand you're on your honeymoon."
   "Who told you that?" said the man, frowning. The girl hugged his arm and
giggled. She had a hairdo that looked like a sneeze that had backfired into her
hair. There was some kind of shiny-looking hair spray on it that had matted it
together in long, ribbony sheets, like the New Year's Eve whistles that unroll
when you blow into them.
   "So you didn't think he'd make it?" said the announcer.
   "We've never been to Georgia before," said the girl.
   "I *knew* he wouldn't make it," said the man.
   "Yes," said the announcer, ". . . and you came all the way from Saginaw,
Michigan?"
   "Who told you that?" said the man. Then he turned to the girl. "You got a
big mouth," he said.
   The announcer turned to face the camera. "Good luck to our visitors from
Saginaw, Michigan," he said. "Let's see if we can get some other reactions."
   ". . . Are you a member of Mr. Fisco's church?" he said.
   "I been some," said the young man. He wore a checkered shirt, and his wet
hair was plastered down over his eyes.
   "Well," said the announcer, "and what is your name?"
   "What?" said the man.
   "What is your name?" said the announcer. "Speak into the microphone,
please."
   "Dee Witt," said Dee Witt.

"Well, Mr. Witt," said the announcer, "what did you think?"

"What?" said Dee Witt.

"I said, what did you think about Mr. Fisco's miracle?"

Dee Witt looked into the camera. "I'll tell you, mister," he said, pulling his hair out of his eyes. "He's full of shit as a Christmas turkey."

"You're on the *air*," said the announcer. "You're on the *air* . . ."

The sun was going down when Brother Fisco got to the Rainbow Pool. He had left the oyster-shell road from the public landing and cut across through the swamp to keep from meeting people. For five or six hours he had wandered around. For about two hours he had really been lost. Then he had gotten his bearings again and walked out to the pool. While he was walking around in the swamp a thunderstorm had blown up. It drenched him, but it made the air bright and clear.

He saw the Ford parked off under the trees, but he didn't go up to it to speak to Della. He was even afraid of what she would say. Instead, he walked down to the edge of the water.

The orange sky reflected on the surface of the pool, with the black trunks of the cypress trees cutting across the orange. Under the overhanging branches were serried black patterns, thrown by the leaves. The moss hung in dark festoons, no wind moving them.

For a moment he looked over the black-and-orange surface — still as polished metal — reflecting the sky. Then he walked out into the water and knelt down, holding his hands clasped before him under the water.

He heard the car door slam, but he couldn't hear Della's footsteps until she started into the pool.

"I ain't up to it," he said, not looking around at her.

For a moment she didn't answer. "I know it," she said. There was another pause. "What you want for supper?" she said.

"I ain't hungry," he said.

"I reckon not," she said. "You got to eat."

"I felt the power, Della," he said after a while. "I felt the *real* power."

"I know you did," she said. "I never took you for no liar."

He could hear her walking in the water behind him. Then he felt her hands on his shoulders.

"Jesus God," he said.

She patted him. For several minutes neither of them spoke. "It's pretty this time of the day," she said. "All black and red."

The ripples from her walking spread out in front of him, widening gently on the glassy surface of the pool.

"It's my favorite time of the day," she said.

"Jesus God," he said. "What we going to do, Della?"

He felt her hand patting his shoulder again. "I don't know, Garnet," she said. "It'll be all right. I didn't never take you for no liar."

He shook his head, sawing it from side to side.

Around the rim of the pool the frogs and crickets had started. Fish rising to feed broke the surface with slow, plopping sounds, like pebbles dropping into the water. In the eastern swamp — where night had already arrived — an owl yodeled mellow and soft. The evening noises coming up as the light was going away. Crooning, distant sounds. Overhead, streams of high red clouds ran in a vortex westward, coming down into the furnace glow behind the trees.

For a long time neither of them spoke to break the stillness. Garnet kneeling in the water, his head sawing slowly from side to side. Della standing behind him, looking up at the westering clouds. Then slowly he began to hear another sound, low and near. Gliding out of the evening sounds and climbing up beyond them. He stopped his head and raised his eyes, tilting back to listen. Behind him his wife's clear, sweet alto began to rise, singing the words of the baptizing song. Going away above his head like the trace of a shooting star in the rain-clear air. Over the calm, red waters and into the westering sky. Out of the cypress shadows . . . black . . . and still. . . .

Some Notes on McAfee County

McAFEE (mak´ · ä · fē — rhymes with *blacker we*) COUNTY: An imaginary coastal county of the state of Georgia. Bounded on the north by the Oconee River, on the south by the Altamahatchee River, and on the west by a surveyor's line running SSW from Fork Shoal on the Oconee River to Spratt's Landing on the Altamahatchee. On the east it touches Kallisaw Sound and the Atlantic Ocean.

County Seat: Kose (kōz — rhymes with *rose*) — population 1,017. There are four other communities in the county that are unincorporated and of unknown size — less than a hundred. These are Two-Oak, Rainbow, Willie, and Fork Shoal. They are pretty much the kind of a place they sound like they would be, though the people in them have their good times too.

The county covers a land area of 428 square miles, at a mean elevation of 16.8 feet above sea level. Population density is 14.3 per square mile.

Selling gasoline is about the leading industry of McAfee County, and there are more Standard Oil pumps than any other kind. But the Shell stations are nicer, on the average.

The 1960 census report put the population at 6,254 — the fourth-highest count in the history of the county. (Highest was in 1900, when there were 6,427.) Currently the percentage of Negroes in the population is down to 58%. In 1900 it was 80%. They seem to be drifting away.

There is not a single feed store in the county, but there are three hardware stores — all of which are doing a good business. The average adult male consumes 1.8 cartons of shotgun shells per year, 21 pounds of twelvepenny nails, 149 inches of galvanized chain, 1/3 of a shovel, and 1/16 of a submersible pump.

Fifty percent of the population are twenty-one years of age or older. About 18% have completed high school, but on the average they drop out after the seventh grade. The McAfee Alligators (the high-school football team — colors green and yellow) have won only three games in the last five years. The coach is pretty depressed about it, but the team doesn't seem to mind. They like the green-and-yellow uniforms and the trips they get to take.

At present the literacy rate is 64%, but it is rising.

The county has a total of fifty-seven churches, two-thirds of them Baptist. The Presbyterians are the smallest denomination, but their church in Kose is the most elegant.

There are 1,334 families, with an average income of $2,431 a year (1960 census figure). The number of rooms per house is 4.3, and the number of people per house is 4.2 — or one person per room. Thirty-nine percent of the houses have running water with indoor plumbing, but the ground water has a high mineral content, and the fixtures tend to corrode in a hurry. The sulfur in the water makes it taste and smell like hard-boiled eggs.

Between 1950 and 1960 there was a net loss by migration of 755 people. No one knows where they went. Probably to Savannah or Jacksonville. None of them ever came back to tell about it.

The average temperature for January is 55.6° Fahrenheit, and for July 82.5°. Rainfall is 55.73 inches per year.

In 1960 there were 71 deaths and 174 live births.

That's about it for statistics.

But there are other ways you could look at McAfee County.

If it were there, latitude 31° 30′ N. and longitude 81° 30′ W. would intersect at Shotford's Grocery Store and Filling Station.

If you could leap up into the air and hang there for a day while the world rolled around underneath you, you would see that it shares a parallel of latitude with Jesup, Georgia; Greenville, Alabama; Laurel, Mississippi; Nacogdoches, Waco, and Odessa, Texas; Enseñada, Mexico; Nagasaki, Japan; Nanking, China (Red China); Lahore, Pakistan; Bagdad, Iraq; Haifa, Israel; Alexandria, Egypt; and Marrakesh, Morocco.

Run a meridian of longitude up through the North Pole and around again, and it would pass through Spartanburg, South Carolina; Charleston, West Virginia; Cleveland, Ohio; Moosonee, Canada; Hudson Bay; Novosibirsk, Russia; Lucknow, India; Colombo, Ceylon; Paita, Peru; the isthmus of Panama; Havana, Cuba; and Cape Kennedy, Florida.

Those are the main places.

If only it were there, McAfee County would have a hell of a good location. Practically a crossroads of the wide world.

But, God damn it, it's not.

McAfee County, Georgia, isn't real.

So always remember. None of this is true.

I thought you ought to know.

The BLACK PRINCE

& *Other* *Stories*

By

Shirley Ann Grau

White Girl, Fine Girl

There are these two places — Stanhope and Kilby — and there are seven miles between. These are the only two towns that state records list in Clayton County. One of them is the state capital and the liveliest little place in the South: the pine ridges around town, the back yards of outlying houses, hold dozens of stills. And from them come the best corn likker in the state: smooth and the color of good Scotch. The legislators always manage to take a few gallons home with them. (After a man's got used to the doings of the capital, there's nothing so tedious as months spent at his home way out in the counties somewhere.) And for the three months when the two houses or the state supreme court are in session, the price of the likker always rises until it is beyond the reach of the colored people. The wise ones, of course, have laid by a supply, if they have had the money to do that; and those who haven't must sweat out the time sober. The police have learned to be vigilant during this time: extra squad cars circle around the colored part of town, which on these nights hums with a restless aimless anger. The state police come in, too, and their white-painted new shiny cars move up and down the streets. There are more fights this time of year than any other. More knifings. The price of burial insurance goes up. And the warden's desk at Kilby is full of yellow tissue-paper triplicate records of new prisoners.

That's what Kilby — the other place in Clayton — is, the big colored prison. It's a town: just three or four buildings for a grocery; and a railroad platform with the name KILBY painted in white letters on a green board and hung from the edge of the roof, right over the room that has a smaller sign:

Post Office; and a few houses around, the biggest one with the yellow clapboard walls and the green shutters for the warden's wife, and the smaller ones painted all yellow for the guards' wives. (The men rarely come down to these houses; they spend most of their time inside the walls; it is as if they have a sentence to serve.) There are other houses for the colored washwomen and the cleaning women and their men and their children. This is the town of Kilby; this is what the county records show. But the real Kilby is half a mile north: the white brick walls and the machine-gun turrets, two on each side, and the men inside: the white guards and the colored prisoners.

You can't see Kilby from any point inside the limits of Stanhope, though if you stood on the capitol steps, on the spot where Jeff Davis took his first oath, you'd be staring in the right direction, and if your eyes were sharp enough, you'd see. But you don't.

But you can see the town from Kilby. On clear days in broad daylight the smoke from the mills comes up plain and still and fans out like a branch in the sky. And the white guards prop their rifles between their knees and the parapet wall and lean on their elbows and watch. And the colored trusties dangle their billies between limp fingers and fold their arms and watch the branch bloom out in the sky.

At night you can see even plainer. During the war, when the mills worked full time on army contracts for tents and sheets and bandages, you could see the smoke come up red against the black sky. After the war, when the mills closed down at night, you could still see a glow — a different one — over where the town was. The lights from the cafés and the clubs: sometimes low under clouds before a storm, sometimes rising straight up, soft like cotton into a clear black sky, sometimes a yellow and small circle under the moonlight. Just lights, from seven miles away over blue pines and fallow patches and little streams that have water in them only during the spring rains; and whole hillsides of hackberries with thorns thick as a rooster's spur; and one river, slow, yellow, and without a bottom; and red dust that any wind — summer or winter — is going to lift and send sliding off down the air. And there is always a wind and the dust moving.

It was a flat hot sun in a powdery white sky when Jayson Paul Evans walked out of Kilby prison. He leaned against the white brick building and hitched up his belt.

The guard behind him at the gate said: "Waiting for a car to come along and pick you up?"

Jayson moved his mouth in slow chewing circles: "Don't reckon I expect none."

From the top wall another guard called "Get started there." He was directly overhead looking down.

Jayson stood clear of the wall and bent his head back to see. In the light his wide black eyes turned shiny like the sun.

"Sweet Jesus," the man at the gate said. "Ain't you ever gonna get out of here?"

Jayson stopped looking at the guard directly above him. "I reckon I will," he said to the man behind him. "I reckon I will now."

There was a strip of asphalt to the town, black asphalt with a white painted line down the center. A carefully painted line. He had done some of the work himself a couple of days earlier. That was how he'd cut down his twenty years for manslaughter, working it out in the road gangs.

He did not see a single white person in the town of Kilby; only the colored washwomen hanging out clothes on fences and bushes. The white wives would be inside. He thought of them briefly: in their slips, lying on beds, with shades drawn, fanning themselves slowly, waiting for the evening to come.

Beyond Kilby on the main highway he turned south, the sun beating hot against his left cheek and his eyes beginning to water from the dust. After he had walked nearly a mile, after the white walls were out of sight, he left the road, cutting across the fields, walking in a straight line for Stanhope. These were old fields; the plowed ground had hardened with rain and frost and sun until it was solid as boards, only a little uneven. And it was easy walking.

"I got no cause to hurry," Jayson told a dusty black crow that scratched on the bare red earth. "No cause to hurry." The crow looked at him sideways out of a light yellow eye and hopped into the protection of the barberry bushes.

Jayson laughed and pulled off his shirt. "Scared of me?" He hooked the shirt through his belt and went off at a jogging trot, his heels striking hard against the ground: a big man making long steps. The dust that came up white from the red ground settled on his skin, and sweat ran crisscross lines in it.

There were trees along the low places away to the right; he could have skirted through them. They were pines: no underbrush to make rough going, just a soft floor of needles and a clean smell when his feet crushed them.

He stood and looked at the trees, and wet his lips with his tongue and spit out the dirt taste. But he kept going, the quickest way, right across the old fields that had been plowed wrong first years ago and that nobody would bother with now and that each year got drier and darker and more washed into gullies and more full of powder, so that each time the wind blew across them, summer or winter, their dust would come swinging up on it. Jayson went on, stumbling a little on the sharpest gullies, swinging his arms wide for balance, and singing for company:

> *"The sun is real hot,*
> *Oh Lord. The sun is real hot*
> *And the wind is hot*
> *And the dust is rolling around,*
> *Oh Lord, Oh Lord, Oh Lord."*

The old plowed bare ground went down across two hills like a ribbon trailing and ended up on a line of staggering fence posts and dragging wire. Jayson kicked at one post; it crumbled without sound: the center had dried away. Jayson wiped one hand across his bare chest, leaving a black streak in the red-white dust. Then he began to push his way through the bushes. They were elderberry mostly, green and yielding. When his fingers touched the soft round stalks, they bent aside smoothly. From a single laurel he pulled a broad leaf and chewed it slowly, bit by bit, until he had eaten it up the stem.

He was going downhill now. He had to work his way along sideways to keep from falling. The rocks — granite most of them, with sparks of fire in the light — rolled under his feet and he had to hold to the elder stems, pale and smooth. For just a moment he stopped and looked at one and rubbed his thumb up and down its length, from the ground up to as high as he could reach.

The thicket ended as a sharp gully, in its bottom during the summer months just a thin trickle of water, so narrow he could almost straddle its breadth. Jayson scrambled down one of the sharp crevices of the side and put his fingers in the water. Then he knelt down and carefully reached in his arm, feeling for bottom; he stretched out his fingers and touched nothing. He drew back his arm and wiped fingers across his lips to taste the water. It was warm from the sun and strong with leaf taste. But he was thirsty and he drank from his cupped hands.

A train whistled to his right. He lifted his head and listened, cocking just a bit to guess the distance. Then he moved off in that direction, following along the bottom of the gully. The tracks, he remembered, were on the far side of the Scantos River, and the whistle had been close, not more than a mile. He had to walk much farther in the twisted gully — two, maybe three miles; but it was easier going than across the fields of the thickets. (You never could tell when you would have to walk miles around a batch of hackberries all tangled together.)

He was beginning to be hungry by the time he reached the river — the broad yellow river moving slowly under the afternoon sun, moving so slowly that you could swear it was solid like ground; moving slowly because it had no bottom.

Jayson tossed a stone out as far as he could, almost to the other bank. "Sweet Jesus," he said, "I reckon you can just rest quiet, you old hungry man inside me. There ain't nothing I can do."

He followed the river south, looking for a way across, looking for a sandbar or a skiff. On the other bank a train went past, a diesel, shining silver in the sun, going all the way to New Orleans.

The heat of the day was beginning to make him sleepy so that he did not see the boys until he could bend over and touch them: squatting on the sands, peeling willows for fishing poles. They turned heads up to him, mouths open with surprise, eyes popping.

"Why," he told them, "if it ain't two nice little boys; two nice little boys my color."

They got to their feet very slowly and began to back away, feeling carefully behind them for each step. The bigger one, light-brown colored, had a hunting knife at his belt. His fingers unsnapped the guard and took hold of the handle.

Jayson laughed. "That a mighty big knife you got there, boy."

The boy held the leather sheath in his left hand; the right loosened the blade.

"You acting like a real man there," Jayson told him. The little one, who had been standing next to him, had disappeared. There wasn't even a sound when he slipped away. "You might could be thinking that you a man."

The knife was out now. The boy held it crosswise in front of him.

"I can see you ain't so foolish to go throwing that thing," Jayson said. He bent down and picked up a brown paper bundle with the grease markings that food leaves. He smelled it briefly. His eyes did not move from the boy, who was on tiptoe now, swaying back and forth, balancing himself for a fight: afraid, but holding his knife steady. And when his lower lip began to tremble, he took it firmly in his teeth.

"I reckon you think you a man," Jayson said. Out of the corner of his eye he had seen the skiff, pulled up on the river sand. He backed toward it, tossing the food package inside, and began pushing it out. Once he stumbled on the uneven bottom, but recovered his balance without taking his eyes from the boy.

The boy shifted his grip on the knife; he held it lightly with two fingers on the blade.

"Ain't no knife gonna stop me," Jayson said, "and I come back and kill you with it."

The muddy yellow water reached his knees. He climbed into the boat and picked up the long pole. He gave two hard shoves and the pole no longer touched solid ground. Then Jayson stood in the boat, the pole held crosswise in his two hands, and looked down at the river and waited until he could drift across the bottomless part and could use the pole again.

On the other side, he left the skiff on the sands and, holding the package of food in his left hand, scrambled up the bluff: the going would be easier along the bed of the railroad. At the top he turned and looked across the yellow river. On the other side the boy had not moved; he was still standing there, the knife ready. And the second boy, the little one, like a black monkey slid down the trunk of the bay tree where he had climbed to be out of the way.

Jayson Paul saw the tall twin chimneys of the cotton mill that was on the outskirts of town. "Right over that little bunch of pines." His shoes, which he had tied together by the laces, he swung in circles around his finger. "Right over yonder." He sat down on the ground and crossed his feet under him. A big yellow and black spider dangled from a honeysuckle bush, sliding up and down on its web. Carefully, with one finger, Jayson Paul shifted the thread to another branch. "That ought to mix you up some, Mr. Spider," he said. Then he stretched himself out full along the ground and sang into the heat of the late evening.

> *"I been in the pen so long,*
> *Yes, I been in the pen so long,*
> *I been in the pen so long, baby,*
> *Baby, that where I been so long."*

He drew his knees up close to his chin and wrapped long arms around them.

> *"I been in the pen so long, baby,*
> *Too long, baby,*
> *I gonna stop lying alone, baby,*
> *Baby, I been away so long."*

For a while after he stopped singing he lay there, his eyes closed thinking how it would be.

Jayson Paul leaned against the tarred black wood of a lamppost and began to put on his shoes. Smoke from the trash incinerator of the mill made him shake his head and sneeze.

"Sweet Jesus," he said. "I done forgot how to breathe."

The mills had closed down for the day. There was no one on the streets; they would be inside eating now. Over the burning the smell of frying was heavy on the beginning night.

"I be mighty glad to get home," he told himself. "For sure. It be real fine.

> *I'm working my way back home,*
> *Oh Baby,*
> *Working my way back home,*
> *Oh Baby,*
> *Working my way back home."*

He recognized the neighborhood: it hadn't changed. First the scattered houses with stretches of bumpy weedy places between them and a few cart horses and a cow or two pulling the tops off the longest grasses. Then houses closer and closer together until at last there was no space or grass between them, just dirt alleys and dirt streets and dogs licking the dirt off their paws on front porches and dust lying over everything; a church, brown-painted with a crooked steeple: they had had a still in the basement once; he wondered if there was any there now — he would have to find out. (Once he could have told you exactly where every batch of brew could be found. It would take time to learn all the new spots again.)

The street lights went on. He looked up at them, strung out yellow against a sky that wasn't dark yet. Jayson remembered them looking that way. He hadn't forgotten anything.

Over to the left was the Pair-a-Dice Bar with its green-painted door and on each side the full-length posters of white girls drinking Jax beer. He pushed open the door and went in. There was only one light burning, a small one without a shade over the bar. The first table was so near the bar he stumbled into it and stood for a minute blinking. He saw that they had added more tables but that nothing much had changed. Behind the bar, the cracked mirror framed in scrolled black wood; the pin-up pictures stuck into the frame and pasted on the glass; the three peacock feathers — red and blue and black — dangling by a cord from the ceiling and turning around and around in each draft — he had seen all this before.

The man behind the counter leaning on his elbows reading the funny page of last Sunday's paper was coffee-colored and young — too young for Jayson to remember him. And his eyes when he looked up at Jayson were the same color as his skin.

"Man," Jayson told him, "I come looking for somebody."

The light eyes blinked twice. "Who for?"

Jayson pulled out a chair and sat down, backwards so that he could lean his folded arms on the back. "I come looking for somebody but I ain't got no idea where she living at."

"That right?" The young man bent his head toward the funny paper again.

"I ain't seen her in quite a while and now I got to find her."

The years in prison had made him careless. He hadn't noticed Joe standing across the room. Joe, with the red and green baseball cap and the light kinky brown hair that stood up straight in front, almost as high as the snapped-up visor; a short man but very heavy and with the curved baling hook of a warehouseman stuck in his belt. Jayson stood up so quickly that the chair caught against his leg and fell over.

"Hey," the light-colored young man said and lifted his funny paper straight up. "What you doing?"

"I done thought I was seeing wrong but I reckon I ain't," Joe said.

"How you?" Jayson told him quietly. He didn't have a knife or a razor, so he kept his hand on the back of the nearest chair and he bent his knee against the edge of the table, ready to send it over.

"Hey," the young man said, and rubbed his light hairless chin with a quick nervous hand. "What you all doing?"

"You was looking for Aggie." Joe leaned back against the wall, his fingers rubbing the wood cross handle of the hook.

"I might could be doing that." Jayson hunched his back and waited.

"You ain't gonna do no fighting in here," the young man said, and pulled at his fingernails. "You ain't gonna do nothing like that."

Joe turned and looked at him and laughed. "No," he said. "We ain't gonna do nothing like that. Iffen he wants to find Aggie, I reckon I ain't gonna stand in his way."

"You ain't used to talk like that," Jayson said softly.

Joe kept on laughing. "Man, I ain't got no more interest in Aggie. I done had it and finished there."

Jayson stood watching him until he stopped laughing.

Joe said: "I reckon I gonna buy us a couple of beers." He sat down and Jayson took a chair about ten feet away. "Ain't got no cause to be scared of me," Joe said, and rubbed his round black face with his hands. "Ain't carrying no meanness for you for the time you like to kill me."

The young man pulled two bottles out of the rattling ice and brought them over, still dripping, and stuck out his thin yellow hand until Joe paid him.

"Why, Jay, man." Joe turned his head around and pulled off his baseball cap; the base of his skull was crossed by thick white scars. "You like to kill me right. Like you did to Mannie."

"Yes," said Jayson. "I done thought about that time." *He couldn't remember it though. Not very clearly. He had been fighting, but he couldn't swear who he was fighting with. He had killed Mannie and he didn't remember it. Nights in Kilby he had tried to call it back and couldn't. All he could remember was fighting and his mouth open and dry and the taste of dust in it.*

"I done thought about it," he said.

Joe tipped back his head and put the bottle to his lips. When he put it down again, he shook his head and rubbed his hand across his mouth. "I used to could take off a whole bottle one gulp that way."

"I remember," Jayson said. *And he did remember that. His mind was full of pictures of Joe emptying a bottle at one gulp. In some of them there'd be a girl in his lap or hanging around his shoulders. He remembered the feel of their skins, soft and moist.*

"I remember," Jayson said.

"A whole bottle," Joe said. "I used to could do."

"I remember," Jayson said. *He remembered: the stuff they'd made. The best corn likker there was: smooth and sweet on the tongue. They could make their own price for it and find buyers any time.*

It was Mannie who found buyers in the white people from the houses on Capitol Hill, the most important people, who had money and a taste for good corn. Mannie had sold to all of them. That's what he did best — sell. With his broad black face that was always shiny with perspiration even in winter, he had a way with white people; they were always glad to buy from him. He was chauffeur to Senator Winkerston's family, but his money did not come from that job. He only used their car to deliver the likker. It was a plan the police never would have caught on to.

"Never in a million years," Jayson said aloud. They had to go ruin it themselves, the three of them. And because of Aggie.

Mannie spent most of his time up at the Winkerston house. He had a room over the garage. Mrs. Winkerston had had it specially painted for him because he was such a splendid driver. He spent most of his time up there (when he was not actually driving the car or washing it) stretched out on his bed, wearing the silk pajamas he always bought with his share of the likker money.

Jayson had never seen the room, but he had seen the pajamas when they had just come and were still in the box that had the name in fancy Old English letters of the store in New Orleans. And when he saw them he wished for a moment that he had some, too, but just for a moment, because he was wishing for other things.

Mannie had a wife, whom he married in church on Easter Sunday — a tall light-brown woman whose name was Aggie. She lived in the colored section of town because at the Winkerstons' with Mannie there was no room for her and their son.

Jayson remembered: a tall woman, light-colored, a thin face, pinched almost; darkness under the cheekbones; and long eyes set wide apart. A thin woman with full nursing breasts. He saw her sitting on the steps of the house in the colored section that Mannie rented and hardly ever lived in. Mannie preferred his room over the garage with the white family. He knew where his wife was; he could find her when he needed her. When he did, he would take one of the Senator's cars and drive down (the family had no objections to his keeping the car overnight), certain that he would know where to find her. And one time he found Jayson, too.

He was surprised. Even Jayson saw that. His round black face (the smiling affable face that the white people liked) was completely blank with surprise. And he staggered a little bit; he had had a few drinks coming down, the best of the stuff they made.

"I remember," Jayson said. *But he did not remember exactly what happened after he looked up and saw Mannie. He had fought and there had been the blood taste in his mouth and there had been the screaming of Aggie somewhere: he heard it far off. His head was swinging from the whisky and excitement of the fight. And when Mannie's razor slashed along the side of his neck, he felt the blood run but no pain. There wasn't anything but breath coming short and not air enough and dust taste and smell. And from the corner of his eyes he saw the icepick on the table and grabbed for it.*

He remembered: *after he had finished with Mannie and was straightening up for breath there had been a short jab along his ribs. He had spun aside and brought down a bottle on Joe's neck. (Joe, who was Mannie's friend and the third partner, who had driven over with him and stayed out in the car to keep an eye on the stuff they had in the back seat).*

Joe held the bottle up to the light. "Used to could take off a whole bottle that way once. Used to once."

"I remember," Jayson said.

"Can't no more. Getting old, maybe. All us getting old."

"Maybe," Jayson said.

"Now you come back looking for Aggie."

"That right." Jayson said.

"She ain't gonna have nothing to do with you."

Jayson grinned. "Just tell me where she at."

Joe shook his head. "She ain't gonna have nothing to do with you." He looked up quickly as Jayson shifted in his chair. "Don't be getting riled up, man. I just telling you what's going on."

Jayson put both hands on his knees and bent forward. "What going on?"

"Drink you beer, man."

"What going on?" Jayson said slowly. "You tell me what going on."

"That what I trying to do." Joe sighed and reached for Jayson's bottle. "Iffen you can let me."

"Go head," Jayson said.

"Aggie ain't having nothing to do with no men."

"Go head." Jayson said, staring at him. He ran his tongue briefly over his lips; they tasted dry and dusty.

"She ain't had no luck with them, the three or four. They just give her kids and no money."

"She got three — all of them girls. The boy, the one that was Mannie's, the one that got baptized in the church, he went and drunk some lye water that his ma was washing clothes in and died. The biggest girl, she yours all right. Looks like you.

"And Aggie got plain mad. So she ain't having nothing to do with no men. She don't let anybody come in her house no more. And she got the kids so they don't let their daddies walk down the street. They got to go round the next block or the kids throw rocks at them. And they big enough to hurt." He grinned and poked one finger down the neck of the beer bottle. "You ought to seen what they done to me, walking past. Just walking past. Not noticing Aggie. Not even studying her. Just walking past."

The street was narrow and without sidewalks. On the north side a brick wall began at the edge of the gravel; the late evening sun struck color off the broken glass on the top. Behind the wall and out of sight were the low brick buildings and the vegetable gardens of the white poorhouse. On the south side of the street ran another wall — of houses, mustard color; in front of each, four wooden steps. A solid wall: wood house, alley gate, wood house, and so on for the entire block. Aggie lived in the second one from the corner with her three girls, who were all half sisters.

Evenings it rains in Stanhope. Not hard. Not hard enough to make it any cooler; not hard enough to settle the dust really. The drops mostly stay as they fall and roll around the top layer of dirt in round blobs until they dry away. Althea, who was the second girl and was eleven, walked up and down in the street, breaking the heavy drops with her bare toe. Anna, who was five, sat cross-legged on the top step, the broadest one, the one with the pile of brick fragments. Alice Mary, who was the oldest and Jayson's child, was sitting on the bottom step. She was thirteen, big for her age, with the beginnings of a heavy woman's body. She sat with her head bent into her hands, dozing in the heat of the late evening.

Althea skipped back in from the street with her quick skip and jammed sharp little fingers into Alice Mary's side. "There he come," she said.

The sun was still so bright: Alice Mary blinked and rubbed her eyes. The piece of brick she had fell into her lap. "Who coming?"

"My Daddy Joe." Althea picked up the brick and juggled it in her hand. "I reckon I could hit him way off where he at." She was big for eleven, with the broad shoulders and back of an older boy.

"There he come," little Anna said. "There come Althea's Daddy Joe."

Alice Mary leaned back against the wood steps. "I sure see him now. Come right slam down the middle of the street."

"I can hit him now for sure." Althea did not stand up, but her right hand snapped forward and the piece of brick hit the man squarely in the stomach.

He gave a quick growl of pain and cupped his hands over the sore spot. The three girls laughed.

"Sweet Jesus" — he rubbed his square chin with one hand — "iffen I ever get my hands on you."

Althea stood up, another rock in her hand, and shouted: "Go off, Daddy Joe. You can't walk down our street. You can't walk by our house."

The three girls called: "Go off, Daddy Joe. Go off, Daddy Joe. Go off, Daddy Joe." Then they stood up and, fast as they could, threw the rocks at him. He dodged around the corner at a scuttling run.

Alice Mary stuck her head in the front door and told her mother: "Daddy Joe was coming down the street."

"I reckon I know," Aggie said. She was lying on the bed in the first room, in her slip to be cooler. She worked as a cook in one of the big houses on Madison Street and when she got home she always lay down for a while before she looked for supper. "I reckon I heard all the racket."

While Joe stood around the corner watching them, Alice Mary helped Althea and Anna find other pieces of brick. They always kept a pile on the front top step.

Joe rubbed his hands over his face and stared at Jayson. "That plain what happened."

Jayson grinned and did not answer.

"That it, all right."

"Let kids chase you," Jayson said.

Joe chewed his underlip. "It ain't worth getting you face bashed none. Just to walk down a street."

"I reckon I best visit her for a spell," Jayson said.

"They ain't gonna let you near the house."

Jayson was still grinning when he stood up.

Joe pointed one finger at the Jax beer poster: a girl, a white girl with red hair and green eyes and a mouth open and waiting. "You ought to go looking for one like that."

Jayson hooked thumbs in his belt and studied the poster. "Hell, man," he said. "Where I gonna find something like that?"

Joe grinned.

"You ain't knowing where."

"Sure," said Joe. "I reckon I know where there one looks like that."

"Jesus," Jayson chewed his lower lip. "Why ain't you got her?"

Joe grinned and made crisscross lines on the wet table oilcloth. He was embarrassed. "She won't have nothing to do with me. She says she don't go for nobody little."

"She ain't white."

"Plain near almost," Joe said.

"She ain't like that." Jayson was staring at the poster.

"I done said she is. Hair and all. You plain got to go take a look."

"Where I got to look?"

Joe grinned. "Iffen you went walking through the houses back of Lansford Mill, she come walking up to you."

Sweat tickled down the side of Jayson's neck and he rubbed at it with the back of his hand. "You reckon she would?"

"Iffen she took a liking to you. You wouldn't even need no money."

"You reckon she would?"

"Hell, man," Joe said. "She there almost like she waiting for you."

Jayson swung his leg in wide circles. "I reckon I better see Aggie first."

Joe rubbed his chin and pulled at a stray hair on his cheek. "She a lot better-looking than Aggie."

"Maybe," Jayson grinned. On the upper left-hand side of his mouth most of the teeth were missing. "But I reckon I will all the same."

"I plain don't study you."

"Man," Jayson said. "I go to Kilby account of Aggie and I sure gonna want her now I out."

"Now you out," Joe said. "What you planning for money?"

"Don't figure trouble getting none, long as people still drinking."

Joe rubbed his hands and grinned. "Like it used to be. Before the fight where Mannie got killed."

"Maybe," Jayson said. "But I got something else I want now."

Joe shook his head and rubbed his teeth with his knuckles. "Aggie ain't young no more."

"Don't reckon I am neither."

"Hell, man," Joe said. "There ain't no use fussing with a woman when she get old."

Jayson grinned. "She was a mighty lot of woman, I remember."

"Okay," Joe said, and tipped back his chair. "You go head. But I'm telling you. She got religion now. She ain't gonna have nothing to do with you."

"Ain't no woman not going to have nothing to do with me," Jayson said. "Now where she living at?"

Over in the direction of the river the chimney sweeps were swinging wide across a sky that was filling with faint summer-night haze. The night wind was beginning to stir the first top dust of the streets.

Inside the mustard-colored wood house Aggie had got up and was beginning to fix supper. The kitchen was two rooms away from the front steps but the noises carried plainly: the banging of pots and singing, a hymn:

> *"King Jesus lit the candle by the waterside*
> *To see the little children when they truly baptized.*
> *Honor, honor*
> *Unto the dying Lamb."*

In the house where she worked on Madison Street she was very quiet; here she listened to the sounds of pots with pleasure. On Madison Street she was an elaborate cook (to the joy of her employers); here she boiled potatoes and tossed a chunk of bacon in a frying-pan. Then she wiped her face with her hands and went back into the front room to lie down again on the bed with the week-old copy of *Life* she had brought from the house on Madison Street.

Outside, Anna had gone back to sleep, her head pillowed on the step above. Althea was building a little arch of the pieces of rock; whenever it reached a certain height Alice Mary would laugh and poke it with her finger.

The arch of rocks collapsed. "You plain got to stop that," Althea said.

"Why I got to stop?" Alice Mary said. "Why I got to stop?"

"You plain got to stop."

"You build it up," Alice Mary said, "and I knock it down." She reached out, but her hand stayed in mid-air. She had seen Jayson coming toward them, coming down the middle of the street, the wood walls of houses on one side and on the other the brick wall with the pieces of glass on top shining faintly under the street lamp. Jayson stopped in the round circle of light and stood looking at them, his fingers hooked in his belt.

"What you looking for?" Alice Mary called. She had her head turned sideways and she was frowning.

"I come looking for somebody called Aggie," Jayson said.

Anna woke up and reached for the nearest little rock.

"Nobody here called that," Alice Mary said.

Althea tossed a rock from one hand to the other.

Jayson stood still in the circle of light, without moving, and grinning.

"Why you want to find her?" Alice Mary's voice hesitated slightly.

Jayson stretched out one arm to the lamppost and leaned against it. "You got no cause to ask," he said. "You got no cause to ask."

From the lowest step Anna stood up. "Iffen you come up on our sidewalk we're gonna bash you."

Jayson laughed. "Ain't no little rock gonna stop me when I pull you head right off you neck."

Anna threw the rock. It struck Jayson's shoulder and bounced into the street, lifting a little cloud of dust.

"Ain't no little rock gonna stop me," Jayson said, and stood clear of the lamppost, hitching up his pants.

"Pitch him one." Anna pulled at the skirt of Alice Mary's dress. "You pitch him one that'll make his head spin."

"Like I did to my Daddy Joe," Althea said.

Alice Mary did not answer. She was staring at him, and her face was puzzled. A thin face, a girl's face twisted into a woman's.

"Come ahead," they said. "Pitch one. Reckon he you daddy. Pitch him one."

He took one step, grinning.

"Reckon I better," she said.

Her aim was good. He ducked as the rock passed his shoulder. But the second one, the one she threw from her left hand, caught squarely on the head. In dodging one, he had walked squarely into the force of the other.

"Sweet God Almighty." He put his hand to his head and then looked at the blood on his fingers. The ground was shifting under his feet like the trick floors at sideshows.

Another rock hit his shoulder. And another the center of his chest; the pain flashed hot through the length of his body. Objects were passing him, missing him and striking into the ground.

Inside his head was the sound of rocks falling. And all around him dust was heavy in the air, so heavy he couldn't see clearly because of it. But then he saw Aggie.

She was calling to the girls through the front window. "Pitch some more," she kept calling. "Pitch some more."

He decided then. He held his arms in front of his face and started walking toward them. Not running. Not hurrying. But walking. The rocks hurt, but as long as they did not hit his head it was not too bad.

Aggie was screaming. He did not look up but he recognized the sound. He had heard it before, the night Mannie was killed. A door slammed somewhere close. He had heard that sound, too, the same night. She had run away then like she'd be doing now. But there was a difference now. And he could not be sure of it.

He could not see where he was going, with his head covered by his arms. He walked straight into the steps, stumbled and sprawled out full-length on them, one of his hands squarely on the pile of rocks. He wondered what had happened to the kids who had been standing there.

He turned his head slowly, looking up. Alice Mary stood on the porch, her hands raised over her head, and in them a whole brick. He jerked his body aside and the brick gouged a piece out of the wood steps.

He remembered she was his kid when he caught her shouder and pushed her off the porch. She stumbled backwards and sat down and a little cloud of dry dust rose.

He went through the house. Aggie was not there. In the kitchen a pot of potatoes was boiling on the stove. He knocked it to the floor and then rubbed the side of his hand where the pot had burned it. The potatoes were over-cooked. They burst on the floor. He stepped into one; it made it hard for him to walk without slipping.

The bacon was burning. The smoke at the bottom of the pan was so thick he could not see the meat. He knocked that pot off, too, and kicked it into a corner.

He walked all the way through the house, back to the kitchen. He opened the door and stood looking out into the back yard. Behind the shed, through a crack of the boards he caught sight of white cloth. Aggie was out there, hiding and watching him as he was watching her.

And suddenly he began to laugh. The white cloth disappeared. He thought of her running away, dodging along in the alleys between the houses; and he laughed still harder. He stood in the doorway and laughed until he had to hold to the door for support.

He turned and walked back to the front of the house, kicking at whatever came in his way. In the room he yanked the mattress off the bed and the effort made him stagger. He would have liked to smash the house to bits, but

suddenly he felt too tired. And he was very hot. He felt the perspiration run
down his face and drop with a pulling tickle from his chin. The perspiration
ran in his eyes, his vision blurred; he could have sworn that the walls swayed
inward, ready to fall on him. He lunged for the door and the safety outside.

He stood on the front steps breathing hard, blinking, until he could see
again. Then he remembered the hurting and began to rub the spots on his head
and body where the rocks had hit him. He noticed his girl still sitting where
she had stumbled on the bare ground of the front yard. She was leaning back
on her hands, staring at him. "Don't you know you daddy?" he asked her. It
was too dark to see much of her face, but her mouth was open and she was
staring up at him. He held on to the porch rail and laughed at her. He let his
body swing back and forth as he laughed.

There was a song going through his head. And because he knew Aggie
would be close enough to hear, he sang it aloud:

> *"Head is like a coffee pot,*
> *Nose is like a spout,*
> *Mouth is like an old fireplace*
> *With the ashes all raked out.*
> *Oh Aggie, po gal,*
> *Oh Aggie, po gal,*
> *Oh Aggie."*

The railing was rotten and cracked under his weight. He went down the steps
with the tune of the songs in his ears.

He stood in the street under the lamp and rubbed his head with both hands;
there was a kind of buzzing in it. He could have sworn that the mill was
working, but it was all in his head. There was blood on his hand too; he wiped
it across the front of his shirt.

He turned so that his heel grated against the asphalt street and looked back
at the house where Aggie lived. The two little girls were still gone: they would
be hiding under the house. His kid was standing up now, on the steps, her foot
raised in mid-air as if she were about to come down and was not sure where the
next step was, while it was there, right in front of her. She stood watching him,
with her foot out stiff and not too steady. He could hear Aggie calling her:
"Alice Mary, you come in here. Alice Mary!"

Alice Mary came down one step as if she hadn't heard. Aggie opened the
front door a crack and put her arm through, trying to reach her. "You come in
here." Just an arm waving up and down in the air, trying to reach something
that wasn't in reach.

He saw that and laughed. He said aloud: "Man, you ain't got no call to be laughing," and shook his head. But he only laughed harder and his voice slid off down the lengths of evening air.

He turned and walked down the street, chuckling and singing.

> *"Mouth is like an old fireplace*
> *With the ashes all raked out.*
> *Oh Aggie, po gal,*
> *Oh Aggie."*

He stumbled a couple of times and caught himself just before falling. Once his knee brushed the ground. "Man, you ain't got no call to be singing," he said aloud. But he only sang louder so that he could hear himself over the buzzing in his head.

Joe called to him: "You, Jayson!" But he did not stop.

Joe came running alongside. "Christ sake, man," Joe shouted at him, "what you yelling for?"

Jayson stopped singing. His mouth was so heavy that he let it hang open.

"Christ sake, man," Joe said, "the police pick you up sure, with you going around acting like that."

Jayson looked at him, and slowly lifted his left hand and pushed up his lower jaw and closed his mouth. His hand stayed on his chin, rubbing it slightly.

"Man," Joe said, "you sure a mess."

Jayson blinked at him, his vision clearing slowly.

"You got blood all over you face."

Jayson rubbed his sleeve across his face and winced at the soreness.

"Come on inside." Joe took his arm and pointed to the Pair-A-Dice Bar. "And get cleaned up some."

"No," Jayson said, and pulled free. "No."

Joe smiled and tugged at his arm again, persuasively. "You just come on in and have a drink, man."

"No," Jayson said, and swayed on his feet.

There was another man standing beside Joe, a younger man, not much past twenty, tall and thin. Jayson's eyes fastened first on the blue and red print of his sport shirt and then lifted to his face. There was something familiar in it and he stared, trying to remember.

"This here is Al," Joe said. "You remember Al."

Jayson crinkled up his lips with the effort.

"He wasn't nothing but a boy," Joe said. "Before. You remember. Nothing but a little boy."

"I remember," Jayson said. A little boy. Tall even then and skinny. Black legs, running, in short trousers, running up and down, fetching and carrying. And two black eyes, shiny as oil in the light, watching. "I remember," Jayson said.

Al stuck out his hand without a word. Jayson stared at it a moment, then took it.

Joe said: "I been telling him how you come back. I been telling him we going in business again. And get the stuff really flowing."

Al said: "That right?" He was wearing a hat, a brown straw with a red flower-printed band. "You gonna do that?"

Jayson did not answer. He turned away from them. He let his eyes swing in a circle around the street, looking.

"What you looking for?" Joe asked.

Jayson did not answer. He took a deep breath and began to move off. Joe and Al walked with him.

"Where you going?" Joe asked him again.

"That right," Al said. "Where?"

Jayson did not answer. He kept walking slowly.

Suddenly Joe chuckled. "Jesus," he said. "Ain't we plain stupid?" He chuckled again.

"How we stupid?" Al said quickly and, frowning, hunched his shoulders. "What call you got to say we stupid?"

"Don't get riled up, man." Joe was still grinning. He patted Jayson on the back. "We gonna fix you up, man. We sure gonna."

Jayson shook his head and looked at him.

Joe said to Al: "Go tell Nancy what we got for her. You tell her we got somebody here who used to be the biggest fellow around here and he aiming to be it again. That what you tell her."

Al opened his mouth in a quick smile and went off, almost at a run. Jayson stared at his legs, moving like a boy's had, back and forth, on errands.

"Sure," said Joe, and patted him on the back again. "That what you want."

"What?" said Jayson. "What I want?"

He swung his eyes around until they rested on the posters on either side of the bar door, the Jax posters of white girls drinking beer and smiling; girls with long red hair, and mouths open just a little.

"I done told you I know where to find one like that," Joe said. "I done told you that. And now I got to show you."

"Show me," Jayson said.

"That what I fixing to do, man," Joe said. "That what I plain fixing to do."

Jayson remembered the part of town back of the Lansford Mill. It had been a low stretch, marsh almost. He remembered catching frogs there. It was filled with houses now, the yellow painted barracks that the government had built for workers at the cotton mill when they were doing three shifts a day on army orders. The barracks were mostly empty now; a few almost white people had slipped into one of the buildings so quietly that no one had seen them come: three or four families with over a dozen kids and heavy-bellied pregnant women.

Jayson stopped and rubbed his head in both hands. He could see again, almost clearly. But it seemed like the ground was a long way off. His feet scarcely touched it.

"Where I got to look?" Jayson asked.

"Down there," Joe said. "Second one from the end on this here side."

"Ain't no call for you to come," Jayson said. "I reckon I can find it."

Joe grinned. "She know you coming. Al done run all the way to tell her."

"No call for you to come."

"Okay," Joe said. "I'm leaving." He turned around and noticed for the first time that Alice Mary had followed them. "Jay, man," Joe said, "look what we got here."

Jayson turned and noticed his girl for the first time. "You been following me?" he called. She did not answer. Looking at him, her eyes were wide open, so wide open that they did not seem to have any lids. And they weren't brown anymore; they were two flat round pieces of silver.

He walked over and took hold of her shoulder. He shook her so that her body struck into the hardness of his thigh. She was perfectly limp; even her arms flapped.

"You ma say for you to follow me?"

She shook her head but did not answer. The pressure of his arm was steadily increasing. She kicked at his shins sharply and pulled free; he grabbed at her as she slipped back out of reach. He grabbed for her again and his hand brushed her dress, but she was too quick. She stood just beyond his hand, body bent forward slightly, waiting, ready.

"Why you coming after me now, when I ain't want nothing to do with you?"

He studied her for a while between half-closed lids and then turned away. "You quit following me or I fix you good." He walked away and, glancing over his shoulder, saw that she had not moved. He searched with the toe of his shoe in the weeds by the side of the road until he found a rock: a piece of concrete, white, with round brown pebbles in it. Even in the dark he could have hit her easy when he threw the rock, but he did not want to, suddenly. The piece of concrete hit the ground a little to one side of her. She disappeared.

He looked around for Joe, and he was gone, too. Jayson straightened up and took a deep breath: the air was full of night and damp. He rubbed his hands down his sides. His eyes, dark and shiny as oil, moved down the row of barracks on the left side of the street.

He began to walk along slowly, dragging his feet in the dirt road. It was completely dark now; over the broken stand of a street light, the evening star was tangled in the electric wires. The night wind caught the top layer of dirt from the road and spun it in slow circles.

He walked until he saw her. She was standing in the doorway of one of the barracks, the second from the end. Like Joe said, she was white or nearly white, and she had red hair, bright red hair. It hung over her shoulders in long perfect waves, like water when the wind passes over it. Red hair like a curtain that would draw down like a shade.

She came down the two steps and walked toward him — slowly, putting one foot in front of the other so that her walk was wavy as her hair. The light from the corner shone on the luminous green shadow of her eyelids. She leaned against the gatepost which was all that was left of the fence the government had built. And she waited for him.

Looking at her he began to grin. The skin on his face felt dry and hard and he could imagine it cracking when his mouth moved as wide, bright, he began to grin. "You waiting on me?"

"I might could be," she said.

The Black Prince

*"How art thou fallen from heaven,
O Lucifer, son of the morning!"*

Winters are short and very cold; sometimes there is even a snow like heavy frost on the ground. Summers are powdery hot; the white ball sun goes rolling around and around in a sky behind the smoke from the summer fires. There is always a burning somewhere in summer; the pines are dry and waiting; the sun itself starts the smoldering. A pine fire is quiet; there is only a kind of rustle from the flames inside the trunks until the branches and needles go up with a whistling. A whole hill often burns that way, its smoke rising straight up to the white sun, and quiet.

In the plowed patches, green things grow quickly: the ground is rich and there are underground rivers. But there are no big farms: only patches of corn, green beans, and a field or two of cotton (grown for a little cash to spend on Saturdays at Luther's General Store or Willie's Café; these are the only two places for forty miles in any direction). There is good pasture: the green places along the hillsides with pines for shade and sure water in the streams that come down from the Smokies to the north; even in the burnt-out land of five seasons back, shrubs are high. But in the whole county there are only fifty cows, gone wild most of them and dry because they were never milked. They are afraid of men and feed in the farthest ridges and the swamps that are the bottoms of some littlest of the valleys. Their numbers are slowly increasing because no one bothers them. Only once in a while some man with a hankering for cow meat takes his rifle and goes after them. But that is not often; the people prefer pork. Each family keeps enough razorbacks in a run of bark palings.

It is all colored people here, and it is the poorest part of the smallest and worst county in the state. The place at the end of the dirt road leading from the state highway, the place where Luther's Store and Willie's Café stand, does not even have a name in the county records.

The only cool time of the summer day is very early, before the mists have shriveled away. There is a breeze then, a good stiff one out of the Smokies. During the day there is no sound: it is dead hot. But in the early mornings, when the breeze from the north is blowing, it is not so lonesomely quiet: crickets and locusts and the birds that flutter about hunting them, calling frantically as if they had something of importance to settle quick before the heat sets in. (By seven they are quiet again, in the invisible places they have chosen to wait out the day.)

A pine cone rattled down on Alberta's head and bounced from her shoulder. She scooped it from the ground and threw it upward through the branches. "You just keep your cone, mister birds. I got no cause to want it." With a pumping of wings the birds were gone, their cries sliding after them, back down the air. "You just yell your head off. I can hit you any time I want. Any time I want." There was a small round piece of granite at her feet and she tossed it, without particular aim, into the biggest of the bay trees: a gray squirrel with a thin rattail tumbled from the branches and peeped at her from behind the trunk with a pointed little rat face. She jammed her hands in the pockets of her dress and went on, swaggering slightly, cool and feeling good.

She was a handsome girl, taller than most people in her part of the county, and light brown — there had been a lot of white blood in her family, back somewhere, they'd forgot where exactly. She was not graceful — not as a woman is — but light on her feet and supple as a man. Her dress, which the sun had bleached to a whitish color, leaving only a trace of pink along the seams, had shrunk out of size for her: it pulled tight across her broad, slightly hunched, muscled back, even though she had left all the front buttons open down to the waist.

As she walked along, the birds were making even more of a row, knocking loose cones and dry pine needles and old broad bay leaves, and twice she stopped, threw back her head, and called up to them: "Crazy fool birds. Can't do nothing to me. Fool jackass birds." Up ahead, a couple of minutes' walk, was the field and the cotton, bursting white out of the brown cups and waiting to be picked. And she did not feel like working. She leaned against a tree, stretching so that the bark crumbled in her fingers, listening to the birds.

Something different was in their calling. She listened, her head bent forward, her eyes closed, as she sorted the sounds. One jay was wrong: its long sustained note ended with the cluck of a quail. No bird did that. Alberta opened her eyes and looked slowly around. But the pines were thick and close and full of blue night shadow and wrapped with fog that moved like bits of cloth in the wind.

Leaving the other bird calls, the whistle became distinct, high, soaring, mocking, like some rare bird, proudly, insolently.

Alberta moved a few steps out from the tree and turned slowly on her heels. The whistle was going around her now, in slow circles, and she turned with it, keeping her eye on the sound, seeing nothing. The birds were still calling and fluttering in the branches, sending bits of twig and bark tumbling down.

Alberta said: "A fool thing you doing. A crazy fool jackass thing." She sat down on a tumbled pile of bricks that had been the chimney of a sugarhouse burned during the Civil War. She spoke in her best tone, while the whistling went round and round her faster. "I reckon you got nothing better to do than go around messing up folks. You got me so riled up I don't reckon I know what way I'm heading in." The sound went around her and around her, but she held her head steady, talking to the pine directly in front of her. "I don't reckon there's nothing for me but set here till you tires out and goes away." The whistle circled her twice and then abruptly stopped, the last high clear note running off down the breeze. Alberta stood up, pulling down her faded dress. "I am mighty glad you come to stopping. I reckon now I can tell what direction I got to go in."

He was right there, leaning on the same pine she had been staring at, cleaning his front teeth with a little green twig and studying her, and she told him to his face: "That was a crazy mean thing, and you ain't got nothing better to do."

"Reckon not," he said, moving the little green twig in and out of the hole between his lower front teeth.

She pushed her hands in the pockets of her dress and looked him over. "Where you come from?"

"Me?" The little green twig went in and out of his teeth with each breath. "I just come straight out the morning."

She turned and walked away. "I be glad to see you go."

He stood in front of her: he had a way of moving without a sound, of popping up in places. "I be sorry to see you go, Alberta Lacy."

She studied him before she answered: tall, not too big or heavy, and black (no other blood but his own in him, she thought). He was dressed nice — a leather jacket with fringe on the sleeves, a red plaid shirt, and new blue denim pants. "How you know what I'm called?" she asked him politely.

He grinned, and his teeth were white and perfect. "I done seen it in the fire," he said. "I done seen it in the fire and I read it clear: Alberta Lacy."

She frowned. "I don't see as how I understand."

He blew the little green twig out of his mouth. "I might could be seeing you again real soon, Alberta Lacy." Then he slipped around the tree like the last trail of night shadow and disappeared.

Alberta stood listening: only the birds and the insects and the wind. Then everything got quiet, and the sun was shining white all around, and she climbed down the slope to the field.

A little field — just a strip of cotton tucked in between two ridges. Her father and her two biggest brothers had planted it with half a morning's work, and they hadn't gone back to tend it once. They didn't even seem to remember it: whatever work they did was in the older fields closer to home. So Alberta had taken it over. Sometimes she brought along the twins: Sidney and Silvia; they were seven: young enough for her to order around and big enough to be a help. But usually she couldn't find them; they were strange ones, gone out of the house for a couple of days at a time in summer, sleeping out somewhere, always sticking together. They were strange little ones and not worth trouble looking for. So most times Alberta worked with Maggie Mary Evans, who was Josh Evans's daughter and just about the only girl her age she was friendly with. From the field there'd be maybe three bales of real early stuff; and they'd split the profit. They worked all morning, pulling off the bolls and dropping them in the sacks they slung crosswise across their shoulders. They worked very slowly, so slowly that at times their hands seemed hardly to move, dozing in the heat. When it got to be noon, when they had no shadow anymore, they slipped off the sacks, leaving them between the furrows, and turned to the shade to eat their lunch.

He was waiting for them there, stretched out along the ground with his head propped up on the slender trunk of a little bay tree. He winked lazily at Alberta; his eyes were big and shiny black as oil. "How you, Miss Alberta Lacy?"

Alberta looked down at him, crooking her lips. "You got nothing to do but pester me?"

"Sure I got something to do, but ain't nothing nice like this."

Alberta looked at him through half-closed lids, then sat down to the lunch.

"You hungry, mister?" Maggie Mary asked. She had stood watching, both hands jammed into the belt of her dress, and her eyes moving from one to the other with the quickness and the color of a sparrow.

The man rolled over and looked up at her. "Reckon I am."

"You can have some of our lunch," Maggie Mary said.

Crazy fool, Alberta thought, standing so close with him on the ground like that. He must can see all the way up her. And from the way he lay there, grinning, he must be enjoying it.

"That real nice," he said to Maggie Mary, and crawled over on his stomach to where the lunch bucket was.

Alberta watched his smooth, black hand reaching into the bucket and suddenly she remembered. "How you called?"

He put a piece of cornbread in his mouth, chewed it briefly, and swallowed it with a gulp. "I got three names."

"No fooling," Maggie Mary said, and giggled in her hand. "I got three names, too."

"Stanley Albert Thompson."

"That a good-sounding name," Alberta said. She began to eat her lunch quickly, her mouth too full to talk. Stanley Albert was staring at her, but she didn't raise her eyes. Then he began to sing, low, pounding time with the flat of his hand against the ground.

> *"Alberta, let you hair hang low,*
> *Alberta, let you hair hang low,*
> *I'll give you more gold than you apron can hold*
> *If you just let you hair hang low."*

Alberta got up slowly, not looking at him. "We got work to finish."

Stanley Albert turned over so that his face was pressed in the grass and pine needles. "All you get's the muscles in you arm."

"That right." Maggie Mary nodded quickly. "That right."

"Maggie Mary," Alberta said, "Iffen you don't come with me I gonna bop you so hard you land in the middle of tomorrow."

"Good-by, Mr. Stanley Albert Thompson," Maggie Mary said, but he had fallen asleep.

By the time they finished work he was gone; there wasn't even a spot in the pine needles and short grass to show where he had been.

"Ain't that the strangest thing?" Maggie Mary said.

Alberta picked up the small bucket they carried their lunch in. "I reckon not."

"Seemed like he was fixing to wait for us."

"He ain't fixing to wait for nobody, that kind." Alberta rubbed one hand across her shoulders, sighing slightly. "I got a pain fit to kill."

Maggie Mary leaned one arm against a tree and looked off across the little field where they had spent the day. "You reckon he was in here most all morning watching us?"

"Maybe." Alberta began to walk home. Maggie Mary followed slowly, her head still turned, watching the field.

"He musta spent all morning just watching."

"Nothing hard about doing that, watching us break our back out in the sun."

Maggie Mary took one long, loping step and came up with Alberta. "You reckon he coming back?"

Alberta stared full at her, head bent, chewing on her lower lip. "Maggie Mary Evans," she said, "you might could get a thought that he might be wanting you and you might could get a thought that you be wanting him —"

Maggie Mary bent down and brushed the dust off her bare feet carefully, not answering.

"You a plain crazy fool." Alberta planted both hands on her hips and bent her body forward slightly. "A plain crazy fool. You wouldn't be forgetting Jay Mastern?" Jay Mastern had gone off to Ramsey to work at the mill and never come back, but left Maggie Mary to have his baby. So one day Maggie Mary took her pa's best mule and put a blanket on it for a saddle and rode over to Blue Goose Lake, where the old woman lived who could tell her what to do. The old woman gave her medicine in a beer can: whisky and calomel and other things that were a secret. Maggie Mary took the medicine in one gulp, because it tasted so bad, waded way out into Blue Goose Lake so that the water came up to her neck, then dripping wet got up on the mule and whipped him up to a good fast pace all the way home. The baby had come off all right: there wasn't one. And Maggie Mary nearly died. It was something on to three months before she was able to do more than walk around, her arms hanging straight down and stiff and her black skin overtinged with gray.

"You wouldn't be forgetting Jay Mastern?"

"Sure," Maggie Mary said, brushing the dust off her bare feet lightly. "I clean forgot about him."

"Don't you be having nothing to do with this here Stanley Albert Thompson."

Maggie Mary began to walk again, slowly, smiling just a little bit with one corner of her mouth. "Sounds like you been thinking about him for yourself."

Alberta jammed both hands down in the pockets of her dress. "I been thinking nothing of the sort."

"Willie'll kill him."

Alberta chewed on one finger. "I reckon he could care for himself."

Maggie Mary smiled to herself softly, remembering. "I reckon he could; he's real fine-appearing man."

"He was dressed good."

"Where you reckon he come from?" Maggie Mary asked.

Alberta shrugged. "He just come walking out of the morning fog."

That was how he came into this country: he appeared one day whistling a bird call in the woods in high summer. And he stayed on. The very first Saturday night he went down to Willie's and had four fights and won them all.

Willie's was an ordinary house made of pine slabs, older than most of the other houses, but more solid. There were two rooms: a little one where Willie lived (a heavy scrolled ironwork bed, a square oak dresser, a chest, a three-footed table, and on its cracked marble top a blue-painted mandolin without strings). And a big room: the café. Since anybody could remember, the café had been there with Willie's father or his grandfather, as long as there had been people in these parts. And that had been a long while: long before the Civil War even, runaways were settling here, knowing they'd be safe and hidden in the rough, uneven hills and the pines.

Willie had made some changes in the five or six years since his father died. He painted the counter that was the bar with varnish; that had not been a good idea: the whiskey took the varnish off in a few weeks. And he painted the walls: bright blue. Then he went over them again, shaking his brush so that the walls were flecked like a mockingbird's eggs. But Willie used red to fleck — red against blue. And the mirror, gilt-edged, and hanging from a thick gold cord: that had been Willie's idea, too. He'd found it one day, lying on the shoulder alongside the state highway; it must have fallen from a truck somehow. So he took it home. It was cracked in maybe two dozen pieces. Anyone who looked into it would see his face split up into a dozen different parts, all separate. But Willie hung it right over the shelves where he kept his whisky and set one of the kerosene lamps in front of it so that the light should reflect yellow-bright from all the pieces. One of them fell out (so that Willie had to glue it back with flour and water) the night Stanley Albert had his fourth fight, which he won like the other three. Not a man in the country would stand up like that, because fighting at Willie's on Saturday night is a rough affair with razors, or knives, or bottles.

Not a man in the country could have matched the way Stanley Albert fought that night, his shirt off, and his black body shining with sweat, the muscles along his neck and shoulders twisting like grass snakes. There wasn't a finer-looking man and there wasn't a better: he proved that.

The first three fights were real orderly affairs. Everybody could see what was coming minutes ahead, and Willie got the two of them out in the yard before they got at each other. And everybody who was sober enough to walk went out on the porch and watched Stanley Albert pound first Ran Carey's and then Henry Johnson's head up and down in the dust. Alberta sat on the porch (Willie had brought her a chair from inside) and watched Stanley Albert roll around the dust of the yard and didn't even blink an eye, not even during the third fight when Tim Evans, who was Maggie Mary's brother, pull a razor. The razor got Stanley Albert all down one cheek, but Tim didn't have any teeth left and one side of his face got punched in so that it looked peculiar always afterward. Maggie Mary went running down into the yard, not bothering with her brother, to press her finger up against the little cut across Stanley Albert's cheek.

The fourth fight came up so suddenly nobody had time hardly to get out of the way: Joe Turner got one arm hooked around Stanley Albert's neck from behind. There wasn't any reason for it, except maybe that Joe was so drunk he didn't see who he had and that once there's been a couple of fights there's always more. Stanley Albert swung a bottle over his shoulder to break the hold and then nobody could see exactly what was happening: they were trying so hard to get clear. Willie pulled Alberta over the bar and pushed her down behind it and crouched alongside her, grinning. "That some fighter." And when it was all over they stood up again; first thing they saw was Joe Turner down on the floor and Stanley Albert leaning on a chair with Maggie dabbing at a cut on his hand with the edge of her petticoat.

He got a reputation from that Saturday night, and everybody was polite to him, and he could have had just about any of the girls he wanted. But he didn't seem to want them; at least he never took to coming to the houses to see them or taking them home from Willie's. Maggie Mary Evans swore up and down that he had got her one day when she was fishing in Scanos River, but nobody paid her much attention. She liked to make up stories that way.

He had a little house in a valley to the east. Some boys who had gone out to shoot a cow for Christmas meat said they saw it. But they didn't go close even if there was three of them with a shotgun while Stanley Albert only carried a razor. Usually people only saw him on Saturday nights, and after a while they got used to him, though none of the men ever got to be friendly with him. There wasn't any mistaking the way the girls watched him. But after four or five Saturdays, by the time the summer was over, everybody expected him and waited for him, the way you'd wait for a storm to come or a freeze: not liking it, but not being able to do anything either. That's the way it went along: he'd buy his food for the coming week at Luther's Store, and then he'd come next door to Willie's.

He never stood up at the counter that was the bar. He'd take his glass and walk over to a table and sit down, and pull out a little bottle from his pocket, and add white lightning to the whisky. There wasn't anything could insult Willie more. He made the whisky and it was the best stuff in the county. He even had some customers drive clear out from Montgomery to buy some of his corn, and, being good stuff, there wasn't any call to add anything: it had enough kick of its own; raw and stinging to the throat. It was good stuff; nobody added anything to it — except Stanley Albert Thompson, while Willie looked at him and said things under his breath. But nothing ever came of it, because everybody remembered how good a job Stanley Albert had done the first night he came.

Stanley Albert always had money, enough of it to pay for the groceries and all the whisky he wanted. There was always the sound of silver jingling in his trouser pocket. Everybody could hear that. Once when Willie was standing behind the bar, shuffling a pack of cards with a wide fancy twirl — just for amusement — Stanley Albert, who had had a couple of drinks and was feeling especially good, got up and pulled a handful of coins out of his pocket. He began to shuffle them through the air, the way Willie had done with the cards. Stanley Albert's black hands flipped the coins back and forth, faster and faster, until there was a solid silver ring hanging and shining in the air. Then Stanley Albert let one of his hands drop to his side and the silver ring poured back into the other hand and disappeared with a little clinking sound. And he dropped the money into his pocket with a short quick laugh.

That was the way Stanley Albert used his money: he had fun with it. Only thing, one night when Stanley Albert had had maybe a bit too much and sat dozing at his table, Morris Henry slipped a hand into the pocket. He wouldn't have ever dared to do that if Stanley Albert hadn't been dozing, leaning back in his chair, the bottle of white lightning empty in one hand. And Morris Henry slipped his little hand in the pocket and felt all around carefully. Then he turned his head slowly in a circle, looking at everybody in the room. He was a little black monkey Negro and his eyes were shiny and flat as mirrors. He slipped his hand back and scurried out into the yard and hid in the blackberry bushes. He wouldn't move until morning came; he just sat there, chewing on his little black fingers with his wide flaring yellow teeth. Anybody who wanted to know what was happening had to go out there and ask him. And ever afterwards Morris Henry swore that there hadn't been anything at all in Stanley Albert Thompson's pocket. But then everybody knew Morris Henry was crazy because just a few minutes later when Stanley Albert woke up and walked across to the bar, the change jingled in the pocket and he laid five quarters on the counter. And the money was good enough because Willie bounced it on the counter and it gave the clear ring of new silver.

Stanley Albert had money all right and he spent it; there wasn't anything short about him. He'd buy drinks for anybody who'd come over to his table; the only ones who came were the girls. And he didn't seem to care how much they drank. He'd just sit there, leaning way back in his chair, grinning, his teeth white and big behind his black lips, and matching them drink for drink, and every now and then running his eyes up and down their length just to let them know he was appreciating their figures. Most often it was Maggie Mary who would be sitting there, warning all the other girls away with a little slanting of her eyes when they got near. And sometimes he'd sing a song: a song about whisky that would make everyone forget they didn't like him and laugh; or a song about poor boys who were going to be hanged in the morning. He had a good voice, strong and clear, and he pounded time with the flat of his hand on the table. And he'd always be looking at Alberta when he was singing until she'd get up, holding her head high and stiff, and march over to where Willie was and take hold of his arm real sweet and smile at him. And Willie would give Stanley Albert a quick mean look and then pour her a drink of his best whisky.

Stanley Albert had a watch, a big heavy gold one, round almost as a tomato, that would strike the hours. (That was how you could tell he was around sometimes — hearing his watch strike.) It was attached to a broad black ribbon and sometimes he held it up, let it swing before the eyes of whatever girl it happened to be at the time, let it swing slowly back and forth, up and down, so that her head moved with it. He had a ring too, on his right little finger: a white-colored band with a stone big as a chip of second coal and dark green. And when he fought, the first time he came into Willie's, the ring cut the same as a razor in his hand; it was maybe a little more messy, because its edges were jagged.

Those were two things — the watch and the ring — that must have cost more than all the money around here in a year. That was why all the women liked him so; they kept thinking of the nice things he could give them if he got interested. And that was why the men hated him. Things can go as smooth as glass if everybody's got about the same things and the same amount of money knocking around in a jean pocket on Saturday night. But when they don't, things begin happening. It would have been simpler maybe if they could have fought Stanley Albert Thompson, but there wasn't any man keen to fight him. That was how they started fighting each other. A feud that nobody'd paid any mind to for eight or ten years started up again.

It began one Sunday morning along toward dawn when everyone was feeling tired and leaving Willie's. Stanley Albert had gone out first and was sitting aside the porch railing. Jim Mastern was standing on the lowest step not moving, just staring across the fields, not being able to see anything in the dark, except maybe the bright-colored patterns the whisky set shooting starwise before his eyes. And Randall Stevens was standing in the doorway, looking down at his own foot, which he kept moving in a little circle around and around on the floor boards. And Stanley Ablert was looking hard at him. Randall Stevens didn't lift his head; he just had his razor out and was across the porch in one minute, bringing down his arm in a sweeping motion to get at Jim Mastern's neck. But he was too drunk to aim very straight and he missed; but he did cut the ear away so that it fell on the steps. Jim Mastern was off like a bat in the daylight, running fast, crashing into things, holding one hand to the side of his head. And Randall Stevens folded up the razor and slipped it back in his pocket and walked off slowly, his head bent over, as if he was sleepy. There wasn't any more sense to it than that; but it started the feud again.

Stanley Albert swung his legs over the railing and stretched himself and yawned. Nobody noticed except Alberta, they were so busy listening to the way Jim Mastern was screaming and running across the fields, and watching Randall Stevens march off, solemnly, like a priest.

And the next night Randall Stevens tumbled down the steps of his cabin with his head full of scatter shot. It was a Monday night in November. His mother came out to see and stepped square on him, and his blood spattered on the hoarfrost. Randall Stevens had six brothers, and the next night they rode their lanky burred horses five miles south and tried to set fire to the Mastern house. That was the beginning; the fighting kept up, off and on, all through the winter. The sheriff from Gloverston came down to investigate. He came driving down the road in the new shiny white state police patrol car — the only one in the county — stopped in Willie's Café for a drink and went back taking two gallons of home brew with him. That wasn't exactly right, maybe, seeing that he had taken an oath to uphold the law; but he couldn't have done much, except get killed. And that was certain.

The Stevenses and their friends took to coming to Willie's on Friday nights; the Masterns kept on coming on Saturday. That just made two nights Willie had to keep the place open and the lamps filled with kerosene; the crowd was smaller; shotguns were leaning against the wall.

That's the way it went all winter. Everybody got on one side or the other — everybody except Stanley Albert Thompson. They both wanted him: they had seen what he could do in a fight. But Stanley Albert took to coming a night all by himself: Sunday night, and Willie had to light all the lamps for just him and stand behind the counter and watch him sit at the table adding lightning to the whisky.

Once along toward the end of February when Cy Mastern was killed and the roof of his house started burning with pine knots tossed from the ground, Stanley Albert was standing just on the rim of the light, watching. He helped the Masterns carry water, but Ed Stevens, who was hiding up in top of a pine to watch, swore that the water was like kerosene in his hands. Wherever he'd toss a bucketful, the fire would shoot up, brighter and hotter than before.

By March the frosts stopped, and there weren't any more cold winds. The farmers came out every noon, solemnly, and laid their hands on the bare ground to see if it was time to put in their earliest corn and potatoes. But the ground stayed cold a long time that year so that there wasn't any plowing until near May. All during that time from March till May there wasn't anything doing; that was the worst time for the fighting. In the winter your hand shakes so with the cold that you aren't much good with a gun or knife. But by March the air is warmer and you don't have any work to get you tired, so you spend all the time thinking.

That spring things got bad. There wasn't a crowd any more at Willie's though he kept the place open and the lights on for the three nights of the weekend. Neither the Stevenses nor the Masterns would come; they were too easy targets in a house with wall lamps burning. And on Sunday night the only person who ever came was Stanley Albert Thompson. He'd sit and drink his whisky and lightning and maybe sing a song or two for the girls who came over to see him. By the end of April that was changed too. He finally got himself the girl he wanted; the one he'd been waiting around nearly all winter for. And his courting was like this:

Thomas Henry Lacy and his sons, Luke and Tom, had gone for a walk, spoiling for a fight. They hadn't seen anything all evening, just some of the cows that had gone wild and went crashing away through the blueberry bushes. Alberta had taken herself along with them, since she was nearly as good as a man in a fight. They had been on the move all night but keeping in the range of a couple of miles and on the one side of the Scanos River. They were for Stevens and there was no telling what sort of affair the Masterns had rigged up on their ground. They rested for a while on the bluff of the river. Tom had some bread in his pocket and they ate it there, wondering if there was anybody in the laurels across the river just waiting for them to show themselves. Then they walked on again, not saying very much, seeing nothing but the moon flat against the sky and its light shiny on the heavy dew.

Alberta didn't particularly care when they left her behind. She turned her head to listen to the plaintive gargling call of a night quail, and when she looked again her father and the boys were gone. She knew where she was: on the second ridge away from home. There was just the big high ridge there to the left. The house was maybe twenty minutes away, but a hard walk, and Alberta was tired. She'd been washing all day, trying to make the clear brook water carry off the dirt and grease from the clothes, her mother standing behind her, yelling at each spot that remained, her light face black almost as her husband's with temper, and her gray fuzzy hair tied into knots like a pickaninny's. The boys had spent the whole day dozing in the shed while they put a new shoe on the mule.

Alberta listened carefully; there was nothing but night noises; her father and the boys would be halfway home by now, scrambling down the rain-washed sides of the ridge. For a moment she considered following them. "Ain't no raving rush, girl," she told herself aloud. The night was cool, but there wasn't any wind. With her bare feet she felt the dry pine needles, then sat down on them, propping her back against a tree. She slipped the razor from the cord around her neck and held it open loosely in the palm of her hand; then she fell asleep.

She woke when the singing started, opening her eyes but not moving. The moon was right overhead, shining down so that the trunks of the pines stuck straight up out of the white shiny ground. There wasn't a man could hide behind a pine, yet she didn't see him. Only the singing going round and round her.

> "*Alberta, what's on you mind?*
> *Alberta, why you treat me so unkind?*
> *You keep me worried; you keep me blue*
> *All the time,*
> *Alberta, why you treat me so unkind?*

She pushed herself up to a sitting position, still looking straight ahead, not following the song around and around. She let the hand that held the razor fall in her lap, so that the moon struck on the blade.

> *"Alberta, why you treat me so unkind?"*

Nothing grows under pines, not much grass even, not any bushes big enough to hide a man. Only pine trees, like black matches stuck in the moonlight. Black like matches, and thin like matches. There wasn't a man could hide behind a pine under a bright moon. There wasn't a man could pass a bright open space and not be seen.

> *"Alberta, let you hair hang low,*
> *Alberta, let you hair hang low.*
> *I'll give you more gold*
> *Than you apron can hold."*

"That ain't a very nice song," she said.

> *"I'll give you more gold*
> *Than you apron can hold."*

She lifted her right hand and turned the razor's edge slowly in the light. "I got silver of my own right here," she said. "That enough for me."

The song went round in a circle, round and round, weaving in and out of the pines, passing invisible across the open moon filled spaces.

> *"Alberta, let you hair hang low,*
> *I'll give you more gold*
> *Than you apron can hold*
> *If you just let you hair hang low."*

There wasn't a man alive could do that. Go round and round.

> *"Alberta, why you treat me so unkind?"*

Round and round, in and out the thin black trees. Alberta stood up, following the sound, turning on her heel.

> *"You keep me worried, you keep me blue*
> *All the time."*

"I plain confused," she said. "I don't reckon I understand."

> *"I'll give you more gold*
> *Than you apron can hold."*

"I ain't got no apron," she said.

> *"Alberta, let you hair hang low,*
> *Just let you hair hang low."*

The song stopped and Stanley Albert Thompson came right out of a patch of bright moon ground, where there were only brown pine needles.

Alberta forgot she was tired; the moon-spotted ground rolled past her feet like the moon in the sky — effortless. She recognized the country they passed through: Blue Goose Lake, Scanos River, and the steeper rough ground of the north part of the country, toward the Tennessee border. It was a far piece to walk and she wondered at the lightness of her feet. By moonset they had got there — the cabin that the boys had seen one day while they were hunting cows. She hesitated a little then, not afraid, not reluctant, but just not sure how to go on. Stanley Albert Thompson had been holding her hand all evening; he still held it. Right at the beginning when he had first taken her along with him, she'd shook her head, no, she could walk; no man needed to lead her. But he'd grinned at her, and shook his head, imitating her gesture, so that the moon sparkled on his black curly hair, and his black broad forehead, and he took her hand and led her so that the miles seemed nothing and the hours like smooth water.

He showed her the cabin, from the outside first: mustard color, trimmed with white, like the cabins the railroad company builds. One room with high peaked roof.

"A real fine house," she said. "A real fine house. You work for the railroad?"

"No."

He took her inside. "You light with candles," she said.

"I ain't ever been able to stand the smell of lamps," he said.

"But it's a real nice house. I might could learn to like it."

"No might could about it." He smoothed the cloth on the table with his fingers. "You going to like it."

She bent her head and looked at him through her eyelashes. "Now I don't rightly know. Seems as how I don't know you."

"Sure you do," he said. "I'm standing right here."

"Seems as how I don't know nothing. You might could have a dozen girls all over this here state."

"I reckon there's a dozen," he said.

She glared at him, hands on hips. "You old fool jackass," she said. "I reckon you can just keep everything."

He jammed his hands into the back pockets of his denim pants and bent backward staring at the ceiling.

"Ain't you gonna try to stop me?"

"Nuh-uh."

She leaned against the doorjamb and twisted her neck to look at him. "Ain't you sorry I going?"

"Sure." He was still staring upward at the ceiling with its four crossed beams. "Sure, I real sorry."

"I don't see as how I could stay though."

"Sure you could." He did not look at her.

"I don't see as how. You ain't give me none of the things you said."

"You a driving woman," he said, and grinned, his mouth wide and white in the dark of his face.

Then he sat down at the table. There were five candles there, stuck in bottles, but only one was lighted, the one in the center. Wax had run all down the side of the candle and down the bottle in little round blobs, nubby like gravel. He picked one off, dirty white between his black fingers. He rolled it slowly between his flat palms, back and forth. Then he flipped it toward Alberta. It flashed silvery through the circle of lamplight and thudded against her skirt. She bent forward to pick it up: a coin, new silver. As she bent there, another one struck her shoulder, and another. Stanley Albert Thompson sat at the table, grinning and tossing the coins to her, until she had filled both pockets of her dress.

He pushed the candle away from him. "You all right, I reckon, now."

She held one coin in her hands, turning it over and over.

"That ain't what you promised. I remember how you came and sang:

> 'I give you more gold
> Than you apron can hold.'"

"Sure," he said and lifted a single eyebrow, very high. "I can do that all right, iffen you want it. I reckon I can do that."

She stood for a moment studying him. And Stanley Albert Thompson, from where he still sat at the table, curled up one corner of his mouth.

And very slowly Alberta began to smile. "I might could like it here," she said. "If you was real nice."

He got up then and rubbed her cheek very gently with his first finger. "I might could do that," he said. "I don't reckon it would be too heavy a thing to do."

The candle was on the table to one side. It caught the brightness of Alberta's eyes as she stood smiling at Stanley Albert Thompson. The steady yellow light threw her shadow over his body, a dark shadow that reached to his chin. His own shadow was on the wall behind. She glanced at it over his shoulder and giggled. "You better do something about your shadow there, Mr. Thompson. That there is a ugly shadow, sure."

He turned his head and glanced at it briefly. "Reckon so," he said.

It was an ugly shadow, sure. Alberta looked at Stanley Albert Thompson and shook her head. "I can't hardly believe it," she said. "You a right pretty man."

He grinned at her and shook himself so that the shadow on the wall spun around in a wild turn.

"I don't reckon you can do anything about it?"

"No," he said briefly. "I can't go changing my shadow." He hunched his back so that the figure on the wall seemed to jump up and down in anger.

She stepped over to him, putting her hands behind her, leaning backward to see his face. "If he don't do any more than dance on a wall, I ain't complaining."

Stanley Albert stood looking down at her, looking down the length of his face at her, and rocking slowly back and forth on his heels. "No," he said. "He ain't gonna do more than wiggle around the wall sometimes. But you can bet I am."

The coins weighed down the pockets of her dress, and his hands were warm against her skin. "I reckon I'm satisfied," she said.

That was the way it began. That was the courting. The woman was young and attractive and strong. The man could give her whatever she wanted. There were other courtings like that in this country. Every season there were courtings like that.

People would see them around sometimes; or sometimes they'd only hear them when they were still far off. Sometimes it would be Stanley Albert Thompson singing:

> *"Alberta, let you hair hang low,*
> *Alberta, let you hair hang low.*
> *I'll give you more gold*
> *Than you apron can hold*
> *If you just let you hair hang low."*

He had a strong voice. It could carry far in a quiet day or night. And if any of the people heard it, they'd turn and look at each other and nod their heads toward it, not saying anything, but just being sure that everyone was listening. And whenever Willie heard it, he'd close his eyes for a minute, seeing Alberta; and then he'd rub his hands all over his little black kinky head and whistle: "Euuuu," which meant that he was very, very sorry she had left him.

And sometimes all you could hear of them would be the chiming of Stanley Albert's watch every quarter-hour. One night that August, when the moon was heavy and hot and low, Maggie Mary was out walking with Jack Belden. She heard the clear high chime and remembered the nights at Willie's and the dangling gold watch. And she turned to Jack Belden, who had just got her comfortable in one arm, and jammed her fingers in his eyes and ran off after the sound. She didn't find them; and it wouldn't have much mattered if she had. Stanley Albert was much too gone on Alberta to notice any other woman in more than a passing appraising way.

And sometimes people would come on them walking alone, arms around each other's waist; or sitting in a shady spot during the day's heat, his head on her lap and both of them dozing and smiling a little. And everybody who saw them would turn around and get out of there fast; but neither of them turned a head or looked up: there might not have been anyone there.

And then every night they'd go down to Willie's. The first night they came — it was on a Thursday — the place was closed up tight. There wasn't ever anybody came on Thursday. Stanley Albert went around back to where Willie lived and pounded on the door, and when Willie didn't answer he went around to the front again where Alberta was waiting on the steps and kicked in the front panel of the wood door. Willie came scuttling out, his eyes round and bewildered like a suckling's and saw them sitting at one of the tables drinking his home brew, only first putting lightning into it. After that they came every night, just them. It was all most people could do to afford a drink on Saturday or the week-end, but some of them would walk over to Willie's just to look at Stanley Albert and Alberta sitting there. They'd stand at the windows and look in, sweating in the hot summer nights and looking. Maybe a few of them would still be there waiting when Stanley and Alberta got ready to go, along toward morning.

That's what they did every single night of the year or so they were together. If they fell asleep, Willie would just have to stand waiting. They'd go out with their arms around each other's waist, staggering some, but not falling. And an hour or so later, people who were going out before dawn to get a little work done in the cool would see them clear over on the other side of the county, at Goose Lake, maybe, a good three hours' walk for a man cold sober. Willie had his own version of how they got around. They just picked up their feet, he said, and went sliding off down the winds. Once, he said, when they were sitting over on the bench against the wall, Stanley Albert flat on it with his head on her lap, when the whisky made the man in him come up sudden, so he couldn't wait, they went straight out the window, up the air, like a whistle sound. Willie had the broken glass to show the next morning, if you wanted to believe him.

Willie hated them, the two of them, maybe because they broke his glass, maybe because they made him stay up late every single night of the week, so that he had to hold his eyes open with his fingers, and watch them pour lightning into his very best whisky, maybe because he had wanted Alberta mighty bad himself. He'd been giving her presents — bottles of his best stuff — but he just couldn't match Stanley Albert. Those are three reasons; maybe he had others. And Maggie Mary hated them; and she had only one reason.

Once Pete Stokes shot at Stanley Albert Thompson. He hadn't wanted to: he was scared like everybody else. But Maggie Mary Evans talked him into it. She was a fine-looking girl: she could do things like that. He hid behind the privy and got a perfect bead on Stanley Albert as he came out the door. The bullet just knocked off a piece of Willie's doorframe. When Pete saw what happened he dropped the gun and began to run, jumping the rail fence and crashing face-first through the thick heavy berry bushes. Stanley Albert pursed his lips together and rubbed his hands on his chin, slow, like he was deciding what to do. Then he jumped down from the porch and went after Pete. He ran through the hackberries too; only with him it did not seem difficult: none of the crackling and crashing and waving arms. Stanley Albert just put his head down and moved his legs, and the sprays of the bushes, some of them thick as a rooster's spur, seemed to pull back and make way. Nobody saw the fight: the brave ones were too drunk to travel fast; and the sober ones didn't want to mix with a man like Stanley Albert, drunk and mad. Alberta, she just ran her hand across her mouth and then wiped it along the side of her green satin dress, yawning like she was tired. She stood listening for a while, her head cocked a little, though there wasn't anything to hear, then walked off, pulling down the dress across her hips. And the next night she and Stanley Albert were back at Willie's, and Pete never did turn up again. Willie used to swear that he ended up in the Scanos River and that if the water wasn't so yellow muddy, that if you could see to the bottom, you would see Pete lying there, along with all the others Stanley Albert had killed.

At the last it was Willie who got the idea. For a week, carefully, he put aside the coins Stanley Albert gave him. There were a lot of them, all new silver, because Stanley Albert always paid in silver. Then one morning very early, just after Stanley Albert and Alberta left, Willie melted the coins down, and using the molds he kept for his old outsized pistol, he cast four bullets.

He made a special little shelf for the pistol under the counter so that it would be near at hand. And he waited all evening, sometimes touching the heavy black handle with the tips of his fingers; and he waited, hoping that Stanley Albert would drink enough to pass out. But of course nothing like that happened. So Willie poured himself three or four fingers of his best stuff and swallowed it fast as his throat would stand, then he blinked his little eyes fast for a second or so to clear his vision, and he reached for the gun. He got two shots over the bar, two good ones: the whole front of Stanley Albert's plaid shirt folded together and sank in, after the silver bullets went through. He got up, holding the table edge, unsteady, bending over, looking much smaller, his black skin gray-filmed and dull. His eyes were larger: they reached almost across his face — and they weren't dark any more; they were silver, two polished pieces of silver. Willie was afraid to fire again; the pistol shook where he held it in his two hands.

Then Stanley Albert walked out, not unsteady any more, but bent over the hole in his chest, walked out slowly with his eyes shining like flat metal, Alberta a few steps behind. They passed right in front of Willie, who still hadn't moved; his face was stiff with fear. Quietly, smoothly, in a single motion, almost without interrupting her step, Alberta picked up a bottle (the same one from which he had poured his drink moments before) and swung it against Willie's head. He slipped down in a quiet little heap, his legs folded under him, his black kinky head on top. But his idea had worked: over by Stanley Albert's chair there was a black pool of blood.

All that was maybe eight or ten years ago. People don't see them any more — Stanley and Alberta. They don't think much about them, except when something goes wrong — like weevils getting in the cotton, or Willie's burning down and Willie inside it — then they begin to think that those two had a hand in it. Brad Tedrow swore that he had seen Stanley Albert that night, just for a second, standing on the edge of the circle of light, with a burning faggot in his hand. And the next morning Brad went back to look, knowing that your eyes play tricks at night in firelight; he went back to look for footprints or some sign. All he found was a burnt-out stick of pine wood that anybody could have dropped.

And kids sometimes think they hear the jingle of silver in Stanley Albert's pocket, or the sound of his watch. And when women talk — when there's been a miscarriage or a stillbirth — they remember and whisper together.

And they all wonder if that's not the sort of work they do, the two of them. Maybe so; maybe not. The people themselves are not too sure. They don't see them around any more.

Miss Yellow Eyes

Pete brought Chris home one evening after supper. I remember it was early spring, because the Talisman rosebush by the kitchen steps had begun to blossom out. For that time of year it was cool: there was a good stiff wind off the river that shook the old bush and creaked it, knocked the biggest flowers to bits, and blew their petals into a little heap against the side of the wood steps. The Johnsons, who lived in the house next door, had put their bedspread out to air and forgot to take it in. So it was hanging out there on the porch railing, a pink spread with a fan-tailed yellow peacock in the middle. I could hear it flapping — loud when the wind was up, and very soft when it fell. And from out on the river there were the soft low tones of the ships' whistles. And I could hear a mockingbird too, perched up on top the house, singing away, forgetting that it was nighttime. And in all this, Pete's steps in the side alley, coming to the kitchen door.

"Hi, kid!" Pete held open the door with one arm stretched behind him. Chris came in.

I thought at first: that's a white man. And I wondered what a white man would do coming here. I got a second look and saw the difference, saw I'd made a mistake. His skin wasn't dark at all, but only sun-tanned. (Lots of white men were darker.) His eyes were a pale blue, the color of the china Ma got with the Octagon soap coupons. He had brown hair — no, it was closer to red, and only slightly wavy. He looked like a white man, almost. But I saw the difference. Maybe it was just his way of carrying himself — that was like a Negro.

But he was the handsomest man I'd ever seen, excepting none. I could feel the bottom of my stomach roll up into a hard ball.

"This here's Celia," Pete said.

Chris grinned and his blue eyes crinkled up into almost closed slits. He sat down at the table opposite me, flipping shut the book I'd been reading. "Evening's no time to be busy, kid."

Pete picked up the coffeepot from where it always stood on the back of the stove and shook it gently. "There's some here all right," he said to Chris as he reached up to the shelf for a couple of cups. "You want anything in yours? I reckon there'd be a can of milk in the icebox."

"No," Chris said. "I like it black."

Pete lit the fire under the speckled coffeepot. "Where's Ma?"

"They having a dinner tonight . . . she said she'll be real late." Ma worked as a cook in one of the big houses on St. Charles Avenue. When there was a dinner, it meant she'd have to stay around and clean up afterwards and wouldn't get home till eleven or twelve maybe.

She'll get tomorrow off, though," I told Chris.

"Good enough." He grinned and his teeth were very square and bright.

They sat down at the table with me and stretched out their legs. Holding the coffee cup to his mouth, Chris reached out one finger and rubbed the petals of the big yellow rose in the drinking glass in the center of the table. "That's real pretty."

"Lena's been putting them there," Pete said.

"That's sure the one I want to meet," Chris said, and grinned over at Pete, and I knew that he'd been talking about Lena.

She was the sort of girl you talk about, she was that beautiful — with light-brown hair that was shoulder-length and perfectly straight and ivory skin and eyes that were light brown with flecks of yellow in them. She was all gold-colored. Sometimes when she stood in the sun you could almost think the light was shining right through her.

She was near seventeen then, three years older than I was. The boys in high school all followed her around until the other girls hated her. Every chance they got they would play some mean trick on her, kicking dust in her lunch, or roughing her up playing basketball, or tearing pages out of her books. Lena hardly ever lost her temper; she didn't really seem to care. "I reckon I know who the boys are looking at," she told me. She was right. There was always a bunch of them trying to sit next to her in class or walk next to her down the hall. And when school was through, there was always a bunch of them waiting around the door, wanting to take her home, or for rides if they had cars. And when she finally came sauntering out, with her books tucked up under one arm, she wouldn't pay them much attention; she'd just give them a kind of little smile (to keep them from going to the other girls) and walk home by herself, with maybe a few of them trailing along behind. I used to wait and watch her leave and then I'd go home a different way. I didn't want to interfere.

But, for all that, she didn't go out very much. And never with the same boy for very long. Once Hoyt Carmichael came around and stood in the kitchen door, asking for her, just begging to see her. She wouldn't even come out to talk to him. Ma asked her later if there was something wrong and Lena just nodded and shrugged her shoulders all at once. Ma hugged her then and you could see the relief in her face; she worried so about Lena, about her being so very pretty.

Pete said: "You sure got to meet her, Chris, man."

And I said to Chris: "She's over by the Johnsons'." I got up and opened the door and yelled out into the alley: "Lena!"

She came in a few minutes. We could hear her steps on the alley bricks, slow. She never did hurry. Finally she opened the screen and stood there, looking from one to the other.

I said: "This is my sister, Magdalena."

"And this here is Chris Watkin," Pete said.

Chris had got up and bowed real solemnly. "I'm pleased to meet you."

Lena brushed the hair back from her forehead. She had long fingers, and hands so thin that the veins stood out blue on the backs. "Nobody calls me Magdalena," she said, "except Celia, now and then. Just Lena."

Chris's eyes crinkled up out of sight the way they had before. "I might could just call you Miss Yellow Eyes. Old Miss Yellow Eyes."

Lena just wrinkled her nose at him. In that light her eyes did look yellow, but usually if a man said something like that she'd walk out. Not this time. She just poured herself a cup of coffee, and when Chris pulled out a chair for her, she sat down, next to him.

I looked at them and I thought: they look like a white couple. And they did. Unless you had sharp trained eyes, like the people down here do, you would have thought they were white and you would have thought they made a handsome couple.

Chris looked over at me and lifted an eyebrow. Just one, the left one; it reached up high and arched in his forehead. "What you looking so solemn for, Celia?"

"Nothing."

And Lena asked: "You work with Pete at the railroad?"

"Sure," he said, and smiled at her. Only, more than his mouth was smiling. "We go swinging on and off those old tenders like hell afire. Jumping on and off those cars."

"I reckon that's hard work."

He laughed this time out loud. "I ain't exactly little." He bent forward and hunched his shoulders up a little so she could see the way the muscles swelled against the cloth of his shirt.

"You got fine shoulders, Mr. Watkin," she said. "I reckon they're even better than Pete there."

Pete grunted and finished his coffee. But she was right. Pete's shoulders were almost square out from his neck. Chris's weren't. They looked almost sloped and hunched the way flat bands of muscles reached up into his neck.

Chris shrugged and stood up. "Do you reckon you would like to walk around the corner for a couple of beers?"

"Okay," Pete said.

Lena lifted one eyebrow, just the way he had done. "Mr. Watkin, you do look like you celebrating something."

"I sure am," he said.

"What?" I asked.

"I plain tell you later, kid."

They must have been gone near two hours because Ma came home before they did. I'd fallen asleep. I'd just bent my head over for a minute to rest my eyes, and my forehead touched the soft pages of the book — *Treasure Island*. I'd got it from the library at school; it was dog-eared and smelled faintly of peanuts.

Ma was saying: "Lord, honey, why ain't you gone to bed?"

I lifted my head and rubbed my face until I could see Ma's figure in the doorway. "I'm waiting for them," I said.

Ma took off her coat and hung it up on the hook behind the door. "Who them?"

"Lena," I said, "and Pete. And Chris." I knew what she was going to say, so I answered first. "He's a friend of Pete, and Lena likes him."

Ma was frowning very slightly. "I plain wonder iffen he belong to that club."

"I don't know."

It was called the Better Days Club and the clubroom was the second floor of a little restaurant on Tulane Avenue. I'd never gone inside, though I had passed the place: a small wood building that had once been a house but now had a sign saying LEFTY'S RESTAURANT AND CAFÉ in green letters on a square piece of board that hung out over the sidewalk and creaked in the wind. And I'd seen something else too when I passed: another sign, a small one tucked into the right center corner of the screen door, a sign that said "*White* Entrance to *Rear*." If the police ever saw that they'd have found an excuse to raid the place and break up everything in it.

Ma kept asking Pete what they did there. Most time he didn't bother to answer. Once when she'd just insisted, he'd said, "We're fixing to have better times come." And sometimes he'd bring home little papers, not much more than book-size, with names like *New Day* and *Daily Sentinel* and *Watcher*.

Ma would burn the papers if she got hold of them. But she couldn't really stop Pete from going to the meetings. She didn't try too hard because he was so good to her and gave her part of his pay check every week. With that money and what she made we always had enough. We didn't have to worry about eating, way some of our neighbors did.

Pete was a strange fellow — moody and restless and not happy. Sometimes — when he was sitting quiet, thinking or resting — there'd be a funny sort of look on his face (he was the darkest of us all): not hurt, not fear, not determination, but a mixture of all three.

Ma was still standing looking at me with a kind of puzzled expression on her face when we heard them, the three of them, coming home. They'd had a few beers and, what with the cold air outside, they all felt fine. They were singing too; I recognized the tune; it was the one from the jukebox around the corner in that bar.

Ma said: "They got no cause to be making a racket like that. Somebody might could call the police." Ma was terribly afraid of the police. She'd never had anything to do with them, but she was still afraid. Every time a police car passed in the street outside, she'd duck behind the curtain and peep out. And she'd walk clear around a block so she wouldn't come near one of the blue uniforms.

The three came in the kitchen door, Pete first and then Lena and Chris.

Pete had his arms full of beer cans; he let them all fall out on the table. "Man, I like to drop them sure."

"We brought some for you, Ma," Lena said.

"And Celia too," Chris added.

"It's plenty late," Ma said, looking hard at Chris.

"You don't have to work tomorrow," I said.

So we stayed up late. I don't know how late. Because the beer made me feel

fine and sick all at once. First everything was swinging around inside my head
and then the room too. Finally I figured how to handle it. I caught hold and let
myself ride around on the big whooshing circles. There were times when I'd
forget there was anybody else in the room, I'd swing so far away.

"Why, just look at Celia there," Ma said, and everybody turned and
watched me.

"You sure high, kid," Chris said.

"No, I'm not." I was careful to space the words, because I could tell by the
way Ma had run hers together that she was feeling the beer too.

Pete had his guitar in his lap, flicking his fingers across the strings. "You an
easy drunk." He was smiling, the way he seldom did. "Leastways you ain't
gonna cost some man a lotta money getting you high."

"That's absolutely and completely right." Ma bent forward, with her hands
one on each knee, and the elbows sticking out, like a skinny football-player.
"You plain got to watch that when boys come to take you out."

"They ain't gonna want to take me out."

"Why not, kid?" Chris had folded his arms on the tabletop and was leaning
his chin on them. His face was flushed so that his eyes only looked bluer.

"Not after they see Lena." I lifted my eyes up from his and let them drop
over where I knew Lena was sitting. I just had time to notice the way the
electric light made her skin gold and her eyes gold and her hair too, so that she
seemed all one blurry color. And then the whole world tipped over and I went
skidding off — but feeling extra fine because Chris was sitting just a little bit
away next to Lena and she was looking at him like she'd never looked at
anybody else before.

Next thing I knew, somebody was saying: "Celia, look." There was a
photograph in front of me. A photograph of a young man, in a suit and tie,
leaning back against a post, with his legs crossed, grinning at the camera.

I looked up. Ma was holding the photograph in front of me. It was in a wide
silver-colored frame, with openwork, roses or flowers of some sort.

Pete began laughing. "Just you look at her," he said; "she don't even know
her own daddy."

"I never seen that picture before," I said, loud as I could.

I'd never seen my daddy either. He was a steward on a United Fruit Lines
ship, a real handsome man. He'd gone ashore at Antigua one day and forgot to
come back.

"He looks mighty much like Chris," Ma said as she cleared a space on the
shelf over between the windows. She put the picture there. And I knew then
that she'd got it out from the bottom of a drawer somewhere, because this was
a special occasion for her too.

"Chris," I said, remembering, "you never did tell us what you celebrating."

He had twisted sideways in his chair and had his arms wrapped around the back. "I going in the army."

Out of the corner of my eye I saw Pete staring at him, his mouth twisting and his face darkening.

Ma clucked her tongue against her teeth. "That a shame."

Chris grinned, his head cocked aside a little. "I got to leave tomorrow."

Pete swung back and forth on the two legs of his tilted chair. "Ain't good enough for nothing around here, but we good enough to put in the army and send off."

"Man" — Chris winked at him — "there ain't nothing you can do. And I plain reckon you gonna go next."

"No." Pete spoke the word so that it was almost a whistle.

"I'm a man, me," Chris said. "Can't run out on what I got to do." He tipped his head back and whistled a snatch of a little tune.

"I wouldn't like to go in the army," Lena said.

Chris went on whistling. Now we could recognize the song:

> Yellow, yellow, yellow, yellow, yellow gal,
> Yellow, yellow, yellow, yellow, yellow gal,
> She's pretty and fine
> Is the yellow gal. . . .

Lena tossed her head. "I wouldn't like to none."

Chris stopped whistling and laughed. "You plain sound like Pete here."

Pete's face all crinkled up with anger. I thought: he looks more like a Negro when he loses his temper; it makes his skin darker somehow.

"Nothing to laugh about," he said; "can't do nothing around here without people yelling nigger at you."

"Don't stay around here, man. You plain crazy to stay around here." Chris tilted back his chair and stared at the ceiling. "You plain crazy to stay a nigger. I done told you that."

Pete scowled at him and didn't answer.

Lena asked quickly: "Where you got to go?"

"Oregon," Chris was still staring at the ceiling and still smiling. "That where you cross over."

"You sure?"

"Chris looked at her and smiled confidently. "Sure I'm sure."

Pete mumbled something under his breath that we didn't hear.

"I got a friend done it," Chris said. "Two years ago. He working out of

Portland there, for the railroad. And he turn white."

Lena was resting her chin on her folded hands. "They don't look at you so close. Or anything?"

"No," Chris said. "I heard all about it. You can cross over if you want to."

"You going?" I asked.

"When I get done with the stretch in the army." He lowered his chair back to its four legs and stared out the little window, still smiling. "There's lots of jobs there for a railroad man."

Pete slammed the flat of his hand down against the table. Ma's eyes flew open like a door that's been kicked wide back. "I don't want to pretend I'm white," he said. "I ain't and I don't want to be. I reckon I want to be same as white and stay right here."

Ma murmured something under her breath and we all turned to look at her. Her eyes had dropped half-closed again and she had her hands folded across her stomach. Her mouth opened very slowly and this time she spoke loud enough for us all to hear. "Talking like that — you gonna do nothing but break you neck that way."

I got so sleepy then and so tired, all of a sudden, that I slipped sideways out of my chair. It was funny. I didn't notice I was slipping or moving until I was on the floor. Ma got hold of my arm and took me off to bed with her. And I didn't think to object. The last thing I saw was Lena staring at Chris with her long light-colored eyes. Chris with his handsome face and his reddish hair and his movements so quick they almost seemed jerky.

I thought it would be all right with them.

I was sick the whole next day from the beer; so sick I couldn't go to school. Ma shook her head and Pete laughed and Lena just smiled a little.

And Chris went off to the army, all right. It wasn't long before Lena had a picture of him. He'd written across the back: "Here I am a soldier." She stuck the picture in the frame of the mirror over her dresser.

That was the week Lena quit school. She came looking for me during lunch time. "I'm going home," she said.

"You can't do that."

She shook her head. "I had enough."

So she walked out of school and didn't ever go back. (She was old enough to do that.) She bought a paper on her way home and sat down and went through the classified ads very carefully, looking for a job. It was three days before she found one she wanted: with some people who were going across the lake to Covington for the summer. Their regular city maid wouldn't go.

They took her on right away because they wanted to leave. She came back with a ten-dollar bill in her purse. "We got to leave in the morning," she said.

Ma didn't like it, her quitting school and leaving home, but she couldn't really stop her.

And Lena did want to go. She was practically jumping with excitement after she came back from the interview. "They got the most beautiful house," she said to Ma. "A lot prettier than where you work." And she told me: "They say the place over the lake is even prettier — even prettier."

I knew what she meant. I sometimes went to meet Ma at the house where she worked. I liked to. It was nice to be in the middle of fine things, even if they weren't yours.

"It'll be real nice working there," Lena said.

That next morning, when she had got her things together and closed the lid of the suitcase, she told me to go down to the grocery at the corner, where there was a phone, and call a taxi. They were going to pay for it, she said.

I reckon I was excited; so excited that I called the wrong cab. I just looked at the back cover of the phone book where there was a picture of a long orange-color cab and a number in big orange letters. I gave them the address, then went back to the house and sat down on the porch with Lena.

The orange cab turned at the corner and came down our street. The driver was hanging out the window looking for house numbers; there weren't any except for the Stevenses' across the way. Bill Stevens had painted his number with big whitewash letters on his front door. The cab hit a rut in the street and the driver's head smacked the window edge. He jerked his head back inside and jammed the gears into second. Then he saw us: Lena and me and the suitcase on the edge of the porch.

He let the car move along slow in second with that heavy pulling sound and he watched us. As he got closer you could see that he was chewing on the corner of his lip. Still watching us, he went on slowly — right past the house. He said something once, but we were too far away to hear. Then he was down at the other corner, turning, and gone.

Lena stood and looked at me. She had on her best dress: a light-blue one with round pockets in front. Both her hands were stuffed into the pockets. There was a handkerchief in the left one; you could see her fingers twisting it.

White cabs don't pick up colored people: I knew that. But I'd forgot and called the first number, a white number, a wrong number. Lena didn't say anything, just kept looking at me, with her hand holding the handkerchief inside her pocket. I turned and ran all the way down to the corner and called the right number, and a colored cab that was painted black with gold stripes across the hood came and Lena was gone for the next four months, the four months of the summer.

It could have been the same cab brought her back that had come for her: black with gold stripes. She had on the same dress too, the blue one with round pockets; the same suitcase too, but this time in it was a letter of recommendation and a roll of bills she'd saved, all hidden in the fancy organdy aprons they'd given her.

She said: "He wanted me to stay on through the winter, but she got scared for their boy." And she held her chin stiff and straight when she said that.

I understood why that woman wanted my sister Lena out of the house. There wasn't any boy or man either that wouldn't look at her twice. White or colored it didn't seem to make a difference, they all looked at her in the same way.

That was the only job Lena ever took. Because she hadn't been home more than a few days when Chris came back for her.

I remember how it was — early September and real foggy. It would close down every evening around seven and wouldn't lift until ten or ten thirty in the morning. All night long you could hear the foghorns and the whistles of the boats out on the river; and in the morning there'd be even more confusion when everybody tried to rush away from anchor. That Saturday morning Lena had taken a walk up to the levee to watch. Pete was just getting up. I could hear him in his room. Ma had left for work early. And me, I was scrubbing out the kitchen, the way I did every Saturday morning. That was when Chris came back.

He came around to the kitchen. I heard his steps in the alley — quickly coming, almost running. He came bursting in the door and almost slipped on the soapy floor. "Hi, kid," he said, took off his cap, and rubbed his hand over his reddish hair. "You working?"

"Looks like," I said.

He'd grown a mustache, a thin line. He stood for a moment chewing on his lip and the little hairs he had brushed so carefully into a line. Finally he said: "Where's everybody?"

"Lena went up on the levee to have a look at the river boats."

He grinned at me, flipped his cap back on, gave a kind of salute, and jumped down the two steps into the yard.

I sat back on my heels, picturing him and Lena in my mind and thinking what a fine couple they made. And the little picture of my father grinned down at me from the shelf by the window.

Pete called: "Seems like I heard Chris in there."

"He went off to look for Lena."

Pete came to the door; he was only half dressed and he was still holding up his pants with his one hand. He liked to sleep late Saturdays. "He might could have stayed to say hello."

"He wanted to see Lena, I reckon."

Pete grinned briefly and the grin faded into a yawn. "You ought to have let him look for her."

"Nuh-uh." I picked up the bar of soap and the scrubbing brush again. "I wanted them to get together, I reckon."

"Okay, kid," Pete said shortly, and turned back to his room. "You helped them out."

Chris and Lena came back after a while. They didn't say anything, but I noticed that Lena was kind of smiling like she was cuddling something to herself. And her eyes were so bright they looked light yellow, almost transparent.

Chris hung his army cap on the back of a chair and then sprawled down at the table. "You fixing to offer me anything to eat?"

"You can't be hungry this early in the morning," Lena said.

"Men are always hungry," I said. They both turned.

"You tell 'em kid," Chris said. "You tell 'em for me."

"Let's us go to the beach," Lena said suddenly.

"Sure, honey," Chris said softly.

She wrinkled her nose at him and pretended she hadn't heard. "It's the last night before they close down everything for the winter."

"Okay — we gonna leave right now?"

"Crazy thing," Lena smiled. "Not in the morning. Let's us go right after supper."

"I got to stay here till then?"

"Not less you want to."

"Reckon I do," Chris said.

"You want to come, Celia?" Lena asked.

"Me?" I glanced over at Chris quickly. "Nuh-uh."

"Sure you do," Lena said. "You just come along."

And Chris lifted one eyebrow at me. "Come along," he said. "Iffen you don't mind going out with people old as me."

"Oh, no," I said. "Oh, no."

I never did figure out quite why Lena wanted me along that time. Maybe she didn't want to be alone with Chris because she didn't quite trust him yet. Or maybe she just wanted to be nice to me. I don't know. But I did go. I liked the beach. I liked to stare off across the lake and imagine I could see the shore on the other side, which of course I couldn't.

So I went with them, that evening after supper. It took us nearly an hour to get there — three changes of busses because it was exactly across town: the north end of the city. All the way, all along in the bus, Chris kept talking, telling stories.

"Man," he said, "that army sure is something — big — I never seen anything so big. Just in our little old camp there ain't a space of ground big enough to hold all the men, if they called them all out together. . . ."

We reached the end of one bus line. He put one hand on Lena's arm and the other on mine and helped us out the door. His hand was broad and hard on the palm and almost cool to the touch.

In the other bus we headed straight for the long seat across the back, so we could sit all three together. He sat in the middle and, leaning forward a little, rested both hands on his knees. Looking at him out the corner of my eye, I could see the flat broad strips of muscle in his neck, reaching up to under his chin. And once I caught Lena's eye, and I knew that on the other side she was watching too.

"All together like that," he said. "It gives you the funniest feeling — when you all marching together, so that you can't see away on either side, just men all together — it gives you a funny sort of feeling."

He turned to Lena and grinned; his bright square teeth flashed in the evening dusk. "I reckon you think that silly."

"No," she said quickly, and then corrected herself: "of course I never been in the army."

"Look there," I said. We were passing the white beach. Even as far away as the road where we were, we could smell the popcorn and the sweat and the faint salt tingle from the wind off the lake.

"It almost cool tonight," Lena said.

"You ain't gonna be cold?"

"You don't got to worry about me."

"I reckon I do," he said.

Lena shook her head, and her eyes had a soft holding look in them. And I wished I could take Chris aside and tell him that he'd said just the right thing.

Out on the concrete walks of the white beach, people were jammed so close that there was hardly any space between. You could hear all the voices and the talking, murmuring at this distance. Then we were past the beach (the driver was going fast, grumbling under his breath that he was behind schedule), and the Ferris wheel was the only thing you could see, a circle of lights like a big star behind us. And on each side, open ground, low weeds, and no trees.

"There it is," Chris said, and pointed up through the window. I turned and looked and, sure enough, there it was; he was right: the lights, smaller maybe and dimmer, of Lincoln Beach, the colored beach.

"Lord," Lena said, "I haven't been out here in I don't know when. It's been that long."

We got off the bus; he dropped my arm but kept hold of Lena's. "You got to make this one night last all winter."

She didn't answer.

We had a fine time. I forgot that I was just tagging along and enjoyed myself much as any.

When we passed over by the shooting gallery Chris winked at Lena and me. "Which one of them dolls do you want?"

Lena wrinkled her nose. "I reckon you plain better see about getting 'em first."

He just shrugged. "You think I can do it, Celia?"

"Sure," I said. "Sure, sure you can."

"That's the girl for you," the man behind the counter said. "Thinks you can do anything."

"That my girl there all right." Chris reached in his pocket to pay the man. I could feel my ears getting red.

He picked up the rifle and slowly knocked down the whole row of green and brown painted ducks. He kept right on until Lena and I each had a doll in a bright pink feather skirt and he had a purple wreath of flowers hung around his neck. By this time the man was scowling at him and a few people were standing around watching.

"That's enough, soldier," the man said. "This here is just for amateurs."

Chris shrugged. We all turned and walked away.

"You did that mighty well," Lena said, turning her baby doll around and around in her hands, staring at it.

"I see lots of fellows better."

"Where'd you learn to shoot like that?" I tugged on his sleeve.

"I didn't learn —"

"Fibber!" Lena tossed her head.

"You got to let me finish. Up in Calcasieu parish, my daddy, he put a shotgun in my hand and give me a pocket of shells. . . . I just keep shooting till I hit something or other."

It was hard to think of Chris having a father. "Where's he now?"

"My daddy? He been dead."

"You got a family?"

"No," Chris said. "Just me."

We walked out along the strip of sand, and the wind began pulling the feathers out of the dolls' skirts. I got out my handkerchief and tied it around my doll, but Lena just lifted hers up high in the air to see what the wind would do. Soon she just had a naked baby doll that was pink celluloid smeared with glue.

Lena and Chris found an old log and sat down. I went wading. I didn't want to go back to where they were, because I knew that Chris wanted Lena alone. So I kept walking up and down in the water that came just a little over my ankles.

It was almost too cold for swimmers. I saw just one, about thirty yards out, swimming up and down slowly. I couldn't really see him, just the regular white splashes from his arms. I looked out across the lake, the way I liked to do. It was all dark now; there was no telling where the lower part of the sky stopped and the water began. It was all the one color, all of it, out beyond the swimmer and the breakwater on the left where the waves hit a shallow spot and turned white and foamy. Except for that, it was all the same dark until you lifted your eyes high up in the sky and saw the stars.

I don't know how long I stood there, with my head bent back far as it would go, looking at the stars, trying to remember the names for them that I had learned in school: names like Bear and Archer. I couldn't tell which was which. All I could see were stars, bright like they always were at the end of the summer and close; and every now and then one of them would fall.

I stood watching them, feeling the water move gently around my legs and curling my toes in the soft lake sand that was rippled by the waves. And trying to think up ways to stay away from those two who were sitting back up the beach, on a piece of driftwood, talking together.

Once the wind shifted a little suddenly or Chris spoke too loud, because I heard one word: "Oregon."

All of a sudden I knew that Lena was going to marry him. Just for that she was going to marry him; because she wanted so much to be white.

And I wanted to tell Chris again, the way I had wanted to in the bus, that he'd said just the right thing.

After a while Lena stood up and called to me, saying it was late; so we went home. By the time we got there, Ma had come. On the table was a bag of food she had brought. And so we all sat around and ate the remains of the party: little cakes, thin and crispy and spicy and in fancy shapes; and little patties full of oysters that Ma ran in the oven to heat up; and little crackers spread with fishy-tasting stuff, like sugar grains only bigger, that Ma called caviar; and all sorts of little sandwiches.

It was one nice thing about the place Ma worked. They never did check the food. And it was fun for us, tasting the strange things.

All of a sudden Lena turned to me and said: "I reckon I want to see where Oregon is." She gave Chris a long look out of the corner of her eyes.

My mouth was full and for a moment I couldn't answer.

"You plain got to have a map in your schoolbooks."

I finally managed to swallow. "Sure I got one — if you want to see it."

I got my history book and unfolded the map of the whole country and put my finger down on the spot that said Oregon in pink letters. "There," I said; "that's Portland there."

Lena came and leaned over my shoulder; Pete didn't move; he sat with his chin in his hand and his elbows propped on the table.

"I want to stay here and be the same as white," he said, but we weren't listening to him.

Chris got out of the icebox the bottles of beer he had brought.

"Don't you want to see?" Lena asked him.

He grinned and took out his key chain, which had an opener on it, and began popping the caps off the bottles. "I looked at a map once. I know where it's at."

Ma was peering over my shoulder. "It looks like it mighty far away."

"It ain't close," Chris said.

"You plain want to go there —" Ma was frowning at the map, straining to see without her glasses.

"Yes," Chris said, still popping the tops off bottles.

"And be white," Lena added very softly.

"Sure," Chris said. "No trouble at all to cross over."

"And you going there," Ma said again. She couldn't quite believe that anybody she was looking at right now could ever go that far away.

"Yea," Chris said, and put the last opened bottle with the others in a row on the table. "When I get out the army, we sure as hell going there."

"Who's we?" I asked.

"Lena and me."

Ma looked up at him so quickly that a hairpin tumbled out of her head and clicked down on the table.

"When we get married," he said.

Lena was looking at him, chewing her lower lip. "We going to do that?"

"Yea," he said. "Leastways if that what you want to do."

And Lena dropped her eyes down to the map again, though I'd swear this time she didn't know what she was seeing. Or maybe everywhere she'd look she was seeing Chris. Maybe that was it. She was smiling very slightly to herself, with just the corners of her lips, and they were trembling.

They got married that week in St. Michel's Church. It was in the morning — nine thirty, I remember — so the church was cold: biting empty cold. Even the two candles burning on the alter didn't look like they'd be warm. Though it only took a couple of minutes, my teeth were chattering so that I could hardly talk. Ma cried and Pete scowled and grinned by turns and Lena and Chris didn't seem to notice anything much.

The cold and the damp had made a bright strip of flush across Lena's cheeks. Old Mrs. Roberts, who lived next door, bent forward — she was sitting in the pew behind us — and tapped Ma on the shoulder. "I never seen her look prettier."

Lena had bought herself a new suit, with the money she'd earned over the summer: a cream-colored suit, with small black braiding on the cuffs and collar. She'd got a hat too, of the same color velvet. Cream was a good color for her; it was lighter than her skin somehow, so that it made her face stand out.

("She ought to always have clothes like that," Mayme Roberts said later, back at our house. She was old Mrs. Roberts's daughter, and seven kids had broken her up so that she wasn't even jealous of pretty girls any more. "Maybe Chris'll make enough money to let her have pretty clothes like that.")

Lena and Chris went away because he had to get back to camp. And for the first time since I could remember, I had a room all to myself. So I made Lena's bed all nice and careful and put the fancy spread that Ma had crocheted on it — the one we hardly ever used. And put the little pink celluloid doll in the middle.

Sometime after the wedding, I don't remember exactly when, Pete had an accident. He'd been out on a long run, all the way up to Abiline. It was a long hard job and by the time he got back to town he was dead tired, and so he got a little careless. In the switch yards he got his hand caught in a loose coupling.

He was in the hospital for two weeks or so, in the colored surgical ward on the second floor of a huge cement building that said Charity Hospital in carved letters over the big front door. Ma went to see him on Tuesdays and Saturdays and I just went on Saturdays. Walking over from the bus, we'd pass Lefty's Restaurant and Café. Ma would turn her head away so that she wouldn't see it.

One time, the first Saturday I went with Ma, we brought Pete a letter, his induction notice. He read it and started laughing and crying all at once — until the ward nurse got worried and called an intern and together they gave him a shot. Right up till he passed out, he kept laughing.

And I began to wonder if it had been an accident. . . .

After two weeks he came home. We hadn't expected him; we hadn't thought he was well enough to leave. Late one afternoon we heard steps in the side alley; Ma looked at me, quick and funny, and rushed over to open the door: it was Pete. He had come home alone on the streetcar and walked the three blocks from the car stop. By the time he got to the house he was ready to pass out: he had to sit down and rest his head on the table right there in the kitchen. But he'd held his arm careful so that it didn't start to bleed again. He'd always been afraid of blood.

Accidents like that happened a lot on the road. Maybe that was why the pay was so good. The fellows who sat around the grocery all day or the bar all had pensions because they'd lost an arm or a hand or a leg. It happened a lot; we knew that, but it didn't seem to make any difference.

Ma cried very softly to herself when she saw him so dizzy and weak he couldn't stand up. And I went out in the back yard, where he couldn't see, and was sick to my stomach.

He stayed in the house until he got some strength back and then he was out all day long. He left every morning just like he was working and he came back for dinner at night. Ma asked him once where he went, but he wouldn't say; and there was never any trouble about it. A check came from the railroad every month, regular; and he still gave Ma part of it.

Pete talked about his accident, though. It was all he'd talk about. "I seen my hand," he'd tell anybody who'd listen. "After they got it free, with the blood running down it, I seen it. And it wasn't cut off. My fingers were moving. I seen 'em. Was no call for them to go cut the hand off. There wasn't any call for them to do that, not even with all it hurting." (And it had hurt so bad that he'd passed out. They'd told us he just tumbled down all of a sudden — so that the cinders along the tracks cut in his cheek.)

He'd say: "Iffen it wasn't a man my color they wouldn't done it. They wouldn't go cut off a white man's hand."

He'd say: "It was only just one finger that was caught, they didn't have cause to take off the whole hand."

And when I heard him I couldn't help wondering. Wondering if maybe Pete hadn't tried to get one finger caught. The army wouldn't take a man with one finger missing. But just one finger gone wouldn't hamper a man much. The way Pete was acting wasn't like a man that had an accident he wasn't expecting. But like a man who'd got double-crossed somehow.

And looking at Ma, I could see that she was thinking the same thing.

Lena came home after a couple of months — Chris had been sent overseas.

She used to spend most of her days lying on the bed in our room, reading a magazine maybe, or writing to Chris, or just staring at the ceiling. When the winter sun came in through the window and fell on her, her skin turned gold and burning.

Since she slept so much during the days, often in the night she'd wake up and be lonesome. Then she'd call me. "Celia," she'd call real soft so that the sound wouldn't carry through the paperboard walls. "Celia, you awake?" And I'd tell her yes and wake up as quick as I could.

Then she'd snap on the little lamp that Chris had given her for a wedding present. And she'd climb out of bed, wrapping one of the blankets around her because it was cold. And she'd sit on the cane-bottomed old chair and rock it slowly back and forth while she told me just what it would be like when Chris came back for her.

Sometimes Pete would hear us talking and would call: "Shut up in there." And Lena would only toss her head and say that he was an old grouch and not to pay any attention to him.

Pete had been in a terrible temper for weeks, the cold made his arm hurt so. He scarcely spoke any more. And he didn't bother going out after supper; instead he stayed in his room, sitting in a chair with his feet propped up on the windowsill, looking out where there wasn't anything to see. Once I'd peeped in through the half-opened door. He was standing in the middle of the room, at the foot of the bed, and he was looking at his stub arm, which was still bright-red-colored. His lips were drawn back tight against his teeth, and his eyes were almost closed, they were so squinted.

Things went on this way right through the first part of the winter. Chris was in Japan. He sent Lena a silk kimono — green, with a red dragon embroidered across the back. He didn't write much, and then it was just a line saying that he was fine. Along toward the middle of January, I think it was, one of the letters mentioned fighting. It wasn't so bad, he said; and it wasn't noisy at all. That's what he noticed most, it seemed: the quietness. From the other letters we could tell that he was at the front all the rest of the winter.

It was March by this time. And in New Orleans March is just rain, icy splashing rain. One afternoon I ran the dozen or so blocks home from school and all I wanted to do was sit down by the stove. I found Ma and Pete in the kitchen. Ma was standing by the table, looking down at the two yellow pieces of paper like she expected them to move.

The telegram was in the middle of the table — the folded paper and the folded yellow envelope. There wasn't anything else, not even the big salt-shaker which usually stood there.

Ma said: "Chris got himself hurt."

Pete was sitting across the room with his chair propped against the wall, tilting himself back and forth. "Ain't good enough for nothing around here," he said, and rubbed his stump arm with his good hand. "Ain't good enough for white people, but sure good enough to get killed."

"He ain't killed," Lena said from the next room. The walls were so thin she could hear every word. "He ain't got killed."

"Sure, Lena, honey," Ma said, and her voice was soft and comforting. "He going to be all right, him. Sure."

"Quit that," Ma told Pete in a fierce whisper. "You just quit that." She glanced over her shoulder toward Lena's room. "She got enough trouble without you adding to it."

Pete glared but didn't answer.

"You want me to get you something, Lena?" I started into our room. But her voice stopped me.

"No call for you to come in," she said.

Maybe she was crying, I don't know. Her voice didn't sound like it. Maybe she was though, crying for Chris. Nobody saw her.

Chris didn't send word to us. It was almost like he forgot. There was one letter from a friend of his in Japan, saying that he had seen him in the hospital there and that the nurses were a swell set of people and so were the doctors.

Lena left the letter open on the table for us all to see. That night she picked it up and put it in the drawer of her dresser with the yellow paper of the telegram.

And there wasn't anything else to do but wait.

No, there were two things, two things that Lena could do. The day after the telegram came, she asked me to come with her.

"Where?"

"St. Michel's." She was drying the dishes, putting them away in the cupboard, so I couldn't see her face, but I could tell from her voice how important this was.

"Sure," I said. "Sure, I'll come. Right away."

St. Michel's was a small church. I'd counted the pews once: there were just exactly twenty; and the side aisles were so narrow two people could hardly pass. The confessional was a single little recess on the right side in the back, behind the baptismal font. There was a light burning — Father Graziano would be back there.

"You wait for me," Lena said. And I sat down in the last pew while she walked over toward the light. I kept my head turned so that she wouldn't think I was watching her as she went up to the confessional and knocked very softly on the wood frame. Father Graziano stuck his gray old head out between the dark curtains. I didn't have to listen; I knew what Lena was asking him. She was asking him to pray for Chris. It only took her a minute; then she walked quickly up to the front, by the altar rail. I could hear her heels against the bare boards, each one a little explosion. There were three or four candles burning already. She lit another one — I saw the circle of light get bigger as she put hers on the black iron rack.

"Let's go," she said, "let's go."

Father Graziano had come out of the confessional and was standing watching us. He was a small man, but heavy, with a big square head and a thick neck. He must have been a powerful man when he was young. Chris had a neck like that, muscled like that.

For a minute I thought he was going to come over and talk to us. He took one step, then stopped and rubbed his hand through his curly gray hair.

Lena didn't say anything until we reached the corner where we turned to go home. Without thinking, I turned.

"Not that way." She caught hold of my arm. "This way here." She went in the opposite direction.

I walked along with her, trying to see her face. But it was too dark and she had pulled the scarf high over her head.

"We got to go to Maam's," she said and her voice was muffled in the collar of her coat.

"To what?" not believing I'd heard her right.

"To Maam's."

Maam was a grisgris woman, so old nobody could remember when she'd been young or middle-aged even. Old as the river and wrinkled like it too, when the wind blows across.

She had a house on the *batture*, behind a clump of old thick hackberries. There was the story I'd heard: she had wanted a new house after a high water on the river had carried her old one away. (All this was fifty years ago, maybe.) So she'd walked down the levee to the nearest house, which was nearly a mile away: people didn't want to live close to her. She'd stood outside, looking out at the river and calling out: "I want a house. A fine new house. A nice new house. For me." She didn't say anything else, just turned and walked away. But the people inside had heard her and spread the word. Before they even began to fix the damage the flood had done to their own houses, the men worked on her house. In less than a week it was finished. They picked up their tools and left, and the next day they sent a kid down to spy and, sure enough, there was smoke coming out of the chimney. Maam had moved in: she must have been watching from somewhere close. Nobody knew where she had spent the week that she didn't have a house. And everybody was really too scared to find out.

She was still living in that house. It was built on good big solid pilings so that flood waters didn't touch it. I'd seen it once; Pete had taken me up on the levee there and pointed it out: a two-room house that the air and the river damp had turned black, on top a flat tin roof that shone in the sun. At the beginning of the dirt path that led down to the house I saw a little pile of food people had left for her: some white pieces of slab bacon, some tin cans. Pete wouldn't let me get close. "No sense fooling with things you don't understand," he said.

Maam didn't leave her house often. But when she did, when she came walking down the streets or along the levee, people got out of her way. Either they slipped down into the *batture* bushes and waited until she passed by on the top of the levee, or, in town, they got off the banquette and into the street when she came by — an old woman with black skin that was nearly gray and eyes hidden in the folds of wrinkles, an old woman wearing a black dress, and a red shawl over her head and shoulders, a bright red shawl with silver and black signs sewed onto it. And always she'd be staring at the girls; what she liked best was to be able to touch them, on the arm or the hand, or catch hold of a little piece of their clothes. That didn't happen often, everybody was so careful of her.

And still Lena had said: "We going to Maam's."

"Lord," I said, "why?"

"For Chris."

There wasn't anything I could answer to that.

It was still early, seven thirty or eight, but nights don't seem to have time. The moon wasn't up yet; the sky was clear, with hard flecks of stars. Out on the river one ship was moving out — slipping between the riding lights of the other anchored ships that were waiting their turn at the docks below the point. You could hear the steady sound of the engines.

On top the levee the river wind was strong and cold and heavy-wet. I shivered even with a coat and scarf. There was a heavy frost like mold on the riverside slant of the levee. I stopped and pulled a clover and touched it to my lips and felt the sting of ice.

There was a light in Maam's house. We saw that as we came down the narrow little path through the hackberry bushes, the way that Pete wouldn't let me go when I was little. She must have heard us coming — walking noisy on a quiet night — because without our knocking Maam opened the door.

I never did see her face. She had the red scarf tied high around her head so that it stuck out far on the sides. She mightn't have had a face, for all I could tell. The house was warm, very warm; I cold feel the heat rush out all around her. She was wearing a black dress without sleeves, a green cord tight around her middle. Under it her stomach stuck out like a pregnant woman.

"I came to fetch something," Lena said. Her voice was tight and hard.

Inside the house a round spot was shining on the far wall. I couldn't see more than that because there wasn't much light; just a single kerosene lamp standing in the middle of the room, on the floor. Being low like that, it made the shadows go upward on the walls so that even familiar things looked strange.

"I came to fetch something," Lena said. "For somebody that's sick."

Maam didn't move.

"To make him well," Lena added.

Maam turned around, made a circle back through her cabin, ending up behind her half-open door, where we couldn't see. I suppose we could have stepped inside and watched her — but we didn't. And in a couple of seconds she was back at the doorway. She was holding both arms straight down against her sides, the hands clenched. And she kept looking from Lena to me and back again.

Lena took her left hand out of her coat pocket and I could see that she was holding a bill and a couple of coins. She moved them slowly back and forth; Maam's eyes followed but she did not move.

"You got to give it to me," Lena said. Her voice was high-pitched and rasping. I hadn't known it could be as rough as that.

Maam held out her hand: a thin black arm, all the muscles and tendons showing along the bone. She held out her arm, palm down, fist clenched. Then slowly, so that the muscles under the thin skin moved in twisting lines, she turned the arm and opened the fingers. And in the palm there was a small bundle of cloth, white cloth. As we stared at it the three edges of the cloth, which had been pressed down in her hand popped up slowly until they stuck straight up.

Lena reached out her right hand and took the three pointed edges of the cloth while her other hand dropped the money in its place. I could see how careful she was being not to touch the old woman.

Then we turned and almost ran back up the path to the top of the levee. I turned once near the top and looked back. Maam was still standing in the door, in her thin black sleeveless dress. She seemed to be singing something; I couldn't make out the words, just the sound. As she stood there, the lamplight all yellow behind her, I could feel her eyes reach out after us.

Lena had done all she could. She'd gone to the church and she'd prayed and lit a candle and asked the priest for special prayers. And she'd gone to the voodoo woman. She'd done all she could. Now there wasn't anything to do but wait.

You could see how hard waiting was for her. Her face was always thin, a little long, with fine features. And now you could almost see the strain lines run down her cheeks. The skin under her eyes turned blue; she wasn't sleeping. I knew that. She always lay very quiet in her bed, never tossing or turning. And that was just how I knew she was awake. Nobody lies stiff and still like that if they're really asleep; and their breathing isn't so shallow and quick.

I'd lie awake and listen to her pretending that she was asleep. And I'd want to get up and go over there and comfort her somehow. Only, some people you can't comfort. You can only go along with their pretending and pretend yourself.

That's what I did. I made out I didn't notice anything. Not the circles under her eyes; not the way she had of blinking rapidly (her eyes were so dry they burned); not the zigzag vein that stood out blue on her left forehead.

One night we had left the shade up. There was a full moon, so bright that I woke up. Lena was really asleep then. I looked over at her: the light hadn't reached more than the side of her bed; it only reached her hand that was dangling over the edge of the bed, the fingers limp and curled a little. A hand so thin that the moonlight was like an X-ray, showing the bones.

And I wanted to cry for her if she couldn't cry for herself. But I only got up and pulled down the shade, and made the room all dark so I couldn't see any more.

Chris died. The word came one Thursday late afternoon. Ma was out sweeping off the front steps and she took the telegram from the boy and brought it to Lena. Her hand was trembling when she held it out. Lena's thin hand didn't move even a little bit.

Lena opened the envelope with her fingernail, read it, cleared the kitchen table, and put it out there. (We didn't need to read it.)

She didn't make a sound. She didn't even catch her breath. Her face didn't change, her thin, tired face, with the deep circles under the eyes and the strain lines down the cheeks. Only there was a little pulse began to beat in the vein on her forehead — and her eyes changed, the light eyes with flecks of gold in them. They turned one color: dark, dull brown.

She put the telegram in the middle of the table. Her fingers let loose of it very slowly. Their tips brushed back and forth on the edges of the paper a couple of times before she dropped her arm to her side and very slowly turned and walked into the bedroom, her heels sounding on the floor, slow and steady. The bed creaked as she sat down on it.

Ma had been backing away from the telegram, the corner of her mouth twitching. She bumped into a chair and she looked down — surprised at its being there, even. Then, like a wall that's all of a sudden collapsing, she sat down and bent her head in her lap. She began to cry, not making a sound, her shoulders moving up and down.

Pete was balancing himself on his heels, teetering back and forth, grinning at the telegram like it was a person. I never saw his face look like that before; I was almost afraid of him. And he was Pete, my brother.

He reached down and flicked the paper edge with his fingers. "Good enough to die," he said. "We good enough to die."

There was a prickling all over me, even in my hair. I reckon I was shivering.

I tried to think of Chris dead. Chris shot. Chris in the hospital. Lying on a bed, and dead. Not moving. Chris, who was always moving. Chris, who was so handsome.

I stood and looked at the yellow telegram and tried to think what it would be like. Now, for Chris. I thought of things I had seen dead: dogs and mice and cats. They were born dead, or they died because they were old. Or they died because they were killed. I had seen them with their heads pulled aside and their insides spilled out red on the ground. It wouldn't be so different for a man.

But Chris . . .

"Even if you black," Pete was saying, "you good enough to get sent off to die."

And Ma said: "You shut you mouth!" She'd lifted her head up from her lap, and the creases on her cheeks were quivering and her brown eyes stared — cotton eyes, the kids used to call them.

"You shut you mouth!" Ma shouted. She'd never talked that way before. Not to Pete. Her voice was hoarser even, because she had been crying without tears.

And Pete yelled right back, the way he'd never done before: "Sweet Jesus, I ain't gonna shut up for nobody when I'm talking the truth."

I made a wide circle around him and went in the bedroom. Lena was sitting there, on the bed, with the pillows propped behind her. Her face was quiet and dull. There wasn't anything moving on it, not a line. There was no way of telling if she even heard the voices over in the kitchen.

I stood at the foot of the bed and put both hands on the cold iron railing. "Lena," I said, "you all right?"

She heard me. She shifted her eyes slowly over to me until they were looking directly at me. But she didn't answer. Her eyes, brown now and dark, stared straight into mine without shifting or moving or blinking or lightening. I stepped aside. The eyes didn't move with me. They stayed where they were, caught up in the air.

From the kitchen I could hear Pete and Ma shouting back and forth at each other until Ma finally gave way in deep dry sobbings that slowed and finally stopped. For a second or so everything was perfectly still. Then Ma said what had been in the back of our minds for months, only I didn't ever expect to hear her say it, not to her only boy.

"You no son of mine." She paused for a minute and I could hear the deep catching breath she took. "You no man even." Her voice was level and steady. Only, after every couple of words she'd have to stop for breath. "You a coward. A god-damn coward. And you made youself a cripple for all you life."

All of a sudden Pete began to laugh — high and thin and ragged. "Maybe — maybe. But me, I'm breathing. And he ain't. . . . Chris was fine and he ain't breathing."

Lena didn't give any sign that she'd heard. I went around to the side of the bed and took her hand: it was cold and heavy.

Pete was giggling; you could hardly understand what he was saying. "He want to cross over, him."

Ma wasn't interrupting him now. He went right ahead, choking on the words. "Chris boy, you fine and you brave and you ain't run out on what you got to do. And you ain't breathing neither. But you a man. . . ."

Lena's hand moved ever so slightly.

"Lena," I said, "you all right?"

"Chris boy . . . you want to cross over . . . and you sure enough cross over . . . why, man, you sure cross over . . . but good, you cross over."

"Lena," I said, "don't you pay any mind to him. He's sort of crazy."

In the kitchen Pete was saying: "Chris, you a man, sure . . . sure . . . you sure cross over . . . but ain't you gonna come back for Lena? Ain't you coming back to get her?"

I looked down and saw that my hand was shaking. My whole body was. It had started at my legs and come upward. I couldn't see clearly either. Edges of things blurred together. Only one thing I saw clear: Chris lying still and dead.

"It didn't get you nowhere, Chris boy," Pete was giggling. "Being white and fine, where it got you? Where it got you? Dead and rotten."

And Lena said: "Stop him, Chris."

She said: "Stop him, Chris, please."

I heard her voice, soft and low and pleading, they way she wouldn't speak to anyone else, but only her husband.

Chris, dead on the other side of the world, covered with ground.

Pete was laughing. "Dead and gone, boy. Dead and gone."

"Stop him Chris," Lena said, talking to somebody buried on the other side of the world. "Stop him, Chris."

But I was the only one who heard her. Just me; just me.

You could see her come back from wherever she'd been. Her eyes blinked a couple of times slowly and when they looked at me, they saw me. Really saw me, her little sister. Not Chris, just Celia.

Slowly she pushed herself up from the bed and went into the kitchen, where Pete was still laughing.

Ma was sitting at the table, arms stretched out, head resting on them. She wasn't crying any more; it hardly looked like she was breathing.

"Dead and gone, man." Pete was teetering his chair back and forth, tapping it against the wall, so that everything on the little shelf over his head shook and moved. He had his mouth wide open, so wide that his eyes closed.

Lena hit him, hard as she could with the flat of her hand, hit him right across the face. And then she brought her left hand up, remembering to make a fist this time. It caught him square in the chest.

I heard him gasp; then he was standing up and things were falling from the shelf overhead. Lena stumbled back. And right where her hand struck the floor was the picture of our father, the picture in the silver metal frame, the one Ma had got out the night Chris first came.

She had it in her hand when she scrambled back to her feet. She was crying now, because he was still laughing. From far away I could hear her gasping: "Damn, damn, damn, damn." And she swung the picture frame in a wide arc at his laughing mouth. He saw it coming and forgot for just a moment and lifted his arm to cover his face. And the frame and glass smashed into his stub arm.

He screamed: not loud, just a high pitched gasp. And he turned and ran. I was in the way and he knocked me aside as he yanked open the door. He missed his footing on the steps and fell down into the alley. I could hear him out there, still screaming softly to himself with the pain: "Jesus, Jesus, Jesus, Jesus."

Lena stood in the middle of the room, her hands hanging down empty at her sides. Her lip was cut; there was a little trickle of blood down the corner of her mouth. Her tongue came out, tasted, and then licked it away.

The Girl with the Flaxen Hair

There were only two houses in our block because we lived on the edge of town. There was our house and there was the old Fitzhugh house and about four hundred feet of weedy place between. The Fitzhugh house had been empty ever since I could remember. Only tramps slept in it sometimes, and once a doper had got in. But not real people.

That's why I was so surprised when I saw crazy Willie begin to open all the windows and sweep out the place. It wasn't any use going over to ask him — he had been born peculiar and couldn't talk right. But I could see for sure that real people were moving in.

That night at supper my mother said: "Willie cleaned out the place today."

My father looked out the kitchen window to where the house was over the weeds. "I heard it's somebody named Ramond."

"Ramond," my mother repeated, tapping her fingers on the table. She was thinking back through all the people she knew, trying to find some called Ramond. It took a while because she knew nearly everybody in four counties. "They from here?"

"No," my father said, still staring at the house. The sun had turned all its windows bright yellow.

My mother reached out and broke a loose thread off his shirt. "Wouldn't it be lovely to have nice people in the old place? I hope they're nice people."

The next morning a truck came, not a regular moving-truck but an open one with latticed wood sides, the sort you'd move stock in. It was full too, and all covered up with canvas.

"Lily!" my mother called. "Lily, you come down here right away."

I slid down the banisters. Usually I got a talking-to if Mother saw me, but this time she was too excited to notice.

"What's the letter on the truck license?" She patted my shoulder and pointed to the old house. "I can't make it out."

It was hard to see a little letter at that distance in the bright sun. Finally I said: "It's a C."

Mother sat down and pushed back her hair. "That's Jefferson County. That must be where they're from." My father was coming downstairs then and she said to him: "It's a Jefferson license — I bet they're from Jefferson City."

"That right?" my father said, yawning.

"What ever do you suppose brought them way out here? Why do you suppose they ever left?" Mother had lived in Jefferson City once, and she remembered it as the most wonderful place on earth.

My father rubbed his cheeks. "Damn that water," he said. He had a very heavy beard and he couldn't get enough lather with the soap, so nearly every day he'd come down with his face stinging and red. That was why he didn't ever say much in the morning.

"I'm going to go over there this evening to kind of welcome her," Mother said, staring at the closed door of the pantry. "I reckon she'd like it if I brought her some of that quince serve."

"Look at your daughter, Becca," my father said, staring hard at me. I was only supposed to have one cup of coffee in the morning and that half milk, but this morning when everybody was so excited, I'd poured myself another — regular strength. She wouldn't have noticed either, but there wasn't much you could get by my father.

My father put his glasses on in a solemn way. "Coffee will make your skin turn yellow." I thought that was funny. You couldn't see if my skin was yellow under my sunburn.

"Don't fuss at the child, Claude," Mother said from the pantry. "She just wanted to celebrate. And you don't get neighbors every day from Jefferson City."

I didn't get to see them right away, because that was the day I had to go spend with my grandmother. She came driving up and I had to go run out to the car and spend the rest of the day with her over at Pine Bluffs.

That evening coming home we passed the old Fitzhugh place, which was now the Ramond place. They had old Willie out in the yard, cleaning it up, and though it was nearly dark, he was still working. I wondered how they got him to do it. Ordinarily Willie was the laziest colored man around here.

"Did you get to see them?" I asked my mother.

"You wait now," she said; "when your father comes down I'll tell you just exactly what happened."

When my father did come he had a bandage around his right hand. "Claude," my mother said, "I didn't notice that when you came in."

"Well" — my father glared at her like he always did when she'd said the wrong thing — "it was there all right."

Mother looked hurt. She pulled her shoulders closer together and shriveled up. I never saw anybody else who could do that. "Yes, Claude," she said very low.

My father's face got red; he patted her shoulder and kissed her cheek. Then my mother unshriveled and stood upright and smiled.

"It was the Crawford kid," my father said. "I was looking at that big cavity he's got in one of his laterals and he was behaving, then, wham —" he hit the table with his left hand — "he bit me. Just clamps down his jaws on the flat part of my hand."

My mother was staring at the bandage, making little clucking sounds of worry.

"Just like that," my father said, "when I'm trying to fill that tooth. I had to near shake his head off to make him let go."

My mother picked up his bandaged hand and felt it carefully. "Oh, Claude —" she said.

My father laughed. "It's not broken, Becca. And I ought to expect things like that."

My mother looked up at him and smiled quick. "You need something to eat," she said. She could worry one minute and forget the next.

Later on, when she and my father were drinking their coffee and I was eating my second dessert, she told about her visit to the Ramonds.

"They've got the old place looking real nice," she said. "I wouldn't thought it possible. It's a big place for just them. Just the three of them. They only got one little girl about our Lily's age."

"That right?" my father said. I could tell that he wasn't really listening to her. He was thinking about his aching hand. But my mother went on.

"We talked for such a long time. She sure likes to talk, Mrs. Ramond. With the little girl sitting quiet on her chair and listening and never saying a word. She has beautiful manners, that one."

I looked out the window at the Ramond house. The upstairs bedrooms were lighted. Old Willie was burning trash out back. You could see him moving against the fire.

"They don't put much furniture out in summer, and they keep it covered up with white denim slips so it'll be cooler." my mother said. "But they got lots and lots of ferns — not just wood ferns either, but maidenhair and Lady Anne and other kinds I never did see before. They keep them right in the house. You can smell how cool the mud is."

She said a lot more, but I didn't listen: I was watching old Willie throw gasoline to make the fire burn better.

Then my father was laughing, and so hard that he hit his sore hand against the table. "Damn," he said and then: "Sorry," to my mother. He leaned back in his chair and chewed his lip. "What a line she gave you!"

Mother looked flustered. "Well I never —"

"What she said was true enough," said my father with a laugh; "she just didn't go far enough. Her father was Senator Winslow, all right. But Senator Winslow had to resign fast to keep from being indicted for bribery. I don't know anything about the rest of her family, but I bet there are people who could tell you plenty in Jefferson City."

My mother just sat and looked at him. She always thought of Jefferson City like she remembered it — its main street full of cars and wagons on Saturday and the Bermuda grass lawns and the brick walls around the capitol. She didn't remember what it would be like with people.

"Oh, Claude," she said, and you could tell she was feeling sad.

"Now I'll tell you the rest of it, so you can get it all straight." My father leaned forward, resting his elbows on the table. "No sense your falling for all their talk; you know what Ramond is? A barber. That's all. He cuts hair and shaves and takes tips."

"Claude, please — Lily'll hear." My mother looked anxiously down at me.

"Let her," my father said. "Let her find out just what they are so she won't be taken in." You could tell from the pitch of his voice that he was determined to talk. My mother settled back in her chair with a little sigh. "He's a barber and he works that extra chair in the hotel shop."

"All right, Claude," my mother said patiently. "All right."

"When they don't have much furniture around it's not because it's stylish and the way they're doing it in Jefferson City — it's because they don't have any furniture." He began to laugh. He found the sound of his own voice funny, and he kept on laughing until the table shook under his arms. Finally he stopped, gasping for breath. "Ferns are the cheapest things there are and dirt's for free."

"All right, Claude," my mother said. "But I'll tell you this — they had an air — Mrs. Ramond and her little girl. It's not just good manners; lots of people have that. It's something more." She looked out the window to the Ramond house. Willie's fire was still smoldering red in the back yard and all the upstairs lights had gone out. "They have an air."

The next morning I was climbing up the rose trellis along the side of our house just to see how high I could get. It was easy going; the roses didn't have too many thorns. From the trellis I thought I could reach the crossbeams under the eaves and from then it was only a little swing up to the roof. But this particular time I didn't make it.

The door at the Ramond house slammed hard and a woman came out, running along the street at a dead run. She held something wrapped in pink in her arms. Before I could do more than get turned around and start climbing down, she had got to our porch and was pounding on the door, though the bell was right there under her elbow. My mother opened the door. "Thank God," the woman said. "I didn't know if you'd be home."

I heard my mother's murmur of surprise as they went inside and quick footsteps the length of the house to the kitchen. Then I ripped open the back of my hand on a splinter. It began to bleed; I felt it run warm down my arm. I was still high up, above the second-story windows. My mother didn't hear me yell, she was so busy inside. I just stayed there on the trellis until the funny bleeding feeling stopped. Then when I wasn't so scared I climbed down.

Mother turned around when I opened the screen door. I put my hand inside the pocket of my overalls. "Don't let the flies in, Lily."

"Yes'm." I closed the door carefully behind me, all the while looking at the woman who had come to live in the only other house on our block. She was big: that was the first thing I thought. Not fat, maybe, but big. I thought of my father somehow when I saw her.

"And so this is your daughter," she said.

"Yes," Mother said. "This is Lily." She looked at me with a kind of half smile. "She's something of a tomboy."

Mrs. Ramond smiled at me. She had very white skin and her eyes were light blue. "How are you, my dear?" I gave a little curtsy Mother had taught me. "I have a little girl about your age," she said and then to my mother: "She takes after you, my dear — that black hair."

"Yes," said my mother. "Except for one thing. I didn't ever go around in coveralls with my face dirty. Lily is rather wild."

My mother had never talked like that before. I couldn't make it out. I began to feel uncomfortable.

"Your mother has been being an angel," Mrs. Ramond said, smiling at me. There was gold far back in her mouth. "My Rose got stung by some wasps. And I didn't know what to do, but she fixed everything wonderfully."

"Well" — my mother smiled — "we're very used to all sorts of stings out here."

"Oh, dear," Mrs. Ramond said. "Are there other stinging insects?" She pulled a little bit of lace out of the neck of her dress and pressed it to her mouth. "We never had to worry about things like that in Jefferson City."

"No," said my mother, "not there."

Mrs. Ramond nodded then. "Have you been there?"

"Oh, yes," my mother said quickly. "I grew up there." That wasn't quite true. She had stayed there only until she was eight. She'd told me that story over and over again.

"Not really?" Mrs. Ramond looked up with more excitement than she had shown yet. "Not really?" My mother smiled yes. "We must spend a long time together talking over our memories. I'm homesick for it sometimes and Rose misses it so very much."

"The dear child," my mother said vaguely and she glanced to the far corner of the kitchen, which was behind me and out of sight. "Do the stings hurt any more? Shall I put more ice on them?"

"No, thank you."

She had been sitting on the straight wooden chair by the window, and she had been watching me ever since I came in. There was one of our blue-checked towels wrapped around her leg where the wasps had gotten her and there was another one on her arm. She was sitting there with the bandaged leg stuck out straight and holding one bandaged arm with the other. But what I noticed first was her hair. It was yellow and it was wrapped around her head in plaits like an old woman's would be.

Mrs. Ramond stood up; she was the tallest woman I'd ever seen. "No," she said. "We won't take up any more of your time. Mornings are so busy, I know."

"My husband comes home for dinner."

Mrs. Ramond smiled and picked up Rose. She stood holding her wrapped in a pink blanket and smiling. "I had best put the child to bed. She'll probably have fever."

"Oh, I don't think so," my mother said. "There wasn't enough for that. Lily got stung all over last summer on a picnic and she didn't get much fever."

Mrs. Ramond nodded. "But Rose is very delicate. We came here partly for her health, you know."

"Is that right?" My mother clucked sympathetically. "I know — I'll go back with you, to see if there's anything I can do. It's always such work moving."

"How sweet of you!" Mrs. Ramond said. "Isn't it, Rose? She must know how nervous I've been with that crazy old colored man pottering around out in the yard."

"Hilda — that's our cook — she should be coming," Mother said. "She'll fix dinner and I'll be back soon. You stay here, Lily." She reached out her hand

and patted my shoulder; then she was gone.

I stayed in the kitchen until I saw Hilda come walking up the street. She stopped at the back gate and put her can of snuff on the top of the gatepost, because Mother wouldn't let her chew while she was around the house. I went out to meet her. "Mother's gone," I said. "She went over to the Ramond's."

"Sure enough?" Hilda leaned on the gate, taking a last slow chew of her snuff.

"They're from Jefferson City," I said.

Hilda sighed and blew the mouthful of snuff out into the grass. "Your ma say what she wanted for dinner?"

"Nuh, nuh. Hilda," I said, "my hand hurts."

She did not stop walking toward the house. She had to get away from that can or she'd take another mouthful. "Have a look," she said.

I held out my hand. The blood had run up my arm in long streaks; it had hardened in drops on my fingernails. And it had turned black. I saw it and began to cry, though it did not hurt very much any more.

"Christ sake," Hilda said, "lemme wash that."

My father came home early because there hadn't been many patients in his office that morning. He came home before my mother got back. When he saw my hand his face got dark and set all over. "What'd you do that on?" I didn't answer; I didn't want to say that I had been climbing the trellis up the side of the house. "Looks like a nail to me. Was it?" I nodded, beginning to cry at the thought of the nail ripping open the back of my hand. "Hush, now," he said, and picked me up in his arms like Mrs. Ramond had done with Rose. "Tell my wife," he said to Hilda, "that we've gone to Dr. Smither's."

Hilda nodded, impressed by the angry sound in his voice. "It ain't looked that bad to me."

"She's going to take a tetanus," my father said, "just in case."

When we came home, my mother was out in the front yard waiting for us. She'd been doing a little digging in the garden to make the time pass; you could see that she'd uprooted the nasturtiums. They had a fight then, my mother and father. And it ended the way it always ended, with my mother crying and my father patting her shoulder and telling her not to.

"It was just an accident, Becca," he told her.

She twisted her handkerchief. "I should have been here," she said. "I'll never talk to them again if you don't want me to."

My father laughed. "Don't go making promises you can't keep, honey."

"They are lovely people," my mother said slowly. "It's so nice to know people like that."

"All right, then," — my father looked out the window to the old house —

"talk to them. Just don't let Lily get killed in the process."

My mother looked relieved because the anger was all gone from his voice. She laughed. "Don't be ridiculous, Claude. Nothing will happen to Lily. She's always getting cut up, you know. If only she wasn't such a tomboy."

My father laughed and ran his fingers through my hair. "Don't you mind, pigeon," he told me. "You'll be a fine lady soon enough."

My mother didn't hear him; she was looking down at me, "I do hope that you and Rose get to be friends. It would be so good for you." Then she turned to my father. "Why, Claude, isn't that nice? — their names fit together. Lily and Rose. Isn't that nice?"

"Yes," said my father. "That's just swell."

The very next day Mother took me to see Rose. She was sitting on their porch, her leg still bandaged over the stung spot, though the ache would have been gone a long time.

"How are you, honey?" my mother asked.

"Much better, thank you." She had blue eyes, lighter than any I'd seen. There was no other color in them like yellow or black. They were plain blue like the sky in the water color in the dining-room that Mother had done years ago.

Rose was looking at me solemnly, without smiling. "You remember Lily?" my mother said.

"Oh, yes." She smiled then. "You came in yesterday after your mother attended to my stings —" she turned back to my mother. "That was very neighborly of you. Thank you."

"That's all right, honey. I was glad to," my mother said. "Your mother home?"

"Of course," Rose said. "She's probably heard your voices, but I'll call her." Then she reached out and with her knuckles tapped four times on the wall behind her. "In this old house," she said "every little sound travels. You might say that was our signal."

"How cute!" my mother said.

Rose said to me: "Wouldn't you like to sit over here and talk to me?"

I guess in all the time I knew her she must have asked me that question a hundred times. It was her favorite one. "Come talk to me" — of course, she didn't mean that at all. She meant that she wanted to talk, wanted somebody to listen to her. And I did.

I thought she was the most beautiful thing I ever saw. And she was used to being admired. Her mother said, "There was a gentleman once — in Jefferson City, when we used to live there — a Mr. Clayton, who told me that Rose had a face like a Botticelli angel."

An angel — no, that wasn't what her face reminded me of. I had seen too many pictures of angels not to know. For one thing, her hair was too heavy, her yellow hair, which she wrapped in braids around her head like an old woman's. And angels' eyes were darker.

She had a way of telling stories, though. She would lean forward, her elbows on the arms of her chair, both her hands pressed to the braids around her head. She would tell the stories quickly, the words rushing out. And yet you never missed a word somehow. My mother would always stop and listen to her; and Mrs. Ramond, too, if she were there, would nod her head and smile as if she were hearing all this for the first time, while she had told the stories to Rose in the first place. They sounded better somehow when Rose told them. There were many stories, but Rose talked so much that sometimes she told the same one twice. I didn't mind.

"Once," she would say, beginning a story about her grandfather, Senator Winslow, and most of the stories were about him, "when he was just married a little while and his first child was only nine days old, some robbers came into the house. Muriel, that was his wife, a tall woman with hair like mine, woke him up saying: 'Save me and the baby.' And so he got his pistol out of the drawer of the little table by the bed. It was a French table, gilt and silvered; he'd brought it back with him on his last trip to Europe. He took the pistol out of the drawer and saw that it was loaded; then he went out in the hall to the stairs. Muriel took the baby from the cradle and hid with it behind the big walnut armoire. When he got to the head of the stair, he saw the robbers in the front hall. 'What are you doing in my house?' he called. The robbers looked up and they were afraid. He shot the leader, and the rest ran out the door. They never could get the stain off the rug in the front hall. And he wouldn't change the rug, because he said it was a warning to other thieves to stay away from his house."

She paused and I broke in: "Did he kill the robber?"

Mrs. Ramond laughed behind me. "He never missed a shot. He had the truest eye in the state."

I nodded and closed my eyes to see better the picture that was in my mind: a tall man, but not very broad or heavy, with hair light like Rose's. He was wearing a blue coat with silver buttons, and high boots that shone like water in the sun.

"Once he went campaigning in the back counties of the state. And the crackers saw his fine clothes (he always wore beautiful clothes; he brought them from France), and they began to laugh. He saw them laughing and he got very angry. His eyes would flash and his face would get dark and his hair would rumple up. If he was at home and he got angry, his wife, Muriel, would send all the servants out of the room quickly. Then she would come up to him gently and ask him to sit down. And when he did, she would sit on the arm of his chair and rub his forehead with her cool white fingers, humming his favorite tune very softly. And the anger would go all out of him. She was the only one who could make the anger all go out of him like that.

"But that time when he went campaigning in the back counties of the state he got angry and there was nobody there who knew how to stop him. 'I see you are laughing, sir' he said to one of the men. 'And may I ask at whom?' And the man, thinking that anyone who wore such fine clothes must be weak, laughed even harder. Until the Senator hit him and he lay out on the ground. Then the Senator took off his blue coat and rolled up the sleeves of his cambric shirt and fought with the whole crowd. When it was over, there were fourteen men lying on the ground; four of them had broken jaws. And he had only a little scratch on his cheek from a man who had drawn a knife and stabbed at him from behind. Then he unrolled his sleeves and put on his blue coat and rode twenty miles to the next place he was to speak."

Always when Rose had finished her story she would sit there, nodding her head with the heavy yellow plaits. Usually I'd get too restless and say something or scrape my chair. Then she'd look up frowning slightly and shaking her head. She was so sorry when a story was finished.

One day she talked longer than usual. The shadow from her house reached nearly across the street; it was time for dinner. I was starting to say that, when I saw her father had come home. He stood leaning against one of the porch pillars and looking at Rose with a kind of twisted smile. "Oh, yes," he said softly. "He was a most remarkable man. Most remarkable. And so very honest a one."

He was a short man, and fat, and dark. His wife was much bigger. He had a strange accent, too, because he had come from France. "Has she ever told you stories about me, Lily?" I shook my head. "No? That is such a pity! How naughty of you, Rose, not to tell stories about your own father!" He looked down at her and twisted the corners of his mouth even more. I thought it was a funny way to smile. "You must ask her sometimes to tell stories about me, Lily. About how I shaved the King of France."

I wondered if I should believe him; but he was French and he was a barber, so I asked: "What — what did the King say?"

He looked at me solemnly. "The King had a very tough beard. And though I had sharpened my razor especially for him, it was not enough. All he said was: 'Ouch.'"

Rose was looking down at her hands folded in her lap. I thought for a moment she was crying. He looked at her, then turned to me. "Do you know what 'flaxen' means?" I shook my head. "Well, it means yellow, like the color of her hair there." Mrs. Ramond came out on the porch and stood staring at him. "Good evening, my dear," he said. She didn't answer and he shrugged and asked me: "Have you ever heard of *The Girl with the Flaxen Hair*?"

I saw the way Mrs. Ramond was looking at him, and I wondered what I should do. "No, sir," I said. I wondered if I should have told the truth.

He was smiling again, twisting the corner of his mouth. "It's a piece of music I wrote," he said. "I used to be a musician, too. Come inside and I'll play it for you. You come, too, Rose."

I stood by the piano and listened while he played. I thought I had never heard anything as smooth as the way the sounds came. But it didn't remind me of Rose somehow. When he finished he smiled again and said: "It's a lovely piece, isn't it? I wrote it especially for Rose, my daughter, the girl with the flaxen hair."

I saw Rose; she was sitting by the window and this time there was no doubt of it. She was crying. Just sitting there, not making a sound, the tears falling into the hands in her lap. My stomach knotted up and my legs got shaky. I began to back to the door. "My mother told me not to be late for supper. She told me that." I made a little bow Mother had taught me. "Thank you."

"You are very polite." He stood up and bowed very slowly. "You must come back and I will play some other of my compositions for you. Au revoir."

I jumped down the steps and ran all the way home, but I heard Mrs. Ramond's voice come hissing out the windows, soft and full of hating: "Raoul, how could you —"

I wasn't afraid of him exactly; my father was the only one who could scare me really, when his face got dark and he scowled. No, I wasn't afraid of Rose's father. But I didn't know what to make of him. I'd never heard anybody play piano in the smooth rippling way he did, his fingers so fast on the keys they were just a blur. I only heard him play that once: *The Girl with the Flaxen Hair*. Because he went away.

"He's gone back to France to study music," my mother said one night. It was hot like always in summer, without a bit of breeze. It was dry too. There hadn't been rain in ages. There was only a mist high up by the stars that made them shine brighter. Like pieces of ice in the hot sky.

"The hell he did." My father gave a quick laugh. He never got so angry and used words like that in front of my mother unless they were talking about the Ramonds.

"Claude, please —" my mother said.

He took a couple of quick draws on his pipe and blew rings into the air.

Then he turned and looked at the Ramond house. The lights were on upstairs although the bedrooms must have been terribly hot.

"Maybe he went to France," my father said, "but it wasn't to study music. And I'll bet my bottom dollar he won't be coming back."

"He just couldn't desert them."

"Why not?" My father laughed again. "It's happened before. Maybe it wasn't such a bad idea. Not after years of that Amazon over there and her background and her stories of the Senator who was just a crook after all. And the girl that looks like she's half dead with that mess of tow hair."

Like my father said, Mr. Ramond didn't come back. If anybody asked Mrs. Ramond where he was, she'd say he was studying music in France. But unless there was a question she didn't talk about him.

"I wonder what they live on, the poor dears," my mother said.

"Go ask her," my father said, grinning.

"Oh, no." My mother looked horrified. "I couldn't ever. You just don't talk about things like that."

"Well, I wouldn't worry," my father said. "She probably has enough from her father, the Senator. After all, he stole enough to have something left over. And they're living on that."

I heard him, though I wasn't supposed to, but I didn't believe him. I knew the Senator too well. He was tall, but not heavy, and he wore a blue coat with silver buttons, and boots shiny as water in the light.

"By the way," my father said, "Rose came to my office this afternoon. She's got an abscessed tooth; one of her second ones. I'm going to pull it for her tomorrow."

Mother and I went to the office with Rose and Mrs. Ramond and sat waiting in the little outside room. My father glared when he saw that we had come, but Mother just looked him up and down and sat down by Mrs. Ramond and put her hand on her arm.

Rose didn't make a sound. My father said afterward that she was just about a perfect patient. When it was finished, she opened the door herself and came out to where we were waiting. My father put his head around the door and said: "You want to keep the tooth as a souvenir?"

"No, Claude, no," my mother whispered to him, and then to Rose: "Come on, honey. We'll drive you home."

She'd got out of the chair too soon: the bleeding hadn't stopped. There was a little trickle of blood out the corner of her mouth. She stopped it with her handkerchief just like it was a drop of perspiration.

She kept her mouth pressed tight closed as we walked down the street to where the car was parked. I guess the sun was too hot, because Mrs. Ramond nearly fainted. She staggered a little bit, and my mother got her around her waist, holding her up, and started sort of dragging her to the car. Rose let her lips open and the blood came out and down her chin. My mother looked over her shoulder. "Oh, my God," she said. "You grab her, Lily, and get her in the car."

I got one arm around Rose and pulled her to the car. She wasn't making any attempt to stop the blood now. It was all down the front of her dress and some had got on me, too. Her blood was red — red as mine — even if she was so pale and light-haired.

Until Rose got killed they went on living next to us. I was just crazy about Rose. There wasn't ever anybody like her. They didn't seem to ever know many people in town except us; they didn't seem to want to. I remember, after they had been living there a couple of weeks, Mother asked Mrs. Ramond to come to her club meeting, but she just shook her head and smiled and said no very politely. And my mother smiled back at her, and I had the feeling she was very glad Mrs. Ramond wasn't going.

"They just wouldn't appreciate her," she told me as we walked back home. "They're nice enough people, but they just wouldn't appreciate her."

I thought of the club: Mrs. Farland, the doctor's wife, who was old and fat and had five girls and wanted to be president and was furious when my mother got elected instead; Mrs. Cullers, who ran the drugstore and grocery; Mrs. Henderson, who was little and pretty almost as my mother and who ran the other drugstore and grocery across town; and my grandmother, who drove in from Pine Bluffs for the meetings. And the others, ten or twelve of them, who came from the farms around.

"Yes," said my mother, and she took hold of my hand, swinging it slowly back and forth. "They wouldn't appreciate her."

So most of the ladies in town made one call on the Ramonds, because it was polite. And that was all. They weren't ever friendly with anybody but us; but we were real good friends — my mother and Mrs. Ramond and Rose and I.

My father couldn't ever stand the sight of them, though he was always polite, and it was only afterward that he said what he thought to my mother and me. And he was the one who found out about Rose at last. He told us one morning two winters later. He was sitting in the breakfast room with his chair tilted back against the wall. He hadn't shaved yet; the beard's darkness made his face look strange. He had made coffee, and the pot was on the table in front of him.

"Why, Claude," my mother said, "how nice! You must have got up real early."

"Since around four thirty."

I'd never been up that early in my life. If it was winter like now, the sun wouldn't be up; and it would be freezing cold with the night fog still all over.

"What ever for?" my mother asked.

"Well" — my father craned his neck to look out the window at the other house. "Looks like they went back to bed."

"They haven't got up yet," my mother said.

"Oh, yes, they have," my father said. "You know, last night — or this morning — when you woke me up because the room was chilly? You went right back to sleep, so you didn't notice. But I went over to Lily's room to turn up her radiator. And then I happened to look out the window and I saw a light in the house over there."

"Maybe Rose was sick," my mother said.

My father didn't answer her. "It wasn't a bright light at all. It was sort of yellow and flickering like a flashlight. I thought it was burglars —"

"Was it?" I said. "Was it?"

He looked at me and rubbed his eyes; you could tell that he was sleepy. "I'm talking to your mother," he said. "Go get some milk." I didn't move because he went on talking. "Well, I got to thinking how helpless they'd be if it was burglars." He shrugged and looked at my mother. "You'd have sense enough to get my gun out of the drawer, but her" — he jerked his head backwards to the house — "she'd probably come running down without a thing and get herself hurt or killed. I got to thinking that and I began to get worried." He laughed and twisted his lips. "You know, I guess I got as much chivalry in me after all as the great Senator."

I tried to imagine him in the blue coat with the silver buttons and the high shining boots. I closed my eyes to try the harder, but all I could see him in was the high collared white smock he wore in his office.

"I got on my clothes because it was cold. Nasty cold, with a heavy wet mist. But by the time I got halfway over there the back door popped open and the girl came out. She was all dressed with a coat and a scarf around her head. And her mother I saw in the door behind her holding a flash with her fingers across the beam to shade it. Then she closed the door and the girl went off at a run."

He stopped and yawned; neither my mother nor I said anything.

"I went after her. After all, a kid like that wandering around alone in the dark of the morning with all the tramps that get thrown off trains here — so I went along. I thought at first I'd catch up with her and tell her what a fool thing she was doing. But I didn't; I got too curious. I just went along behind, close enough if there was any trouble, but not close enough for her to notice.

But now that I remember, I don't think she would have noticed no matter how close I got. She didn't notice anything. Just kept going at a run, her head bent a little. Right straight to the railroad yards.

"That's where we went. It's quite a way and I'd been doing a trot and was winded. She'd been running and she didn't seem tired at all. You know the pile of coal where they load the trains. Well, she made straight for that, without hesitating even. And then I saw that she was carrying one of these flexible baskets. They're made out of straw, I think. She filled it up with coal; filled it right to the very top, too, because pieces kept rolling off when she walked. I wonder how much it weighed, that basket. It was maybe a half a bushel or a little more. You wouldn't think she'd have strength like that, her being so little and light."

He looked at my mother. "Well," he said. "That's all —"

My mother sat very quietly, chewing on one fingernail. "Claude," she said, "they must be terribly poor."

My father let his breath go out in a whistling sigh. "I reckon the Senator didn't steal enough, after all."

The very next afternoon Rose sat in our front parlor. I looked down at her shoes, expecting almost to see some of the cinder dust from the railroad yards on them, but they were dusted clean. She had brought an old album over to show us and was turning the pages slowly. "That's my great-aunt and her husband. He was wounded at Siloe and when they were bringing him home he died." She turned the page. "This was my grandmother. Her dress is lovely, isn't it? Pale yellow — she was married in it."

My mother took the book from her and examined it closely. "It really is," she said.

"My dress will be just like that — yellow, you know, and with that little high neck. He'll give me a brooch and that will be my only ornament."

I wondered who he was. My mother smiled. "Isn't it early for planning, dear?" she said to Rose. "You don't know who your groom is going to be."

"No," Rose said. "Mother and I have talked it over."

They talked over a lot of things. Sometimes when they left the shade up, we could see them at night, sitting in the parlor, talking. And even when the shade was down, we could see the light from behind it and know that they were in there, talking.

"I don't think I'll want any flowers," Rose said. "I'll just brush out my hair and let it hang, perfectly plain. The church will be full of flowers, though. In all shades of yellow — pale like asters — or bright like jonquils or gold like tiger lilies."

(When we told my father about it later, he just laughed. "It'd look nice, all right, but you couldn't ever get all those flowers to bloom at the same time.")

"It'll be all in Jefferson City. Do you remember Trinity Church?"

My mother nodded. "But it's still so far off, dear."

Rose shook her head. "Not so far. I'll be eighteen then and I'm twelve now. That isn't far."

I thought of the light every evening in the parlor and their talking, just the two of them, and Rose's straight blond hair. And for the first time in ages I thought of her father, the man with the accent, who had played a piece called *The Girl with the Flaxen Hair* and said it was a picture of her. He was gone; he had been gone nearly two years. And they didn't seem to miss him. But they were poor, so poor they stole coal from the railroad yards in the winter.

Rose was killed that spring in the railroad yards. It was the Comet, the express to Birmingham. They had changed its schedule, so that it came racing through town four hours earlier than usual.

Rose got on the tracks; she wasn't looking and didn't notice: she didn't ever seem more than half awake at that time of morning anyway.

The people on the train didn't know anything, or if they did they didn't stop or give a sign. It was Pete Lafferty, going out to start up the boiler on the switch engine around five o'clock, found her a little to one side of the track. She was still holding on to the wicker basket, which had a couple of pieces of coal in it. She must have just gotten started.

And Pete left her where she was lying and ran back and got Tim Maybeck, the station manager, and Tim took one look and called the sheriff and the doctor and my father because he lived next door. And the sheriff woke up his deputy and all of them together — all six of them — wrapped her up in an army-colored blanket and brought her home. They all helped carry her into the house, carrying her gently and slowly.

Mrs. Ramond didn't make a sound. She just thanked them and locked the door behind them. If she cried, nobody saw her.

For a while all the men stood around on the porch, wondering if there was something else they should do. Then they walked across to our house and my father opened a bottle of whisky.

There wasn't a wake. Mrs. Ramond packed everything into two valises and left. My mother and I went down to the station with her and watched while they put Rose in the baggage car; she was going to her grandfather's plot in Jefferson City. Mrs. Ramond watched the door of the baggage car close and then, not turning or speaking, she got into the day coach. She never came back; she never wrote.

When we got home, my mother cried for hours. "The poor little thing. The poor little dead thing."

My father sat very quietly holding her. "God forgive me," he said very softly, "but it's best. They just couldn't go on."

"Why'd she go?" my mother asked with her head buried in the cloth of his shoulder. "You don't need coal in spring. Why'd she go?"

He shook his head. "I don't know. She just did, that's all. Maybe she got in the habit. Maybe she thought about putting it aside for next winter. Maybe she didn't think at all." He rubbed his forehead slowly. Outside the window a little breeze ran a shadow across the yellow weeds. "All she did was get killed."

I tried to think what it would be like to get killed. I tried to think what it must be like for Rose right now in the baggage car going to Jefferson City.

My father reached over and patted my shoulder. "Don't you grieve, honey. It's over; you'll forget."

He was wrong there. I didn't ever forget. Always I could sit down and think and see her so clear, like she was standing by me. Even years later, even after my father died, even all the way through high school. By that time, by the time I finished school, it was sort of hard for me to remember my father: his face was blurry and I'd have to look at a picture to be sure. I forgot him.

I forgot him. But I didn't ever forget them. And it wasn't Mrs. Ramond I remembered. It was Rose and the Senator. Always there'd be the Senator with his boots shiny as water in the sun and his blue coat with the silver buttons. And Rose would be standing next to him, smiling at him, wearing the yellow dress. And he'd give her a round pin that sparkled with diamonds and she'd fix it to the neck of her yellow dress. And all around them would be yellow flowers — asters, jonquils, tiger lilies. She'd have her hair loose: the way I'd never seen it. Not in braids around her head, but brushed back and hanging down.

The Bright Day

"Finish, good lady; the bright day is done,
And we are for the dark."

It was quite a summer. It was hot: the sun, even when it had just come up, was yellow hot and small as a quarter. There hadn't been any rain in nearly two months, and outside of town only the early cotton had come up; and the corn had rust.

It was quite a summer, all right. And then, in July, there was a hailstorm: the same morning we heard the news about Pamela Langley coming.

I remember I had been wondering what I should have for supper. Andrew only got to come home from camp on week-ends and I wanted something specially good. I had gone down to the cellar to see what I could find. Half the junk in the cellar was new to me, because Andrew and I had only been married a little over a year.

So I didn't see the hailstorm at all. First I heard of it Cousin Roger was standing at the head of the cellar steps calling. And there they were on the grass, the hailstones, some of them big as a golf ball, most of them the size of marbles, some of them small and white as drops of wax — in little drifts like the light snow we had in winter.

"Every single pane in the greenhouse is broken," Cousin Roger said. "Who would have thought it was going to hail — in July? It hasn't since I was a boy. A little boy."

"Yes," I said without listening. I was thinking about Andrew coming and wondering if this would make any difference in his coming home. Outside I could see Aunt Mayme walking around and around the greenhouse. Then she came in and said to me: "There's fifty panes broken, best I could count.

Melton will be heartbroken when he comes home."

"I was down in the cellar," I said. "I didn't hear anything."

The front door slammed and Uncle Melton's voice was calling: "Mayme, Mayme, where are you?"

He went into the dining-room first and we heard him speak to Cousin Roger. Finally he came in and sat down, pulling the lapel of his linen suit away from his hot body. "What happened to the greenhouse?"

Aunt Mayme lifted her eyebrows. "I reckoned you knew: the hail smashed it up some."

"Oh God," Uncle Melton said. "There just isn't anything left to go wrong."

They were twins and they looked it. The same yellow-red hair, the same white skin that fifty or fifty-five years had creamed up like fine old paper.

"Pamela's coming," Uncle Melton said. "She isn't dead. She's coming home."

Cousin Roger came hurrying into the room. "I found it," he said. "We haven't had hail in summer since 1916 — July 23, 1916. I found the record I made then."

"1916," Uncle Melton said slowly. "It must have been about then that Pamela went away."

"No," Aunt Mayme said. "It was later. A little later. Just after the war. Because we all wondered if there wasn't a soldier in it somewhere."

I sat listening, wondering who they were talking about. I didn't ask then and there about Pamela. When Andrew got home, he told me.

"We thought Pamela was dead. There hadn't been news from her in so long." He turned and sat down on the bed — heavily and slowly as if he were tired. I stood over by the dresser, brushing out my hair.

"I never saw her," he said. "She was before my time. She's first cousin to Mayme and Melton and second to me — and you." He grinned briefly. "Follow me?"

"I guess so."

"Pamela had a sister, Josephine Fredericks. Now do you see? Josephine married well — very well. Fredericks had money when they married. And he got more. In tobacco. Mrs. Fredericks was Pamela Langley's sister. And Pamela is her heir if there's no valid will. And next to Pamela we're the only relatives. See?"

"But Pamela's turned up again. So she gets it all."

The stem of the pipe he was smoking cracked. He had bitten it through. I hadn't realized he was so angry about the whole thing. Andrew was quiet usually; it was very hard to tell what he was thinking. "She gets the whole damn lot," and he got up and went downstairs.

I suppose it was funny, the way Uncle Melton and Aunt Mayme and even Andrew had worked and paid to give Pamela Langley title to a lot of money. I suppose it was very funny. You see, Pamela had been gone so long they were certain she was dead and that they were the heirs. And they set out to prove their title.

The trouble was that old widowed Josephine Fredericks, Pamela's sister, had made a will. Or at least that's what John Woodville said.

He was a doctor of sorts. Josephine had picked him up and moved him into her big house and told everybody that he was her doctor and her best friend. And when she died they found a will leaving everything to John Woodville.

First Uncle Melton and Aunt Mayme and Andrew set out to prove that she wasn't sane when she wrote the will. (Uncle Melton, for all his silly little ways and his red hair, is a pretty good lawyer.) Then they discovered the will wasn't genuine. They had a handwriting expert examine it and he was sure: he swore out a statement and gave it to Uncle Melton, who locked it up in his office safe downtown to wait out the time for the case to come up. So everything was all fixed.

Then Pamela came back after all those years, and all the scheming had done was give her a clear claim to her sister's money.

Pamela was a wanderer. She was in her mid-thirties, not married, when one day she just decided to leave. Since she didn't have any family, except her sister, Josephine, there wasn't anything to stop her. Later she'd sent postcards from places like Detroit and New York and Liverpool. They thought she'd died in one of those places. If she'd stayed away just a little longer, until after the court had decided, it would have been all right for us. But now everything went to Pamela.

At breakfast Uncle Melton said: "Pamela will be in today. After church we will drive down to the station and meet her."

Andrew said: "Charlotte and I will stay home."

"I have a headache," I said.

That was how Pamela Langley came home, after thirty-something years: Mayme and Melton brought her back and I knew they'd be just as nice and hospitable to her as any two humans could be. I didn't see her the first day she came because I was really sick. Andrew, of course, saw her, but he didn't seem to want to talk when he sat with me, and I didn't feel well enough to ask.

Andrew went back to camp early that Monday morning. He kissed me and said: "It'll be all right, honey." He'd hardly got out the front door before Aunt Mayme came in.

"How are you, dear?"

"I'm all right, thank you," I said.

"Are you starting a baby?"

I felt myself go red at her abrupt question. "No," I said awkwardly, "I don't think so."

"Well," she said, "that's good. Better that the family waits for happy times." She stood over against the open windows, over against the gray light of the first dawn. The room was lightening fast.

"You really should get up, dear," she said. "You have to meet Pamela."

Of course I had to. I went down and let Aunt Mayme introduce me to Pamela Langley.

She was old, much older than I had expected, in her late sixties. She was tall, about my size, and heavy, and her corsets weren't too good. And you could tell she'd never been even passably nice-looking.

What I noticed most was the material of her dress. When I first came in I thought: she's wearing a gray dress. But it wasn't; over the gray was a close-woven design, tiny threads of red, blue, and yellow. When I told her how lovely the silk was, she only said yes in a vague kind of way and that she'd forgotten where she'd got it.

She'd forgotten a great many things about her travels; I found out that soon enough, because she was always wanting to tell me stories. There was the time she'd been in Athens as the governess in an official's family.

"What sort of official?" I asked her.

"I don't remember." She frowned, just slightly. "But he was dark, I remember, very dark, with heavy black hair. And both of his children were fair. Isn't that strange? But then their mother was English. I never knew her. She was dead when I came; that's why I came: to take care of the children. . . ."

She talked on and on — cities like Athens, Cairo, Paris, whose streets were all tangled like a boy's fish net — and at the end was home. That was the thing she remembered most clearly.

The morning I met her, the very first morning she was back, she insisted on taking a walk, with the sun blazing and getting along toward noon.

"Why, Cousin Pamela" — Aunt Mayme pressed one hand to her throat — "it's killing hot out there."

Pamela laughed. "I reckon I can survive. I lived through a lot hotter in Algiers."

Aunt Mayme lifted her eyebrows.

"If you're going," I said, "I'll come along."

Aunt Mayme looked at me out of the corner of her eyes. "You better take a sunshade, dear," she said. "You haven't been to Algiers."

Pamela touched my shoulder, briefly, smiling. "She hasn't missed very much; it was a dirty place."

"Yes," Aunt Mayme said. "I imagine it was. Let me give you my big shade. I'll help you get it out of the closet."

In her room she said with a kind of whistling sigh of annoyance: "Charlotte, you can be most trying."

"I want to go for a walk," I said, reaching for the sunshade hanging on the closet door. "I want to get out the house for a little exercise."

She was holding the sunshade's handle. "Pamela only knows that her sister left a will in Woodville's favor."

"But that wasn't genuine."

She closed the door and leaned on it for a minute. "You are not to tell her that. You understand?" Her face was perfectly blank, not excited, not nervous. "Now take your hot morning walk."

Pamela stayed with us two weeks. She liked me, maybe because I'd sit quiet and listen to her stories.

She had been all over the world: to England first, then China, Japan, and home. It took her nearly thirty years. And then she'd come back at last.

That's what she'd talk about most — coming home. I asked her once: "Why did you leave, then?"

"Why?" she said. "I don't think I know, really. I wasn't unhappy here. There was enough money from Papa's estate; Josephine didn't need any." I caught my breath at the mention of Josephine and wondered if she was going to ask about the will, but she went on: "There wasn't any real reason for me to stay either. I reckon I wanted to see what other places looked like."

I smiled at her, making a little joke at Aune Mayme's expense. "Aunt Mayme says there's a soldier in the story."

"A soldier?" She laughed. "Mayme is romantic at heart. It's a pity she didn't get married. . . . I didn't have any soldier to make me run away. I just left because I wanted to. And I knew I could come home when I wanted to."

I understood her. She could come home — just as if she'd never been away. She could go all around the world and come back without remembering anything. And she could come back to Josephine's money. She could come back and ruin all the plans we'd made.

Then Aunt Mayme found the perfect little house for Pamela. It was a pleasant place, only four rooms, but that was more than enough. It had been empty for nearly two years, ever since old Mrs. Sherwood had died there; but it was nicely furnished and the only thing to do was give it a good cleaning.

·   ·   ·

Aunt Mayme and Uncle Melton didn't want me to know what was going on. They didn't quite trust me yet. They didn't intend for me to know what they were planning to do. Nor did Andrew, I felt.

But they had to get me out of the house. So Andrew insisted that I accept an invitation from the Robinsons; they weren't particularly old or close friends, but still they invited us to spend a couple of weeks with them.

One night, while with them, Andrew let something slip. He said it was a great pity we had to go shares at all in the money.

One thing about Andrew: when he's caught he knows he's caught. So when I made him sit down and explain what he'd said about sharing the money, he told me the truth.

When he got through, I didn't say anything. He came over and kissed me and said: "You know how it is, honey. You understand." And I nodded because I did understand. He smoked one cigarette over by the window, then he came to bed. He patted my shoulder once, and soon I could tell he was asleep.

I don't think I got much sleep that night. I kept thinking over and over what they had done.

It was this way: Pamela knew her sister had left a will in Woodville's favor. But she didn't know that there was proof that it was false. She didn't even seem particularly interested — she and Josephine had scarcely been friends, and thirty years had taken all of the feeling out of the relationship. And Pamela had money enough from her father; so it was unlikely she would question the will.

Uncle Melton had had a talk with John Woodville and had made a bargain. The will would not be contested. Uncle Melton would withdraw his charge — for a price. And the price was two thirds of what Woodville would get.

I can see what it was like, that scene. John Woodville trying to bargain, knowing that he had to take what was offered to him. So it was settled with Woodville getting one third; the rest Aunt Mayme and Uncle Melton and Andrew would share. Everything had worked beautifully — except that Andrew told me.

In the morning Andrew said I still looked tired and maybe we'd better go home. All the way back, all the long drive through the heat and dust. In one place the brush fires had worked clear up to the road. There was nothing unusual about them, only maybe there were a few more this year. But they were part of the summer along with the dryness and the heat. And the sun bright and yellow through the smoky sky.

Andrew had turned on the radio because the quiet rustling sound of fire burning under pine bark puts your nerves on edge. When we had driven through the burning strip, Andrew flipped off the radio. "God, that's a relief."

"Yes," I said without really hearing him. All through the trip I hadn't really listened to him. Once in a while I'd notice him looking at me out of the corner of his eye and once he'd asked me if I felt all right. But I was too busy thinking to notice very much. I kept thinking about Pamela and knowing I ought to do something.

We were nearly home when I said to Andrew: "I'm going to tell her."

"Tell her?" There was a puzzled look in his eyes.

"I've got to tell Pamela."

He stared straight ahead at the road. "That'd be a hell of a thing to do." We turned left down the street that was ours. "With everything settled, Pamela could charge us with conspiracy to defraud or something like that."

"I know." I'd gone over and over the whole thing.

There were little beads of sweat forming around his mouth, and under the tan his face was white.

"I'm sorry, Andrew," I said. "But we just couldn't. . . . And I just can't stand the thought of that Woodville creature getting any of the money. He did forge the will."

In two more blocks we would be home. "He won't get much," Andrew said. "We'll get most of it like we should."

I shook my head and didn't answer.

He looked full at me. "You won't do anything."

"There's a car coming," I said, as calmly as I could, though I was beginning to be frightened a bit: I knew how much the thing meant to him. "You better watch the road . . . and how could you stop me?"

He didn't answer. When we turned up our driveway and stopped, he lifted the bags from the back seat and went in the house first. I thought that I would drive over at once and speak to Pamela. I slipped over into the driver's seat, but Andrew had taken the ignition keys with him. I had to stop and look for my set in my purse.

It's funny how a little thing like not being able to find keys right away can change just about everything. If my purse had been in order I would have slipped the key in the ignition and been off down the street and told Pamela. And I guess that I wouldn't have had a husband any more. But it doesn't matter, because it took a couple of minutes to find the keys and by that time Andrew had put down the bags and was coming out again and Uncle Melton was with him. They saw me sitting on the left side of the car and they ran the rest of the way. I heard their feet coming across the grass when I flipped on the ignition. Then Andrew's arm reached in and pulled out the keys and the engine stopped. I looked up and saw the smear of my lipstick on the sleeve of his khaki shirt.

"I'm sorry, dear," he said. "I didn't mean to knock into you like that. Is your lip hurt?"

I glanced in the rear-view mirror. The lipstick was smeared down across my chin.

"I look like something out of *Treasure Island*," I said, with a smile, hoping all the while that the edges of my mouth would not tremble. "Give me the keys now."

Uncle Melton slipped into the seat beside me. His round white face was dripping with perspiration, and his tie was knocked just a bit crooked. "Perhaps we should go in the house, Charlotte."

"Give me the keys," I said to Andrew. "Don't stand there looking so foolish."

I heard a shade being raised and Aunt Mayme was looking out the dining-room window. My heart was beginning to thump so loud I wondered if Uncle Melton, sitting close beside me, could hear it. "Andrew," I said, and my voice shook though I tried to keep it even, "give me the keys."

He opened the door quickly and slipped behind the wheel, pushing me over along the slick plastic seat-covers. My shoulder nudged against Uncle Melton's starched coat.

"Andrew," I said, "I made up my mind."

He pulled the keys out of his breast pocket and drove the car back through the yard to the garage. "Now," he said, "let's go in the house."

He took hold of my arm, pulling me out after him. For one moment I caught hold of the steering wheel. "No."

With his other hand he lifted my fingers, gently enough. "Don't make me lose my temper, dear."

He kept hold of my arm as we started across the yard and Uncle Melton appeared on my other side. "Please," he said, "no scenes. It's too hot to be violent."

We went inside to the living-room, the three of us, three abreast, down the hall. They both kept hold of my arms, not roughly but very gallantly.

Cousin Roger was in the living-room. He was reading a heavy red book. Uncle Melton dropped my arm. "Roger," he said, "do you remember where we stored last year's orange wine?"

Cousin Roger took off his glasses and rubbed his bald head. "I reckon it was in the north corner of the cellar. We planning to use some?"

Uncle Melton winked at him. "We could be having a celebration tonight, if you could find it."

That got rid of Cousin Roger. After he found the bottle, he'd drink most of it; then he'd take himself upstairs to his room and lay himself out straight on

his bed. And if anyone came into the room he'd swear up and down that he
was dead and embalmed and he'd be buried on Sunday coming after the best
wake the town had ever seen.

Andrew dropped my arm and took out his pipe. "Andrew Conners," I told
him, so mad now that my voice shook, "you are the biggest coward I have ever
known."

"Don't blame the boy, Charlotte," Uncle Melton said. "And don't make a
scene. They give me a headache."

I sat down in the nearest chair. My face must have been bright red by this
time, and with the lipstick smear down my chin I must have looked pretty
silly, but I was furious and a little afraid too.

"I can see what you're doing," I told them. "One of you standing by the
window and the other one by the door. And Aunt Mayme's just outside the
other door."

Andrew laughed but did not move.

"I will tell Pamela."

Uncle Melton said softly: "That would be very foolish, child."

"That would be very very foolish, dear," Aunt Mayme said as she came into
the room.

They looked much alike, the two of them, saying practically the same
thing.

"Pamela does not need the money," Uncle Melton said.

"She has enough from her father," Aunt Mayme said.

"She is very old."

"She will die soon."

"She has enough to be more than comfortable."

"She would not be able to handle a large amount."

They kept talking like that, first one, then the other, so that I got dizzy
twisting my head back and forth between them. All the while Andrew stood
in front of me, not saying anything, just watching.

"We are only getting what is ours."

"Had she stayed away a little longer —"

"Things would have been settled this way."

"They are settled now."

My head began to hurt; it was hard for me to turn back and forth, so I stared
straight ahead at Andrew.

"We're doing it for you and Andrew."

"For your children."

"But we don't have children," I said.

"But we will," Andrew said.

Uncle Melton said: "You've never met John Woodville."

Aunt Mayme said: "He's a nice man."

"We wanted you to meet him."

"I don't want to," I said, staring at Andrew.

"Wipe the lipstick from your chin," Aunt Mayme said, and held out a handkerchief.

"I've got a compact in my bag."

Andrew handed me the leather pouch. My head was going in wide, singing circles. Little sleep the night before; the long hot ride; the excitement. I put the lipstick on in a wavering line.

"That looks terrible," I said.

"It looks beautiful on you," Andrew said.

He was kneeling on the floor beside me, holding the ridiculous huge purse with all my junk inside. He moved and it rattled. At the shoulders his khaki shirt was wet through, and his face was shiny with perspiration.

"Do you want the money so very much?"

"Very much."

He had loved me very much; he had married me over the objections of his family: I remembered that.

"But some will go to Woodville."

"He deserves something," Uncle Melton said.

"For the three years of service to poor old sick Josephine," Aunt Mayme said.

"Yes," I said. "Yes."

"There isn't as much as we expected," Andrew said.

"And you don't have to worry about Pamela."

"Not about her. She'll be all right," Andrew said. "You know that."

His arm brushed across my head. He must have made a gesture to Uncle Melton and Aunt Mayme to leave the room. He slipped his arm around me. I was very tired and let my head rest on his chest. I could hear his heart: slow and regular. He knew I would agree. And so I did.

Andrew went back to camp the next day. After he had gone, I began to think what I had done. Without Andrew I was not so sure. Lying there in bed alone, in the half dark (we'd kept the shutter fast closed to hold in some of the night's coolness for a little part of the day), I began to wonder at what I had done. And I decided that I should go speak to Pamela.

I dressed and went to look for breakfast. Aunt Mayme was in the kitchen, reading the papers. She looked up and nodded; "Good morning." And I had the feeling she had been waiting there for me ever since Andrew left. I drank one cup of coffee quickly, almost choking, wondering whether I should simply go out without saying anything. In the end I decided to tell her and dare her to stop me.

I said: "How's Pamela?"

She took off her glasses and looked at me slowly. "She's fine, I believe — though the weather is so oppressive for her."

"Really." I lifted my eyebrows as she herself would have done. "I thought she'd seen a lot hotter."

Aunt Mayme shrugged and didn't answer.

"I think," I said, "I'll drop in on her this evening when it's cooler."

She began to wipe the glasses slowly on her handkerchief. "You must be tired, dear. You should stay home."

I could feel the back of my neck getting red. I was angry — at her or maybe at myself. "I'm not tired," I said. "I think I'll go and see her right now."

Aunt Mayme put the glasses into their velvet case. "If you like, dear."

I went out. I went out with a lot of noise and a slamming of the front door. I walked down the street toward Pamela's house, but when I got there, I went on past her door. Then I remembered that when Aunt Mayme had looked at me, there had been a smile on her face.

She was right to smile. Because I wouldn't have any more walked in and told Pamela than she herself would, or Uncle Melton, or Andrew. And when I came back, hot and dizzy from the sun, she put one arm around me and said: "My dear," and hugged me. "After all, we are one family." And I knew she was right.

I told Andrew once: "I'm glad there isn't so very much. I'm glad there isn't the house."

And he kissed me on the cheek, lightly, and smiled. "You're just tired, honey."

And I let him think that. But I was glad, because that small disappointment made the whole thing more honest somehow. Of course, it wasn't more honest and I knew it. But I was part of it along with Aunt Mayme and Uncle Melton and Andrew. I could say it was right, like they did, but I might just as well have told the sun to stop shining in that bright dry summer.

I think we've used the money very practically. We've a farm now, a beautiful place with some of the sweetest stretches of pasture I ever saw. We've a lovely house too, built like an old plantation manor, on the highest ground for miles around. Sometimes when we are coming home very late, and the night mists still hug to the ground, it is a fairy castle that will blow away with morning. But of course it won't. It is beautiful and solid. And we love it, all of us,

Mayme and Melton and Andrew and I and even Cousin Roger, whom we took along because there wasn't anything else to do with him. He still gets drunk occasionally and is sure that he is dead. Mayme and Melton have changed very little; if anything, they have grown to look more alike. Andrew is out of the army; he threw away all his uniforms, but he keeps the Purple Heart and the Silver Star in a little glass frame hung on the wall next to his dresser. He's put on a little weight, but it's becoming.

And I don't change at all. Aunt Mayme tells me: "Dear, you look as young as the day you married."

So I tell her: "I take care of myself."

And she always shakes her head again. "And you keep your figure — even after Andrew and little Melton."

Pamela lives in town: the same little old-fashioned comfortable house Aunt Mayme and Uncle Melton found for her. She seems quite comfortable on the income from her father; year before last she bought the house. She's made very few changes in the six years: a new sink in the kitchen, and she's torn down the old warped cistern. She is content to live out the rest of her life. But I've noticed that she's feebler. The heat worries her; she uses a palmetto fan constantly now. And she stays in the house nearly all the time.

This morning I stopped in for a minute or two. We talked for a while and she made me a cup of jasmine tea. The supply she brought back from China seems to be without an end. Then I said that I must be leaving because there was a long drive before home.

She kissed me good-by and her lips were as dry and faint as her tea leaves. "It's nice to go home," she said. "It's the best part of being away." Like all old ladies, she is a little too sweet. "No matter where I was, I always wanted to come back here. It is so wonderfully peaceful to come home."

I drove faster than usual going home. And when the house finally came in sight, I felt relieved. It was as though I had expected it to be that fairy mist castle and blow away. But it was of timber and bricks and cement and it would be standing when I was dead. I parked the car and walked across the gravel court. For just a minute I thought I was going to faint, the sun was so hot.

Fever Flower

Summers, even the dew is hot. The big heavy drops, tadpole-shaped, hang on leaves and stems and grass, lie on the face of the earth like sweat, until the spongy sun cleans them away. That is why summer mornings are always steamy. The windows of the Cadillacs parked in car ports are frosted with mist. By ten the dew is gone and the steam with it, and the day settles down to burn itself out in dry heat.

In the houses air-conditioning units buzz twenty-four hours a day. And colored laundresses grumble at the size of washes. And colored cooks work with huck towels tied around their necks and large wet spots on their black linen uniforms — until by mid-July they refuse to come in the mornings and fix any sort of breakfast. It is a mass movement. None of the white people can do anything about it. But then it is not serious. No one needs breakfast in summer. Most people simply skip the meal; the men, those of them who have strict bosses, grumble through the mornings empty-stomached or gulp hasty midmorning coffee; the women lie in bed late — until it is lunch time and the cooks have come. Nurses feed children perfunctory breakfasts: cold cereals and juices at eleven o'clock. Summer mornings no one gets up early.

By eight thirty Katherine Fleming was sitting alone in the efficient white and yellow tiled kitchen at breakfast: orange juice and instant coffee. She had somehow spilled the juice and she was idly mopping up the liquid from the stainless-steel counter top when the phone rang. Her hands were sticky when she picked up the receiver.

"Why, Jerry —" She swallowed the last of the coffee. "I really didn't think you'd be up this early. . . . Sure I'm all right."

She leaned her elbow on the counter, remembered the spilled juice and lifted her arm hastily, as she listened. She shook her head. "Let's not try lunch, honey. I'm supposed to run out and say hello to Mamma."

She listened another moment, frowning a bit with the beginnings of irritation. "Don't tease me, honey. I'm going because she's lonesome for me. I ought to, you know. Even if I'd rather be with you. And, anyway, there's tonight."

She listened a moment more, said good-by, and stood up, irritably ruffling the back of her hair with one hand.

It always annoyed her to lie. But it would never have done to tell Jerry Stevenson to his face that she did not want to see him; she felt she owed him that much, because he had been fun the night before. Last night she had adored him; this morning all that was left was a feeling of well-being. She stretched, arching her back. She felt wonderful, soft and rested and fine. He was part of last night; he would be part of tonight. But this sudden intrusion into the morning left her vaguely annoyed, though she knew she could forget about him.

Katherine Fleming went upstairs and dressed quickly: a summer suit of white linen, a pale-green blouse that would bring out the color of her eyes. She finished her make-up and studied herself in the mirror, nodding just a bit in approval: nice brown hair, very nice gray eyes, a figure Grable needn't have been ashamed of. And furthermore, she told herself, she had years in her favor. She was twenty-five: she looked twenty-two. She picked up her handbag and went quickly down the hall to tell her daughter good-by.

Four years ago Katherine had been married; two years ago she had been divorced. A house that was new and very modern, a daughter whose name was Maureen, and a sizable check that came every month on the third: these were left of her marriage.

She did not regret anything. She did not look back on her marriage with anger or any feeling stronger than a kind of vague relief that it was finished at last. She was not angry with Hugh; she had never been. Not even when she heard of his remarriage to one of her college friends. Not even that last time when they had called it quits.

Hugh had sat quietly in the armchair over by the window and listened while she told him that nothing between them was ever going to work. He sat facing her, his eyes lifted a little and focused on the spot of wall slightly above her head, so that he was at once looking at her and not seeing her. He had gray eyes, large ones, with lashes for a man ridiculously long and curly. In the light from the window the gray eyes turned shiny as silver and as hard. When she had finished, he got up and left without a word. He hadn't even stopped to pack. The next morning he called and told the maid to send his things to the hotel. Katherine remembered that the only thing she had felt was a kind of wonder that it had all been so easy.

She had never seen him again. But she was sure that had they met, she could have talked amicably with him. He, however, made very certain that they did not meet. Even on the one day a week when he came to see his daughter, she was not allowed to be in the house. His lawyers had insisted on that during the settlement. She was to have the child and a regular check; he was to have the one day a week when she would not be in the house.

Katherine Fleming walked quickly down the hall to tell her daughter good-by, her bag swinging idly from her fingers. A stupid arrangement, she thought, but then Hugh had been a strange fellow, full of odd ideas. One time he had gotten fascinated by sculpture. He had even considered lessons from Vittorio Manale, who was making a name for himself as one of the moderns. Hugh would always have the best of everything. But Hugh was also a practical man. He never could quite convince himself that money spent for lessons would have been well spent, so he never took any. But he never quite gave up the idea. He spent his Saturday afternoons — just about the only free time he had — in the museums, walking around and around the figures that interested him, figures in white marble, in polished brown granite. He stared at them with his eyes half-shut, trying to imagine how they had been done.

He couldn't work in marble, of course: he couldn't have used a chisel. But he always had been a marvelous whittler — he kept a row of different knives in his desk drawer — so he went to work in soap. That was when Katherine first knew him, the summer she finished college. The first piece he did was a dog, with the ears of a spaniel and the body of a terrier. He had given the little bit of carved soap to her mother. (Her mother still kept it on the whatnot shelves along with the other things of china and straw and the little basket of true Italian marble that they had sent her from Naples on their honeymoon.)

Katherine thought the whole thing was more than a little silly. A grown man, in his late thirties, and as handsome as Hugh Fleming, ought not to be whittling like a boy. But there were many things about him that were boyish: his clothes dropped all over the room at night (even four years in the navy had not cured him of that habit); the quick brushing back of his hair when he was angry; the open joy in new money or a new car or a new house or a new and beautiful wife. Or his whittling. But then Katherine had to admit that some of the things he made were lovely. As he caught the knack, his products came to have the look of marble; one in particular, a woman's head. He said it was she;

he had her sit as a model for him, while he worked, but it did not look much like her. She was not that beautiful: her features were somewhat irregular, her eyes not large enough to be so striking, her hair not so perfectly waved. His work had the perfection of line and contour of the face on a cameo. Perhaps, though, he really saw her like that. After all, by the time the figure was completed they were engaged. In any case, that bit of her was undoubtedly the finest thing he ever did. After they had separated she dropped the head into a pan of water and watched its slow disintegration, which took several days.

A crazy idea, Katherine thought, having me leave the house. But like him, she admitted. She went into her daughter's room. Maureen was three, but the room in which she slept was not a nursery. It was a young girl's room with pale-blue ruffled organdy curtains and an organdy skirt around the vanity table and a blue-chintz-lined closet; a long mirror on one wall — the extra wide kind in which one surveys an evening dress's lacy folds; small colored balls of perfume atomizers: red and gold, empty and waiting for the scent their owner would choose when she got old enough to care for such things.

Katherine had insisted that the room be furnished in this manner a few months ago. She did not quite realize why, why it had seemed very necessary to her that the changes be made at once. Perhaps it was only her longing to get through the awkward growing years, the child years.

Perhaps an unconscious admission that the only real contact between herself and Maureen would come during the four or five years of the girl's first beauty, years that would be terminated by her marriage. They would not see each other very often: Marueen must go away to college; at home her time would be occupied by her friends. Yet for mother and daughter it would be the happiest time, although an uneasy one, for they would both realize that they did not really like each other very much.

Katherine leaned over and kissed her daughter. "I'm leaving now, honey."

Maureen stared at her solemnly. "'By." She had been drinking orange juice (briefly Katherine recalled her own breakfast): her upper lip with the soft invisible hairs now sported an orange mustache.

"Messy." Katherine picked up a napkin from the tray beside the bed. "Now wipe your mouth."

Solemnly Maureen scrubbed the napkin across her lips, then turned her attention to the bowl of cereal in front of her.

"She's eating, ma'am," Annie said, rolling pale-blue eyes behind her rimless glasses. "And it isn't easy to get her to eat in the morning."

Katherine shrugged. She had come in at the wrong time; she admitted the mistake to herself. "I'm glad her appetite's better," she said sweetly. "I was worried."

"Yes, ma'am," Annie said. Her voice had no inflection to give the words a second and ironic meaning.

She's angry, Katherine thought, because I interrupted the routine. And now she's thinking I don't care a bit what happens to my daughter. But I do. I do.

Then because she did not quite believe herself, she leaned over and kissed Maureen on top of the head. "Good-by, honey. I'll see you tonight, I reckon."

She did not say good-by to Annie. She turned and picked up her gloves and bag from the chair and left quickly.

There was nothing else to do. She had to be out of the house. And she didn't like going downtown: shopping, eating lunch alone, going to a movie. And she didn't like to go with any of the women she knew. What they thought showed so plainly on their stupid faces (and Katherine was not stupid by any means). And what they thought was a combination of admiration and pity: she has got rid of her husband; she looks happy over it; and today by court order she cannot go home; it is her husband's house again. Katherine saw these things plainly in their faces and she did not go out with these women who were her best friends and whom she liked on other days of the week.

It was not that she minded being out. Not at all. Her friends and her club work took up all her time. But she could have gone home, had she wanted. On these days she could not, not and keep the settlement. Hugh would be strict on that point, she knew. Katherine was furious, but she was too sensible to object. So she usually drove the thirty-five miles over to Barksfield and visited her mother. It seemed the best thing to do.

After a few more years she would find that she much preferred a solitary day in town. After a few years she would find a positive pleasure in being alone.

Perhaps that was why she never remarried. Not that she did not have a chance to. She was a very beautiful woman. She dressed superbly; she went out a great deal and had hundreds of friends. She could have remarried a dozen times, but she said, No, thank you, in a polite way that left no room for argument or doubt. She did not take lovers either, except in the first few years after the divorce, for she was confused then and afraid of loneliness. But she freed herself from them when she realized she could be happiest alone. Each day she experienced a great pleasure when she woke to her beautiful appointed house, her beautiful daughter. Her own lovely body delighted her. She liked to lie in the tub and feel the water move over her and pour half a vial of bath oil over her shoulders. She also found that it was a delicious pleasure to walk around her room naked and feel her body move. She had a perfect body; she was a superb animal. But she was not quite human. She did not need anyone.

Hugh Fleming unlocked the front door and came into the hall. He still kept his door key, though he used it only one day in the week. He kept it in the leather case along with his other keys — the car, the office, the other house. It was a silver key with his initials on the head, the sort that had to be specially made. Katherine had given it to him for Christmas the first year of their marriage. He folded up the leather case, put it in his pocket, and went upstairs to see his daughter. He was earlier than usual: she was just finishing her breakfast.

"I have not done a thing to getting her dressed, Mr. Fleming," Annie told him, lifting her eyebrows in polite annoyance. "You came on us a bit early."

Hugh picked up his daughter, who hugged him delightedly, one hand grabbing his ear, the other holding his tie. "How's my girl?" he said. "How's my big girl?"

She giggled in her thin high-pitched voice and reached for his coat pocket where he always kept a present for her. She let herself hang limp across his arm while she reached into his left-hand pocket, then straightened up, triumphantly holding a green and white bead necklace.

"Now, that is pretty for sure," Annie said. "And isn't he a nice daddy to be remembering you?"

Hugh brushed the rumpled brown hair with his fingertips and twisted it into ringlets. He was holding his daughter, he thought. It was hard to realize that sometimes, she looked so much like her mother.

The awkward squarish child body in his arms squirmed and shifted; a little hand dug into the cloth of his coat as Maureen climbed up to sit atop his shoulder. Tenderness, a great protecting tenderness, burst its soft petals. "I'll give her the bath, Annie. You go start the water."

"Sure, she splashes like a baby whale, Mr. Fleming," Annie said warningly. "And you'll be ruining your suit."

"She's my daughter." He hugged Maureen tighter and she squealed a little at the sudden pressure. "To hell with the suit. I want to."

Annie lifted her eyebrows slightly. She would have given Mr. Fleming the same lecture on blaspheming and evil words that she gave her nephews but for one fact: he paid her salary. So she went and filled the tub and spread the towels and handed Mr. Fleming Maureen's slip and panties. "I will leave her dress on the bed." She spoke with dignity, her conscience still smarting under his affront. "It would only be wilting up in the steaming bathroom."

"Okay," said Hugh, not noticing the iciness of her tone. "Come on, honey," he told Maureen, "your old man's going to give you a bath."

Contrary to Annie's dour prediction, Maureen did not splash in the tub. She was a bit awed at the unaccustomed turn of events and sat very still, staring up into her father's face with neither anger nor friendliness but only a kind of surprise. Hugh washed his baby carefully, an aching pleasant tenderness in his heart. It was not a usual feeling for him; he had not experienced it often before and it never lasted long. It would fade and be replaced by the vaguely angry, dissatisfied stirring with which he usually viewed his daughter. It was not that he disliked her. Not at all. He was being a very good father to her; he was supporting her well. And that was the point — although Hugh would never have admitted it. He was a businessman, one of the shrewdest; he knew a good deal when he saw one. He was spending quite a bit of money on his daughter and he could not quite convince himself that it was worth it.

Of course, it was, in the long run. Maureen turned out to be a lovely young woman. She had a truly magnificent wedding, and Hugh, circulating among the guests, his head buzzing a little from the champagne, finally realized how fine an investment his daughter had been. After all, it was none of his fault that the man she married turned out to be no good, even though he was handsome and came from a fine family.

At her wedding Hugh could be happy in his investment, and it was a great satisfaction to him.

But it was not the same sort of pleasure he felt that morning when against the sour disapproving looks of Annie he bathed and dressed his daughter. And that emotion, perhaps because more rare, is more precious.

They went to the park that particular morning. "Just like I promised you last week," he reminded her. She stared at him without understanding, her dark eyes puzzled: she had long ago forgotten his promise. For a moment he was annoyed that she had not looked forward to it, as he had done. Then he laughed and told her: "You're only a baby yet," and hugged her soft little body. And all day he was very careful of her.

Toward the end of the afternoon, just as they were walking back to the parked car, they passed the tropical gardens. Through the glass door Maureen caught sight of the huge silver reflecting globe and pointed to it with an insistent nod.

"You don't want to go in there, honey," Hugh told her. But she was already hanging on the chrome handle, trying to pull open the glass door.

They went inside. Hugh had always found the air too humid to be comfortable; he found himself taking shallow quick breaths, panting almost. But Maureen loved the heat and the dampness. She smiled up at him, her dark eyes impish and full of life. She tugged at his hand and would have run off, had he not tightened his grip. Finally she stood on tiptoe, swaying back and forth, her nose crinkling with the heavy scents.

He walked slowly up and down the paths with her, past broad wax-leaved plants dripping moisture, and heavy pollened red flowers, and vines carefully propagated by hand and bound up with straw. And then the orchids, a whole wall of them with their great spreading petals reaching into the heat. "See," Hugh told Maureen. "Pretty. Just the color of your dress." The blooms were forced to grow to gigantic size in half the time; they were beautiful and exotic and they did not last.

"Now let's go," Hugh said, for he was beginning to be very tired himself. He picked up Maureen and carried her to the car. She protested, crying, and then suddenly fell asleep. He watched her with faint stirrings of the tenderness whose great upsurge he had experienced that morning.

And it was the last time he would have such a joy in his daughter, Maureen. That afternoon his wife, his second wife, whose name was Sylvia, decided not to go for a drive as she usually did. Even with a cape she thought she looked just too big; and with the anxiety of the novice, she was desperately afraid that her baby would come on her suddenly and indecently in a field or on a road. In the late afternoon she called Hugh and asked him to come home.

By that time Hugh's pleasant affection for his daughter had worn off and had left only the sense of viewing a not particularly successful venture. They had just come back and were still in the front hall when the phone rang. Hugh shifted Maureen to his left arm and answered it himself, saying yes quickly.

Maureen was still dozing. He carried her upstairs to the room her mother had designed with expensive good taste. Then he left quickly, calling out a brief good-by to Annie, and thinking only of Sylvia, wondering if anything could go wrong. (Sylvia bore him three more children: three boys after the first girl. All of them grew up prosperous and healthy. She was a very fine wife for him. And after his death — she found him one evening, sitting on the porch, erect but not breathing — she discovered that she did not want to live either.)

Annie left Maureen to sleep undisturbed in her clothes. The house was very quiet and empty: Hugh had gone and Katherine had not returned. (She would be just now beginning the drive back, her face white and strained from the effort of being polite, her make-up a little streaked by the heat.) Outside on the dry lawns sprinklers were beginnning to throw out fan-shaped streams of water.

Annie went down the hall to her own room, leaving the door ajar in case Maureen should call. She opened the blinds and sat down by the window, the late afternoon heat against her face, and, taking a stiff bound Bible from the table, began to read. She was a very religious woman and read in the Bible every day for a half-hour. She did not like the Old Testament; she could never quite convince herself that its heroes (with their bloody swords and many wives) were men of God. And although she always began the New Testament at the Gospel of St. Matthew — she felt that she should begin at the beginning — she found that she preferred the epistles. (She could make no sense of the Apocalypse at all.) Today it was Paul to the Galatians. "Walk in the spirit and you shall not fulfil the lusts of the flesh. . . . The fruit of the Spirit is joy." She heard the front door open, then slam shut, as Katherine came home.

Annie stood up. Joy. The lusts of the flesh. The chaff which shall be cast in the fire. Hell fire. Which was like summer sun, but stronger seven times. In her mind she saw clearly: Katherine and Hugh revolving slowly in a great sputtering, leaping fire while she stood on the edge, watching, dressed in some sort of luminous stuff which all the righteous wore in the hereafter, holding Maureen by the hand.

(Annie died while Maureen was on her honeymoon, just a week after there'd been a card from Hawaii signed: "Love from your little girl, Maureen.")

No one suspected then that Maureen's husband would turn into the sort of fellow he did. No one guessed that she would have two more ex-husbands when, as a middle-aged, strikingly handsome woman, she took a very beautiful, very expensive apartment for one on the west coast. . . .

Annie found Katherine sprawled on the couch in the living-room. "Is something wrong, ma'am?" she asked politely.

"I've had some day," Katherine said. "Lord, but my head aches."

"Maureen is sleeping." Annie stood with her hands in the pockets of her white apron, holding herself stiffly erect. "She is very tried."

"That's fine," Katherine said. "I knew her father would take good care of her." She rubbed her temples gently. "Annie, go get me an aspirin. What a day I've had!"

"Yes, ma'am," Annie said.

Katherine stretched herself on the couch, one arm across her eyes. "You damn old Puritan," she said. "See if the air-conditioner's working. It's hot as hell."

Later that evening Maureen woke, fretful, and began to cry. Lying on her bed in the orchid pinafore she had worn to the park, she began to cry — softly at first, then louder so that Annie could hear.

"You eat something wrong, lamb?" Annie asked. "Did that father of yours feed you something wrong?"

Maureen spread out her arms and legs and stretched, as if she would grow suddenly, grow to fill the bed, which was too big for her.

"We'll take off your dress, lamb. And you'll rest better."

But Maureen shook her head and dug her fingers into the bed. The orchid dress was wet through in spots with perspiration.

"Annie won't move you, then, lamb. But we'll cool off this old room for you." She walked over to the door and glanced at the thermostat dial: it was as low as it could go. "You're running a fever, lamb."

Annie stood looking down at her. "My pretty little one. My pretty, pretty one."

Annie rubbed her hands together slowly. "Sure," she said, "and you look like a young lady already, there."

Maureen did not answer. She lay on the bed, staring up at the ceiling, her eyes wide.

"Don't look like that, lamb." Annie moved over and sat on the edge of the bed. Half under her breath she began a lullaby, a soft, plaintive little air, with a wide tonal range — too wide, for her voice faltered on the high notes. But the Gaelic words came out soft and clear:

> "My little lady, sleep
> And I will wish for you: A love to have,
> A true heart,
> A true mind,
> And strong arms to carry you away."

Her fingers brushed away the hair from Maureen's forehead: it was damp and sticking to the skin in little wisps. The child pulled away. The sun had left her cheeks flushed — bright color, high across the cheekbones. Fever sparkled her eyes and enlarged them. Tiredness gave lines to her face and shadows and the illusion of age.

"Sure," Annie repeated, "and you look like a young lady, a lovely young lady already, there,"

Maureen lay on her side, the clear lines of her profile showing against the pink spread. She did not turn again: she had stopped crying. And lay there, beautiful and burning.

The Way of a Man

For five years the boy lived with his old father in the house on Bayou St. Philippe.

It was a good house, snug and tight against the brief cold winds of the tumbled gray January sky and the hard quick squalls of August. The house was built on good solid ground, a high bank of shells, that stuck up out of the marsh like the back of an alligator: a great alligator extending nearly two miles from the state highway, winding and twisting out into the Gulf marsh where the tides were salty and sea fish came up into the bayou mouths. The house stood at the end of the winding shell ridge, farthest away from the highway, the end where Bayou St. Philippe made a circle in from the east and let its slow yellow-green waters into the Gulf.

It was a comfortable clapboard house with one room and a lean-to kitchen. Inside was a double bed; a cylinder-shaped oil stove for winter; and a chest that the man had brought from New Orleans once when he was young and had gone into the city for a spree: a low chest and of some light wood — cedar or maple, it was hard to tell after so many years. And tacked carefully to the wall over the chest was a colored lithograph of the Virgin, tall and serene in a bright blue gown; from the same nail dangled a black-bead rosary, its cross missing.

None of the walls were painted — inside or out — but time had given the boards a uniform black stain. Outside, also blacked by time and weather, were racks for drying nets, the small kind that a single man could handle, for he always fished alone; and racks for drying the muskrat pelts when he trapped during the season.

The boy, whose name was William, had been born in this house and until he was five years old had played among the racks and breathed the smell of nets and of drying pelts and watched wind shadows roll over the marsh grass.

He had been born in the house — one hot September afternoon. The sky was a still high arch of bright blue: the sun slid down it like a silver dime. In the south a mass of thunderclouds sat low on the horizon; the waters of the Gulf moved with the peculiar nervous tremor of a storm on them somewhere.

He was not long being born. His mother cried quietly and briefly in the hot afternoon, saw that her child was a man, and fell asleep. No one seemed particularly concerned. When the work was done, his grandmother rolled down the sleeves of her long-sleeved cotton print dress, nodded to her daughter, and began the walk back across the marsh. As she went she saw the old man who was her daughter's husband coming back from a day's fishing.

When the boy was two, his mother left. She was a young woman, not more than twenty then, with a long lithe body and quick darting eyes. She had married the old man because of two mistakes. She thought he was too old to give her a child and she thought that he was rich. Within a year she had a child growing in her body. And she never saw his money.

A government pension check came regularly each month on the third. They held it for him at the post office over in Port Allen; he walked in to fetch it. He had done this for so many years that the two men who sorted the mail looked specially for his envelope — light brown with the blue check showing through the strip of cellophane — and put it up on a little shelf beside the general-delivery window to wait for him.

"Say, Uncle," one of them asked him once, "how come the government's sending you money?"

The old man took the check in his knotted black fingers. "Account I was in the war."

"Which war?" the man said. "There's been a lot of them."

The old man blinked his eyes slowly.

"It couldn't a been the Civil War," the white man said. He had hold of one end of the envelope. "You ain't that old."

His partner came and leaned on the counter beside him. "I bet it was the Spanish War, wasn't it, Uncle?"

"You in the fighting, Uncle?" the other one asked.

"I done press the pants and shine the shoes for them that's done the fighting," the old man said with dignity and pulled his envelope from the white man's hand.

Holding his check carefully in two fingers, he always went directly across the street to the bank to cash it. When he had the bills in his hand, he would buy food for the month and fishing gear or some new traps, and on his way home he'd pick up a jug of corn likker.

That was it. His young wife never saw his money. She was convinced he had hidden it somewhere; she spent days searching and found nothing. But she was certain he was rich.

It wasn't any life for a young woman, a pretty woman. One day she was gone. When the old man came home, there was only his son in the house, a fuzzy-headed black boy with bright brown eyes and a constant smile. The old man called for his wife once and walked once around the house, looking over the marsh on all sides. Then he went in and began supper himself. The boy followed him inside, climbed on the edge of the table, and waited for food.

The next morning the old man sat in the sun and mended his nets. The boy crouched on the edge of the bayou and tried to catch the little water lizards with his hands.

William was young and agile as a black monkey and noisy. And his father was very old and slow. And so one day the man took down the boy's cap from the nail where it had been hanging and put it on the nervous kinky head, and folded the boy's clothes in a brown paper bag. Then he took his son by the hand and walked into town to give him back to his mother. He stopped only once — in the grocery to ask where she was living — and then went directly to the house. There he knocked on the door and she herself came to answer it — a young woman wearing a pink print dress stretched tight across full hips and heavy breasts. The old man pointed down to the boy and dropped his hand and turned around without a word and walked away. The woman looked down at her son — at his thin long black limbs and his thin quick monkey face — and then up at the broad heavy stooped back of the man as he walked away. And she asked her son: "Don't he feed you none, the old man?"

The boy nodded and grinned. The upper row of his front teeth was missing.

"He can afford to, him," the woman said. "He can sure afford to, him." Then she turned and walked back into the house, leaving the door open behind her. Her son followed her, stopping to pick up the brown paper parcel of clothes that his father had dropped on the steps.

That was how he came to his mother, after his father had shown that he would have no more to do with him. And he lived with her until he was fourteen and the police caught him stealing tires. Then he was sent up to the north part of the state to the reform school.

Three years later he was back knocking on his mother's door. And she opened it and stood leaning against the doorjamb studying him. "You a man grown," she said. "I used to could look down at you and you was a boy. But now I got to look up because you a man."

"Reckon so," he said.

He was a man grown. Not tall but broad: his father's build. There were such muscles across his back that he almost seemed to be stooping. He had the same quick nervous face of his childhood, the same nervous up-twitching of the left corner of the mouth.

Because he was a man, he did not live in his mother's house. She fixed him a bed in the kitchen (her house had only two rooms), a pillow and a blanket rolled up to be out of the way; and she kept it there in case the officer who was in charge of his parole should come around looking. He did come occasionally — a slight dark Negro, whose dark-blue police uniform did not fit him, whose name was Matthew Pettis. The first time he came she met him at the door and asked him in and offered him some coffee and said that her son was working on the oyster boats because he was so strong — for all that he was just seventeen, he was a man grown. She showed him the bed. And Pettis nodded and rubbed his black kinky hair, and his little shiny black eyes danced all over the room.

The next time Pettis came, William happened to be there and he and his mother sat side by side on the bed in the front room and answered yes sir and no sir to the questions and looked with quiet brown eyes into Pettis's restless quick ones.

When the policeman had gone, William stood up and stretched and pulled on his cap and sauntered slowly out of the house. His mother did not notice he was gone until she called to ask him if he wanted anything to eat. She opened the front door and called for him out into the street. Then she went back and began to eat herself. She did not think of him again. She did not know where he had gone or where he was living. She did not wonder about it. A man could make his own way.

He was living in Bucktown, a double line of colored houses strung out along a dirt road and only a couple of miles from the oyster docks. He had a girl there, short, plump, and high-brown colored. Her name was Cynthia Lee. She was always laughing, always showing her short square teeth and her dull red gums. She worked at the shrimp plant that was a little farther down the shore. He'd worked there too, once, when he'd first come back. He'd quit because the work was too light, for a man. And he went to the oyster boats, where the pay was better and the work was enough to try the muscles of a strong back.

He'd been saying hello to her for over a week before he got the nerve to ask her to have a beer with him on Saturday night. She said, "I reckon so," with her quick bright grin and a little jerk of her head.

They went to the Smile Inn, which was the closest bar for Negroes, and they had three beers each, and then, because it was Saturday and the place got very crowded and men kept bumping into her round little body and saying: "Excuse me," with a grin, he pointed to the door.

"It too crowded," he said. "I don't study getting all mashed up by people none."

She just laughed and pushed her way to the door.

He walked her home. It was night and there weren't any lights along the dirt road. They stumbled in ruts and held on to each other, laughing. The moon came up finally over the straggling thin pines and they could see the road in front of them.

"I ain't used to coming home this late," she said.

"Ain't you?"

"No," she said. "Ma'll give me hell."

"Seems like you could handle her with no trouble." He rubbed his chin with the back of his hand. "Seems like you'd better be worrying about your pa."

She grinned; in the uncertain moon glow her little square teeth flashed white in the darkness of her face. "He done picked up and gone a long time ago."

"That right?" William said.

"Ma don't miss him none." She laughed again and stumbled in a deep rut. He caught her around the waist.

"Cynthia Lee," he said, "seems like you can't even walk none. You sure must be drunk."

"Me?" Her laugh went up and down the dark. "I can't ever hold no likker."

He tightened his arm. "I reckon I know one kind you could." He kissed her. Her square white teeth clamped on his lower lip. He hissed with the pain and slapped her away from him. She stumbled backwards and sat down. Her body made a soft sound against the ground. He rubbed his lip for a few moments and then bent over her. He had thought she was crying; but she was only laughing softly.

It was settled after that. He lived with her in her mother's house in Bucktown. And since her mother was a big fat jolly woman who worked as a cook in one of the white houses on the beach, and who thought William was a fine handsome man, things went well.

One evening after work he went out to see his father. He had not been there since he was a little boy and he wondered if he remembered the way. He began to walk down the highway, the highway that led into the city. It was a dry time. The wheels of the cars on the asphalt strip stirred up dust and he coughed and covered his nose and mouth with one hand. He rubbed the other hand across his face and felt the grit of the dust on it. He pulled a handkerchief out of his pocket and wiped his face carefully, for he knew that his skin was black and that the light dust would streak it. And he did not want to appear before his father with a face streaked up like the clowns he had seen in a circus once. (At the reform school once for good behavior they had given him a pass to the circus and had let him go alone. He had been so fascinated and dazed by all that he had seen that he had returned to the school, forgetting his plan to break parole and run away. When it was too late, he remembered with a sick feeling in his stomach. He was calling himself all the names he could think of, whispering them clearly to himself, when the chaplain, a fat little man with a bald pink head, came and shook his hand and told him that he was proud of him, that he had behaved like a man.)

When William saw the white shell road leading off the highway, he knew that he would remember the way, even if it had been years since his father had taken him by the hand and, walking so fast that he had to run and stumble after, had brought him over to his mother.

The shell road ran south and ended with a small wharf where some white fishermen kept their boats dragged up above the tides on slips of rough wood. Just before the road's end a footpath went off straight eastward through the waist-high grasses that moved in any wind. At the end was Bayou St. Philippe and his father's house. Long before he got close, he could see the house on the ridge of high ground, a square little weathered building with a slanting lean-to for a kitchen and a slanting little pile of firewood. Though it was warm spring weather, his father had built a little fire outside on the grass-free stretch of ground. He was sitting alongside it now on a straight-back cane chair he had brought from inside.

William remembered the chair; he was sure it was the same one that had been there when he was a boy. He remembered trying to climb the ladder back and stumbling to the floor with the chair over him like a tent. And his father had pulled him free with one hand and with the other had given him a slap across the head that made his eyes blur and his ears sing. William stopped and stared at the old man and wondered how he had been able to hit so hard.

He wore tennis shoes; the old man had not heard him come up. He had not lifted his head from the redfish he was cleaning. Very slowly, eyes squinting with the effort, he was removing the fish scales.

"Hi," said William.

The old man looked at him slowly over the smoke and haze of the fire. Slowly he put the fish back in the wicker basket at his side.

"You remember me?" William asked, and stepped closer, his hands jammed down in his pockets, wondering if he had got all the road dust off his face, for he did not want his father to laugh at him.

The old man looked at him slowly, up and down, without answering. His face in the firelight in the dusk was very old and very lined. Even the blackness of his skin was beginning to gray — like a film of dust was gathering over it.

"You remember me?" William repeated.

The old man nodded slowly, very slowly. "You a man grown now. A man grown."

"I past seventeen," William said, and squared his shoulders.

He stepped up to the fire and took the fish out of the basket and held out his hand for the scaling knife, and when the old man gave it to him he finished the cleaning in a few quick movements. "I been working on the oyster boats," he said.

"I worked the boats," his father said, and folded his hands together and rested his chin on them.

"You did?" William studied his father. He was a big man, big as his son, or he had been once. He was stooped now so that he always seemed to be huddling into himself.

The old man took the cleaned fish and went inside. William picked up the chair and followed him.

"You want I should put it on to cook?" William asked.

The old man shook his head.

"You ain't changed nothing," William said. The room was just as he remembered it. He opened the wood shutter on the side that looked out on the bayou and, beyond that, a quarter mile away, the Gulf. "It's rough out there," he said. "It's gonna be a rough night."

It began to rain while they were eating. "First come in over a month." His father did not stop chewing, his jaws moved slowly up and down.

"Lay the dust a little," William said.

In one corner the roof leaked; water ran down the wall. But neither of them noticed. The old man went and lay on his bed and almost immediately fell asleep. William stretched on the floor, pillowed his head on a pile of nets, listened to the rain, and thought about his girl until he fell asleep too.

The water that had leaked in through the roof ran down the smooth boards of the floor and touched his cheek. He lifted his head, rubbing at his face, and saw that it was morning.

The door was open. William rolled over and peered out of it. His father was standing there right on the edge of the bayou, looking down toward its mouth and the Gulf.

When William stood up he saw the skiff too: overturned, half awash, caught just inside the bayou. He jammed hands in his pockets and looked around. The squalls of the past night had not changed the appearance of the marsh; but then the grasses never changed from summer to winter. Even after a hurricane had whipped through them they rose fresh and untouched.

"I plain don't see nobody," he told his father.

The old man swung his head slowly back and forth as if he were looking for somebody.

"Look," William said, "iffen you don't want that boat, I sure enough do."

The old man kept his skiff pulled up alongside the house. William shoved it down into the water. Then quickly he got the oars, which were leaning against the wall; and when he turned he found that his father was sitting in the boat waiting.

"That all right with me," William said. "You just plain remember that my boat."

"Who done seen it?" his father said. "I plain ask you."

"That don't matter." William picked up the oars and fitted them into the locks. "I the one to get it in, and it mine."

"I plain ask you: who done seen it first?"

"Jesus," William said. "I plain telling you: that mine."

His father did not answer. He did not seem to hear.

"I plain telling you," William said. "I done spoke out first."

He began to row down to the overturned skiff. The water was rough and occasionally he felt a wet slap in his face — cool for all the warmth of the day. As he rowed he stared up at the sky, which was low and hazy, and thought about the things he could do with a boat of his own. After a coat of paint nobody would recognize it.

"Look," his father said. "They got a net out."

He lifted his oars and rested them and turned his head. Strands of net were caught across the skiff and a few feet out were five colored cork floats.

"That net ain't gonna be worth nothing," his father said.

"Jesus," William told him, "I ain't wanting that net. I plain wanting the boat."

His father stared at him. His old face was lined with determination. "Who seen it first?"

"I ain't arguing," William said. "I telling you. That mine."

They came alongside the skiff. Their own prow nosed into the reeds. The old man reached out and touched the other hull, tapping it softly with his fingers. Using one of the oars for a pole, William pushed against it.

"Jesus," he said. "She's fast. She caught up fast."

"She ain't gonna come loose that way," his father said.

"I know that, man." William felt his ears get hot with anger. "I plain know that."

"There ain't no way but get out and push her off."

William stood up and walked down to the prow of the skiff. With the oar he tested the depth of the water. "Jesus," he said when he lifted the oar, "that near waist deep."

He took the pack of cigarettes out of his shirt pocket and put it carefully in a dry place under the seat. Then he swung himself over the side. "I only doing this," he told his father, "account of it my boat. I gonna get it and it mine."

His father did not answer.

"I don't want no trouble with you," William said.

His father did not appear to hear.

William looked at him and knew that he would have trouble and did not care.

The water came to his waist, and it was cold. He felt his clothes hamper his movements and he wished he could have taken them off. But there might be jellyfish about, and even though he knew that their red stinging marks were harmless he was afraid of them.

And because he was afraid and did not want to be, he splashed noisily and quickly around to the other skiff. The bayou floor was a tangled mass of seaweed; he stumbled and his face touched the water. He spluttered and wiped the green weed taste away with the back of his hand. He saw that the stern of the boat was caught on a mound of sand; he climbed up beside it, pushing down the reeds. The water scarcely came to his ankles here.

He stopped and looked at his father, who was sitting without moving and watching him.

"I the one who pushed this loose," William said, "you remember."

The old man blinked his eyes slowly.

William said: "You ain't strong enough to push this off."

The eyes kept blinking at him.

"I got this, so it mine. Man's got a right to what he can get."

His father still did not answer. William felt his ears sing with anger. He bent and hooked his fingers under the stern handles, lifting and pushing. The muscles across his shoulders and back tensed against his shirt. He heard the wet cloth tear as the boat floated free.

They towed the skiff back up the bayou. "There's net all over her," the old man said.

"She pulls heavy," William said.

On the shore William sat down and began to take off his shoes. He shook them and stood them carefully aside to dry out. His father could pull up the skiff, he thought.

He noticed something strange. For a minute he wasn't sure what it was. Then he realized: the quiet. Before, up to a minute before, there had been the sounds of his father moving about the skiff. Then suddenly everything stopped. He lifted his head abruptly and saw his father standing there, his back to him, and looking down at the skiff. And William sat where he was, wiping his face slowly with one hand, and stared at the skiff they had found.

It was right side up now. And he saw that there were more nets tangled around it than he had thought. And through their black crisscross he saw a yellow dress and white skin.

He got to his feet slowly and walked over and stood beside his father and looked down at the snarl of black net — and the girl tangled in it, caught in it, lying there, face down on the shells, one arm pulled up, twisted and broken over her head.

"Sweet Jesus," William said. His heart was beating so fast he could hardly talk. "Sweet Jesus Christ."

"She caught up under the seats," his father said.

"She been to a party," William said very slowly. She was wearing an evening dress, bright yellow, with a full skirt that the water had shredded and wrapped around her legs.

William looked down at her and rubbed his chin and fought down the sickness in his throat. "Maybe she done took too much to drink and went out fishing for a joke."

"That might could be," his father said.

She had red hair, short red hair, bright in the sun. The yellow dress had fallen to her waist, and her back and shoulders shone white and slender. He had never seen such white skin.

There was a quivering in his stomach, but he said calmly, the way a man should: "I done reckon she went out cause she got a little too much, and the storm caught her up and killed her."

"That might could be," his father said.

There was one thing a man had to do. William pulled his heavy knife from his pocket and went to work cutting through the nets, slowly. The tips of his fingers rubbed against the yellow taffeta underskirt. He stared at the white curve of her back and saw that the skin was not so perfect. It had been torn in some places, but the water had washed all the blood away.

He cut through the last of the nets and folded up the knife and put it away

and sat back on his heels and tried to get courage to turn her over. He had seen
the face of the drowned before.

His father's black old hand took her shoulder and turned her. She was not
quite stiff yet; he let her fall on her back. William jerked his head aside and
closed his eyes so that he should not see. He got to his feet, stumbling, and
walked away.

He heard his father say: "Ain't you a man grown?" But he kept walking until
he got to the house and sat down on the steps.

"A man's got a call not to look at some things," he said aloud. His breath was
coming short and quick. When he'd been little and breathed like that, he'd
been crying. But he was not crying now.

A man didn't have to look at some things just to prove he was a man. "A
man's got no call like that," he said aloud.

He could imagine what her body would look like. The picture had flashed
in his mind when he saw his father turn her over, even though he shut his eyes
so that he would not see. The picture came into his mind and stayed there —
her body shining white and perfect, shining wet and dead.

He felt dizzy suddenly. His head kept going in wide swinging circles,
circles that left streaks of color behind them. He reached down both hands
and held tightly to the steps. But that did not help any. He lifted both hands
and took hold of his head. He held the outside of his head steady, but the
inside behind his eyes kept turning.

He was almost afraid . . . he did not know what was happening to him.
Then his head was all right. He opened his eyes. And lifted his head and even
looked over at the shore where his father had stood. He saw that the girl's boat
was still there, but his father's boat was gone. He stood up and saw his father
out at the bayou's mouth. He saw the yellow of the dress too, and then his
father changed the course of the boat and began to row southward, paralleling
the shoreline. William sat down again and listened. And although he knew
better, he felt that if he listened hard enough he could hear the splash when his
father found a spot that was far enough away and pushed the girl's body over.

"A man's got no call to do some things," he said aloud. "Iffen he don't want
to." He straightened up, folded his arms and felt the muscles of his back
stiffen. A man had muscles like that.

He sat and stared at the ground that was bare of grass and that last night's
rain had crisscrossed with thin little lines. He sat and thought about the things
a man could do. And gradually he lifted his eyes until he was staring across the
uncertain ground, the marsh, and the straight grasses that moved in the
slightest wind.

Finally he heard his father come back. When he turned around, the old man had his skiff up on the bank and was standing looking at the other one. He held his chin in one wrinkled black hand as he studied the boat.

William got up slowly and walked over to him. "It done take you a long while."

"I done went quite a ways." The hand kept rubbing the chin, the thin black chin with the irregular tufts of white whiskers.

William felt in his shirt pocket for the cigarettes, remembered where they were, and walked over to the boat to look for them.

He had put the pack under the bow seat. He remembered very distinctly. He remembered the smooth slick feel of the cellophane on his fingers when he put it there.

"I plain see what happened," he said to the bottom of the skiff. "I plain see what happened." He straightened up and turned to his father. And held out his hand.

The old man did not move.

William hunched his shoulders slightly. "I ain't no kid," he said, "to get things taken from me. I a man grown that can take what his."

Slowly the old man took the pack of cigarettes out of his trouser pocket and handed it to his son. Slowly William lit one.

The old man put a foot up on the gunwale of the second skiff. "I got me a mighty pretty skiff here."

William looked at him from under his brows. "I wouldn't have a dead skiff for no amount of money."

The old man reached down and scratched his ankle. "Yes, sir, a real pretty skiff."

"Listen," William said. Always when he was angry his ears began to hurt and burn. "Iffen I wanted that boat there . . ."

"Yes, sir," the old man said, and rubbed his foot up and down the gunwale. "A sweet boat. This here is plain my lucky day."

"I a man can take what he wants," William said. "And I plain wouldn't have nothing to do with that there boat."

The old man reached down and pulled off a strip of grass that had caught inside the boat. "Got myself a new boat."

"You damn keep it," William said. Holding the cigarette between his lips, he began to walk away. "I ain't arguing with you."

From behind him the old man spoke. "And you supposed to be a man grown."

"A man don't have to do every single thing. Some things he don't do."

He went to his mother's house. He was very angry. And he was hungry. The door of the icebox stuck. He jerked at it so savagely that it crashed open against the wall. He heard his mother come and stand in the doorway behind him.

"I looking for something to eat," he said, and glanced at her over his shoulder. She had just got up; she still wore a red flower-printed housecoat.

"There ain't nothing there. Stan come in and I fix him a real supper last night." Stan was her husband, a railroad waiter with a lean, hungry black face, who always drew long runs and was very seldom in town.

William slammed shut the door. "I reckon I better go find something."

"You been fishing?" his mother asked. She was staring at his trousers, which were still wet at the seams.

"I been to see the old man." He began to walk toward the door.

She caught his arm, stopping him. "He ain't give you no breakfast?"

"I ain't one to ask," he said.

She hooked both thumbs in the belt of her housecoat and spread her palms downward against her hips. "With all that money he got —"

Stan called sleepily: "That William you talking to, honey?"

"Nobody else," she said. "Don't you go getting jealous." She turned back to her son, but all she saw was the screen door closing behind him.

She called after him: "Why ain't you got him to give you something?"

"I ain't wanted nothing from him," he said.

William did not see his father again for nearly four months. At night sometimes the old black face, its cheeks and jaw studded with tufts of white hair, floated through his dreams. During the day he did not think of him. He had his job on the oyster boats (it was a good season and a heavy one) and he had his girl, whose name was Cynthia Lee.

One Friday evening in November he stood drinking his beer in Jack's Café with some of the other fellows from his boat. Cynthia Lee came up to him and pulled at his arm. Her mouth was open, but this time not smiling. She told him that Matthew Pettis and another policeman were asking for him at his mother's.

He put the glass down on the bar and turned it around and around slowly. He could guess what had happened. Something had gone wrong in the deal he had with Clarence Anderson and Mickey Lane. He thought briefly of the newspaper-wrapped package hidden in his room and the brown dry weeds inside. He wondered if the police had found that. They did not know where he lived; he was supposed to stay with his mother. But there were always people who would tell them.

Maybe he could get to the package before they did. . . . He wondered how much the police knew; maybe they had the package already. They would find it soon if he didn't get back to it. But maybe they were waiting for him there. . . . Maybe . . .

Cynthia jiggled his arm. "What you aiming to do? What you studying to do?"

"I getting out," he said.

She called after him as he left — "William!" — but he did not bother to answer. He did not have time.

He turned away from the houses and the lights in the windows and, running, twisted and turned down back alleys until he found himself in the open country. He stopped for a moment and caught his breath and listened. There were nothing but pines, thin straggling pines growing in the sandy ground; there wasn't even a wind to rustle their needles. But he saw Matthew Pettis's quick black face behind every tree and every hackberry bush. A quivering began deep down in his stomach. "A man got no call to be afraid," he said.

He left the pine ridge and made his way through the swampy grounds. He was tired from a day's work on the oyster boat, but he made himself move at a trot. The close damp night odor was beginning to come up from all around him.

He did not know exactly where he was going until he saw the square boards of his father's house right in front of him over the reeds. Then he stopped and thought for a minute. "There's things a man can ask for," he said. And he knew he would ask the old man for money, for enough money to get him to the city, to New Orleans.

He walked closer. The sun was down, but the light was still good enough for him to see the second boat, the girl's boat, pulled up high against the north side of the house. The old man had painted it dark green, but William still recognized it, and from four months past the memory of the girl flashed into his mind. He shook his head to be rid of it. Death frightened him.

As he had done before, he ate with the old man — fish and canned beans. And because it was near to the time the pension check came (on the third of every month), William began to wonder if the old man would have any money at all.

William sat very still, thinking, rubbing his underlip with his tongue and wondering how he should ask. Finally he said: "I done got myself in trouble."

The old man dunked the two plates up and down in a bucket of water and wiped them on the sleeve of his shirt. "That right?"

"You might could sound more interested," William said. "You might could."

"Ain't no interest to me," his father said. His thick nubby black fingers reached for the package of cigarettes on the shelf beside the door, the shelf that was nothing but a board resting on two wood blocks fastened to the wall with tenpenny nails.

"I gonna need some money."

The old man lit his cigarette slowly and did not answer.

"I gonna need just enough money to get me to New Orleans."

The old man tipped his chair back against the wall and smoked slowly.

"I shoulda been paid tomorrow. So I ain't got any money."

"I ain't got none either."

"Sure you got it," William said. "Everybody know you got it."

"Everybody but me," the old man said.

"I got to get to New Orleans," William said, and rubbed his fingers up and down the edge of the table, bending them and pressing on them hard as he could.

"You can walk."

"It eighty-odd miles," William said.

The ashes from the old man's cigarette dropped to the floor.

"A man's got a right to ask some things," William said.

The old man did not answer.

"Iffen I stay around here the police catch me sure."

"That right?" his father said, and closed wrinkled lids over his eyes.

William got up and stood in the door, looking across the grasses. All he could see was Pettis's thin face under the blue cap. He closed his eyes and shook his head, but the image followed him. His jaw began to tremble and he held it with his hand.

"And you supposed to be a man," his father said softly; his lips scarcely moved. "You supposed to be a man and you afraid. You plain afraid."

William spun around. The rubber soles of his tennis shoes squeaked on the boards. "I ain't afraid." He felt quick tears spurt down his cheeks. "I got a right to ask."

His father laughed, soundlessly as old people always do, and doubled up on his chair. His father opened his mouth and laughed at him. "And you a man . . ."

The tears filmed his eyes and wet his mouth as he stumbled across the room. His hip struck something that must have been the edge of the table; his head was filled with the echo of his own sobbing as he went stumbling toward his father. "A man got a right to some things."

He felt his arm go up, but it was not his arm moving. He could not see when

his fist came down, but he felt something crumble. "A man got a right . . ."
He stood there crying until the tears were all used up.

His father was dead. He had gone down like an old wall that has been dry
and toppling for years, waiting for someone to push it over. He had fallen from
his chair and lay on his side, one arm stretched out gently.

William shook his head slowly, back and forth. Unbelieving. He had forgot
that old bones were brittle from wear. He had forgot that the bigness of a man
meant nothing against age, that old men die easily.

William held up his hand and looked at it. There was no blood on it. He
looked down at his father. In the dusk he could see no marks on the black old
face. The boy rubbed his knuckles slowly with the fingers of his left hand. He
had not meant to: the old man had died so easily.

After a while William lifted his head and listened, sniffling back the last of
the tears. He walked over to the window, pushed open the shutter a bit, and
looked out. The night was going to be foggy. You could see it beginning
already in the reeds at the edge of the bayou, white fog lying along the ground
like a strip of bandage. It would be thick, come night — even thicker when the
smoke came down from the cypress stumps they were burning to the north.

He stood looking out the window, squinting his eyes, thinking. He wondered where he should go. There was his mother's; he would trust her. But the
police would be sure to watch there. There was Cynthia Lee and the house in
Bucktown. But they would have found out about that by now. He had friends,
but he did not want to trust them. Not now.

William looked down at the old man lying on the boards of the floor with
the chair fallen over him and he shook his head. He had not meant to kill him.
He lifted his arm and held it in the same position. He felt the muscles in his
shoulder and along the arm. They had killed the old man. He had not done it.
Not with his mind. He had lifted his arm, and his muscles and his strength and
his youth had done it. He swung his arm outward, repeating the blow. Then
he rubbed his head and turned from his father to the window and the stretch of
bayou and Gulf and the fog that was coming up slowly.

He would have to sleep out. There were plenty of places of high ground
near the road. Most nights he would not have minded that. But tonight with
the fog, the fog that was mixed with cypress smoke, with sweet fleshy cypress
smoke . . .

There was no help for it. He pulled closed the shutter and turned back to the
room. Like a man should, he straightened his shoulders and looked down at
his father. Already it was so dark that he could not see the face at all, only the
vague outline of the body. It might have been anyone lying there. It might have

been — but he knew it wasn't. He knew that it was his father lying dead with the side of his skull crushed in. Maybe even the mark of a fist along the side of his head.

There was no help for that either. He had not intended to, but he had done it, and now there was no use standing shivering like a baby. A man did what he did and didn't study about it afterwards.

If he were to sleep out, William knew that he would need a blanket. The fog would be cold and the night was going to be long. He stepped over his father and reached for the blanket on the bed. It was tucked in tightly, and when he jerked at it the light mattress came loose. Something hit the floor with the quick sound of metal and rolled toward him and struck his foot. He jumped, then bent down and felt around on the dark floor with his fingers to see what it was that had come jumping out toward him, as if it had been meant for him. His fingers touched and recognized it and lifted it up: a silver dollar.

Then William remembered what he had come for. And what he had nearly forgotten. He reached into his pocket for a lighter. The first two tries the flint did not spark. He shook it, saying softly: "Damn!" Then he was holding a small yellow flame in his hand. He checked the coin in his fingers: a dollar. And he bent down over the bed to see what else was hidden under the mattress.

The light caught the sheen of the round silver pieces lined up on one of the slats of the bed. He held the light down and counted them slowly, using his finger as a pointer. There were six of them, and the one he held in his hand made seven.

One by one he picked them up and dropped them in his pocket. That was all: seven of them.

There was a kerosene lamp by the window. He lit it and searched carefully around the bed. And found nothing. He began to get angry. He jerked the bed from the wall and looked behind it. He yanked open the drawers of the chest and went through them, tossing the stuff on the bed. He felt behind the window frame and found nothing. His anger increased, anger at the old man lying on the floor, the old man who kept only seven silver dollars.

William went out to the lean-to kitchen. There was only a single rough shelf holding four cans; he knocked them to the floor. There was a pot on the stove; he knocked that over too. He noticed a loose floor board. Using the handle of the pot, he pried it open; there was only ground underneath. He put his hand through the opening and pulled up a handful of dry musty earth. He threw it against the wall with disgust.

"God damn, God damn, God damn," he whispered softly to himself. He looked out, this time on the side away from the bayou. Fog was thicker there over the marsh, making the grasses silvery, translucent almost, floating. It was like the fog sucked away all color.

Fog was always sucking away, William thought. When you walked through it you could feel it sucking at your skin, sucking away at your skin, trying to wither you up. When he slept he could cover himself all up with the blanket, head and all, so that it could not reach him.

There were two other loose floor boards. He pried them up and found only ground under them. He broke the boards across his knee and tossed them into a corner.

He went through his father's pockets carefully: three nickels and two pennies and a smooth brown rabbit's foot on a key chain with a single heavy key. William held the key up to the lamp and turned it slowly in the light. Then he looped the chain around his fingers, snapped it, and let the key roll to the floor. The rabbit's foot he put in his pocket with the nickels.

He picked up the chair that had been knocked over and put it against the wall and sat down. He sat and thought what he should do and where he should go. He began to wish he could stay right where he was; but already he thought he could begin to smell the dead. There was always a smell; the girl had had it too, young as she was and as washed clean with salt water.

He would have to go. He stood up, held the chair by the back, and smashed it to pieces against the wall. The wood splintered and cut his hand. He sucked at the palm until there was no longer any blood taste.

If he could only stay where he was — he would be safe. He glanced out at the fog that was thickening by the moment. The road from town would be almost blocked up by now; a police car couldn't get through.

He could stay where he was and be safe . . . but he couldn't stay. He looked down at his father. The lamp wasn't bright enough to show his face. It might have been anybody lying there. Anybody who was dead.

William leaned against the wall and rubbed his head slowly with both hands. Then he picked up the quilt and folded it around his shoulders to keep the fog away from him. And he opened the door.

The fog was very heavy now, but low: a white strip that covered the grass and the ground and cut the trees in half. William hunched the quilt high over his head.

A man did what he had to do. . . .

Sometimes he did not intend to, but things came to him and he did them.

He did not mean to kill the old man. He looked back into the room. The lamp was running out of oil; the wick was burning with a sputtering blue flame. The light did not reach down to the floor. There mightn't have been anyone lying there at all.

William stared at the dark floor and tried to remember how the old man had looked. And could not.

The police would remember; Matthew Pettis would remember. William saw the smooth black face under the peaked visor of the blue cap, the short slim body, the nervous fingers, and the quick black eyes, shiny as oil in the sunlight. Pettis would remember, and he would follow him; it would be his job to follow him.

William pulled closed the door behind him and hugged the quilt tighter around his body. He would find a place to sleep tonight near the highway. In the morning he would flag down the first bus; there would be enough money for the fare. And even Pettis would have a hard time finding him in a city as big as New Orleans.

He turned around slowly. In another hour the fog would be too heavy to walk in, even. He would have to be near the road before it got that thick, so thick that he could not move. He fingered the quilt: a good heavy one. He would need it, sitting by the road waiting for the sun to come with morning. It was a big quilt too, wide and long; he would wrap himself up in it so that the fog could not reach him, the sucking fog that was heavy with the sweet smoke of cypress.

He leaned back against the wall for a minute, shivered, and was afraid, the way a boy is afraid playing a game in the dark. Then he remembered and stood up straight and walked off as quickly as he could with the quilt hunched around his shoulders: the things a man has done he must abide with.

One Summer

You forget most things, don't you? It's even hard to remember in the hurry and bustle of spring what the slow unwinding of fall was like. And summer vacations all blur one into the other when you try to look back at them. At least, it's that way for me: a year is a long time.

But there's one summer I remember, clear as anything; the day, a Thursday in August.

It had been a terrific summer, the way it always is here. There was dust an inch thick on everything. The streams were mostly all dry. Down in the flaky red dust of the beds — where the flood in spring was so fast you couldn't cross it and where now there was just a foot or two of slimy smelling water — you could find the skeletons of fishes so brittle that they crumbled when your foot touched them. The wells were always dug extra deep just for summers like this: there's always water if you go down deep enough for it. There was plenty of water for drinking and washing and even maybe enough to keep the gardens watered, but nobody did; most of the plants withered and crumbled away. By August, cracks were beginning to show in the ground, too, crisscross lines maybe half an inch wide showing under the brown dead grass.

So that when this big pile of thunderheads came lifting out of the south everybody watched them, wondering and hoping.

I was sitting on Eunice Herbert's porch, over in the coolest part, behind the wooden jalousies. There was a swing there, and an electric fan on a little black iron table, and two or three black iron stands of ferns, all different kinds — her

mother was crazy about them. Maybe it wasn't cooler there, but with the
darkness from the closed jalousies and the smell of wet mud from the fern
pots, it seemed comfortable.

Eunice was the prettiest girl in town, there wasn't any doubt of that. She
had hair so blond that it looked almost silver white. All summer long she kept
it piled up on top of her head with a flower stuck right on top; she got the idea
from the cover of *Seventeen*, she said. Whenever she was at a party, there was
nearly always a fight between some boys. It was just sure to happen, that's all;
I was in enough to know. I almost had got thrown out of school because of one
of them: at the spring party in the gym of the big yellow-brick high school. I
don't remember how it started. I was just dancing with some girl when over at
the table where Eunice was sitting two fellows started to fight. I remember
dropping the girl's arm and walking over. Not wanting to fight, not really, but
somehow I did; and somehow I got a Coke bottle in my hand and started
swinging. It was the bottle that nearly got me expelled. My father had to do an
awful lot of talking so I could go on and finish the year with the rest of my
class.

One thing though — it set things up fine between Eunice and me. In those
two months she hadn't had a date with another fellow.

That hot Thursday afternoon in August we were sitting on her porch swing,
holding hands under the wide skirt of her dress, which she had spread out so
that her mother wouldn't see anything but two people sitting and talking. Her
mother was inside, doing something, I never found out what, but every ten
minutes or so she'd stick her head out the door and ask: "You children want
something?" And Eunice would say: "Oh, Mamma, no," with her voice
going up a little on the last word.

We were just sitting there swinging back and forth, staring at the green little
leaves of the ferns. I was feeling her soft thin fingers. There was a kind of
shivering going up and down my back that wasn't just the electric fan blowing
on my wet shirt.

Then her mother stuck her head out the front door to the porch for maybe
the fifteenth time that afternoon — she was a little woman with a tiny face that
reminded me of a squirrel somehow, with a nervous twitching nose. "Children," she said (and I could feel Eunice's fingers stiffen at the word), "just you
look out there —" she pointed to the south; "here's a big pile of rain clouds,
coming right this way."

"Yes, ma'am," I said. We'd noticed the clouds come up half an hour past.

And then because she kept staring at us we had to get up and walk over and
peer out though the little open squares in the jalousies and look at the sky.

"It looks like rain," I said, because somebody had to say something.

Without turning around I heard Mrs. Herbert take a seat in one of the wicker chairs. I heard the cane creak and then the rockers begin to move softly back and forth on the wood flooring. Alongside me I could feel Eunice stiffen like a cat that's been hit by something. But there wasn't anything she could do: her mother was going to sit and talk to us for the rest of the afternoon. I might just as well go sit in one of the single chairs.

The afternoon was so quiet that from my house — just across the street and one house down — you could hear our cook, Mayline, singing at the top of her voice:

> *"Didn't it rain, little children,*
> *Didn't it rain, little children,*
> *Didn't it rain?"*

So she'd noticed that big mass of clouds too.

"Is that Mayline I hear?" Mrs. Herbert said. The words came out slowly, one for each creak of her rocker.

"Yes, ma'am," I said and sat down in the red-painted straight chair.

Eunice dropped down in the middle of the swing and folded her hands on her lap and didn't say anything.

"Well," her mother said with just an edge of annoyance, "if you children are doing anything you don't want me to see . . ."

"Oh, Mamma," Eunice said, staring down at her hands.

"Yes, ma'am," I said, and then changed it to "No, ma'am," and all the while I was thinking of a way to get us out of there.

From the corner of my eye I saw that Eunice's mother was getting that hurt bewildered look all mothers use.

And then — just at that right minute — we heard Morris Henry come running down the street. He was a poppy-eyed little black monkey Negro, no taller than a twelve-year-old, but strong as a man and twice as quick. He had little hands, like a child's or a girl's maybe, with nails that he always chewed down to the quick. Even when there wasn't anything more to bite on, he'd keep chewing away at the fingers with his wide flaring yellow teeth.

He came running down the road — you could hear the sound of his bare feet on the dirt road quite a ways in front of him. He took a short cut through the empty lot at the corner and came bursting through the high dry grass that went up like a puff of smoke all around him.

With the dust in his nose he started sneezing, but he didn't stop. He tore down the middle of our street at top speed, both hands holding to his trousers so they wouldn't fall off. He took our fence with a one-hand jump, made a straight line through the yard to the kitchen door, and was up the steps two at a time. The door slammed after him.

It was quiet then with him inside my house. All you could see was the path he'd broken for himself through the dry stalks of the zinnias in the front yard.

"My goodness," Mrs. Herbert said. "Hadn't you better go see what's wrong?"

"Yes, ma'am," I said.

"I'll come with you," Eunice said quickly.

We yanked open the screen door and we were all the way down the steps and halfway to the front gate before we heard it slam, we were running that fast.

"The front way," I said. And we rushed up the front steps and in the front door.

We had to stop for a minute: the parlor was always kept with the blinds drawn, and coming out of the sun we couldn't see a thing. I could hear Eunice breathing heavily alongside me. She was so close it was the easiest thing in the world to put my arm around her. I kissed her hard, and for as long as I dared with people so close — the voices in the kitchen sounded excited.

"You hurt," she said.

And I just grinned at her; it was the sort of hurt she liked.

And then we went into the kitchen to see what had happened.

Little Morris Henry was sitting in a red-painted kitchen chair and my mother was holding his thin little shoulder, that was all bulged and lumpy with muscle. Over in a corner Mayline stood with her mouth open and a streak of flour on her black face.

Next to my shoulder I could hear Eunice let her breath out with a quick hissing whisper. No one seemed to have noticed that we had come in. Mayline was looking over in our direction and her eyes rested right on us, but there wasn't any recognition in them. They were just empty brown eyes; only they weren't brown any more, but bright live metal. They were eyes like flat pieces of silver.

Because we didn't know what to do, we stood very still and waited.

In a minute my mother looked around. She seemed to feel that we were there; she couldn't have seen us, we were behind her. But she looked over. Keeping her hand on Morris Henry's shoulder she twisted her head around and looked at us.

"He says there's something wrong with the old gentleman. . . ." Her voice wandered off. She had spoken in such a whisper and the words had slipped so gradually that you couldn't quite tell when she stopped. I wondered if I had really heard anything at all.

She seemed to realize this, because she repeated louder this time, in a way that you couldn't mistake: "He says there's something wrong with the old gentleman."

That would be my grandfather. Everybody called him that. They never did use his name. When they were talking about him it was "the old gentleman" and to his face they always said "sir."

"The old gentleman's gone fishing on the Scanos River," they'd say. And that would mean he'd taken his little power boat out in the middle of the muddy red yellow river and stopped the motor and thrown over his line and was sitting there waiting for the fish to bite; and they always did; he was a fine fisherman.

Or maybe Luce Rogers, who was Mayline's husband — of a sort and not a legal sort — would stick his head in the kitchen door and wipe his shiny face with his broad hand and look at Mayline and shake his head and say sadly: "Baby, I can't sit with you this morning. I got to go to work." And Mayline would look at him from under her lids, not quite believing him because he didn't like to work and he sure had a wandering eye. So she would suck in one corner of her mouth and hold it between her teeth and stare at him, nodding her head just a little. And he would open his eyes very wide and shake his head and say: "You ain't got no cause to suspicion me, baby. I was just plain walking past the place when the old gentleman yells at me from the porch."

And Mayline would relax for a little while anyhow, because that would mean that my grandfather had found some work for him to do, like mowing the grass maybe or washing the windows, or doing some other work that the regular girl, whose name was Wilda Olive, couldn't do. It was just about the only time Luce Rogers worked — when my grandfather caught him.

That Thursday afternoon in the kitchen, it was Eunice who moved first. She slipped around me — she was standing almost half behind me in the doorway — and went up to my mother and put her arms around her.

"You better sit down, Mrs. Addams," she said. She had the chair all pulled out from the table and ready. "You look a little pale."

That wasn't true; my mother looked perfectly all right. But that was Eunice's way — she'd used that line in the high-school play a couple of months before and she didn't see any reason not to use it again. Or maybe it was because she didn't really know what to say either.

Anyhow, my mother did sit down. And she leaned one arm against the table and beat a little tattoo on it with her fingers.

The minute she sat down, Morris Henry bounced up and went over and stood by the window, chewing his little knuckles. Eunice stood next to my mother and looked over at me. And I looked down at the ground.

My mother began tapping the heel of her shoe against the floor. That was a sure sign she was thinking. Finally she said to me: "MacDonald —"

"Yes, ma'am," I said.

She was the only one who ever used my full name like that. To most people I was just Mac. But she liked that full name, maybe because it had belonged to her family. Or maybe she just liked the sound of it.

"Go see if there's a car in the neighborhood we can borrow. . . . Go outside and look.

"Eunice," she was giving orders now, "put in a call for Dr. Addams. . . . I've got to put on a regular dress." She only wore a kind of smock-like affair around the house, because of the heat.

I went out in the yard and looked up and down the block. There wasn't a single car in any driveway. It wasn't surprising, because most people either took the car down to the business section with them if they were going to work, or if they left them at home their wives took them to the market or the movies. I had known that I wasn't going to find anything when I went out.

I went back up the stairs into the hall. Eunice had finished calling and had put the phone back on the little black wood table that teetered if you touched it too hard. She was leaning against the wall, at an angle with it, and her legs were crossed. The way she had hunched her shoulders her peasant blouse was slipping way down on one side.

Eunice waved at me to come back. She had just called my father's office. He wasn't there. Nobody had expected that he would be. He was out making his calls. He had a big practice — he was probably the most popular doctor in the county or maybe even in this part of the state — and there was no telling exactly where he was.

Eunice put down the phone for a minute. "Isn't it just dreadful, Mac?" she said in a whisper; "about your grandfather, I mean."

"Yeah," I said. I was looking at the smooth stretch of her shoulder.

She saw my gaze and pulled up the cloth.

"You the prettiest girl in this town," I said, "bar none." I had told her that before, and she always answered the same way.

She gave a little giggle and said: "Men . . ."

My mother came out into the hall. She just looked at us and walked over and took the phone off the hook. There was somebody on the party line. She broke through that in a minute and had the operator. "Can you find Dr. Addams?" she said. "Tell him it's his father."

That was the way you located either of the two doctors in this town, if you needed them fast. You just called up Shirley Williams, who was the operator, and told her. And sooner or later my father would make a call and she'd recognize his voice and give him the message. It worked fast that way; much faster than you'd think. I was sure that in about half an hour my father would know about it wherever he was.

She hung up the phone and looked at us. "This is just no time for you to behave like children. . . . MacDonald, is there a car we can borrow?"

"No, ma'am," I said.

"I'll just have to walk then." She took a sunshade out of the closet and slammed the door. She was halfway down the walk before she turned to look at me.

"I reckon you better come along," she said slowly. "I might need you to take a message."

My grandfather wouldn't ever have a telephone in his house. There was always somebody passing by soon enough to take a message for him, he said.

She pointed me back into the house. "Go get a hat," she said. "It's killing out here."

On the way out I said to Eunice: "I'll see you tonight."

It was an agreement we had. During the last two months, almost every night I'd slip out of my room and throw one small piece of gravel against her window screen. And then when she looked out I'd blink my flashlight real quick, just once. And she would slip down. . . . If her folks ever found out, there'd really be a row. Though they didn't have to worry. Eunice wasn't that sort of girl. We'd just stand out in the dark, not even talking, so no one would notice us. Until the mosquitoes got too bad; and then I'd kiss her good-night.

"I'll see you tonight," I told her as I grabbed my hat and rushed out after my mother.

The sun was so hot you could feel it tingling your skin right through the clothes. It was so hot you didn't sweat any more. My mother went right on walking very fast, so that we covered the five blocks to my grandfather's house in maybe two minutes. And all the while I had my eyes on the big pile of thunderheads, the ones that had just come up and were hanging there in the sky promising rain. The people we passed, sitting on their shaded porches, who nodded or waved to us, were watching them too and they called out to ask us if we had seen them.

My mother answered them, hardly politely sometimes, we were walking so fast.

As it turned out we needn't have been in such a hurry after all.

My grandfather had died that hot afternoon in August, while everybody for miles around was watching the big pile of thunderheads. And nobody was paying much attention to an old man.

He had tumbled out of his chair in the living-room and died there on the floor with his mouth full of summer dust from the green flowered carpet. Wilda Olive, the colored woman who kept house for him, found him there about an hour later. She'd been puttering around in the back yard, making like she was sweeping off the walk, but really, just like everybody else, keeping an eye on those clouds.

She came in to tell him about the rain that might be coming and found him where he'd done a jackknife dive into the carpet. For a while she just stood looking at him, with his seersucker coat rumpled up in back and his bald head buried under his arm, bald head that was getting just a little dusty on the floor. She took a couple of steps backwards (she didn't even go near or touch him) and she lifted up her apron and put it over her head and began to cry. It was one of those long aprons that wrap all around and it was big enough to cover up her head. She just stood there, bent over in the dark from the heavy linen folds, and wailing. Not high, not the way a white woman would cry, but a kind of flat low tone that you could almost see curling its way up through the layers of heat in the day.

Morris Henry, who happened to be passing by in the street, had heard it and gone in to look. After one look his poppy eyes stuck out even more than usual; and he headed straight for our house, at a run. And my mother and I came rushing over in the full heat of the afternoon sun. . . .

Minute we stepped through the front gate we began to hear Wilda Olive's moaning. My mother nodded toward the pecan tree in the north corner of the yard. "You just sit down there and wait for me," she said.

Of course, I didn't do anything of the sort. I followed her right inside.

She pushed past Wilda Olive and bent over the old man and stretched out her hand but didn't quite touch him and pulled back her hand and straightened up and just stood there. Finally she reached over and pulled the apron from Wilda Olive's head. "Stop that," she said sharply.

Wilda Olive didn't seem to hear her. My mother held up her own hand, with fingers outspread, and looked at it carefully. Then slapped Wilda Olive hard as she could. That hushed her.

"We'll need some ice water," my mother told her. "It's perishing hot out, walking."

Wilda Olive went to the kitchen. And my mother came and stood out on the porch. "MacDonald," she said when she saw me, "I thought I told you to stay out in the yard under the tree."

She wasn't really paying any attention to me; I could tell that from her tone; so I didn't move. She took one of the cane rockers from where it was leaning backwards against the porch wall and turned it around and sat down, very slowly. Very slowly, with one hand she rubbed the left side of her face, the two skins rubbing together smoothly and squeaking just a little from the wet of the perspiration.

Wilda Olive brought the ice water and disappeared. "Let's hope she doesn't start that racket again," my mother said, and listened carefully. But everything was quiet. "We'll just wait for your father," she said.

I sat down on the edge of the porch, my feet stuck through the railing and hanging down. It was so hot it was hard to breathe.

There was a little bead of sweat collecting very slowly on my neck, right over the little hump of bone there. I hunched my shoulders so that the shirt would not touch and break it. I felt it getting bigger and bigger until it had enough force to cross the bone and begin to wiggle slowly down my back. It was all the way down to within an inch of my belt when my father came driving up.

My mother jumped up and went out to meet him. Her feet in their white sandals went by me very fast and I noticed for the first time how small they were and how brown and smooth the turn of her ankle. I'd never thought of my mother as having nice legs before. . . .

My mother stood against the side of the car, leaning in through the window, the sun full and hard on her white print dress. I saw the line of her thighs and her narrow hips. It was funny for me to be thinking of my mother that way now, with my grandfather lying all doubled up on the floor inside and dead. I saw something I'd never seen before: she had as good a figure as Eunice Herbert.

When my father went inside, she sat down, not saying anything to me, rocking herself slowly, her foot beating out the time. There was a fuzz of yellow hair all up her leg; I saw that out of the corner of my eye.

Then my father came out and sat on the arm of her chair. I looked up and saw how she sat there with her eyes tight closed. My father was writing out the death certificate, the way he had to; I recognized the form. I'd seen them lying around his office enough.

And I thought how he was writing his father's name: Cecil Percival Addams. I could see his hand printing out the name, slow and steady. He was writing out his father's name on a death certificate.

Just the way it would be for me someday. What he was doing now, I would be doing for him someday. I would sit where he was now; and there would be my wife alongside me, crying a little bit and trying not to show it. I would be a doctor, too, writing just the way he was now. And he would be lying dead inside.

And then we'd all move up one step again. And it would be my son who'd be looking down at me, lying still and dusty. I'd never thought of that before.

The trickle of sweat reached to my belt, broke, and spread, cold on my hot skin. I shivered. The thunderheads were still piled up in the south, shining gray-bright in the sun. They struck me as being very lonesome.

My father signed the paper and laid it out on the railing. "Jeff'll need that," he said quietly. Jeff was the undertaker, a little man, quick and nervous and bald, who wore black suits in the winter and white linen ones in the summer. His wife had run off with a railroad engineer and disappeared. He had a married daughter over to the north in Birmingham and he visited her twice a year.

My mother bent her head over in her lap with a quick sharp movement. My father slipped his arm around her.

"Honey," he said, "don't. Let's go home."

He lifted her up and they walked to the car. I could tell from the way he braced himself that he was almost carrying her. And even a small woman like my mother is a heavy load in one arm. I hadn't thought my father was that strong.

My mother slipped in the front seat and made room for me alongside her.

"No," my father said. "Let him stay here."

My mother shook her head doubtfully.

"Somebody's got to," my father said as he got behind the wheel. "He's almost a man. And there isn't going to be anything for him to do."

My mother didn't look convinced.

"Look," my father said shortly, "he's staying."

"There's a phone next door in the Raymond place," my mother said faintly, "MacDonald, if you want to call."

"Yes, ma'am," I said.

"Stay on the porch, son, if you want to," my father said. "Just see that Jeff gets the certificate. And keep an eye on Wilda Olive."

"Yes, sir," I said.

As they drove off, my mother rubbed her face deep down in my father's shoulder, the way a girl does sometimes on a date coming home.

And just for a second I could really feel Eunice's cheek rubbing against my shoulder and hear the soft sound it made on the cloth. And there was the tickle of her hair on my chin. And the far faint odor that wasn't really perfume — though that was part of it — but was the smell of her hair and her skin.

Then all of a sudden I didn't have that picture any more. I was back on my grandfather's porch, watching my father drive off with my mother. She had her face buried deep down in his shoulder. My father's arm went up and around to pull her closer to him. Then I couldn't see any more, the dust on the road was so thick.

I looked around. In the whole afternoon there wasn't a thing moving, except me. Except my breathing, up and down. And that seemed sort of out of place.

For a while I sat on the porch. Then I thought that maybe I ought to have a look at Wilda Olive. I didn't want to go through the house, so I walked all the way around it, outside, around to the kitchen door. "Wilda Olive." I thought I called loud but my voice softened in the heat until it was just ordinary speaking tone.

She was in the kitchen, scouring out the sink, quietly, like nothing had happened. She looked up and saw me. "Yes, sir," she said.

She'd never said "sir" to me before. The old man's death had changed that. I had moved up one step. I was in my father's place. It was funny how quick it all happened.

"Yes, sir," she said.

"You all right?" That sounded silly. But I'd said it, so I stuck my hands down deep in my pockets and lifted up my jaw and waited for her to answer.

"Yes, sir." She dropped her eyes. Ordinarily she would have gone back to her work and let me stand there to do what I wanted. But that had changed, too. Now she stood waiting for me. Not going on with her work because of me.

"You were cutting up pretty bad when we came," I told her.

"Yes, sir," she said. There wasn't the slightest bit of expression in her face now.

"Well," I said, "I'll be out front if you want me — on the porch, because it's too hot inside." That wasn't the reason. I didn't want to stay inside with the old man. But she mustn't know that. I wanted to go around, the way I'd come — through the garden — but I knew she was expecting me to go straight through the house. And so I did, walking fast as I could without seeming to hurry.

I had hardly got back out on the porch before I saw Eunice coming. She had a red ruffled parasol held high against the sun and she was carrying something wrapped in a checked kitchen towel in her other hand. I watched her open the gate and come up to the porch.

"I thought you'd be steaming hot," she said, "so I brought you over a Coke." She unwrapped the towel and there it was, the open bottle, still with ice all over the outside.

"Thanks," I said. I drank the Coke, but I couldn't think of anything else to say. Somehow she didn't belong here. Somehow I just didn't want her here.

She took the bottle from me when I had finished. "I got to get back," she said. "I promised Mamma to help with dinner."

"Thanks," I said again.

At the foot of the steps she turned. "I'm awful sorry."

The sun was shining on her just the way it had on my mother.

"It's okay," I said. "It's okay."

She was gone then. And there was only the Coke taste in my mouth to remind me that she had been there. And that was gone soon, and there was just the dust taste. And there wasn't a trace of her. I just couldn't believe that she had been there . . . it was funny, the way things were beginning not to seem real.

That evening they came, the little old people who had been my grandfather's friends . . . or maybe his enemies. Time sort of evened out all those things.

Jeff, the undertaker, had come and gone and the house was really and truly empty now; I found I could breathe better. (That was another strange thing: I had never feared my grandfather, living and moving; but dead, he made me afraid. . . .)

Matthew Conners was the first. I saw him way off down the road, coming slowly, picking his way carefully between the ruts, testing the deepest ones with his cane, lifting himself carefully over them.

The sun had gone down but the sky was still full of its light, hard and bright. The rain clouds hadn't moved.

Matthew came up the walk and stood at the foot of the steps. "He come back yet?"

"No, sir," I said. "Jeff'll have him along soon."

Matthew Conners nodded. His head bobbed quickly up and down on the sinewy cords of his neck. He'd been a handsome man once, they said; the bad boy of the southern counties. There was a picture of him in an album of my grandfather's; very tall, very thin, with hair carefully pompadoured in front. Even in the picture you could see how bright the stripes of his tie were. He'd never married. He'd gone on living in the two rooms behind his hardware store (which was on the busiest corner in town, next to the post office). Until one day he sold the business to a nephew. He kept the rooms, though, and lived there. He spent most of his days there, sitting on the doorstep, not saying much to people who were passing, just sitting there, as if he were waiting.

Matthew Conners climbed slowly up the porch steps and sat down on the chair where my mother had sat and put the cane down between his knees and crossed his hands on it and waited.

I saw those hands, blue spots and heavy-veined, crossed and folded together, and I thought how maybe at that very minute Jeff was pressing my grandfather's hands together. . . .

They came all evening, the old people. After Matthew Conners came Vance Bonfield and the short, very fat woman who was his wife, Dorothy, her double chins dripping with perspiration.

I said: "Good evening." They nodded but didn't answer.

And then Henry Carmichael, walking because he didn't live far at all. By this time the porch chairs were all filled — there were only three of them. I started to bring out another chair, but the old man just shook his bald shiny head in my direction and went in the house. Slowly and with great care he began bringing out a dining-room chair, his old hands trembling with its weight. He brought two chairs, out, stopped and counted them carefully with one finger. Then he took a handkerchief out of his coat pocket, wiped his face carefully, and with a tired sigh sat down with the others.

They didn't seem to talk to each other at all, beyond the first hello, just sat there waiting, with their hands folded.

So I sat down on the steps and waited, too. Only thing is, I was careful not to fold my hands. I put them out flat, one on each knee.

The long summer twilight had just about worn out when Jeff and his four Negro helpers brought my grandfather back, in a shining wood coffin this time, and put him in the living-room. I heard Wilda Olive begin to cry, softer this time; so I didn't bother to stop her. I don't think I could have anyway. The old men didn't seem to notice; they didn't turn their heads or say anything. They just sat staring out at the front lawn.

I moved out into the side yard and sat down under the locust tree. The dry ground had cracked up, pulling apart the tangled grass roots. In one of the cracks there was a lily bulb, shriveled and dry. I tried to think what kind it must have been, but I couldn't ever remember seeing a flower in that spot.

My father came back. He parked his car, came in the gate, and walked straight up to me. He held out his hand. I wasn't sure whether he wanted to shake mine or give me a pull to my feet. I reckon he did both.

"Go ahead home, son," he said, still holding my hand.

I found myself saying very softly and slow and sure, as if I wasn't in a bit of a hurry: "Don't you reckon you going to need me here?"

"That's all right," my father said.

"You be all right?"

"Sure," my father said, and turned away, walking toward the house. "You just hurry. Your mother's waiting supper on you."

I couldn't help feeling that my father wanted me to stay, that he wanted company somehow, but couldn't have it. So I left, walking as fast as I could.

When I caught sight of our house, even if it was so hot, I began to run.

My mother was sitting very quietly in the parlor waiting for me. She had a copy of the *Ladies' Home Journal* in her hands, but she wasn't reading it. She was just using it for something to hold on to. She was wearing the same light print dress she had on before, but now the fresh starchness was gone. The lace on the organdy collar wasn't standing out stiff any more and there were perspiration spots on the shoulders.

She didn't look up from the book when I came in. "Just wash your hands down here, MacDonald. Mayline won't mind if you use the kitchen sink this once."

"Yes'm," I said.

"And we'll eat dinner right away — and then get dressed."

"Yes'm," I said.

"We can keep fresher that way — for the evening." She hesitated over the last words. It was one thing about my mother; wakes always scared her a lot; she'd said so once.

"You hungry, MacDonald?" she asked finally, standing up and putting the magazine back on the table under the lamp.

"No'm," I said. "Not much, just sort of."

After supper my mother and I walked back over to the house. She was wearing a black chiffon dress; and the dye gave off a peculiar smell in the heat: not sour like perspiration, nor sweet like some flowers, nor bitter like Indian grass, but a mixture of all three. I had got dressed too, because I had to: a white suit and a tie, a black tie that had been part of my father's navy uniform. Under the coat I could feel the cotton of the shirt get wet and stick to my body.

Mrs. Herbert was out in the front yard cutting zinnias with a big shiny pair of scissors. She was the only woman I ever knew who kept her house filled with zinnias, and the strong woody odor of them was in all the rooms. Standing there in the half dark she looked like one of those flowers, with her thin body and her frizzy ragged-looking red-brown hair. (Eunice said her mother never had her hair just cut, but singed; she thought it was good for it.)

Eunice was sitting on the top step of the porch. When my mother stopped to say a word to Mrs. Herbert, she came down and stood a little way farther down the fence, leaning on the top rail, her fingers crumbling the dry heads of cornflowers.

"You look nice, all dressed up like that," Eunice said to me softly.

"It's plenty hot," I said. "With a tie and all."

"It makes you look different."

"How?"

"I don't know," she said. "Just different."

My mother had turned around now and was standing waiting for me.

"I got to go," I said. "I got to be there. . . ."

Eunice nodded. It was funny how, being a blonde like she was, her eyelashes were almost black. And when she stood looking down the way she did now, they were just a black semicircle on her cheeks. Usually I would have spent the evening on her porch or at a movie with her. And now I couldn't because my grandfather had to have a wake.

"Look," I said. "I won't be all that late tonight. . . . I'll let you know when I get home."

She nodded, still looking down, the eyelashes still making that dark mark on her cheeks.

I turned around and walked off quick as I could after my mother. And all the way over — in the first dark, which was dusty and uncertain to the eye — I was angry. I kept asking myself why I had to be a part of the old man's dying.

My mother took my arm, formally, and I wondered suddenly if I did look different or something.

The windows of the house were all wide open, it was so hot, and there was a light in every room. Very dim light, from a single bulb that was either small or shaded over with brown paper. The rooms were crowded and full of talk, buzzing whispers that didn't seem to say anything, and vague nodding heads. There were people here who'd come from all parts of the county and some from Montgomery, even. All people I knew, but I had a hard time recognizing them, their faces were so different in the half light.

Out in the kitchen there were two new colored women, working under Wilda Olive's direction. They were cooking everything, emptying out the cupboards. There wasn't any reason to watch the larder any more; the stuff had to be used up. Wilda Olive had never had anyone to help her before; she'd never had anyone to boss about — the way she did now. And she was really fixing a supper, for all the people who'd come. Not even the white women stopped or interfered with her. The smell of cooking was all over the house, making the air so heavy I couldn't catch my breath. I had to go outside.

There was only one light globe burning with all its brightness, full away — the one out in the yard. The summer moths were flying around in big swooping circles, and two little kids — a boy and a girl — were standing in the

circle of light, swatting them down with pieces of folded newspaper. Each time
they hit one, it would disappear with a tiny popping sound and a puff of
something like smoke.

The whole yard was full of kids, the youngest ones who were not allowed in
the house. They were wandering around, making up games to play or fighting
or just sitting, or calling for their mothers in hushed uncertain voices. Mamma
Lou Davis, a big fat colored woman, had posted herself at the front gate, to
make sure that they didn't wander away.

In the far corner of the garden, next to the row of leathery old live-forever
bushes, a bunch of the kids had begun to play funeral. They'd found a trowel
somewhere and they dug a little hole. Then very carefully they filled it and
heaped it so that the mud came to a mound on top. The sticks they'd tied
together like a cross wouldn't stand up in the loose dry ground, so they pulled
off the silvery leaves from bushes and stuck them all over the mound, like
feathers. Then they stood in a circle, solemn all of them, with their hands
folded behind their backs, and sang:

> *"We will gather by the river,*
> *The beautiful, beautiful river,*
> *We will gather by the river . . ."*

There were more verses, dozens of them, but they only seemed to know those
three lines. So they sang them over and over again.

There was one — a girl with a fat round race — who was sitting on the
ground a foot or two away from the group. Her fresh starched pinafore dress
was getting all dusty and rumpled, and every time the group paused for
breath, in that second or two of quiet, she'd ask: "Which river? Which river?
Where?" Not paying any attention to her, they'd go on singing:

> *"Gather by the beautiful river."*

Their voices together were thin and high-pitched and ragged.

Eunice and her mother came (her father was the druggist and had to stay at
the store until it closed at eleven); they didn't see me. I could tell from the
polite and cautious way Eunice was looking around that she was searching for
me as she followed her mother inside.

I just stood there in the far corner of the yard, not thinking much of
anything, just sort of letting my mind float out on the heavy waves of jasmine
odor. It couldn't have been long — not much more than a half-hour — when I
saw Eunice come out on the porch again. She walked right straight over to the

railing this time and stood there, with her right hand rubbing up and down her throat. You could see that she wasn't steady on her feet. Almost immediately her mother came rushing out of the door and put her arm around her and whispered in her ear, and then the two of them came down the steps and got in their car and drove away.

Mamma Lou Davis spoke to me from her stand near the gate: "That little girl sure got plenty sick, green sick. . . ."

"Yeah," I said.

"It plain affect some people that way, dying does." One of the kids, a little boy, made a dash for the gate and the street beyond. Mamma Lou's broad black hand caught him neatly on the top of the head and turned him back into the yard.

"She weren't in there long," Mamma Lou said. "But she got plenty sick."

"Yes," I said, "I could tell that."

I looked over on the porch and saw the extra chairs had been filled. Asa Stevenson had come, a short man, almost a midget. (They said he had killed three wives with his children. He had ten or eleven kids, all told, and every one of them was big and strapping; every one of them was exactly his image.) And Mrs. Martha Watkins Wood, a big woman with yellow wrinkled skin stretched tight across her heavy bones, and with the long sad face of a tired old horse, had come out from Montgomery.

Now in the circle on the porch, all the chairs were filled. Old Carmichael had known just who was coming, had expected them. With the arrival of Mrs. Wood the circle was complete. You could almost see it draw up on itself and close — a solid circle of wooden chairs. And at that precise moment I noticed that the silence was gone. They began talking, their voices light and rustling in the hot night air. Nobody went near them.

Over in the corner of the yard one of the kids was still singing:

> "We will gather at the river,
> Gather at the beautiful river. . . ."

By ten o'clock it had turned very quiet. The kids had fallen asleep — most of them — on the porch steps or out on the grass. A couple of them were using the little grave they had dug for a pillow. Mamma Lou was still at the gate, but she was sitting now, on a camp stool somebody had brought her from the house. I recognized the stool — it was the one my grandfather used when he went fishing.

Inside, the people seemed to have no more to say. They sat in the chairs that had been brought from all parts of the house for them, and looked at each other, and occasionally one of the women managed a smile, a kind of hesitant one, that seemed even littler in the half light.

From her position on the lowest step little Trudy Wilson shivered with a nightmare and began to cry. Her mother's heels made a kind of running clatter on the straw matting of the hall. They were the first to leave, the Wilsons, even though Trudy had waked up from her dream and was smiling again. The people with the children left first, and then the people who had a distance to drive. And then the people who had a business day coming with tomorrow. Until there were only my parents and me and the old people on the porch.

"Do you suppose they'll stay all night?" my mother asked.

"How could I know?" my father said. "They'll leave when they get ready and not before."

That was true enough. Hoyt Stevenson, who'd driven over with his wife and their three daughters and his father, had tried to get the old man to drive back with them. He tried for at least ten minutes, talking to the man in a low voice. And the old man just didn't answer, just kept shaking his head.

That's the way it was with all of them. So their families got together and figured out a way that they could get home to bed and not worry about the old people's getting home. Jim Butts, who owned the sawmill and who could afford a big car and a chauffeur, offered to ride home with somebody and leave his car and the colored driver. That's the way they did it. Finally there was just Butts's big light-yellow-colored Cadillac parked out front with the fuzzy-haired Negro asleep at the wheel, his arms wrapped all around it. And our car, which was parked up the drive, next to the house.

"Ruby, honey," my father said, "why don't you go to bed?"

My mother smiled at him limply. "I reckon I will. . . ."

Wilda Olive came in softly, carrying a round wicker tray with small cups of coffee.

My father took two. "I'll need them to stay awake."

"Thank you," my mother said. "I nearly forgot you were here, Wilda Olive."

"Yes'm," she said softly, gave me my cup of coffee, and went out on the porch to bring the rest to the old men.

I tasted the coffee. It had brandy in it.

"Say," my father said, "she sure made this a stiff dose."

"I'm so tired," my mother said. "It'll make me light-headed as anything."

"You can be in bed by that time," my father told her; "go ahead."

She stood up. "Come on, MacDonald," she said to me.

"I'm staying."

She appealed to my father. "I couldn't ever walk home alone at this time of night."

"MacDonald," my father said.

"Okay." I got up.

My father put his coffee cup down slowly. "What did you say?"

"Yes, sir."

My mother was tugging at my arm.

"Can I come back?"

My father shook his head.

"Don't you want company?"

"Go home," my father said.

My mother pulled my arm. "MacDonald, please —" And outside she gave a sigh of annoyance. "I'd think you'd have some sense. Can't you see your father's all upset without you pestering him?"

"Yes, ma'am," I said.

When we were almost home I asked her: "Why do you suppose he didn't want company?"

"Sometimes you want to be alone, MacDonald."

"I wouldn't," I said.

I saw her staring at me with a funny kind of look. I rubbed my hand quick all over my face to wipe off whatever expression she was worried about.

On our porch I stopped and took off my coat and tie. I dropped them on a chair. Meanwhile she had opened the door.

"Come on in, son."

I shook my head. "I reckon I need a walk." I started down the steps.

"MacDonald," my mother said, "you aren't coming to bed?"

"No'm."

"Your father said —"

"I don't care —" and because I didn't want to hear her answer to that, I bolted around the corner of the house. I didn't quite know where I wanted to go, so I just stood for a minute, just looking around. There was a thin flat hard sliver of moon pasted up in the west. The sky was almost bright blue and there were piles of thunderheads all over it now, shining clear in the light. There wasn't a bit of air. The dust wasn't even blowing. Everything was still and moldy and hot in the moonlight.

It was the sort of night when you breathe as shallow as you can, hoping to keep the heat out of your body that way, because your body is hot enough already. And you feel like you have a fever and maybe you do — on a thermometer — but you know it's just summer, burning.

I began to walk, not going anywhere, just wading through the dark and the heat. There were mockingbirds singing, like it was day. In the houses all the windows were wide open, and even out in the streets you could hear the hum of electric fans.

I passed a couple of colored boys walking, in step down the sidewalk. They rolled big white eyes at me as they went past. They were wearing sneakers; you couldn't hear their steps at all even in the quiet.

I wasn't thinking of anything. I was just moving around feeling how good the little breeze that made was. I walked through the town, through the business section, the closed stores and the grocery and the movie house; and the railroad station, open, but empty; and the rails shining white in the light, but empty too. I kept on walking until I had swung back through town in a circle and started back toward home. And the first thing I knew I was passing my grandfather's house. I saw the big jasmine bush at the corner of the lot — dusty but full of yellow flowers.

I went around to the side yard out of the reach of the street light and climbed over the fence. It was just a wire and wood fence and I had to swing over quick before my weight brought it down.

I was right by the kitchen window, so I looked in. Wilda Olive was standing there, at the kitchen table. She was dressed in a black linen dress so starched that it stood out all around her like stiff paper. And her hair was just combed and pulled straight on top her head and shining with lacquer. She wasn't asleep; her eyes were open.

Out in the yard, so close that I could almost put my hand down and touch it, a mockingbird was singing. I looked around carefully trying to see him. I saw a spot of gray close by the back porch that could have been the bird, but I wasn't sure.

My father was in the dining-room — I slipped over and looked through that window. He was sitting in one of the armchairs, all hunched down in it so that his head rested against the back. He was facing toward the living-room doors. My grandfather was in the first room, the one with the curtains drawn and the light shining dull brown through them.

And the old people were still on the porch. I could hear their voices, light and rustling.

I walked around the house and stood on the front steps, listening to them.

"There was plenty of timber for a house," Vance Bonfield was saying. He was a little wrinkled man, with a full head of clear black hair, which he dyed carefully every week. "But Cecil Addams wouldn't have any of plain pine. He had to have that cypress brought out from Louisiana."

"Wasn't him," Matthew Conners said. "His wife wanted it. Wanted a house just like she used to have. That's what it was."

Vance looked at him, blinking his pale-blue eyes slowly.

"Her name's plain gone from my memory," he said. "Do you happen to recall it?"

"Linda," Mrs. Wood said.

"Louise." Mrs. Bonfield's double chin quivered with the word.

"It was Lizette," Matthew Conners said.

"Ask him," Vance said, and lifted his thin old hand to point to me. (I jumped; I hadn't really thought they'd noticed me.)

"Ask him," Henry Carmichael said; "young people always remember better."

"Not so," Matthew Conners said, and banged with his cane on the porch boards. "They just got less to remember."

And then I said as loud as I could, because some of them were deaf: "Her name was Eulalie."

They looked at me and slowly shook their heads.

And I added quickly: "Lalia for short."

They sighed together: "Aahh"; they looked relieved.

"That's a bright young boy," Matthew Conners said. "A bright young fellow."

They looked at me. "He's a fine young fellow."

"Looks like his grandpa," Vance said. "A man's looks goes on in his sons."

Wilda Olive brought out a round of whiskies.

Looking at her, Vance said: "I can remember when she was the prettiest high-brown girl in this part of the state."

Matthew Conners cackled to himself, remembering. "And wasn't it a hell of a to-do when he brought her home after his wife died."

"I remember," they said.

I stood looking at them, wondering what it was they remembered, all of them together. Something I didn't know, something I couldn't know. Nor my father. Something my grandfather had known, who was dead.

Wilda Olive served them the drinks as if she never heard.

Vance held the glass in his hand, which shook so that the ice tingled. "Yes, sir," he said. "She was the prettiest thing you ever laid eyes on. Skin all yellow and burning."

Wilda Olive went inside. I looked after her and tried to see how she had looked years ago, when she had been pretty, so pretty that she'd caught my grandfather's eye. But all I saw was a colored woman, middle-aged and getting sort of heavy, with grieving lines down her cheeks.

"Prettiest thing," Vance said. "Sort of thing a young man can have, if he wants it."

"Man can't have anything long," Matthew Conners said.

They were looking at me. I began backing away.

"He's got a girl already," Asa Stevenson said, and hunched his dwarfed shoulders. "He got in a fight over her and near got thrown out of school."

"Who?" Mrs. Bonfield's fat chin lifted up and stared at me.

And Vance put in: "The Herbert girl, what's her name?"

I was backing off. They called to me: "Wait."

I had to stop.

"What's her name?" Matthew Conners leaned forward and rested his thin wrinkled chin on his cane. "What's her name?"

"I don't know," I said. The words sounded stupid and I knew they heard that too, but the only thing I could do was repeat: "I don't know."

"Not know your girl's name," Carmichael said, shaking his head. "Not know your girl's name . . ." His voice trailed off. "How do you call her to come out to you?"

Matthew Conners cackled softly. "You plain got it twisted, man. He's the one that come out. . . ."

"She's a pretty girl," Mrs. Wood said, her voice high and shrill in her solemn long face.

"You're right to pick a pretty girl," Vance said. "While you can."

I saw the hate in their eyes and I began to be sick. I backed away, down the steps and around the corner of the porch. This time they didn't seem to notice and let me go.

"It isn't long a man has anything," Matthew Conners was saying, and the ice cubes in his glass rattled. "It isn't long."

I climbed back over the fence, and the wire squeaked with my weight. I walked along the other side, slowly, curling my toes in the hard dry grass at each step.

Finally I sat down under the big locust tree near the street; I knew they couldn't see me there.

There was a funny sort of quivering in my stomach. I leaned back against the rough bark of the tree and looked up through the leaves at the sky that was almost bright blue. Out of the corner of my eye I could catch the sheen of the moon on the car waiting in the street. And that same moon made little blobs of light all around me. It was hot; I just sat there with my arms wrapped around my knees, feeling the sweat run down my back. I noticed a movement over on the porch. I looked more carefully. One of the old men, my grandfather's friends, was wiping his face slowly on a white handkerchief.

I sat under the locust tree and stared up at the sky that was so bright the stars looked uncertain and dim. I don't know how long I sat there before I began to notice something different. The rustling of voices was changing. I shifted my eyes from the sky to the porch.

Their talk was drying up quickly. The words got fewer and farther apart. They began watching each other with a quick sidewise slanting of eyes. And mouths came to a stiff closed line. They began to fidget nervously in their chairs.

Then one by one, with an imperceptible murmur, they slipped away. Singly, each singly, they left. I watched them leave, quiet and alone, and I thought: that's how they came.

The road ended here. They had to walk one way. And soon there were five of them, scattered down the length of the road, poking their way along, feeling the way with their sticks, black on a bright road.

I got up and went over and woke Claude, the chauffeur. He pushed his cap back on his head and rubbed his face with one hand.

"Claude," I said, "there they go."

"Huh?" He held his hand pressed to his face so that his stub nose was all pushed to one side.

"There they go," I repeated. "You better catch them."

He opened his eyes and looked down the road. "Christ Almighty," he said, starting the engine, "they plain near got away."

He swung the car around and went after them. I stood leaning on the gatepost watching. He drove up to the last man, drove a little past him and stopped, got out, opened the door quick. The old man never stopped walking, just kept walking until he was right abreast of the car, and then Claude stepped up and took his arm and almost lifted him into the car. Then he closed the door, quietly (I couldn't hear a sound), and went on after the next one. He did that until they were all safely in the car.

I started home then, and all the way I kept thinking of the picture of the old people moving down the road.

And suddenly I remembered the last time I had seen my grandfather — two days ago. We had both gone to the same place fishing. In deep summer there was only one place around here that you could fish in, only one place where the water stood deep and cool. He'd showed it to me himself the summer past — in an old gravel pit, way back behind the worn-out holes and the sandy ridges. It was quite a trick getting into it; it's hard climbing in loose gravel. I got to the top of the ridge and stood looking down at the line of aspens and willows and red honeysuckle bushes that grew around the pool. Then I noticed that my grandfather was already there, sitting on his camp stool, his rod in his hand. And at first I grinned and thought how surprised he would be to see me; and how much better it was to fish with company, even though you never say a word.

I started to climb down to him, and some loose gravel rolled away under my feet. He looked up and saw me. And he got up and grabbed his stool and his bait box and hurried away up the other side of the ridge. And I noticed a funny thing: his line wasn't out. He'd been sitting there, holding his rod, and waiting, but he hadn't cast out his line. He'd just been sitting there, waiting. . . .

And I understood then. . . . Why Matthew Conners had sold his store and didn't seem to notice the people passing by who talked to him. Why Mrs. Martha Watkins Wood wouldn't keep a servant full time in the big old empty house of hers in Montgomery, just day help. Why Vance Bonfield and his wife suddenly took separate rooms after sleeping in the same bed for forty-six years. Why Henry Carmichael shouted at the noisy grandchildren who climbed the wisteria vines to peer into the windows of his room. Why old people wanted to be left alone. . . .

There was the fear in my grandfather's eyes the day at the gravel pool. Even from a distance I had seen it. The fear that had made the old man pick up his bait basket and scurry off as fast as his stiffening legs could go.

The fear of dying . . . the fear that grows until at last it separates you from the people you know: the dusty-eyed old people who want to be left alone, who go off alone and wait. Who fish without a line.

One day I'll be that afraid. . . . All of a sudden I knew that. Knew that for the first time, I'll be old and afraid.

I'll be old and restless in company and want to be alone. Because loneliness is more bearable than company, when you are waiting; because it's a kind of preparation for that coming final loneliness.

I could feel it starting, just the beginning of fear.

I'll be old and sit on porches and talk in dry rattling whispers and remember the past and the things that I had when I was able to have them. And in the shaded parlors, in the faces of dead friends, see the image of my fear. The fear that will live with me: will follow me through the day and lie down with me at night and join me again in the morning, until there isn't any more morning and I don't get up at all. . . .

I began to run, not knowing where I was going, not caring. And there was the fear running with me, just with me.

It was so hot, I was running through a blank solid wall. I had to breathe and I kept trying, but there wasn't any air, just heat.

From far away there was the pounding of my own feet on the ground. I looked down at them, moving. I could hear the strangling sound of my own breathing, but that was far away too.

Only, the mockingbird was singing louder and louder and there was a spot of gray flying alongside me. Like it was laughing at me, trying to run away from it.

I was getting tired, so tired; I tried but I couldn't keep up the pace. It was hard too to keep my balance; I kept falling forward. I stretched out my arms; they touched something and I held on to it tightly. I stood shaking my head until my eyes cleared.

It was a fence, a picket fence. And just beyond was our house. I had come home. Not thinking about it, I had come home. All the hot noisy outside had come down to this: our green-painted clapboard house with the olive-colored shutters and the big black screen porch all around it. But somehow I couldn't go inside.

I lifted my eyes. And there were the thunderheads. They were right behind the house, right in line with it, but miles up in the sky. Just where they'd been all day. They'd turned red with the sunset and disappeared with the first dark and then reappeared silver-white with the moon. And there they were, hanging cool-looking and distant.

I looked away from them, down and across the street, to the light in the side window of the Herbert's house. That would be Eunice, waiting for me. For just a minute I saw her face and her eyes that crinkled at the corners and the way her hair was piled up on top of her head with a flower stuck in it.

I thought of all these things and I just turned away from the yellow square of light. And took a couple of steps backward until I pressed up against the big thick barberry hedge. One of the crooked thorns scratched my hand; I looked at it, bleeding slightly; it didn't hurt. Somehow nothing much seemed real — not Eunice, nor my house, nor the hedge that had cut me. Nothing but the pile of thunderheads up in the sky and the fear that had caught up with me, was running circles around me.

Circles and circles around me. Like the mockingbird that was singing louder and louder. The brown-gray bird.

Very slowly I sat down, leaning my back against the sharp thorns of the hedge. And listened.

Joshua

outh of New Orleans, down along the stretch that is called the Lower Coast, the land trails off to a narrow strip between river and marsh. Solid ground here is maybe only a couple of hundred feet across, and there is a dirt road that runs along the foot of the green, carefully sodded levee. It once had state highway markers, but people used the white painted signs for shotgun targets, until they were so riddled they crumbled away. The highway commission has never got around to replacing them. Maybe it doesn't even know the signs are gone; highway inspectors hardly ever come down this way. To the east is the expanse of shifting swamp grass, and beyond that is the little, sheltered Bay Cardoux, and farther still, beyond the string of protecting islands, is the Gulf. To the west is the Mississippi, broad and slow and yellow.

At intervals along the road there are towns — scattered collections of rough, unpainted board houses with tin roofs, stores that are like the houses except that they have crooked painted signs, and long, flat, windowless warehouses to store the skins of muskrats that are taken every year from the marsh. Each building perches on stilts two or three feet high; in the spring the bayous rise. The waters always reach up to the roadbed and sometimes even cover it with a couple of inches of water.

There is no winter to speak of. Sometimes there is a little scum of ice on the pools and backwaters of the bayous and a thin coating over the ruts in the road. But the temperature never stays below freezing more than a day or two, and the little gray film of ice soon disappears under the rain.

For it rains almost constantly from October to March. Not hard; not a storm; there is never any lightning. There is just a steady, cold rain.

The river is high. The trees that grow out on the *batture* — on the land between the river's usual bed and the levee, on the land that all summer and fall has been dry and fertile — are half-covered with water.

The inside walls of the houses drip moisture in tiny beads like sweat, and bread turns moldy in a single day. Roofs begin to leak, and the pans put under the leaks have to be emptied twice a day. From the bayous and the swamps to the east come heavy, choking odors of musk and rotting grasses.

It is mostly all colored people here in the lower reaches. Poor people, who live on what they find in the river and the swamps and the Gulf beyond them.

Joshua Samuel Watkin sat at the kitchen table in one of the dozen-odd houses that make up Bon Secour, Good Hope, the farthest of the towns along the dirt highway, which ends there, and the nearest town to the river's mouth.

Joshua Samuel Watkin leaned both elbows on the table and watched the way his mother used her hands when she talked. She swung them from her wrist, limply, while the fingers twisted and poked, way off by themselves.

His small, quick, black eyes shifted from her hands to her lips, which were moving rapidly. Joshua stared at them for a moment and then went back to the hands. He had the ability to shut out sounds he did not wish to hear. His mother's flaming, noisy temper he could shut out easily now; it had taken the practice of most of his eleven years.

He glanced at the doorway, where his father was standing. He had just come in. The shoulders of his light-gray jacket were stained black by the rain, and the tan of his cap had turned almost brown. Joshua glanced briefly down at his father's hands. They were empty; he would have dropped the string of fish outside on the porch. Pretty soon, Joshua knew, one of his parents was going to remember those fish and send him outside to clean them for supper. It was a job he had never liked. No reason, really. He would have to squat outside, working carefully, so that most of the mess fell over the side into the yard, where the cats could fight for it.

His father yanked one of the wooden chairs from under the table and sat down on it heavily. He was answering now, Joshua noticed, and his face was beginning to get the straight-down-the-cheek lines of anger. He tilted his chair back against the wall and jammed both hands down deep into his pockets.

From the way things were beginning to look, Josh thought, it might be just as well if he got out for a while. But he'd better stay long enough to see if there was going to be any supper. He still hadn't bothered to listen to them, to either of them; he knew what they were saying. He balanced his spoon across the top of his coffee cup and then tapped it with his finger gently, swinging it. He miscalculated, and the spoon hit the oilcloth with a sharp crack.

His father's chair crashed down and with an extra rattle one of the rungs came loose. "Christ Almighty," his father said. "Ain't I told you a million times not to do nothing like that?"

"He ain't done nothing," his mother said, and, reaching out her limp black hand, balanced the spoon across the cup again.

Joshua smiled to himself, though his face did not move. It was one sure way to get his mother on his side — just let his father say a word against him. It worked the other way, too; let his mother fuss at him and his father would be sure to take his part. It was as if they couldn't ever be together.

His father let his breath out with a high-pitched hiss.

"He ain't done nothing," his mother repeated. "Just drop his spoon a little."

His father kept on staring at her, his head bent a little, the dark eyes in his dark face glaring.

"Leastways he ain't just sitting around the house on his tail end, scared to stick his nose outside."

"Woman," his father said, "iffen you ain't the naggingest —"

"Scared." His mother stuck out her underlip. "You just plain scared."

"I ain't scared of nothing a man ain't got cause to be scared of."

"I hear you talking," his mother said. "Only I plain don't see you moving nohow."

"Nagging bitch," his father said, almost gently, under his breath.

His mother's underlip stuck out even farther, and she whistled sharply, derisively, through her teeth.

His father bent forward, slapping a hand down, one on each knee. "Sure I scared!" he shouted in her face. She did not even blink. "Everybody scared!"

Joshua turned his eyes toward the window. All he could see was gray sky. Raining, solid, gray sky in all four directions — east over the swamps and west over the river and north to the city and south to the Gulf, where the fishing boats went, and the U-boats were hiding.

His father was saying: "Like Jesse Baxter, you want me to plain get blown to bits."

Joshua did not take his eyes off the square of gray sky, but he was seeing something else. The fishing boats from Bon Secour, three of them, had come on the two U-boats, surfaced in the fog and together, exchanging supplies. And one of the ships had lobbed a couple of shots from its deck gun square into Baxter's boat. There wasn't anything but pieces left, and the two other fishing boats hadn't even time to look for them, they were so busy running.

All they'd heard, just for a second or two, was the men around the gun laughing. The two surviving boats had not gone out again. Nobody would take them out.

Joshua had heard the story and he had dreamed about it often enough. He would wake up sweating even in the cold and shaking with fear. He couldn't quite imagine a U-boat, so its outline and shape changed with each dream. But the action was always the same — the gun pointing at him and the laughing.

With a little shudder, Joshua turned his eyes back to his parents. "That been a week and a half," his mother was saying, "and how you think we gonna eat? How you think we gonna eat iffen you don't find a boat?"

"We been eating." His father had his chin pressed down against the rolled collar of his gray wool sweatshirt. "Ain't we been eating?"

His mother snorted. "Why, sure," she said. "You man enough to go sneaking out in the little old back bayous and catch us a couple of fish."

"Fish ain't bad," his father said. "Ask *him* iffen he going hungry."

Joshua felt their eyes focused on him, and he squirmed.

"Don't go putting words in the boy's mouth," his mother said.

"Just you ask him."

"Ask him iffen there ain't things you got to have money to buy. Ask him iffen he don't got no coat to wear with the cold. Ask him iffen he don't need a new coat." She turned to Joshua. "You tell him what you want. You tell him what you plain got to have." Her voice ended in a kind of ragged shriek.

"I get him a coat," his father said.

"When that gonna be? He plain gonna freeze first."

"Ain't no son of mine gonna freeze," his father said.

"You plain scared," his mother taunted. "You just plain scared."

Joshua got to his feet and slipped around the edge of the table and outside. On the porch he found a square of black canvas and wrapped it around himself, letting it make a cowl above his head. It had been used to cover an engine, and it smelled of grease and was slippery to the touch, but it would keep him dry and very warm.

He noticed the string of fish that his father had brought home. With the toe of one blue canvas sneaker, he kicked the string down into the yard. It hit the soggy ground with a little splash. The cats would be coming around at dark.

He walked down the road, stepping carefully, watching for the biggest puddles, keeping to the levee side, where the ground was highest. The rain was falling noisily on his square of tarpaulin. With the steady, quick, clicking sound of drops all around him, falling on his head but not touching him, tapping on his shoulders but not really being there, after a while he wouldn't be sure of his balance any more, or his direction, there would be such an echo in his head. He kept blinking to steady himself, but that didn't seem to do much good. He had heard men say they would rather get drenched to the skin and maybe get the fever than spend hours under a tarpaulin with a slow, steady winter rain falling.

The wind blew in swirling eddies — like puffs of smoke, almost, the drops were so fine. Joshua rubbed the wet from his eyes. Over the noise of the rain he heard the faint sound of the river against the levee, a sound that went on day and night, winter and spring, until you got so used to it you had to make a special effort to hear it. Squinting, he looked up. The tops of water aspens on the other side of the levee shuddered under the rain, showing the frightened white underside of their leaves.

Joshua hunched the tarpaulin higher over his head and walked faster. Over to the right now he could see the landings where Goose Bayou swung in close and deep. And there were the boats, moored and wet under the rain, and empty, just where they'd been for the last week or more, and, at the far end of one of the landings, the empty space where Jesse Baxter's boat belonged.

Joshua stopped and stared at the empty space, at the muddy, rain-specked water and Baxter's mooring posts with the ropes still around them but dragging down into the water. Like it was in his dreams, he thought, when, cold and sweating, he saw the shape of a ship in the fog and heard the sound of a deck gun.

He reached the shelter of the overhang of a building and let the tarpaulin drop from his head. He still kept it wrapped around his shoulders, because he was shivering. In the middle of the board platform in front of the building, a yellow dog with black-marked flanks was scratching behind one ear, slowly, limply, and overhead a double-board sign hung upside down at a sharp angle. On one side of it was painted, in white letters: "Bourgeois Store." Years ago the wind had lifted it and turned it on its hook, and it had jammed that way, with only the blank side showing. Nobody ever seemed to notice. Maybe because nobody ever looked up.

Joshua peeped in through the window. A single electric-light bulb way up against the ceiling in the center of the room was burning, because the day was so dark. It was a little bulb and almost worn out — you could see the red, glowing coils of wire inside it; and it wasn't much brighter inside the store than out.

Joshua rubbed his fingers against the glass and stared harder. There were two tables set together lengthwise across the front of the room, and behind them two more. They were covered with clothes in neat little piles, according to size and color. There were wall shelves, too, filled with a clutter of hardware. There were so many things in the room that you couldn't find any single object quickly, even if the thing you were looking for was as big as a man.

Joshua finally located Claude Bourgeois at the side of the room, over by the stove, almost hidden behind small crab nets that were hanging by long cords from the ceiling. There were two men sitting with him. Joshua could have known he would be there; he hardly ever moved from that spot during the winter, his bones ached so. Now that he was old, he'd stopped fighting the rain and the cold; he just let them have their way outside the store. He didn't move outside at all. His wife, Kastka, who was part Indian, rubbed his arms and legs with liniment and kept the fire going full away in the silver-painted potbellied stove.

Joshua opened the door. Just inside he let his tarpaulin fall in a heap. Claude and the two men with him turned and looked, and Claude said: "Close that there door quick, boy," and they went back to their talking.

Joshua recognized the two other men: Oscar Lavie and Stanley Phillips. Lavie ran Claude's fishing boat for him now that he was too old to go out, and Phillips was never very far away from Lavie. They always worked together; it had been that way since they were kids.

Joshua walked over to the small glass case that stood against the left wall, the case that was filled with knives. He stood looking down at them, at one in particular, one in the middle of the case. It had a blade at least six inches long, and its handle was of some white stuff, white and iridescent and shining as the inside of an oyster shell that is wet and fresh. Someday, he told himself, when he had money of his own, he would buy that. If just nobody got to it first.

Not that he needed a knife; his father had bought him one a month or less ago, with the money from the last haul the men had made. He remembered how angry his mother had been. "God Almighty," she'd said. "Iffen you ain't plain crazy, you. Buying that there trash when the boy needs a coat."

His father had just winked at him and said: "You don't hear him complaining none."

"Maybe he ain't got no more sense than you," his mother had said, "but he gonna be mighty cold this winter without no coat."

"Woman," his father had said, "ain't you got but one idea in you head?"

Little Henry Bourgeois came and stood alongside of Joshua. He was Claude's son, the son of his old age, the son of the woman who was part Indian. Henry had the round Negro features of his father and the skin color of his mother, a glowing red, deep and far down, so deep that it wasn't so much a skin color as a color under that. It was almost like seeing the blood.

"You heard the news?" Henry asked. His father had a radio in the store, a small one in a square green case. It was the only radio in Bon Secour.

"No," Joshua said.

"They come almost up the river," Henry said. "They sink one of the freighter ships again."

The war and the shooting and the submarines. And just a little way off. Joshua felt his breath catch in the middle of his chest, catch on the lump that was so big and cold that it hurt. And he remembered all his dreams: the fog, and the other ship, and himself in the gray, rain-speckled water, dying, in a million pieces for the fish to chew. His face did not change. He kept on looking at the knife. "That right?" he said.

"Josh," old Claude Bourgeois called to him. "You come over here."

He turned and crossed through the maze of tables and ducked under the hanging skeins of nets.

"Boy," Claude Bourgeois said, "iffen you don't quit leaning on that there glass it gonna crack through, sure as anything."

Joshua looked down at his feet in the blue canvas sneakers, blue stained darker by the water he had been walking through. He wiggled his toes, and they made little bumps on the outside of the canvas.

"You papa home?" Claude Bourgeois asked.

Joshua nodded.

"He wanting to go out fishing?"

"I reckon — it Ma wanting him to go out."

Oscar Lavie shifted in his chair, lifted one bare foot, and hooked it between his cupped hands. "Iffen you want you boat out," he told Claude Bourgeois, "I reckon you plain better take it out yourself."

Claude opened his mouth, and then, thinking better of whatever he was about to say, closed it again.

"I seen that there ship popping up out of the fog," Oscar went on, "and it ain't nobody's fault it ain't blown me up, place of Jesse Baxter."

Stanley Phillips nodded his head slowly. He stuttered badly, and when he talked people hardly ever understood him. So he let others do the talking. But his lack of speech had given him an air of confidence. Sometimes when he stood leaning against the corner of a building, his hands jammed down in his pockets, his slight body arched back and braced for balance, he seemed to own everything he looked at — the streets and the houses and the people. All the women liked him; some of them got a dreamy look in their eyes when he passed. "He don't have to talk, him," they would say. Only last year Stanley Phillips had married — all proper, in the church over at Petit Bayou — a wife, by far the prettiest colored girl anywhere along the river. And when he'd been out fishing, gone for maybe a couple of days or a week, he'd always head straight for home, and when he got within fifty yards of his house, he'd stop and give a long, loud whistle and then walk on slowly, counting his steps, and every fifth step giving another whistle, so his wife would have time to get ready for what was coming.

"Iffen you was in the army," Claude Bourgeois said softly, "you wouldn't have no chance to say no."

Neither Stanley nor Oscar had bothered registering for the army. They just disappeared whenever any stranger came around asking questions, which wasn't very often.

"You figure on anything there?" Oscar asked, his eyes resting on the fat, lumpy body of the old man.

"Not me," Claude Bourgeois said hastily. "Not me."

"That real fine of you," Oscar said. "Then I reckon I ain't gonna have to slice up all you fat and feed it to the gators."

"Me?" Claude rolled his eyes around so that they almost disappeared. "I ain't gonna do nothing like that."

"That nice of you," Oscar said.

"Why, man," Claude said, changing the subject quickly, "you plain got to go out eventually."

"That ain't yet," Oscar said, and Stanley nodded. "It ain't worth nothing going out to get blown to pieces."

"How they gonna find you in all that water out there?"

"It ain't worth the chance," Oscar said.

Joshua stared over at the pot of coffee on the stove top, where it always stood to keep warm. Nobody offered him any, so he looked away.

"Why, man" — Claude was holding his hand outspread in front of him — "you can't go on living on bayou fish forever; there other things you got to have money for." He nodded at Joshua. "This here boy need a coat, only his daddy ain't working to give him none."

"Leastways his daddy ain't lying in pieces all over the bottom of the Gulf, with the fishes eating him," Oscar said. "Leastways, iffen you are so concerned, you plain can give him a coat. Just you give him one on credit now."

"You gonna do that?" Joshua asked.

Claude coughed. "There ain't no cause to do nothing like that," he said. "This here a matter of business, and this ain't good business, any way you looks at it. There all sort of money waiting for his daddy out there, iffen you wasn't too scared to go get it."

Joshua drifted away toward the door. He picked up the tarpaulin, studied it for a minute, then flipped it around himself and went outside. Little Henry

Bourgeois followed right behind him. The low gray sky was thickening with the evening. In the branches of a chinaberry tree a hawk and a catbird were fighting. "Where you going?" Henry asked.

Joshua went down the steps and out into the road. The mud was soft and gummy, and stuck to the bottom of his shoes in heavy cakes. Each step was a sucking sound.

"Damn gumbo mud," he said. He could hear Henry's steps behind him.

They walked about a block, with their heads bent way down, so they really couldn't see where they were going. Henry gave a quick little squishing skip and came abreast of Joshua. "Where you going?" he asked again. "You going there?"

Joshua nodded.

They came to the warehouse. The fur-trading company had put it up maybe ten years ago, when they first discovered all the muskrat around here. There'd been need for extra space then. But things had changed; a couple of hurricanes had drowned out the animals, and they were coming back slowly. It hardly paid for a man to set his traps during the season, since he had to take the skins up to Petit Bayou now to sell them.

But the old warehouse still stood, at the north end of the string of houses. It was a rough building with plain, unpainted wood sides that time and rain and fogs had stained to an almost uniform black. On the far side, behind some low bushes — barberry bushes, with thick thorns and pronged leaves — Joshua had discovered a loose board. It had taken him nearly three hours to work it loose.

The two boys wiggled through the bushes, pried down the board, and slipped inside. They shook themselves like wet puppies and kicked off their shoes. The building was unheated, but somehow it always seemed warm, maybe only because it was dry. The floor boards were double thickness and carefully waterproofed with tar. It was a single room, big and almost empty. There were no windows, and when Henry put the board back in place, the only light came from the thin cracks between the boards. The two boys had been here so often that they knew their way around the room; they did not need to see.

They both walked straight out into the center of the room, until their bare feet felt the familiar rough texture of burlap. There had been a big heap of old bags in the warehouse, and the boys had carefully piled them in a circle, leaving a clear place about four feet across in the middle. When they sat there, the bags were higher than their heads and kept off drafts and cold. In the corners of the warehouse they had found a few furs — tattered, mangy things, too poor to be sold — and they used these as seats or beds, for sometimes they slept here, too. Their families did not miss them; after all, a boy should be able to look out for himself.

Joshua and Henry settled themselves, and Joshua lit the kerosene lantern he had brought a couple of days before. His mother had stomped and raged for a whole day after she discovered it was missing. Joshua did not even have to lie about it; before she had thought to ask him, his father came home and her anger turned on him, and they argued long and hard, and ended as they always did, going in their room to make love.

"I done brought something this time," Henry said. He pulled a paper-wrapped package from under his jacket. The greasy stains of food were already smearing the brown paper. "This here is our supper."

They divided the cold fried fish and the bread, and then Joshua put out the lamp — it was hard to get kerosene for it — and they ate in the darkness, with just the sound of rain on the tar-paper roof and the sound of their own chewing and the occasional scurry of a rat or maybe a lizard or a big roach.

"Man," Joshua said slowly. "This is fine, no?"

"Sure," Henry agreed, with his mouth full. "Sure is."

"Look like they gonna be a fog tonight."

"Sure do," Henry said. "It a good night to be right in here. It a fine night to be in here."

Joshua's fingers brushed the surface of one of the moldy-smelling pelts with a faint scratching sound. "You might even could make a coat outa these here, iffen you had enough," he said.

"No," Henry said scornfully.

Joshua did not argue.

They fell asleep then, because it was dark and warm and they weren't hungry any longer. And Joshua dreamed the same dream he dreamed almost every night. There was a thing that he knew was a submarine. Even the way its shape kept changing — from long, like a racing boat only a hundred times bigger, to narrow and tall, like the picture postcards of the buildings in New Orleans. But it was always fog-colored. At times it slipped back into the fog, and when it came out again, it was a different shape. And he was always there, too, in a boat sometimes, a pirogue or a skiff, hunched down, trying not to be seen, or on foot in the marsh, in knee-high water, crouched down behind some few, almost transparent grasses. Hiding where he knew there was no hiding place.

Joshua shook himself, turned over, bent his other arm and pillowed his head on it, and went back to the dream. He did not wake again, but from time to time he whimpered.

That night one of the submarines was destroyed. The patrol boats found it almost a quarter mile inside the pass, heading for the shipping upriver. The heavy, cold, raining night exploded and then exploded again. Joshua woke up and couldn't be sure he wasn't still in his dream, for the waking was like a dream. Alongside him, Henry was whispering: "Sweet Jesus. Sweet Jesus." With fumbling fingers and a quick sharp scratch of matches, Joshua lit the lantern. The light raced to the roof and stayed there, holding back the darkness. Quickly, afraid, he glanced around the room. He was almost surprised to find it empty.

"What that?" Henry asked. His eyes caught the light and reflected it - bright, flat animal eyes.

Joshua did not answer. His throat was quivering too much. He looked around the empty room again and shook his head slowly.

"What that?" Henry repeated.

Joshua turned up the wick high as it would go. The top of the glass chimney began to cloud with smoke, but he did not lower the flame.

Henry jiggled his elbow persistently. "What that go up out there?" he asked.

"Ain't nothing."

Outside, people were yelling, their voices frightened and sleepy. Their words were muffled and garbled by the walls.

"You reckon maybe we ought to go out and see?" Henry asked.

"I reckon not," Joshua said, and there was a flat note of decision in his voice. "I reckon we best stay right here."

A plane flew by, close overhead. The building shook and the lamp flame wavered.

"I reckon the war come plain close," Joshua said.

"It quiet now," Henry said, and even managed to smile.

Joshua moved his lips but no sound came out. His tongue fluttered around in his throat.

The shouting outside was stopping. There were now just two voices, calling back and forth to each other, slower and slower, like a clock running down. Finally they stopped, too.

Henry said: "It smoking some."

Joshua turned the lampwick down. The circle of light around them contracted. He watched it out of the corner of his eye and quickly turned the wick back up again.

"Ain't you better put that out?" Henry said. "We ain't got all that much kerosene."

"We got enough," Joshua said.

"You scared."

"Me?" Joshua said. "Me? No." Even he did not believe this. He tried hard to stay awake, knowing that just as soon as he fell asleep, just as soon as he stepped over that line, the indistinct shape, gray like the fog, would be waiting to kill him.

Suddenly it was broad daylight. The lamp had burned out; its chimney was solid black. Henry pointed to it. Joshua nodded. "You left the lamp burning till it run out of oil," Henry said.

Joshua walked slowly across the room. "Me?" he said. "No."

"I heard you talking in you sleep."

"I don't talk in my sleep, me." Joshua put his shoulder to the loose board and pushed. He felt the cold, damp air in his face. He blinked and looked out at the gray day.

"You was crying," Henry said. "You was crying and saying 'Don't.' That what you was doing."

Joshua wriggled through the opening without answering.

Henry stuck his head out after him. "You was scared," he shouted.

Joshua kept going steadily. He could feel a trembling behind his knees, and he had to concentrate with all his might to keep his walk straight.

As he went up the splintered wooden steps of his house, he could hear his father singing:

> "Mo parle Simon, Simon, Simon,
> Li parle Ramon, Ramon, Ramon,
> Li parle Didine,
> Li tombe dans chagrin."

Sober, his father wouldn't even admit to understanding the downriver version of French. He'd near killed a man once who'd called him a Cajun. Drunk, he would remember that he knew hundreds of Cajun songs.

Joshua opened the door and went inside. His father and Oscar Lavie were in the kitchen, sitting at opposite ends of the table. Stanley Phillips was not around; he wasn't ever one for leaving his wife before afternoon.

In the middle of the green-checked oilcloth table cover were two gallon jugs of light-colored orange wine. One was already half empty. And on the table, too, next to the big wine bottles, was the small, round bottle of white lightning. Just in case they should need it.

They were so busy with their song they did not notice Joshua. He looked at them, wondering where his mother was. Then he went looking for his food.

He found some beans on a plate at the back of the stove, and a piece of bread in the wall cupboard. He ate them, standing up in a corner.

Slowly his father swung his head around to him and said: "Look who come in."

Oscar Lavie said: "We celebrating way they blow up everything last night."

"You ma gone rushing out of here like the devils of hell hanging on her petticoat."

"I ain't done nothing of the kind." His mother popped her head in through the narrow little door that led to the lean-to at the back of the house. "I just went to get some kindling wood, so you crazy fool drunks ain't gonna freeze to death."

Oscar began singing, almost to himself:

> *"Cher, mo l'aime toi.*
> *Oui, mo l'aime toi.*
> *Vec tou mo coeur*
> *Comme cochon l'aime la bou."*

"Ain't I told you to get out?" his father said softly to his mother. "Ain't I told you I sick and tired of looking at you?"

Joshua finished eating silently. Oscar gave a deep sigh. "Us all gonna starve to death," he said. "Us all."

His father poured himself another glass of wine. Joshua's mother did not move. She stood in the doorway holding the kindling in her arms.

His father's heavy-lidded eyes focused on Joshua and lifted a little. "What you gonna eat tonight?" his father asked.

The boy turned and put the dish back where he had found it, on the stove. "I don't know, me," he said.

His father began to laugh. He laughed so hard that he had to put his head down on the tabletop, and the table shook, and the wine in the bottle swished back and forth. When he spoke, it was from under his arms. "You hear him, Oscar, man," he said. "He don't know what he going to eat. He don't know."

Oscar did not even smile as he stared off into space. The black of his skin seemed almost blue under the morning light.

"He don't know what he going to eat. I don't know either, me."

Joshua stood watching them.

"I ain't going out today, me, to look for nothing," his father said. "I plain sick of catching a couple of fish or shrimp with a hand net."

"Han Oliver, he got a pig," Lavie said, with a dreamy look on his face.

"Man," Joshua's father said, "Han plain swears he gonna kill anybody what tried to touch his pig, and he been sitting guard on it."

"I seen a dog out front there."

"I just ain't that hungry yet."

Lavie sighed deeply. "It ain't gonna hurt us none not to eat for one day."

"No," his father said, and was silent for so long that Joshua began walking toward the door. He had no clear idea what he would do outside; he only felt he had to leave. His father's head jerked up. "Unless *he* go out."

Joshua stopped short. "Me?" he said.

Oscar looked at him. His eyes faltered, focused again, and held. "He a fine little boy," he said. "He can go run my lines."

"No," Joshua said.

"He ain't gonna do that," his mother said. She came into the room now and dumped her armload of kindling alongside the stove.

"That kindling plain all wet," Oscar said vaguely, scowling.

"You ain't never found nothing dry in winter," his mother snapped.

"It gonna smoke," Oscar said plaintively.

"No skin off my nose," his mother said.

"Ain't I told you to get out?" his father said.

"You done told me a lot of things," his mother said.

"I tired of hearing you —"

"You ain't sending that little old boy out where you scared to go."

"Ain't scared," Oscar corrected. "Drunk."

"Woman," his father said, "I plain gonna twist you head around till you sees where you been."

He stood up, a little uncertain on his feet, and his chair fell over. His mother turned and ran out. They could see her through the window, scurrying over to the Delattes' house, next door. She was yelling something over her shoulder; they couldn't make out what.

His father looked at Joshua, his eyes traveling up and down every inch of his body. "You going out," he said.

"I ain't," Josh whispered.

"You going out and save you poor old papa some work," his father said. "Or I gonna twist up every bone in you body till you feels just like a shrimp."

Joshua edged his way carefully to the door.

"You know I mean what I done said."

Joshua ducked out the door. Behind him he heard his father laugh.

Henry was down at the landing, leaning against one of the black tar-coated pilings and teasing a big yellow tomcat with a long piece of rope. Joshua walked past without a word, and righted his father's pirogue and pushed it into the water.

"You going out?" Henry asked, and his voice quivered with interest.

"Reckon so." Josh bent down to tie the lace of one of his sneakers.

"Why you going out?"

"Reckon somebody got to see about getting something to eat."

"Oh," Henry said.

"My papa, he gonna stay drunk today."

"I heard."

"I reckon I could let you come along."

"That okay. We ain't needing no fish at my house."

"You afraid." Joshua looked at him and lifted his eyebrows. "You plain afraid."

"No-o-o," Henry said, and scowled.

"Why ain't you come along with me, then?"

"I ain't said I ain't coming." Henry tossed the piece of rope away. The cat pounced on it in spitting fury. "I ain't said nothing like that."

"Let's get started, then."

"I tell you what," Henry said. "I gonna go borrow my daddy's shotgun. Maybe we see something worth shooting at. I seen a couple of ducks yesterday or so."

Joshua nodded. It would feel better, having a shotgun with them. Wasn't much good, maybe, but it was something. In his nightmares, he'd wished often enough that he had one with him.

While he waited, he got down in the pirogue and took his place in the stern. Carefully he wrapped the grease-stained black tarpaulin around him. "It cold, all right, man," he said aloud. The yellow tomcat turned his head and watched him. For a minute Joshua stared into the bright yellow eyes and at the straggling broken tufts of whiskers.

Joshua made the sign of the cross quickly. "If you a evil spirit, you can't touch me now," he said. The cat continued to look at him, its black pupils widening slightly and then contracting. Joshua began to wonder if maybe this wasn't one of his nightmares, if this wasn't all part of something he was dreaming. Maybe when he woke up he'd just be back in his bed, and maybe his mother would be shaking him and telling him to stop yelling and his father would be laughing at him for a coward. He took one of his fingers, cracked and almost blue with the cold, between his teeth. He bit it so hard the tears came to his eyes. But he'd done that before in dreams and still he hadn't waked up. No matter how scared he was, he had to finish it out, right to the end.

He held the lightly moving pirogue in place with his paddle and waited for Henry, impatiently, humming a little tune under his breath — the one he'd heard his father singing:

> *Mo Parle Simon, Simon, Simon,*
> *Li parle Ramon, Ramon, Ramon . . .*

and told himself that the cold in his stomach was the weather outside.

He noticed something different. He lifted his head, sniffing the air; it had stopped raining. The sky had not cleared or lifted, and the air was still so heavy you could feel it brushing your face. Everything was soaked through; the whole world was floating, drenched, on water. But for a little while there was not the sound of rain.

And he missed that sound. He felt lonesome without it, the way he always did in spring — suspended and floating. For there isn't any real spring here — just a couple of weeks of hesitation and indecision between the rainy winter and the long, dry summer. There are always more fights and knifings then.

Henry came running back, a shotgun in one hand and four or five shells in the other. "I done got it," he said.

"Don't you point that there thing at me," Joshua said, and jerked his head aside.

"Us can go now," Henry said. He laid the gun in the bottom of the boat and then quickly got in the bow and wrapped a narrow blanket around his shoulders and knees. "I feel better with that along, me."

Joshua shrugged. "It don't matter to me."

They paddled out, following the curve of Goose Bayou, grinning to themselves with the fine feel of the pirogue — the tight, delicate, nervous quiver of the wood shell, the feel of walking across the water the way a long-legged fly does.

A couple of hundred yards down Goose Bayou they turned south, into a smaller bayou, which, for all anybody knew, had no name. It circled on the edge of a thick swamp, which nobody had bothered to name, either, though most people at one time or other had gone exploring in the tangle of old cypress and vines and water aspens and sudden bright hibiscus plants. Way back in the center somewhere, so that people hardly ever saw them, some cats lived — plain house cats gone wild and grown to almost the size of a panther, living up in the tangled branches of the trees, breeding there. Some nights you could hear their screaming — pleasure or maybe pain; you couldn't tell.

Nobody had ever had the courage to go all the way through the swamp. It wasn't all that big; people simply went around it. Except for one man, and that was an old story, maybe true, maybe not. Anyhow, it had been on to fifty years past. There'd been a white man with yellow hair, the story said, and he'd jumped ship out there in the river. He'd had a long swim in from the channel to the levee, but by the time he climbed up the muddy *batture*, he wasn't as tired as he should have been. Maybe he was hopped up on dope of some sort. Anyhow, when he came walking out of the river, just a little above Bon Secour, his clothes dripping and sticking to his body, his yellow hair all matted and hanging down over his face, there was a girl walking on the levee top. She stopped, watched him stumbling and slipping on the wet, slimy river mud, waved to the people she was with to wait a little, and went down to help him, making her way carefully through the tangle of aspens and hackberries, so that her dress wouldn't get torn.

It was torn clear off her, almost, when they found her half an hour later — those people she'd been walking with. They'd finally got tired waiting for her and gone down to see. They'd have killed him, white man or not, if they'd found him. For nearly two days the men hunted for him while the women went ahead with the funeral. They trailed him at last to the small stretch of swamp, and then they stopped, because none of them wanted to go in there themselves and they couldn't ever have found him in there, in a stretch about four miles long and maybe a mile wide. They did look in the outer fringes — in the part they knew. They could see the signs of where he'd been; they could see that he was heading right straight for the middle of the swamp. Nobody ever saw him again. Maybe he fought his way out and went on like he intended to, though the way he went crashing around, he didn't seem to know where he was going. Or maybe he kept on living in there; it wouldn't have been hard. He had a knife, he'd killed the girl with it. Or maybe he just died, and the fish and the ants and the little animals cleaned his bones until they were left shining white and shreds of his hair shining yellow.

Joshua and Henry paddled past the thick swamp and remembered the story, and listened for the screaming of the cats, but since it was daylight, they heard nothing.

"It good to get out, man," Joshua said.

Henry did not answer, but then nobody talked much in the swamps. People got suddenly embarrassed and shy of their words and spoke only in whispers when they said anything at all, because the swamp was like a person listening. The grasses and bushes and trees and water were like a person holding his breath, listening, and ready to laugh at whatever you said.

Joshua and Henry found the trotlines that Oscar Lavie had set out the day before across a little cove that the bayou made in the swampy island. Oscar had tied a red strip of handkerchief to the end of a vine to mark the place. Henry reached up and unknotted the cloth. "Man," he said, "this wet through." He squeezed the rag over the side of the pirogue.

"It been raining," Joshua said. He gave the pirogue a quick shove up among the cypress knees to the one the line was tied to. "Iffen you loose that, we see what all we got." A sudden swinging vine hit his cheek. He jumped slightly, then grinned.

They worked their way back across the little cove, checking each of the seven single lines. The first three were empty, the bait gone. The next two held only the heads of catfish; the bodies were eaten clean away. "That plain must have been a gar," Henry said, and Joshua nodded.

They could tell by the drag of the lines that the last two were full. Joshua coaxed the lines slowly to the surface — two catfish with dripping whiskers, and gigs, sharp and pointed and set.

"Watch 'em," Josh said. "They slice you up good."

"You ain't gonna worry about me," Henry said. "You just bring 'em up where I can get at 'em." He picked up the steel-pointed gaff from the bottom of the boat and jabbed it through the whiskered bottom jaw of one of the fish. While Joshua steadied the boat, Henry held the fish until its convulsive movements had all but stopped.

When they had finished, Joshua coiled up the trotline and dropped it in the center of the boat with the fish. "Granddaddies, them, all right," he said.

Henry nodded, breathless from exertion.

Joshua turned the pirogue back out into the bayou and paddled rapidly. Soon they passed the swampy island and were in the salt marshes, miles of grasses rustling lightly and stretching off flat on both sides, with just a few *chênières* — shell ridges with dwarfed, twisted water oaks — scattered on the trembling, shifting surface.

"Man, it cold!" Joshua said. "Sure wish I had me a big old heavy coat."

"Look there," Henry said. From a *chênières* away to the left, four or five shapes pumped heavily up into the air.

"Too far away to do us no good."

"Leastways they still got some duck around."

"That a bunch of pintails," Joshua said.

"How you tell?"

"I just plain know, man. I just plain can tell, that all."

Henry was staring over where the indistinct shapes had faded into the low sky. "It mighty late for them to be around."

Joshua dug his paddle deeper in the water. The pirogue shuddered and shot ahead.

"You can't tell what they are from way over here," Henry said.

"I plain can."

Henry turned his head and studied him. "What the matter with you?"

"I hope to God that that there moccasin chew out you wagging tongue," Joshua said.

Henry jerked around; the pirogue swayed wildly. "Where a moccasin?"

"There." Joshua pointed to a long, dark form that was disappearing among the reeds and the Spanish-fern bushes. "And, man you plain better stop jumping or you have us in this here water."

"I ain't liked snakes."

"You plain scared," Joshua said softly.

"Maybe we get in shooting range of some ducks," Henry said.

Joshua snorted.

Henry said: "Wonder why they all afraid to come out. Ain't nothing out here."

After a moment Joshua said: "I aim to have a look at where all the trouble was. I aim to keep on going till I can plain see the river." He had been afraid last night; and Henry had seen him. Now there was something he had to prove.

For a while Henry was quiet. Then he said: "Man, I'm colding stiff. Let's go back."

"Ain't no use to yet," Josh said.

"I'm freezing up."

"Me, too," Josh said. "But there ain't no use to turn back yet."

They moved steadily south, in a twisting line through the narrow waterways, following the pattern of a curve that would bring them to the river, far down where it met the Gulf.

In about an hour they were there, in a narrow passage of water sheltered by a curve of reeds from the full force of the river, but where they could see into the broad stream and across to the faint, low line of grasses on the other side. Here the river was just a yellow-brown pass flowing between banks of sifting mud and reeds and tough, tangled bushes and twisted, dead trees brought down years ago and left far up out of the usual channel by the flood waters.

The wind was high. The grasses all around bent with a small screaming sound. The water was swift and almost rough. The pirogue shuddered and bounced. They let their bodies move with it, balancing gently. "Watch that old alligator grass there," Henry said as the craft swung over near the tall reeds. "They plain cut you up like a knife."

Joshua turned the pirogue crosswise in the channel. Behind them a pair of ducks rose, hung for a minute, and then began a quick climb up the strips of wind.

"God Almighty!" Henry said. "There more duck!"

Joshua stood up in the pirogue, following the sweep of their flight. They disappeared almost at once in the low sky. He sat down.

"You reckon we ever gonna get close enough for a shot?" Henry said.

Joshua did not answer. Out of the corner of his eye he had seen something — something blue-colored. And that was one color you did not see down here in the marsh, ever. There were browns and greens and yellows, but never blue — not even the sky in winter. Still, when he had stood up in the pirogue, so that he was taller than the surrounding reeds, and had followed the flight of the ducks, his eyes had passed over a bright blue. He stood up again, balancing himself gently in the moving boat, and let his eyes swing back — carefully this time.

He found it. Down a way, on the other side of the stretch of reeds, right by the open stream of river. There must be a little shell mound there, he thought, a little solid ground, because bushes grew there, and there was one bare, twisted, dead chinaberry tree. The river was always throwing up little heaps like that and then in a couple of years lifting them away. His eyes found the spot of blue color again. "Look there," he said.

Henry got to his feet slowly, carefully. The wooden shell rocked and then steadied. Henry squinted along the line of the pointing finger. "Sweet Jesus God!" he whispered. "That a man there!"

They were still for a long time. The pirogue drifted over to one side of the channel and nudged gently against the reeds. They took hold of the tops of the grasses, steadying themselves. The water got too rough; they had to sit down quickly.

Joshua found a small channel opening through the grass. He pushed the pirogue through it until there was only a dozen yards or so of low oyster grass ahead of them. The river there was full of driftwood, turning and washing down with the slow force of a truck.

"We plain can't get around the other side," Joshua said.

"Ain't no need to get closer," Henry said.

"I plain wonder who he is."

They could see so clearly now: bright-blue pants and a leather jacket.

They were bent forward, staring. "He got yellow hair," Henry said. The water made a sucking sound against the hull, and he looked down at it with a quick, nervous movement. "Water sound like it talking, times," he said.

"I plain wonder who he is."

"Ain't been here long, that for sure," Henry said. "Ain't puffed up none."

"That right," Joshua said.

"Remember the way it was with the people after the hurricane? And they only out two days?" Henry's voice trailed off to a whisper.

"I remember," Joshua said.

The man had been washed up high into the tough grasses. He was lying face down. He would stay here until the spring floods lifted him away — if there was anything left then.

"He got his hands stuck out up over his head," Henry said. They could not see the hands, but the brown, leather-clad arms were lifted straight ahead and pointing into the tangle of hackberries.

"His fingers is hanging down so the fishes nibble on them," Joshua said, and felt his shoulders twitch.

"I done felt fish nibble on my fingers," Henry said.

"Not when you was dead."

They were quiet again. All around them the sound of the miles of moving water was like breathing.

Suddenly Henry remembered. "I bet I know who he is."

"Who?" Joshua did not turn his eyes.

"I bet he off that there submarine that got sunk out in the river."

"Maybe," Joshua said.

"Or maybe he off one of the ships that got sunk."

"It don't make no difference, none."

"It ain't no use to hang around here," Henry said finally. "What we hanging around here for?"

Joshua did not answer. Henry turned and looked at him. Joshua was rubbing his chin slowly. "He got a mighty nice jacket there," he said.

"Ain't no use hanging around admiring a dead man's clothes, none."

"I might could like that jacket, me," Joshua said.

Henry stared back over his shoulder.

"You think I scared," Joshua said.

"No," Henry said. "I ain't thinking that."

"I ain't scared of going over there and getting that coat that I like," Joshua bragged.

Henry shook his head.

"Him there — he ain't gonna need it no more," Joshua said.

"You ain't gonna do that."

"You think I afraid. I reckon I just gonna do that."

"You plain could get killed going on that riverside, with all the driftwood coming down."

"Ain't going on that side," Joshua said. "I gonna climb over from this here side."

"Iffen you ain't drown yourself," Henry said, "you gonna get cut to pieces by sword grass or get bit by one of them snakes we seen a little while ago."

"I ain't afraid," Joshua said.

He handed Henry the paddle. "You steady it now, man," he said. He got to his feet, and the pirogue did not even tremble with his movement. He took a firm grasp on the top of the toughest grasses and jumped over the side. The boat dipped heavily and the yellow, cold water splashed in.

"God Almighty," Henry said. "You like to upset us for sure."

Joshua fought his way through the twenty feet or so of matted oyster grass and waist-high water until he reached the little shell mound. The water was shallower there; it came only a little above his ankles. He began to move slowly along through the tangle of bushes, working his way across to the riverside. A heavy branch snapped away from his shoulders and clipped him in the face. He jerked his head back and clapped his hand to the cut spot.

"What that?" Henry called. "A snake ain't got you?"

"No," Joshua said. "I ain't afraid of no snakes when I sees something I want, me."

He could feel a quivering deep down inside himself. But he said aloud: "That just the cold, just the cold water, boy. I can just think how warm and fine it gonna be with a nice coat, me."

He took his hand away and looked at it. There was blood all over the palm. The branch must have cut his cheek deeply.

"It beginning to rain again," Henry called.

"I ain't afraid of no little rain," Joshua called back.

The ground under his feet must have been covered with moss, for it was slippery walking. He lost his balance once and almost fell. He felt the water splash cold up to his shoulders.

"That a gator got you?" Henry's voice was thin and ragged.

"I ain't afraid of no gators," Joshua called back. He had reached the man now. He bent down and touched the soft brown leather of the jacket. From the feel, he knew that it was buttoned across the chest. He'd have to turn the body over. He tugged at one shoulder, but the arms were caught somehow.

"You come help me," he told Henry, and, getting no answer, he looked around quickly. "Iffen you got any ideas of getting scared and running off, I just gonna peel you hide off."

He spread his legs and braced himself and pulled harder and harder. The body turned over stiffly, with a swish of water. Joshua did not look at the face. He stared at the two buttons, and then his cold fingers fumbled with them. They would not loosen.

"What you doing?" Henry called.

Joshua took out his knife, the one his father had given him, and cut off the buttons. One fell in the water. The other he caught between two fingers and dropped in his own pocket.

"Ain't you near got it?"

Joshua looked up and over at Henry when he pulled the jacket off.

"Come on," Henry said, and waved the paddle in the air.

Joshua, still without looking down, turned and worked his way back, dragging the jacket from one hand, in the water.

By the time they got home, it was almost dark and the rain was falling heavily. All the color had washed out of the country, leaving it gray and streaked and blurry, like the clouds overhead. The marshes off a little way looked just like the lower part of the sky.

Joshua picked up the fish with one hand, and with the other he tossed the jacket over his right shoulder.

He could feel the leather pressing cold against his neck. It had a smell, too. He crinkled his nose. A slight smell, one you wouldn't notice unless you were taking particular notice of such things. Faint, but distinct, too — like the way the swamp smelled, because it had so many dead things in it.

There was a cold wind coming up with the night; you could hear its angry murmuring out in the marshes. Wet as he was, and shivering, Joshua stopped for just one moment and turned and looked back the way they had come, down Goose Bayou, across the gray grasses, and he blinked and shook his head, because he couldn't quite see clear. It had gotten that dark.